ROBERT CRAIS
Three Great Novels: featuring Elvis Cole

Robert Crais

Three Great Novels: featuring Elvis Cole

Free Fall
Voodoo River
Sunset Express

ORION

First published in Great Britain in 2002 by
Orion
An imprint of Orion Books Ltd
Orion House, 5 Upper St Martin's Lane, London WC2H 9EA

ISBN 0 75285 356 2 (hardback)
ISBN 0 75285 357 0 (trade paperback)

A CIP catalogue record for this book is available
from the British Library

Typeset by Deltatype Ltd, Birkenhead, Merseyside
Printed and bound in Great Britain by
Clays Ltd, St Ives plc.

Contents

Free Fall

AN ELVIS COLE NOVEL

For my father,
Robert Emmett Crais,
called away before the show.
A seat remains empty.

Free Fall

1

Jennifer Sheridan stood in the door to my office as if she were Fay Wray and I was King Kong and a bunch of black guys in sagebrush tutus were going to tie her down so that I could have my way. It's a look I've seen before, on men as well as women. 'I'm a detective, Ms Sheridan. I'm not going to hurt you. You may even find that you like me.' I gave her my best Dudley Do-Right smile. The one with the twinkle.

Jennifer Sheridan said, 'Is what we say privileged, Mr Cole?'

'As in attorney-client?' I was holding the door, but Jennifer Sheridan couldn't seem to make up her mind whether to come in or leave.

'Yes.'

I shook my head. 'No. My records and my testimony can be subpoenaed, and under California law, I must provide them.'

'Oh.' She didn't like that.

'But there is latitude. I sometimes forget things.'

'Oh.' She liked that better, but she still wasn't convinced. I guess there's only so much you can do with the Dudley.

Jennifer Sheridan said, 'This isn't easy for me, Mr Cole. I'm not sure I should be here and I don't have much time. I'm on my lunch hour.'

'We could talk over sandwiches, downstairs.' There was a turkey and Swiss on a French baguette waiting for me in the deli on the ground floor. I had been thinking about it for most of the morning.

'Thank you, no. I'm engaged.'

'That wasn't a sexual proposition, Ms Sheridan. It was a simple offer to share lunch and perhaps more efficiently use both our times.'

'Oh.' Jennifer Sheridan turned as red as a beating heart.

'Also, Ms Sheridan, I'm getting tired of holding the door.'

Jennifer Sheridan made up her mind and stepped past me into the office. She walked quickly and went to one of the two director's chairs across from my desk. There's a couch, but she didn't even consider it.

Jennifer Sheridan had sounded young on the phone, but in person she looked younger, with a fresh-scrubbed face and clear healthy skin and dark auburn hair. Pretty. The kind of happy, innocent pretty that starts

7

deep inside, and doesn't stop on the way out. That kind of pretty. She was wearing a light blue cotton skirt with a white blouse and a matching light blue bolero jacket and low-heeled navy pumps. The clothes were neat and fit well, and the cuts were stylish but not expensive. She would have to shop and she would have to look for bargains, but she had found them. I liked that. She carried a black imitation leather purse the size of a Buick, and when she sat, she sat with her knees and her feet together, and her hands clutching the purse on her lap. Proper. I liked that, too. I made her for twenty-three but she looked eighteen and she'd still be carded in bars when she was thirty. I wondered if I looked old to her. Nah. Thirty-nine isn't old.

I closed the door, went to my desk, sat, and smiled at her. 'What do you do, Ms Sheridan?'

'I'm a secretary for the law firm of Watkins, Okum, & Beale. We're in Beverly Hills.'

'Is that how you found me?' I work for Marty Beale, time to time. A little skip-tracing, a little missing persons. That kind of thing.

'I peeked in Mr Beale's reference file. He thinks highly of you.'

'You don't say.'

'They don't know that I'm here and I would appreciate it if you didn't say anything.'

I nodded. 'On the phone you said something about your boyfriend.'

'My fiancé. I think that he's mixed up in some kind of criminal thing. I've asked him, and he denies it, but I know that something's going on. I think he's scared, and that worries me. My fiancé is not scared of very much.'

I nodded again and tucked that away. Fearless Fiancé. 'Okay. What kind of crime are we talking about?'

'I don't know.'

'Is he stealing cars?'

'I don't think so.'

'Is he embezzling?'

'No. It wouldn't be that.'

'How about fraud?'

She shook her head.

'We're running out of choices, Ms Sheridan.'

She glanced into the big purse as if there were something inside it that she was hoping she wouldn't have to show me, as if the purse were somehow a point of no return, and if she opened it and let out whatever was inside, she would never be able to close it again or return the elements of her life to a comfortable or familiar order. Pandora's Purse. Maybe if I had a purse like that, I'd be careful of it, too.

I said, 'I know it's hard, Ms Sheridan. If it was easy, you wouldn't need

8

me. But if you don't tell me about him, or what you think he is up to, I can't help you. Do you see that?'

She nodded and held the purse tighter.

I took out a yellow legal pad, a black SenseMatic pencil, and made as if I were poised to copy the rush of information she was about to provide. I drew a couple of practice marks on the page. Subliminal prompting. 'I'm ready. Fire away.'

She swallowed.

'Anytime.'

She stared at the floor.

I put the pad on the desk and the pencil on the pad. I put my fingertips together and looked at Jennifer Sheridan through the steeple, and then I looked at the Pinocchio clock that I've got on my wall. It has eyes that swing from side to side as it tocks, and it's always smiling. Happiness is contagious. It was twelve twenty-two, and if I could get down to the deli fast enough, the turkey would still be moist and the baguette would still be edible. I said, 'Maybe you should go to the police, Ms Sheridan. I don't think I can help you.'

She clutched the purse even tighter and gave miserable. 'I can't do that.'

I spread my hands and stood up. 'If your fiancé is in danger, it is better to get in trouble with the police than it is to be hurt or killed.' Twelve twenty-three. 'Try the police, Ms Sheridan. The police can help you.'

'I can't do that, Mr Cole.' The misery turned into fear. 'My fiancé *is* the police.'

'Oh.' Now it was my turn. I sat down.

Jennifer Sheridan opened the purse and took out a 3x5 color snapshot of herself and a tall good-looking kid in a navy blue LAPD summer-weight uniform leaning against a squad car. They were smiling. 'His name is Mark Thurman. He doesn't work uniform anymore. Last year he was chosen for a plainclothes position at the Seventy-seventh Division in South Central Los Angeles.'

'What kind of plainclothes?'

'They call it a REACT team. They monitor career criminals and try to stop them before they hurt people. It's an elite unit, and he was the youngest man chosen. He was very proud of that.' She seemed proud of it, too. 'Everything was fine for the first few months, but then he changed. It happened almost overnight.'

'What kind of change?' I was thinking Kevin McCarthy. *Invasion of the Body Snatchers.*

'He became anxious and scared and secretive. We never keep secrets from each other and now there are things that he won't talk about with me.'

I looked closer at the picture. Thurman had long forearms and a ropey neck and a country boy's smile. He must've been fourteen inches taller than Jennifer Sheridan. I said, 'I know a lot of police officers, Ms Sheridan. Some of them are even my friends. It can be a hard job with unusual hours and you see too much of what's wrong with people. You don't want to go home and chat about it.'

She shook her head, telling me that I didn't get it. 'It isn't just him not talking about the job. He was in uniform for three years and I know to expect that. It's the way he acts. We used to talk about getting married, and having children, but we don't anymore. I ask him what's wrong, he says nothing. I say tell me about your day, he says that there's nothing to say. He was never like that before. He's become irritable and snappish.'

'Irritable.'

'That's right.'

'He's irritable, and that's why you think he's involved in crime?'

She gave me exasperated. 'Well, it isn't just that.'

'Have you seen him perform a criminal act, or heard him speak of it, or seen the results of it?'

'No.'

'Has he exhibited signs of an income other than his police salary?'

'No.'

I tapped the desk. 'Sounds like you think he's up to something because he's irritable.'

She gave me more of the impatience. 'You don't understand. Mark and I have known each other since the seventh grade. We fell in love in the ninth grade. That's how long we've been going together. I love him and he loves me and I know him better than anyone else in all the world.'

'All right,' I said. 'Do you have any clues?'

She frowned at me.

'Clues,' I said. 'An overheard snatch of conversation. A subrosa glimpse of a secret bank account. Something that I can use in ascertaining the nature of the crime.' I hadn't used *ascertaining* in three or four weeks.

She said, 'Are you making fun of me?'

I was getting one of those headaches that you get when your blood sugar starts to drop. 'No, I'm trying to make you consider what you want and why you want it. You claim that Mark Thurman is involved in criminal activity, but you have no direction in which to point me. That means that you're asking me to surveil an active-duty police officer. Police officers are paranoid by nature and they move around a lot. This will be expensive.'

She looked uncertain. 'How expensive?'

'Two thousand dollars. In advance.'

You could see her swallow. 'Do you take Visa?'

'I'm afraid not.'

She swallowed a second time. 'That seems an awful lot.'

'Yes,' I said. 'It is.'

She put the photograph of Mark Thurman back in her purse and took out a red doeskin wallet. She dug in the wallet and got a faraway look like she was working with numbers. Then she pulled out two twenties and put them on my desk. 'I can pay you forty dollars now, and forty dollars per month for forty-nine months.'

I said, 'Jesus Christ, Ms Sheridan.'

She clenched her jaw and brought out another ten. 'All right. Fifty dollars.'

I raised my hands, got up, and went to the glass doors that lead out to the little balcony. The doors that came with the office were aluminum sliders, but a couple of years ago I had them changed to a nice set of double-glazed French doors with brass handles. I opened the doors, set them so that the breeze wouldn't blow them closed, and that's when I saw two guys sitting across the street in a brown unmarked sedan four stories below. A tall guy with shaggy, thick-cut hair sat behind the steering wheel and a shorter guy with a ragged face slouched in the passenger's side. The tall guy had long forearms and a ropey neck and looked a lot like Mark Thurman. Sonofagun. I turned away from the doors and looked at Jennifer Sheridan. Nope. She didn't know that they were out there. 'Mark work today?'

She looked surprised that I'd ask. 'That's right. He works Monday through Friday, from eleven until six.'

'He let his hair grow since he went to REACT?'

Jennifer Sheridan smiled, trying to figure me. 'Why, yes. He had to, for the undercover work.'

Thurman, all right.

I walked back to the desk and looked at her. You could see how much she loved him. You could see that she trusted him, and that she'd never think that maybe he was following her. I said, 'Do you and Mark live together?'

She made a tiny headshake and a bit of the red again touched her cheeks. 'We've talked about it, but we decided to wait.'

'Uh-huh. So you believe that he's hiding something, and you want me to find out what.'

'Yes.'

'What if I find out that Mark Thurman isn't who you think he is? What if I look, and I find something that changes the way that you feel about him, and the way that he feels about you?'

Jennifer Sheridan made a little move with her mouth, and then she cleared her throat. 'Mark is a good man, Mr Cole. If he's involved in something, I know it's not because he wants to be. I trust him in that, and I love him. If we find out that he is in trouble, we will help him.' She had thought about these things. Probably lay awake with them.

11

I went back to the doors and pretended to adjust them. Thurman and the other guy were still in the sedan. Thurman had been looking up, but ducked back when he realized that I had come back onto the balcony. Fast moves are bad. Another couple of years on the job and he'd know better. You just sort of casually look away. Shift the eyes without moving the head. Eye contact can kill you.

I went back into the office and sat, and Jennifer Sheridan said, 'Will you help me, Mr Cole?'

I said, 'Why don't we do this? I'll nose around and see if there is anything worth pursuing. If there is, I will work for you and pursue it. If there isn't, I will return your money, and you won't owe me anything.'

Jennifer Sheridan said, 'That will be fine,' and then she smiled. Her tanned skin dimpled and her white teeth gleamed and there came a quality of warmth to the room as if a small sun had risen from beneath my desk. I found myself returning the smile. I wrote a receipt in her name for the amount of forty dollars, and noted that it was paid against a due balance of one thousand, nine hundred sixty dollars, payable in monthly installments. I gave back the extra ten with her receipt, then put the forty dollars into my wallet. My wallet didn't feel any fatter than it had without the forty. Maybe if I went down to the bank and had the forty changed to ones, it would feel like more.

Jennifer Sheridan took a folded sheet of paper from the huge purse and handed it to me. 'This is where Mark lives, and his home phone number, and his license plate, and his badge number. His partner's name is Floyd Riggens. I've met Floyd several times, but I don't like him. He's a mean-spirited man.'

'Okay.' Riggens would be the other guy in the car.

She took back the paper and scribbled something on the back. 'This is where I live and this is my work number. It's a direct line to Mr Beale's office, and I answer his phone, so I'll be the one who picks up when you call.'

'Fine.'

She stood, and I stood with her. She put out her hand. I took it. I think we were in a contest to see who could smile the most. She said, 'Thank you, Mr Cole. This is very important to me.'

'Elvis.'

'Elvis.' She smiled even wider, and then she gathered her things and left. It was twelve forty-six, and I stopped smiling. I sat at my desk and looked at the paper that she had given me with the information about Mark Thurman and herself, and then I put it into the desk's top right-hand drawer along with my copy of the receipt.

I leaned back and I put my feet up, and I wondered why Mark Thurman and his mean-spirited partner Floyd Riggens were following

Jennifer Sheridan while they were on duty. I didn't like the following, but I didn't have very long to wonder about it.

At twelve fifty-two, Mark Thurman and Floyd Riggens came in.

2

They didn't kick the door off its hinges and they didn't roll into the office with their guns out like Crockett and Tubbs used to do on *Miami Vice*, but they didn't bother to knock, either.

The guy I figured for Floyd Riggens came in first. He was ten years older than Thurman and maybe six inches shorter, with a hard, squared-off build and weathered skin. He flashed his badge without looking at me and crossed to Joe Pike's office. I said, 'It's empty.' He didn't pay attention.

Mark Thurman came in after him and went out onto the balcony, like maybe a couple of Colombian drug lords had ducked out only seconds ago and were hanging off the side of the building with grappling hooks and Thurman wanted to find them. He looked bigger in person than he had in the pictures, and he was wearing faded khaki fatigue pants and a red jersey that said LANCASTER HIGH VARSITY. Number 34. He looked younger, too, with a kind of rural innocence that you rarely find in cops, sort of like *Dragnet* as played by Ronnie Howard. He didn't look like a guy who'd be into crime, but then, what does a criminal look like? Boris Badenov?

Riggens came out of Pike's office and scowled at me. His eyes were red and swollen and I could smell the scotch on his breath even though he was standing on the other side of the chairs. Hmm. Maybe he didn't have the weathered look, after all. Maybe he had the drunk look. Riggens said, 'We need to talk about the girl.'

I gave him innocent. 'Girl?'

Riggens squinted like I'd spit on his shirt and grinned out the corner of his mouth. Mean-spirited. 'Oh, I like it when jerks like you get stupid. It's why I stay on the job.'

'What are you drinking to get eyes like that – Aqua Velva?'

Riggens was wearing a baggy beachcomber's shirt with the tail out, but you could still make out the butt of his piece riding high on his right hip. He reached up under the shirt and came out with a Sig 9-mil and said, 'Get your ass against the goddamned wall.'

I said, 'Come on.'

Mark Thurman came in off the balcony and pushed the gun down. 'Jesus Christ, Floyd, take it easy. He doesn't know what this is about.'

'He keeps dicking with me, he won't make it long enough to find out.'

I said, 'Let me guess. You guys work for Ed McMahon and you've come to tell me that I've won the Publisher's Clearing House sweepstakes for a million bucks.'

Riggens tried to lift his gun but Thurman kept the pressure on. Riggens's face went red to match his eyes and the veins swelled in his forehead, but Thurman was a lot stronger, and sober, so it wasn't much of a problem. I wondered if Riggens acted like this on the street, and if he did, how long he had been getting away with it. Stuff like this will get you killed. Thurman said, 'Stop it, Floyd. That's not why we're here.'

Riggens fought it a little longer, then gave it up, and when he did Thurman let go. Riggens put the Sig away and made a big deal with the hand moves and the body language to let everyone know he was disgusted. 'You want to do it, then do it, and let's get out of here. This asshole says she wasn't even here.' He went to the couch and sat down. Petulant.

Thurman sort of shook his head, like he couldn't figure Riggens out, like he had tried for a long time and was maybe getting tired of trying. He turned back to me. 'My name is Mark Thurman. This is my partner, Floyd Riggens. We know she was up here because Floyd followed her up.'

I glanced at Floyd again. He was staring at the Pinocchio clock. 'Maybe Floyd got confused. There's an insurance office across the hall. Maybe she went there.'

Floyd said, 'Okay, she wasn't here. We're not here, either, you want to play it that way. You fell asleep and you're dreaming all this.' He got up and went to the clock for a closer look. 'Hurry up, Mark. I don't wanna spend the day.' Like a little kid.

Thurman looked nervous, but maybe he was just uncomfortable. His partner was looking bad and that made him look bad. He said, 'We called in about you and the word is that you're a straight shooter, so I thought we should talk.'

'Okay.'

'Jennifer and I are having some trouble.'

'You mean, this isn't official police business?'

Riggens went back to the couch and sat down. 'It could be, you want. We could have information that you been up to something. We could even find a snitch to back it up. That would look real good for your license.'

Thurman's face went dark and he said, 'Shut up, Floyd.'

Riggens spread his hands. What?

Thurman came to the front of my desk and sat in the right-side director's chair. He leaned forward when he sat and stared at me the way you stare at someone when you're trying to figure out how to say something you don't want to say. 'I'm here for personal reasons, and they have to do with me and Jennifer. You want to pretend she wasn't here, that's fine. I understand that. But we still have to talk. See?'

'Okay.'

Riggens went, 'Jesus Christ, get on with it.'

Thurman's face clouded again and he once more looked at Riggens and said, 'If you don't shut the fuck up, I'm going to clock you, Floyd.' Enough's enough.

Riggens frowned and crossed his arms and drew himself into kind of a knot. Drunk enough to be pissed, but sober enough to know that he'd stepped over the line. These guys were something.

Thurman turned back to me and sat there, his mouth working. He was having trouble with it, and he didn't strike me as a guy who'd have trouble with a lot. He made a little blowing move with his lips, then laced his fingers and leaned forward. 'We followed her because she's been pressing me pretty hard about some stuff, and I knew she'd try something like this. She's pretty strong-willed, and she gets a head on about things, if you know what I mean.'

Riggens made a snorting sound, then recrossed his arms and put his feet up on the little coffee table I have in front of the couch. I didn't like it, but I didn't say anything.

Thurman said, 'Jennifer and I have been going together since we were kids. I've been acting kind of distant with her for the past couple of months and I haven't told her why, and Jennifer has it figured that I'm mixed up in something. I know that's what she talked to you about, because that's what she talks to me about. Only, that isn't it at all.'

'No?'

'No.' Mark Thurman looked down at his feet and worked his jaw harder and then he looked up at me. 'I've got another girlfriend.'

I stared at him.

'I knew that if she hired someone, they'd find out and tell her, and I don't want that. Do you see?'

I said, 'Another woman.'

He nodded.

'You've been seeing another woman and Jennifer knows something is up, but she doesn't know what. And you're trying to head me off so I won't blow the whistle.'

He nodded again.

Riggens uncurled his arms and pushed up from the couch. 'You don't need to know anything else. The word is that you're a straight shooter and we're looking for a break. It was me I'd slap the bitch down and

16

move on, but he doesn't want to play it that way. Why don't you give the kid a hand?'

I said, 'Jesus Christ, Riggens, why'd you come along? Moral support?'

Riggens said, 'No one's trying to muscle you, smart guy. Everyone's playing straight up.' Riggens jerked his head toward Thurman. 'Tell him we're playing straight up.'

Mark Thurman looked back at me, only now there was a lost quality to his eyes. 'I didn't want you telling Jennifer. When it comes, it's got to come from me.' He was leaning forward so far I thought he'd fall out of the chair. 'Do you see?'

'Sure. I see.'

'It's personal. That's how it should stay.'

'Sure.'

Riggens said, 'No one's asking you to turn down the fee. Just play it smart. Do us the favor and someday you'll get a payback.'

'But I can keep the fee.'

'No problem.'

I looked at Thurman. 'Some right guy you've got as a partner, Thurman, saying it's okay for me to stiff your girlfriend.'

Riggens said, 'Fuck you,' and banged out. Thurman sat in the director's chair, not saying anything, and then he pushed himself up. He was twenty-four years old and he looked like a baby. When I was twenty-four I looked a million years old. Vietnam. He said, 'You do what you want, Cole. No one's telling you what to do. But I'm asking you not to tell her what I said. I get ready, I should be the one tells her. Shouldn't I?'

'Sure.'

'I just got to work this out, that's all I'm saying.' Like he was in the principal's office, like he had been caught throwing eggs at the class geek's house, and now he was ashamed of it. He went to the door. Riggens was already down the hall.

I said, 'Thurman.'

He stopped and looked back at me with his right hand on the handle.

'Why don't you just tell her?'

He didn't answer. He stood there, sort of staring, like he didn't know what to say. Maybe he didn't.

I said, 'She didn't say anything to me about crime. She said that she thought you were seeing another woman. She said that she always knew you were that way.'

Mark Thurman went as red as Jennifer Sheridan when I told her that I hadn't been making a pass. He stared at me with the sort of look you'd have if you were in a hurry one day and backed out your drive without looking and ran over a child. Like someone had pushed an ice spike through your heart. He stared at me like that, and then he went out. He didn't close the door.

I went to the little balcony and stood back from the rail and watched the street. Mark Thurman and Floyd Riggens came out of my building, climbed back into the brown sedan, and drove away. Neither of them spoke, as far as I could tell, and neither of them looked particularly happy. It was six minutes after one, and it looked as if my case was solved.

I closed the glass doors, sat on my couch, and thought about what I might say when I was inducted into the Detective's Hall of Fame. Perhaps they would bill me as *Elvis Cole, World's Fastest Detective*. Wouldn't Jennifer Sheridan be pleased. She could say *I knew him when*. At six minutes after one, Jennifer Sheridan would be sitting in Marty Beale's outer office, not expecting a phone call in which the detective that she had hired only moments before would crush her heart with one fell blow, service with a smile, *thank you, ma'am, and the bill is in the mail*. Of course, since I had made such a big deal to Jennifer Sheridan about her lack of proof, she might enquire as to mine, and I had none. I had only Mark Thurman's word, and maybe he had lied. People do.

I put aside my thoughts of the Hall of Fame and called a guy I know named Rusty Swetaggen. For twenty-four years he drove a black-and-white in and around the city of Los Angeles, then his wife's father died and he inherited a pretty nice restaurant in Venice, about four blocks from the beach. He likes it better than being a cop. He said, 'Rusty's.'

I made hissing and cracking noises into the phone. 'I'm calling from the new car phone. Pretty good, huh?'

Rusty Swetaggen said, 'Bullshit, you got a car phone.' Then he yelled at someone in the background. 'It's the big-time op, making like he's got a car phone.' Someone said something and then he came back on the line. 'Emma says hey.'

'Hey back. I need to find out about an officer and I don't want him to know.'

'This guy active duty?'

'Yeah. His name is Mark Thurman. He works a REACT team out of the Seventy-seventh.'

Rusty didn't say anything. I guess he was writing. Then he said, 'Is this guy dirty?' He didn't like asking. You could hear it in his voice. You ride the black-and-white for twenty-four years and you don't like asking.

'I want to find out. Can you do this for me?'

'Sure, Elvis. I'd do anything for you. You know that.'

'I know. I'll be by in a couple of hours. That okay?'

'Fine.'

Rusty Swetaggen hung up, and then I hung up.

I took the shoulder holster out of my bottom left drawer and put it on. It's a nice brushed-leather Bianchi rig that cost a fortune, but it's comfortable, and it's made for the Dan Wesson .38 revolver that I carry.

18

Stylish detectives often carry automatics, but I have never been a slave to fashion.

I took the Dan Wesson out of its drawer and seated it into the shoulder holster and then I covered the works with a light gray cotton sport coat. It looks great over my black-and-maroon Hawaiian beach shirt, and is ideal for hiding firearms in L.A.'s summer weather. I took the Watkins, Okum, & Beale stationery out of my desk, put it in the inside pocket of the sport coat, then called the deli and asked them if they still had my turkey and Swiss on baguette. They did.

I walked the four flights down to the deli, ate my sandwich at a little table that they have by the door, then left to find out whether or not LAPD Officer Mark Thurman was telling the truth, or telling a lie.

Either way, Jennifer Sheridan wouldn't like it.

3

Driving along Santa Monica Boulevard through West Hollywood and Beverly Hills is a fine thing to be doing in late March, just at the end of the rainy season. It was warmer than it should have been, with highs in the mid-eighties and mare's-tail cirrus streaking the sky with feathery bands, and there were plenty of men in jogging shorts and women in biking pants and Day-Glo headbands. Most of the men weren't jogging and most of the women weren't biking, but everyone looked the part. That's L.A.

At a traffic light in Westwood I pulled up next to a woman in pristine white biking pants and a white halter workout top sitting astride a white Japanese racing bike. I made her for Jennifer Sheridan's age, but maybe she was older. The line of her back was clean and straight, and she leaned to the right, her right toe extended down to kiss the street, her left toe poised on its pedal. Her skin was smooth and tanned, and her legs and body were lovely. She wore a ponytail and bronze-tinted sunglasses. I gave her the big smile. A little Dennis Quaid. A little Kevin Costner. She stared at me through the bronze lenses and said, 'No.' Then she pedaled away. Hmm. Maybe thirty-nine is older than I thought.

At the western edge of UCLA, I climbed the ramp onto the 405 freeway and headed north into the San Fernando Valley. In another week the smog and haze would build and the sky would be bleached and obscured, but for now the weather was just right for boyfriends tailing girlfriends and girlfriends hiring private eyes to check up on boyfriends and private eyes spending their afternoons on long drives into the valley where they would risk life and limb snooping around police officers' apartments. If Randy Newman were here, he'd probably be singing *I Love L.A.*

I edged off the 405 at Nordhoff and turned west, cruising past the southern edge of Cal State, Northridge, with its broad open grounds and water-conscious landscaping and remnants of once-great orange groves. In the prewar years before freeways and super-highways the valley was mostly orange trees, but after the war the orange groves began to vanish and the valley became a bedroom community of low-cost family housing tracts. When I came to L.A. in the early seventies, there were still small bits of orchard dotted around Encino and Tarzana and Northridge, the trees laid out in geometric patterns, their trunks black with age but their fruit still sweet and brilliant with color. Little by little they have melted away into single-family homes and minimalls with high vacancy rates and high-density apartment complexes, also with high vacancy rates. I miss them. Minimalls are not as attractive as orange trees, but maybe that's just me.

Mark Thurman lived in a converted garage apartment in the northwestern part of the San Fernando Valley, about a mile west of Cal State, Northridge, in an older area with stucco bungalows and clapboard duplexes and mature landscaping. Though the structures are old, the residents are not, and most of the apartments are rented to college students or junior faculty from the university or kids out on their own for the first time. Lots of bikes around. Lots of small foreign cars. Lots of music.

I parked across the street from a flat-topped duplex and looked down the drive. The sheet of Watkins, Okum stationery said that Thurman drove a 1983 blue Ford Mustang as his personal car, but the Mustang wasn't around, and neither was the dark brown cop-mobile. Still out fighting crime, no doubt. Or tailing Jennifer Sheridan. A chain-link fence ran parallel to the drive along a row of eight-foot hedges. About halfway back, a little wrought-iron gate ran from the fence to the duplex, cutting the drive in half. Thurman's converted garage was in the rear yard behind the gate, snuggled against the hedges. A set of sliding glass doors had been installed where the garage door used to hang and someone had built a little sidewalk out of stepping-stones that ran around the side of the place by the hedges. A curtain of vertical blinds was drawn across the glass doors and pulled closed. It was a nice, neat, well-kept place, but it didn't look like the kind of place a cop taking down heavy graft would keep. Of course, maybe Mark Thurman was smart, and the outward appearance of his home was just a dodge to throw off unsuspecting PIs. Maybe the inside of the place looked like Uncle Scrooge's money bin and the walls were lined with cash and bricks of gold. Only one way to find out.

I got out of the Corvette, strolled up the drive, and let myself through the little wrought-iron gate. A young German shepherd was lying by the gate beneath the hedges next door. He watched me come and when I let myself through the gate he lifted his head. I said, 'Woof.' He got up and walked with me. Police dog. If Thurman came home I'd have to go over the fence. Hope he didn't bite.

There were three young women lying on towels in the little yard that separated the duplex from the guest house. One was on her belly, the other two were on their backs, and the one nearest to me was up on an elbow, adjusting a radio. U-2. Nobody was wearing very much in the way

21

of clothes, and you could smell the suntan oil. The one with the radio saw me first and made a little gasping noise. I said, 'Hi, ladies. Is Mark around?' Elvis Cole, the Smooth Detective.

The one with the radio relaxed and the other two looked over. The one without the radio was wearing little round sunglasses and the one on her belly smiled. The two on their backs were brunette, the one on her belly a blonde.

The one with the radio said, 'He's at work.'

I glanced at my watch and made a big deal out of looking disappointed. 'He said he'd meet me here. I guess he got hung up.'

The one on her belly said, 'Are you a cop, too?'

I said, 'Do I look like a cop?'

The three of them nodded.

I spread my hands. 'I'd do great undercover, hunh?'

The one on her belly said, 'I don't know. You might.'

The other two laughed.

The one with the little round glasses covered her mouth and said, 'Ohmygod, do you know who he looks like? He looks like Mel Gibson in *Lethal Weapon*. Don't you think so?'

I was liking the one with the glasses just fine. Maybe thirty-nine wasn't so old after all.

The one with the radio said, 'If Mark told you he'd be here, he's probably on his way. He's pretty good about that kind of stuff.'

I said, 'I've just got to drop something off. You think he'd mind?'

Radio said, 'You could leave it with us.'

'Couldn't do that. It's business-related. And it's sort of a surprise.'

The one on her belly looked interested. 'Evidence.'

The one with the little round sunglasses said, 'Allie likes cops. She wants to see your gun.'

Allie slugged Sunglasses in the leg, and all three of them laughed.

The one with the radio said, 'Go ahead. Mark's cool. He keeps a spare key in a little Sucrets box to the left of the landing behind a plant pot.'

'Thanks.'

The German shepherd was waiting for me when I went around the side of the guest house, and followed me to the door. The Sucrets box and the key were exactly where Radio said they'd be. Some neighbors, hunh? I took out the key and let myself in. The German shepherd sat on his haunches and stared after me and whined. Helluva police dog, too.

Mark Thurman's garage had been converted into a pretty nice apartment. The side door opened into a living room, and from the door you could see the kitchen and another door that led to a bedroom and a bath. A brown cloth couch rested against the west wall and a shelving unit stood against the north. The east wall was the glass doors. A CD player and a Sony TV and a VCR and about a zillion CDs were in the wall unit, but the CD player and the VCR were low-end Pioneer and neither was a bank breaker, even on a police officer's take-home. There was an overstuffed chair at either end of the couch, and a coffee table of bright white pine that matched the wall unit. He would've bought the set from one of those discount places. Imported, they would have told him. Danish. There wasn't a sea of gold coins that you could dive into, or mounds of money bags scattered around, but I hadn't yet seen the bedroom. One shouldn't jump to conclusions.

I glanced through the kitchen, then went into the bedroom. It was small, with a single window and a door that led into the bath, and it wasn't any more lavishly appointed than the living room. I went into the bath first, then came back into the bedroom. There was a king-sized bed without a headboard, a nightstand, and a dresser with a large curved mirror that didn't match any of the other furniture. Garage sale. The bed was made and neat, and the spread was pulled tight across its surface. I went through the dresser drawers and then I looked under the bed. Under the bed there was a red Lily of France brassiere. Thirty-six C. I pulled it out and looked at it, but there was nothing to suggest the owner. Jennifer Sheridan might be a thirty-six C, but I hadn't asked and I hadn't thought about it. I put the brassiere back where I had found it, and then I looked in the nightstand. There was a New Balance shoe box in the large cabinet at the bottom of the nightstand with Mark Thurman's diploma from the police academy, a couple of letters from someone named Todd, and Thurman's credit card and banking receipts. Thurman held a checking account and savings account with Cal Fed, one MasterCard, one Visa card, plus gas cards from both Chevron and Mobil. He kept the billing statements from the Visa and MasterCard in a legal-sized envelope marked *VISA*. Neither card showed recent purchases for anything out of the ordinary, but the most recent bill was three weeks old. His savings account held $3,416.28. I copied the account numbers for the Visa and the MasterCard and then I put the box back as I had found it and went to the closet.

A summer-weight LAPD uniform and a set of navy winters hung with the sport shirts and the jeans and the slacks. They hadn't been worn in a while. A single blue suit looked like it didn't get worn much, either. There were shoes and a spinning rod and a set of golf clubs that looked so old they had probably been handed down from father to son. Above the clothes, a high shelf ran around the perimeter of the closet, weighted down with old issues of *Sports Illustrated*, a motorcycle helmet that looked like it had never been used, and a cardboard box containing an outsized scrapbook with yellowed clippings of Mark Thurman playing football and baseball and basketball and track for the Lancaster Wildcats. Four letter man. Mark had played fullback and strong side linebacker, going both ways for sixty minutes a game. There were newspaper photos of Mark in action, and Mark celebrating with teammates, but there were also snapshots of Mark alone and Mark with Jennifer and Jennifer alone, here Mark eating ice cream at the Tastee Freeze, here Jennifer posing shyly in the empty bleachers, here the two of them at the Sophomore Prom and the Junior-Senior and at graduation. I don't know how old they were in the earliest photographs, but they looked like babies. You got the feeling that Jennifer had taken the photos of Mark and Mark had taken the photos of Jennifer, and that there had never been anyone else in their lives, that they had been complete and whole since that moment when they'd fallen in love in the ninth grade, and, in some wonderful way, always would be. But maybe not. The clippings and the photographs began in ninth grade and ended with graduation. Maybe all those years of oneness had become oppressive to Mark and he had decided that there had to be more and, like the photos in the scrapbook, the oneness had to end. Maybe he had told me the truth. Maybe, after all those years, it was finally over.

I put the scrapbook back as I had found it and finished going through his things, but there were no keys to a newly purchased Porsche, no hastily scrawled map to bags of money buried in the high desert, and no unexplained series of numbers for the Swiss accounts. There was only the thirty-six C. That's the way it goes, sometimes.

I made sure the rooms were like I had found them, then I let myself out, locked the door, and went around to the drive. The German shepherd was gone. So was Allie. The other two were still on their backs. I said, 'Allie get bored?'

The one with the radio said, 'She said she was hot. She went in to cool off.'

The one with the little round glasses said, 'What took you so long?'

'Pit stop.' Elvis Cole, Man of a Thousand Lies. 'You guys know Mark's friend, Jennifer?'

'Sure.'

'She come around lately?'

'Not for a couple of weeks, but she used to.'

The one with the glasses said, 'She's so flat. I don't know what he sees in her.'

The one with the radio said, 'Puh-lease, Brittany.' Brittany. Whatever happened to the women's movement?

I said, 'Mark said he's got another friend. Have you met her?'

The one with the radio said, 'We haven't seen her.'

Brittany sat up and wrapped her arms around her knees. 'You mean he's available?'

I shrugged.

Michael Bolton started singing about how much being in love hurt and the one with the radio turned it up. Brittany lay back and stretched,

24

making a thing out of lifting her ribs and showing her body. She looked thoughtful. Making plans, no doubt. Devising strategies.

The one with the radio said, 'Let me get Allie. She wanted to say good-bye.' Then she got up and went into the house. Brittany was mumbling to herself and Allie was probably mumbling, too. I left before they got back.

Women in heat are frightening to behold.

4

I let myself out through the little gate, walked back to my car, and drove two blocks to a 7-Eleven where I used their pay phone to call a friend of mine who works in the credit department of Bank of America. I gave her Mark Thurman's name, social security number, and account numbers from both his Visa and MasterCard. I told her that I wanted to know if the charge totals for the month exceeded two thousand dollars and, if they did, how many separate purchases exceeded five hundred dollars and where and when they had been made. I also told her that I wanted to know if Thurman had applied for or received any additional credit cards during the past year. She asked me who the hell did I think I was, calling up out of the blue and asking for all of that? I told her that I was the guy who was going to take her to see Sting at the Greek Theater, then take her to dinner at Chinois on Main afterwards. She asked if tomorrow was okay, or did I want the information later tonight? She called me Chickie when she said it.

I drove back to the 405, then went south, back across the floor of the valley, then through the Sepulveda Pass and into the basin, heading toward Venice and Rusty Swetaggen's place. I left the freeway at Wilshire and turned west to San Vicente Boulevard in Brentwood. It would've been faster to stay on the 405, but San Vicente was nicer, with interesting shops and elegant cafes and palatial homes that somehow seemed attainable, as if the people within them got there by working hard, and were still the type of folks who would give you a smile if you passed them on the sidewalk. Sort of like the Cleavers or the Ricardos.

Bike paths bordered the east- and westbound lanes, and an expansive center island with a row of mature coral trees divided the traffic. Bicyclists and joggers and power walkers flock to San Vicente for its pleasant surroundings and two-mile straightaway from Brentwood to the ocean. Even at midday, the bike paths were crowded and runners pounded along the center island. A man who might've been Pakistani ran with a dust mask, and a red-haired woman with a Rottweiler stopped to let the dog piddle on a coral tree. The woman kept her legs pumping as she waited for the dog. Both of them looked impatient.

Brentwood became Santa Monica and the nice homes became nice apartment buildings, and pretty soon you could smell the ocean and pretty soon after that you could see it. Santa Monica has rent control, and many of the apartment buildings had little signs fastened to their walls that said PEOPLE'S REPUBLIC OF SANTA MONICA. Protest by the apartment owners.

San Vicente ended at Ocean, which runs along a sixty-foot bluff separating Santa Monica proper from the sand and the water and Pacific Coast Highway. Most of the joggers turned back at Ocean, but most of the riders turned left to continue on the bike paths that run along the top of the bluff. I turned with the riders. The top of the bluff sports green lawns and roses and a comfortable parklike setting. There are benches, and some of the time you can sit and watch the ocean and the volleyball games down below on the beach. The rest of the time the benches are used by the thousands of homeless who flock to Santa Monica because of its mild climate. Santa Monica encourages this. The People's Republic.

A block and a half up from the Venice boardwalk I aced out a flower delivery van for a parking spot, fed the meter, and walked two blocks inland to Rusty Swetaggen's place between a real estate office and an architectural firm where they specialized in building houses on unbuildable building sites. You could eat at Rusty's during the day, and people did, but mostly they went there to drink. The real estate salespeople were all politically correct women who believed in Liz Claiborne and the architects were all young guys in their thirties who dressed in black and wore little round spectacles. Everyone was thin and everyone looked good. That's the way it is in Venice. Rusty Swetaggen is a short, wide guy with a body like a bulldog and a head like a pumpkin. If you didn't know that he owned the place, you'd think he was there to rob it. Venice is like that, too.

Six years ago, Rusty and Emma's fifteen-year-old daughter, Katy, took up with a guy from the Bay Area who introduced her to the joys of professional loop production and crack-inspired public sex performance. Katy ran away and Rusty asked me to help. I found her in the basement of a three-bedroom house in the San Francisco hills, sucking on a crack bong to kill the pain of the beating that her Bay Area hero had just given her because she wasn't quite enthusiastic enough in the multiple-partner sex she'd just been forced to have in front of a Hitachi 3000 Super-Pro video camera. I got Katy and all copies of the fourteen sex loops she'd made in the previous three days. None of her performances had as yet been distributed. I destroyed the tapes and brought Katy to a halfway house I know in Hollywood. After eight months of hard family therapy, Katy moved back home, returned to high school, and began to put her life on track. She met a guy named Kevin in a support group during her second year of college, and fourteen months later they were married. That was seven months ago, and now she was finishing a business degree at Cal State, Long Beach. Rusty Swetaggen cried for a week after I brought her back, said he'd never be able to repay me, and refused to let me or anyone who was with me pay for a drink or for anything else that he might provide. I stopped going to Rusty's because all the free drinks were embarrassing.

Rusty was sitting at the bar, reading a copy of *Newsweek*, when I walked in. It was twenty-six minutes past two, but the place was still crowded with the lunch-hour rush. The real estate salespeople and the architects were vying for bar space with a lot of businessmen sporting bow ties and very short hair. The real estate people were getting the best of it. More practice, I guess. I pushed in beside Rusty and said, 'I can't believe a guy with your money hangs around the job. I had your bucks, I'd be on the beach in Maui.'

Rusty squinted at the kid who worked the bar and said, 'It's a cash business, Hound Dog. You don't watch'm, they'll rob you blind.'

The kid showed Rusty his middle finger without looking up. 'I don't have to steal it. I'm going to own it one day.' The kid's name was Kevin. Rusty's son-in-law.

Rusty shook his head and looked back at me. 'The day I get any respect around here I'll drop dead and be buried.'

I said, 'Eat the food around here and it'll happen sooner rather than later.'

Rusty Swetaggen laughed so hard that an architect looked over and frowned.

Kevin said, 'You want a Falstaff, Elvis?'

'Sure.'

Rusty told him to bring it to the table and led me to an empty window booth where someone had put a little *Reserved* sign. People were waiting by the maitre d', but Rusty had saved the booth.

After Kevin had brought the beer, I said, 'You get anything on my guy?'

Rusty hunkered over the table. 'This guy I talked to, he says the people from the Seventy-seventh like to hang at a bar called Cody's over by LAX. It's a shitkicker place. They got dancers in little chicken-wire cages. They got secretaries go in to get picked up. Like that.'

'Is Thurman a regular?'

'He didn't give it to me as a fact, but a REACT unit is a tight unit, sort of like SWAT or Metro. They do everything together, and that's where they've been hanging.'

'You got the address?'

He told me and I wrote it down.

'Your guy know if Thurman is mixed up in anything dirty?'

Rusty looked pained, like he was letting me down. 'I couldn't push it, Hound Dog. Maybe I could've gotten more, but you want Mr Tact. The rest is going to take a couple days.'

'Thanks, Rusty. That's enough for now.'

I finished the Falstaff and took out my wallet. Rusty covered my hand with his. 'Forget it.'

I said, 'Come on, Rusty.'

Rusty's hand squeezed. 'No.' The squeeze got harder and Rusty's jagged teeth showed and suddenly the pumpkin head looked like a jack-o'-lantern from hell and you could see what had kept Rusty Swetaggen alive and safe for twenty-four years in a black-and-white. It was there for only a second and then it was gone, and he gently pushed my wallet toward me. 'You don't owe me anything, Elvis. I'm glad to help you, and I will always help you in any way I can. You know that.' There was something in his voice and his eyes and the way he held his hand that said that my not paying was profoundly important, as profound as anything had been or ever would be in his life.

I put the wallet away and stood. 'Okay, Rusty. Sure.'

He looked apologetic. 'I've got a couple more calls to make, and I'm waiting to hear from a guy. You want tact.'

'Sure.'

'You hungry? We got a pretty good halibut today.' Like nothing would make him happier than to feed me, to give to me.

'I'll see you around, Rusty. Thanks.'

One hour and forty minutes later I parked in a McDonald's lot about three-quarters of a mile from LAX and walked across the street to Cody's Saloon. Mid-afternoon was late for lunch and early for quitting time, but a dozen men were lining the bar and sipping cold beer out of plain glasses. There weren't any female real estate agents and none of the guys at the bar looked like architects, but you never know. Maybe they were politically incorrect and wanted to keep it a secret. There was a big sign on the roof of a neon cowgirl riding a bucking horse. The cowgirl looked sort of like a cheerleader from Dallas. Maybe she was politically incorrect, too.

A young guy with a lot of muscles was behind the bar, talking with a couple of women in skimpy cheerleader outfits who were hanging around at the waitress station. A red-haired woman in an even skimpier outfit danced without enthusiasm in a chicken-wire cage behind the bar. Neither the bartender nor the waitresses were looking at the dancer, and neither were most of the guys lining the bar. Guess it's tough to get motivated with the chicken wire. They were playing Dwight Yoakam.

I went to a little table across from the dancer's cage and one of the waitresses came over with her little pad. I ordered another Falstaff. When you've got a forty-dollar retainer, the sky's the limit.

29

When she came back with it, I said, 'What time do things pick up?' I gave her the nice smile. The Kevin Costner.

She smiled back and I saw her eyes flick to my hands. Nope. No wedding ring. I made the smile wider. She said, 'Mostly after dinner. We get a lot of cops in here and they don't get off until later.'

I nodded. 'You know an officer named Mark Thurman?'

She tried to remember. 'What's he look like?'

'Big. Like a jock. He probably comes around with a guy named Floyd Riggens. They work together.'

Now she remembered and her face grew hard. 'I know Floyd.' Floyd must be a real pip all the way around.

I grinned like it was an old joke. 'That Floyd is something, isn't he?'

'Uh-huh.' She wasn't seeing much humor in it.

'What time do they usually get here?'

'I don't know. Maybe eight. Something like that.' Like she was getting tired of talking about it. Maybe even pissed. Floyd must be something, all right. 'Look, I've got to get back to work.'

'Sure.'

She went back to the bar and I sipped the beer and pretty soon I ordered another. There didn't seem to be a lot to do until eight o'clock, so sipping Falstaff seemed like a good way to pass the time.

Dwight Yoakam stopped and Hank Williams, Jr, came on and pretty soon the day-shift waitresses left and the night shift cranked up the Garth Brooks and the Kentucky Headhunters. The night-shift dancers were younger and moved better in the cage, but maybe that was because of the music. Or maybe it just seemed that way because of the Falstaff. Maybe if you drank enough Falstaff your personal time scale would grind to a stop and everyone around you would move faster and faster until they looked like a Chip'n Dale cartoon running at fast forward and you looked like a still picture frozen in time. Maybe they would continue to age but you would stay young and pretty soon they'd be dead and you'd have the last laugh. That Falstaff is something, isn't it? Maybe I was just drunk. Occupational hazard.

By seven o'clock the crowd had grown and I didn't want to be there if Riggens or Thurman walked in early, so I paid for the beer, went back to the McDonald's, and bought a couple of cheeseburgers to eat in the car.

At fourteen minutes after eight, Mark Thurman's blue Ford Mustang turned into Cody's parking lot. There were three other people in the car. A brown-haired woman was sitting in the front passenger seat beside Thurman. Riggens and an overweight blonde were shoehorned into the back. The overweight blonde was loud and laughing and pulling at Riggens's pants as they got out of the car. The brown-haired woman was tall and slender and looked like a thirty-six C. They walked across the parking lot, Riggens and the blonde together, Thurman and the brunette together, and then the four of them went into the bar.

I sat in my car for a long time after they disappeared, smelling the McDonald's and tasting the beer and watching the neon cowgirl blink. My head hurt and I was tired from all the sitting, but I wasn't anxious to get home. Getting home meant going to bed and sleep wouldn't come easy tonight. Tomorrow I would have to speak with Jennifer Sheridan and tell her what I had found.

Sleep never comes easy when you're going to break someone's heart.

5

I woke the next morning with a dull ache behind my right eye and the sound of finches on my deck. I have a little A-frame off Woodrow Wilson Drive in Laurel Canyon, in the hills above Hollywood. I don't have a yard because the A-frame is perched on a hillside, but I've got a deck, and a nice view of the canyon. A woman I know gave me a build-it-yourself bird-feeder kit for Christmas, so I built it, and hung it from the eave of my roof high enough to keep the birds safe from my cat. But the birds scratch the seed out of the feeder, then fly down to the deck to eat the seed. They know there's a cat, but still they go down to pick at the seed. When you think about it, people are often like this, too.

I rolled out of bed, pulled on a pair of shorts, then went downstairs and out onto the deck. The finches flew away in a gray, fluttery cloud.

I did twelve sun salutes from the hatha-yoga to loosen my muscles, then moved to the tai chi, and then to the tae kwon do, first the Tiger and Crane *katas*, and then the Dragon and Eagle. As I worked, the finches returned to eat and watch as if I were now elemental to their world and no longer a threat. I worked for the better part of an hour, driving through the *katas* faster and faster, breathing deep to well my energy, then unloading that energy with long explosive moves until my muscles burned and the sweat spotted the deck as if there had been a passing rain shower. I finished with another twelve sun salutes, and then I went in. Penance for the Falstaff. Or maybe just client avoidance.

My cat was staring at the finches. He's large and he's black and he carries his head sort of cocked to the side from when he was head-shot by a .22. He said, 'Naow?'

I shook my head. 'Not now. Got a call to make.'

He followed me into the kitchen and watched while I called my friend at B of A. You know you're serious when you call after an hour's worth of *katas* before you shower. Good thing we don't have smell-o-phones.

I said, 'You get anything out of the ordinary on Mark Thurman?' The detective makes a desperate last-ditch attempt at linking Mark Thurman to Criminal Activity.

'Doesn't look like it. Thurman's outstanding credit charges on both Visa and MasterCard appear typical. Also, he has not applied for higher credit limits nor additional credit cards through any facility in the state of California.' The desperate attempt fails.

'That's it, huh?'

'You sound disappointed.'

'What's disappointment to a hard guy like me?'

'Tell me about it. Are these good seats for Sting, or are we going to camp in the back of the house like last time?'

'Did I mention that you're not aging well?'

She hung up. So did I. These dames.

I took a deep breath, let it out, and then I called Jennifer Sheridan at Marty Beale's office. She answered on the second ring. 'Watkins, Okum, & Beale. Mr Beale's office.'

'This is Elvis Cole. I have uncovered some things, and we should speak.' The cat came over and head-bumped me.

'Well. All right.' She didn't sound happy about it, like maybe she could hear something in my voice. 'Can you tell me now?'

'It's better if we meet for lunch. Kate Mantilini's is very nice.'

More of the pause. 'Is it expensive?'

'I'll pay, Ms Sheridan.'

'Well, I only have the hour.' Nervous.

'I could pick up a couple of cheeseburgers and we could sit on the curb.'

'Maybe the restaurant would be all right. It's only a few blocks from here, isn't it?'

'Three blocks. I'll make a reservation. I will pick you up in front of your building or we can meet at the restaurant.'

'Oh, I don't mind walking.'

'Fine.'

I put the receiver down and the cat looked up at me. He said it again. 'Naow?'

I picked him up and held him close. He was warm against me and his fur was soft and I could feel his heart beat. It was good to hold him. He often doesn't like it, but sometimes he does, and I have found, over the years, that when I most need to hold him, he most often allows it. I like him for that. I think it's mutual.

I scrambled two eggs, put them in his bowl, then went upstairs to shower and dress. At seven minutes after twelve, I walked into Kate Mantilini's and found Jennifer Sheridan already seated. The waiters were smiling at her and an older woman at the next table was talking to her and all the lights of the restaurant seemed focused on her. Some people just have lives like that, I guess. She was wearing a bright blue pant suit with a large ruffled tie and black pumps with little bows on them, and she looked even younger than the first time I'd seen her. Maybe she wasn't twenty-three. Maybe she was seventeen and the people around us would think I was her father. If she looked seventeen and I looked thirty-eight, that would work out. Bummer.

She said, 'I hope this won't take long.'

'It won't.'

I motioned to the waiter and told him that we were in a hurry and would like to order. He said fine and produced a little pad. I ordered the niçoise salad with sesame dressing and an Evian water. Jennifer Sheridan had a hamburger and french fries and a diet Coke. The waiter smiled at me when she ordered. Probably thought I was a lecher. When the waiter had gone, Jennifer Sheridan said, 'What have you found out, Mr Cole?' The mister.

'What I have to tell you will not be pleasant, and I want you to prepare yourself for it. If you'd rather leave the restaurant so that we might go someplace private, we can do that.'

She shook her head.

I said, 'Typically, when an officer is profiting from crime, it shows up in his lifestyle. He'll buy a boat or a time-share or maybe a high-end sound system. Something like that.'

She nodded.

'Mark hasn't. In fact, I checked his bank balances and his credit card expenses and there is no indication that he has received any undue or inordinate sums of money.'

She looked confused. 'What does that mean?'

'It means that he has not been acting strangely because he's involved in crime. There's a different reason. He's seeing another woman.'

Jennifer Sheridan made a little smile and shook her head as if I'd said three plus one is five and she was going to correct me. 'No. That's not possible.'

'I'm afraid that it is.'

'Where's your proof?' Angry now. The older woman at the next table looked over. She frowned when she did. She had a lot of hair and the frown made her look like one of those lizards with the big frill.

I said, 'Five minutes after you left my office yesterday, Mark came to see me. He had been following you. He explained to me that he was seeing someone else, and that he had not been able to bring himself to tell you. He asked me not to tell you this, but my obligation and my loyalty are to you. I'm sorry.' The detective delivers the death blow.

Jennifer Sheridan didn't look particularly devastated, but maybe that was just me.

The waiter brought our food and asked Jennifer Sheridan if she'd like catsup for her french fries. She said yes and we waited as he went to the counter, found a bottle, and brought it back. Neither of us said anything and Jennifer Sheridan didn't look at me until he had gone away. He seemed to know that something was wrong and frowned at me, too. The woman with the big hair was keeping a careful eye on our table.

When the waiter was gone, Jennifer Sheridan ate two french fries, then said, 'For Mark to come to you and make up a story like this, he must be in bigger trouble than I thought.'

I stared at her. 'You think he's making it up?'

'Of course.'

I put down my fork and I looked at the niçoise. It was a good-looking salad with freshly grilled ahi tuna, and I think I would've enjoyed eating it. Jennifer Sheridan had asked me for proof and I told her about my visit from Mark Thurman, but I hadn't told her the rest of it and I hadn't wanted to. I said, 'He's not making this up.'

'Yes, he is. If you knew Mark, you'd know that, too.' Confident.

I nodded, and then I looked at the salad again. Then I said, 'What size bra do you wear?'

She turned a deep shade of crimson. 'Now you're being ugly.'

'I put you at a thirty-four B. I went into Mark's apartment to look through his bank papers and I found a thirty-six C-cup brassiere.'

She looked shocked. 'You broke into his apartment? You went through his things?'

'That's what private detectives do, Ms Sheridan.'

She put her hands in her lap. 'It isn't real.'

'It was a red Lily of France brassiere. I held it. It was real.'

She shook her head. 'That's not what I mean. They knew you would look so they planted it there to make you think he was seeing another woman. What do they call it? A false lead?'

'Later that evening, I staked out a country-and-western bar called Cody's. It's a place where the police officers who work with Mark tend to gather. At a little bit after eight last night, Mark and his partner Floyd Riggens arrived. Mark was with a tall woman with dark brown hair.' I felt bad telling her and the bad feeling was oily and close, but there didn't seem to be any other way.

'And?'

'I wish I had better news, but there it is. I have looked into the matter and this is what I have found. I think my work here is done.'

'You mean you're quitting?'

'The case is solved. There's nothing left to do.'

Jennifer Sheridan's eyes welled and her mouth opened and she let out a long loud wail and began to cry. The woman with the big hair gasped and looked our way and so did most of the other people in the restaurant.

I said, 'Maybe we should leave.'

'I'm all right.' She made loud whooping sounds like she couldn't catch her breath and the tears rolled down her cheeks, making dark tracks from the mascara. The waiter stormed over to the maitre d' and made an angry gesture. The woman with the big hair said something to an elderly man at an adjoining table and the elderly man glared at me. I felt two inches tall.

'Try to see it this way, Jennifer. Mark being involved with another woman is better than Mark being involved in crime. Crime gets you in jail. Another woman is a problem you can work out together.'

Jennifer Sheridan wailed louder. 'I'm not crying because of that.'

'You're not?'

'I'm crying because Mark's in trouble and he needs our help and you're *quitting*. What kind of crummy detective are you?'

I spread my hands. The maitre d' said something to the waiter and the waiter came over.

'Is everything all right, sir?'

'Everything is fine, thank you.'

He looked at Jennifer Sheridan.

She shook her head. 'He's a quitter.'

The waiter frowned and went away. The woman with the big hair made a *tsk*ing sound like she thought they should've done something.

Jennifer said, 'I want to be sure, that's all. If he's seeing this other woman, then who is she? Do they work together? Does he love her? Did you follow them home?'

'No.'

'Then you don't know, do you? You don't know if they slept together. You don't know if he kissed her good night. You don't even know if they left the bar together.'

I rubbed my brow. 'No.'

The woman with the big hair whispered again to the elderly man, then stood and went to three women sitting in a window booth. One of the women stood to meet her.

Jennifer Sheridan was crying freely and her voice was choking. 'He needs us, Mr Cole. We can't leave him like this, we *can't*. You've *got* to help me.'

The woman with the big hair shouted, 'Help her, for God's sake.'

The three women at the window booth shouted, 'Yeah!'

I looked at them and then I looked back at Jennifer Sheridan. She didn't look seventeen anymore. She looked fifteen. And homeless. I dropped my napkin into the niçoise. I'd had maybe three bites. 'You win.'

Jennifer Sheridan brightened. 'You'll stay with it?'

I nodded.

'You see how it's possible, don't you? You see that I'm right about this?'

I spread my hands. The Defeated Detective.

She said, 'Oh, thank you, Mr Cole. Thank you. I knew I could depend on you.' She was bubbling now, just like Judy Garland in *The Wizard of*

Oz. She used her napkin to dry her eyes, but all she did was smear the mascara. It made her look like a raccoon.

The woman with the big hair smiled and the elderly man looked relieved. The waiter and the maitre d' nodded at each other. The three women in the window booth resumed their meal. The restaurant returned to its normal course of lunchtime events, and Jennifer Sheridan finished her hamburger. Everybody was happy.

'Jesus Christ,' I said.

The waiter appeared at my elbow. 'Is something wrong with the niçoise, sir?'

I looked at him carefully. 'Get away from me before I shoot you.'

He said, 'Very good, sir,' and he got.

6

At twelve fifty-five, I gave Jennifer Sheridan a lift the three blocks back to her office and then I headed back toward mine, but I wasn't particularly happy about it. I felt the way you feel after you've given money to a panhandler because the panhandler has just dealt you a sob story that both of you knew was a lie but you went for it anyway. I frowned a lot and stared down a guy driving an ice cream truck just so I could feel tough. If a dog had run out in front of me I probably would've swerved to hit it. Well, maybe not. There's only so much sulking you can do.

The problem was that Jennifer Sheridan wasn't a panhandler and she wasn't running a number on me. She was a young woman in pain and she believed what she believed, only believing something doesn't make it so. Maybe I should spend the rest of the afternoon figuring out a way to convince her. Maybe I could rent one of those high-end, see-in-the-dark video cameras and tape Mark Thurman in the act with the brown-haired woman. Then we could go back to Kate Mantilini's and I could show everyone and what would the woman with the big hair think then? Hmm. Maybe there are no limits to sulking, after all.

I stopped at a Lucky market, bought two large bottles of Evian water, put one in my trunk, then continued on toward my office. Half a block later two guys in a light blue four-door sedan pulled up behind me and I thought I was being followed. A Hispanic guy in a dark blue Dodgers cap was driving and a younger guy with a light blond butch cut was riding shotgun. His was the kind of blond that was so blond it was almost white. I looked at them, but they weren't looking at me, and a block and a half later they turned into a Midas Muffler shop. So much for being followed.

When I got up to my office I opened the French doors off the little balcony, then turned on the radio, and lay down on my couch. KLSX on the airwaves. Howard Stern all morning, classic rock all afternoon. We were well into classic rock and I liked it just fine. Lynyrd Skynyrd. What could be better than that?

It was a cool, clear afternoon and I could be at the beach but instead I was here. Portrait of a detective in a detective's office. When a detective is in a detective's office, shouldn't he be detecting? One of life's imponderables. The problem was that I didn't suspect Mark Thurman of a crime, and crime still didn't look good to me as the answer to Jennifer Sheridan's problems. If you're talking cops and crime, you're talking motive, and I didn't see it. I had been in Thurman's home and I had talked to his fiancée and his neighbors, and the crime part just didn't fit. When you're talking cops and crime, you're talking conspicuous consumption. Cops like to buy cars and they like to buy boats and they like to buy vacation homes and they explain it all by saying that the wife came into a little money. Only Thurman didn't have a wife and, as near as I could tell, he didn't have any of the other things, either. Of course, there could always be something else. Debt and dope are popular motives, but Thurman didn't seem to fit the profile on those, either. I had witnessed events and gathered evidence, and an examination of same had led to certain conclusions which seemed fair to me but not to the client. Maybe the client was crazy. Maybe I was crazy. Maybe the client was just confused and maybe I should have done more to alleviate her confusion, but I had not. Why? Maybe she should be the detective and I should be the client. We couldn't be any more confused than we were now.

Sometime later the phone rang. I got up, went to my desk, and answered it. 'Elvis Cole Detective Agency. We never lie down on the job.'

'Caught you sleeping, huh?' It was Rusty Swetaggen.

'Ha. We never sleep.'

Rusty said, 'I talked to a guy who knows about REACT.'

'Yeah?' I sat in the chair and leaned back and put my feet up. It was quiet in the office. I looked at the water cooler and the couch and the two chairs opposite my desk and the file cabinet and the Pinocchio clock and the closed door to Joe Pike's office. The water machine hummed and little figures of Jiminy Cricket and Mickey Mouse stared back at me and the coffee machine smelled of old coffee, but something was missing.

Rusty said, 'Maybe I shouldn't even mention this.'

'You've rethought our friendship and you want me to pay for lunch?'

'Nothing that important. This guy I talked with, he said something that's maybe a little funny about the REACT guys down at Seventy-seven.'

'Funny.' I have seen these things in my office ten thousand times, and today something was different.

'Yeah. It's like he wouldn't've even mentioned it if I hadn't pushed him, like it's one of those things that doesn't matter unless you're looking, and it probably doesn't matter even then.'

'Okay.' I was only half listening. I picked up the phone and carried it around to the file cabinet and looked back at my desk. Nope. Nothing was off with the desk.

'He says their arrest pattern is maybe a little hinky for the past few months, like maybe these guys aren't making the arrests that they should be, and are making a lot of arrests that they shouldn't.'

'Like what?' I looked at the file cabinet. I looked at the Pinocchio clock.

'REACT was always big on dope and stolen property, and they've always posted high arrest rates, but the past couple of months they haven't been making the big numbers. They've mostly been booking gang-bangers and stickup geeks. It's a different level of crime.'

'We're not just talking Thurman? We're talking the team?'

'Yeah. It's a team thing. What I hear, Thurman's got a great record. That's why he got the early promotion.' I looked at the French doors. I looked at the little refrigerator. Nope.

Rusty said, 'Hell, Elvis, maybe it's just the off-season. I hear anything else, I'll let you know.'

'Sure, Rusty. Thanks.' I looked back at the Pinocchio clock.

Rusty Swetaggen hung up and then I hung up and that's when I saw it. The Pinocchio clock was still. Its eyes weren't moving. It wasn't making the tocking sound. The hands were stopped at eleven-nineteen.

I followed the cord to where it plugs into the wall behind the file cabinet. The plug was in the socket, but not all the way, as if someone had brushed the cord and pulled it partway out of the wall and hadn't noticed. I stood very still and looked around the office and, in the looking, the office now felt strange, as if an alien presence were a part of it. I went back to my desk, opened each drawer and looked at it without touching it. Everything appeared normal and as I had left it. Ditto the things on the desk top. I got up again and opened the file cabinet and looked at the files without touching them and tried to recall if they were positioned as I had last seen them, but I couldn't be sure. I keep all active files in the office cabinet as well as all cases in the current quarter. At the end of every quarter I box the closed files and put them in storage. There were twenty-seven files in the cabinet drawer. Not much if you're the Pinkertons but plenty if you're me. Each file contains a client sheet and day book entries where I've made notes along the way, as well as any photographs or paperwork I accumulate, and a conclusion sheet, which is usually just a copy of the letter I write to the client when the job is over. I hadn't yet made a file for Jennifer Sheridan. I fingered through the twenty-seven files that were there, but nothing seemed to be missing. I closed the cabinet and looked at the little figurines of Jiminy Cricket and Mickey Mouse and Pinocchio on my desk and on top of the file cabinet. Jiminy doffing his top hat had been moved, but Mickey and Minnie riding in a Hupmobile had not. Sonofagun. Someone had searched my office.

I put Jiminy in his proper place, plugged in the Pinocchio clock and set it to the correct time, then went back to my desk and thought about Mark Thurman. The odds were large that whoever had come into my office wasn't Mark Thurman or anyone who knew Thurman, and that the timing had just been coincidental, but the timing still bothered me. I had thought the case was over, but apparently it wasn't. I wasn't exactly sure that the case was still on, but maybe that's what I had to prove. Hmm. Maybe I should ask Jennifer Sheridan to be a partner in the firm. Maybe she gave detective lessons.

I called this reporter I know who works for the *Examiner* named Eddie Ditko. He's about a million years old and he loves me like a son. He said, 'Jesus Christ, I'm up to my ass in work. What the fuck do *you* want?' You see?

'I need to find out about the REACT unit deployed out of the Seventy-seventh Division down in South Central L.A.'

Eddie said, 'You think I know this shit off the top of my head?' Isn't Eddie grand?

'Nope. I was thinking maybe you could conjure it in your crystal ball.'

'You got crystal balls, always imposing like this.' Eddie went into a coughing fit and made a wet hacking noise that sounded like he was passing a sinus.

'You want I should call 911?'

'That's it. Be cute.' I could hear keys tapping on his VDT. 'This'll take some time. Why don'tchu swing around in a little while. I might have something by then.'

'Sure.'

I put on my jacket, looked around my office, then went to the door and locked up. I had once seen a James Bond movie where James Bond pasted a hair across the seam in the doorjamb so he could tell if anyone opened the door while he was gone. I thought about doing it, but figured that someone in the insurance office across the hall would come out while I was rigging the hair and then I'd have to explain and they'd probably think it was stupid. I'd probably have to agree with them.

I forgot about the hair and went to see Eddie Ditko.

7

The *Los Angeles Examiner* is published out of a large, weathered red-brick building midway between downtown L.A. and Chinatown, in a part of the city that looks more like it belongs in Boston or Cincinnati than in Southern California. There are sidewalks and taxis and tall buildings of cement and glass and nary a palm tree in sight. Years ago, enterprising developers built a nest of low-rise condominiums, foolishly believing that Angelenos wanted to live near their work and would snap the places up to avoid the commute. What they didn't count on is that people were willing to work downtown but no one wanted to live there. If you're going to live in Southern California, why live in a place that looks like Chicago?

I put my car in the lot across the street, crossed at the light, then took the elevator up to the third floor and the pretty black receptionist who sits there. 'Elvis Cole to see Eddie Ditko. He's expecting me.'

She looked through her pass list and asked me to sign in. 'He's in the city room. Do you know where that is?'

'Yep.'

She gave me a peel-and-stick guest badge and went back to talking into the phone. I looked at the badge and felt like I was at a PTA meeting. *Hello! My name is Elvis!* I affixed the badge to my shirt and tried not to look embarrassed. Why risk the hall police?

I went through a pair of leather upholstered swinging doors, then along a short hall that opened into the city room. Twenty desks were jammed together in the center of the room, and maybe a dozen people were hanging around the desks, most of them typing as fast as they could and the rest of them talking on the phone. Eddie Ditko had the desk on the far left corner, about as close to the editors' offices as you could get without being one of the editors. A woman in her late twenties was working at a terminal next to him. She was wearing huge round glasses and a loud purple dress with very wide shoulders and a little purple pillbox hat. It was the kind of clothes you wore when you were establishing your identity as a retro-hip urban intellectual. Or maybe she was just odd. She glanced up once as I approached, then went on typing. Eddie was chewing on an unlit Grenadiers cigar and scowling at his VDT when I got there. He had to be forty years older than her. He didn't bother glancing up. 'Hey, Eddie, when are they going to make you an editor around here and get you off the floor?'

Eddie jerked the cigar out of his mouth and spit a load of brown juice at his wastebasket. He never lit them. He chewed them. 'Soon's I stop saying what I think and start kissing the right ass, like everybody else around here.' He said it loud enough for most of the room to hear. The purple woman glanced over, then went on with her typing. Tolerant. Eddie grimaced and rubbed at his chest. 'Jeez, I got chest pains. I'm a goddamned walking thrombo.'

'Lay off the fats and exercise a little.'

'What're you, my fuckin' mother?' Eddie leaned to the side and broke wind. Classy.

I pulled up a chair and sat on it backwards, hooking my arms over its back. 'What'd you find on the REACT guys?'

Eddie clamped the wet cigar in his teeth, leaned toward the VDT, and slapped buttons. The little VDT screen filled with printing. 'I put together some stuff from our morgue files, but that's about it. REACT is an elite surveillance unit, and that means the cops block their files. They can't do their jobs if everybody knows who they're surveilling.'

'How many guys we talking about?'

'Five. You want the names?'

'Yeah.'

He hit a couple of buttons and a little printer beside his VDT chattered and spit out a page. He handed it to me. Five names were listed in a neat column in the center of the page.

LT. ERIC DEES
SGT. PETER GARCIA
OFF. FLOYD RIGGENS
OFF. WARREN PINKWORTH
OFF. MARK THURMAN

I looked over the names. They meant nothing. 'They any good?'

Eddie grinned like a shark with his eye on a fat boy in baggy shorts. 'They wouldn't be a REACT team if they weren't any good. They target felons and they've got a ninety-nine-point-seven per cent conviction rate. Dees has been down there almost six years, along with Garcia and Riggens. Pinkworth joined a couple of years back and they picked up Thurman a year ago. He's the baby.'

'How'd Thurman make the squad?'

Eddie hit more buttons and the printing on the screen changed. 'Same as everybody else. Top ten of his academy class, a string of outstandings in his quarterly evaluations, Officer of the Month four times. You remember that nut pulled a gun on the RTD bus and threatened to start killing people unless Madonna gave him a blow job?'

'Sort of.'

The purple woman looked over. Interested.

'Hell, I wrote about that one. Guy stops the bus in the middle of Hollywood Boulevard, and Thurman and a guy named Palmetta were the first cops on the scene. Thurman was, what, maybe twenty-two, twenty-three years old?'

The purple woman shrugged.

'Yeah, he was just a kid. That was part of the story. Anyway, the nut shoots this fat guy in the leg to make his point, then grabs this nine-year-old girl and starts screaming he's going to do her next. He wants Madonna, right? Palmetta puts the call in for a hostage negotiator and the SWAT team but Thurman figures there ain't time. He takes off his gun and goes into the bus to talk to the guy. The nut tries to shoot him twice but he's shaking so bad both shots miss, so he puts the gun to the girl's head. You know what happened then?'

The purple lady was leaning forward, frowning because she wanted to know.

Eddie said, 'Thurman tells the guy he's had Madonna and Madonna's a lousy lay, but he knows Rosanna Arquette and Rosanna Arquette is the best blow job in town. Thurman tells the guy if he puts down the gun, as soon as he's out on bail, he'll set it up with Rosanna Arquette 'cause she owes him a couple of favors.'

The purple woman said, 'And he went for that?'

Eddie spread his hands 'Here's a nut believes he's gonna get Madonna, why not? The guy says only if she blows him *twice*. Thurman says, okay, she'll do it twice, but not on the same day, she's got a thing about that. The nut says that's okay with him 'cause he's only good for once a week anyway, and puts down the gun.'

The purple lady laughed, and she didn't look so odd anymore.

Eddie was smiling, too. 'That was, what, a couple years ago? Thurman gets the Medal of Valor and six months later he wins the early promotion to plain-clothes and the REACT team. They're top cops, pal. Every one of those guys has a story like that in his file else he wouldn't be on the team.'

'Eddie, what if I didn't want the good stuff? What if I was a reporter and I was looking for something that maybe had a smell to it?'

'Like what?'

'Like maybe I'm looking to see if they've crossed over.'

Eddie shook his head and patted the VDT. 'If it's in here, it's already public record. Someone would've had to lodge the complaint, and it would've had to come out through LAPD PR or one of the news agencies or the courts. It wouldn't be a secret and no one would be trying to hide it.'

'Okay. Could you check for allegations?'

'Substantiated or otherwise?'

I looked at him.

'Reporter humor. It's probably over your head.' Eddie hit more keys and watched the screen, and then did it again. When he had filled and wiped the screen three times, he nodded and leaned back. 'I had it search through the files keying on the officers' names for every news release during the past year, then I threw out the junk about them saving babies and arresting the Incredible Hulk and just kept the bad stuff. This is pretty neat.'

I leaned forward and looked at the screen. 'What's it found?'

'Excessive-force complaints. "Suspect injured while resisting arrest." "Suspect filed brutality charges." Like that. 'Course, these guys are busting felons and felons tend to get nasty, but check it out, you've got twenty-six complaints in the past ten months, and eleven of them are against this guy Riggens.'

'Any charges brought?'

'*Nada.* IAD issued letters of reprimand twice, and dealt a two-week suspension, but that's it.'

I read the list. Twenty-six names ran down the left side of the page, and next to each name there was a booking number and the arresting charge and the claims levied by the defendants and the accused officer or officers. Riggens had all or part of eleven of the charges, and the remainder were divided pretty evenly between Pinkworth and Dees and Garcia and Thurman. Thurman had part of three.

Eddie said, 'You've got to understand, cops on these special tac squads get charges filed all the time, so most of these really are garbage, but if I'm looking for tuna I'm looking for losers, and that's Riggens.'

'Thanks, Eddie.'

Eddie stuck the cigar in his mouth and rolled it around and looked at me. 'What you got going here, kid? It any good?'

'I don't know. I'm still just running down the leads.'

He nodded and sucked on the cigar, and then he gazed at the editors' offices. He wasn't getting any younger. 'If there's a story here, I want it.'

'You bet, Eddie.'

Eddie Ditko spread his hands, then hacked up something phlegmy and spit it into the basket. No one looked and no one paid any mind. I guess seniority has its privileges.

I went back the way I came, took the elevator down to the lobby, then used the pay phone there to call Jennifer Sheridan in Marty Beale's office. I asked her for Floyd Riggens's address. She said, 'Which one?'

'What do you mean, which one?'

45

'He's divorced. He used to live in La Cañada, but now he's got a little apartment somewhere.'

I told her that if she had them both, I'd take them both. She did. She also told me that Riggens's ex-wife was named Margaret, and that they had three children.

When I had the information that I needed, I said, 'Jennifer?'

'Yes?'

'Did Mark ever complain to you about Floyd?'

There was a little pause. 'Mark said he didn't like having Floyd as a partner. He said Floyd scared him.'

'Did he say why?'

'He said Floyd drank a lot. Do you think Floyd is involved in this?'

'I don't know, Jennifer. I'm going to try to find out.'

We hung up and I went out of the building and across the street to my car.

8

Floyd Riggens was living in a small, six-unit stucco apartment building on a side street in Burbank, just about ten blocks from the Walt Disney Studio. There were three units on the bottom and three on top, and an L-shaped stair at the far end of the building. It was a cramped, working-class neighborhood, but working class was good. Working class means that people go to work. When people go to work, it makes things easier for private eyes and other snoopers who skulk around where they shouldn't.

I parked three houses down, then walked back. Riggens had the front apartment, on top. Number four. None of the units seemed to belong to a manager, which was good, but the front door was open on the bottom center unit, which was bad. Light mariachi music came from the center unit and the wonderful smells of simmering *menudo* and fresh-cut cilantro and, when I drew closer, the sound of a woman singing with the music. I walked past her door as if I belonged, then took the stairs to the second level. Upstairs, the drapes were drawn on all three units. Everybody at work. I went to number four, opened the screen, and stood in Riggens's door with my back to the street. It takes longer to pick a lock than to use a key, but if a neighbor saw me, maybe they'd think I was fumbling with the key.

Floyd Riggens's apartment was a single large studio with a kitchenette and a closet and the bath along the side wall. A sleeping bag and a blanket and an ashtray were lined against the opposite wall and a tiny Hitachi portable television sat on a cardboard box in the corner. A carton of Camel Wides was on the floor by the sleeping bag. You could smell the space, and it wasn't the sweet, earthy smells of *menudo*. It smelled of mildew and smoke and BO. If Floyd Riggens was pulling down graft, he sure as hell wasn't spending it here.

I walked through the bathroom and the closet and the kitchenette and each was dirty and empty of the items of life, as if Riggens didn't truly live here, or expect to, any more than a tourist expects to live in a motel. There was a razor and a toothbrush and deodorant and soap in the bathroom, but nothing else. The sink and the tub and the toilet were filmed with the sort of built-up grime that comes of long-term inattention, as if Riggens used these things and left, expecting that someone else would clean them, only the someone never showed and never cleaned.

There were four shirts and three pants hanging in the closet, along with a single navy dress uniform. Underwear and socks and two pairs of shoes were laid out neatly on the floor of the closet, and an empty gym bag was thrown in the far back corner. The underwear and the socks were the only neat thing in the apartment.

An open bottle of J&B scotch sat on the counter in the kitchenette, and three empties were in a trash bag on the floor. The smell of scotch was strong. A couple of Domino's pizza boxes were parked in the refrigerator along with four Styrofoam Chicken McNuggets boxes and half a quart of lowfat milk. An open box of plastic forks and a package of paper plates sat on the counter beside the sink. The sink was empty, but that's probably because there were no pots or pans or dishes. I guess Riggens had made the choice to go disposable. Why clutter your life with the needless hassle of washing and cleaning when you can use it and throw it away?

It had taken me all of four minutes to look through Riggens's apartment. I went back into the main studio and stood in the center of the floor and felt oily and somehow unclean. I don't know what I expected, but it wasn't this, and it left me feeling vaguely depressed, as if this wasn't a place where someone lived, but more a place where someone died. I went to the sleeping bag and squatted. A photograph had been pushpinned to the wall. It was an older picture and showed Riggens with a plain woman about his age and three kids. A boy and two girls. The boy looked maybe fourteen and sullen. The oldest girl was maybe twelve, and the youngest girl was a lot younger. Maybe four. She was tiny compared to the others, with a cute round face and a mop of curly hair and she was holding up a single bluegill on a nylon cord. She looked confused. Riggens was smiling and so was his wife. Margaret. They were standing in front of the bait shop at Castaic Lake, maybe twenty miles north of L.A. in the Santa Susana Mountains. The picture looked worn around the edges, as if it had been handled often. Maybe it had. Maybe Riggens lived here but maybe he didn't. Maybe he brought his body here, and drank, and slept, but while the body was here he looked at the picture a lot and let his mind go somewhere else. Castaic, maybe. Where people were smiling.

I closed the apartment as I had found it, went down the stairs, and picked up the Ventura Freeway east through the Glendale Pass and into La Cañada in the foothills of the Verdugo Mountains.

It was mid-afternoon when I got there, and knots of junior high school kids were walking along the sidewalks with books and gym bags, but no one looked very interested in going home or doing homework.

Margaret Riggens lived in a modest ranch-style home with a poplar tree in the front yard in the flats at the base of the foothills. It was one of those stucco-and-clapboard numbers that had been built in the mid-fifties when a developer had come in with one set of house plans and an army of bulldozers and turned an orange grove into a housing tract to sell 'affordable housing' to veterans come to L.A. to work in the aerospace business. The floor plan of every house on the block would be the same as every other house. The only differences would be the colors and the landscaping and the people within the houses. I guess there is affordability in sameness.

I parked at the curb across the street as a girl maybe thirteen with limp blonde hair walked across the Riggenses' front lawn and let herself into their home without knocking. That would be the older daughter. A white Oldsmobile Delta 88 was parked in the drive. It needed a wash. The house looked like it needed a wash, too. The stucco was dusty and the clapboard part was peeling and needed to be scraped and painted. I crossed the street, then went up the drive to the front door and rang the bell. It would have been shorter to cut across the lawn, but there you go.

A tired woman in a sleeveless sun shirt and baggy shorts opened the door. She was smoking a Marlboro. I said, 'Hello, Ms Riggens. Pete Simmons, Internal Affairs, LAPD.' I took out my license and held it up. It would work, or it wouldn't. She would read the ID, or she wouldn't.

Margaret Riggens said, 'What'd that sonofabitch do now?' Guess she didn't bother to read it.

I put the license away. 'I'd like to ask you a couple of questions. It won't take long.'

'Ain't that what they all say.' She took a final pull on the Marlboro, then flipped it into the front yard and stepped out of the door to let me in. I guess visits by guys like Pete Simmons were an inevitable and expected part of her life.

We went through the living room into an adjoining dining area off the kitchen. The girl who had come in before me was sitting cross-legged on the living room floor, watching *Geraldo* and reading a copy of *Sassy* magazine. There was a hard pack of Marlboros beside her and a green Bic lighter and a big clay ashtray that looked like she'd made it in pottery class. She was smoking. Loud music came from the back of the house, but there was a muffled quality to it as if a door was closed. The music suddenly got louder, and a boy's voice screamed, 'I told you to stay out of my room, you little shit! I don't want you here!' Then the boy came out of the back hall, pulling the younger girl by the upper arm. He was maybe sixteen now, with most of his father's growth, and she was maybe six. The

49

little girl's face was screwed up and she was crying. The boy shouted, 'Mom, make her stay out of my room! I don't want her back there!'

Margaret Riggens said, 'Jesus Christ, Alan.'

I said, 'You're holding her too tight. Let go.'

Alan said, 'Who in the hell are you?'

The little girl was staring at me. 'You're hurting her,' I said. 'Let go.'

Margaret Riggens said, 'Hey, I don't need any help with my kids.'

I was looking at Alan and Alan was looking at me, and then he suddenly let go and bent over the little girl and screamed, 'I *hate* you!' He stomped back down the hall and the music went soft as the door closed. The little girl didn't seem too upset by what had happened. Guess it happened so often she was used to it. Probably even a game by now. She rubbed at her arm and ran back down the hall. The music didn't change pitch, so I guess she went into her own room.

Margaret Riggens said, 'These kids,' then stooped down, took a cigarette from her older daughter's pack, and turned away to sit at the dining room table.

I said, 'Maybe it'd be better if we had a little privacy.'

Margaret Riggens used a book of paper matches to light the Marlboro, and put the spent match in a little beanbag ashtray she had on the table. 'Is Floyd going to get fired?' Guess the privacy didn't matter.

'No, ma'am. This is just follow-up on a couple of things.'

'That alimony is all I have. He pays it on time. Every month.'

I took out the little pad I keep in my jacket and made a big deal out of taking that down. 'That's good to hear. The Department frowns on a man if he ducks his responsibility.'

She nodded and sucked on the cigarette. Out in the living room, the oldest girl was sucking on a cigarette, too.

I tried to look sly. 'We hear enough good things like that, and it makes it easy to overlook a bad thing. Do you see?'

She squinted at me through the smoke. 'I don't understand.'

I made a little shrugging move. Conversational. 'Everybody thinks we're looking to chop heads, but that's not true. We hear a guy does right by his family, we don't want to throw him out in the streets. We find out he's gotten himself into trouble, we'll try to counsel him and keep him on the payroll. Maybe suspend him for a while, maybe demote him, but keep him employed. So he can take care of his family.'

She drew so hard on the Marlboro that the coal glowed like a flare. 'What kind of trouble?'

I smiled. 'That's what I want you to tell me, Ms Riggens.'

Margaret Riggens turned toward her older daughter. 'Sandi. Shut off the TV and go to your room for a little while, okay?'

Sandi gathered up her things, then went down the same hall the other kids had used. Margaret turned back to me. 'I don't know what you're talking about.'

'You and Floyd talk?'

'Maybe once a week. There's always something with one of the kids.'

'He's supporting two households, Ms Riggens. Kids need things. So do adults.'

'Jesus Christ, have you seen where he lives?'

I spread my hands. 'Has money seemed a little easier to come by?'

'Ha.'

'Has Floyd maybe hinted around that he has something going?'

'Absolutely not.'

I leaned forward and I lowered my voice. 'If an officer crosses the line and someone aids and abets in that crossing, they can be charged. Did you know that, Ms Riggens?'

She drew on the cigarette and now her hands were trembling. 'Are you telling me that Floyd has stepped over the line?'

I stared at her.

She stood up, dribbling cigarette ash. 'I've had enough with that sonofabitch. I really have. I don't know anything about this. I don't know what the hell you're talking about.'

'Sit down, Ms Riggens.'

She sat. Breathing hard.

'I'm making no accusations. I'm just curious. Floyd has a problem with the drinking. Floyd has a problem with the excessive-force complaints. Floyd has money problems. Pretty soon problems become a way of life. You see how these things add up?'

She crushed out the cigarette in the little beanbag ashtray and lit another. The first continued to smolder.

'I'm not accusing Floyd, and I'm not accusing you. I'm just wondering if maybe you've heard anything, or noticed a change in Floyd's behavior, that's all.'

She nodded. Calmer, now, but with eyes that were still frightened and weak. The look in her eyes made me feel small and greasy, and I wanted to tell her it had all been a mistake and leave, but you don't learn things by leaving. Even when the staying smells bad.

She said, 'He's been out of his mind ever since that guy died. The past couple of years have been tough, but since then has been the worst. That's when he went back to the bottle.'

I nodded like I knew what she was saying.

'He was in AA before that, and he was getting better, too. He'd come over sometimes, we'd have dinner, like that.'

'But then the guy died?'

She rolled her eyes. 'Well, everyone's still thinking about Rodney King and this black guy dies when they're trying to arrest him and then the family files a lawsuit and it was awful. Floyd started drinking worse than ever. He was angry all the time, and he'd blow up over the tiniest thing. They told me it was a stress reaction.'

'About how long ago was that?'

She gestured with the cigarette. 'What was it? Three or four months?'

I nodded. 'Did Floyd feel responsible?'

She laughed. 'Floyd doesn't feel responsible for hitting the bowl in the morning. I thought he was worried about the suit, but then the suit went away and I thought he'd relax. You know those suits cost a fortune. But he still stayed drunk all the time. Eric would call and check on him to make sure he was holding it together. Things like that. Eric was a godsend.' Eric Dees.

I nodded.

'Floyd hasn't been acting right since then. If he's gotten himself mixed up in something, I'll bet that's why. I'll bet it's all part of the stress reaction.'

'Maybe so.'

'That should qualify for disability, shouldn't it?'

There were about ten million questions I wanted to ask, but I couldn't ask them without tipping her that I wasn't from LAPD. I patted her hand and tried to look reassuring. 'That'll be fine, Ms Riggens. You've been a big help, and that will be in the record.'

'Why don't you people make him go back to AA? When he was in AA he was doing a lot better.'

'Let's just keep this our little secret, all right, Ms. Riggens? That way it looks better for you all the way around.'

She crushed out the cigarette into the over-full ashtray and pushed ashes out onto the table. 'Look, I don't know what Floyd's mixed up with, and I don't want to know. I'm not aiding and abetting anything. I got enough to worry about.'

'Sure. Thank you for your time.'

I got up and went to the door. Margaret Riggens stayed at the table and lit another Marlboro and drew the smoke deep off the match and stared out through the windows into her shabby backyard. You could hear the kids screaming over the loud bass throbbing of the music and I imagined that it went on without end, and that her living hell wasn't a whole lot different from Floyd's.

Out in the living room there was an upright Yamaha piano that looked like it hadn't been played in a long time. A schoolbag was sitting on one end of it, and half a dozen wilting yellow roses were floating in a glass jar on the other end. Between the two was a framed picture of Floyd and Margaret Riggens standing together at his police academy graduation. They were fifteen years younger, and they were smiling. It was a photograph very much like the one that Jennifer Sheridan had, only

52

Jennifer and Mark still looked like the people in their picture, and Floyd and Margaret didn't.

I guess romance isn't for everyone.

9

When I pulled away from the house that Floyd Riggens once shared with
his wife and children, the sun was low in the west and the ridgeline along
the Verdugo Mountains was touched with orange and pink. I worked my
way across the valley, letting the rush hour traffic push me along, and
enjoyed the darkening sky. I wondered if Margaret Riggens found much
in the mountains or the sky to enjoy, but perhaps those things were too
far away for her to see. When you're hurting, you tend to fix your eyes
closer to home.

I cut across the northern edge of Burbank and Pacoima, and then
dropped down Coldwater to a little place I know called Mazzarino's that
makes the very best pizza in Los Angeles. I got a vegetarian with a side of
anchovies to go and, when I pulled into my carport fifteen minutes later,
the pizza was still warm.

I opened a Falstaff and put out the pizza for me and the anchovies for
the cat, only the cat wasn't around. I called him, and waited, but he still
didn't come. Off doing cat things, no doubt.

I ate the pizza and I drank the beer and I tried watching the TV, but I
kept thinking about Margaret Riggens and that maybe I had come at all of
this from the wrong direction. You think crime, and then you think
money, but maybe that wasn't it. Maybe Mark Thurman had gotten
himself involved in another type of crime. And maybe it wasn't Mark
alone. Maybe it was Mark and Floyd. Maybe it was the entire REACT
team. For all I knew, it was the full and complete population of the state
of California, and I was the only guy left out of the loop. Me and Jennifer
Sheridan. I was still thinking about that when I fell asleep.

At ten oh-six the next morning I called this cop I know who works in
North Hollywood. A voice answered the phone with, 'Detectives.'

'Is that you, Griggs?' It was this other cop I know, Charlie Griggs.

'Who's this?'

'Guess.'

Griggs hung up. Some sense of humor, huh?

I called back and Griggs answered again. I said, 'Okay, I'll give you a hint. I'm known as the King of Rockin' Detectives, but I wasn't born in Tupelo, Mississippi.'

'I knew it was you. I just wanted to see if you'd call back. Heh-heh-heh.' That's the way Griggs laughs. Heh-heh-heh.

'Lemme speak to Lou.'

'What's the magic word?'

'C'mon, Charlie.'

'What do you say, wiseass? You wanna speak to Lou, tell me what you say? Heh-heh-heh.' This guy's an adult.

'I'm going to get you, Griggs.'

'Heh-heh-heh.' Griggs was killing himself.

'I'm going to give your address to Joe.'

The laughing stopped and Griggs put me on hold. Maybe forty seconds later Lou Poitras picked up. 'I don't pay these guys to goose around with you.'

'Griggs hasn't done a full day's work in fifteen years.'

'We don't pay him to work. We keep'm around because he's such a scream. Sort of like you.' Another comedian.

I said, 'Four months ago, a guy died during a REACT arrest down in South Central. You know anyone I can talk to about it?'

'Hold on.' Poitras put me on hold again and left me there for maybe eight minutes. When he came back he said, 'Suspect's name was Charles Lewis Washington.'

'Okay.' I wrote it down.

'There's a guy working Hollywood named Andy Malone used to be a partner of mine. He's a uniform supervisor on the day shift. He just came out of the Seventy-seventh. You wanna go down there now?'

'Yeah.'

'I'll call him and set it up.'

'Thanks, Lou.'

'You got that twelve bucks you owe me?'

I made a staticky noise and pretended we had been cut off. Works every time.

Forty minutes later I parked in a diagonal parking place outside the glass front door of the Hollywood Police Division, and went past three black women who were standing on the sidewalk into a trapezoidal public room with a high ceiling and a white tile floor. There was a pay phone on the wall up by the front glass and padded chairs around the perimeter of the wall for your waiting comfort. The walls were aqua, the glass was bulletproof. A Formica counter cut off the back third of the room, and three uniformed officers sat on stools behind the counter. Two women and a man. One of the women and the man were talking on telephones, and the other woman was writing in a small black notebook. A Hispanic man and woman sat in the chairs under the pay phone. The Hispanic man sat with his elbows on his thighs and rocked steadily. He looked worried. The Hispanic woman rubbed his back as he rocked and spoke softly. She looked worried, too.

I went past them to the officer writing in the little black notebook and said, 'Elvis Cole to see Sergeant Malone.'

'He expecting you?'

'Yes.'

'Have a seat.'

She left the counter and went back through a door into the bowels of the station house. There was another door on the customer side of the counter. It was heavy and dense and if no one buzzed you through it'd probably take a rocket launcher to get past it. I sat opposite the door and waited. In a couple of minutes the female officer reappeared behind the counter and said, 'He's finishing up a couple of things. He'll be with you in a minute.'

'Sure.'

I waited some more.

A well-dressed black woman came in and asked the people behind the counter if Officer Hobbs was in. The same officer who had gone to see Malone said something into a phone, and a couple of minutes later a tall muscular black officer came through the heavy door. He smiled when he saw the woman and she smiled when she saw him. He offered his hand and she took it and they went out through the glass door to hold hands in the privacy of the sidewalk. Love at the station house. Two Pakistani men came in past the lovers. One of them was maybe in his fifties and the other was maybe in his forties. The older one looked nervous and the younger one wore a loud pink shirt and leather sandals. The younger one went to the counter and said, 'We would like to speak with the chief of police.' He said it so loud the Hispanic man stopped rocking. The two desk officers glanced at each other and smiled. The desk officer on the phone kept talking like it was nothing. Guess you work the desk at Hollywood, nothing surprises you. The male desk officer leaned back on his stool and looked through the doorway behind the counter and yelled, 'We got a citizen out here wants to see the chief.' A uniformed lieutenant with silver hair came out and stared at the Pakistanis, then frowned at the desk officer. 'Knock off the shit and take care of these people.'

The younger Pakistani said, 'Are you the chief?'

The lieutenant said, 'The chief's busy with the city council. How can I help you?'

Just as he said it the heavy door opened and a hard-shouldered uniformed sergeant looked out at me. 'You Cole?'

'Yeah.' He had sandy hair and thick, blocky hands and a deep tan because most of his time would be spent on the street. He wore a little red and green and gold Vietnam service ribbon beneath the badge on his left breast and a marksmanship pin beside the ribbon.

'Andy Malone,' he said. 'We can talk back here.' He put out his hand and I stood and took it, and then I followed him through the door.

We went down a long hall past three candy machines and a soft-drink machine and a couple of rest rooms for people who weren't cops to use. At the far end of the hall there was a booking desk where a couple of cops were processing a tall skinny black kid. The kid's hands were cuffed. One of the cops was white and the other was black, and they both were thick across the chest and back and arms, like they spent a lot of time in the gym. Guess you work in a war zone, you want to be as threatening as possible. The white cop was trying to unlock the cuffs and the black cop was shaking his finger about two inches from the kid's nose, saying, 'Are you listening to me?' The kid was giving with attitude and you knew he wasn't listening and wasn't going to. Your bad guys are often like that.

There were a couple of varnished wood benches in the hall opposite a door that said SERGEANT'S OFFICE. We went into the office and Malone closed the door. 'You want coffee?'

'Sure. Thanks.'

Malone filled a couple of paper cups, handed one to me, then went behind a cluttered desk and sat. He didn't offer cream or sugar. Maybe they didn't have any.

I sat across from him in a hard chair, and we looked at each other and sipped our coffee. He said, 'My buddy Lou Poitras says you want to know about Charles Lewis Washington.'

'Uh-huh.'

'You're a private investigator.'

'That's it.' The coffee was hot and bitter and had probably been made early this morning.

'Make any money at it?'

'No one's getting rich.'

He took more of the coffee and made a little smile. 'The wife's been after me to leave the force since the riots. All this time, she's still after me.' He made a shrugging move with his head, then set the cup on his desk. 'So tell me why you're digging around Charles Lewis.'

'His name came up in something I'm working on and I want to run it down.'

Malone nodded and had more of his coffee. He didn't seem to mind the taste, but then, he was used to it. 'How do you know Poitras?'

'Met on the job. Got to know each other.'

He nodded again and leaned back. When he did, the old swivel squealed. 'Lou says you pulled time in Vietnam.'

'Yep.'

He put down his coffee and crossed his arms. 'I was there in sixty-eight.'

'Seventy-one.'

The chair squealed again. The nod. 'People think the Nam they think the sixties. Lot of people forget we still had guys there till March twenty-nine, 1973.'

'Lot of people don't care.'

He made a little smile. 'Yeah. We kicked ass in Saudi. That sort of makes up for things.'

'Don't forget Panama and Grenada.'

The smile got wider. 'Kick enough ass, and pretty soon you forget the losers. Who wants to remember losers when you got so many winners running around?'

I said, 'Hell, Malone, we're not that damned old, are we?'

Malone laughed, uncrossed his arms, and said, 'What do you want to know about Washington?'

I told him.

Malone went to a battered gray cabinet, took out a manila folder, and brought it back to the desk. He skimmed through it for a couple of minutes, then he closed it. He didn't offer to let me see. 'Washington worked in a pawnshop over on Broadway, down in South Central. We had information that the shop was being used as a fence drop for some of the guns looted during the riots, so REACT put eyes on the place, then went in with a sting.'

'And it went bad.'

'That's a way to say it. Washington thinks he's making a buy on ten thousand rounds of stolen ammo, the officers think it's under control, but when they flash the badges he goes a little nuts and decides to resist. Washington dives behind a counter, and comes up with a piece, but our guys are thinking Rodney King, so they don't shoot him. There's a scuffle and Washington hits his head and that's it.'

'I hear it was controversial.'

'They're all controversial. This one less than most.'

'What do you have on Washington?'

Malone checked the report again. 'Twenty-eight. A longtime Double-Seven Hoover Crip with multiple priors.'

'He there alone in the store?'

'Sure. The family went nuts. We had the pickets, the wrongful-death suit, all of that, but they backed off.'

'Did the city settle?'

'Nope. They dropped it.'

'Can I read the report?'

Malone stared at me for a while and you could tell he didn't like it, then he shrugged and shoved it across the desk at me. 'Here in my presence. I can't let you copy it and I can't let you take it.'

'Sure.'

I read the report. It told me what Malone had told me, only with more words. Lieutenant Eric Dees, the REACT team leader, had written the report. Garcia and Pinkworth and Riggens had gone in to front the sale, and Thurman and Dees were the outside men. When it was clear that the transaction would be consummated, Garcia identified himself as a police officer, told Washington that he was being placed under arrest, and Dees and Thurman entered the premises. As the cuffs were being applied, Washington broke free from Pinkworth and Riggens and lunged for a weapon. The officers attempted to subdue the suspect without the use of deadly force, and Pinkworth and Riggens received substantial injuries. Washington was struck repeatedly by all officers involved, but refused to succumb, and died when team leader Eric Dees tackled him, causing his head to strike the corner of a metal display case. Dees assumed full responsibility. There were copies of the IAD investigation report and a letter of final disposition of the case. The letter of disposition released the officers involved from any wrongdoing. Copies of the death report, the coroner's findings, and Charles Lewis Washington's arrest record were appended to the finding.

'What about Riggens?'

'What can I say? Riggens has his problems, but you read the report. It was a team effort.'

I said, 'Does it seem odd to you that five officers couldn't apprehend this guy without letting him kill himself?'

'Hell, Cole, you know what it's like out there. Shit happens. This kid was a felon gangbanger and he picked the wrong time to pull a gun. Our guys tried to do the right thing, but it went wrong. That's all there is to it. Nobody wants another Rodney King.'

I nodded. 'Mind if I copy down Washington's address?'

'No problem.'

'Any idea why they dropped the suit?'

Malone shrugged. 'People down there are tired. I spent four years in South Central. God knows I can tell you *we* are.' He made the shrug again. 'Nobody ever drops a wrongful death against LAPD. Too many shysters are willing to take the case on a contingency, and the city council's always ready to settle out, but who can tell.'

'Yeah. Who can tell. Thanks, Malone. I appreciate it.'

I handed back the file and went to the door. He said, 'Cole.'

'Yeah?'

'I know the kind of press South Central gets, but the people down there, most of the people down there are good people. That's why I stayed the four years.'

'Most folks everywhere are good people.'

He nodded. 'I don't know what you're doing, or where you're going, but watch yourself around the gangs. LAPD owns the streets, but the gangs keep trying to take'm away. You understand?'

'More than I want.'

I showed myself out, picked up my car, and took the long drive down to South Central Los Angeles.

Home of the body bag.

10

I dropped down through West Hollywood and the southwest corner of Beverly Hills through La Cienega Park to the I-10 freeway, then picked up the 10 east to the Harbor, then went south on the Harbor past USC and Exposition Park, and into South Central.

Even on the freeway, the world begins to change. The cinderblock sound walls and ramp signs show more graffiti, and, if you know how to read it, you can tell that it isn't just young Hispanic taggers out to get famous all over town, it's gangbangers marking turf and making challenges and telling you who they've killed and who they're going to kill. Just the thing you want to see when you're looking for an exit ramp.

I left the freeway at Florence, looped under to Hoover, then turned south to Eighty-second Street. Broadway and Florence show liquor stores and neighborhood groceries and gas stations and other businesses, but Hoover and the cross streets are residential. Up by the businesses you get out-of-work men hanging around and a lot of graffiti and it looks sort of crummy, but the residential streets will surprise you. Most of the houses are stucco or clapboard bungalows, freshly painted and well maintained, with front yards as neat and pretty as anything you'd find anywhere.

Elderly people sat on porches or worked in yards trimming roses and, here and there, small children played on tricycles. Satellite dishes sprouted from poles like black aluminum mums and clean American cars sat in the drives. There were a lot of the dishes, and they looked identical, as if a satellite-dish salesman had gone door-to-door and found many takers.

There was no graffiti on the houses and there was no litter in the streets or the yards, but every house had heavy metal bars over windows and door fronts and sometimes the bars encircled a porch. That's how you knew there was a war on. If there wasn't a war, you wouldn't need the protection.

According to the police report, Charles Lewis Washington had lived with his mother in a rose-colored bungalow on Eighty-second Street, just west of Hoover. His mother, Ida Leigh Washington, still lived there. It was a nice-looking place, with a satellite dish on a tower in their backyard and a well-kept Buick LeSabre in the drive. An open-air front porch was boxed in by a redwood trellis and bright yellow vine roses. The vine roses were healthy and vibrant.

I parked at the curb in front of their home, went up the narrow walk, and onto the porch. The roses threw off a heavy scent and smelled wonderful. The front door opened before I got there, and a slender young black man looked out at me. I could hear music, but it was coming from another house, not this one. He said, 'May I help you?'

I gave him the card. 'My name is Elvis Cole. I'm a private investigator, and I was hoping to speak with Mrs Ida Leigh Washington.' He was wearing a plain white crewneck tee shirt and blue Navy work pants and white sneakers and an imitation gold watchband. The band was bright against his dark skin. He read the card and then he looked back at me.

'About what?'

'Charles Lewis Washington.'

'Lewis is dead.'

'I know. That's what I want to talk about.'

He stared at me a couple of seconds longer, like he had to make up his mind, but like he was making it up about things that had nothing to do with me. After a little of that, he stepped back out of the door and held the screen. 'All right. Please come in.'

I went past him into a small, neat living room. An old man maybe three hundred years old and a young woman who couldn't have been more than sixteen were watching TV. The girl was sitting on a burgundy velveteen couch and the old man in a hardwood rocker. He was holding a can of Scrapple. They both looked at me with a sort of curious surprise. The white man comes to call. A little boy maybe three years old pulled at the girl's legs, but she ignored him. Crocheted doilies were spread on the arms of the couch and the headrest, but you could make out the worn spots through the gaps in the doilies. The girl didn't look a whole hell of a lot older than the baby, but there you go. Toys appropriate to a three-year-old were scattered about the floor. I smiled at them. 'Hi.'

The old man nodded and the girl picked up a remote control and clicked off the TV.

The younger man said, 'Go tell Mama we got company.'

The girl slipped off the couch and went down a little hall into the back of the house. I said, 'Your wife?'

'Lewis's girlfriend, Shalene. This is their son, Marcus, and this is my grandfather, Mr Williams. Say hello, Marcus.'

Marcus covered his eyes with his fingers and sat down on the floor, then rolled over onto his belly. He giggled as he did it. The old man started rocking.

Lewis's girlfriend came back with a heavy, light-skinned woman in her fifties. Ida Leigh Washington. There was a friendly half smile on her face, and a fine film of perspiration as if she'd been working.

The younger man held the card toward her. 'Man wants to ask you about Lewis.'

The older woman froze as if someone had put a gun to her head, and the half smile died. 'Are you with the police?'

'No, ma'am. I'm a private investigator, and I had some questions about what happened to Charles Lewis Washington. I was hoping you could help me.'

She looked at the card, and then she looked at me, and then she looked at her son. He crossed his arms and stared at her with the sort of look that said you're on your own. She shook her head. 'I'm very sorry, but you've come at a bad time.'

'Please, Mrs Washington. This won't take long, and it would be terribly inconvenient to come back later.' I thought about saying *aw, shucks*, but I figured that would be overboard.

She fingered the card and looked at the younger man. 'James Edward, did you offer the man a cool drink?'

James Edward said, 'You want a Scrapple?'

'No, thank you. I won't take any more of your time than necessary.'

Mrs Washington offered me a seat in the overstuffed chair. It was worn and comfortable and probably had belonged to Mr Washington. She sat on the couch with the girl and the baby. James Edward didn't sit.

I said, 'Was Lewis in a gang, Mrs Washington?'

Her foot began to move. Nervous. 'No, he was not. The police said he was, but that wasn't so.'

'I saw his arrest record. He was arrested for stealing electronics equipment with three other young men when he was sixteen years old. All four kids, including Lewis, admitted to being members of the Double-Seven Hoover Crips.'

'When he was a baby.' The foot stopped moving and she made an impatient gesture. 'Lewis got out of all that. That Winslow Johnston was the troublemaker. They put him in the penitentiary and he got killed there and Lewis gave it up. He joined the Navy and got away from all this. When he came back he found Shalene.' Mrs Washington reached out and patted Shalene on the thigh. 'He was trying to make something of himself.'

Shalene was staring at me the way you stare at someone when you're thinking that a good time would be punching little holes in their head with an ice pick.

'The report also said Lewis owned the pawnshop.'

'That's right.'

'Where'd he get the money to buy an ongoing business like that, Mrs Washington?'

There were lovely crocheted doilies on the couch's arms. She straightened the one nearest her, then began to twist it. 'He had money from the Navy. And I co-signed some papers.'

Marcus climbed down off the couch and toddled out of the living room and into the kitchen. Mrs Washington leaned forward to see where he was going but Shalene didn't. Mrs Washington straightened and looked at her. 'You'd better see where he's going.'

Shalene went into the kitchen after him.

I said, 'Mrs Washington, I don't want to offend you, and I promise you that nothing you say to me will be repeated to police or to anyone else. Was Lewis fencing stolen goods?'

Her eyes filled. 'Yes,' she said. 'I believe that he was. But that gave them no call. Lewis didn't carry no gun. Lewis wouldn't have done what they said.'

'Yes, ma'am.'

'I know my boy. I know him the way only a mother can know a son. They had no call to hurt my boy.' Jennifer Sheridan knowing Mark Thurman.

'Yes, ma'am.' She was twisting the crocheted doily into a high, tight peak.

I said, 'If you believe that, then why did you drop the wrongful-death suit against the officers who killed him?'

Mrs Washington closed her eyes against the tears, and the old man spoke for the first time. He said, 'Because Lewis was always looking for trouble and he finally found it. There's nothing else to it, no reason to keep it alive.' His voice was deep and gravelly, and more like a bark than a voice. His eyes blinked rapidly as he said it. 'It was right to let it go, just let it go and walk away. Let the dead lie. There's nothing more to say to it.' He put the Scrapple can carefully on the floor, then, just as carefully, he pushed himself up and walked from the room. He took very short steps, and used first the couch and then the wall to steady himself. Shalene had come back with Marcus in her arms to stand in the door to the kitchen, staring at me and hating me. Mrs Washington was staring into the folds of her lap, eyes clenched, her body quivering as if it were a leaf in the wind. I sat there in the warm living room and looked at them and listened and I did not believe them. Mrs Washington said, 'You should go. I'm sorry, now, but you should go.'

'You really, truly believe he was murdered.'

'You have to go.'

I said, 'Did the officers threaten you?'

'Please, go.'

'The officers who shot Lewis. Did they come here and threaten you and make you drop the suit?'

'Please leave.'

James Edward said, 'What're you going to tell him, Mama?'

'Don't you say anything, James Edward. There's nothing more to say.' Ida Leigh Washington pushed to her feet and waved me toward the door. 'I want you out of my house. You're not the police and you have no paper that says you can be here and I want you out.'

Marcus began to wail. For a moment, everything was still, and then I stood. 'Thank you for your time, Mrs Washington. I'm sorry about your son.'

James Edward went to the door and followed me out. Mrs Washington hurried after us, but stopped in the door. 'Don't you go out there with him, James Edward. They'll see you, out there.'

James Edward said, 'It's all right, Mama.'

He pushed her gently back into the house and closed the door. It was cooler on the porch, and the rose smell was fresh and strong. We stood like that for a moment, then James Edward went to the edge of the porch and peered out between the roses and looked at his neighborhood. He said, 'I wasn't here when it happened.'

'The Navy?'

He nodded. 'Missed the riots, too. I was away for four years, first in the Med, then the Indian.'

'How long have you been out?'

'Five weeks, four days, and I gotta come back to this.' He looked at me. 'You think it's the cops, huh?'

I nodded.

He gave disgusted, and moved into the shade behind the trellis. 'The cops killed my brother, but a nigger named Akeem D'Muere made'm drop the suit.'

I gave him stupid. 'Who's Akeem D'Muere?'

'Runs a gang called the Eight-Deuce Gangster Boys.'

'A black gang made your family drop the suit?' I was taking stupid into unexplored realms.

'You're the detective. I been away for four years.' He turned from the street and sat on the glider and I sat next to him.

'So why's a black gang force a black family to drop a wrongful-death suit against a bunch of white cops?'

He shook his head. 'Can't say. But I'm gonna find out.'

'There has to be some kind of connection.'

'Man, you must be Sherlock fuckin' Holmes.'

'Hey, you get me up to speed, I'm something to watch.'

He nodded, but he didn't look like he believed it.

I said, 'This is your 'hood, James Edward, not mine. If there's a connection between these guys, there's going to be a way to find out, but I don't know what it is.'

'So what?'

'So they don't have a detective's-mate rating in the Navy, and maybe I can help you find out. I find out, and maybe we can get your mother out from under this thing.'

James Edward Washington gave me a long, slow look, like maybe he was wondering about something, and then he got up and started off the porch without waiting for me. 'C'mon. I know a man we can see.'

11

We walked out to the Corvette and James Edward Washington gave approval. I got in, but James Edward took a slow walk around. 'Sixty-five?'

'Sixty-six.'

'I thought private eyes were supposed to drive clunky little cars like Columbo.'

'That's TV.'

'What about if you follow somebody? Don't a car like this stand out?' James Edward was liking my car just fine.

'If I was living in Lost Overshoe, Nebraska, it stands out. In L.A., it's just another convertible. A lot of places I work, if I drove a clunker it'd stand out more than this.'

James Edward smiled. 'Yeah, but this ain't those places. This is South Central.'

'We'll see.'

James Edward climbed in, told me to head east toward Western, and I pulled a K-turn and did it.

We drove north on Western to Slauson, then turned east to parallel the railroad tracks, then turned north again. James Edward told me that we were going to see a guy he knew named Ray Depente. He said that Ray had spent twenty-two years in the Marine Corps, teaching hand-to-hand down at Camp Pendleton before tendering his retirement and opening a gym here in Los Angeles to work with kids and sponsor gang intervention programs. He also said that if anyone knew the South Central gang scene, Ray did. I said that sounded good to me.

Four blocks above Broadway I spotted the same two guys in the same blue sedan that I'd suspected of following me two days ago. They stayed with us through two turns, and never came closer than three cars nor dropped back farther than six. When we came to a 7-Eleven, I pulled into the lot and told James Edward that I had to make a call. I used the pay phone there to dial a gun shop in Culver City, and a man's voice answered on the second ring. 'Pike.'

'It's me. I'm standing in a 7-Eleven parking lot on San Pedro about three blocks south of Martin Luther King Boulevard. I'm with a black guy in his early twenties named James Edward Washington. A white guy and a Hispanic guy in a dark blue 1989 sedan are following us. I think they've been following me for the past two days.'

'Shoot them.' Life is simple for some of us.

'I was thinking more that you could follow them as they follow me and we could find out who they are.'

Pike didn't say anything.

'Also, I think they're cops.'

Pike grunted. 'Where you headed?'

'A place called Ray's Gym. In South Central.'

Pike grunted again. 'I know Ray's. Are you in immediate danger?'

I looked around. 'Well, I could probably get hit by a meteor.'

Pike said, 'Go to Ray's. You won't see me, but I'll be there when you come out.' Then he hung up. Some partner, huh?

I climbed back into the car, and fourteen minutes later we pulled into a gravel parking lot on the side of Ray Depente's gymnasium. James Edward Washington led me inside.

Ray's is a big underground cavern kind of place with peeling paint and high ceilings and the smell of sweat pressed into the walls. Maybe forty people were spread around the big room, men and women, some stretching, some grinding through *katas* like formal dance routines, some sparring with full-contact pads. An athletic woman with strawberry hair was on the mats with a tall black man with mocha skin and gray-flecked hair. They were working hard, the woman snapping kick after kick at his legs and torso and head, him yelling c'mon, get in here, c'mon, I'm wide open. Every time she kicked, sweat flew off her and sprayed the mat. Each of them was covered with so many pads they might've been in space suits. James Edward said, 'That's Ray.'

I started fooling around with the martial arts when I was in the Army and I got pretty good at it. Ray Depente was good, too, and he looked like an outstanding teacher. He snapped light punches and kicks at the woman, making her think defense as well as offense. He tapped them on the heavy pad over her breasts and taunted her, saying stop me, saying Jesus Christ protect yourself, saying you mine anytime I want you. She kicked faster, snapping up roundhouse kicks and power kicks, then coming in backwards with spin kicks. He blocked most of the kicks and slipped a few and taunted her harder, saying he ain't never had a white woman but he was about to get one now. As fast as he said it she hooked his left knee and he stumbled to catch himself and when he did she got off a high fast spin kick that caught him on the back of the head and bowled him over and then she was on him, spiking kicks hard at his groin pad and his spine and his head and he doubled into a ball, covering up, yelling that he gives, he gives, he gives, and laughing the big deep laugh. She helped him up and they bowed to each other, both of them grinning, and then she gave a whoop and jumped up to give him a major league hug. Then she hopped away to the locker rooms, pumping her fist and yelling 'Yeah!' Ray Depente stepped off the mat, unfastening the pads, and then he saw us standing on the hardwood at the edge of the mat. He grinned at James Edward and came over, still pulling off the pads. He was two inches taller than me and maybe fifteen pounds heavier. 'Welcome back, Admiral. I've missed you, young man.'

He grabbed James Edward in a tight hug, and the two men pounded each other on their backs. When James Edward stepped back, he said, 'You ain't never had a white woman but you're about to get one now?'

Ray grinned. 'Thirteen months ago two assholes followed her into a parking lot in Rancho Park. One of them raped her in the backseat of her MB. The second one was just getting ready to mount up when a couple of women came along and scared'm off. What you think would happen if those guys came back today?'

'Testicular transplant?'

'Uh-huh.'

I said, 'She's come along fast.'

'Motivation, baby. Motivation is all.'

James Edward said, 'Ray, this is Elvis Cole. He's a private investigator.'

'Do tell.' We shook. Ray Depente had a hand like warm steel. 'What do you investigate?'

'I'm working with something that's bumped up against a gang called the Eight-Deuce Gangster Boys. James Edward says that you know about those guys.'

Ray peeled away the rest of his body pads and used his sweatshirt to wipe his face and neck. Everybody else in the place was wearing heavy canvas karate *gies*, but not Ray. Ray wore desert-issue combat pants and an orange Marine Corps tee shirt. Old habits. 'Bumping up against the Crips isn't something you want to do if you can help it. Crips got sharp edges.'

I gave him shrug. 'Occupational hazard.'

'Uh-huh. Be tough and see.'

'The Gangster Boys a Crip set?' People hear Crips or Bloods and they think it's just two big gangs, but it isn't. Both the Crips and the Bloods are made up of smaller gang sets. Eight-Deuce Gangster Boys, Eight-Trey Swan Crips, Rolling Sixties Crips, Double-Seven Hoover Crips, East Coast Crips, like that.

Ray nodded. 'Yeah. From down around Eighty-second and Hoover. That's where they get the name. You want to be a Gangster Boy, you got to do a felony. You want to be OG, you got to pull the trigger. It's as simple as that.'

James Edward said, 'O.G. means Original Gangster. That's like saying you're a made man in the Mafia.'

'Okay.'

Ray said, 'What are you messing around with that's got you down here in South Central with a goddamned Crip set?'

'Charles Lewis Washington.'

Ray's smile faded and he looked at James Edward. 'How's your mama doing, son?'

'She's okay. We got a little problem with the Eight-Deuce, though.'

Ray looked back at me. 'You working for the family?'

'Nope. But maybe what I'm doing gets us to the same place.'

Ray looked at James Edward and James Edward nodded. Ray said, 'I hadn't seen Lewis for a couple years, but when I heard about him dying, I didn't like it, and I didn't like how it happened. I worked with that boy out of youth services. It was a long time ago and he didn't stay with it, but there it is. Once you're one of my young men, you're one of my young men. Just like this one.' Ray Depente put a warm steel hand on James Edward's shoulder and gave him a squeeze. 'I tried to point this one toward the Marines but he liked the idea of ships.' Ray and James Edward grinned at each other, and the grins were as warm as the hand.

I said, 'The cops say that Lewis was a Double-Seven gangbanger. His mother says no.'

Ray frowned. 'Lewis used to mess around with the Double-Sevens, but that was years ago. That's how he came to me.'

'He ever have anything to do with the Eight-Deuce Gangster Boys?'

'Not that I know.'

'The family filed a wrongful death after Lewis was killed, but James Edward here tells me that a guy named Akeem D'Muere made them back off.'

Ray looked at James Edward again. 'You sure?'

James Edward nodded.

I said, 'Why would Akeem D'Muere go to bat for a bunch of white LAPD officers?'

Ray shook his head. 'I know Akeem. Akeem D'Muere wouldn't go to bat for anybody unless there's something in it for him.'

'When Lewis Washington died, every news service in town was looking into it, smelling Rodney King all over again. Maybe Akeem D'Muere wanted all the looking to stop. Maybe there was something going on at the Premier Pawn Shop that he didn't want anyone to find out.'

'You think?'

I shrugged. 'I think there's a connection. I just don't know who to ask to find out.'

James Edward said, 'That's why I brought him here, Ray. Figured you'd be the guy to know.'

Ray Depente smiled at James Edward. 'You want me to ask around, young mister, I can do that. Know a man who'll probably be able to help. But you stay away from those Eight-Deuce. The Navy doesn't teach you what you need to know to mess with that trash.'

James Edward said, 'Hell Ray.'

The strawberry-haired woman came out of the dressing room, showered and changed, and gave Ray a ten-megawatt smile as she bounced out of the gym and into the sunshine. I said, 'Pretty.'

Ray said, 'Uh-huh.'

An older woman pushed her head out of a little glass cubicle that served as an office at the rear of the gym. She called, 'Ray, it's somebody from Twentieth Century-Fox. They say it's some kind of emergency and they need you to come over and show Bruce Willis how to do something for a movie they're making.'

James Edward grinned. 'Bruce Willis. Damn.'

Ray didn't look as thrilled with Bruce Willis as did James Edward. 'Now?'

'They said right away.'

James Edward said, 'These studio dudes hire Ray to set up fight scenes and teach his moves to their actors. Arnold been here, man. Sly Stallone useta come here.'

Ray shook his head. 'I can do it tonight, but I can't do it now. I've got a class coming in, now.'

The woman said, 'They said right away.'

Ray shook his head. 'Movie people.' He called back to her. 'Tell'm I gotta pass.'

James Edward Washington gave impressed. 'Is this fuckin' righteous or what? Tellin' Bruce Willis to pass.'

The older woman went back into the glass cubicle.

Ray said, 'Jesus Christ, James Edward. It ain't no big thing.' Ray Depente looked my way and gave embarrassed. 'These kids think this movie stuff is a big deal. They don't know. A client's a client.'

'Sure.'

'I've got a class.'

'Sure.'

A dozen little girls came in, shepherded by a tall erect black woman in a neat dress suit. Most of the little girls were black, but a couple were Hispanic. They all wore clean white karate *gies* and tennis shoes. They took off their shoes before they stepped onto the mat. Ray uncrossed his arms and smiled. 'Here they are, now.'

James Edward Washington laughed and said, 'Damn.'

Ray Depente squeezed James Edward's shoulder again, then told me that it had been a pleasure to meet me, and that if he learned something he would give James Edward a call. Then he turned away and walked out onto the mat to face his class.

The little girls formed a neat line as if they had done it a thousand times before and bowed toward Ray Depente and shouted *kun hey* with perfect Korean inflection. Ray said something so quietly that I could not hear, and then he bowed to them.

Ray Depente gets five hundred dollars an hour from movie stars, but some things are more important.

12

James Edward Washington wanted to chill with Ray for a while, so he stayed, and I walked out to my car, making a big deal out of taking off my jacket so that I could look up and down the street and across the intersections. Joe Pike drives an immaculate red Jeep Cherokee, and I was hoping to spot him or the blue sedan, but I saw neither. Of course, maybe they weren't there. Maybe the blue sedan hadn't really been following me and I was making a big deal with the jacket for nothing. Elvis Cole, Existential Detective. On the other hand, maybe the guys in the blue sedan were better than me and I wasn't good enough to spot them.

Not.

I climbed the ramp to the I-10 freeway and went west, changing lanes to avoid slower traffic and speeding up when the traffic allowed and trying to play it normal. Just another Angeleno in the system. It paid off. A quarter mile past the La Brea exit I spotted the blue sedan hiding on the far side of a Ryder moving van, two lanes over. The guy with the Dodgers cap was still driving and the guy with the butch cut was still riding shotgun.

I took the La Cienega exit and went north, timing the lights to get a better view, but always just missing. They were good. Always three or four cars back, always with plenty of separation, and they didn't seem worried that they'd lose me. That meant they knew they could always pick me up again, or that they were working with a second car. Cops always use a second car.

La Cienega is four lanes, but Caltrans was at it again, and as La Cienega approached Pico, the two northbound lanes became one. There's a 20/20 Video in a large shopping center on the northeast corner, and the closer I got to the 20/20, the slower I drove. By the time I cleared the work in the intersection, a guy behind me in a Toyota 4x4 had had enough and roared past, giving me the finger. I stayed in the right lane as I crossed Pico, and the remaining two cars behind me turned. Then there was just me and the blue sedan. The driver swung right, making the turn with the two other cars as if they had never intended anything else, and that's when I picked up the slack car. Floyd Riggens was driving his dark brown sedan two cars back, sitting in traffic behind a couple of guys on mopeds. My, my.

I stayed north on La Cienega and three blocks later the blue sedan sat at a side street ahead of me, waiting. As soon as they made the turn onto Pico they must've punched it like an F-16 going into afterburner, then swung north on a parallel side street to come in ahead of me. Floyd would've radioed that he still had me in sight, and that we were proceeding northbound, and that's how they'd know where to wait. Floyd hung back, and after I passed, the blue sedan pulled in behind me again. Right where I wanted them.

I turned east on Beverly, then dropped down Fairfax past CBS Television City to the Farmer's Market. The Market is a loose collection of buildings surrounded on all sides by parking lots used mostly by tour buses and people from Utah, come to gawk at CBS.

I turned into the north lot and made my way past the buses and about a million empty parking spots toward the east lot. Most of the traffic stays in the north lot, but if you want to get from the north lot to the east, you have to funnel through a cramped drive that runs between a couple of buildings where people sell papayas and framed pictures of Pat Sajak. It's narrow and it's cramped and it's lousy when you're here on a Saturday and the place is jammed with tourists, but it's ideal for a private eye looking to spring an ambush.

When I was clear of the little drive, I pulled a quick reverse and backed my car behind a flower truck. A teenaged girl in a white Volkswagen Rabbit came through the gap after me, and, a few seconds later, the blue sedan followed. It came through at a creep, the guy in the passenger seat pointing to the south and the driver sitting high to see what he was pointing at. Whatever he saw he didn't like it, because he made an angry gesture and looked away and that's when they saw me. I jumped the Corvette into their path and got out of the car with my hands clear so they could see I had no gun. The kid with the butch bounced out and started yelling into a handi-talkie and the Hispanic guy was running toward me with his badge in one hand and a Browning 9mm in the other. Floyd Riggens was roaring toward us from the far end of the lot. Thurman wasn't with him. Thurman wasn't anywhere around.

The Hispanic guy yelled, 'Get your hands up. Out and away from your body.' When the guns come out there's always a lot of yelling.

The guy with the butch ran over and patted me down with his free hand. I made him for Pinkworth. The other guy for Garcia. While Pinkworth did the shakedown, some of the people from the tour buses began to gather on the walk and look at us. Most of the men were in Bermuda shorts and most of the women were in summer-weight pant suits and just about everyone held a camera. Tourists. They stood in a little group as they watched, and a fat kid with glasses and a DES MOINES sweatshirt said, 'Hey, neat.' Maybe they thought we were the CBS version of the Universal stunt show.

Garcia said, 'Jesus Christ, we've got a goddamned crowd.'

I smiled at him. 'My fans.'

Pinkworth looked nervous and lowered his gun like someone might see it and tell. Garcia lowered his, too.

Riggens's car screeched to a stop and he kicked open the door. His face was flushed and he looked angry. He also looked drunk. 'Stay the fuck away from my wife.'

Garcia yelled, 'Floyd,' but Floyd wasn't listening. He took two long steps forward, then lunged toward me with his body sort of cocked to the side like he was going to throw a haymaker and knock me into the next time zone.

He swung, and I stepped outside of it and snapped a high roundhouse kick into the side of his head that knocked him over sideways.

The fat kid said, 'Look at that!' and the fat kid's father aimed a Sony video camera at us.

When Riggens fell, Garcia's gun came up and Pinkworth started forward, and that's when Joe Pike reared up from behind their car, snapped the slide on a 12-gauge Ithaca riot gun, and said, 'Don't.'

Garcia and Pinkworth froze. They spread their fingers off their pistol grips, showing they were out of it.

The crowd went, 'Ooo.' Some show, all right.

Joe Pike stands six-one and weighs maybe one-ninety, and he's got large red arrows tattooed on the outside of each deltoid, souvenirs from his days as a Force Recon Marine in Vietnam. He was wearing faded blue jeans and Nike running shoes and a plain gray sweatshirt with the sleeves cut off and government-issue sunglasses. Angle the sun on him just right, and sometimes the tattoos seem to glow. I think Pike calls it his apparition look.

I said, 'Gee, and I thought you'd got lost in traffic.'

Pike's mouth twitched. He doesn't smile, but sometimes he'll twitch. You get a twitch out of Pike, he's gotta be dying on the inside. In tears, he's gotta be.

I took Garcia's and Pinkworth's guns, and Pike circled the blue sedan, finding a better angle to cover Riggens. When he moved, he seemed to glide, as if he were flowing over the surface of the earth, moving as a panther might move. To move was to stalk. I'd never seen him move any other way.

Garcia said, 'Put down that goddamned gun. We're LAPD officers, goddamn it.'

Pike's shotgun didn't waver. An older woman with a lime green sun hat and a purse the size of a mailbag looked at the other tourists and said, 'Does the bus leave after this?'

I pulled Riggens's gun and then I went back to Pinkworth and Garcia and checked their IDs. Pinkworth said, 'You're marked fuck for this, asshole. You're going down *hard.*'

'Uh-huh.'

Riggens moaned and sort of turned onto his side. His head was bleeding where it had bounced on the tarmac, but it didn't look bad. I took the clips out of the three police guns, tossed them into the blue sedan's backseat, then went back to Riggens. 'Let me see.'

Riggens pushed my hand off and tried to crab away, but he didn't do much more than flop onto his back. 'Fuck you.'

Pinkworth said, 'You're in a world of shit. You just assaulted a Los Angeles police officer.'

I said, 'Call it in and let's go to the station. Maybe they'll give Riggens a Breathalyzer while you guys are booking me.' You could smell it on him a block away.

Garcia said, 'Quiet, Pink.'

A green four-door sedan identical to the other two cop sedans came toward us across the lot. Riggens was still trying to get up when the green car pulled in behind him and a tall guy with short gray hair got out. He was wearing chino slacks and a striped short-sleeve shirt tucked neatly into his pants and short-topped Redwing trail shoes. He was tanned dark, like he spent a lot of time in the sun, and his face was lined. I made him for his mid-forties, but he could've been older. He looked at Riggens, then the two cops by the blue sedan, and then at Joe Pike. He wasn't upset and he wasn't excited, like he knew what he'd find when he got here and, when he got here, he knew that he could handle it. When he saw Joe Pike he said, 'I didn't know you were in on this.'

Pike nodded once.

I gave them surprised. 'You guys know each other?'

Pike said, 'Eric Dees.'

Eric Dees looked at me, then looked back at Pike. 'Pike and I rode a black-and-white together for a couple of months maybe a million years ago.' Pike had been a uniformed LAPD officer when I'd met him. 'Put away the shotgun, Joe. It's over, now. No one's going to drop the hammer.'

Pike lowered the shotgun.

Pinkworth craned around and stared at Pike. 'This sonofabitch is Joe Pike? *The* Joe Pike?' Pike had worn the uniform for almost three years, but it hadn't ended well.

Riggens said, 'Who?' He was still having trouble on the ground.

Dees said, 'Sure. You've just been jumped by the best.'

76

Pinkworth glowered at Pike like he'd been wanting to glower at him for a long time. 'Well, fuck him.'

Joe's head sort of whirred five degrees to line up on Pinkworth and Pinkworth's glower wavered. There is a machine-like quality to Joe, as if he had tuned his body the way he might tune his Jeep, and, as the Jeep was perfectly tuned, so was his body. It was easy to imagine him doing a thousand pushups or running a hundred miles, as if his body were an instrument of his mind, as if his mind were a well of limitless resource and unimaginable strength. If the mind said start, the body would start. When the mind said stop, the body would stop, and whatever it would do, it would do with precision and exactness.

Dees said, 'Long time, Joe. How's it going?'

Pike's head whirred back and he made a kind of head shrug.

'Talkative, as always.' Dees looked at the people from Des Moines. 'Pink, move those people along. We don't need a crowd.' Pinkworth gave me tough, then pulled out his badge and sauntered over to the crowd. The fat kid's father didn't want to move along and made a deal out of it. Dees turned back to me. 'You're this close to getting stepped on for obstruction and for impersonating an officer, Cole. We drop the hammer, your license is history.'

I said, 'What's your connection with Akeem D'Muere and the Eight-Deuce Gangster Boys?'

Dees blinked once, then made a little smile, like maybe he wasn't smiling at me, but at something he was thinking. 'That's an official police investigation. That's what I'm telling you to stay away from. I'm also telling you to stay the hell out of Mark Thurman's personal life. You fuck with my people, you're fucking with me, and you don't want to do that. I'm a bad guy to fuck with.'

Riggens made a sort of a coughing sound, then sat up, squinted at me, and said, 'I'm gonna clean your ass, you fuck.' He got most of his feet under himself but then the feet slipped out and he sort of stumbled backwards until he rammed his head into the green sedan's left front wheel with a *thunk*. He grabbed at his head and said, 'Jesus.'

Dees stared hard at me for another moment, then went to Riggens. 'That's enough, Floyd.'

Floyd said, 'He hit me, Eric. The fuck's takin' the ride.' There was blood on Riggens's face.

Dees bunched his fingers into Riggens's shirt and gave a single hard jerk that almost pulled Riggens off the ground and popped his head back against the sedan. 'No one's going in, Floyd.'

Riggens got up, took out a handkerchief, and dabbed at his head. The handkerchief came back red. 'Shit.'

I said, 'Better get some ice.'

'Fuck you.'

Dees made a little hand move at Garcia. 'Pete, take Floyd over there and get some ice.'

Floyd said, 'I don't need any goddamn ice. I'm fine.'

Dees said, 'You don't look fine. You look like a lush who got outclassed.' When he said it his voice was hard and commanding and Floyd Riggens jerked sideways as if he had been hit with a cattle prod. Garcia went over to him and took him by the arm. Floyd shook his hand off but followed him into the Market.

Joe Pike said, 'Elite.'

Eric Dees's face went hard. 'They're good, Joe. They didn't cut and walk away.'

Pike's head whirred back to lock onto Eric Dees.

I said, 'That's the second time I've seen Riggens and the second time I've seen him drunk. Your people always get shitfaced on duty?'

Dees came close to me. He was a little bit taller than me, and wider, and maybe six or eight years older. He reminded me of a couple of senior NCOs that I had known in the Army, men who were used to leading men and taking care of men and exercising authority over men. He said, 'I take care of my people, asshole. You'd better worry about taking care of you.'

Joe Pike said, 'Easy, Eric.'

Eric Dees said, 'Easy what, Joe?' He looked back at me. 'This is your wake-up call, and you're only going to get one. The little girl's problems with Mark are going to be solved. She's not going to need you anymore. That means you're off the board.'

'Is that why four LAPD officers have nothing better to do than follow me around?'

'We followed you to talk to you. It was either talk to you or kill you.'

'I'm shaking, Dees.' The detective plays it tough. 'What did Akeem D'Muere have to do with Lewis Washington's death?'

When I said Lewis Washington, Dees's eyes went hard and I wondered if I'd pushed too hard. 'I'm trying to play square with you, Cole. Maybe because of Joe, or maybe because I'm a square guy, but if you're not smart enough to listen, there are other ways I can solve the problem.'

'Where's Mark Thurman? You give him the day off?'

Dees looked at the ground like he was trying to think of the magic word, and then Pinkworth came back with Riggens and Garcia. As soon as Pinkworth turned away, the crowd came back. The fat kid's father was smiling. Riggens got into his sedan and Pinkworth and Garcia went back to the blue. Dees looked up at me with eyes that were profoundly tired. 'You're not helping the girl, Cole. You think you are, but you're not.'

'Maybe she has nothing to do with it anymore. Maybe it's larger than her. Maybe it's about Lewis Washington and Akeem D'Muere and why five LAPD officers are so scared of this that they're living in my shorts.'

Dees nodded. Like he knew it was coming, but he wasn't especially glad to see it arrive. 'It's your call, bubba.'

Then he went back to his car and drove away.

Riggens cranked his sedan and took off after him with a lot of tire squealing. Garcia fired up the blue, and as they pulled out after Riggens, Pinkworth gave me the finger. When he gave me the finger the fat kid in the DES MOINES sweatshirt laughed and shook his dad's arm so that his dad would see.

A Kodak moment.

13

Thirty-five minutes later I pulled up the little road to my house and saw Pike's red Jeep Cherokee under the elm by the front steps. I had left the Farmer's Market before Pike, and I had made good time, but when I got home, there he was, as if he had been there for hours, as if he had been both here and there at the same time. He does this a lot, but I have never been able to figure out how. Teleportation, maybe.

Pike was holding the cat and the two of them were staring at something across the canyon. Looking for more cops, no doubt. I said, 'How'd you beat me?'

Pike put down the cat. 'I didn't know it was a race.' You see how he is?

I turned off the alarm and let us into the kitchen through the carport. I was uncomfortable moving into and through the house, as if I expected more cops to be hiding in a closet or behind the couch. I looked around and wondered if they had been in the house. People have been in my house before. I didn't like it then, and I liked it even less, now.

Pike said, 'We're clear.'

One minute he's across the room, the next he's right behind you. 'How do you know?'

'Went down to the end of the road. Checked the downslope and the upslope. Walked through the house before you got here.' He made a little shrug. 'We're clear.'

A six-thousand-dollar alarm, and it's nothing to Pike.

He said, 'You want to tell me about this?'

I took two Falstaffs out of the refrigerator, gave one to Pike and kept one for myself, and then I told him about Jennifer and Thurman and Eric Dees's REACT team. 'Four months ago Dees's team was involved in an arrest in which a man named Charles Lewis Washington died. Washington's family filed a suit against Dees and the city, but they dropped it when a street gang called the Eight-Deuce Gangster Boys pressed them.'

Pike took some of the Falstaff and nodded. 'So what's the connection between a street gang and Eric Dees?'

'That's the question, isn't it?'

I went upstairs, got the notes I had made on the case, and brought them down. 'You hungry?'

'Always.'

'I've got some of the venison left.'

Pike made a face. 'You got something green?' Two years ago he had gone vegetarian.

'Sure. Tuna, also, if you want.' He'll sometimes eat fish. 'Read the notes first, then we'll talk after.'

Pike took the notes, and I went into the freezer for the venison. In the fall, I had hunted the hill country of central California for blacktail deer and had harvested a nice buck. I had kept the tenderloins and chops, and had the rest turned into smoked sausage by a German butcher I know in West L.A. The tenderloins and the chops were gone, but I still had three plump sausage rings. I took two of the rings from the freezer, put them in the microwave to thaw, then went out onto the deck to build the fire. The cat was sitting out there, under the bird feeder. I said, 'Forget the birds. We're making Bambi.'

The cat blinked at me, then came over and sat by the grill. Venison is one of his favorite things.

I keep a Weber charcoal grill out on the deck, along with a circular redwood picnic table. The same woman who had given me the bird feeder had also helped me build the picnic table. Actually, she had done most of the building and I had done most of the helping, but that had probably worked out better for the table. I scraped the grill, then built a bed of mesquite coals in the pit and fired them. Mesquite charcoal takes a while, so you have to get your fire going before you do anything else.

When the coals were on their way, I went back into the kitchen.

Pike looked up from the report. 'We're squaring off against five LAPD officers, and all we're getting paid is forty bucks?'

'Nope. We're also getting forty dollars per month for the next forty-nine months.'

Pike shook his head.

'Think of it as job security, Joe. Four years of steady income.'

Pike sighed.

I opened another Falstaff, drank half of it on the way upstairs to the shower, and the other half on the way back down. When I got back down, Pike had built a large salad with tuna and garbanzo beans and tomatoes and onions. We brought the salad and the venison out onto the deck.

The sky had deepened, and as the sun settled into a purple pool in the west, the smells of budding eucalyptus and night-blooming jasmine mingled with the mesquite smoke. It was a clean, healthy smell, and made me think, as it always does, of open country and little boys and girls climbing trees and chasing fireflies. Maybe I was one of the little boys. Maybe I still am. There are no fireflies in Los Angeles.

I put the venison on the grill, then sat with Pike at the table and told him about Charles Lewis Washington and the Washington family and what I had learned from Ray Depente about Akeem D'Muere and the Eight-Deuce Gangster Boys.

Pike sipped his beer and listened. When I finished he said, 'You think the family was telling the truth about Charles Lewis going straight?'

'They believed it.'

'Then where'd a guy like that get the cash to buy a solvent business?'

'There is that, yes.'

'Maybe he had a partner.'

I nodded. 'D'Muere funds the pawnshop to front a fence operation, and Lewis's working for D'Muere. I can see that, but why does D'Muere front off the Washington family from pressing their lawsuit? The pawnshop is shut down. The fence operation is history.'

'If there's a suit, there's an investigation. There was something else there that he wants to hide.'

'Something that Eric Dees knows?'

Pike shrugged.

'If Dees knows about it, it's not hidden.'

Pike angled his head around and stared at me. 'Unless it's something Eric wants hidden, too.'

'Ah.' I turned the sausages. Fat was beginning to bubble out of the skin and they smelled wonderful. 'Akeem D'Muere and Eric Dees are sharing a secret.'

Pike nodded.

'The question arises, how far will they go to protect it?'

Pike stared at me for a moment, then got up and went into the house. I heard the front door open, then I heard his Jeep's door, and then he came back out onto the deck. When he came back, he was wearing his pistol. It's a Colt Python .357 with a four-inch barrel. Eternal vigilance is the price of freedom. I said, 'Guess that means they'll go pretty far.'

Pike said, 'If five cops are on you, then it's important to them. If they're with you, then they're not doing the work they're supposed to be doing, and that's not easy to cover. Dees's people can't just go to the beach. He has to account for their time to his boss, and he has to produce results with whatever cases they're working.'

'And all five guys have to be on board with it.'

Pike nodded. 'Everybody has to be on board.'

I turned the sausages again. The skins were taking on a crunchy texture and the cat had hopped up on the rail that runs around the edge of the deck so he could be as close to the sausage as possible. Any closer and we could serve barbecued cat.

Pike said, 'Eric was nervous. That's not like him. Maybe even scared, and that's not like him, either.'

82

'Okay.'

'Scared people do atypical things. He was thinking maybe that he could scare you off. Now that he knows that I'm in, it will change what he thinks. He knows that I won't scare.'

'Great. That will make him all the more dangerous.'

'Yes,' Pike said. 'It will.'

'Maybe Dees is telling the truth. Maybe we're just stepping on a case and he's pissed.'

Pike shook his head. 'He wants you out, it's easy. He tells his boss and his boss calls you in and you sit down together. You know that.' The sky darkened and the hillside below us grew speckled with lights. Pike adjusted his sunglasses, but did not remove them. He never removes them. Even at night. 'If he's not playing it straight, then he can't play it straight. That's the first rule every cop learns.'

I turned the sausage rings a last time, then took them off the grill and put them onto a maple cutting board. I sliced them at an angle, then put half the meat on my plate and a serious portion on a saucer for the cat. I blew on his to cool it. Pike went into the house and came out with two more Falstaffs and what was left of a loaf of rosemary bread. I took some of the salad and tasted it. Pike had made a dressing of soy sauce, rice vinegar, and minced garlic. I nodded. 'Good.'

He nodded back.

We ate without speaking for several minutes, and Pike didn't look happy. Of course, since Pike never smiles, it's sometimes tough to tell when he is happy, but there are ways. I said, 'What?'

Pike picked up a piece of tuna with his fingers, took a small bite, then held out the rest to the cat. The cat stepped forward and ate with enthusiasm. Pike said, 'I haven't seen Eric in many years.'

'Was he good?'

'Yes.'

'Was he honest?'

Pike turned his head and the dark lenses angled toward me. 'If I saw it any other way, I wouldn't have ridden with him.'

I nodded. 'But people change.'

Pike wiped his fingers on his napkin, then turned back to his meal. 'Yes. People change.'

We ate the rest of the meal in silence, and then we brought the dirty dishes into the kitchen and flipped a nickel to see who would wash. I lost. Midway through the load the phone rang and Joe Pike answered. He said, 'Jennifer Sheridan.'

I took the phone and said, 'Elvis Cole, Personal Detective to Jennifer Sheridan.'

Jennifer Sheridan said, 'Floyd Riggens just left me. He was here with another officer. They said that I was going to get Mark killed. They said that if I didn't make you stop, something bad would happen.' Her voice was tight and compressed and the words came quickly, as if she were keeping a close rein, but just.

'Are you all right?'

'I called Mark, but he's not home.'

'What about you? Are you all right?'

I could hear her breathe. She didn't say anything for a time, and then she said, 'I'd like someone with me, I think. Would you mind?'

'I'm leaving now.'

I hung up. Pike was staring at me, his glasses reflecting the kitchen lights. 'Riggens paid her a visit. I'd better go over there.'

Pike said, 'This isn't going to work out the way she wants it to.'

I spread my hands. 'I don't know. Maybe we can make it work out that way.'

'If Dees and Thurman and these guys are mixed up with Akeem D'Muere, it'll be ugly. She may find out something about him that she wished she didn't know.'

I spread my hands again. 'Maybe that's the price for being in love.'

Pike said, 'I'll finish the dishes.'

I told him thanks, then I put on the Dan Wesson and drove to see Jennifer Sheridan.

14

Twenty-six minutes later I parked on the street across from Jennifer Sheridan's apartment building and buzzed her number on the security phone. The speaker came to life and Jennifer Sheridan said, 'Who is it?'

'Elvis Cole.'

The door lock buzzed open and I went in and took the elevator to the third floor.

Jennifer Sheridan lived in one of those stucco ant farms just off the freeway in Woodland Hills that caters to attractive young singles, attractive young couples, and the not-so-young-but-almost-as-attractive newly divorced. There would be a lot of grabass around the pool and something called a 'fitness room' where men and women would watch each other work out, but I guess it was a fair trade for a secure building at an affordable price in a low-crime area. Unless the cops were doing the crime.

Apartment 312 was down a long hall with a lot of shag carpeting and textured wallpaper and cottage-cheese ceilings. Jennifer Sheridan was peeking out of a two-inch crack in her door, waiting for me. When she saw me, she closed the door to unhook the chain, then opened it again. 'I'm sorry for calling you like that, but I didn't know what else to do. I feel so silly.'

I gave her the benevolent detective smile. 'It's no trouble and you did the right thing by calling me.' Maybe it was the six-pack-of-Falstaff smile.

She stepped out of the door and led me through an entry past her kitchen and into the living room. She was wearing an oversized white sweatshirt that hung low over black tights and white Keds tennis shoes. Comfortable. Just the kind of thing to be lounging around in in the apartment when Floyd Riggens came to call. She said, 'I tried calling Mark again, but there's still no answer. I left a message on his machine.'

'Okay.'

'There was another man with Floyd, but I don't know his name. He was a police officer, also.'

'What did he look like?'

'Bigger than Floyd, with very short hair. Blond.'

'Pinkworth.'

She nodded. 'Yes, that's right. Floyd called him Pink but I didn't realize that was a name.' She was trying to be brave and she was doing a good job.

'Did Floyd threaten you?'

She nodded.

I said, 'Did they hurt you?'

'Not really.' She made an uneasy smile, as if she didn't want to say anything that would cause trouble. 'He sort of grabbed me a little, that's all. I think he'd been drinking.' When she said it, she sort of brushed at her right arm. She wore the sweatshirt with the sleeves pushed above her elbows and on her forearm where she brushed there were angry red marks, the way there might be if someone grabbed hard and twisted.

I touched her forearm and turned it to look at the marks and a sharp pain throbbed behind my eyes. I said, 'Floyd.'

She took her arm back, and made a sort of dismissive laugh. 'I don't think he meant to. It just surprised me, that's all.'

'Of course.' The throbbing pain was worse.

It was a nice apartment, with inexpensive oak furniture and the kind of large overstuffed couch and matching chairs that you would buy on sale at Ikea or Home Club. A Sony television sat on a long white Formica table opposite the couch, along with a lot of plants and a portable CD player. A little forest of photographs stood between the plants and Mark Thurman was in most of the photographs. Many of the shots were duplicates of ones I had seen in Mark Thurman's album but many were not. An enormous stuffed Garfield stood sentry by the dining room table and a half-dozen smaller stuffed animals rested on the couch. Everything was neat and clean and in its proper place. I said, 'Why don't you sit, and I'll get something for us to drink, and then we can figure out what to do.'

She shook her head. 'I'm not helpless. Besides, the activity is good. Would you like a diet Coke or a glass of wine? I've got a Pinot Grigio.'

'The Pinot.'

She said, 'You sit, and I'll be right back.'

'Yes, ma'am.'

She smiled and went into the kitchen.

There was a pass-through between the kitchen and the living room so you could see from one into the other. I sat in the overstuffed chair at the far end of the living room and watched her get the wine. Jennifer Sheridan stood on her toes to reach two flute glasses out of her cupboard, then put them on the counter beside her sink. She opened the fridge, took out the bottle of Pinot, and worked out the cork. The Pinot had been opened earlier and was missing maybe a glass. She worked with her back to me. I watched the shape of her calves when she went up onto her toes and the line of her thighs and the way the oversized sweatshirt hung low over her bottom and draped from her shoulders. She didn't look so young from the back and I had to turn away to make myself stop looking at her. Jesus Christ, Cole. Portrait of the detective as a lecher. I looked at the pictures on the white table instead. Mark Thurman. Watching me. I crossed my eyes and made a face at him. Screw you, Mark. I looked at the Garfield, instead. Maybe you shouldn't drink a six-pack of Falstaff before you visit a client.

Jennifer Sheridan came out with the two glasses of wine, handed one of them to me, and went to the couch. She must've seen me looking at the Garfield. 'Mark won that for me. Isn't it cute?'

'How nice.' I smiled. 'Tell me about Riggens and Pinkworth. Tell me everything they said. Don't leave anything out.'

She shook her head. 'The other guy didn't say very much. He just stood by the door, and every once in a while said something like "You oughta listen to him" or "We're only trying to help."'

'Okay. Then tell me about Floyd.'

She sipped her wine and thought about it, as if she wanted to be very careful and get it right. As she told me she picked up a stuffed lion from the couch and held it. 'He told me that Mark didn't know they were here, but that he was Mark's partner and he said that someone had to straighten me out because I was going to get Mark killed. I asked him to tell me what was going on but he wouldn't. He said that I didn't love Mark and I said that I did. He said I had a funny way of showing it. I told him to get out, but he wouldn't. He said that I never should have hired you because all you're doing is making trouble.'

'Floyd and I had a run-in today.' I told her about the Farmer's Market.

She blinked at me. 'You hit him?'

'No. I kicked him.'

She said, 'Kicked?'

'Yeah. Like Bruce Lee. You know.'

'You can get your foot up that high?'

I spread my hands. 'I am a man of profound talents.'

She touched her left cheek between the ear and the eye. 'He had a bruise right here.' Sort of awed.

I spread my hands again and she smiled, maybe thinking how he had grabbed her. When she smiled I wanted to drop one wing and run in a circle. Guess we aren't so mature, after all.

I said, 'You don't get four active-duty REACT cops on your tail unless they're very scared of what you're doing. They didn't want me to know that they were on me, and now they know that I do, and they didn't want you to know that something is going on, and now Riggens has come here and threatened you. They've been trying to control the program but that isn't working, and things are beginning to fall apart. The gloves are coming off.'

She nodded, and looked thoughtful, like maybe whatever she was thinking wasn't easy to think about. She said, 'Was Mark there? At the Market?'

'No.' I was watching her. The thing that was hard to think about was even harder to say.

'He said Mark was in trouble. He said that they've been trying to help Mark, but that I was messing everything up and Mark was going to be hurt. He started yelling. He said maybe somebody ought to show me what it was like. I got scared then, and that's when he grabbed me.' She suddenly stopped speaking, went into the kitchen, and came back with the bottle of Pinot. She added more to her glass, then put the bottle on the table. 'Do you think Mark knew that Floyd was coming here?'

'I don't know. Probably not.' The detective answers a cry for support with a resounding maybe.

'I asked him why he was doing this. I asked him to tell me what had happened or what was going on. I told him I would help. He thought that was funny. He said that I didn't want to know. He said that Mark had done bad things and now they were fucked. I said Mark wasn't like that and he said I didn't know anything about Mark.' She stopped as if someone had pulled her plug, and stared into the forest of photographs.

I said, 'And you're scared he's right?'

She nodded.

'You're scared that you don't know anything about Mark, and that if you find out, you might not love him anymore.'

She pursed her lips and shook her head, then looked directly at me. 'No. I will always love him. No matter what. If he did something, it's because he believed he had to. If I can help him, then I will help him. I will love him even if he no longer loves me.' She blinked hard several times, and then took more wine. I watched her drink, and I wondered what it would be like to have someone love me with that commitment and that intensity, and, in that moment, I wished that it were me.

I said, 'Jennifer, did Mark ever mention someone named Lewis Washington?'

'No.'

'It might've been three or four months ago.'

'Maybe he said the name in passing and I wasn't paying attention, but I don't think so.'

I said, 'Four months ago, Mark's REACT team went into a place called the Premier Pawn Shop to arrest Lewis Washington for fencing stolen goods. There was a struggle, and Lewis Washington died of massive head injuries.'

She stared at me.

'The REACT team statement is that Washington pulled a gun and the head injuries resulted accidentally when team members tried to subdue Washington without the use of firearms. Washington's family said that Lewis didn't own a gun and was trying to go straight. The Washingtons sued the city and the LAPD, claiming wrongful death. The LAPD investigated, but found that there had been no wrongdoing.'

Jennifer Sheridan didn't move. She was staring at the far pictures. Mark and Jenny at the prom. Mark and Jenny after the big game. See them smile. See them laugh. 'Was it Mark?'

'The REACT team statement was that it was a combination of all five officers present, though Eric Dees, the team leader, took responsibility.'

She took a deep breath. 'Mark never told me any of that.'

'How about the name Akeem D'Muere?'

'No.'

'Akeem D'Muere is a gangbanger in South Central Los Angeles. He bosses a street gang called the Eight-Deuce Gangster Boys. Lewis Washington's family dropped their lawsuit because Akeem D'Muere told them that he'd kill them if they didn't.'

'He didn't tell me any of this. You think Mark has something to do with these people?'

'I don't know if these two things are connected or not. Maybe they're not. Maybe Mark didn't tell you about Akeem D'Muere because he doesn't know.'

'He didn't tell me about any of this.' She was shaking her head.

'This isn't going to be easy, Jennifer. What we find out about Mark might be a bad thing, just like Riggens said. It might be something that you'll wish you didn't know, and what you find out might change forever what you feel about Mark and about you with Mark. Do you see that?'

'Are you telling me that we should stop?'

'I'm not telling you one way or the other. I want you to know what you're dealing with, that's all.'

She turned away from me and looked at the pictures on the white Formica table, the pictures that had charted her life from the ninth grade until this moment. Her eyes turned pink and she rubbed at them. 'Damn it, I didn't want to cry anymore. I'm tired of crying.' She rubbed her eyes harder.

I leaned forward and touched her arm. The arm that Riggens had hurt. I said, 'Crying is dangerous. It's wise of you to avoid it this way.'

She said, 'What?' Confused.

'First, there's the dehydration, and then the lungs go into sob lock.'

She stopped the rubbing. 'Sob lock?'

I nodded. 'A form of vapor lock induced by sobbing. The lungs lose all capacity to move air, and asphyxiation is only moments away. I've lost more clients to this than gunshot wounds.'

'Maybe,' she said, 'that doesn't so much speak to the clients as to the detective.'

I slapped a hand over my chest. 'Ouch.'

Jennifer Sheridan laughed, forgetting about the tears. 'You're funny.'

'Nope. I'm Elvis.' You get me on a roll, I'm murder.

She laughed again and said, 'Say something else funny.'

'Something else funny.'

She laughed again and made a big deal out of giving me exasperated. 'No. I meant for you to *say* something funny.'

'Oh.'

'Well?' Waiting.

'You want me to say something funny.'

'Yes.'

'Something funny.'

Jennifer Sheridan threw the stuffed lion at me but then the laughter died and she said, 'Oh, my God. I am so scared.'

'I know.'

'I've got a college education. I have a good job. You're supposed to go out a lot, but I don't do that. You're supposed to be complete and whole all by yourself, but if I can't have him I feel like I'll die.'

'You're in love. People who say the other stuff are saying it either before they've been in love or after the love is over and it hasn't worked out for them, but no one says it when they're in the midst of love. When you're in love, there's too much at stake.'

She said, 'I've never been with anyone who makes me feel the way that he makes me feel. I've never tried to be. Maybe I should've. Maybe it's all been a horrible mistake.'

'It's not a mistake if it's what you wanted.' I was breathing hard and I couldn't get control of it.

She stared down into her flute glass, and she traced her fingertip around its edge, and then she stared at me. She didn't look sixteen, now. She was lean and pretty, and somehow available. She said, 'I like it that you make me laugh.'

I said, 'Jennifer.'

She put down the flute glass. 'You're very nice.'

I put down my glass and stood. She went very red and suddenly looked away. She said, 'Ohmygod. I'm sorry.'

'It's all right.'

She stood, too. 'Maybe you should go.'

I nodded, and realized that I didn't want to go. The sharp pain came back behind my eyes. 'All right.'

'This wine.' She laughed nervously, and still didn't look at me.

'Sure. Me, too.'

I backed away from her and went into the entry hall by the kitchen. I liked the way the tights fit her calves and her thighs and the way the sweatshirt hung low over her hips. She was standing with her arms crossed as if it were cold. 'I'm sorry.'

I said, 'Don't be.' Then I said, 'You're quite lovely.'

She flushed again and looked down at her empty glass and I left.

I stood in the street outside her apartment for a long time, and then I drove home.

Pike was gone and the house was cool and dark. I left it that way. I took a beer from the refrigerator, turned on the radio, and went out onto my deck. Jim Ladd was conning the air waves at KLSX. Playing a little George Thorogood. Playing a little Creedence Clearwater Revival. When you're going to listen to radio, you might as well listen to the best.

I stood in the cool night air and drank the beer and, off to my left, an owl hooted from high in a stand of pine trees. The scent of jasmine now was stronger than it had been earlier in the evening, and I liked it. I wondered if Jennifer Sheridan would like smelling it, too. Would she like the owl?

I listened and I drank for quite a long while, and then I went in to bed.

Sleep, when it finally came, provided no rest.

15

At ten-forty the next morning I called my friend at B of A. She said, 'I can't believe this. Two calls in the same week. I may propose.'

'You get that stupid, I'll have to use the Sting tickets on someone else.'

'Forget it. I'd rather see Sting.' These dames.

'I want to know who financed the purchase of a place called the Premier Pawn Shop on Hoover Street in South Central L.A.' I gave her the address. 'Can you help me on that?'

'You at the office?'

'Nope. I'm taking advantage of my self-employed status to while away the morning in bed. Naked. And alone.' Mr Seduction.

My friend laughed. 'Well, if I know you, that's plenty of company.' Everybody's a comedian. 'Call you back in twenty.'

'Thanks.'

She made the call in fifteen. 'The Premier Pawn Shop was owned in partnership between Charles Lewis Washington and something called the Lester Corporation. Lester secured the loan and handled the financing through California Federal.'

'Ah ha.'

'Is that "ah ha" as in this is important, or "ah ha" as in you're clearing your throat?'

'The former. Maybe. Who signed the papers?'

'Washington and an attorney named Harold Bellis. Bellis signed for Lester and is an officer in that corporation.'

'Bellis have an address?'

'Yeah. In Beverly Hills.' She gave it to me, then I hung up, showered, dressed, and charged off to deepest, darkest Beverly Hills. Portrait of the detective in search of mystery, adventure, and a couple of measly clues.

The Law Offices of Harold Bellis were on the third floor of a newly refurbished three-story office building a half block off Rodeo Drive and about a million light-years from South Central Los Angeles. I found a parking space between a Rolls-Royce Corniche and an eighty-thousand-dollar Mercedes two-seater in front of a store that sold men's belts starting at three hundred dollars. Business was brisk.

I went into a little glass lobby with a white marble floor and a lot of gold fixtures and took the elevator to the third floor. Harold Bellis had the front half of the building and it looked like he did very well. There was a lot of etched glass and glossy furniture and carpet about as deep as the North Atlantic. I waded up to a receptionist seated behind a semicircular granite desk and gave her my card. She was wearing one of those pencil-thin headphones so she could answer the phone and speak without having to lift anything. 'Elvis Cole to see Mr Bellis. I don't have an appointment.'

She touched a button and spoke to someone, then listened and smiled at me. There was no humor in the smile, nor any friendliness. She said, 'We're sorry, but Mr Bellis's calendar is full. If you'd like an appointment, we can schedule a time next week.'

I said, 'Tell him it's about the Premier Pawn Company. Tell him I have a question about the Lester Corporation.'

She said it into the microphone, and a couple of minutes later a rapier-thin woman with prominent cheeks and severely white skin came out and led me through a long common office where secretaries and aides and other people sat in little cubicles, and then into her office, and then into his. Her office held a bank of designer file cabinets and fresh-cut tulips and the entrance to his office. You want to see him, you've got to get past her, and she wouldn't be easy to beat. She'd probably even like the fight.

Harold Bellis had the corner office and it was big. She said, 'This is Mr Cole.'

Harold Bellis stood up and came around his desk, smiling and offering his hand. He was short and soft with pudgy hands and a fleshy face and thinning gray hair that looked as soft as mouse fur. Sort of like the Beverly Hills version of Howdy Doody. 'Thanks, Martha. Harold Bellis, Mr Cole. Martha tells me you're interested in the Premier Pawn Shop. Would you like to buy it?' He sort of laughed when he said it, like it was an obvious joke and we both knew it. Ha ha.

'Not today, Mr Bellis, thanks.'

Martha looked down her nose at me and left.

Harold Bellis's handshake was limp and his voice was sort of squeaky, but maybe that was just confidence. An original David Hockney watercolor and two Jésus Leuus oils hung on the walls. You don't get the Hockney and the Leuus by being sissy in the clinches. 'I'm working on something that brought me across the Premier and I learned that you're an officer in the company that owns it.'

'That's correct.' Bellis offered me a seat and took the chair across from me. The decor was Sante Fe, and the seating was padded benches. Bellis's chair looked comfortable, but the benches weren't. He said, 'I have a meeting with a client now, but she's sorting through records in the conference room, so we can squeeze in a few minutes.'

'Great.'

'Does this involve Mr Washington's death?'

'In part.'

Bellis gave me sad and shook his head. 'That young man's death was a tragedy. He had everything in the world going for himself.'

'The police say he was fencing stolen goods. His family suspects that, too.'

'Well, that was never established in a court of law, was it?'

'Are you saying he wasn't?'

'If he was, it was unknown to the co-owners of the shop.' Bellis's smile grew tighter and he didn't look so much like Howdy Doody now.

I smiled at him. 'Who are the co-owners, Mr Bellis?'

Harold Bellis looked at my card as if, in the looking, something had been confirmed. 'Perhaps if you told me your interest in all of this.'

'Mr Washington's family implied that he was the sole owner of the Premier, but upon checking, I found that something called the Lester Corporation arranged the financing and carried the paper.'

'That's right.'

'Since Mr Washington had no credit history, and was working at a minimum-wage job at the time, I was wondering why someone would co-sign a loan with him for such a substantial sum of money.'

Harold Bellis said, 'The Lester Corporation provides venture capital for minority businessmen. Lewis Washington made a proposal, and we agreed to enter into partnership. That's all there is to it.'

'To the tune of eighty-five thousand dollars.'

'Yes.'

'You co-signed a loan for a man with no formal education, a criminal record, and no business experience, because you like to help underprivileged entrepreneurs?'

'Someone has to, don't you think?' He leaned forward out of the Sante Fe chair and the Howdy Doody eyes were as hard as a smart bomb's heart. Nope, he wouldn't be sissy in the clinches.

I said, 'Does Akeem D'Muere own the Lester Corporation?'

Bellis didn't move for a long moment and the eyes stayed with me. The smart bomb acquiring its target. 'I'm afraid I'm not at liberty to discuss the Lester Corporation or any other client, Mr Cole. You understand that, don't you?'

'I understand it, but I was hoping that you'd make an exception.'

The hard eyes relaxed and some of the Howdy Doody came back. Howdy Doody billing at a thousand dollars an hour. 'Do you suspect that this Mr D'Muere has something to do with Lewis Washington's death?'

'I don't know.'

94

'If you suspect someone of criminal activity, you should report it to the police.'

'Perhaps I will.' Elvis Cole makes his big threat.

Harold Bellis glanced at his watch and stood up. The watch was a Patek Philippe that wholesaled out at maybe fourteen thousand dollars. Maybe if you could blow fourteen grand on a watch and keep Hockney originals around for office decorations, you didn't think twice about giving eighty-five thousand to a total stranger with no credentials and a spotty past. Of course, you didn't get rich enough for the watch and the Hockneys by not thinking twice. Harold Bellis said, 'I'm sorry I couldn't be more help to you, Mr Cole, but I really have to see my client now.' He looked at my card again. 'May I keep this?'

'Sure. You can have a couple more, if you want. Pass'm out to your friends. I can use the work.'

Harold Bellis laughed politely and showed me to the door. The thin woman reappeared and led me back through the office and out to the lobby. I was hoping she'd walk me down to my car, but she didn't.

Outside, my car was still bracketed by the Rolls and the Mercedes, and gentlemen of indeterminate national origin were still going into Pierre's to buy three-hundred-dollar belts and twelve-hundred-dollar shoes. Slender women with shopping bags and tourists with cameras crowded the sidewalks, and foreign cars crept along the outside lanes, praying for a parking space. I had been inside maybe fifteen minutes and not much had changed, either with Beverly Hills or with what I knew, but I am nothing if not resourceful.

I fed quarters into the parking meter and waited. It was eleven twenty-five.

At sixteen minutes after noon, Harold Bellis came out of his building and walked north, probably off to a business lunch at a nearby restaurant. Eleven minutes later, his assistant, Martha, appeared out of the parking garage driving a late-model Honda Acura. She turned south.

I ran back across the street, rode the elevator up to Bellis's floor, and hurried up to the receptionist, giving her the Christ-my-day-is-going-to-hell smile. 'Hi. Martha said she'd leave my calendar with you.'

She gave confused. 'Excuse me?'

'When I was here this morning, I left my date book in Harry's office. I called and Martha said she'd leave it with you for me.'

The receptionist shook her head. 'I'm sorry, but she didn't.'

I gave miserable. 'Oh, man. I'm screwed. It's got all my appointments, and my account numbers. I guess it just slipped her mind. You think it'd be okay if I ran back there and checked?' I gave her expectant, and just enough of the little boy so that she'd know my fate in life rested squarely on her shoulders.

'Sure. You know the way?'

'I can find it.'

I went back past the assistants and the cubicles to Martha's office. It was open. I went in and closed the door, then looked over the files until I found the client index. It took maybe three minutes to find the client index and twenty seconds to find the Lester files.

The articles of incorporation of the Lester Corporation, a California corporation, were among the first documents bound in the Lester Corp files. The president of the Lester Corporation was listed as one Akeem D'Muere. D'Muere's address was care of The Law Offices of Harold Bellis, Attorney-at-Law. Sonofagun.

I flipped through the files and found records of the acquisitions of nine investment properties throughout the South Central Los Angeles area, as well as two properties in Los Feliz and an apartment building in Simi Valley. The purchases included two bars, a laundromat, and the pawnshop. The rest were residential. I guess the weasel-dust business pays.

The Premier Pawn Shop location was purchased nine months and two days prior to Charles Lewis Washington's death. There was a contract with a property management firm for six of the businesses, as well as receipts from contractors for maintenance and renovation work performed on seven of the businesses. Each property had a separate file. The Premier showed plumbing and electrical work, as well as a new heating and air conditioning unit, and there was also a receipt from something called Atlas Security Systems for the installation of an Autonomous Monitoring System, as well as a Perimeter Security Alarm. Similar systems had also been purchased for the two bars. I wasn't sure what an Autonomous Monitoring System was, but it sounded good. The cost of these things and their installation was $6,518.22, and there had been no mention of them in the police reports. Hmm.

I wrote down the phone number of Atlas Security Systems, then closed the file, and borrowed Martha's phone to call them. I told a guy named Mr Walters that I was a friend of Harold Bellis's, that I owned a convenience store in Laguna Niguel, and that I was thinking of installing a security system. I told him that Harold had recommended Atlas and something called an Autonomous Monitoring System, and I asked if he could explain it. Mr Walters could. He told me that the Autonomous Monitoring System was perfect for a convenience store or any other cash business, because it was an ideal way to keep an eye on employees who might steal from you. The AMS was a hidden video camera timed to go on and off during business hours, or whenever a motion sensor positioned to my specifications told it to. He gave me cost and service information, and then I thanked him and told him that I'd get in touch.

I hung up the phone, returned the files to their cabinets, left the door open as I had found it, then walked out past the receptionist and drove to my office.

As I drove, I thought about the video equipment.

No one shot at me on the way, but maybe they were saving that for later.

16

When I got to my office at five minutes past one, there was a message on my machine from James Edward Washington, asking me to call. I did.

James Edward said, 'You know a taco stand called Raul's on Sixty-five and Broadway?'

'No.'

'Sixty-five and Broadway. I'm gonna be there in an hour with a guy who knows about what's going on. Ray came through.'

'I'll meet you there.'

I hung up, then called Joe Pike. He answered on the first ring. 'Pike.'

'I'm going to meet James Edward Washington at a place called Raul's on Sixty-five and Broadway in about one hour. He says he's got a guy who maybe knows something.'

'I'll be there.'

'There's more.' I told him about the Lester Corporation and Harold Bellis and the contract with Atlas Security. I told him about the video equipment.

Pike grunted. 'So Akeem D'Muere saw what happened to Charles Lewis.'

'It's possible.'

'And maybe it shows something different than the police report claims.'

'Yeah. But if that's the case, why doesn't Akeem use it to fry these guys? Why is he protecting them?'

Pike fell silent.

'Joe?'

'Watch your ass out there, Elvis. It's getting too hot for these guys to sit by. They're going to have to move.'

'Maybe that's how we finally crack this. Maybe we make it so hot that they've got to move, and when they move we'll see what they're doing.'

'Maybe. But maybe their idea of a move is to take us out.'

Nothing like a little inspiration.

Thirty-two minutes later I exited the freeway and turned north on

Broadway past auto repair shops and take-out rib joints and liquor stores that had been looted in the riots and not yet rebuilt.

Raul's Taco was a cinderblock stand on the west side of Broadway between a service drive and an auto parts place that specialized in remanufactured transmissions. You ordered at a little screen window on one side of the stand, then you went around to the other side to wait for your food. There was a tiny fenced area by the pick-up window with a couple of picnic benches for your more elegant sit-down diners and a couple of little stand-up tables on the sidewalk for people in a rush. A large sign over the order window said WE HAVE SOUL-MAN TACOS. An hour before noon and the place was packed.

I drove up to Sixty-fourth, pulled a U-turn at the light, then swung back and parked at the curb in front of the transmission place. James Edward Washington and a young black guy maybe Washington's age were sitting across from each other at one of the picnic tables, eating tacos. The second guy was wearing a neon orange hat with the bill pointed backwards, heavy Ray Ban sunglasses, and a black Los Angeles Raiders windbreaker even though it was ninety degrees. Washington saw me and nodded toward the table. The other guy saw him nod and turned to watch me come over. He didn't look happy. Most of the other people in Raul's were watching me, too. Guess they didn't get many white customers. Washington said, 'This is the guy Ray was talking about. Cool T, this is the detective.'

Cool T said, 'You say his name Elvis I thought he a brother.'

I said, 'I am. Amazing what a marcel and skin lightener will do, isn't it?'

Cool T shook his head and gave disgusted. 'And he think he funny, too.'

Cool T started to get up but Washington put a hand on his forearm and held him down. 'He's white, but he's trying to help about Lewis. That means he can be all the funny he wants.'

Cool T shrugged without looking at me. Aloof.

Washington took a taco wrapped in yellow paper out of the box and offered it to me. He said, 'This is a Soul-Man taco. These Mexicans grill up the meat and the peppers and put barbecue sauce on it. You like barbecue?'

'Sure.' I unwrapped the taco. The paper was soaked through with oil and barbecue sauce, but it smelled like a handful of heaven. The taco was two handmade corn tortillas deep-fried to hold their shape, and filled with meat and chili peppers and the barbecue sauce. The sauce was chunky with big rings of jalapeño and serrano peppers.

Cool T finished off the rest of his taco, then pointed out the peppers. 'It's pretty hot, you ain't used to it. They probably make one without the peppers, you ask.' He was showing a lot of teeth when he said it.

99

I took a bite, and then I took a second. It was delicious, but it wasn't very hot. I said, 'You think they'd give me more peppers?'

Cool T stopped showing the teeth and went sullen. Shown up by the white man.

Washington said, 'Cool T's been living on these streets while I've been swabbing decks. He's seen what's going on.'

Cool T nodded.

'Okay. So what's Cool T know?' I finished my taco and eyed the box lustily. There were three more tacos in it. Washington made a little hand move that said help yourself. I did.

Cool T said, 'Those cops ain't cops no mo'. They just passin'.'

'What's that mean?'

'Mean they in business and they use the Eight-Deuce as what we call sales representatives.' He grinned when he said it.

I looked at Washington. 'Is this for real?'

Washington shrugged. 'That's what his girlfriend says.'

Cool T said, 'I friendly with this bitch used to live with a Gangster Boy.'

I said, 'Are you telling me that these officers are in the crack trade?'

Cool T nodded. 'They in the everything trade. Whatever the Eight-Deuce in, they in.' He selected another taco. 'Ain't been an Eight-Deuce home boy locked down in four or five months. Pigs take off the Rolling Sixties and the Eight-Trey Swans and all these other nigguhs, but not the Eight-Deuce. They look out for each other. They share the wealth.'

'The cops and the Eight-Deuce Gangster Boys.'

'Uh-hunh. They in business together.' He finished the taco and licked his fingers. 'Eight-Deuce point out the competition and the cops take it down. You wanna see it happen, I can put you onto something.'

'What?'

Cool T said, 'Nigguh been sellin' dope out a ice cream truck over by Witley Park. He at the park every Thursday and the park in Eight-Deuce turf and they tired of it. The cops going over there today to run him off.'

Washington said, 'I figured we could go over there and see what's what. I figure if it's our guys, maybe we can do something with it.'

I was liking Washington just fine. 'Okay.'

Cool T said, 'Not me. Anybody see me over there and something happen, I be meetin' up with Mr Drive-By.'

Cool T stood up. Washington held out his fist and Cool T brushed his own fist against it, back and top and sides, and then he walked away.

I looked at Washington. Well, well. 'You did okay.'

Washington nodded. Cool.

17

When we walked out to the car, I saw Joe Pike parked at a fire hydrant a block and a half north. We made eye contact, and he shook his head. No one was following.

James Edward said, 'What're you looking at?'

'My partner.'

'You work with someone?' He was looking up Broadway.

'If you look for him like that, people will know someone's there.'

James Edward stopped looking and got into the car. I slid in after him. 'Use the mirror. Angle it so that you can see. He's in a red Jeep.'

James Edward did it. 'Why's he back there?'

'The men who killed your brother have been following me. He's there to follow the followers.'

James Edward readjusted the mirror and we pulled away. 'He any good?'

'Yes.'

'Are you?'

'I get lucky.'

James Edward settled back and crossed his arms. 'Luck is for chumps. Ray knows a couple of people and he asked them about you. He says you're a straight up dude. He says you get respect.'

'You can fool some of the people some of the time.'

James Edward shook his head and stared at the passing buildings. 'Bullshit. Any fool can buy a car, but you can't buy respect.'

I glanced over, but he was looking out at the streets.

James Edward Washington told me where to go and I went there and pretty soon we were on streets just like James Edward Washington's street, with neat single-family homes and American cars and preschool children jumping rope and riding Big Wheels. Older women sat on tiny porches and frowned because teenagers who should've been in school were sitting on the hood of a Bonneville listening to Ice Cube. The women didn't like the kids being on the Bonneville and they didn't like Ice Cube but they couldn't do anything about it. We drove, and after a while I knew we weren't just driving, we were taking a tour of James Edward Washington's life. He would say turn, and I would turn, and he would point with his chin and say something like *The girl I took to the prom used to live right there* or *Dude I knew named William Johnston grew up there and writes television now and makes four hundred thousand dollars every year and bought his mama a house in the San Gabriel Valley* or *My cousins live there. I was little, they'd come to my street and we'd trick-or-treat, and then I'd come back here with them and we'd do it all over again. The lady that lived right over there used to make caramel-dipped candy apples better'n anything you ever bought at the circus.*

We drove and he talked and I listened, and after a while I said, 'It has to be hard.'

He looked at me.

I said, 'There are a lot of good things here, but there are also bad things, and it's got to be hard growing up and trying not to let the bad things drag you down.'

He looked away from me. We rode for a little bit longer, and then he said, 'I guess I just want you to know that there's more to the people down here than a bunch of shiftless niggers sopping up welfare and killin' each other.'

'I knew that.'

'You think it, maybe, but you don't know it. You're down here right now cause a nigger got beaten to death. We're driving to a park where a nigger gonna be selling drugs and niggers gonna be buying. That's what you know. You see it on the news and you read it in the papers and that's all you know. I know there's people who work hard and pay taxes and read books and build model airplanes and dream about flying them and plant daisies and love each other as much as any people can love each other anywhere, and I want you to know that, too.'

'Okay.' He wasn't looking at me, and I wasn't looking at him. I guess we were embarrassed, the way men who don't know each other can get embarrassed. 'Thanks for telling me.'

James Edward Washington nodded.

'It's important.'

He nodded again. 'Turn here.'

At the end of the block was a playground with a basketball court and six goals, and, beyond the court, a softball diamond with a long shallow outfield. A few teenaged guys were on the court, but not many, and a guy in his early thirties was running wind sprints in the outfield, racing from second base to the far edge of the outfield, then walking back, then doing it all again. A row of mature elms stood sentry along the far perimeter of the outfield, then there was another street and more houses. A sky blue Sunny Day ice cream truck was parked at the curb in the shade of one of the elms and a tall guy in a Malcolm X hat was leaning against it with his arms crossed, watching the sprinter. He didn't look interested in selling ice cream.

James Edward Washington said, 'That's our guy.'

We turned away from the park, made the block, and came back to a side street that gave an unobstructed view of the basketball players and the outfield and the ice cream truck on the far street. I parked on the side street so we'd have an easy, eyes-forward view, and then I shut the engine. If the neighbors saw us sitting there, maybe they'd think we were scouting for the NBA.

Maybe eight or nine minutes later four guys in a white Bel Air turned onto the far street, slowed to a stop, and the guy with the X hat went over to them. One of the guys in the backseat of the Bel Air gave something to the X, and the X gave something to the guy in the Bel Air. Then the Bel Air drove away and the X went back to his leaning. A little bit later a kid on a bike rolled up the sidewalk, jumped the curb down to the street, and skidded to a stop. The kid and the X traded something, and the kid rode away. Washington said, 'Cool T better be giving it to us straight about those cops.'

I pointed at the X. 'He's here, isn't he?'

'He's here, but will the cops come, and if they come are they coming because they're cops or because they're working with the Eight-Deuce?'

'We'll find out.'

'Yes. I guess we will.' James Edward shifted in the seat, uncomfortable, but not because of the seat. 'They don't come and run this muthuhfuckuh off, maybe I'll do it myself.'

'Maybe I'll help you.'

Washington glanced at me and nodded.

A couple of minutes later Joe Pike came up along the sidewalk and squatted beside my window. I said, 'Joe Pike, this is James Edward Washington. James, this is my partner, Joe Pike.'

Pike canted his head to lock onto James Edward Washington and reached in through the window. You can't see his eyes behind the dark glasses, but it's always easy to tell where he's looking. His whole being sort of points in that direction, as if he were totally focused on you. James Edward took his hand, but stared at the tattoos. Most people do.

I told Pike about the X at the ice cream truck and what Cool T had said about Thurman's REACT team and their involvement with the Eight-Deuce Gangster Boys.

Pike nodded. 'Dees and his people are supposed to thump this guy?'

James Edward said, 'That's the word.'

Pike looked at the X. 'It's a long way across the playground to the ice cream truck. If Dees moves the action away from us, we've got too much ground to cover to catch up. We might lose them.'

I said, 'Why don't you set up on that side, and we'll stay here. If Dees moves that way, you've got them, and if he moves in this direction, we've got him.'

Pike stared behind us up the street, then twisted around and looked at the park. 'You feel it?'

'What?'

Pike shook his head. 'Doesn't feel right.'

He stepped away from the car and stood without moving for a time and then he walked away. I thought about what Joe had said. *They're going to have to make a move.*

James Edward watched Pike leave. 'He's sorta strange, huh?'

'You think?'

A few minutes later we saw Pike's Jeep pass the ice cream truck and turn away from the park. James Edward looked at me. 'You don't think he's strange?'

We moved deeper into the afternoon, and business was good for the man in the ice cream truck. Customers came by in cars and trucks and on motorcycles and bicycles and on foot. Some of the cars would slow as they passed and the X would stare and they would make the block a couple of times before they finally stopped and did their deal, but most folks drove up and stopped without hesitating. The X never hesitated, either. Any one of these people could've been undercover cops but no one seemed to take that into consideration. Maybe it didn't matter. Maybe business was so good and profits were so large that the threat of a bust was small relative to the potential gain. Or maybe the X just didn't care. Some people are like that.

Once, two young women pushing strollers came along the far sidewalk. The X made a big deal out of tipping his cap with a flourish and giving them the big smile. The women made a buy, too. The one who did the talking was pregnant. Washington rubbed his face with both hands and said, 'Oh, my Jesus.'

School let out. More players joined the basketball games. The guy running wind sprints stopped running, and the time crept past like a dying thing, heavy and slow and unable to rest.

James Edward twisted in the seat and said, 'How you stand this goddamn waiting?'

'You get used to it.'

'You used to be a cop?'

I shook my head. 'Nope. I was a security guard for a while, and then I apprenticed with a man named George Fieder. Before that I was in the Army.'

'How about that guy Pike?'

'Joe was a police officer. Before that, he was a Marine.'

James Edward nodded. Maybe thinking about it. 'You go to college?'

'I had a couple years, on and off. After the Army, it was tough to sit in a classroom. Maybe I'll go back one day.'

'If you went back, what would you study?'

I made a little shrug. 'Teacher, maybe.'

He smiled. 'Yeah. I could see you in a classroom.'

I spread my hands. 'What? You don't think there's a place for a thug in the fourth grade?'

He smiled, but then the smile faded. Across the park, a girl who couldn't have been more than sixteen pulled her car beside the ice cream truck and bought a glassine packet. She had a pretty face and precisely cornrowed hair in a traditional African design. Washington watched the transaction, then put his forearms on his knees and said, 'Sitting here, seeing these brothers and sisters doing this, it hurts.'

'Yes, I guess it does.'

He shook his head. 'You aren't black. I see it, I see brothers and sisters turning their backs on the future. What's it to you?'

I thought about it. 'I don't see brothers and sisters. I don't see black issues. Maybe I should, but I don't. Maybe because I'm white, I can't. So I see what I can see. I see a pretty young girl on her way to being a crack whore. She'll get pregnant, and she'll have a crack baby, and there will be two lifetimes of pain. She'll want more and more rock, and she'll do whatever it takes to get it, and, over time, she'll contract AIDS. Her mother will hurt, and her baby will hurt, and she will hurt.' I stopped talking and I put my hands on the steering wheel and I held it for a time. 'Three lifetimes.'

Washington said, 'Unless someone saves her.'

I let go of the wheel. 'Yes, unless someone saves her. I see it the only way I can see it. I see it as people.'

Washington shifted in the bucket. 'I was gonna ask you why you do this, but I guess I know.'

I went back to watching the X.

James Edward Washington said, 'If I wanted to learn this private eye stuff, they got a school I could learn how to do it?'

James Edward Washington was looking at me with watchful, serious eyes. I said, 'You want to learn how to do this, maybe we can work something out.'

He nodded.

I nodded back at him, and then Floyd Riggens's sedan turned onto the far street and picked up speed toward the ice cream truck.

I said, 'Camera in the glove box.'

Mark Thurman was in the front passenger seat and Pinkworth was in the backseat. The sedan suddenly punched into passing gear and the X jumped the chain-link fence and ran across the outfield toward the basketball court. He was pulling little plastic packs of something out of his pockets and dumping them as he ran.

James Edward opened the glove box and took out the little Canon Auto Focus I keep there. I said, 'You see how to work it?'

'Sure.'

'Use it.'

I started the Corvette and put it in gear in case the X led Riggens across the park toward us, but it didn't get that far. Riggens horsed the sedan over the curb and cut across the sidewalk at the far corner where there was no fence and aimed dead on at the running X and gunned it. The X tried to cut back, but when he did, Riggens swung the wheel hard over and pegged the brakes and then Riggens and Thurman and Pinkworth were out of the car. They had their guns out, and the X froze and put up his hands. Thurman stopped, but Riggens and Pinkworth didn't. They knocked the X down and kicked him in the ribs and the legs and the head. Riggens went down on one knee and used his pistol, slamming the X in the head while Pinkworth kicked him in the kidneys. Mark Thurman looked around as if he were frightened, but he didn't do anything to stop it. There were maybe a hundred people in the park, and everybody was looking, but they didn't do anything to stop it, either. Next to me, James Edward Washington snapped away with the little Canon.

Riggens and Pinkworth pulled the X to his feet, went through his pockets, then shoved him away. The X fell, and tried to get up, but neither his legs nor his arms were much use. His head was bleeding. Pinkworth said something sharp to Mark Thurman and Thurman walked back across the park, scooping up the little plastic envelopes. Riggens climbed the chain link and went into the ice cream truck and that's the last we saw of it because a burgundy metal-flake Volkswagen Beetle and a double-dip black Chevrolet Monte Carlo playing NWA so loud that it rocked the neighborhood pulled up fast next to us and three guys wearing ski masks got out, two from the backseat of the Monte Carlo and one from the passenger side of the Volkswagen. The guy from the Volkswagen was wearing a white undershirt maybe six sizes too small and baggy pants maybe forty sizes too big and was carrying what looked to be a Taurus 9mm semiautomatic pistol. The Taurus fit him just right. The first guy out of the Monte Carlo was tall and wearing a black duster with heavy Ray Ban Wayfarers under the ski mask and was carrying a sawed-off double-barrel 20-gauge. The second guy was short and had a lot of muscles stuffed into a green tee shirt that said LOUIS. He was holding an AK-47. All of the guns were pointed our way.

James Edward Washington made a hissing sound somewhere deep in his chest and the tall guy stooped over to point the double twenty through my window. He looked at me, then James Edward, and then he gestured with the double twenty. 'Get out the muthuhfuckin' car, nigger.'

James Edward got out of the car, and then the tall guy pointed the double twenty at me. 'You know what you gonna do?'

'Sure,' I said. 'Whatever you say.'

The tall guy smiled behind the ski mask. 'Tha's right. Keep doin' it, and maybe you see the sun set.'

18

The guy with the Taurus brought James Edward Washington to the metal-flake Beetle and put him in the right front passenger seat. The Beetle's driver stayed where he was, and the guy with the Taurus got into the back behind Washington.

The guy in the long coat said, 'They gonna take off and you gonna follow them and we gonna follow you. You get outta line, they gonna shoot your nigger and I gonna shoot you. We hear each other on this?'

'Sure.'

'M'man Bone Dee gonna ride with you. He say it, you do it. We still hear each other?'

'Uh-huh.' While the tall guy told me, the shorter guy in the Louis Farrakhan tee shirt walked around and got into my car. When he walked he held the AK down along his leg, and when he got in, he sort of held the muzzle pointed at the floorboard. The AK was too long to point at me inside the car. The guy in the long coat went back to the Monte Carlo and climbed into the back. There were other guys in there, but the windows were heavily tinted and you couldn't see them clearly. If Pike was here, he might be able to see them, but Pike was probably on the other side of the park, still watching the cops. But maybe not.

Bone Dee said, 'You got a gun?'

'Left shoulder.'

Bone Dee reached across and came up with the Dan Wesson. He didn't look under my jacket when he did it and he didn't look at the Dan Wesson after he had it. He stared at me, and he kept staring even after he had the Dan Wesson.

I said, 'I always thought the AK was overrated, myself. Why don't you buy American and carry an M-16?'

More of the staring.

I said, 'You related to Sandra Dee?'

He said, 'Keep it up, we see whether this muthuh-fuckuh overrated or not.'

No sense of humor.

The Beetle started rolling and the guy in the shotgun seat of the Monte Carlo motioned me out. I tucked in behind the Bug and the Monte Carlo eased in behind me. I stayed close to the Beetle, and the Monte Carlo stayed close to me, too close for another car to slip between us. There was so much heavy-bass gangster rap coming out of the Monte Carlo, they shouldn't have bothered. No one would come within a half mile for fear of hearing loss.

We went west for a couple of blocks, then turned south, staying on the residential streets and avoiding the main thoroughfares. As we drove, Bone Dee looked through the glove box and under the seats and came up with the Canon. 'Thought you liked to buy American?'

'It was a gift.'

Bone Dee popped open the back, exposed the film, then smashed the lens on the AK's receiver and threw the camera and the exposed film out the window. So much for visual evidence.

The Bug drove slowly, barely making school zone speeds, and staying at the crown of the street, forcing oncoming cars to the side. Rolling in attack mode. Kids on their way home from school clutched their books tight to their chests and other kids slipped down driveways to get behind cars or between houses in case the shooting would start and women on porches with small children hurried them indoors. You could see the fear and the resignation, and I thought what a helluva way it must be to live like this. *Does South Central look like America to you?* A short, bony man in his seventies was standing shirtless in his front yard with a garden hose in one hand and a can of Pabst Blue Ribbon in the other. He glared at the guys in the Bug and then the guys in the Monte Carlo. He puffed out his skinny chest and raised the hose and the Pabst out from his sides, showing hard, letting them have him if they had the balls to take him and saying it didn't scare him one goddamn bit. Dissing them. Showing disrespect. An AK came out of the Volkswagen and pointed at him but the old man didn't back down. Hard, all right. We turned again and the AK disappeared. With all the people running and hiding, I began to think that running and hiding was a pretty good idea. I could wait until we were passing a cross street, then backfist Bone Dee, yank the wheel, and probably get away, but that wouldn't work too well for James Edward Washington. Not many places to hide inside a Volkswagen Beetle.

Two blocks shy of Martin Luther King Boulevard we turned into an alley past a '72 Dodge with no rear wheels and stopped at a long, low unpainted cinderblock building that probably used to be an auto repair shop. The alley ran behind a row of houses along to a train track that probably hadn't been used since World War II. Most of the railroad property was overgrown with dead grass, and undeveloped except for the cinderblock building. The houses all had chain-link fences, and many had nice vegetable gardens with tomato plants and okra and snap beans, and most of the fences were overgrown with running vines so the people who lived there wouldn't have to see what happened in the alley. Pit bulls stood at the back fences of two of the houses and watched us with small, hard eyes. Guess the pit bulls didn't mind seeing what happened. Maybe they even liked it.

The guy in the long coat got out of the Monte Carlo and went to one of four metal garage doors built into the building and pushed it open. No locks. There were neither cars nor signs nor other evidence of human enterprise outside the building, but maybe inside was different. Maybe this was the Eight-Deuce clubhouse, and inside there would be pool tables and a soda fountain and clean-cut kids who looked like the Jackson family playing old Chubby Checker platters and dancing like the white man. Sure. Welcome to The Killing Zone.

When the door was open the Bug drove into the building.

Bone Dee said, 'Follow him.'

I followed. The Monte Carlo came in after me and then the guy in the long coat stepped through and pulled the door down. Nothing inside, either. The building was as empty and as uncluttered as a crypt.

When the door was down Bone Dee reached over, turned off the ignition, and took the keys. The guy in the long coat came over with the double-barreled twenty. There were no lights and no windows in the place, and the only illumination came from six industrial skylights built into the roof. No one had washed the skylights since they had been installed, so the light that came down was filtered and dirty and it was hard to see. One of the skylights was broken.

The guy in the coat made a little come-here finger gesture with his free hand and said, 'Get outta there, boy.'

I got out. Bone Dee got out with me.

The guy in the coat said, 'I like that old Corvette. You get dead, can I have it?'

'Sure.'

He ran his hand along the fender as if it were something soft, and would appreciate tenderness.

The doors on the Beetle opened and the two guys in there got out with James Edward Washington and pushed him toward me. The Monte Carlo opened up at the same time and three guys came out of there, two from the front and one from the back. The guy from the Monte Carlo's backseat was holding a Benelli combat shotgun and the two from the front were carrying AKs like Bone Dee. The guy who'd been in the backseat of the Beetle had put away the Taurus and come up with an old M-I carbine. You count the double twenty and figure for handguns, and these guys were packing serious hurt. I spent fourteen months in Vietnam on five-man reconnaissance patrols, and we didn't carry this much stuff. Of course, we lost the war.

I said, 'Okay, are you guys going to give up now or do I have to kick some ass?'

Nobody laughed. James Edward Washington shifted his weight from foot to foot and looked as tight as a hand-me-down shirt. A fine sheen of sweat slicked his forehead and the skin beneath his eyes, and he watched the Monte Carlo like he expected something worse to get out. Something worse did.

A fourth guy slid out of the back of the Monte Carlo with the lethal grace of an African panther. He was maybe a half inch shorter than me, but with very wide shoulders and very narrow hips and light yellow skin, and he looked like he was moving in slow motion even though he wasn't. There was a tattoo on the left side of his neck that said *Blood Killer* and a scar on the left side of his face that started behind his eye, went back to his ear, then trailed down the course of his cheek to his jaw. Knife scar. He was wearing a white silk dress shirt buttoned to the neck and black silk triple-pleated pants and he looked, except for the scar, as if he had stepped out of a Melrose fashion ad in *Los Angeles Magazine*. Bone Dee handed him the Dan Wesson. The other three guys were watching me but were watching the fourth guy, too, like maybe he'd say jump and they'd race to see who could jump the highest. I said, 'You Akeem D'Muere?'

D'Muere nodded like it was nothing and looked at the Dan Wesson, opening the chamber, checking the loads, then closing the chamber. 'This ain't much gun. I got a nine holds sixteen shots.'

'It gets the job done.'

'I guess it does.' He hefted the Dan Wesson and lined up the sights on my left eye. 'What's your name?'

'Elvis Cole.'

'What you doin' here?'

'My buddy and I were looking for a guy named Clement Williams for stealing a 1978 Nissan Stanza.' Maybe a lie would help.

Akeem D'Muere cocked the Dan Wesson. 'Bullshit.' Nope. Guess a lie wasn't going to help.

I said, 'Why'd you force the Washington family to drop their wrongful-death suit against the LAPD?'

He decocked the Dan Wesson and lowered it. 'How much you know?'

I shook my head.

D'Muere said, 'We see.' He wiggled the Dan Wesson at Bone Dee and the other guy with an AK. 'Get on this fool.'

Bone Dee hit the backs of my knees with his AK and the other guy rode me down and knelt on my neck. Bone Dee knelt on my legs. The guy on my neck twisted my head around until I was looking up, then put the muzzle of his AK under my ear. It hurt.

Akeem D'Muere stood over me. 'It be easy to kill you, but easy ain't always smart. The people I know, they say you got friends at LAPD and you turnin' up dead maybe make'm mad, maybe make things even worse.'

Something moved across the skylights. Pike, maybe.

'Still, I can't let you keep runnin' around, you see? Things gettin' outta hand and they got to stop. *You* got to stop. You see that?'

'Sure.' It was hard to breathe with the guy on my back.

Akeem D'Muere shook his head. 'You say that, but it just talk, so I gotta show you how things are.' Akeem D'Muere went over to James Edward Washington, touched the Dan Wesson to James Edward's left temple, and pulled the trigger. The explosion hit me like a physical thing and the right side of James Edward Washington's face blew out and he collapsed to the concrete floor as if he were a mechanical man and someone had punched his off button. He fell straight down, and when his face hit the cement, a geyser of blood sprayed across the floor and splattered onto my cheeks.

I went as stiff and tight as a bowstring and pushed against the men on my back but I could not move them. James Edward Washington trembled and twitched and jerked on the floor as a red pool formed under his head. His body convulsed and something that looked like red tapioca came out of his mouth. The guy in the long coat who had opened and closed the big door went over to James Edward and squatted down for a closer look. He said, 'Look at this shit.'

The convulsing peaked, and then the body grew still.

Akeem D'Muere came back, squatted beside me, and opened the Dan Wesson's chamber. He shook out the remaining cartridges, then wiped down the Dan Wesson and dropped it next to me. He said, 'The fuckin' bitch next. She started this.'

I blinked hard five or six times, and then I focused on him. It was hard to focus and hard to hear him, and I tried to think of a way to shake off the men on my back and get to him before the AKs got to me.

Akeem D'Muere smiled like he knew what I was thinking, and like it didn't really worry him, like even if I tried, and even if I got out from under the men and past the AKs, he still wouldn't be worried. He looked over at the others. 'You got the keys?'

Bone Dee said, 'Yeah,' and held up my keys.

Akeem sort of jerked his head and Bone Dee went to the guy with the carbine and they went out of my field of view to my car.

Maybe thirty seconds later Bone Dee came back and Akeem D'Muere went over to James Edward Washington's body. He touched the body with his toe, then shook his head and looked at me. 'Don't matter none. This just another dead nigger.'

I tried to say something, but nothing came out.

Akeem D'Muere turned away. 'Let's get the fuck out of here.'

Bone Dee and the guy with the carbine got back into the Volkswagen and Akeem D'Muere and the guy with the Benelli riot gun went to the Monte Carlo. The guy on my shoulders stayed there and another guy with an AK went to the Monte Carlo and stood by the open passenger door, ready to cover me. The tall guy with the double twenty opened the big doors. When he did, something outside made a loud BANG and the tall guy was kicked back inside and Joe Pike came through fast, diving low and rolling toward the Volkswagen, then coming up and snapping off one shot at the guy on my shoulders and two shots through the Volkswagen's driver's-side window. The bangs were loud and would've been Pike's .357. The first bullet rolled the guy off my shoulders and the two in the Volkswagen pushed the driver over into the passenger side on top of Bone Dee. Pike yelled, 'Down.'

I stayed down.

The guy standing guard by the Monte Carlo dove into the open passenger door, and the big Benelli came out over the top of him and cut loose, putting most of its pellets into the Volkswagen. Pike popped two fast shots at the Monte Carlo, and then the Monte Carlo roared to life and fishtailed its right rear into the Volkswagen and then into the side of the garage door and then it was gone.

I ran forward and pulled Bone Dee out of the VW. The driver was dead. Bone Dee screamed when I grabbed him and yelled that he'd been shot and I told him I didn't give a damn. I pushed him down on the cement and made sure he wasn't armed and then I went to James Edward Washington but James Edward Washington was dead. 'Jesus Christ.'

Pike said, 'You okay?'

I shook my head. I took a deep breath and let it out and then I began to shake.

Pike said, 'We're going to have company.' He put his Python down carefully, so as not to mar the finish. 'You hear them?'

'Yes.'

I think Pike heard them before me, but maybe not. The sirens came in from both sides of the alley and then people were yelling and two cops I'd never seen before leapfrogged through the door. They were in street clothes and were carrying shotguns, and one took up a position in the doorway and the other rolled in and came up behind the Volkswagen's left front fender, much as Pike had. They screamed POLICE when they made their advance and told us to put down our weapons. Habit. Our weapons were already down. I said, 'Guy by the Volkswagen is wounded. The other three are dead.'

A third cop appeared in the opposite side of the door with another shotgun. 'Keep your hands away from your body and get down on the ground. Do it *now*.' He had long hair tied back with a blue bandana.

Pike and I did what they said, but they came in hard anyway, like we knew they would, one of them going to Pike and one of them coming to me and the third going to Bone Dee. The one who went to Bone Dee was short. More cars pulled up outside, and you could hear the *whoop-whoop* of the paramedics on their way in.

The cop who came to me put his knee into my back and twisted my hands around behind me and fit me with cuffs. You get knees in your back twice at the same crime scene, and you know it's not shaping up as a good day. I said, 'My wallet's on the floorboard of the Corvette. My name is Elvis Cole. I'm a private investigator. I'm one of the good guys.'

The cop with the bandana said, 'Shut the fuck up.'

They cuffed Pike and they cuffed Bone Dee and then the short cop said, 'I got the keys,' and went to my Corvette. The cop with the bandana went with him. They moved with clarity and purpose.

The other cop picked up my wallet and looked through it. He said, 'Hey, the sonofabitch wasn't lying. He's got an investigator's license.'

The cop with the bandana said, 'Not for long.'

A couple of bluesuits came in and said, 'Everything cool?'

The cop with the bandana said, 'We'll see.'

The short cop fumbled with the keys, then opened the trunk and made one of the world's widest grins. You'd think he'd won Lotto. 'Bingo. Just where they said.' He reached into the trunk and pulled out a baggie of crack cocaine worth about eight thousand dollars and tossed it to the cop with the bandana. What Bone Dee and the guy with the carbine had been doing behind me.

I looked at Joe Pike and Pike's mouth twitched.

I said, 'It isn't mine.' I pointed at Bone Dee. 'It's his.'

The cop with the bandana said, 'Sure. That's what they all say.' Then he took out a little white card, told us we were under arrest, and read us our rights.

After that he brought us to jail.

19

The cop with the bandana was named Micelli. He put Pike into a gray sedan and me into a black-and-white, and then they drove us to the Seventy-seventh. Micelli rode in the sedan.

The Seventy-seventh Division is a one-story red brick building just off Broadway with diagonal curbside parking out front and a ten-foot chain-link fence around the sides and back. The officers who work the Double-seven park their personal cars inside the fence and hope for the best. Concertina wire runs along the top of the fence to keep out the bad guys, but you leave personal items in your car at your own risk. Your car sort of sits there at your own risk, too. The bad guys have been known to steal the patrol cars.

We turned through a wide chain-link gate and rolled around the back side of the building past the maintenance garage and about two dozen parked black-and-whites and up to an entry they have for uniformed officers and prospective felons. Micelli got out first and spoke with a couple of uniformed cops, then disappeared into the building. The uniforms brought us inside past the evidence lockers and went through our pockets and took our wallets and our watches and our personal belongings. They did me first, calling off the items to an overweight property sergeant who noted every item on a large manila envelope, and then they did Pike. When they did Pike, they pulled off the hip holster for his .357, the ankle holster for his .380, an eight-inch Buck hunting knife, four speed-loaders for the .357, and two extra .380 magazines. The overweight sergeant said, 'Jesus Christ, you expecting a goddamned war?'

The uniform who did Pike grinned. 'Look who it is.'

The sergeant opened Pike's wallet, then blinked at Pike. 'Jesus Christ. You're him.'

The uniformed cop took off Pike's sunglasses and handed them to the sergeant. Pike squinted at the suddenly bright light, and I saw for the first time in months how Pike's eyes were a deep liquid blue. My friend Ellen Lang says that there is a lot of hurt in the blue, but I have never been able

115

to see it. Maybe he just hides it better with me. Maybe she sees his eyes more often than I.

Micelli came back as they were finishing and I said, 'Play this one smart, Micelli. There's a detective sergeant in North Hollywood named Poitras who'll vouch for us, and an assistant DA named Morris who'll back Poitras up. Give'm a call and let's get this straight.'

Micelli signed the property forms. 'You got connections, that what you telling me?'

'I'm telling you these guys know us, and they'll know we've been set up.'

Micelli grinned at the property sergeant. 'You ever hear that before, Sarge? You ever hear a guy we're bringing in say he was set up?'

The sergeant shook his head. 'No way. I've never heard that before.'

I said, 'For Christ's sake, Micelli, check me out. It's a goddamned phone call.'

Micelli finished signing the forms and glanced over at me. 'Listen up, pogue. I don't care if you've been hamboning the goddamned mayor. You're mine until I say otherwise.' He gave the clipboard to the property sergeant, and then he told the uniforms to bring us to interrogation. He walked away.

Pike said, 'Cops.'

The uniforms brought us through a heavy metal door and into a long sterile hall that held all the charm of a urinal in a men's room. There were little rooms on either side of the hall, and they put Pike into the first room and me into the second. The rooms sported the latest in interrogation-room technology with pus-yellow walls and water-stained acoustical ceilings and heavy-duty soundproofing so passing liberals couldn't hear the rubber hoses being worked. There was a small hardwood table in the center of the floor with a single straight-backed metal chair on either side of it. Someone had used a broken pencil to cut a message into the wall. *In interrogation, no one can hear you scream.* Cop, probably. Detainees weren't allowed pencils.

They kept me waiting for maybe an hour, then Micelli and a cop in a gray suit came in. The new cop was in his late forties and looked to be a detective lieutenant, probably working out of homicide. Micelli took the chair across the table from me and the guy in the suit leaned against the wall. Micelli said, 'This conversation is being recorded. My name is Detective Micelli, and this is Lieutenant Stilwell.' You see? 'I'm going to ask you questions, and your answers will be used in court. You don't have to answer these questions, and if you want a lawyer, but can't afford one, we can arrange for a public defender. You want someone?'

'No.'

Micelli nodded. 'Okay.'

'Did you call Poitras?'

Micelli leaned forward. 'No one's calling anyone until we get through this.'

Stilwell said, 'How do you know Lou Poitras?'

Micelli waved his hand. 'That doesn't mean shit. What's it matter?'

'I want to know.'

I told him about me and Poitras.

When I finished, Stilwell said, 'Okay, but what were you doing down here?'

'I got a tip that a REACT cop named Eric Dees is involved with a gangbanger named Akeem D'Muere and I'm trying to find out how.'

Micelli grinned. Stilwell said, 'You got proof?'

'A guy named Cool T gave me the tip. He was a friend of James Edward Washington. Washington is one of the dead guys.'

Micelli said, 'That's fuckin' convenient.'

'Not for Washington.'

Micelli said, 'Yeah, well, we got a little tip, too. We got tipped that an asshole fitting your description and driving your car was down here trying to move a little Mexican brown to the natives. We got told that the deal was going down in an abandoned building off the tracks, and we went over there, and guess what?'

'Who gave you the tip, Micelli? Dees? One of the REACT guys?'

Micelli licked the corner of his mouth and didn't say anything.

I said, 'Check it out. Twenty minutes ago I saw Akeem D'Muere put a gun to James Edward Washington's head and pull the trigger. I'm working for a woman named Jennifer Sheridan. Akeem D'Muere has a mad on for her, and he said that she's next.'

Stilwell crossed his arms. 'Two of the dead men found in the garage were named Wilson Lee Hayes and Derek La Verne Dupree. Both of these guys had a history of trafficking in narcotics. Maybe you were down here to meet them and the deal went bad. Maybe you and your buddy Pike tried to rip those guys off.'

I spread my hands.

Micelli said, 'You own a 1966 Corvette?' He gave me the license number.

'Yeah.'

'How come there was a half kilo of crack in the trunk?'

'Akeem D'Muere's people put it there.'

'They dumped eight thousand dollars' worth of dope, just to set you up?'

'I guess it was important to them.'

'Eight-Deuce Gangster Boys buy and sell dope, they don't give it away. No profit in it.'

'Maybe it wasn't theirs. Maybe Dees gave it to them. Maybe it came from the LAPD evidence room.'

Micelli leaned forward across the table and gave me hard. 'You're holding out for nothing. Your buddy's already come clean.'

'Pike?'

Micelli nodded. 'Yeah. He gave it to us. He said you guys found a connection for the dope. He said you thought you could turn the trick with the Eight-Deuce for a little extra cash. He said that after you set the deal you got the idea that you could just rip these guys off, then you'd have the cash and the dope. Maybe sell it three or four times. Really screw the niggers.'

I gave them the laugh. 'You guys are something Micelli.'

Stilwell said, 'If you don't like our take on it, how about yours?'

I gave it to them. I told them about Mark Thurman and Eric Dees and Charles Lewis Washington. I described how I had been followed, and how Pike and I had boxed Riggens and Pinkworth at the Farmer's Market. I told them about Dees warning me off. I told them about the meeting with Cool T, and Cool T putting us onto the park, and the Eight-Deuce Gangster Boys lying in wait for us. Micelli squirmed around while I said it, like maybe he was bored with the nonsense, but Stilwell listened without moving. When I ran out of gas, Stilwell fingered his tie and said, 'So you're saying that Dees set you up to get you out of the way.'

'Yeah.'

'Why doesn't he just bump you?'

'Maybe he knows that if I get bumped, guys like Joe Pike and Lou Poitras will stay with it, and he doesn't want that. He wants to buy time so he can regain control of things.'

'But if he gets you jugged, he's got to know you're going to talk. He's got to know we're going to call him in and ask him about it.'

I said, 'He knows I'm going to be sitting here with a guy like Micelli. He knows I can't prove anything and all it looks like is that I'm trying to dodge the charge. If I'm alive, he's still got control. If I'm dead, guys like Pike and Poitras are a couple of loose cannons.'

Micelli made a big deal out of throwing up his hands. 'He's wasting our time with this crap. I got tickets to the Dodgers tonight. I want to get there before the stretch.'

I said, 'Listen to me, Stilwell. D'Muere said he's going for the girl. Even if you guys don't buy my end of it, send a car around to her apartment. What's that cost you?'

Stilwell stared at me another couple of seconds. Then he pushed away from the wall. 'Finish up, Paul.' Then he left.

Micelli and I stayed in the interrogation room for another hour. I would go through my story and then Micelli would ask me who was my connection and how much was I going to get for the dope, as if I had said one story but he had heard another. Then he would have me go through my story again. The room was bugged and there were probably a couple of guys listening in. They would be taking notes and a tape recorder would be recording everything I said. They'd be looking for discrepancies and Micelli would be waiting for my body language to change. He'd keep trying out scenarios until I seemed comfortable with one, even if it was one I denied. Then he'd know he struck pay dirt. Of course, since I was telling the truth, he wasn't going to get the body language when and where he wanted it. He probably wasn't too concerned about that, though. Time was on his side. Maybe I shouldn't have passed on the lawyer.

After about the sixth time through, the door opened and Stilwell came back, only this time Eric Dees was with him. Micelli said, 'You been listening to this stuff?'

Dees grinned. 'Yeah. He's pretty good at this.'

Stilwell said, 'You arrest the guy in the park?'

Dees nodded. 'Sure. He's down in cell four.'

'Cole said you ripped off his dope.'

Dees smiled wider. 'Gathered it for evidence, duly logged and checked in.'

I said, 'Come off it, Stilwell. He knew I was going to be in here. He knew I was going to be talking.'

Stilwell stayed with Dees. 'You got anything going with these gangbangers?'

Dees spread his hands. 'Trying to bust'm. Cole's been nosing around and I tried to warn him off and maybe that's when he got the idea for the dope deal. I don't know. I don't want to talk about an ongoing investigation in front of a suspected felon.'

Stilwell said, 'Sure.'

Dees said, 'I've got to go wrap it up with my guys. You need anything else?'

'That's it, Eric. Thanks.'

Dees left without looking at me.

I said, 'Jesus Christ, Stilwell, what do you expect him to say?'

'Just about what he said.'

'Then what are you going to do about it?'

Stilwell grabbed my upper arm and lifted. 'Book you on three murder counts and a dope. I think you're guilty as sin.'

20

They took me out into the detectives' squad room and began the booking process. Dees wasn't around, and after Micelli spoke to a couple of uniforms, he and Stilwell left.

The processing cops had already begun with Pike and, as I watched, they used paraffin on his hands and took his picture and fingerprinted him and asked him questions so that they could fill out their forms. He nodded once and I nodded back. It was strange to see him without the glasses. He seemed more vulnerable without them. Less inviolate. Maybe that's why he wears them.

They led Pike away through a hall toward the jail and then they started with me. A uniform cop named Mertz led me from station to station, first using the paraffin, then getting my prints, and then taking my picture. I crossed my eyes when they took the picture and the cop who worked the camera said, 'No good, Mertz. He crossed his goddamned eyes.'

Mertz picked up a baton and tapped it against his thigh. 'Okay, smart ass. Cross'm again and I'll smack you so hard they'll stay crossed.'

They took the picture again but this time I didn't cross them.

When Mertz was filling out my personal history form, I said, 'When do I get a bail hearing?'

'Arraignment's tomorrow. One of the detectives ran over to the court to get a bail deviation so we could bind you over.'

'Jesus Christ. Why?'

'You see the crowding down there? You're lucky they'll arraign you by next Monday.'

When the processing was finished, Mertz turned me over to an older uniform with a head like a chayote squash and told him to take me to felony. The older uniform led me back along a hall to a row of four-by-eight-foot cages. Each cage had a seatless toilet and a sink and a couple of narrow bunks, and it smelled of disinfectant and urine and sweat, sort of like a poorly kept public men's room. 'No place like home.'

The older uniform nodded. Maybe to him it was home.

There were two black guys in the first cage, both of them sitting in the shadows of the lower bunk. They had been talking softly when we approached, but they stopped when we passed and watched us with yellow eyes. Once you were in the cells, there was no way to see who was in the next cell, and no way to reach through the bars and twist your arm around to touch someone in the next cell, even if someone in the next cell was reaching out to touch you. I said, 'Which one's mine?'

The uniform stopped at the second cell, opened the gate, and took off my handcuffs. 'The presidential suite, of course.'

I stepped in. A Hispanic guy in his early thirties was lying on the lower bunk with his face to the wall. He rolled over and squinted at me, and then he rolled back. The uniform closed the gate and locked it and said, 'You wanna make a call?'

'Yeah.'

He walked back down the hall and out the heavy door and was gone. One of the black guys in the cell next to me said something and the other laughed. Someone in one of the cells on the other side of me coughed. I could hear voices, but they sounded muted and far away. I said, 'Joe.'

Pike's voice came back. 'Fourth cell.'

Someone yelled, 'I'm trying to sleep, goddamn it. Shut the fuck up.' It was a big voice, loud and deep, and sounded as if it had come from a big man. It also sounded about as far away as Joe Pike.

I said, 'D'Muere said he's going for Jennifer Sheridan.'

Joe said, 'Dees wouldn't go for that.'

'Dees may not know. D'Muere wasn't talking like a guy who was worried about what Eric Dees thought.'

The big voice yelled, 'Goddamn it, I said shut up. I don't want to hear about your goddamn –' There was a sharp meat-on-meat sound and the voice stopped. Joe continued, 'Maybe he isn't. Maybe things aren't the way we were told.'

'You mean, maybe they aren't partners.'

Pike said, 'Maybe Dees is an employee. Maybe D'Muere is the power, and Eric Dees is just trying to control him. Maybe putting us in here is part of that.'

'Only maybe while we're in, Jennifer Sheridan gets offed.'

Pike said nothing.

The heavy door opened and the cop with a squash for a head came back pushing a phone that was bolted to a kind of a tripod thing on heavy rollers. The cop pushed it down to my cell and parked it close enough for me to reach the buttons. 'You can make as many calls as you want, but it won't take long distance, okay?'

'Sure.'

He went out and left the door ajar because of the phone cable.

I called Marty Beale's direct line and a male voice answered. It wasn't

Marty, and it wasn't Jennifer Sheridan. 'Watkins, Okum, & Beale. Mr Beale's office.'

'Jennifer Sheridan, please.'

'She didn't come in today. May I take a message?'

'I'm a friend, and it's important that I speak with her. Do you know where I can reach her?'

'I'm sorry, sir. I'm an office temp, and I didn't get here until this afternoon.'

'Do you know why she didn't come in?'

'I'm sorry, sir.'

I hung up and called Jennifer Sheridan's apartment. On the third ring, the phone machine answered. After it beeped, I said, 'It's Elvis. If you're there, pick up.'

No one picked up.

I called Lou Poitras. A woman's voice answered, 'Detectives.'

'Lou Poitras, please.'

'He's out. You want to leave a message?'

'How about Charlie Griggs?'

'Hold on.' I heard her ask somebody in the background about Griggs. She came back on the line. 'He's with Poitras. You want to leave a message or not?'

I hung up and leaned against the bars. 'She didn't go to work and she's not at home.'

Pike said, 'Could mean anything.'

'Sure.' Mr Optimism.

'We could help her.'

'In here?'

Pike said, 'No. Not in here.'

'Joe.' I knew what he was saying.

'Wait.'

The cop with the squash head came back for the phone, and forty minutes after that the heavy door opened again and in came the squash with a Hispanic cop sporting a flattop crew cut. The squash said, 'You guys are going to be bused over to County. On your feet.'

You could hear the men in the cells coming off their bunks.

The squash went down the row, unlocking the doors and telling the prisoners to step out into the hall. When the squash got down to Pike's cell, he said, 'What in hell happened to you?'

The big voice said, 'Fell.'

Pike was three people behind me.

They lined us up and led us down another corridor past the booking area. The young Hispanic cop brought up the rear.

We went down another short hall and then out into a kind of outdoor alcove. Two uniformed cops were walking into the maintenance building to our right and a third uniformed cop was coming in from the parking lot to our left. A large blue bus that said SHERIFF on the side was parked maybe sixty feet away. The deputy sheriff who drove the thing was talking to a guy in the maintenance building. The cop coming in from the parking lot walked past us and went inside through the same door that we had just come out of. The deputy sheriff yelled, 'Hey, Volpe,' and went into the maintenance building. Pike said, 'Now,' then stepped out of the line and launched a roundhouse kick into the side of the Hispanic cop's head. The Hispanic cop went down. The squash heard it and turned and I hit him two fast straight rights low on the jaw, and he went down, too. The Hispanic guy who had shared my cell said, 'The fuck you guys doing?' He looked surprised.

The black guys with the yellow eyes held on to each other and smiled. The big guy who'd been with Pike said, 'Fuckin' A,' and ran to the right past the maintenance building and toward the front gate. Two other guys ran after him. Pike and I went to the left through the parking lot, keeping low and moving toward the street. We made the fence just as men began shouting. The fence ran back along the side of the building past a trash dumpster and maybe half a dozen fifty-five-gallon oil drums and a motorcycle that looked like somebody's personal property. We followed the fence back toward the oil drums, and pretty soon we were on the side of the building. The shouts got louder and there were the sounds of men running, but all of the noise seemed behind us.

We went up onto an oil drum, chinned ourselves to the roof, then jumped back across the concertina wire to the street. A couple of kids on mountain bikes watched us with big eyes.

We walked toward the houses just as an alarm buzzer went off at the police station. An older man rocking on a porch stood and looked at us. 'What's going on?'

I told him they were running tests.

We stayed on the street until he couldn't see us, and then we cut between two houses and started to run.

Somewhere behind us, there came the sound of sirens.

21

We went over fences and through vegetable gardens and between houses. We checked each street for police, then crossed steadily and with purpose as if two white guys on foot were an everyday thing in South Central Los Angeles. Twice we had to pull back between houses for passing patrol units, and once we surprised an elderly woman coming out of her home with a basket of wet laundry. I gave her my best Dan Aykroyd. 'Gas company. We've had reports of a leak.' The Aykroyd works every time.

We moved from her yard to the next, and worked our way north.

More black-and-whites roared past, and sirens that started far away drew close. The cops knew that anybody who made it through the gates would be on foot, so they'd concentrate their people within a close radius. More and more cops would flood into the surrounding streets, and pretty soon there would be helicopters. Pike said, 'We need wheels.'

'They impounded my car. You think they got the Jeep?'

'I was on the next street over. They didn't know about it.'

'That makes it, what, ten or twelve blocks from here? Might as well be in Fresno.'

Pike said, 'If we have limits, they are self-imposed.' Always count on Pike for something like that.

Two black-and-whites sped east on Florence under the freeway. After they passed, we trotted west into an Arco station that had one of those little Minimart places. A couple of cars sat at the pumps, and a Hostess delivery van sat at the Minimart. A young black guy in his early twenties got out of the van with a box of baked goods and went into the Minimart. Pike said, 'Wheels.'

'Maybe he'll give us a ride.'

Pike frowned.

The delivery guy came out of the Minimart, threw his box into the van, and climbed in after it. I went up to his window and said, 'Excuse me. We need a lift about ten blocks west of here. Think you could help?'

The delivery guy said, 'Hey, sure. No problem.'

Only in L.A.

Maybe ten minutes later he dropped us off at Joe Pike's Cherokee. Joe keeps a spare key duct-taped to the inside of the front fender. He found it, unlocked the cab, and we climbed inside. Joe dug under the dash and came out with a plastic bag containing five hundred dollars in cash, a driver's license that said his name was Fred C. Larson, a Visa card in the same name, and a Walther TPH .22-caliber pocket gun. *Be prepared.*

I said, 'Fred?'

Pike headed toward the freeway. 'They'll cover our houses and our businesses.'

'We don't go home. We try for Jennifer Sheridan. We've got to get her off the street before D'Muere finds her.'

'Where does she live?'

I told him. Pike drove quickly, and neither of us spoke during the ride.

We parked in front of her building maybe forty minutes later and pressed her call button, but no one answered. We pressed more buttons until someone finally buzzed open the glass door and we went up to the third floor.

We were knocking on her door when a woman with two small children came out of the apartment across the hall. The woman was maybe in her forties and heavy across the hips. She made a *tsking* sound when she saw us and said, 'I'd appreciate it if you ask her not to make so much noise tonight. All the hammering woke up Teddi.'

I looked at her. 'What hammering?'

She pulled the door shut and locked it. The two children ran down the hall. I guess one of them was Teddi. 'Well, the knocking. It was so loud it woke Teddi and Teddi woke me and I had to look. It was after two.' She squinted at Pike. 'Was it you?'

Pike shook his head.

I said, 'Someone was hammering at her door after two in the morning?'

The woman nodded, but now she wasn't interested in talking. Her children had disappeared around a corner and she wanted to go after them. 'Yes, and someone got quite loud, too. It was very inconsiderate.'

'More than one voice?' I was thinking D'Muere.

'I don't believe so.' She glanced at Pike again. 'Well, I thought it was him but I guess not. Her boyfriend. That big guy. I think he's a police officer.'

'Mark Thurman?'

'I don't know his name. We just see him in the hall.'

'He was here at two this morning?'

She nodded. 'Making a terrible racket. Then they left together.' Now she frowned at me and looked at my hair.

I said, 'What?'

She gave embarrassed, and then she hurried away down the hall. 'I've got to find those damn kids.'

I looked at Pike. He said, 'You've got something in your hair.'

I touched my hair and felt something crusty. My fingers came away speckled red. James Edward Washington's blood. 'If she's with Thurman, she's running. If she's running, that means she's safe.'

'Until she gets found.'

'Yeah.'

Thirty minutes later we checked into a motel Pike knew two blocks from the beach in Santa Monica. It was called the Rising Star Motel. Fred C. Larson signed the register.

The room was simple, but functional, with two double beds and a bath and cheap wall paneling that had been scarred by years of transient use. There was a little round table and two chairs by the window, and a TV bolted to a dresser. The bolts looked thick and heavy enough to pin down a Saturn Five.

Pike left after a couple of minutes, and I went into the bathroom and inspected myself.

I went out to the ice machine, brought back a bucket of ice, then peeled off my shirt, put it in the sink, covered it with the ice, and ran in cold water. I wanted to call Mrs Washington and tell her about James Edward, but I didn't. James Edward Washington's blood was on my shirt and in my hair. How could I tell her about that? When the shirt was soaking, I took off the rest of my clothes, went into the shower, and let the water beat into me. The water was hot. I used the little motel soap and a washcloth, and I scrubbed hard at my face and my neck and my hands and my hair, and then at the rest of me. I washed my hair twice. The police had let me wash off; but that had been with Handi Wipes and paper towels and Borax soap. There's only so much you can do with a Handi Wipe. I scrubbed until my skin was pink and my scalp stung with the hot water, and then I got out to see about the shirt. I rubbed the fabric as hard as I had rubbed my skin, but it was too late. The bloodstains were set, and would always be there. How could I tell Ida Leigh Washington about that?

Twenty minutes later there was a double rap at the door and Joe Pike let himself in. He was carrying an olive green Marine Corps duffel and a large grocery bag and he was wearing new sunglasses. The sunglasses would've been the first thing he bought. He put the grocery bag on the little round table and the duffel bag on the bed. He looked at me and nodded. 'Better.'

'You went by the gun shop?'

He took waist holsters and handguns from the duffel. 'Called one of the guys and had him pick up some things. We met at the market.'

'Have the cops been by your shop?'

Pike nodded. 'They've got an undercover van parked down the block. It'll be the same at your place, too.'

126

Great.

Pike unwrapped the holsters and inspected them, and then tossed one to me. Clip holsters. We could snap them to our waistbands and wear our shirts out over them for that Miami thug look. Pike handed me a Smith & Wesson .38. He counted four hundred dollars out of a plain white envelope, handed half to me. 'There's food in the bags.'

He'd bought soap and deodorant and toothbrushes and paste and razors and the things you need to keep yourself up. He'd also bought a six-pack of cold Thai beer. I put the toiletries in the bathroom, and then we ate. While we ate I called my office to check for messages, but there were none. I called my home next and there were two messages from Jennifer Sheridan. In the first message she identified herself and asked if I was there and, when I didn't answer, she hung up. In the second, she again asked if I was there, but this time when I didn't answer she said that she would call back later tonight. She said that it was very important that she speak with me. She was speaking softly and she didn't sound happy.

Pike watched me listen. 'Jennifer?'

'She's going to call later tonight.'

Pike stared at me.

'I've got to be there, Joe.'

Pike's mouth twitched, and he stood up, ready to go. 'If it were easy, it wouldn't be fun.'

22

We cruised the Mulholland Snake from Cahuenga Pass to Laurel Canyon, and then back again. It was after ten, and the traffic was light and getting lighter, mostly affluent stragglers who'd put in extra hours at the office or in the bar and were only now cresting the mountain in their effort toward home.

When we saw that there were no police stationed at either end of Woodrow Wilson Drive, Pike shut the lights and pulled over. 'You want me to take you in closer?' The turnoff to my house was maybe a mile in along Woodrow Wilson.

'Nope. Too easy to get boxed if we meet a black-and-white coming the other way.'

Pike nodded. 'I know. Just thought I'd offer.'

'There's a turnout about a mile and a half east that the kids use as a parking place, on the valley side overlooking Universal Studios. Wait there. If the police come I'll work my way downslope, then come back around onto Mulholland and meet you there.'

'If you don't get caught.'

Some support, huh?

I slipped out of the Jeep, then trotted off Mulholland and onto Woodrow Wilson Drive, taking it easy and slipping into bushes or shadows or behind parked cars whenever headlights showed around a curve. Woodrow Wilson Drive is narrow and winding and affects sort of a rural quality, even in the midst of high-density housing and fourteen million people. There are trees and coyotes and sometimes even deer, and, though there are many homes in the area, the houses are built for privacy and are often hidden from view. Frank Zappa lives there. So does Ringo Starr. Smaller streets branch off of Woodrow Wilson, and, like mine, lead to areas often more private, and even more rustic. If the police were waiting for me, or came while I was there, it would be easy to work my way downslope, then loop around and work back to Mulholland. Of course, it's always easy if you don't get caught.

I passed three joggers and, twice, couples walking dogs, once a man and woman with an Akita, and once two men with a black Lab. I nodded at them and they nodded back. Elvis Cole, the Friendly Felon, out for an evening's stroll.

I left Woodrow Wilson and turned up my road and moved into the trees. The mountain shoulders up there, and the road follows the shoulder into a little canyon. I crept through the scrub oak until the road curved around to my house, and then I saw the plain unmarked sedan sitting in the shadows beneath a willow tree, maybe sixty yards past my front door. I kept the trunk of an oak between myself and the car and I waited. Maybe eight minutes later someone on the passenger's side moved, then the driver moved, and then they were still again. Shadows within shadows. If there were cops outside the house, there might be cops inside the house. The smart thing to do would be to leave and forget about being in my living room when Jennifer Sheridan called. Of course, if I wasn't there when she called, maybe she'd never call again. For all I knew, Akeem D'Muere was closing in on her at this very moment and her last call would be a call for help and I wouldn't be there to answer it because I'd be off doing the smart thing. Whatever that was.

Across the canyon, headlights moved on mountain roads and someone somewhere laughed and it carried on the night breeze. A woman. I thought about it some more and then I moved down the slope toward my house. Sometimes there is no smart move.

I worked through the trees and the brush until I was beneath my house, and then I climbed up to the deck. There were no police posted along the back and, as best I could tell, none within the house. Of course, I wouldn't know that for sure until I went in, would I?

I checked to see if the two cops were still in their sedan, and then I went back downslope and found the spare key I keep beneath the deck. I moved back across the slope to the far side of the house, climbed up onto the deck, and let myself in through the glass doors.

The house was still and dark and undisturbed. No cops were lying in wait, and the SWAT team didn't rappel down from my loft. If the police had been here, they had come and gone without breaking the door and without abusing my possessions.

The message light on my machine was blinking. I played it back, worried that it was Jennifer and that I had missed her call, but it was Lou Poitras. He called me an asshole, and then he hung up. You've got to love Lou.

I went into the kitchen, opened a Falstaff, and drank some. The moon was waxing three-quarters, and blue light spilled through the glass steeples at the back of my A-frame to flood the living room. I didn't need the light. Behind me the cat door clacked and the cat walked into the kitchen. He went to his food bowl.

I said, 'It's been a pretty crummy day. The least you could do is say hello.'

He stared at his bowl.

I took out his dry food and fed him. I watched as he ate, and then I took down a larger bowl and put it on the floor and emptied the box into it. I didn't know when I would get back, so I figured that this would have to do. I turned on the kitchen tap just enough to drip. He could hop up and drink.

I went to each door to make sure it was locked, then found a nylon overnight bag and packed it with toiletry items and three changes of clothes. The police had my wallet and all the things in it, but I had spare American Express cards and Visa cards in my dresser, along with gas cards and three hundred dollars in cash. I packed that, too.

When I was done I called Charlie Bauman, a lawyer I know who has an office in Santa Monica. I called him at home. Charlie answered on the fourth ring and said, 'Hey, Elvis, how's it going, buddy?' There was music somewhere behind him and he sounded glad to hear from me.

I said, 'I'm sitting on the floor in my living room, in the dark, and I'm wanted on three murder counts and a dope charge.'

Charlie said, 'Shit, are you out of your nut?' He didn't sound so happy to hear from me anymore.

I told him about it. When I got to the arrest and the questioning, he stopped me.

'You should've called me. Never give up your right to an attorney. That was bush.'

'I'm calling you now, Charlie.'

'Yeah, yeah. *After* you fuck up.'

I gave him the rest of it. When I finished, he didn't say anything for a while.

'Charlie?'

'You assaulted a police officer, and you escaped?'

'Pike and I. Yeah.'

'Shit.'

I didn't say anything.

Charlie said, 'Okay. You've got to come in. Come to my place, and we'll go in together. I'm sure we can pull bail, even after this.'

'No.'

'What do you mean, no?'

'I can't come in yet, Charlie. There's something I've got to do.'

Charlie went ballistic. 'Are you *fucked*?'

I hung up.

The house was quiet with a stillness that went beyond the auditory or the visual. Outside, a police helicopter tracked across the horizon, overflying Hollywood. Closer, cars wound their way along mountain roads. The phone rang, but I did not answer it. The machine caught it, and Charlie said, 'Okay, so you're not going to go in. Shit, pick up, willya?'

I picked up.

He made a sigh. 'All right. I'll talk to the DA. I'll start trying to work things out.'

'Sure.'

'Shit, don't get killed.' He hung up. What a way to say good-bye.

I went back to the aloneness of my house and wondered if in fact Jennifer Sheridan was going to call. Maybe I was just wasting my time, and risking my freedom.

The cat came out of the kitchen and watched me for a while, the way cats will, but then he tired of it and left. I thought that, were I a cat, it might be nice to go with him. Creep through a little grass, stalk a few field mice, maybe hang with a couple of nice lady cats. I guess cats grow weary of human pursuits. So do humans.

Thirty-six minutes later gravel crunched outside my front door and a light played through the entry windows. The cops from the sedan, come to take a look-see.

Footsteps moved to the carport and a second light tracked along the opposite side of the house. I scrambled behind the couch, and tried to wedge myself under it. The footsteps came out onto the deck, and now both lights raked over the couch and the living room and the stairs that lead up to my loft. There was maybe eight feet and a couple of dust bunnies between me and the two cops. I held my breath. The lights worked over the couch again and then the footsteps went away. My, my. Nothing like an adrenaline jolt to help you wile away the hours.

Seventy-two minutes after the cops had come to call, the phone rang again, and this time it was Jennifer Sheridan. When I picked up, she said, 'Thank God you're there.'

'Where are you?' Her voice was low, as if maybe she were calling without Mark knowing. Or maybe because she was just tired.

'I'm with Mark.'

'Where with Mark?'

'I made a mistake getting you involved in this. You have to stop, now. You have to leave us alone.'

'It's too late to leave you alone, Jennifer.' I told her about the Eight-Deuce Gangster Boys. I told her about Eric Dees working through the Eight-Deuce to set me up and I told her about James Edward Washington getting his brains blown out. I said, 'They're killing people. That means Mark is involved. They set us up with the Eight-Deuce and Akeem D'Muere killed James Edward Washington and that's the same as if they had ordered him killed. They're accessories before the fact, and if you're a part of it now, then you're an accessory after the fact. Do you understand that?'

She was breathing hard, but she didn't sound frantic. She sounded resolved. 'We can't come back, yet. We have to stay away.'

'Because of Mark?'

'It's not like what you think. Eric is going to work everything out. We only have to be up here a little while.' Up here.

I said, 'Eric isn't going to work it out, Jennifer. D'Muere is out of control. You need to come in. Tell me where you are.'

'I can't do that. I'm calling to ask you to stop. I want you to leave us alone.'

'I can't do that. It's larger than you now, Jennifer. There's James Edward.'

Jennifer Sheridan hung up.

I stood in the dark with the phone in my hand, and then I replaced the receiver and reset the answering machine. I made sure all of the windows were locked and the alarm was armed and the faucet still dripped for the cat, and then I picked up the overnight bag, let myself out, and moved back down the slope to the trees.

It took just under an hour to work my way back to Mulholland and to the turnout where Joe Pike was waiting. It was a broad, flat area looking out on the valley. Pike's Jeep was there. So were a Toyota Celica and a Chevy van. Music came from the van.

I slipped into the passenger side of the Jeep and Pike looked at me. The smell of coffee was strong. 'She call?'

'Yes. She wouldn't tell me where she is.'

'You think she's in danger?'

'I think they're all in danger. I'm just not sure who they're in danger from.'

Pike's mouth twitched. 'It's often like that, isn't it?'

'Yes. Often.' I stared at the lights of the San Fernando Valley and listened to the music from the van. It sounded Spanish. I said, 'If we can't find her, then we have to stop Akeem. That means we go back to the source.'

Pike nodded. 'The guy who set us up.'

'Cool T. Cool T might know.'

Pike shook his head. 'What a name.'

Pike started the Jeep and we drove back down into the city and to the motel, and the next day we went for Cool T.

23

Joe Pike and I left the motel for Ray Depente's place at five minutes after eight the next morning. We drove to Ray's much as you would drive anywhere. SWAT wasn't waiting on the roof, and the police hadn't cordoned off the area, and a squadron of black-and-whites with screaming sirens didn't give chase. We were just two guys in a Jeep. Wanted for murder, maybe, but there you are.

We stopped at a Denny's for breakfast, and while we were eating, two uniformed cops came in and sat in the smoking section. Pike and I paid, and walked out past them, but they never looked our way. Detective material.

At seven minutes before nine, we pulled into the little parking lot next to Ray Depente's, and went inside.

Ray Depente was sitting at his desk in the little glass cubicle, talking on the phone and leaning back with his feet up. The older woman who managed the office was behind him, peering into a file cabinet. When we stepped out of the door, Ray saw us and put down his feet and stood up. He mumbled something into the phone, then hung up and came around the desk and out onto the floor. The cops would've been here. They would've talked to him.

I said, 'Hi, Ray. This is a buddy of mine. Joe Pike.'

Ray stopped just outside of striking range and looked over Joe Pike and then squinted back at me. You could see him braining out what he'd have to do and how he'd have to do it to neutralize us. Pike slid two steps to the side, giving himself room if Ray made the move. There weren't many people in the gym. A young Asian guy sporting a black belt worked three women and a man through an intermediate *kata*, and a young Hispanic guy practiced roundkicks on a heavy bag in the far corner. Some of his leg moves were so fast you couldn't follow them.

Ray said, 'You've got no business here. Leave now, before I call the police.'

'I didn't kill James Edward, Ray. Akeem D'Muere set me up for the bust and D'Muere pulled the trigger.'

'Ain't the way the police tell it.' Ray took a half step back and turned so that his shoulders were angled to the plane of attack. 'Why don't we give'm a call, let everybody sit down and talk about it.' He made a little head move toward his office.

Pike said, 'That won't happen.'

Ray shifted again, adjusted his angle more toward Joe. 'Maybe not, but you never know.' Behind him, the class grunted and worked through their *kata*, and the heavy bag snapped with deep coughing *whumps*. 'I won't tell you again to leave, then we'll see what happens.' The woman in the little office closed the file and looked out at us and then came around the desk to stand in the door as if she could somehow read the tension.

I said, 'You don't know me, but you know James Edward. You think he was digging for a deal?'

Ray Depente canted his head like he'd been trying not to think of that, and his eyes flicked from me to Pike, then back. There was a physical quality to time, as if it were suddenly still, and moving through it was like moving through something dense and unyielding. 'Maybe you used him for a fool. Maybe you thought you could come down here and rip off the brothers, but it didn't work out that way. The police said you escaped. An innocent man don't escape.'

'Bullshit. James Edward and I came here to find out what happened at the Premier Pawn Shop. James Edward is dead because the cops involved didn't want us to find out, and neither does Akeem. Your man Cool T set us up.'

'I know you're lying. Cool T's righteous.'

'He set us up. He told us when and where to be, and the Eight-Deuce were there waiting for us.'

Ray was fighting it. You could see him starting to think that maybe I was being square. He wet his lips. 'Why in the hell did you come back here?'

'Because Akeem wants to kill a woman named Jennifer Sheridan, and I can't let that happen.'

'I don't know anything about it.'

'You don't, but maybe Cool T does, or knows somebody who does.'

Behind us, the Hispanic kid launched a flurry of kicks at the heavy bag, then collapsed to the mat, sweat falling like rain from the dark cloud of his hair. Ray Depente abruptly straightened from his fighting stance. 'I've got a class due in forty-five minutes.'

'This won't take long.'

'All right. Let's talk about it. If what you say makes sense, I'll see what I can do.'

Ray led us back across the wide parquet floor to the little cubicle and said, 'Miriam, I need maybe a few minutes alone with these gentlemen. Would you excuse us, please?' Miriam moved out of the door when she saw us coming and stood beside her desk. She peered at me and at Pike with obvious distaste. 'Who's going to answer the phones?'

'I will, Miriam. I remember how they work.'

'That fella from NBC is supposed to call.' She didn't like this at all.

'I can handle it, Miriam. Thank you.'

She *humphed* and bustled out, and then he closed the door, and went behind his desk. He took the phone off the hook.

A couple of hard chairs sat against a wall that was mostly pictures and mementos of Ray Depente's Marine Corps years. I took one of the chairs, but Pike stayed on his feet, looking at the pictures. Ray in fatigues showing gunnery-sergeant stripes. An older Ray showing master sergeant. An 8×10 of Ray Depente screaming at a platoon of recruits. Another of him smiling and shaking hands with President Reagan. Ray in dress blues with enough ribbons on his chest to make him walk sideways. Pike shook his head at the pictures, and said, 'Jarhead.'

Ray Depente's eyes flashed. 'You got a problem with that?'

Pike's mouth twitched. 'I went through Pendleton.'

Depente's eyes softened and he settled back, maybe looking at Pike with a little more respect. *There are two basic types of individuals: Marines, and everybody else.* He gave a thin, tight smile. 'Yeah. You got the look, all right.' He crossed his arms and looked at me. 'Okay, we're here and I'm listening.'

I told him about Eric Dees and the REACT team, and that these guys were now apparently involved with the Eight-Deuce Gangster Boys. I told him about the meeting at Raul's Taco, and what Cool T had told us. 'Cool T said that the REACT cops were in business with the Eight-Deuce. He told us that the Eight-Deuce would hip the REACT cops to the competition, and the cops would bust the dealers. He knew we were looking for a connection, and that's what he gave us. He told us that the REACT cops were going to step on a dope dealer in the park. The cops showed up, but so did the Eight-Deuce. They knew that we were there, and they were looking for us.'

Ray shook his head. 'I believe what you say, but I know Cool T to be a right brother. If he told you this, it's because he believed it.'

I spread my hands.

Ray gave me certain. 'Bet your life on it.'

Pike said, 'James Edward did.'

Ray's jaw flexed and he shifted in the chair. 'Yeah. I guess he did.' He fixed the sharp eyes on me again. 'Least, that's what you say.'

I said, 'Cool T said that the Eight-Deuce are working for the REACT cops, but it's not tracking out like that. These cops are acting like they're scared of Akeem, and they're trying to handle him, but they don't have the horsepower. That puts a woman I know in jeopardy. She's hiding with one of the officers involved, and if she's hiding, it's because the cops don't think they can control Akeem. I need to find out how this thing fits together. If I find out how it fits, maybe I can find her, or maybe I can stop Akeem.'

'And you think Cool T's the way.'

'Yes.'

Ray rubbed at the hard ridges above his eyes and looked out at the students on his mat. A couple of men in their forties had come in and were watching the class spar. Two of the women were sparring, and the remaining woman and man were doing the same. They danced forward and back, punching and kicking and blocking, but none of the punches and kicks landed. They weren't supposed to land. Ray shook his head. 'My goddamned Christ, first Charles Lewis, and now James Edward. How long you figure Akeem D'Muere and these officers been lying down together?'

'Since Charles Lewis.' I told him about the video equipment. I told him how, after Charles Lewis, the REACT team stopped arresting members of the Eight-Deuce Gangster Boys, and that they hadn't arrested any since.

'You figure those officers wrongfully killed that boy, and Akeem got it on tape, and he's holding it over them.'

'I'm not sure, but that's what I think.'

Ray Depente picked up his phone and punched a number. He stared at me while it rang, and kept his eyes on me when he spoke. 'This is Ray. Cool T over there?'

I crossed my arms and tilted back the chair and watched Ray Depente watch me.

He made seven calls, and when Ray Depente found what he was looking for, he put down the phone, stood up, and said, 'I know where he is. Let's go find out what the fuck is going on.'

24

The three of us took Pike's Jeep, and drove south on Hoover to a row of low industrial buildings on the west side of the street. A two-way alley ran from the street between the buildings to a little truck yard in the rear. Ten-wheel trucks like they use for local deliveries moved in and out of the alley, but a couple of eighteen-wheelers were parked at the curb. Guess the big trucks wouldn't fit through the little alley.

The eighteen-wheelers had their sides open, and men with hand trucks moved between the trucks and one of the warehouses, going into the eighteen-wheelers empty and coming out full like ants raiding a pantry. Ray said, 'Park across the street. Cool T got him a temp job unloading those things. If he's here, we'll see him.'

Pike drove past, made a U-turn, and parked so that we had a clear view of the action.

Maybe ten minutes later Cool T came out of the warehouse with an empty hand truck. I nodded. 'That's him.'

Cool T still wore the neon orange cap turned backwards, but the sunglasses were gone, and he had a little yellow Sony Walkman clipped to his belt and a set of headphones in place over the cap. His lips were moving, singing along with something on the Sony. He pushed the hand truck up a long metal ramp and disappeared into the near truck, but a couple of minutes later he reappeared with maybe eight cases of power steering fluid and went back down the ramp and into the warehouse. I said, 'Let's go.'

We trotted across Hoover, then around the side of the warehouse and up a little flight of stairs onto the loading platform. Freestanding metal industrial shelves towered maybe fifteen feet high, jammed with crates of shock absorbers and air filters and transmission fluid. Guys with loaded hand trucks were coming in through a big door on the side and working their way down the long aisles between the shelves. Once they got inside, everybody seemed to be going in different directions, but I guess they knew what they were doing. The crates already stacked on the shelves looked neat and orderly.

A bald guy maybe in his late fifties was sitting at a little desk, digging through receiving forms with a rat-tail file, and shouting at the men with the hand trucks. He looked over when he saw us and said, 'I got all the muscle I need. Come back tomorrow.'

Ray said, 'Myron Diggs is expecting us.'

Pike said, 'Myron.'

Ray looked at Joe. 'You think Cool T is his Christian name?'

The guy at the desk said, 'Oh. Well, if Myron is expecting guests, who am I to object?' Everybody's a comedian. Everybody's got an act they want to sell. 'I hire a guy to do a full day's work. He don't want to work, he can find himself another goddamn job. That's all I got to say about it.' A peach, this guy.

Ray said, 'It won't take long.'

The bald guy didn't look satisfied. 'Yeah, right. It never takes long.' He made a gesture toward the back quarter of the warehouse. 'Try over around E-16. He's doin' auto parts.'

We moved past the bald guy and into the aisles and back toward E-16. The warehouse covered maybe twelve thousand square feet, and most of it was mazed with shelves and aisles that had little letters and numbers on them just like the sections in a parking garage. When we found the *Es*, Pike said, 'Better if we split up.'

'Okay.'

Ray and Joe Pike turned off at the first intersection, and I continued back to the third. I had gone maybe six aisles when I found Cool T wrestling the eight cases of power steering fluid off of his hand truck. I said, 'Hey, Cool T. Let's take a walk.'

Cool T made a noise when he saw me, and then he looked nervous and pulled off the headset. 'What you doin' here?' He began backing away. 'I don't wanna be seen with you, man. Lot of these guys are gangbangers.'

Joe and Ray came into the aisle behind him, cutting him off. When he saw Ray he frowned. 'Ray, what you doin' here?' He looked back at me. 'What the fuck goin' on?'

Ray said, 'We've got to talk, Cool.'

Cool T was waving us away. 'You tryin' to get my ass killed? This muthuhfuckuh after the Eight-Deuce. They see I with him, they'll be treatin' me to Mr Drive-By.' He was looking down the other aisles, seeing who was there. 'You know better'n this, Ray. James Edward know better than this.' He tried to push past me.

I grabbed his arm. 'James Edward died yesterday.'

It stopped him the way a heavy caliber rifle bullet will stop you. It brought him up short and his breath caught and his eyelids fluttered and he sort of blinked at me. 'Fuck you sayin'?'

'We went over to the park, like you said. We saw the ice cream guy selling dope, and then the cops came, but the Eight-Deuce came, too. They knew we were there, Cool. They were gunning for us.'

'Bullshit.'

'They took us to a little place by the railroad tracks. Akeem D'Muere put a Dan Wesson thirty-eight-caliber revolver to James Edward's temple and blew his brains out.'

Cool T's mouth opened and closed and his eyes made little jerky moves. 'That's a fuckin' lie.'

I said, 'You fed us a bullshit story to get us there so they could set us up for a phony dope bust. It was a setup.'

'You a muthuhfuckin' liar.' Cool T lunged at me and threw a straight right hand. I stepped to the outside and hooked a left up and inside under his ribs. He stumbled sideways and when he tried to come back at me Ray Depente tied him up and twisted his arms behind his back. 'That's enough, boy.'

Cool T's eyes were red and he struggled against Ray, but a Sherman tank could probably struggle against Ray and it wouldn't do any good. Cool T said, 'He fuckin' lyin'. I didn't set'm up. I love James Edward like a goddamned brother.' The red eyes began to leak.

Ray Depente looked at me. 'He didn't know. He wasn't part of it.'

'No. I guess he wasn't.'

Ray Depente turned Cool T loose, and Cool T wiped at the wet around his eyes and smeared it over his cheeks. He shook his head. 'James Edward dead because of me.'

'You didn't know.'

'This shit ain't happenin'.'

I said, 'It's happening.'

'They feedin' me stuff to set you up, that means they know I with you. They know I was askin' about them, and that means they'll be comin' for me. They'll kill me just like they killed James Edward.'

There didn't seem to be a whole lot to say to that.

He shook his head. 'I can't believe the goddamned bitch lied to me. I got all that stuff from a woman I diddle. She run around with some of those niggers in the Eight-Deuce. She get rock from some of those niggers.'

I said, 'We need to talk to her, Cool T.'

Cool T looked at Joe. 'Who this guy?'

'This is Joe Pike. He's with me.'

Cool T nodded. 'Then he gonna die, too.'

Pike's mouth twitched.

I said, 'Akeem wants to kill a woman named Jennifer Sheridan. I've got to find out what Akeem knows and doesn't know, and if he has a line on the woman. Do you see?'

'Okay.'

'Maybe the girl who set us up, maybe she knows.'

Cool T put his hands together and pressed them against his mouth like he was praying. He looked tall and gaunt, and the sort of loose-jointed energy that he'd had only a few minutes ago seemed gone, as if he had pulled himself inward and, in the pulling, had made himself hard and fierce. He let his hands drop to his sides. 'She a sister named Alma Reeves.'

'You know where to find her?'

'I know.' He turned back to the hand truck and wrestled it from under the stack of boxes and rolled it to the side of the aisle and left it neatly against the wall. 'I take you over there.'

'What about your job?'

'Fuck the job. This for James Edward.'

25

Alma Reeves lived in a small stucco bungalow with a nice flagstone walk and a single car in the drive and a little picket fence that needed painting. We cruised the block once so that we could check out the house and the street. I said, 'Does she live alone?'

Cool T was sitting behind me, next to Ray Depente. 'She live with her mama and sister. The sister got a pretty good job with State Farm, so she won't be around, but the mama be there. She old.'

'Okay.'

Across the street and two houses down, three teenaged guys in cutoff baggies and gold chains and backwards baseball caps sat on a low brick wall, laughing about something. Pike said, 'What about the three guys on the wall?'

'The one in the middle Eight-Deuce. The other two are wanna-bes.'

Pike didn't like it. 'No good. They see us go in, it'll be bad for the family.'

Cool T said, 'Fuck'm.'

Pike looked at him.

Cool T said, 'These niggers used to me. I here all the time.'

Ray said, 'Don't use that word again.'

Cool T gave hands. 'What?'

Ray put hard eyes on him. 'I'm looking where you're looking, and I don't see any. I'm looking in this car, and I don't see any in here, either.'

The hard eyes got heavy and Cool T looked away.

Ray said, 'I just want to get that straight.'

Cool T nodded.

I cleared my throat. 'Oh, boys.'

They both looked at me. Pike looked at me, too.

'Sorry. That didn't come out right.'

Pike shook his head and turned away. You can't take me anywhere. I said, 'If Joe and I go in through the front, it won't take a rocket scientist for those guys to figure out who we are. We can let Cool T out here like

141

we're dropping him off, then we'll park on the next street over and come in through the backyard.' I looked at Cool T. 'Will she let you in?'

'I get in.'

Pike stopped at the drive and Cool T got out, and then Pike kept going. One of the guys on the low wall pointed at Cool T and Cool T pointed back, and then we turned the corner. Pike turned right, then right again, and we counted houses until we were in front of a tiny saltbox that would butt against the back of Alma Reeves's place. Joe said, 'Here,' and pulled to the curb.

Ray said, 'Let me get out first and go up to the house. Folks inside see a couple of white men sneaking up the drive, they'll call the police for sure.'

Ray got out and walked up the drive to the front door and knocked. After a little bit, Ray shook his head and motioned us forward. Nobody home.

We went up the drive and through a neatly kept backyard and over a low chain-link fence and onto Alma Reeves's property. Cool T was standing in the back door, waiting for us and holding by her left forearm a young woman who couldn't have been more than seventeen. She looked scared.

We trotted past two rows of nicely set tomato plants and across their yard and up three cement steps and into a small yellowed kitchen with a picture of Jesus on the wall. A heavy woman with gray hair was leaning against the doorjamb between the kitchen and the dining room, saying, 'Y'all stop that and get out of here. Y'all get out of here, now.'

Cool T pulled the door closed after us. He locked it. The heavy woman's voice got higher, and she said, 'Cool T! Cool, what you doin', boy? I'm talking to you, Myron.'

Ray Depente said, 'It's all right, Mama. Nothing bad is gonna happen here.'

Cool T jerked Alma Reeves's arm. ''Less it has to.'

I said, 'Cool.'

'Goddamn it. She the reason James Edward dead.' He shook her arm again. 'Fuckin' bitch, set me up like I'm some kinda chump, lie to me like that so a brother gets killed.' Cool T raised his hand and Alma fell back against the refrigerator with a whimper and Pike stepped in and caught Cool T's arm.

'No.'

The heavy woman said, 'Alma, what is he talking about? Alma, you talk to me!' Nobody was looking at the heavy woman.

Cool T glared at Pike, but then he let go of the girl and stepped back. When he let go, she stumbled back and fell. Cool T was so angry that he was trembling. He was so angry that his eyes were rimmed red again, and filled with tears, but the tears weren't because she had lied to him.

'Goddamn it, this outrageous shit has been goin' on too long down here, brother on brother. This shit got to stop.'

Alma Reeves was shouting. 'He *made* me, Cool. He said you was asking and he told me what to say. I didn't know he was gonna *kill* anyone. I swear to *Jesus* I didn't know.'

Alma Reeves was sitting on the floor, looking up at us, and I wondered how frightening it must be for these two women to have four men push into their home and act in this manner. I squatted down by her. 'How did Akeem know that Cool was working with us?'

She jerked away from me. 'I can't be talkin' about all this. Don't you understand anything? I be talkin' about this and it gets back, I'm dead for sure.'

The heavy woman was pulling at her hair. 'What do you mean, dead? Alma, what have you gotten yourself messed with?'

Alma looked at her mother. Then she closed her eyes.

I said, 'Ray, why don't you take Mrs Reeves into the living room.'

Ray took the heavy woman away. She begged us not to do anything to her baby. She said it over and over as Ray pulled her away, and hearing it made me feel small and foul and ashamed of myself. I said, 'Look at me, Alma.'

She didn't move.

I said, 'Akeem doesn't know that we're here. No one but the people in this room knows that we're here, and no one else is going to know. Do you understand that?'

She opened her eyes.

'No one saw us come in, and no one will see us go out. We are going to move against Akeem. If you help us, no one will know. If you don't help us, I'll make sure Akeem believes that you turned on him. Do you see?' Small and foul and mean.

She said, 'Oh, you muthuhfuckuh.'

I nodded.

Alma Reeves said, 'I got what you call a little dependency problem.'

Cool T said, 'She went along with Akeem for the rock. She a crack 'ho.'

She flared at him. 'I ain't no 'ho. Don't you call me that.'

I said, 'Cool.'

He said, 'She say she want to quit, so I got her in a program, but she didn't stay. That's why she diddle around with trash like the Eight-Deuce. 'Ho'ing for the rock.'

Alma Reeves was the kind of unhealthy thin that doesn't come from dieting. Who needs protein and vitamin B when you can suck on a crack bong? Ray came back in the room. I said, 'What did Akeem tell you to say to Cool T?'

'That the cops was gonna lean on a brother be sellin' rock at the park. He say I was supposed to tell Cool, then call him and tell him right away.'

'Alma, this is important. Did Akeem say anything about a girl named Jennifer Sheridan?'

She shook her head. 'I don't know.'

'It's very important, Alma. He's already killed James Edward, and I think he wants to kill her.'

'I don't know. I'm not over there that much. I don't know.'

Pike said, 'Where does Akeem live?'

'He in a place just off Main over here.' She made a little hand wave toward the east. 'Used to be a rock house.' She told us where it was and what it looked like.

Ray said, 'Shit. That means it's built like a fort. There'll be reinforced walls and steel on the doors and windows.'

Cool T laughed. 'What you fools thinkin' about doin', stormin' the 'hood like at Normandy?' He laughed louder.

I said, 'Reconnoiter. We go, we watch, we learn whatever we can learn, and we maybe try to pick up Akeem when he's alone. If someone comes, we follow them. Whatever we can do.'

Cool T said, 'What about Alma?'

We looked at her. 'I didn't know Akeem was gonna kill that boy. I swear I didn't. Why I wanna tell Akeem now I told you?'

Cool T said, 'Crack. Crack 'ho do anything for the rock.'

Alma screamed, 'I can't help it. Don't you call me that.'

Cool T went to the little dinette and pulled out a chair. 'Maybe I'll just set a spell.' He gave me sleepy eyes, eyes that were tired maybe from seeing too many brothers killed by other brothers. James Edward Washington eyes. 'Make sure she don't call up old Akeem.'

Ray said, 'Thanks, Cool.'

I looked back at Alma, and then I found a notepad and a Bic pen on one of the counters. I wrote down a name and a phone number. 'You want to get into a program and try to get off this stuff?'

She stared at me.

I dropped the pad into her lap. 'There's a woman I know named Carol Hillegas. She runs a halfway house in Hollywood. If you want to get into a program, give her a call.' I looked at Cool T. 'If she wants to go, call Carol and take her over there. It won't cost anything.'

Alma Reeves stared down at the pad.

Cool T got up from his chair, came over, and took the notepad out of her lap. 'Crack 'ho ain't gonna do nothin' to help herself. Maybe I'll give a call for her.'

We went out as we came, through the backyard and over the little chain-link and out the rear neighbor's drive to Pike's Jeep. Ray Depente gave directions and we made the short drive to Akeem D'Muere's.

D'Muere's house was maybe five houses from an intersection, and we could see it well. It was a small cinderblock with an ill-kept front lawn

144

and a couple of overgrown roses that looked like they needed water and heavy steel grates over the windows. Rock house. When we edged to a stop at the intersection, Floyd Riggens came out of the house, punched a black guy who was maybe nineteen years old, and knocked him down.

Then Warren Pinkworth was running out of the house and pulling Riggens away, and Eric Dees was coming out of the house, too.

I said, 'Well, well.'

Pike's mouth twitched.

More of the Gangster Boys came out of the house and Pinkworth shook Riggens like he was an idiot. Riggens did a lot of finger jabbing toward the kid, but he didn't try to get back into it. He walked out to the street and got into a sedan. Akeem D'Muere came out after Dees, and the two of them argued, but they probably weren't arguing about Riggens.

Pike said, 'If these guys are willing to risk being seen here, whatever they've got going must be falling apart.'

Ray Depente twisted in his seat. 'What are we going to do?'

'Watch.'

Ray didn't like that. 'There the motherfuckers are, right there. Shouldn't we call the police? They can see for themselves.'

'See what, Ray?' I looked at him. 'Dees is conducting an investigation. He's questioning Akeem D'Muere and other members of the Eight-Deuce Gangster Boys for information they might have as to my whereabouts, or the drug deal James Edward and I were trying to put together.'

Pike said, 'Uh-huh. And these guys might know. Two of them were found dead at the scene. Probably been a parade of cops through here.'

Ray's jaw worked and his eyes were wide.

I said, 'Can you get back from here okay, Ray?'

He looked at me.

'We have to find Jennifer Sheridan, and Dees knows where she is. Dees would've told Thurman to hide her, and he's worried, so he'll make contact. We're going to follow him when he leaves. Do you see?'

Ray Depente didn't move.

Akeem D'Muere said something sharp to Eric Dees, then went back into his house. Dees stood for a moment like he wanted to do something, but then he walked out to the street. Pinkworth and Riggens were out there, sitting in Riggens's sedan. There was another car behind them, but that was probably Dees's.

I said, 'Ray.'

Ray stared past me at the crack house, and then he nodded, maybe more to himself than to me. He said, 'Tell me that this sonofabitch is going to pay for James Edward.'

'He'll pay. I promise.'

Ray Depente turned heat-seeker eyes my way. 'Bet your ass he will.'

Ray Depente got out of the Jeep and walked back the way we had come.

Pike shook his head. 'Hate to have that sonofabitch mad at me.'

'Uh-hunh.'

Eric Dees finished speaking to Pinkworth and Riggens, then climbed into his own car. Pinkworth drove away first, and when Dees drove away, Pike and I followed.

26

It didn't take long.

Eric Dees went west toward LAX, then climbed onto the San Diego Freeway and headed north, up through Los Angeles and the Sepulveda Pass and into the San Fernando Valley.

He left the freeway at Roscoe, turned west again toward Van Nuys Airport, then pulled into the parking lot of a Tommy's hamburger stand where Mark Thurman was sitting at a window table, waiting for him. Jennifer Sheridan wasn't around.

We snapped a turn into a Nissan dealership next to the Tommy's just as Mark Thurman left his window table and came out to meet Eric Dees. Pike eased the Jeep toward them along one of the aisles of new Nissans, and parked behind a row of vans. We got out of the Jeep and moved up between two of the vans and watched.

Dees got out of the car, and Thurman hugged him, and Dees hugged him back, slapping Mark Thurman's shoulder the way you do when you're moved to see someone that you haven't seen in a while and they are someone you care about. Cars moved in and out of the lot, and Hispanic guys who looked like they did yard work and women who looked like they worked in offices came out of or went into the Tommy's, and looked at Dees and Thurman as they did, but Thurman and Dees seemed not to notice, nor to care. Dees put out his hand and Thurman gripped it tight, as if he were using it to anchor himself.

Thurman seemed tired and drawn, but then, so did Eric Dees. They looked nervous, and they looked glad to see each other, and they didn't look like homicidal co-conspirators rendezvousing to foil justice and commit evil. I wasn't sure what they should look like, but they didn't look like that. Pike said, 'What?'

I shook my head. 'I don't know. It's not the sort of meeting I expected.'

Pike nodded and maybe his mouth twitched.

A balding salesman in a bright blue Miles Vandeveer sport coat smiled his way over and said, 'That's an outstanding little van you're looking at there, gentlemen. You wanna trade in this old clunker, I'll give you a fair deal.' He slapped the side of Pike's Jeep. Hard.

Pike's head swiveled toward the salesman. 'Clunker.'

I stepped in front of him. 'We're just looking, thanks. If we have any questions, I'll come get you.'

The salesman gestured at the van. 'Great new five-year, fifty-thousand-mile warranty with these vehicles.' He looked back at the Jeep, and this time slapped the hood. 'Be a big step up from a maintenance hog like this old bitch.'

I said, 'Oh, man.'

Pike leaned toward the salesman and said, 'Look at me.'

The salesman looked.

Pike said, 'Touch the Jeep once more, and I will hurt you.'

The salesman's smile faltered, then failed. He swallowed hard. 'Yes, well. I'll be in the showroom if you gentlemen have any questions.'

I said, 'That will be fine.'

He made a last stab at the smile, couldn't quite manage it, and walked backwards until he bumped into a green Stanza. When he hit the Stanza, the impact turned him around, and the fast walk became a sort of skipping hop, as if he had to go to the bathroom. Then he ducked into the showroom and peered out at us through the glass. A saleswoman with red hair came up beside him, and he started with the big gestures, filling her in.

I said, 'Great, Joe. Nothing like a little restraint. What if he calls the cops?'

Pike gave sullen. 'Clunker.'

Thurman and Dees went into Tommy's and bought a couple of Cokes and returned to Thurman's window table. Eric Dees did most of the talking. Thurman nodded a lot, and occasionally said something, but mostly he just sipped at his drink. Thurman looked scared. He looked like Eric Dees was telling him things that were maybe hard to understand, but necessary to hear. At one point, Thurman got agitated and spread his hands, gesturing broadly, but Dees reached across the table and gripped his shoulder to explain something, and after a while Mark Thurman calmed.

The meeting didn't last long. Ten minutes later they came back into the parking lot and went to Eric Dees's sedan. Dees put his hand on Thurman's shoulder again, and said something else, and this time Mark Thurman smiled. Bucking up. Hanging tough. With Eric Dees telling him everything would be fine if he just hung in a little while longer. You could see it on his face. The pep talk by the old man. Then they shook hands and Eric Dees got into his sedan and drove away. Pike said, 'Now what?'

'We stay with Thurman.'

Mark Thurman crossed the parking lot to his blue Mustang even before Eric Dees had pulled away. He tossed his cup into a big cement trash container, climbed into the Mustang, and pulled out onto Roscoe heading east. Pike and I trotted back to the Jeep and roared through the car dealership and out into traffic after him. The salesman in the blue sport coat watched us go, then made a big deal out of saying something to the saleswoman who'd come up beside him. I think he gave us the finger.

We followed Thurman up onto the 405 and climbed north through the valley past Mission Hills and the Simi Freeway interchange and the San Fernando Reservoir. I kept waiting for him to exit, and maybe head west toward his apartment, but he didn't. We continued north into the Newhall Pass and the Santa Susana Mountains until the 405 became the Golden State, and when we came to the Antelope Valley Freeway just before Santa Clarita, Mark Thurman exited and followed it east, up through the San Gabriels. I said, 'Thurman's from Lancaster.'

Pike glanced at me.

'Mark Thurman is going home.'

The landscape became parched and barren and more vertical than not. Pockets of condominiums clung to the mountains, and fields of low-cost housing spread across creek beds, and huge billboards proclaimed YOU COULD BE HOME NOW IF YOU LIVED HERE. Ten years ago, only rattlesnakes and sagebrush lived here.

Thurman followed the freeway through the mountains past quarries and rock formations and drop sites for dead bodies, and then we were out of the mountains and descending into the broad flat plain of Antelope Valley. The valley up there is high desert, and the communities there grew up around top-secret military projects and government funding. Chuck Yeager broke the sound barrier up there. Edwards Air Force Base is there, with its shuttle landings and Stealth fighters, and, beyond that, the Mojave Desert spreads out to the north and east, a hot dry desolate plain that is ideal for crashing top-secret government hardware. In the foothills of the San Gabriels there is water and fruit orchards, and, in the winter, there is even snow. But the valley is different. In the valley, there is only scrub brush and heat and cactus, and secret things that no one is supposed to know.

Maybe six miles after we descended out of the San Gabriels, Mark Thurman left the highway and turned into a flat middle-class housing tract with stucco houses and azalea bushes and two-car garages so filled with the clutter of life that at least one of the family's cars had to stay in the drive. We turned in after him, and Pike shook his head. 'No traffic and no movement. We follow him in there, he'll make us.'

'Then let him go.'

We let Mark Thurman draw ahead and turn and disappear from sight.

We pulled to the side of the street and waited, and maybe five minutes later we started again. We made the same turn that Mark Thurman made, and then we drove slowly, crisscrossing the subdivision streets, and looking for his blue Mustang.

Two streets over, we found it, parked in the open garage of a pleasant two-story house with a neatly kept lawn and a fig tree in the front yard.

We parked in the drive behind the Mustang, walked up to the front door, and rang the bell. Footsteps came toward the door, the door opened, and Mark Thurman looked out at us. I said, 'Hi, Mark.'

Mark Thurman tried to shove the door shut. He was big, and strong, but he started the move too late and we had the angle.

The door crashed open, and Joe Pike went in first and I went in after him. Thurman threw a fast straight right, but it was high over Joe Pike's left shoulder. Pike hit Mark Thurman three times in maybe four-tenths of a second. Once in the neck and twice in the solar plexus.

Mark Thurman made a choking sound, then sat down and grabbed at his throat.

Somewhere deeper in the house a voice called, 'Who is it, Mark?'

I called back. 'Mark lost his voice, Jennifer. Better come out here and give him a hand.'

27

Jennifer Sheridan came out of a door off the back of the entry and saw Mark Thurman on the floor. When she saw Thurman she ran to him, yelling, 'What did you do to him?'

Pike said, 'Hit him.'

We pulled Thurman to his feet and helped him into the living room. He tried to push away from us, but there wasn't a lot of *umphf* in it. I said, 'Take it easy. We've got the gun.'

Jennifer gave confused. 'What gun?'

Pike showed her Mark's revolver, then stuck it in his belt. 'Is anyone else here?'

Jennifer followed us into the living room, hovering around Mark Thurman as we put him into a green Naugahyde Ez-E-Boy. 'No. The house belongs to Mark's aunt, and she's away. That's why we're using it.'

Pike grunted approval, then pulled the drapes so that no one could see in from the street.

Jennifer Sheridan touched Mark Thurman's face with her fingertips. His face was already starting to puff. 'I'd better get some ice.'

He tried to push her away. 'Goddamn it, why'd you tell them?'

She stepped back. 'I didn't.'

I said, 'I'm a detective, Mark. I did a little detective work and found you.' I told him about watching Akeem D'Muere's, and about picking up Dees and following him to Tommy's.

Thurman tried to act like it was no big deal. 'So what? That doesn't prove anything.' He looked at Jennifer. 'Jesus Christ, Jen, this guy is a wanted fugitive.'

She said, 'No, Mark. He wants to help us. He got into trouble trying to help.'

Mark yelled, 'Don't tell this guy anything.' Panicked. 'He's just making guesses. He doesn't know anything.' He tried to push up from the chair, but Joe Pike shoved him down.

I said, 'I know that the Premier Pawn Shop is owned by Akeem D'Muere. I know that eleven weeks before Charles Lewis Washington

151

died, D'Muere hired a security contractor called Atlas Security to install a hidden surveillance camera at the Premier.' When I said it, his face dropped maybe a quarter of an inch. He tried not to show it, but there it was. 'The camera was there when you guys pulled the sting. It would've recorded what happened.' I felt like Perry Mason, laying out my summation for the court. Did that make Jennifer Della Street? Was Pike Paul Drake? 'Akeem D'Muere has a tape of what happened that night, and because he has the tape he has you.'

Jennifer moved behind him and put her hand on his back. 'It's killing him.'

'For Christ's sake, Jennifer, be quiet.' He was looking scared.

Jennifer said, 'That's why it went so bad for us. They made him swear to keep quiet and he did, but he just isn't like that.'

Mark said, 'Eric's taking care of it. Don't admit anything. What if he's wired?'

Jennifer Sheridan pulled at him, trying to make him see, trying to make him come to his senses. 'He's not wired and Eric's getting you into trouble.' She turned from him and looked at me. 'He thinks he's protecting them. He wasn't part of all that. He's not like the others.'

'Nothing happened, goddamn it.' Thurman pointed at me. 'I'm telling you that nothing happened.'

'Damn it, Mark,' she shouted. 'Stop protecting them. *Stop lying for them.*'

I said, 'Leave him.'

They looked at me as if I'd fired a shot into the floor.

I said, 'He doesn't love you, Jennifer. He's willing to take you down with him, just because he isn't strong enough to stand up to the guys he works with.'

Mark Thurman boiled up out of the chair like an angry bull and hit me with his shoulder, driving me back across the living room. Jennifer Sheridan shrieked and yelled, 'Mark,' but then Pike was next to her, wrapping her in his arms.

I stayed high on Thurman's shoulders and let him carry me across the room and into the wall. He was angry and scared and probably not thinking too well, but he was also large and strong. We hit the wall and he backed away to throw a punch, and when he did I spun left and kicked him on the right side of his face and then I slipped to the side, and kicked him behind the left knee. He went down. I could've kicked him on the outside of his knee and broken the ligaments, but I didn't want to do that. I said, 'Don't be stupid, Mark. You're not helping you and you're not helping Jennifer.'

He shoved his way up and this time he sort of crabbed in sideways, like he wanted to box. He feinted with his left and threw a straight right and when he did, I pushed it past and snapped a side kick to his head that made him stumble back and drop his hands. I kicked him twice more, and punched him hard once in the solar plexus, and he went down. I'd hit him hard enough to keep him there.

I squatted beside him and said, 'You're going to listen to this.'

He shook his head. Like a five-year-old. His nose was swelling and there was a smear of blood along his lower lip.

I said, 'Eric Dees and Akeem D'Muere conspired to set me up for this dope bust. In the course of that action, Akeem D'Muere murdered James Edward Washington. That makes Dees a co-conspirator to murder.'

Thurman was breathing hard. Sucking deep breaths and letting them out.

'You tried to keep all of this from Jennifer, but Jennifer hired me, and you finally brought her in. You told Jennifer about Charles Lewis Washington and Akeem D'Muere, and that means you've implicated her. You're a cop. You know what that means.'

Mark Thurman looked at her.

'She's become an accessory after the fact to murder. She can be charged, and she can be tried. Do you see that? Do you see what you've done to her?'

Jennifer Sheridan frowned. 'Mark?'

I said, 'Who are you going to protect, boy? Eric Dees, or Jennifer?'

Mark Thurman raised his hands as if he were about to say something, but the something didn't come and he lowered them. He looked from me to Jennifer Sheridan, and then back to me. He said, 'It was Floyd.'

You'd know it was Floyd. It'd have to be.

'I'm not even sure what happened. Floyd was hitting him, and then Pinkworth was hitting him, and he just died.' Jennifer Sheridan knelt down beside him and put her hand on his arm.

I said, 'You told yourselves it was an accident. Everybody's thinking Rodney King, and you decide to cover up.'

He nodded. 'Only a couple of days later, here comes the tape. Just like Rodney. Only this time the bad guys had the tape, and not the good guys. Akeem had the tape.'

There was quiet in the small house.

Jennifer Sheridan said, 'He went along because he didn't know what else to do. You can see that, can't you?'

I didn't answer.

'He didn't do it for himself. Don't you see that?'

I looked at Pike and Pike looked at me.

Mark Thurman said, 'What are you going to do?'

I shook my head. 'I don't know.'

He said, 'It was just an accident.' I looked at him and he wasn't a cop anymore. He was a big handsome kid who looked confused and scared, and more than a little bit lost. He said, 'I dream about it every night, and

I just don't know. It got out of hand, and we didn't know what to do. Even Floyd was surprised. Floyd didn't expect to kill him. It just happened.' He tried to think of another way to say it. His mouth opened and closed a couple of more times. His brow knotted. Then he just shook his head.

'So you decided to protect each other.'

'You think I'm proud of this? You think I don't see that poor guy? Jesus God, I don't know what to do.' He was shaking his head. Jennifer Sheridan looked like she wanted to hold him and take care of him and make it all better even though she knew it was wrong. Maybe that's what love is.

I said, 'How many copies of the tape are there?'

'We got one. I don't know how many D'Muere has. Maybe a million.'

'Who has the copy you saw?'

'Eric.' Jennifer Sheridan put out her hand and Mark Thurman took it. Jennifer smiled, and Mark Thurman smiled back at her. They looked relieved, as if by finally sharing this the weight was becoming bearable. Mark said, 'I know where he hides it.'

I took a deep breath and then I let it out. I felt tired and my back hurt where the muscles lace over the shoulder blades. Tension, I guess. Stress.

Jennifer Sheridan said, 'Will you help him?'

I looked at Jennifer Sheridan looking at me and I nodded. 'Okay,' I said. 'I want to see the tape.'

28

Jennifer Sheridan helped Mark Thurman to the couch and sat next to him. He could've made it on his own this time, but he let her help.

I said, 'Has everyone on the REACT team seen the tape?'

'Yeah.'

'Has anyone else?'

He shook his head. 'Not on our side. Who would we show it to?'

Pike went to the window and looked out the curtain. He said, 'Eric would have a plan. Akeem pops up with the tape, says do what I want or I burn you, Eric isn't going to just roll over.'

Thurman nodded. 'Eric said we should play along until we could find something to make Akeem back off.'

'Like what?'

'We started running intelligence on him and doing twenty-four-hour surveillance. We even went out and bought these video cameras. We figured if we got him doing a capital offense on tape, we could trade him. You burn us, we burn you, like that.'

Pike moved to the other side of the window and looked out the curtain from that side. 'Dorks.'

Thurman gave him hard. 'Hey, what would you do?'

Pike didn't bother to look at him. 'I wouldn't be where you are. I wouldn've killed Charles Lewis Washington, and then lied about it. I would've done the right thing.'

Jennifer Sheridan frowned. 'You don't need to be so harsh.'

I said, 'A man died, Jennifer. It doesn't get much harsher than that.'

She put her hand on Mark Thurman's thigh.

I said, 'Okay. So you were looking for something to press Akeem. Did you get anything?'

'Not yet.'

'So the five of you went along with him, committing crimes.'

'That's right.' Thurman made a tiny nod, the kind where your head barely moves, and he wouldn't look at me.

'And Eric figured you guys would keep on like that until you found something to use against Akeem?'

'Yeah.'

'Committing crimes.'

'Yeah.' He stared at the floor and looked even more ashamed. He was a guy with a lot to be ashamed of.

Jennifer said, 'Why do you have to keep asking him about these things? He feels bad enough.'

I said, 'I have to ask him because I don't know the answers. I have to know what he's done so that I'll know how to help him or even if I can help him. Do you see?'

She saw, but she didn't like it. 'I thought you said that you'd help.'

'I'm deciding. Maybe I'll help him, but maybe I won't. Maybe I can't.'

She liked that even less. I looked back at Thurman, and then I stood up. 'Where does Dees keep the tape?'

'He's got it hidden in his garage.'

'You know where?'

'Yeah. If he hasn't moved it.'

'Let's go see.'

We took Thurman's Mustang, and Thurman drove. Joe Pike stayed with Jennifer Sheridan.

Forty-two minutes later we left the freeway in Glendale and turned onto a pleasant residential street lined with mature trees and sidewalks and the sort of modest middle-class houses that more suggested Indiana or Iowa than Southern California. Mark Thurman said, 'Are you sure about this?'

'I'm sure. Which one?'

Thurman pointed out a white frame Cape Cod with a tiny front yard and a couple of nice magnolia trees and lots of surrounding shrubbery. The drive ran along the left side of the house to the garage. Like the rest of the houses on Dees's street, it was prewar, and the garage was detached. Someone had bolted a basketball goal above the garage door, and the net was yellowed and frayed. It had been there a long time. Thurman said, 'We can't just ask him, you know.'

'We're not going to ask him. We're going to steal it.'

Thurman nodded and frowned, like he knew I was going to say that. 'What if it's not there?'

'If it's not there, we'll find out where it is, and then we'll figure a way to get it from there.' A 1984 Nissan 4×4 sport truck sat in the drive beneath the basketball goal. One of those heavy roll bars with a row of lights across the top was mounted in the bed behind the cab, and the suspension was jacked up about eight inches too high so the little truck could sport oversized knobby tires. 'Who belongs to the truck?'

'Eric Junior. I guess he's home from school.'

'How about Mrs Dees? Would she be home?'

Thurman cruised past the house without my having to tell him. 'She works at Glendale General. She's a nurse, but I don't know if she works today, or when she gets home, or any of that.'

'Okay.'

'Would the kid recognize you?'

'Yeah, I think so. I've been here a few times, but not many.'

'How about the neighbors?'

He shook his head. 'No.'

We K-turned in someone's drive, went back, and parked one house away on the driveway side. I said, 'I'm going to see what the boy's up to. You're going to wait for my signal, then go into the garage and get the tape.'

Thurman looked nervous. 'Jesus Christ, it's broad daylight.'

'During the day, we look like we belong. At night, we look like crooks. You're a cop.'

'Well. Sure.'

'Give me the keys.'

He looked at me, then he took out the keys and gave them over. I put them in my pocket, then got out of the car and went up the Deeses' sidewalk to the front door. I pretended to ring the bell, though I didn't, and then I pretended to knock, though I didn't do that, either. If the neighbors were watching, it would look good for them.

I stood at the door and listened, and heard voices deep in the house, but they were the kind of voices that come from a television, and not from real people. The front door was under an overhang, and there was a long brick veranda that ran along the front of the house under the overhang, and a couple of large frame windows. The windows were open to let in the light. I went to the near window and looked in and tried to see the boy and the television, but I couldn't. The way the hall and the entry were laid out from the living room, it was a good bet that the boy and the TV were on the side of the house opposite from the garage. I went back to the edge of the porch and motioned to Thurman. He got out and went down the drive to the garage, and he didn't look happy about it. I stood by the front windows and watched. If the boy came through the house, I could always knock on the door for real and pretend like I was selling aluminum siding. If Mrs Dees drove up, I could pretend I was a real estate agent, and make a big deal out of listing her house, and maybe keep her away from the garage until Thurman made his getaway. If Eric Dees drove up, maybe I could run like hell before he shot me to death. There are always options.

It didn't take Mark Thurman long.

Less than three minutes later he came back along the driveway, and made a short quiet whistle to get my attention. When I looked, he held up an ordinary TDK half-inch VHS cassette. I walked away from the front door and got back into the Mustang maybe ten seconds after Mark Thurman.

He sat behind the wheel in the keyless Mustang with both hands on the cassette. He held it tightly. 'Now what?'

We went to the motel.

The sky had turned a deep violet by the time we got into Santa Monica, and the air was cooling nicely. The room had a VCR hooked to the TV, and that's where we'd screen the tape.

Thurman said, 'Is this where you've been holed up?'

'Yeah.' Like we were outlaws.

When we got into the room, Thurman looked around and saw the four left over Thai beers. They were warm. 'Say, could I have one of those?'

'Sure.'

'You?' He held out a bottle.

'No.'

I turned on the TV. Nightly News with Peter Jennings came on, and I loaded the cassette. Peter Jennings vanished in a flash of static, and a grainy high-angle shot of the interior of the Premier Pawn Shop filled the screen. Black and white. A muscular black guy maybe in his late twenties sat in a swivel chair behind the counter, watching a tiny TV. He wore a white Arrow shirt with the sleeves rolled up, and his hair was cut close with a couple of racing stripes carved above each ear. Charles Lewis Washington. There was no one else in the shop.

As I watched, Mark Thurman came up behind me and drank deep on the beer. He shifted his weight from foot to foot, not fast like he had to pee, but enough to show he wasn't comfortable. He said, 'There's a lot of this kind of stuff at first.'

'Okay.'

'We could maybe fast forward it.'

'Let's just watch.'

He went to the machine and turned it off. 'Look, this isn't easy.'

'I know.'

'You don't have to treat me like a piece of shit.'

I stared at him for maybe ten seconds. 'It doesn't matter if I like you or not, and it doesn't matter how I treat you or not. Whatever it is that I'm doing, I'm doing for Jennifer. Not for you.'

Mark Thurman stared at me for another couple of seconds, then he said, 'Can I have another of those beers?'

I turned on the VCR and watched the rest of the tape. Mark Thurman went into the bathroom and drank.

29

The image was sort of overexposed and blurry, and not nearly as nice as your basic home video. From the angle the camera must've been maybe nine or ten feet up, and was mounted so that it framed the length of the shop.

The tape ran without incident for another couple of minutes before Floyd Riggens and Warren Pinkworth entered from the bottom of the frame. There was no sound. Charles Lewis got out of his chair and went to the counter, and the three of them spoke for a few minutes. Then Pinkworth took two cardboard boxes out of his pocket and put them on the counter. Each box was about the size of a bar of soap, but they weren't Ivory. Washington opened the top box and shook out twenty rounds of what looked to be 5.56mm rifle cartridges. Same kind of stuff you pop in an M-16. He examined the bullets, and then he put them back into the box and pushed both boxes toward Pinkworth. The three of them talked some more, and Riggens left the frame. In a couple of minutes he came back, only now Pete Garcia was with him, carrying a pretty good-sized pasteboard box. It looked heavy. Garcia put the larger box on the counter and Charles Lewis looked inside. Whatever was there, you couldn't see it, but it was probably more of the little cardboard ammo boxes. Washington nodded as if he were agreeing to something, and when he did Riggens and Garcia and Pinkworth were all screaming and pulling out badges and guns. Charles Lewis Washington jumped back so far that he fell over the swivel chair. Riggens went over the counter after him. Riggens raised his pistol twice and brought it down twice, and then he jerked Washington to his feet and moved to hit him again. Washington covered up and pulled away. The narrow aisle behind the counter opened into the shop, and Washington, still holding his arms over his head, stumbled from behind the counter and into Pete Garcia. Maybe you could say it looked like he was attacking Garcia, but it didn't look like that to me. It looked like Washington was trying to get away from Riggens. Garcia hit Washington on the upper back and the arms four times, and then pushed him down. Pinkworth was pointing his gun in a two-handed combat stance, and shouting, and he stomped at Washington's head and back. Riggens came from behind the counter and waded in beside Pinkworth. Garcia was pointing his gun at Washington's head. Washington seemed to reach for him and Garcia kicked at his arm. At the bottom of the screen, Mark Thurman ran in wearing a tee shirt that said POLICE on the front and back. He stopped beside Garcia and aimed his gun, also in the two-handed combat stance. Charles Lewis Washington pushed up to his knees and held out his right arm like maybe he was begging Riggens and Pinkworth to stop. They didn't. Washington rolled into sort of a ball, but Riggens continued to hit him. Thurman started forward, then stopped and said something to Garcia, but Garcia made a hand move telling him to stay back. Thurman lowered his gun and stepped back. He looked confused. Eric Dees ran in then, also wearing a POLICE tee shirt, and stopped midway between Garcia and Pinkworth to assess the situation. Garcia shouted and pointed at Washington, and Dees pulled Pinkworth back. He tried to train his gun on Washington, but Riggens kept getting in the way. Washington was on his stomach now, trying to crawl under a shelf. The white Arrow shirt was streaked with blood. He was moving slowly, the way you might if you were stunned and unable to think clearly. Thurman raised his gun, then lowered it. He looked like he wanted to move forward, maybe do something, but he didn't. Washington again raised his hand as if begging Riggens to stop. Riggens hit his hand. Dees grabbed Riggens's arm and pulled him back, but Washington started crawling away again. I guess if I was hurt bad, and confused, I'd try to crawl away, too. Riggens pointed at him and shouted, and went back to hitting him, and this time he was swinging for the head. Pinkworth moved in and swung for the legs, but he needn't have bothered. Charles Lewis Washington had already stopped moving. Dees pulled Riggens off again and Garcia moved in, gun first as if he thought maybe Washington was faking it and might suddenly jump up and mow them all down. He checked Washington's neck for a pulse, then shook his head. Garcia holstered his gun and said something to Dees, and now he checked Washington's wrist, but he didn't find a pulse there, either. Eric Dees came over and checked for himself. Mark Thurman holstered his gun, leaned against the counter, and threw up. Eric Dees went to him, said something, and then went back to the body. Mark Thurman moved out of the frame.

I let the tape play for another thirty seconds or so, and then I turned it off.

Mark Thurman said, 'Let it play and it shows us figuring out what to do. You can see Floyd planting a gun so we could say he was armed.'

I looked over at him. Thurman was in the bathroom door. I said, 'I've seen enough for now.'

'Yep.' He killed the rest of the beer. 'When I came into it everybody was screaming. I thought maybe the guy had a gun or something. It wasn't like I was scared, I just didn't know what to do.' He went to the little round motel table and took another beer. Twenty-five years old, looking for a friend, and there were no friends around. 'What could I have done?'

'You could have stopped them.'

He pulled at the warm beer and nodded. 'Yes. I'd say that's pretty clear. But I didn't, did I?'

'No. That's something you'll have to live with. You had an opportunity to behave well, but you behaved poorly. Had you behaved well, Charles Lewis Washington might still be alive.'

He sucked down the rest of the beer and you could tell that he was living with that, too.

I said, 'You're going to have to give up Dees and the other guys.'

'I can't do that.' There was one beer left. He went for it.

'You don't have a choice, Mark.'

'The hell I don't.' Angry now. Walled in by circumstances and goddamned tired of it. 'Jesus Christ, I feel bad enough. Now you want me to be a traitor? You want me to sell out my friends?'

'I want you to do what you should've done when it began. I want you to do the right thing.'

He raised his hands like he didn't want to hear it and he turned away.

I took two fast steps toward him, grabbed the back of his shirt, and shoved him across the little table. He said, 'Hey,' and dropped the beer.

I said, 'Charles Lewis Washington was living with a woman named Shalene. They had a baby named Marcus. Now that baby is going to grow up without a father. Do you understand that?'

'Let me up.' He grabbed my wrists, trying to pry my hands off and push up off the table, but I wouldn't let him.

'He had a brother named James Edward and a mother and a grandfather.' The muscles across my back and the tops of my shoulders felt tight and knotted. I dug my fingers into his face and neck and pressed. 'You have been part of something bad. It's unfair, and it's ugly, and you didn't know what you were supposed to do, but now you do, and you have to be man enough to stand up. If you don't, Ida Leigh Washington will have lost two sons for nothing and I will not allow that.'

He wasn't trying to pry me off anymore. He still gripped my wrists, but it was more as if he were holding on than pushing away.

I let go of him and stepped back, but he stayed on the table. He covered his face with his hands and then he sobbed. The sobs grew louder, and his body jerked, and he said things that I could not understand. I think he said that he was sorry.

I went into the bathroom, wet a towel, and brought it out to him. I helped him to sit up and gave him the towel, but it didn't do much good.

He sat in one of the cheap motel chairs, bent over with his face in his hands, crying.

Finally, I held him close.

He would hurt for a long time, though not as long as Ida Leigh Washington. Still, he would hurt, and maybe this was his way of getting used to it.

30

At twelve minutes after seven the next morning, I phoned Lou Poitras at home. Thurman didn't want to listen, so he went outside and stood in the parking lot. Crime is certainly glamorous, isn't it?

Poitras's middle daughter, Lauren, answered and asked who I was. I told her Maxwell Smart. She said, 'Nyuh-uh. You're Elvis Cole.' She's nine, and we'd known each other maybe seven years.

'If you knew who I was, why'd you ask?'

'Mommy told me always ask.' These kids.

'Lemme speak to your daddy.'

'Daddy was talking about you last night. He said you were an asshole.' She giggled when she said it. These kids are something, aren't they?

'Let me speak to him.'

The phone got put down and you could hear her running away, yelling for Lou and yelling that it was me. Lou Poitras came on maybe twenty seconds later, and said, 'Where you calling from?' His voice was tight in a way I hadn't heard it before.

'Why, Lou? You going to have me arrested?'

'Maybe I should. You screwed up bad, Hound Dog.'

'If not me, who? If not now, when?'

'Stop with the goddamn jokes. This isn't funny.' There was a kind of fabric sound that made me think he was moving with the phone, maybe getting away from his family.

I said, 'I need to see you, and I need to be certain that I'm not going to be taken into custody when I do.'

'You gonna turn yourself in?'

'No. I'm going to talk to you about cutting a deal that involves myself and Joe Pike and an LAPD officer, and I need someone to take it up the line to the DA.'

His voice went harder, and low, like maybe he didn't want his wife or kids to hear. 'Are you telling me that an LAPD officer is involved in this?'

'I've got visual proof that Charles Lewis Washington was unarmed when he was beaten to death five months ago. I've also got eyewitness

163

proof that since that time, Eric Dees and his REACT team have been participating with the Eight-Deuce Gangster Boys in an ongoing series of misdemeanor and felony crimes.'

Lou Poitras didn't say anything for maybe forty seconds. Behind him, I heard his wife yelling for the kids to quit dogging it and get ready for school. Lou said, 'You're sure?'

'Sure enough to call you. Sure enough to think I can get the deal.' Nobody a good cop wants to bust more than a bad cop.

Poitras said, 'What kind of visual proof?'

'Videotape from a black-and-white surveillance camera.'

'There wasn't a tape in the Washington thing.'

'It was a hidden camera.'

'And this tape shows the incident?'

'Yes.'

'In its entirety?'

'Yes.'

'Can I see it?'

'You going to come alone?'

'You know better than that.' Giving me pissed. Giving me Had Enough. 'There's a video repair place called Hal's on Riverside just east of Laurel in Studio City. The guy owns it knows me. It's early, but he'll open up to let us use a unit. Can you meet me there in forty minutes?'

'Sure.' Most of the traffic would be coming this way.

Lou Poitras hung up without saying good-bye.

I put the cassette into a plastic Hughes Market bag, locked the room, and went out to the parking lot. Thurman was waiting in his car.

Thirty-five minutes later we pulled off the freeway in Studio City and found Hal's Video in a shopping center on the south side of the street. Lou Poitras's car was in the parking lot, along with a couple of other cars that looked abandoned and not much else. Eight A.M. is early for a shopping center. We parked next to Poitras's car, but Thurman made no move to get out. He looked uneasy. 'You mind if I stay out here?'

'Up to you.'

He nodded to himself and seemed to relax. 'Better if I stay.' It was going to be hard, all right.

I took the plastic bag with the videocassette and went into Hal's. It was a little place, with a showroom for cheap VCRs and video cameras made by companies you'd never heard of and signs that said AUTHORIZED REPAIR. Lou Poitras was standing in the showroom with a Styrofoam cup of coffee, talking to a short overweight guy with maybe four hairs on his head. Hal. Hal looked sleepy, but Lou didn't.

I said, 'Hi, Lou.'

Poitras said, 'This is the guy.' Some greeting, huh?

Hal led us into the back room where he had a VCR hooked to a little

164

Hitachi television on a workbench. The Hitachi had been turned on. Its screen was a bright, motionless blue. Waiting for the tape. 'Everything's set up. You want me to get it going?'

Poitras shook his head. 'Nah. Go have breakfast or something. I'll lock up when we leave.'

'Forget breakfast. I'm gonna go home and go back to sleep.'

Hal left, and when we heard the front door close, Lou said, 'Okay. Let's see it.'

I put the tape in the VCR and pressed PLAY and Charles Lewis Washington appeared in the swivel chair behind the counter at the Premier Pawn Shop. I fast-forwarded the tape until Riggens and Pinkworth entered, and then I let it resume normal play. I said, 'You know those guys?'

Poitras said, 'No. They the officers?'

'There were five guys in Eric Dees's REACT team. Dees, Garcia, Thurman, Riggens, and Pinkworth. That's Riggens. That's Pinkworth.'

'Is there sound?'

'Unh-unh.'

A couple of minutes later Riggens left and came back with Garcia and the case of bullets. I said, 'That's Pete Garcia.'

Poitras's face was flat and implacable as a stretch of highway. He knew where we were going, and he didn't like it.

Charles Lewis Washington nodded to conclude the deal, and the three onscreen officers produced their guns and badges. Riggens went over the counter, and the beating began. I said, 'You see Washington go for a gun, Lou?'

Poitras kept his eyes on the screen. 'They're behind the counter part of the time. You can't see behind the counter.'

Washington came from behind the counter, and Garcia whacked him into Pinkworth. Riggens and Pinkworth beat him as he held up his hand and begged them to stop. If he had a gun behind the counter, he didn't have one now. Thurman entered the picture. 'That's Mark Thurman.'

Poitras nodded.

'Here comes Dees.'

'I know Dees.'

'I don't see the gun, Lou. I don't see any aggressive or threatening behavior.'

'I can see that, Hound Dog.' His voice was soft and hoarse, and the planes of his jaw and temples flexed and jumped and he had grown pale. I quit while I was ahead.

Pete Garcia checked Charles Lewis Washington for a pulse and shook his head, no, there was none.

I pressed the fast-forward again and we watched the men moving and talking at high speed, like in a cartoon. Riggens left the shop, then came back with a paper bag. He took a gun out of the bag. He put it in Charles Lewis Washington's hand. I said, 'There's the gun, Lou.'

Lou Poitras reached out and touched the off button, and the merciful blue reappeared. 'How'd you get this?'

'Mark Thurman and I stole it from Eric Dees's garage.'

'How'd Dees get it?'

'A gangbanger in South Central named Akeem D'Muere has the original. He's using it to blackmail Dees and the REACT team into supporting his drug trade.' I told him how Akeem D'Muere owned the Premier Pawn Shop, how he had had a surveillance camera installed, and how he had forced the Washington family to drop their suit against the city to protect Dees's team.

Poitras said, 'Okay. What's all this got to do with you and the charges against you?'

I gave him the rest of it, from the time Jennifer Sheridan hired me to James Edward Washington and Ray Depente and Cool T, and being set up by Eric Dees and the Eight-Deuce Gangster Boys so it would look like I was trying to pull down a drug deal. Poitras said, 'That's shit. Why set you up? Why not just kill you?'

'Akeem's a killer, but Dees isn't. He got into this mess trying to cover up for his people because of what happened to Charles Lewis Washington, and he's been looking for a way to get out. He's trying to control Akeem. He doesn't want to make it worse. He just wants to survive it.'

Poitras's face split with a feral grimace. 'What a great guy.'

'Yep.'

'So what's the deal?'

'All charges against Joe and myself are dropped, and the city has to do right by the Washington family.'

Poitras shook his head, and the grimace came back. 'You and Pike we can handle, but when you start talking a wrongful-death suit, you're talking the mayor's office and the city council. You know what that's like. They're gonna ask how much. They're going to try to weasel.'

'Weaseling isn't in the deal. They have to negotiate in good faith. No weaseling, no disrespect.'

Lou said, 'Jesus Christ, they're lawyers. Weaseling is all they know how to do.'

'If the Washingtons sue, they'll win big. The city can fight them and drag it out, but they'll still win and the city will look bad because of the fight. So will the department. Do it my way, and no one has to know about the deal. The department can claim they uncovered the tape as a result of an internal investigation, and use going public as proof that the police can be trusted to wash their own dirty laundry. The city makes a big deal out of apologizing to the Washingtons, and everybody ends up looking like a hero. Jesus Christ, Lou, those people have lost two sons.'

Poitras gave a shrug. 'I don't think they'll go for it, but I'll try. What else?'

I said, 'Thurman skates and stays on the job.'

Poitras's face went as flat as a stone wall. 'Every one of these officers is taking the hard fall. Every one of them will do time.'

'Not Thurman. You can fine him, you can demote him, whatever you want, but he stays on the job.'

Poitras's eyes sort of flickered and his sport coat pulled across his shoulders as his muscles swelled. A fine ribbon-work of veins appeared on his forehead. I have known Lou Poitras for almost ten years, and I couldn't recall having seen him so angry. 'These guys shit on the badge, Hound Dog. I don't want guys like this in my department.'

'Thurman's young, Lou. He didn't have a hand in it. You saw.'

'He's sworn to protect. That means you protect even from other officers. He just stood there.'

'He froze. His team is like his family. Dees is like a father. He wants a second chance.'

'Fuck him.'

'You get four out of five, Lou. That's the way it works.'

Lou Poitras's jaw danced and rippled and he looked at the tape in the VCR, maybe thinking he should just take the tape, but maybe not, maybe thinking he should just arrest my ass. But maybe not. He let out a deep, hissing breath and his jacket smoothed as the heavy muscles in his shoulders and chest relaxed. Making peace with it. He said, 'Okay. Maybe we can make it fly. I'll have to run it up the line. It'd help if I had the tape.'

'Sorry, Lou. It's all I've got.'

He nodded and put his hands in his pockets. Wouldn't have to shake hands with me, his hands in his pockets. 'You going to be around?'

'No place in particular. We escaped fugitives lead nomadic lives.'

'Yeah. I guess you do.' He thought about it, then said, 'Call me at one o'clock. If I'm not in the office, Griggs will be there. I should know by then.'

'Okay, Lou. Thanks.' I took the tape from the VCR and we went out to the showroom toward the door. You could look out the glass there. You could see the cars, and who was in the cars. Poitras said, 'Is that Thurman?'

'Yeah.'

He stared at Thurman with empty eyes. He wet his lips and he stared.

I went to the door, but Lou Poitras didn't go with me. I guess there weren't many escaped felons he'd let walk away.

I stopped in the door and looked back at him. 'Tell me the truth, Lou. When you heard about the charges, did you doubt me?'

Lou Poitras shook his head. 'Nope. Neither did Griggs.'

'Thanks, Lou.'

When I turned away, he said, 'Try not to get stopped for a traffic violation. Our orders are shoot to kill.'

Ha ha. That Lou. Some kidder, huh?

31

Thurman said, 'How'd it go?' He didn't look at me when he asked.

'We'll know by one o'clock.'

'I want to call Jennifer.'

'Okay. You hungry?'

'Not especially.'

'I am. We've got to kill time and not get caught until one. We'll grab something to eat. You can call Jennifer. We'll move around.'

'Fine.'

We drove over the hill into Hollywood. I drove, and Thurman sat in the passenger seat. Neither of us said very much or looked at the other, but there wasn't any tension in the car. There was more an awkwardness.

We followed Laurel Canyon down out of the hills, then turned east on Hollywood Boulevard. As we drove, Thurman's eyes raked the sidewalks and the side streets and the alleys, just like they had done when he was riding a black-and-white here, just like they had done when he saved the nine-year-old girl from the nut on the bus. He said, 'Hollywood was my first duty assignment when I left the academy.'

'Yeah.'

'My first partner was a guy named Diaz. He had twelve years on the job and he used to laugh a lot. He used to say, Jesus Christ, why you wanna do this for a living? A good-looking white guy like you, why don't you get a real job?'

I looked over at him.

Thurman laughed at the memory. 'I said I wasn't born on Krypton like Clark Kent and I wasn't good enough to be Batman like Bruce Wayne, so this was the next best thing. You get to wear a uniform and drive around in a fast car and put the bad guys behind bars. Diaz got a kick out of that. He started calling me Clark Kent.' Thurman fell silent and crossed his arms and stared ahead into Hollywood. Maybe remembering Diaz. Maybe remembering other things. 'You think they'll let me stay on the department?'

'We'll see.'

'Yeah.' We rode like that for a while, and then he said, 'I know you're not doing it for me, but I appreciate what you're doing in this.'

'They haven't gone for it yet, Thurman. A lot could go wrong.'

We went to Musso & Frank Grill for breakfast and used the pay phone there to call Lancaster. Mark Thurman spoke to Jennifer Sheridan and I spoke to Joe Pike. I said, 'It's happening fast. We should know by one o'clock.'

'You want us to come down?'

'No. If it goes right, we'll call you, and then we'll come up. Once we turn over the tape, they'll move on Akeem and the Eight-Deuce. I don't want Jennifer down until those guys are off the street.'

'Sounds good.'

We took our time with breakfast and didn't leave Musso's until the waiters and the busboys were giving us the glare treatment. When we left, we walked down Hollywood Boulevard to Vine, and then back again, looking at the people and the second-rate shops and trying to kill time. We passed the place where Thurman had gone onto the bus to save the nine-year-old girl. He didn't bring it up.

We picked up the car and drove east to Griffith Park where you can rent horses and ride along trails or in carefully controlled riding pens. The park was crowded, and most of the trail riders were families and kids, but most of the pen riders were serious young women with tight riding pants and heavy leather riding boots and their hair up in buns. We bought diet Cokes and watched them ride.

At eleven minutes before one that afternoon, we pulled into the parking lot at Griffith Observatory at the top of the Hollywood Hills and went into the observatory's great hall to use their pay phone. I figured it was a pretty safe place from which to make the call. You don't find a lot of cops browsing through the meteorite display or admiring the Chesley Bonestell paintings.

At exactly one o'clock by the observatory's time, I called Lou Poitras at his office. Charlie Griggs answered. Mark Thurman stood next to me, watching people come in and go out of the hall. Griggs said, 'North Hollywood detectives. Griggs.'

'This is Richard Kimball. I've been falsely accused. A guy with one arm did it.'

Griggs said, 'Let's see you smart off like that when they put you in the gas chamber.' Always a riot, Griggs.

'Is Lou there, or do I have to deal with the B team?'

Griggs put me on hold and maybe six seconds later Poitras picked up. 'I brought in Baishe, and we talked to a woman named Murphy at the DA.' Baishe was Poitras's lieutenant. He didn't much like me. 'Murphy brought in someone from the chief's office and someone else from the mayor's office, and we got together on this. Everybody's pretty anxious to see the tape.'

'What about Thurman?' When I said his name, Thurman looked at me.

'They'd like to have him, but they're willing to give him up to get the other guys. They don't like it much.'

'They don't have to like it, they just have to guarantee it. Does he stay on the job?'

'Yeah.'

'Do I have their word?'

'Yes.'

When Poitras said yes, I nodded at Thurman and he closed his eyes and sighed as if the results had just come back negative. I said, 'Are they going to deal square with the Washington family?'

'Shit, this comes out, the Washingtons are going to own City Hall.'

'Are they going to deal square?'

'Yes. That came from the DA's person and the mayor's person.'

'Okay. What's the next step?'

'They want Thurman to come in with the tape. They've made a lot of promises with nothing to go on except my word, and they don't like that. It all hinges on the tape. As soon as they see the tape, they'll move on Dees and those other assholes, and they'll move on Akeem D'Muere and anyone wearing Eight-Deuce colors. Everybody comes in.'

'Okay.'

'We can do it whenever you say. Sooner is better than later.'

I looked at Thurman. We would have to call Jennifer and Pike, and then we'd have to go get them and come down. It was eight minutes after one. 'How about your office at six?'

'Make it Baishe's office. Let him feel like he's in charge.'

'Done.'

I hung up the phone and told Mark Thurman the way it was going to be. I said, 'We have to call Lancaster.'

Thurman said, 'Let's not. I want to be the one to tell Jennifer. I want to see her face when I tell her that it's over.'

'I told her we'd call.'

'I don't care. I want to get flowers. Do you think we could stop for flowers? She likes daisies.' He was like a cork that had been pulled down very far into deep water and suddenly released. He was racing higher and higher, and the higher he got the faster he moved. The sadness and the shame were momentarily forgotten and he was grinning like a kid who'd just won first prize in one of those contests they're always having in the backs of comic books.

I said, 'Sure. We can get daisies.' I guess I was grinning, too.

He said, 'Oh, boy.' Oh, boy.

We took the four-mile drive down out of Griffith Observatory and stopped at a flower shop in Hollywood for the daisies and then we hopped on the freeway and went north toward Lancaster and the house where Mark Thurman and Jennifer Sheridan had been hiding. It didn't take very long at all.

The neighborhood was alive with kids on skateboards and men and women working on their lawns and teenagers washing cars and the varied stuff of a Saturday afternoon. Joe Pike's Jeep was in front of the house where we had left it, and the drapes were still closed. We pulled into the drive and parked and Thurman got out first. He said, 'I want to go in first.' He held the flowers like a sixteen-year-old going to his first prom.

I followed him up the walk and stood beside him when he rang the bell once, then unlocked the door, and went in yelling for Jennifer Sheridan. He needn't have bothered.

Pete Garcia was sitting on the couch and Floyd Riggens was sitting in the green Ez-E-Boy. Riggens had his legs crossed and a cold Pabst in his right hand. He made a nasty grin when we walked in and said, 'Jennifer's not here, asshole. We've got her, and we want the goddamned tape.'

32

No one said anything for maybe three seconds, and in that time you could feel the silence in the house, and the emptiness. There was me and Thurman and Riggens and Garcia, but no one else. I knew without looking. No one else. Garcia seemed nervous.

Thurman squinted, like maybe he hadn't heard right. 'Jennifer?' Loud.

Riggens said, 'You think I'm kidding?'

Thurman yelled toward the back of the house, then went to the foot of the stairs. 'Jennifer?' Getting frantic.

Riggens grinned. 'He thinks I'm kidding, Pete.'

I said, 'What did you do with her, Riggens?'

'Put her someplace safe until we get this straight. There's the copy of the tape, there's the copy of Jennifer. You see where we're going with this?'

'Where's Pike?'

Garcia said, 'Fuck him.' When Garcia moved, he seemed to jerk, and when he wasn't moving he rubbed his palms on his thighs like they were wet.

'What happened to Pike?' Maybe something in my voice.

Riggens made a little shrug, but he'd heard it, too. 'Who the fuck knows. They separated in town and we got her. He's not so much. He wasn't so goddamn much.'

Thurman came back from the stairs, his eyes nervous and his face flushed. 'She's gone.'

Riggens said, 'What did I say?'

'You bastard.' Thurman threw the flowers at Riggens and started for him, but Riggens lifted his left hand and showed a 9-mil Browning. His face went cold as an ax blade. 'You wanna fuck with me? You want to see how far it'll push?'

Thurman stopped. He didn't look like a kid going to the prom anymore. He looked like an oversized street cop with a serious mad on. He looked dangerous.

I said, 'Mark.'

Riggens straight-armed the Browning and told Thurman to back up, but Mark Thurman didn't move.

I said, 'Mark.'

Garcia's eyes flicked from Thurman to me and then to Riggens. Beads of sweat had risen on Garcia's forehead and he wiped his palms again. I didn't like that.

I stepped close behind Thurman, then eased him back.

Riggens said, 'You sold us out, you fuck.'

Mark Thurman said, 'If she's hurt, I'll kill you, Floyd.' He looked at Garcia. 'I'll kill every one of you.'

Floyd nodded. 'You shoulda thought about that before you decided to sell us out, you prick.' He gestured again with the Browning. 'Where's the tape?'

I said, 'What tape?'

Pete Garcia said, 'Oh, fuck this.' He jerked up from the couch so quickly that Mark Thurman stepped back.

Garcia said, 'Just shoot the sonofabitch, Floyd. Jesus Christ.'

I said, 'Oh, that tape.'

Riggens shifted the muzzle from Thurman to me. 'Come on. You guys give us the tape, and we'll give you the girl. That's the way it's going to work.'

I shook my head. 'Too late, Riggens. We gave it to IAD.'

Garcia said, 'Then the broad's dead.' He shouted it, as if what little control he had over himself was going.

Mark Thurman said, 'That's not true. We still have it.'

I looked at him.

Thurman said, 'It's in the car. Floorboard behind the driver's side.' He looked at me. 'I'm not going to risk Jennifer.'

Riggens said, 'Go see, Pete.'

Garcia went outside and came back maybe two minutes later with the tape. 'Got it.'

Riggens cocked his head toward a large-screen Zenith in the corner. 'Check it out.'

Garcia took the tape to the VCR and fumbled with the controls. His hands were shaking so badly that it took him a couple of tries to get the cassette into the machine. I didn't like all the shaking. Garcia wasn't the nervous type, but he was nervous today. I thought about why he might be nervous, and I didn't like that, either.

When the Zenith filled with Charles Lewis Washington and the Premier Pawn Shop, Riggens said, 'Fine. Eric's waiting. We'll take your car.'

The four of us went out to Mark Thurman's Mustang. Floyd Riggens asked if Thurman knew how to get to something called the Space Age

Drive-In, and Thurman said that he did. Riggens told Thurman to drive and me to ride in the shotgun seat. Riggens and Garcia sat in back.

We worked our way out of the subdivision and onto the Sierra Highway, driving up through the center of town. It took maybe ten minutes to cross through Lancaster, and pretty soon we were away from the traffic and the traffic lights and into an area that the local cognoscenti probably called the outskirts of town. Not as many houses out here. Less irrigated lawn, more natural desert.

Maybe a quarter mile past a Tastee-Freez, Floyd Riggens said, 'There it is.'

The high sail of the Space Age Drive-In Movie Theater's screen grew up out of the desert maybe two hundred yards from the highway behind a marquee that said CL SED. It was surrounded by barren flatland and overgrown scrub brush and yucca trees. A narrow tarmac road branched off the highway and ran up past the marquee and a little outbuilding where people had once bought tickets to giant-ant movies, and disappeared along a high fence beside the movie screen that had probably been built so that people couldn't park on the side of the road and watch the movies for free.

Riggens said, 'Turn in just like you were going to the movies.'

We turned up the little road and followed it up past the marquee and the ticket booth and toward the entrance between the screen and the fences. The fences shouldered off of the movie screen and seemed to encircle the perimeter of the drive-in. A chain-link gate had been forced out of the way.

The Space Age Drive-In looked like it had been closed for maybe a dozen years. The tarmac road was potholed and buckled, and the outbuilding had been boarded over, and the fences had wilted and were missing boards. A long time ago someone had painted a cowboy in a space suit riding an X-15 on the back of the screen, tipping his Stetson toward the highway, but like the fences and the ticket booth and the marquee, he hadn't been maintained and he looked dusty and faded. Much of his face had peeled.

We went through the gate and passed into a large open field of crushed rock and gravel with a series of berms like swells on a calm sea. Metal poles set in cement sprouted maybe every thirty feet along the berms, speaker stands for the parked cars. The speakers had long since been cut away. A small cinderblock building sat in the center of the field with two cars parked in front of it. Concession stand. Eric Dees's green sedan and its blue stable mate were parked in front of the stand. The concession stand's door had been forced open.

Riggens said, 'Let's join the party.'

Pinkworth came out of the stand as we rolled up and said, 'They have it?' He was holding a shotgun.

Riggens grinned. 'Sure.'

Garcia got out with the tape and went into the concession stand without saying anything. More of the nervous, I guess.

Pinkworth and Riggens told us to get out of the car, and then the four of us went inside through an open pair of glass double doors. There were large windows on either side of the doors, but they, like the doors, were so heavy with dust that it was like looking through a glass of milk.

The concession stand was long and wide with a counter on one side and a little metal railing on the other. A sort of kitchen area was behind the counter, and a couple of single-sex bathrooms were behind the railing. I guess the railing was there to help customers line up. The kitchen equipment and metalwork had long since been stripped out, but tattered plastic signs for Pepsi and popcorn and Mars candy bars still spotted the walls. There was graffiti on some of the signs, probably from neighborhood kids breaking in and using the place as a clubhouse. Pete Garcia and Eric Dees were standing together by another pair of glass double doors at the back of the stand. Garcia looked angry and maybe even scared. Jennifer Sheridan was sitting on the floor outside the women's bathroom. When Jennifer and Mark saw each other, she stood and he ran to her, and they hugged. They stood together and held hands and she smiled. It was an uneasy smile, but even with all of this, she smiled. Love.

Eric Dees took the tape from Pete Garcia, then grinned at me. 'Sonofabitch if you didn't cause some trouble.'

I said, 'How'd you figure it, Dees?'

'You put in eighteen years on the job, you make a few friends.' As he spoke he put the tape on the floor, then stepped on it. He took a can of Ronson lighter fluid out of his pocket, squirted the fluid on the cassette, then lit it. Once it was going, he used more of the fluid. 'They heard the talk, and they let me know there's an investigation going down. They said there's something about a tape, so I check and find out the tape is gone.' The fire was going pretty good, so he put away the fluid and came over and stood close to Mark Thurman. 'You fucked up bad, Mark. You should've just let it sit.'

Mark Thurman said, 'Jesus Christ, Eric, we were wrong.' The smell of the burning plastic was strong.

Riggens said, 'Hey, we went through that. We agreed. *You* agreed. You gave your word.'

Thurman shook his head. 'It was wrong. We did the bad thing together, and then we covered it up together. We should've stood up together, Floyd. Doesn't that bother you?'

'Going to fuckin' jail bothers me more!' Riggens was yelling. 'Losing the job and the pension and getting raked through the papers bothers me a helluva lot more!'

Garcia was pacing near the doors, glancing out like he expected something.

Dees said, 'You think I like this? You think I want it?' He looked at the fire. It was already dying away. 'You should've trusted me, Mark. I was going to work it out. I'm *still* going to work it out.'

Riggens said, 'Fuckin' A.'

I said, 'How, Dees? You going to bring Charles Lewis Washington back to life?'

Riggens screamed, 'Fuck you. With no tape, no one can prove anything. So maybe you showed it. Big fuckin' deal. Without the tape it's just hearsay, and we can ride that out.'

I nodded. 'Unless there's a copy.'

Garcia stopped the pacing and looked at me. Pinkworth shifted behind Eric Dees and Riggens sort of let his mouth open. Dees said, 'I'm willing to bet that you haven't made a copy. I figure you take the tape, you're thinking about cutting a deal, why do you need a dupe? You got a dupe, why make a big deal out of holding out? You'd just say, okay, here's the tape. You see?' Garcia was looking from Dees to me, Dees to me.

I spread my hands. 'But it's still a bet. You bet, sometimes you lose.'

Dees nodded. 'Yeah, but probably not this time.'

Guess you didn't earn command of a REACT team if you weren't smart. Of course, if you were smart, you didn't get yourself into a fix like this, either.

Mark Thurman said, 'Okay, the tape is gone and you're going to work things out. Let us out of here.'

Dees shook his head. 'Not yet.'

Jennifer said, 'You said if you got the tape back, you'd let us go. You said that.'

'I know.'

The crunching sound of tires over gravel came from outside, and Akeem D'Muere's jet black Monte Carlo eased between the fences and came toward the concession stand. Garcia said, 'He's here.' Pinkworth and Riggens went to the doors.

Eric Dees took out his 9mm Beretta service gun and Mark Thurman said, 'What the hell is D'Muere doing here, Eric?'

Floyd Riggens turned back from the doors. 'Akeem's pissed off about all the trouble. He wants to make sure it don't happen again.'

Jennifer said, 'What does that mean?'

I met Eric Dees's eyes. 'It means that Akeem wants to kill us, and Eric said okay.'

33

Eric Dees said, 'Floyd. Pink. Get on them.'

Riggens drew his gun and Pinkworth worked the slide on his pump gun. Pete Garcia looked like he was about to pee in his pants. Jennifer Sheridan said, 'Oh, shit.'

Thurman shouted, 'Are you nuts? Have you lost your fuckin' mind?'

I took two steps forward, putting myself closer to Riggens and Pinkworth. 'You can't live it out, Dees. We come up dead, they're going to know. They'll backtrack the case and put it in bed with you.'

Dees nodded, but he nodded the way you nod when you're not really thinking about it. 'We'll see.'

Thurman said, '*Dees.*'

Eric Dees went outside and walked toward the Monte Carlo. The front passenger door opened and two black guys slid out with sawed-off Mossberg shotguns. They said something to Dees and the three of them came toward the concession stand.

Thurman yelled, 'Jesus Christ, Riggens. Pete.'

Pete Garcia said, 'Shut up. Just shut up.'

Pike moved across the cloudy glass at the back side of the concession stand. Everyone was looking toward the front, at Eric Dees with the hitters, so nobody saw him but me.

Eric Dees and the two Eight-Deuce hitters came in through the double doors, Dees squinting from the bright desert sun and the hitters stone-faced behind heavy-framed Wayfarer sunglasses. The hitters held their shotguns loosely, right hands on the pistol grips, left hands cradling the slides. Nothing like being comfortable with your work.

I said, 'Think it through, Dees. It's falling apart around you.'

Dees made a little gesture at Pinkworth and Riggens. 'Pink, you and Riggens take off.' He glanced at Garcia. 'Come on, Pete. We're outta here.'

Thurman shook his head, giving incredulous, still not believing that this could be happening. 'You're just giving us to these guys?'

Riggens said, 'Yeah.'

Riggens and Pinkworth holstered their guns and went to the door. Garcia wiped his hands on his thighs and hopped around some more, but he didn't move to leave. 'I can't believe we're doing this, Eric. We can't go along with this.'

Riggens stopped. Pinkworth was already outside, but he stopped, too, when he realized that Riggens wasn't with him.

Garcia looked at Dees, then Riggens. 'We can't do this. This is fuckin' nuts.'

Riggens went red in the face. 'What'd you say?'

Pinkworth came back and stood in the door.

Riggens screamed, 'You losing your fuckin' nut? We got a lot at stake here.'

Garcia screamed back at him. 'We know these people. This is fuckin' conspiracy. Fuckin' cold-blooded murder.'

The taller of the two hitters said, 'Shit.' He racked the slide on his shotgun.

Dees said, 'It's too late to back out, Pete. This is the only chance we have. You know that. Come on. All you have to do is let it happen.'

Pete Garcia said, 'No, Eric,' and reached under his shirt for his gun. When he did, the tall hitter lifted his shotgun and the shotgun went off with a sound that was as sharp and loud as a seismic shock. Pete Garcia was kicked back into the counter and then Joe Pike stepped into the glass doors at the back of the shack and fired his shotgun twice. The milky glass erupted inward and the tall hitter flipped backwards. Dees and Riggens came out with their pieces and fired at Pike, but Pike wasn't there anymore. The short hitter ran under their fire toward the broken doors, boomed his shotgun into the remaining glass, then looked out. 'Muthuhfuckuh gone.'

Something scuffed on the roof, and the short hitter let off another volley through the ceiling.

Warren Pinkworth ran for the blue sedan. Beyond him, the Monte Carlo kicked up a cloud of rocks and sand and fishtailed across the berms. Eric Dees dove out through the double doors and shot at something on the roof, but whatever he shot at he didn't hit. He said, 'Shit.'

I pushed Jennifer Sheridan down, and when I did, Mark Thurman went for Floyd Riggens. I yelled, 'No,' and Floyd Riggens shot him. Thurman spun to the left and sat down and Jennifer Sheridan screamed. She clawed past me, baring her teeth as if she'd like to tear out Riggens's throat.

I pushed her down again, then came up with the tall hitter's shotgun just as the short hitter turned and fired two times. Both of his shots went wide to the right. I shot him in the face, and then I fired out through the double doors at the Monte Carlo and hit it, but then it was behind the fence and away and Floyd Riggens was shooting at me. I dove behind the little wall that shielded the entrance to the bathrooms.

There were more gunshots outside, and then Eric Dees was in the double doors, yelling, 'Floyd, get your ass out here!' Outside, Pinkworth climbed into the blue sedan and ground it to life.

Riggens fired twice more at me, then went for the doors. Riggens's eyes were wide and red and he looked like he was crying, but I wasn't sure why. He stopped over Mark Thurman. Mark Thurman looked up at him, and Riggens said, 'This is all your fault.' Then he raised his gun to fire. Jennifer Sheridan picked up Pete Garcia's pistol and shot Floyd Riggens in the chest. The bullet kicked him back, but he kept his feet. He opened his mouth and looked down at himself and then he looked at Jennifer Sheridan and fell.

Outside, Warren Pinkworth put the blue sedan in gear and sped away. Eric Dees shouted, 'You fuck,' fired two times at me, then dove behind the counter. Everything went still and quiet and stayed that way.

Pete Garcia rolled onto his side and moaned.

Jennifer Sheridan dropped Garcia's gun, then grabbed Mark Thurman by the shirt and dragged him toward the rest rooms. He had to outweigh her by a hundred pounds, but she kicked off her shoes for better traction and made a sort of groaning sound and did what she had to do. The floor was gritty with shattered glass, but she seemed not to notice.

Gravel crunched outside the concession stand, and Joe Pike took a position behind the broken double doors.

I said, 'That's it, Dees. It fell apart. It's over.'

Eric Dees moved behind the counter.

Pike looked in through the broken doors and I pointed at the counter. 'Dees.'

Eric Dees moved behind the counter again.

Pike said, 'Don't be stupid, Eric. Let's go home standing up.'

Dees said, 'What else have I got, Joe?'

Eric Dees charged around the near end of the counter, firing as he came, and when he did, Joe Pike and I fired back.

Dees went down hard, and I ran forward and kicked his pistol away, and then it was over. Dees was on his back, blinking at the ceiling and clutching at his chest. Most of the pellets had taken him there. A dozen feet away, Pete Garcia said, 'Oh, God,' but he didn't say it to anyone in the room.

Pike came up beside me and looked down. 'Hey, Eric.'

Eric Dees said, 'Joe.'

Pike said, 'There a radio in the unit?'

'Yeah.'

'I'll try to raise an ambulance.'

Pike went out to the green sedan.

Dees opened and closed his mouth and blinked up at the ceiling again. He said, 'How's Pete? Is Pete okay?'

I checked Pete Garcia and Floyd Riggens, and then I went to Mark Thurman. Jennifer Sheridan said, 'He's bleeding.'

The bullet had caught him low on the left side. She had ripped away part of her blouse and was using it to press on the wound. There was plenty of blood. Her hands were covered with it.

'Let me see.'

She pulled away the little compress and a steady rhythmic surge of blood pulsed from his abdomen. Artery.

He said, 'I gotta stand up.'

She said, 'You've got to stay down. You're bleeding, Mark. I think it's an artery.'

'I want to get up.' He pushed her off and flopped around and finally I helped him stand. When he was up he pushed me off and tried to walk. It was more of a sideways lurch, but he did okay.

Jennifer said, 'Damn it, Mark, *please*. We have to wait for the ambulance.'

Mark Thurman stumbled sideways. I caught him and helped him stay up. He said, 'You gotta help me.' He had lost a lot of blood.

Jennifer Sheridan said, 'Make him lie down.'

'He's okay.'

I helped Mark Thurman lurch across the concession stand to Eric Dees. Mark Thurman dug a slim billfold out of his back pocket, opened it, and held it out. It was his LAPD badge. He said, 'Do you see this?'

'What in hell are you doing?' Little bubbles of blood came out of Dees's nose when he said it and I wasn't sure if he was seeing the badge or not.

Mark Thurman breathed hard and sort of wobbled to the side but he kept his feet. His shirt and his pants were wet with his own blood. He said, 'I'm doing something that I should've done a long time ago, you sonofabitch. I am an LAPD officer, and I am placing you under arrest. You are under arrest for murder, and conspiracy to commit murder, and because you're a lousy goddamned officer.' Then Mark Thurman fainted.

Eric Dees was dead by the time the ambulance arrived.

34

Jennifer Sheridan rode in the back of the ambulance when they brought Mark Thurman and Pete Garcia to the Lancaster City Hospital. Pike and I followed behind in Mark Thurman's Mustang.

The Lancaster cops assumed that something bad had gone down between a group of gangbangers and a group of LAPD officers, and neither Joe nor I told them different. The Lancaster police, as might be expected, assumed that the police officers on the scene had been there as the representatives of Truth and Justice. We didn't tell them different about that, either. Joe Pike got one of the Lancaster cops to give him a lift back to his Jeep.

The emergency room staff tried to keep Jennifer Sheridan out of the ER, but Mark Thurman woke up enough to say that he wanted her with him, and they relented. I went with him, too. Because of the nature of the bleeding, the ER staff prepared to take Mark Thurman into the operating room. One of the doctors grumbled about having no X rays, but I guess nobody wanted to wait. Pete Garcia was already on the table, and it didn't look good for him.

Jennifer and I stood beside Mark in a green tile hallway and waited for the orderlies to wheel him into the OR. Jennifer held his hand. Mark Thurman smiled at her, then his eyes moved to me. It was a sleepy smile. They had pumped him full of Demerol. 'What do you think will happen now?'

I made a little shrug. 'It'll come out. No way to keep it in.'

Mark looked lost and maybe a little fretful. 'The tape's gone. There's no more proof of what happened that night. They catch Pinkworth, all he's going to do is deny everything. Akeem D'Muere isn't going to offer anything.'

'There's Garcia.'

Mark Thurman sighed. 'If he makes it.'

'There's me and there's Pike.'

'Yeah. But that's just words. You weren't there that night.'

'No. But we'll offer what we can. If no one believes, then there it is.'

A nurse came and told Mark that it would be just a minute more.

I said, 'What do you want to do, Mark?'

He looked at Jennifer, and she nodded, and then he looked at me. 'I don't care about the tape. I want to go forward. I want to tell them what happened to Charles Lewis Washington. Can you set that up?'

I patted his shoulder and the orderlies came and took him away.

Jennifer Sheridan and I went into the little waiting room they have there and I bought her a cup of coffee. Then I went to the pay phone and called Lou Poitras. It was eighteen minutes after six, and he wasn't happy to hear from me. 'You're late. I got half a dozen people sitting here waiting for you and your boy Thurman. You getting cold feet?'

'The tape's gone, Lou. Dees burned it.'

Lou Poitras put me on hold. A couple of minutes later he picked up again. 'I had to change phones. I didn't want those people to see me have an aneurism.'

'Dees is dead. So is Riggens. Garcia and Thurman are under the knife now, and Pinkworth ran. I'd guess he'll go home. He'll think about it for an hour, then call in with a story.'

Lou Poitras said, 'Jesus Christ.'

'Thurman wants to come in, Lou. Tape or no tape. He wants to make a statement about what happened in the pawnshop, and what's been happening since, and he's willing to testify.'

Lou Poitras made a soft sound, but said nothing for several seconds. 'There's no deal without the tape, Hound Dog. None of these people will make a promise on verbal testimony. If he comes forward, he takes his chances.'

'He knows that. He wants to step forward anyway. If Garcia makes it, he'll probably be willing to corroborate.'

'That would help.'

'But even if Garcia doesn't, Thurman comes forward.'

'I understand.' There was maybe just a little bit more respect in Lou Poitras's voice than there had been. 'We're going to have to bring you in. Tell me where you are.'

I told him.

When I hung up, Joe Pike was sitting beside Jennifer Sheridan. He was holding her hand. I sat on the other side of her and took her free hand. She didn't look happy. She said, 'I can't believe I killed a man. I just shot him.'

'Yes.'

'A man I've known and talked to. Before they were divorced, the four of us had dinner once. We ate at the Sizzler.' She was staring at a point in the middle space, somewhere very far from here.

I said, 'You shot a man who was going to murder Mark Thurman. If you hadn't shot him, Mark would be dead. Do you see that?'

She nodded.

'It's what you have, and you must use it. You're going to hurt. You're going to miss sleep, and you're going to feel guilty, and it's going to get worse before it gets better, but you can survive it. You helped Mark survive, and now he will help you. He is alive because of you. When you hear him breathe, when you see him smile, it is because of you. Tell yourself that and know that it's true. Tell it to yourself as often as you need. If you forget, call me and I will tell you.'

She leaned her head against my shoulder and we sat like that. A few minutes later I told them about the call to Lou Poitras and the way it was going to be.

When I finished, Jennifer Sheridan said, 'I don't want to leave Mark.'

I rubbed her hand. Joe still had the other. 'You'll be fine. They're going to want to talk to you, and to Mark, but probably not until later. Joe and I will go now.'

She looked down at our hands, then up again. 'What will I say?'

'The truth.'

'Will they put him in jail?'

'I don't know. I don't think so, but I don't know. A lot of people out there are going to want his head.'

She nodded again, and this time smiled sort of sadly. 'He just wanted to be a police officer.'

'Yes. But now he'll have to move on, and so will you.'

'It's going to be such a big change. What will he do?'

'Something.'

'Well, we still have each other. We can make it.'

'Yes,' I said. 'If you want to make it, you can.'

She smiled again, and this time the smile didn't seem so sad. 'Thanks for sticking it out with me.'

'Jennifer, you're worth it.'

Twenty-two minutes later a couple of California Highway Patrol cops in khaki uniforms came into the waiting room. The shorter of the two said, 'Who's Cole?'

'Me.' I stood, and Pike stood with me. Jennifer got up with Pike and took my hand.

The same cop said, 'We're supposed to take you down to L.A. Is this guy Pike?'

Pike said, 'Yeah.'

'Okay. The both of you.'

The taller guy began to dig out his cuffs, but the shorter guy waved them away. 'We don't need that.'

Jennifer's grip on my hand tightened. I gave her the smile and squeezed her hand back and said, 'Everything's going to be fine.' Mr Confidence.

The high desert sky was turning a nice purple when the state cops

184

loaded us into a black-and-white highway cruiser and blasted off down the Antelope Valley Freeway. Less than an hour later, the sky was dark when we pulled into the parking lot of the Seventy-seventh Division in South Central Los Angeles. I thought they'd take us to Parker Center, but there you go. Criminals always return to the scene of the crime. Even if we have to be taken.

They were expecting us. The Seventy-seventh's halls and squad rooms were jammed with cops and reporters and lawyers and handcuffed young black men who looked like they were Eight-Deuce gangbangers. A couple of them I recognized. I didn't see Akeem D'Muere, but Harold Bellis was talking to the homicide lieutenant, Stilwell. Stilwell looked bored, but Bellis looked confident. He also looked like he had just been called away from dinner. L'Orangerie, no doubt. *Des Oeufs de Poule au Beluga*, no doubt. The appetizer alone would've cost more than Stilwell's take-home for the day.

Stilwell saw me, went to a closed door that said WATCH COMMANDER, then opened the door and stuck in his head. Lou Poitras came out with two women and four men. The squad room was so crowded that if any more people came out of the office, they'd have to kick out the bad guys to make room for the good guys. One of the women was a prosecutor in the DA's office named Murphy, and one of the men was a uniformed captain who was probably the watch commander. I didn't recognize the others.

A guy in a wrinkled pinstripe with no tie said, 'Is this Cole?' He said it like he was in charge.

Lou Poitras pointed at me, then Pike. 'Cole. Pike.'

The pinstripe said, 'Let's go through it. I want to wrap this up.'

The pinstripe was a guy named Garvey from the chief's office and the other woman was a muck-a-muck named Greenberg from the city council. Of the two other guys, one was named Fallon, also from the DA's, and the other was from the mayor's office. The guy from the mayor was named Haywood. Fallon and Haywood took Joe Pike into an office down the hall, and Greenberg went with them. Garvey and everybody else took me into the watch commander's office. When we were settled, Murphy said, 'You're not under arrest at this time, Mr Cole, but we reserve the right to prosecute you for anything that you might admit to or say during this interview.'

Lou Poitras said, 'Jesus Christ, Murphy.'

Garvey made a take-it-easy gesture. 'At ease, Sergeant.'

Murphy said, 'Who's your attorney?'

'Charlie Bauman.'

She nodded. 'I know Charlie. I'd advise you to call him.'

I took her advice. An uncharacteristically smart move.

Everyone left for coffee while I called Charlie, told him where I was, and told him that I wouldn't say anything until he arrived. When I was done, I opened the door and saw Lou Poitras standing in the squad room with his boss from North Hollywood, a lieutenant named Baishe. Baishe has always looked shriveled and tight to me, sort of like a daddy longlegs, and he's never liked me much, but when I opened the door, he was jabbing the street cop Micelli in the chest and telling him that he'd acted like a goddamned bush-league asshole. Micelli said he didn't have to take this shit from some North Hollywood dick and jabbed back, and when he did Lou Poitras slapped his hand to the side and told him to step away. Poitras was maybe five inches taller than Micelli and eighty pounds heavier, and he looked like he was itching to use it. Micelli told Poitras to fuck himself, but he stepped away. Stilwell was over by a couple of uniforms, staying out of it. I said, 'Christ, Baishe, were you defending me?'

When Baishe saw me grinning, he scowled and said, 'Hell, no. I always knew you'd fuck up big time. I'm just surprised it took you this long.' A man with friends is the wealthiest man in the world.

Poitras told me to wait in the office, then asked if I wanted a cup of coffee. I told him that I did and waited in the open doorway for him to bring it. While I was waiting two Hispanic cops brought in Akeem D'Muere. His hands were cuffed, but he walked tall and defiantly, as if he were in some way larger than life, as if he were above all this and impervious to it and amused by it. Harold Bellis went to him, immediately complaining to the officers about the handcuffs. No one jumped to take them off. Stilwell went over to the uniforms, and they led D'Muere and Bellis toward the interrogation rooms. When they led D'Muere past, he saw me. I made my hand into a gun, pointed it at him, and dropped the hammer. He smiled. Amused.

Charlie Bauman came in maybe ten minutes later.

Murphy from the DA and Garvey from the chief saw him before I did, and then Charlie came to me. 'You say anything yet?'

'I learned my lesson last time.'

'Okay. These guys wanna have a powwow, so lemme see what I can work out.'

He went back to them, and pretty soon they were joined by Greenberg and Haywood. When Charlie came back, he said, 'They want a freebie, and I'm willing to give it to them, but it's up to you. You run through what you know and answer their questions, but it'll be off the record. If they decide to prosecute, they can't use your statements against you. Do you agree?'

'Yes.'

We went back into the watch commander's office, and I went through everything from the beginning, just as I had when I'd gone through it with Stilwell and Micelli, only this time there was more of it to tell.

Everyone looked interested except the watch commander, who spent a lot of time saying things like, 'I've known Eric Dees for ten goddamned years. He's a fine officer,' or, 'Talk is cheap, but where's the goddamned evidence?' He said stuff like that until Murphy told him to shut up or leave the room.

I told them how Mark Thurman and I had stolen the tape from Eric Dees's garage, and described what I had seen on the tape and how I had tried to make the deal through Poitras. Poitras confirmed it. Then I told them what had happened at the Space Age Drive-In and what had happened to the tape. Murphy said, 'And the tape is destroyed?'

'Yeah. Dees burned it.'

The watch commander said, 'Ha.' As if that proved something.

Murphy ignored him and looked at Garvey. He shrugged. 'Might be possible to recover some of it. Won't know until we look.' Garvey picked up the phone and punched numbers. 'Where is it?'

I told him.

He repeated it into the phone.

We spent a total of three hours and fourteen minutes on it, and then Murphy said, 'Why don't you kick back for a while. We've got to talk with Pike, and then we've got to see where we stand.'

'Sure.' Mr Kick Back. That's me.

They let me stay in the commander's office. They left the door open and told me to help myself to coffee or the bathroom, but not to leave the building. Charlie Bauman went with them. The squad room had sort of settled down, with most of the reporters and lawyers gone, and most of the Gangster Boys in holding cells or interrogation rooms. It was closing on midnight, and from somewhere along one of the halls I could hear Jay Leno.

Maybe forty minutes later Charlie Bauman and the others came back. The people from the DA and the mayor and the city council stopped in the hall to talk, and Charlie and Pike came over to me. Charlie looked tired. 'There's a lot of little stuff, but they're not going to press on the Washington thing. They believe you didn't do it.'

'What about Lancaster?'

Charlie said, 'Man, Lancaster is nothing compared to this other stuff. They need to talk to Thurman, and they need him to testify, but as long as he backs up what you said, you guys can walk.'

'He will.'

'Then you're done. Go home and get some sleep.'

Lou Poitras broke away from the group and came over and offered his hand. 'Well, you've squeaked through another one, Hound Dog.'

I nodded. ''Tis better to be lucky than good.'

He looked at Joe Pike, and Pike looked back, but neither man offered a hand. 'How're you doing, Joe?'

Pike said, 'Fine. Thank you. And you?'

'Good.'

They stared at each other some more, and then Lou cleared his throat and turned away. Awkward.

Joe Pike and Lou Poitras have hated each other for almost twelve years, and in all of that time, this was the first that they had spoken civilly to each other. Crime makes for strange bedfellows.

Joe and I were walking out with Charlie Bauman when Harold Bellis and Akeem D'Muere came out of the interrogation hall. I thought maybe they were leading D'Muere to booking, but then I realized that no one was leading him and that they were heading for the exit. D'Muere saw me looking at him and made his hand into a pistol and dropped the hammer. He didn't smile. Then he and Bellis were gone. I looked at Murphy and Fallon and the big shots from the city. 'How come that sonofabitch is walking out?'

Murphy said, 'We can't file.' Her jaw was knotted and her mouth was a razor's slash.

Maybe I hadn't heard them right. 'He murdered James Edward Washington. You've got my statement.'

Fallon said, 'We can't use it.' He didn't seem any happier than Murphy.

I looked at Pike. 'Did I suddenly lose my grip on reality?'

Two uniforms came through with a young black kid in cuffs. The kid was smiling. Murphy watched him pass, her face set, and then she said, 'That young man says that he did it.' The kid was maybe fourteen.

'He didn't do it. I was there. I saw it. D'Muere pulled the trigger.'

'Three other young men admitted to being present and also said the kid did it. They pulled him out of a lineup.'

Pike said, 'Come on, Murphy. D'Muere found a kid to play chump. The boy does juvie time and comes home a hero.'

Murphy's hard jaw softened and she suddenly looked like a woman who wanted to go home, take off her shoes, and drink three or four glasses of some nice chardonnay. 'You know it and I know it, but that young man still says he did it and three eyewitnesses say he did it, too. We can't file against D'Muere, Elvis. That's just the way this one's going to work out.' She didn't wait for me or Pike or anyone else to speak. She and Fallon left, walking heavily as if the weight of the city were on them. Greenberg followed after them.

'But he murdered James Edward Washington.' I didn't know what else to say.

Garvey said, 'Go home, Cole. You've done a lot, and you've done it well, but there's nothing more to be done.'

35

The watch commander authorized the release of my car and the personal possessions that had been taken from us at the time of our original arrests. He could have ordered a staff uniform to do it, but he did it himself, and we were out of there faster because of it. I guess that was his way of showing respect.

It was seventeen minutes before two that morning when we walked out of the Seventy-seventh, got into my car, and legally drove off the police grounds and onto the city's streets. We climbed onto the freeway, then worked our way north through the system toward Lancaster. There weren't many cars out, and the driving was easy.

Pike's Jeep was where he had left it, on a little circular drive outside the hospital. I parked behind it, and then we went inside to the waiting room and asked the nurses about Mark Thurman.

A nurse maybe in her early forties with a deep tan and a light network of sun lines checked his chart. 'Mr Thurman came through the surgery well.' She looked up at us, first Pike, then me. 'Are you the gentlemen who brought him in?'

'Yes.'

She nodded and went back to the chart. 'It looks like a bullet nicked a branch of the external iliac artery in his left side. No damage to any of the organs, though, so he's going to be fine.' She closed the chart as she said it.

Pike said, 'Is Jennifer Sheridan still here?'

A black nurse who'd been sitting with a young Chinese orderly said, 'A couple Lancaster police officers came for her. That was at about eleven-thirty. She said to tell you that she would be fine. Mr Thurman was out of surgery by then, and she knew he was okay.'

Pike said, 'What about the other officer? Garcia?'

The two nurses stopped smiling, and the black nurse said, 'Were you close to Mr Garcia?'

'No.'

'He did not survive the surgery.'

We went out, Pike to his Jeep and me to my car, and we headed back through the rough barren mountains toward Los Angeles. The high desert air was cold and the surrounding mountains were black walls against the sky and the desert. At first we drove along together, but as the miles unwound we slowly grew apart, Pike with his drive and me with mine. Alone in my car, I felt somehow unfinished and at loose ends, as if there was still much unsaid, and even more unrealized. I wondered if Pike also felt that way.

I pulled into my carport just after four that morning and found a message on my machine from Ray Depente. He said that James Edward Washington was going to be buried at Inglewood Park Cemetery at eleven A.M. tomorrow, which made it today. He said that he thought I'd want to know.

I stripped off my clothes, showered, and climbed into bed, but the sleeping was light and unsatisfactory and I was up again before seven. I went out onto my deck and breathed deeply of the air and thought how sweet it smelled with a hint of wild sage and eucalyptus. I did twelve sun salutes from the hatha-yoga, then worked through a progression of *asanas* that left me sweating. At five minutes after nine I called Joe Pike and told him of James Edward Washington's funeral. He said that he would come. I called a florist I know in Hollywood and ordered flowers. I thought roses would be nice. It was late to order flowers, but the florist knows me, and promised to deliver the flowers to the church in time for the service.

I ate breakfast, then showered and dressed in a three-piece blue suit that I bought six years ago and have worn as many times. Once to a wedding and five times to funerals. Today would be number six.

It was a warm, hazy day, and the drive along the Harbor Freeway to South Central Los Angeles was relaxed and pleasant. I left the freeway at Florence, then went west to Inglewood, and then through the gates to the cemetery there just north of Hollywood Park. The cemetery is broad and green, with gently sloping grounds and well-kept headstones and winding gravel roads. A dark green canopy had been erected on the side of one of the slopes to protect the casket and the minister and the immediate family from the sun. A hearse and a family limo and maybe twenty cars were parked nearby. They had just arrived, and some of the older people were still being helped up the slope. I parked near Joe Pike's Jeep and moved up the slope to join the mourners. Joe was standing at the back of the crowd, and Cool T was four people away.

Twin rows of folding chairs had been placed under the canopy for the family. Ida Leigh Washington was seated in the center of the front row, with the elderly man to her right, and Shalene with the baby on her left. Ray Depente was behind Mrs Washington with a hand on her shoulder. He was wearing a dark brown herring-bone suit with a U.S.M.C. pin in his lapel. When Ray saw me, he said something into Mrs Washington's ear, then stood and waited for me. I went to Mrs Washington, offered my hand, and told her how sorry I was. She thanked me for the flowers and said, 'Someone from the police called my home this morning, as did one of those people from the city council. I understand that the truth about my boy Charles Lewis is going to come out because of you.'

I told her that I didn't know if it was because of me, but that it was going to come out, yes.

She nodded and considered me for quite a long time, and then she said, 'Thank you.'

I offered my condolences to the old man, and then to Shalene. Marcus said, 'I remember you,' loudly, and with a big smile. Shalene shushed him. She still didn't like me much.

Ray Depente led me away from the grave and Joe Pike drifted up behind us. Cool T watched from the crowd. Ray said, 'How come that bastard D'Muere is walking around free?'

I told him.

Ray listened, his face tight and contained. When I was done, he said, 'You remember what you said?'

'Yes.'

'You said we'd have justice. You said that bastard would pay for killing James Edward. Him getting a fourteen-year-old fool to take his place isn't what I call justice.'

I didn't know what to say. 'The DA's people know what's going on. They'll keep digging for a case against D'Muere, and when they find it, they'll file.'

Ray Depente said, 'Bullshit.'

'Ray.'

Ray said, 'That bastard called the Washingtons. He said that if they open their mouths about this, he'll kill that baby.' He pointed at Marcus. 'He called that poor woman on the day of her son's funeral and said that. What kind of animal does something like that?'

I didn't know what to say.

Ray Depente said, 'Fuck him and fuck the DA, too. I know what to do.' Then he walked away.

Joe said, 'I know what to do, too.'

I looked at him. 'Jesus Christ. Marines.'

Cool T came out of the crowd and met Ray Depente and they spoke for a moment, and then the minister began the service. Maybe five minutes into it, Akeem D'Muere's black Monte Carlo with the heavily smoked windows turned into the graveyard and slowly cruised past the line of parked cars, his tape player booming. The volume was cranked to distortion, and the heavy bass drowned out the minister. The minister stopped trying to speak over the noise and looked at the car, and everyone else looked at the car, too. Ray Depente stepped out from the row of chairs and walked toward the car. The Monte Carlo stopped for a moment, then slowly rolled away. When the car was on the other side of the cemetery, the minister went on with the service, but Ray Depente stayed at the edge of the dark green canopy and followed the car with his eyes until it was gone.

Guard duty. The kind of duty where your orders are to shoot to kill.

When the service was over and the people were breaking up and moving down the slope, Joe and I stood together and watched Ray Depente help Mrs Washington to the family's limo. Joe said, 'He's going to do something.'

'I know.'

'He's good, but there's only one of him.'

I nodded and took a breath and let it out. 'I know. That's why we're going to help.'

Pike's mouth twitched and we went down to our cars.

36

At two oh-five that afternoon, Joe Pike and I found Ray and Cool T together in Ray's office. Cool T looked angry and sullen, but Ray looked calm and composed, the type of calm I'd seen on good sergeants when I was in Vietnam. Ray saw us enter and followed us with his eyes until we were at his door. 'What?'

'Are you going to kill him?'

'I don't know what you're talking about.' Innocent.

'Well, there are ways to do it. Get a good scoped hunting rifle, hang back a couple of hundred yards, and drop the hammer. Another way would be to drive around for a while until you see him, then walk up close with a handgun. There are more apt to be witnesses that way, but it's a matter of personal preference, I guess.'

Cool T shifted in his chair.

Ray leaned back and laced his fingers behind his head. 'Man, do you think I just fell off the watermelon truck?'

'What I think is that you've got a pretty good life doing well by a lot of folks, and you're about to mess it up.'

Ray looked at Cool T and Cool T grinned. Ray didn't. He gave me lizard eyes. 'That's what it is to you, that it?'

I spread my hands.

'So you come down here to point that out? Maybe set me straight?'

'Nope. We came to help.'

'Well, we don't need the white man coming down here to solve the black man's problems. We can manage that just fine, thank you.'

Pike's mouth twitched for the second time that day.

Ray gave the eyes to Pike. 'What?'

Pike shook his head.

I said, 'The DA would file if they thought they could win, and maybe there's a way we can give them that. Maybe not on James Edward, but on something.'

Ray Depente waited.

'If you want Akeem, you're going to have to go to him. That means his home, and it used to be a crack house. It's fortified like a bunker. But once we're in, I'm betting we can find something that the DA can use to put D'Muere away.'

Cool T said, 'Ain't no way we can get in there. Goddamn police use a goddamn batterin' ram to get in a crack house. Where we gonna get that?'

Ray glanced at Cool T. 'There are other ways.' He looked back at me. 'If it was worth it. If it would lead to that sonofabitch getting what he deserves.'

'We won't know until we get there, will we?'

Ray nodded. 'Why are you doing this, Cole?'

'Because I liked James Edward, Ray. Hell, I even like you.'

Ray Depente laughed and then he stood up and put out his hand. 'Okay. You want to help out on this, we'll let you help.'

Forty-two minutes later Joe Pike and I cruised past Akeem D'Muere's fortified home in Joe's Jeep. We parked six houses down on the same side of the street in an alley between a row of flowering azalea bushes and a well-kept frame house with an ornate birdbath in the front yard. Ray Depente and Cool T were one block behind us, sitting in Ray's LeBaron. Akeem D'Muere's black Monte Carlo and the maroon Volkswagen Beetle were parked at the front of his house, and a half-dozen Gangster Boys were hanging around on the Beetle. A couple of young women were with them. I wondered if they called themselves Gangster Girls.

Pike said, 'Brick house across the street. Clapboard two doors down, this side. Check it out.'

I looked at the brick house across the street and then at the clapboard house. A heavy woman with her hair in a tight gray bun was peeking from behind a curtain in the brick house and a younger woman, maybe in her early thirties, was peeking at us from the clapboard. The younger woman was holding a baby. 'They're scared. You live on a street with a gang for your neighbors and I guess peeking out of windows becomes a way of life. Never know when it's safe to venture out.'

Joe shifted in his seat. 'Helluva way to live.'

'Yes,' I said. 'It is.'

A tall kid leaning against the Bug's left front fender looked our way, but then went back to jiving with his buddies. All attitude, no brains.

Pike pulled a pair of Zeiss binoculars from the backseat and examined the front of D'Muere's house. 'Windows set close on both sides of the door. Bars on the windows.'

'What about the door?'

'Solid core with a couple of peepholes. No glass.'

'Does it open outward?'

'Yep.' Pike put down the glasses and looked pleased. Dope dealers often rebuild their doors to open outward instead of inward. Harder for the cops to bust in that way. It was something that we'd been counting on.

Fourteen minutes after we parked in the alley, Cool T turned onto the far end of the street in Ray Depente's LeBaron and drove slowly toward D'Muere's as if he were looking at addresses. He stopped in the middle of the street, and said something to the kids on the Volkswagen.

I said, 'Now.'

Joe and I rolled out of the Jeep and moved through the backyard of the near house and into the next yard toward D'Muere's. We moved quickly and quietly, slipping past bushes and over fences and closing on D'Muere's while Cool T kept the gangbangers' attention. Akeem D'Muere's backyard was overgrown by grass and weeds and thick high hedges that had been allowed to run without care or trimming. A creaky porch jutted off the back of the house, and a narrow cement drive ran back past the house to a clapboard garage. The garage was weathered and crummy and hadn't been used in years. Why use a garage when you can park on the front lawn? Ray Depente appeared from the hedges on the far side of the yard and held up a finger to his mouth. He was wearing a black Marine Corps-issue shoulder sling with a Colt Mark IV .45-caliber service automatic. He pointed to himself, then gestured to the east side of the house, then pointed at us and then at our side of the house, and then he was gone.

Pike took the back of the house and I moved up the drive along the side. The windows along the back and sides of the house were barred, and many had been covered on the inside with tar paper, but there were gaps and tears in the paper and I moved from window to window, trying to see inside. Cool T drove away as I made the front corner of the house, and then I faded back to the rear. The rear was so crummy we could probably pitch a tent back there and no one would notice. Pike and Ray and I crouched in the bushes beside the porch.

Ray said, 'Two rooms and a bath on my side. Three full-sized windows, all barred, and a half-sizer on the bathroom. Someone was in the bathroom but the other two rooms were clear.' He looked at Pike. 'Will the door work?'

Pike nodded. 'No problemo.'

'How about the front?'

'No problemo.'

I said, 'Kitchen and two rooms on my side. I made six people, four male, two female. No children.'

Ray nodded. 'Any way out the windows?'

'Not unless they can squeeze through the bars.'

Ray smiled. 'This is going to work.'

Twelve minutes later Cool T once more turned onto the street and again stopped in front of the house. This time a couple of bangers slid off the Beetle and went toward him. When they did, Joe and I moved up the drive and across the front yard and Ray Depente trotted toward them from the opposite side of the house. One of the girls saw Ray Depente and said, 'What the hell?' and then the others saw me and Joe. The second girl ran and a short guy with too many muscles clawed at his pants for a piece. Joe Pike kicked him in the head with an outside spin kick, and then Ray Depente and I were at the Beetle with our guns out. The two guys out in the street started pulling for hardware, too, but Cool T came out with an Ithaca 12-gauge and they put up their hands. Ray said, 'Down.'

The Eight-Deuce Gangster Boys went down onto their stomachs.

Ray said, 'Make noise, and I'll bleed you.'

A tall skinny kid with a Raiders cap wiggled around and said, 'Why don't you kiss my goddamn ass?'

Ray punched him one time hard in the side of the head and he shut up.

Cool T opened the LeBaron's trunk and tossed me a bag filled with plastic wrist restraints. I passed a couple to Pike, and we tied them off. We worked quickly, and as we tied I glanced at the surrounding houses. You could see faces in the windows and behind doors. Watching. Wondering what in hell these fools were doing.

Ray gave two smoke grenades to Pike, kept two for himself, then pulled three ten-gallon metal gas cans from the trunk and four six-foot lengths of galvanized pipe from the backseat. When we finished with the tying, Pike took two lengths of the pipe and trotted to the back of the house. Cool T hefted the other two and started toward the front. When he was halfway there, the front door opened and a chunky guy with a thick neck and a thick belly stepped out and fired a Beretta 9 millimeter, *bapbapbapbap*. One of the rounds caught Cool T on the outside of his right arm. He screamed and went down, and then I had the Dan Wesson out and I was firing, and the heavy guy fell back. I said, 'Guess they know we're here.'

Ray grunted. 'Mm-hmm. Imagine that.'

Cool T scrambled behind the Monte Carlo and we went to him. Ray said, 'How you doing, Cool?'

'It burns like a sonofabitch.'

Pike examined the wound, then used part of Cool T's shirt to bind it. 'You'll be fine.'

A couple of faces peeked around the jamb, and someone in the house yelled, 'The fuck you doin'? Whatchu want?'

Ray yelled back. 'My name is Ray Depente. We came for Akeem D'Muere and we want to see his chickenshit ass out here.'

A second voice in the house yelled, 'Fuck you.' It was going to be one of those conversations.

Someone pulled the heavy guy out of the door, then a guy in a duster jumped forward, fired two pistol shots, then pulled the door closed.

Ray said, 'You think they'll call the police?'

We left Cool T sitting against the Monte Carlo's wheel and gathered up the pipe and the gas cans and went to the house. We put the pipes across the door and wedged them behind the window bars on either side. As we did it we could hear voices inside. They were trying to figure out what we were up to. Joe Pike came back around the house. 'Back door is sealed.'

'How about the windows?'

'No one's getting out.'

Someone inside yelled, 'The fuck you assholes want? Get away from here.' The closed door muffled the voice.

I stood to the right of the door, reached around, and pounded on it. A shotgun blast ripped through the door about where I should've been standing. I said, 'Hey, Akeem. It's time to pay up for James Edward Washington.'

Another blast came through the door.

'Gunfire is not meaningful discourse, Akeem.'

Another blast came through, this one very low.

I said, 'Here's the way it's going to happen. Everybody's going to put down their guns, and everybody's going to come out one at a time, and then we're going to tell the police what really happened to James Edward Washington. How does that sound?'

Akeem D'Muere shouted, 'Are you on dope? Get the fuck out of my face.'

I said, 'Akeem, I'm going to move in and set up house on your face.'

'You can't get in here. Get the fuck away.'

'It's not a question of us getting in, Akeem. The question is, can you get out?'

Ray Depente popped the top off of one of the gas cans and began splashing gas on the door and the windows and the sides of the house. The smell of it was strong and sharp in the still air.

Akeem said, 'What the fuck you doin' out there? What's that smell?'

'We're pouring gasoline on your house. You told the Washingtons that you were going to burn them out, didn't you? We thought you'd appreciate the poetic justice of the moment.'

A different voice yelled, 'Bullshit. You wouldn't do that.'

Ray Depente said, 'Watch.'

Ray finished with one can and started with another. Pike took the third can around to the rear. We could hear banging at the back of the house, but the pipes would hold. Across the street, a door opened and a man in his early seventies came out onto his porch and watched with his hands on his hips. He was smiling.

Inside, you could hear men moving through the house, and voices, and then the tar paper was abruptly torn off the front window and someone fired most of an AK-47's magazine out into the ground at full auto. Ray Depente looked at me and grinned. 'You think they gettin' scared?'

'Uh-hunh.'

He grinned wider. 'These pukes ain't met scared.'

Joe Pike came back. 'Ready.'

Ray Depente took a big steel Zippo lighter from his pocket, flipped open the top, and spun the wheel. He said, 'Welcome to hell, assholes.' Then he touched the flame to the gasoline.

The eastern front corner of Akeem D'Muere's fortified crack house went up with a *whoosh*. Ray and Pike moved around the house, tossing the smoke grenades in through the windows. The grenades had instant fuses, and in two seconds there would be so much smoke that you'd think you were in an inferno. The fire stayed at just one corner of the house, though, and didn't spread. We'd placed the gasoline so that it would smell, but we'd also placed it so that the fire would be small and controlled. The people inside didn't know that, though. There were shouts, and more shots, and someone banged on the front door, trying to get it open. Someone else started screaming for us to let him out, and smoke began to leak from windows and from around the front door. Across the street, more people came out of their houses to watch.

I shouted over the noise. 'The guns come out first.'

'We can't get the goddamn door open.'

'The window.' The smoke was making them choke.

More tar paper was pulled off the windows, and handguns and shotguns and AK-47s were shoved through the glass. Clouds of thick gray smoke billowed out with the guns.

Ray Depente found a garden hose, turned it on, and sprayed it on the fire. It didn't put out the fire, but it cooled it some.

Someone inside said, 'Let us out. Please.'

I looked at Ray. He nodded. He and Joe took up positions at the corners of the house.

'One at a time. Hands on your heads.'

'Man, I'll put my hands up my ass you let me out of here.'

I unshipped the pipes, pulled open the door, and two men and two women stumbled out, jostling each other to get away from the smoke and the fire. Pike pushed them down and used the plastic restraints. Neither of the two guys was Akeem D'Muere.

Ray Depente yelled, 'You wanna cook, that's up to you.'

No one answered.

Ray looked at me and I held up three fingers and he nodded. Akeem, plus two others. They'd be hard cases, and they would've kept their guns. We could hear coughing.

Pike said, 'Maybe they doubt our sincerity.'

Pike stayed with Cool T to watch the others, and Ray Depente and I went in after Akeem. We went in low and fast, pushing through the oily smoke, and found them in a short hall between the kitchen and a back bedroom. Akeem D'Muere was with a dopey-looking guy with sleepy eyes and another guy who looked like he could have played defensive line for the Raiders. They were coughing and rubbing at their eyes. They heard us, but the smoke was too thick for them to see us. The big guy shouted, 'They're inside,' and started swinging wild. He didn't see anything, he was just swinging, and his first two punches hit the wall. I stepped outside and caught the joint of his left knee with a hard snap kick. The knee went and the big man made a gasping sound and fell. I followed him down and took his gun.

The dopey guy yelled, 'I see the muthuhfuckuhs,' and started firing a Smith .40 somewhere up toward geosynchronous orbit. Akeem D'Muere pushed the dopey guy at us and ran toward the front of the house. Ray Depente slapped the dopey guy's .40 to the outside, then hit him three fast times, twice in the chest and once in the neck, and the dopey guy fell.

Ray said, 'Take his gun.' Ray was already after Akeem.

I grabbed the dopey guy's gun, then used the plastic restraints as quickly as I could. I wanted to get to Akeem D'Muere before Ray got to him, but I didn't make it. Two shots came from the living room, then a third, and I got there just as Ray Depente came up under D'Muere's gun, twisted it free just as he had taught a thousand guys down at Camp Pendleton, then threw Akeem D'Muere through the open front door out into the yard. I went after them.

Akeem D'Muere was standing sort of bent to the side in the front yard, rubbing at his eyes and spitting to try to clear the smoke from his lungs. Ray Depente went down off the little porch, peeled away his shoulder sling, and said, 'Look at me, boy.' Ray didn't wait for him to look. Ray spun once and kicked Akeem D'Muere on the side of the head, knocking him to the ground.

I said, 'Ray.'

Up and down the block, doors opened and people came out onto porches and into yards. Pike and Cool T had the Eight-Deuce Gangster Boys on the ground and out of the play.

Ray Depente went to Akeem and dragged him to his feet. Ray was a couple of inches taller, but thinner, so they probably weighed close to the same. When Ray was lifting him, Akeem tried to grab and bite, but Ray dug his thumbs into Akeem D'Muere's eyes. D'Muere screamed and stumbled back. Ray stood and looked at him and there was something hard and remote in his eyes. Ray opened his hands. 'Hit me. Let's see what you got.'

Akeem D'Muere launched a long right hand that caught Ray high on the cheek and made him step back, but when he tried to follow with a left, Ray blocked it to the inside and drove a round kick into the side of

D'Muere's head. D'Muere stumbled sideways, and Ray reversed and kicked him from the opposite side, and this time D'Muere fell. I put a hand on Ray's shoulder. 'That's enough, Ray.'

Ray slapped away my hand. 'Stand away from me now.'

'Ray, you're going to kill him.' Akeem D'Muere struggled up to his knees.

Ray said, 'And wouldn't that be a shame.' He kicked Akeem D'Muere in the chest and knocked him backwards.

I looked at Pike, but Pike was impassive behind the dark glasses.

Ray walked around behind D'Muere, lifted him by the hair, and said, 'You meet James Edward, you tell'm I said hi.' He spun again, and kicked, and Akeem D'Muere snapped over into the ground.

I took out the Dan Wesson. 'Ray.'

'You wanna shoot me for a piece of garbage like this, go ahead.'

He picked D'Muere up again. D'Muere's mouth and nose and ears were bleeding, and most of his teeth were gone. Ray held him up until D'Muere could stand on his own, then Ray punched him four fast times, twice in the solar plexus and twice in the face. Akeem D'Muere fell like a bag of wet laundry. One of the Gangster Girls screamed, 'You're gonna kill'm.'

Ray said, 'You think?'

I aimed the Dan Wesson. 'I don't have to kill you, Ray. I can do your knee. Be hard to teach after that.'

Ray nodded. 'You're right. But think of my memories.' He lifted D'Muere's head by the hair, aimed, and punched him two hard times behind the ear. Then he let the head drop.

'Damn it, Ray.' I cocked the Dan Wesson.

Pike said, 'He means it, Ray.'

'I know. So do I.'

He reached down and lifted Akeem D'Muere once more.

As he brought D'Muere up, a dark blue Buick stopped in the street by the LeBaron and Ida Leigh Washington got out. She stood in the street, motionless for a time, and then she moved toward us. She was still wearing the clothes that she had worn to her son's funeral. Black.

Ray Depente saw her and let Akeem D'Muere fall to the ground. He said, 'You shouldn't be here, Ida Leigh.'

She stopped about ten feet from him and looked at the smoldering house, and then at the thugs on the ground with their hands bound, and then at me and Joe. She said, 'I wanted to see where he lived. Is that the one killed my son?'

'Yes, ma'am.'

Somewhere far off, a siren sounded. On the way here, no doubt.

Ida Leigh Washington stepped closer and looked down at D'Muere. His face was a mask of blood, but she did not flinch when she saw it. She put a hand on Ray's forearm and said, 'What could turn a boy into an animal like this?'

Ray said, 'I don't know, Ida Leigh.'

She raised her eyes from D'Muere up to Ray. 'This man took my last son. No one could claim my hurt, or my anger. No one could have a greater claim on this one's life.' Her voice was tight and fierce. She patted Ray's arm. 'There's been enough killing down here. We have to find a way to live without the killing.'

Ray Depente didn't move for a minute. Ida Leigh Washington kept her eyes on him. Ray stepped back. He turned away from Akeem D'Muere, and as the police cars began to arrive he helped Mrs Ida Leigh Washington back to her car.

Up and down the street, the people on the porches and in the windows and in the yards began to applaud. It would've been nice to think that they were applauding Ida Leigh Washington, but they weren't. At least I don't think they were. That far away, those people couldn't have heard one woman's softly spoken words, could they?

The cops got out of their cars and looked around and didn't know what to make of it. A Hispanic cop with a butch cut looked at Pike and me and said, 'Weren't you guys at the Seventy-seventh last night?'

'Yeah. We'll probably be there again tonight, too.'

He didn't know what to make of that, either.

37

When the police went into Akeem D'Muere's house, they found $82,000 in crack cocaine in the attic, along with six cases of stolen rifles. Because the police legally entered the house investigating a crime in progress, the evidence found was admissible and resulted in charges brought against D'Muere. The investigators found no copies of the videotape that Eric Dees destroyed, and Akeem D'Muere, for some reason known only to him, denied all knowledge of such a tape.

The DA went easy on Pike and me. They agreed to trade on all charges except the assault on the police guards when Pike and I escaped from the Seventy-seventh. We were allowed to plead to a misdemeanor, served three days in county jail, and then it was over.

Of the five REACT officers involved in the wrongful death of Charles Lewis Washington, only Warren Pinkworth and Mark Thurman survived. Thurman turned state's evidence and sought neither a plea nor mercy. Warren Pinkworth was indicted on five counts of murder. He attempted a plea, but none was allowed.

Sixteen weeks after the events at the Space Age Drive-In Theater in Lancaster, Mark Thurman was fired from the ranks of the LAPD, losing all benefits that had been accrued. He said he didn't mind. He said it could have been worse. He was right. Four days after that, all administrative and criminal charges were dropped against Mark Thurman due to the intercession of Mrs Ida Leigh Washington. Three members of the city council and one member of the DA's staff objected and wanted, for political reasons, to use Thurman as an example, but cooler heads were only too happy to acquiesce to Mrs Washington's wishes. Negotiations were under way in the matter of her wrongful-death suits against the city. She was suing in the names of both of her sons.

Twenty-four weeks and three days after the events in the Space Age Drive-In, after spring had moved into summer, and then into the early part of fall, I was sitting in my office reading last week's newspaper when the phone rang and I answered, 'Elvis Cole Detective Agency, we're on your case for no money down.'

Jennifer Sheridan laughed. It was a good laugh, nice and clear. She and Mark were living together in Lancaster. She had given up her job with Watkins, Okum, & Beale and had taken a new job with a law firm based in Mojave. She had taken a twenty per cent cut in salary to do it, but she said that it was what she wanted. Mark Thurman had applied for a job with both the Palmdale PD and the Lancaster PD, but had been rejected both times. He had decided to return to school and obtain a degree in physical education. He thought he might like to coach high-school football. Jennifer Sheridan was sure that he would be wonderful at it. She said, 'How do you expect prospective clients to take you seriously if you answer the phone that way?'

I gave her Groucho. 'You kiddin'? I wouldn't work for a client who'd hire me.'

She laughed again. 'You do a terrible Groucho.'

'Want to hear my Bogart? That's even worse.' You get me on a roll, I'm a riot.

She said, 'Mark and I are getting married on the third Sunday of next month. We're getting married in the little Presbyterian church in Lake Arrowhead. Do you know where that is?'

'I do.'

'We've sent you an invitation, but I wanted to call. We'd like you to come.'

'I wouldn't miss it.'

'If you give me Joe's number, I'd like to invite him, too.'

'Sure.' I gave her the number.

Jennifer Sheridan said, 'It won't be a big wedding, or particularly formal. Just a few people.'

'Great.'

'We want a church wedding. We like the tradition behind it.'

She was leading up to something. 'What is it, Jennifer?'

She said, 'I'd really like it if you gave me away.'

Something warm formed in the center of my chest, and then I felt it in my eyes. 'Sure. I'd like that, too.'

'I love him, Elvis. I love him so much.'

I smiled.

She said, 'Thank you.'

'Anytime, kid. Romance is my business.'

She said, 'Oh, you,' and then she hung up.

After a bit I put aside the paper and went out the glass doors and stood on my balcony. It was late afternoon, and the fall air was cool and nice. A beauty-supply company has the office next to mine. It is owned by a very attractive woman named Cindy. She is also very nice. Sometimes she will come out onto her balcony and lean across the little wall that separates her space from mine, and look into my office and wave to get my attention. I did that now, leaning across and looking in her office, but her office was empty. It goes like that, sometimes.

I took a deep breath and looked out over the city to the ocean and to Santa Catalina Island, far to the south, and thought about Jennifer Sheridan and her love for Mark Thurman, and I wondered if anyone would love me the way she loved him. I thought that they might, but you never know.

I stood on the balcony, and breathed the cool air, and after a while I went in and shut the door. Maybe I would come out again in a while, and maybe, this time, Cindy would be in her office.

One can always hope.

Voodoo River

AN ELVIS COLE NOVEL

For Steve Volpe,
Proprietor of The Hangar,
trusted friend,
and the best slack man in the business
Semper fidelis.

Voodoo River

1

I met Jodi Taylor and her manager for lunch on the Coast Highway in Malibu, not far from Paradise Cove and the Malibu Colony. The restaurant was perched on the rocks overlooking the ocean, and owned by a chef who had his own cooking show on public television. A *saucier*. The restaurant was bright and airy, with spectacular views of the coast to the east and the Channel Islands to the south. A grilled tuna sandwich cost eighteen dollars. A side of fries cost seven-fifty. They were called *frites*.

Jodi Taylor said, 'Mr Cole, can you keep a secret?'

'That depends, Ms Taylor. What kind of secret did you have in mind?'

Sid Markowitz leaned forward, bugging his eyes at me. 'This meeting. No one is to know that we've talked to you, or what we've discussed, whether you take the job or not. We okay on that?' Sid Markowitz was Jodi Taylor's personal manager, and he looked like a frog.

'Sure,' I said. 'Secret. I'm up to that.'

Sid Markowitz didn't seem convinced. 'You say that now, but I wanna make sure you mean it. We're talking about a celebrity here.' He made a little hand move toward Jodi Taylor. 'We fill you in, you could run to a phone, the *Enquirer* might pay you fifteen, twenty grand for this.'

I frowned. 'Is that all?'

Markowitz rolled the bug eyes. 'Don't even joke about that.'

Jodi Taylor was hiding behind oversized sunglasses, a loose-fitting man's jeans jacket, and a blue Dodgers baseball cap pulled low on her forehead. She was without makeup, and her curly, dusky-red hair had been pulled into a ponytail through the little hole in the back of the cap. With the glasses and the baggy clothes and the hiding, she didn't look like the character she played on national television every week, but people still stared. I wondered if they, too, thought she looked nervous. She touched Markowitz's arm. 'I'm sure it's fine, Sid. Peter said we could trust him. Peter said he's the best there is at this kind of thing, and that he is absolutely trustworthy.' She turned back to me and smiled, and I returned it. Trustworthy. 'Peter likes you quite a bit, you know.'

'Yes. It's mutual.' Peter Alan Nelsen was the world's third most successful director, right behind Spielberg and Lucas. Action adventure stuff. I had done some work for him once, and he valued the results.

Markowitz said, 'Hey, Peter's a pal, but he's not paid to worry about you. I wanna be sure about this guy.'

I made a zipper move across my mouth. 'I promise, Sid. I won't breathe a word.'

He looked uncertain.

'Not for less than twenty-five. For twenty-five all bets are off.'

Sid Markowitz crossed his arms and sat back, his lips a tight little pucker. 'Oh, that's just great. That's wonderful. A comedian.'

A waiter with a tan as rich as brown leather appeared, and the three of us sat without speaking as he served our food. I had ordered the mahi-mahi salad with a raspberry vinaigrette dressing. Sid was having the duck tortellini. Jodi was having water. Perhaps she had eaten here before.

I tasted the mahi-mahi. Dry.

When the waiter was gone, Jodi Taylor quietly said, 'What do you know about me?'

'Sid faxed a studio press release and a couple of articles to me when he called.'

'Did you read them?'

'Yes, ma'am.' All three articles had said pretty much the same thing, most of which I had known. Jodi Taylor was the star of the new hit television series *Songbird*, in which she played the loving wife of a small-town Nebraskan sheriff and the mother of four blond ragamuffin children, who juggled her family with her dreams of becoming a singer. Television. The PR characterized *Songbird* as a thoughtful series that stressed traditional values, and family and church groups around the nation had agreed. Their support had made *Songbird* an unexpected dramatic hit, regularly smashing its time-slot competition, and major corporate sponsors had lined up to take advantage of the show's appeal. Jodi Taylor had been given the credit, with *Variety* citing her 'warmth, humor, and sincerity as the strong and loving center of her family'. There was talk of an Emmy. *Songbird* had been on for sixteen weeks, and now, as if overnight, Jodi Taylor was a star.

She said, 'I'm an adopted child, Mr Cole.'

'Okay.' The *People* article had mentioned that.

'I'm thirty-six years old. I'm getting close to forty, and there are things that I want to know.' She said it quickly, as if she wanted to get it said so that we could move on. 'I have questions and I want answers. Am I prone to breast or ovarian cancer? Is there some kind of disease that'll show up if I have children? You can understand that, can't you?' She nodded hopefully, encouraging my understanding.

'You want your medical history.'

She looked relieved. 'That's exactly right.' It was a common request from adopted children; I had done jobs like this before.

'Okay, Ms Taylor. What do you know about your birth?'

'Nothing. I don't know anything. All I have is my birth certificate, but it doesn't tell us anything.'

Sid took a legal envelope from his jacket and removed a Louisiana birth certificate with an impressed state seal. The birth certificate said that her name was Judith Marie Taylor and that her mother was Cecilia Burke Taylor and her father was Steven Edward Taylor and that her place of birth was Ville Platte, Louisiana. The birth certificate gave her date of birth as July 9, thirty-six years ago, but it listed no time of birth, nor a weight, nor an attending physician or hospital. I was born at 5:14 on a Tuesday morning and, because of that, had always thought of myself as a morning person. I wondered how I would think of myself if I didn't know that. She said, 'Cecilia Taylor and Steven Taylor are my adoptive parents.'

'Do they have any information about your birth?'

'No. They adopted me through the state, and they weren't given any more information than what you see on the birth certificate.'

A family of five was shown to a window table behind us, and a tall woman with pale hair was staring at Jodi. She had come in with an overweight man and two children and an older woman who was probably the grandmother. The older woman looked as if she'd be more at home at a diner in Topeka. The overweight man carried a Minolta. Tourists.

'Have you tried to find out about yourself through the state?'

'Yes.' She handed a business card to me. 'I'm using an attorney in Baton Rouge, but the state records are sealed. That was Louisiana law at the time of my adoption, and remains the law today. She tells me that we've exhausted all regular channels, and recommended that I hire a private investigator. Peter recommended you. If you agree to help, you'll need to coordinate what you do through her.'

I looked at the card: Sonnier, Melancon, & Burke, Attorneys at Law. And under that: Lucille Chenier, Associate. There was an address in Baton Rouge, Louisiana.

Sid leaned forward, giving me the frog again. 'Maybe now you know why I'm making a big deal about keeping this secret. Some scumbag tabloid would pay a fortune for this. Famous actress searches for real parents.'

Jodi Taylor said, 'My mom and dad are my real parents.'

Sid made the little hand move. 'Sure, kid. You bet.'

She said, 'I mean it, Sid.' Her voice was tense.

The tall woman with the pale hair said something to the overweight man and he looked our way, too. The older woman was looking around, but you could tell she didn't see us.

Jodi said, 'If you find these people, I have no wish to meet them, and I

213

don't want them to know who I am. I don't want anyone to know that you're doing this, and I want you to promise me that anything you find out about me or my biological relatives will remain absolutely confidential between us. Do you promise that?'

Sid said, 'They find out they're related to Jodi Taylor, they might take advantage.' He rubbed his thumb across his fingertips. Money.

Jodi Taylor was still with me, her eyes locked on mine as if this was the most important thing in the world. 'Do you swear that whatever you find will stay between us?'

'The card says "confidential", Ms Taylor. If I work for you, I'm working for you.'

Jodi looked at Sid. Sid spread his hands. 'Whatever you want to do, kid.'

She looked back at me, and nodded. 'Hire him.'

I said, 'I can't do it from here. I'll have to go to Louisiana, and, possibly, other places, and, if I do, the expenses could be considerable.'

Sid said, 'So what's new?'

'My fee is three thousand dollars, plus the expenses.'

Sid Markowitz took out a check and a pen and wrote without comment.

'I'll want to speak with the attorney. I may have to discuss what I find with her. Is that okay?'

Jodi Taylor said, 'Of course. I'll call her this afternoon and tell her to expect you. You can keep her card.' She glanced at the door, anxious to leave. You hire the detective, you let him worry about it.

Sid made a writing motion in the air and the waiter brought the check.

The woman with the pale hair looked our way again, then spoke to her husband. The two of them stood and came over, the man holding his camera.

I said, 'We've got company.'

Jodi Taylor and Sid Markowitz turned just as they arrived. The man was grinning as if he had just made thirty-second-degree Mason. The woman said, 'Excuse us, but are you Jodi Taylor?'

In the space of a breath Jodi Taylor put away the things that troubled her and smiled the smile that thirty million Americans saw every week. It was worth seeing. Jodi Taylor was thirty-six years old, and beautiful in the way that only women with a measure of maturity can be beautiful. Not like in a fashion magazine. Not like a model. There was a quality of realness about her that let you feel that you might meet her at a supermarket or in church or at the PTA. She had soft hazel eyes and dark skin and one front tooth slightly overlapped the other. When she gave you the smile her heart smiled, too, and you felt it was genuine. Maybe it was that quality that was making her a star. 'I'm Jodi Taylor,' she said.

The overweight man said, 'Miss Taylor, could I get a picture of you and Denise?'

Jodi looked at the woman. 'Are you Denise?'

Denise said, 'It's so wonderful to meet you. We love your show.'

Jodi smiled wider, and if you had never before met or seen her, in that moment you would fall in love. She offered her hand, and said, 'Lean close and let's get our picture.'

The overweight man beamed like a six-year-old on Christmas morning. Denise leaned close and Jodi took off her sunglasses and the maître d' and two of the waiters hovered, nervous. Sid waved them away.

The overweight man snapped the picture, then said how much everybody back home loved *Songbird*, and then they went back to their table, smiling and pleased with themselves. Jodi Taylor replaced the sunglasses and folded her hands in her lap and stared at some indeterminate point beyond my shoulder, as if whatever she saw had drawn her to a neutral place.

I said, 'That was very nice of you. I've been with several people who would not have been as kind.'

Sid said, 'Money in the bank. You see how they love her?'

Jodi Taylor looked at Sid Markowitz without expression, and then she looked at me. Her eyes seemed tired and obscured by something that intruded. 'Yes, well. If there's anything else you need, please call Sid.' She gathered her things and stood to leave. Business was finished.

I stayed seated. 'What are you afraid of, Ms Taylor?'

Jodi Taylor walked away from the table and out the door without answering.

Sid Markowitz said, 'Forget it. You know how it is with actresses.'

Outside, I watched Jodi and Sid drive away in Markowitz's twelve-cylinder Jaguar while a parking attendant who looked like Fabio ran to get my car. Neither of them had said good-bye.

From the parking lot, you could look down on the beach and see young men and women in wetsuits carrying short pointy boogie boards into the surf. They would run laughing into the surf, where they would bellyflop onto their boards and paddle out past the breakwater where other surfers sat with their legs hanging down, bobbing in the water, waiting for a wave. A little swell would come, and they would paddle furiously to catch its crest. They would stand and ride the little wave into the shallows where they would turn around and paddle out to wait some more. They did it again and again, and the waves were always small, but maybe each time they paddled out they were thinking that the next wave would be the big wave, the one that would make all the effort have meaning. Most people are like that, and, like most people, the surfers probably hadn't yet realized that the process was the payoff, not the waves. When they were paddling, they looked very much like sea lions and, every couple of years or so, a passing great white shark would get confused and a board would come back but not the surfer.

Fabio brought my car and I drove back along the Pacific Coast Highway toward Los Angeles.

I had thought that Jodi Taylor might be pleased when I agreed to take the job, but she wasn't. Yet she still wanted to hire me, still wanted me to uncover the elements of her past. Since my own history was known to me, it held no fear. I thought about how I might feel if the corridor of my birth held only closed doors. Maybe, like Jodi Taylor, I would be afraid.

By the time I turned away from the water toward my office, a dark anvil of clouds had formed on the horizon and the ocean had grown to be the color of raw steel.

A storm was raging, and I thought that it might find its way to shore.

2

It was just after two when I pulled my car into the parking garage on Santa Monica Boulevard and climbed the four flights to my office there in the heart of West Hollywood. The office was empty, exactly as I had left it two hours and forty minutes ago. I had wanted to burst through the door and tell my employees that I was working for a major national television star, only I had no employees. I have a partner named Joe Pike, but he's rarely around. Even when he is, conversation is not his forte.

I took out Lucille Chenier's business card and dialed her office. A bright southern voice said, 'Ms Chenier's office. This is Darlene.'

I told her who I was and asked if Ms Chenier was available.

Darlene said, 'Oh, Mr Cole. Mr Markowitz phoned us about you.'

'There goes the element of surprise.'

She said, 'Ms Chenier's in court this afternoon. May I help?'

I told her that I would be flying in tomorrow, and asked if we might set a time for me to meet with Ms Chenier.

'Absolutely. Would three o'clock do?'

'Sounds good.'

'If you like, I can book you into the Riverfront Howard Johnson. It's very nice.' She sounded happy to do it.

'That would be great. Thank you.'

She said, 'Would you like someone to meet you at the airport? We'd be happy to send a car.'

'Thanks, but I think I can manage.'

'Well, you have a fine flight and we'll look forward to seeing you tomorrow.' I could feel her smiling across the phone, happy to be of service, happy to help, and happy to speak with me. Maybe Louisiana was the Land of Happy People.

I said, 'Darlene?'

'Yes, Mr Cole?'

'Is this what they mean by southern hospitality?'

'Why, we're just happy to help.'

I said, 'Darlene, you sound the way magnolias smell.'

She laughed. 'Oh, Mr Cole. Aren't you the one.'

Some people just naturally make you smile.

I dialed Joe Pike's condo and got his answering machine. It answered on the first ring and Joe's voice said, 'Speak.' You see what I mean about the conversation?

I told him who we were working for and where I would be, and I left both Sid Markowitz's and Lucille Chenier's office numbers. Then I hung up and went out onto the little balcony I have and leaned across to look into the office next door. A woman named Cindy runs a beauty distribution outlet there, and we often meet on the balcony to talk. I wanted to tell her that I would be gone for a few days, but her office was dark. Nobody home. I went back inside and phoned my friend Patricia Kyle who works on the Paramount lot, but she was in a casting meeting and couldn't be disturbed. Great. Next I called this cop I know named Lou Poitras who works detectives out of the North Hollywood division, but he wasn't in, either. I put down the phone, leaned back in my chair, and looked around the office. The only thing moving besides me was this Pinocchio clock I've got. It has eyes that tock side-to-side and it's nice to look at because it's always smiling, but, like Pike, it isn't much when you're trying to work up a two-way conversation. I have figurines of Jiminy Cricket and Mickey Mouse, but they aren't much in the conversing department, either. My office was neat, clean, and in order. All bills were paid and all mail was answered. There didn't seem to be a whole lot of preparation necessary for my departure, and I found that depressing. Some big-time private detective. Can't even scare up a friend.

I shut the lights, locked the door, and stopped at a liquor store on the way home. I bought a six-pack of Falstaff beer from a bald man with a bad eye and I told him that I was going to Louisiana. On business. He told me to have a nice time and to stop in again when I got back. I said that I would, and I told him to have a nice night. He gave me a little wave. You take your friendship where you find it.

At 1:40 the next afternoon I was descending into the Baton Rouge metropolitan area over land that was green and flat and cut by chocolate waterways. The pilot turned over the muddy wide ribbon of the Mississippi River, and, as we flew over it, the bridges and the towboats and the barges and the levee were alive with commerce and industry. I had visited Baton Rouge many years before, and I remembered clear skies and the scent of magnolias and a feeling of admiration for the river, and for its endurance through history. Now, a haze hung low over the city, not unlike Los Angeles. I guess commerce and industry have their drawbacks.

We landed and taxied in, and when they opened the airplane the heat and humidity rolled across me like warm honey. It was a feeling not unlike what I had felt when I stepped out of the troop transport at Bien

Hoa Air Base in 1971 in the Republic of South Vietnam, as if the air was some sort of extension of the warm soupy water in the paddies and the swamps, as if the air wasn't really air, but was more like thin water. You didn't walk through the air down here, you waded. Welcome to Atlantis.

I sloshed down to the baggage claim, collected my bag, then presented myself to a smiling young woman at the Hertz desk. I said, 'Pretty hot today, huh?'

She said, 'Oh, this isn't hot.'

I guess it was my imagination.

I gave her my credit card and driver's license, asked directions to the downtown area, and pretty soon I was driving past petrochemical tank farms and flat green fields and white cement block structures with signs that said things like FREE DIRT and TORO LAWNMOWERS. The undeveloped land gave way to working-class neighborhoods and grocery markets and, in the distance, the spidery structures and exhaust towers of the refineries and chemical plants that lined the river. The chemical plants reminded me of steel towns in the Northeast where everything was built low to the ground and men and women worked hard for a living and the air smelled strange and sulfurous. Most of the men in these neighborhoods would work at the refineries, and they would work in shifts around the clock. The traffic in the surrounding areas would ebb and flow with great whistles announcing the shift changes three times a day, at seven and three and eleven, sounding like a great sluggish pulse, with each beat pumping a tired shift of workers out and sucking a fresh shift of workers in, never stopping and never changing, in its own way like the river, giving life to the community.

The working-class neighborhoods and the refineries gave way to the state's capitol building, and then I was in the heart of downtown Baton Rouge. The downtown area was a mix of new buildings and old, built on a little knoll overlooking the river and the Huey Long Bridge. The river ran below the town, as much as within it, walled off from the city by a great earth levee that probably looks today much as it did over a hundred years ago when Yankee gunboats came down from the North. Even with the commerce and the industry and a quarter-million people, there was a small-town southern feel to the place. Monstrous oak trees laden with Spanish moss grew on wide green lawns, standing sentry before a governor's mansion sporting Greek revival pillars. It made me think of *Gone With the Wind*, even though that was Georgia and this wasn't, and I sort of expected to see stately gentlemen in coarse gray uniforms and women in hoop gowns hoisting the Stars 'n' Bars. *I wish I was in the land of cotton . . .*

At six minutes before three, I walked into an older building in the heart of the riverfront area and rode a mahogany-paneled elevator to the third floor and the offices of Sonnier, Melancon, & Burke, Attorneys at Law. An

African-American woman with gray hair watched me approach and said, 'May I help you?'

'Elvis Cole for Lucille Chenier. I have a three o'clock appointment.'

She smiled nicely. 'Oh, yes, Mr Cole. I'm Darlene. Ms Chenier's expecting you.'

Darlene led me back along a corridor that was solid and enduring, with heavily lacquered pecan walls and art deco sconces and framed prints of plantations and cotton fields and portly gentlemen of an age such that they might have shared cigars with old Jeff David . . . *Old times there are not forgotten* . . . The whole effect was unapologetically Old South, and I wondered what Darlene felt when she walked past the slave scenes. Maybe she hated it, but then again, maybe in a way I might never understand, she was proud the way any person might be proud of obstacles overcome and disadvantages defeated, and of the ties with a land and a people that adversity builds in you. On the other hand, maybe not. Like friendship, you take your paycheck where you find it.

She said, 'Here we are,' and then she showed me into Lucille Chenier's office.

Lucille Chenier smiled as we entered, and said, 'Hello, Mr Cole. I'm Lucy Chenier.'

Lucy Chenier was five-five, with amber-green eyes and auburn hair that seemed alive with sun streaks and a wonderful tan that went well with the highlights. She seemed to radiate good health, as if she spent a lot of time outdoors, and it was a look that drew your eye and held it. She was wearing a lightweight tweed business suit and a thin gold ring on the pinkie of her right hand. No wedding band. She came around her desk and offered her hand. I said, 'Tennis.'

'Pardon me?'

'Your grip. I'll bet you play tennis.'

She smiled again, and now there were laugh lines bracketing her mouth and soft wrinkles at the corners of her eyes. Pretty. 'Not as often as I'd like. I had a tennis scholarship at LSU.'

Darlene said, 'Would you like coffee, Mr Cole?'

'No, thank you.'

'Ms Chenier?'

'I'm fine, Darlene. Thanks.'

Darlene left, and Lucy Chenier offered me a seat. Her office was furnished very much like the reception area and the halls, only the couch and the chairs were covered with a bright flower-print fabric and there were Claude Monet prints on the walls instead of the plantation scenes. A blond wood desk was end on to a couple of double windows, and an iron baker's rack sat in the corner, filled with cascading plants. A large ceramic mug that said LSU sat among the plants. The Fighting Tigers. She said, 'Did you have a nice flight?'

'Yes, I did. Thank you.'

'Is this your first time to Louisiana?' There was a southern accent, but it was slight, as if she had spent time away from the South, and had only recently returned.

'I've visited twice before, once on business and once when I was in the army. Neither was a fulfilling visit, and both visits were hot.'

She smiled. 'Well, there's nothing I can do about the heat, but perhaps this time will be more rewarding.'

'Perhaps.' She went to the blond desk and fingered through a stack of folders, moving with the easy confidence of someone who trusted her body. It was fun watching her.

She said, 'Sid Markowitz phoned yesterday, and I spoke with Jodi Taylor this morning. I'll bring you up to date on what we've done, and we can coordinate how you'll proceed.'

'All right.'

She took a manila folder from the desk, then returned to sit in a wing chair. I continued to watch her, and continued to have a fine time doing it. I made her for thirty-five, but she might have been younger. 'Yes?'

'Sorry.' Elvis Cole, the Embarrassed Detective, is caught staring at the Attorney. Really impress her with the old professionalism.

She adjusted herself in the chair and put on a pair of the serious, red-framed reading glasses that professional women seem to prefer. 'Have you worked many adoption cases, Mr Cole?'

'A few. Most of my experience is in missing persons work.'

She said, 'An adoption recovery isn't the same as a missing persons search. There are great similarities in the steps necessary to locate the birth parents, of course, but the actual contact is a far more delicate matter.'

'Of course.' She crossed her legs. I tried not to stare. 'Delicate.'

'Are you familiar with Louisiana's adoption laws?'

'No.'

She slipped off her right shoe and pulled her foot up beneath her in the chair. 'Jodi Taylor was relinquished to the state for adoption on an unknown date thirty-six years ago. Under the laws of the state at that time, all details of that surrender and all information pertaining to Jodi's biological parents were sealed. When Mr and Mrs Taylor adopted her, their names were entered as parents of record, and Jodi's birth name, whatever that might have been, was changed to Judith Marie Taylor. All records of that name change were also sealed by the state.'

'Okay.' Maybe I should take notes. If I took notes, she might think me professional.

'Louisiana maintains what we call a voluntary registry of birth parents and adopted children. If birth parents or adopted children wish to contact each other, they register with the state. If both the parent and the child

221

are registered, then, by mutual consent, the records are unsealed and an intermediary working for the state arranges a meeting between the two.'

'Did Jodi enter the registry?'

'Yes. That was the first thing we did. Neither of her birth parents is registered. I filed a request for special leave with the state to open the records, but we were turned down.'

'So, legally speaking, that was the end of the road and now it's up to me.'

'That's right. You'll conduct the actual investigation to try to identify Jodi's birth parents or locate a bio-family member who can supply the information she seeks, but you won't make contact with them. If contact has to be made, that will be my job. Do you understand?'

'Sure.' Strong back, weak mind.

She took a folder from the larger file and passed it to me. 'These are local maps with directions to Ville Platte, as well as some tourist information. I'm afraid there isn't much. It's a small town in a rural area.'

'How far away?' I opened the folder and glanced at it. There was a Triple-A map of the state, a Chamber of Commerce map of Ville Platte, and a typed sheet listing recommended restaurants and motels. Everything the visiting private eye needs in order to swing into action.

'A little over an hour.' She closed the larger file and placed it on her lap. 'Our firm is very well established, so if there's any way that we can help with research or access to state agencies, don't hesitate to call.'

'I won't.'

'May I ask how you'll proceed?'

'The only way to ask about a child who was given up for adoption is to ask about a child who was given up for adoption. I'll have to identify people with a possible knowledge of the event, and then I'll have to question them.'

She shifted in the chair, not liking it. 'What do you mean, question them?'

I smiled at her. 'Questions. You know. "Where were you on the night of the fourth?" Like that.'

She nodded twice, then frowned. 'Mr Cole, let's be sure that you appreciate the complexities involved. Typically, the birth parents of a child given for adoption in the nineteen-fifties were young and unmarried, and great pains were taken to keep that birth secret. It's just as typical that, years later, those birth parents are leading lives in which their current friends and families know nothing of that earlier pregnancy and the fact that a child was born. Nothing must be said or done that could possibly give away their secret. It's as much your job to protect the birth parents' confidences as it is to uncover Jodi Taylor's medical history. Jodi wants it that way, and so do I.'

I gave her my most winning smile. 'I just look stupid, Ms Chenier. I can actually spell the word "discretion".'

She stared at me for a surprised moment, and a trace of color crept onto her cheeks and neck. She was wearing a necklace of large silver shells and they stood out against her skin. 'That did sound like a lecture, didn't it?'

I nodded.

'I'm sorry. You don't look stupid at all. Perhaps I should tell you that these issues are important to me. I'm an adopted child myself. That's why I practice this kind of law.'

'No apologies are necessary. You just want to make sure I respect everyone's privacy.'

She was nodding. 'That's right.'

I nodded back at her. 'I guess that rules out the ad.'

She cocked her head.

'Famous actress seeks birth mother! Huge reward.'

The laugh lines reappeared at the corners of her mouth and the flush went away. 'Perhaps we'd be better served with a more conservative approach.'

'I could tell people that I'm investigating an alien visitation. Do you think that would work?'

'Perhaps in Arkansas.' Regional humor.

We grinned at each other for a moment, then I said, 'Would you join me for dinner?'

Lucy Chenier smiled wider, then stood and went to the door. 'It's very nice of you to ask, but I have other plans.'

'How about if I sing "Dixie"? Will that soften you up?'

She opened the door and held it for me. She tried not to smile, but some of it got through. 'There are several fine Cajun restaurants listed in the folder. I think you'll like the food.'

I stood in the door. 'I'm sure I'll be fine. Maybe Paul Prudhomme will see me for dinner.'

'Not even if you sing "Dixie". Paul Prudhomme lives in New Orleans.'

'That makes two fantasies you've destroyed.'

'I don't think I'll ask.'

'Good night, Ms Chenier.'

'Good night, Mr Cole.'

I walked out singing 'The Battle Hymn of the Republic', and I could hear Lucy Chenier laughing even as I rode down in the elevator.

3

I had a fine catfish dinner at a restaurant recommended by Lucy Chenier's office, and then I checked into a Ho-Jo built into the base of the levee. I asked them for a room with a view of the river and they were happy to oblige. Southern hospitality.

I ordered two bottles of Dixie beer from room service and sat drinking the beer and watching the towboats push great strings of barges upstream against the current. I thought that if I watched the river long enough I might see Tom and Huck and Jim working their raft down the shore. Of course, river traffic was different in the 1800s. In the old days, there were just the paddle wheelers and mule-drawn barges. Now, Huck and Jim would have to maneuver between oil tankers and Japanese container ships and an endless gauntlet of chemical waste vents. Still, I trusted that Huck and Jim were up to the job.

The next morning I checked out of the hotel, drove across the river, then turned north and followed the state highway across a wide flat plain covered with cotton and sugarcane and towns with names like Livonia and Krotz Springs. Cotton gins and sugar-processing plants sprouted on the horizon, the sugar plants belching thin smoke plumes that gave the air a bitter smell. I turned on the radio and let the scanner seek stations. Two country outlets, a station where a man with a high-pitched voice was speaking French, and five religious stations, one of which boasted a woman proclaiming that all God's children were born evil, lived evil, and would die evil. She shrieked that evil must be fought with evil, and that the forces of evil were at her door this very moment, trying to silence the right-thinking Christian truths of her broadcasts and that the only way she might stave them off was with the Demon Dollar Bill, twenty-dollar minimum donation please, MasterCard or Visa accepted. Sorry, no American Express. I guess some evils are better than others.

I left the highway at Opelousas, then went north on a tiny two-lane state road following what the map said was Bayou Mamou. It was a muddy brown color and looked more like standing water than something that actually flowed. Cattails and cypress trees lined the far bank, and the near bank was mostly wild grass and crushed oyster shells. A couple in their early twenties poled a flat-bottomed boat along the cypress knees. The man stood in the stern, wearing an LSU T-shirt and baggy jeans and a greasy camouflage ball cap with a creased bill. He pushed the little boat with steady, molasses-slow strokes. The woman wore a pale sundress and a wide straw hat and heavy work gloves and, as the young man poled, she lifted a trotline from the water to see if they had caught fish. The young man was smiling. I wondered if John Fogerty had been thinking of Bayou Mamou when he wrote 'Born on the Bayou'.

I passed a wooden billboard that said THE KNIGHTS OF COLUMBUS WELCOME YOU TO VILLE PLATTE, LA. 'HOME OF THE COTTON FESTIVAL', and then the highway wasn't the highway any more. It was Main Street. I passed gas stations and an enormous Catholic church, but pretty soon there were banks and clothing and hardware stores and a pharmacy and a couple of restaurants and a record store and all the places of a small southern town. A lot of the stores had posters for something called the Cotton Festival. I turned off the air conditioner and rolled down the window and began to sweat. Hot, all right. Several people were standing around outside a little food place called the Pig Stand, and a couple of them were eating what looked like barbecued beef ribs. A million degrees outside, and these guys were slurping down ribs in the middle of the day. Across from the Pig Stand there was a little mom-and-pop grocery with a hand-painted sign that said WE SELL BOUDIN and a smaller sign that said FRESH CRACKLINS. Underneath that someone had written *no cholesterol – ha-ha*. These Cajuns are a riot, aren't they?

I drove slowly and, as I drove, I wondered if any of the people I passed were in some way related to Jodi Taylor. I would look at them and smile and they would smile back, and, with a curious feeling, I searched for Jodi Taylor's reflection. Were those the eyes? Is that the nose? If Jodi Taylor were beside me, and were not familiar from being on television, would one of these people catch a passing glance of her and call her by another name? I realized then that Jodi Taylor must sometimes wonder these same things.

If I was going to find Jodi Taylor's birth family, I would have to interview people, but the question was who? I could check with local medical personnel, but any physician who was a party to the adoption would be legally bound to remain silent. Ditto clergy and members of the local legal community. Also, they would ask questions that I didn't want to answer and would probably notify the cops, who would come around to ask similar questions. Small-town cops are notoriously territorial. Therefore, ix-nay the more obvious sources of information. Perhaps I could forgo interviews altogether and use the concept of familial resemblance to find said birth parents. I could post pictures of Jodi Taylor all over town. *Do you know this woman?* Of course, since she was famous, everybody would know her, but maybe there was a way around that. I could have Jodi wear a Groucho Marx nose when I took the picture. That should fool 'em. Of course, then everybody might think she was Groucho Marx. Ix-nay the nose.

Thirty-six years ago a child had been born and its care relinquished to the state. That would not be a common occurrence in a town of Ville Platte's size. People would talk and, quite possibly, people would remember, even thirty-six years later. Gossip is a detective's best friend. I could randomly question anyone over the age of fifty, but that seemed sort of unprofessional. A professional would narrow the field. All right. Who talks about having babies? Answer: mommies. Task at hand: locate women who delivered on or about 9 July, thirty-six years ago. The detective flies into action and it is awesome to behold. A mind like a computer, this guy. A regular Sherlock Holmes, this guy.

I drove back to the little grocery with the 'boudin' sign, parked at the curb, and went in. A kid in a gray USL Ragin' Cajuns T-shirt was sitting behind the register, smoking a Marlboro and reading a drag boat magazine. He didn't look up when I walked in. In Los Angeles, you walk into a convenience store and the people who work there reach for their guns.

I said, 'Howdy. Is there a local paper?'

He waved the cigarette at a newspaper rack they had off to the side, and I picked up a copy and read the masthead. *The Ville Platte Gazette – established 1908.* Perfect. *Daily.* Even better.

I said, 'Do you have a library in town?'

He sucked on the Marlboro and squinted at me. He was pale, with wispy blond hair and caterpillar fuzz above his lip and a couple of primo zits ripening on his forehead. Eighteen, maybe, but he could've been older.

I said, 'You got a library?'

''Course. Where you think you are, Arkansas?' They're really into that Arkansas thing down here.

'Any chance you'd tell me how to get there?'

He leaned back on his stool and crossed his arms. '*Which* library?' Score one for the yokel.

Six minutes later I circled the town square past a red-brick Presbyterian church and parked at the library. An older African-American gentleman was behind the counter, stacking books onto a gray metal cart. A young woman with braided hair sat at a reading table and a kid with a limp shuffled through the stacks, listing to the right so he could read the book spines. I went to the counter and smiled at the librarian. 'That air conditioning feels good.'

The librarian continued stacking the books. 'That it does. And how are you today, sir?' He was shorter than me and thin, with a balding head and a prominent Adam's apple and very dark skin. He was wearing a plaid short-sleeved shirt and a burgundy knit tie. A little nameplate on the counter said MR ALBERT PARKS.

I said, 'Do you have the *Gazette* on microfiche?' I could have gone by the newspaper offices, but newspaper people would ask questions.

'Yes, sir. We do.' He stopped stacking books and came over to the counter.

I told him the year I wanted, and asked if he had it.

Mr Parks grinned broadly, pleased to be able to help. 'I think we might. Let me run in the back and see.'

He disappeared between the stacks and returned with a cardboard box and had me follow to an ancient microfiche unit on the other side of the card catalogs. He pulled out one of the spools and threaded it into the machine. 'There are twenty-four spools in this box, two spools for each month of the year. I put in January. Do you know how to work the machine?'

'Sure.'

'If the film gets stuck, please don't force the little crank. These kids from the school use this thing and always tear the film.'

'I'll be careful.'

Mr Parks frowned down into the little box and fingered through the spools.

I said, 'What's wrong?'

'Looks like we have a month missing.' He frowned harder, then arched his eyebrows and looked up at me. 'May's gone. Did you need May?'

'I don't think so.'

'Maybe I put it in a different year.'

'I don't think I'll need it.'

He nodded thoughtfully, told me to call him if I needed any help with the little crank, then went back to his book cart. When he was gone I took the January spool out of the microfiche and dug around in the box until I found the two July spools. I threaded in the first and skimmed through until I reached the *Gazette* dated 9 July. The ninth was a Tuesday and had no birth announcements. I searched through the tenth, eleventh, and twelfth, which was the following Friday. Friday's paper had three birth announcements, two boys and twin girls. The boys were born to Charles & Louise Fontenot and William & Edna Lemoine, the twin girls to Murray & Charla Smith. As I was writing their names on a yellow legal pad, Mr Parks strolled by. 'Are you finding everything you need?'

'Yes,' I said. 'Thank you.'

He nodded and strolled away.

I cranked the little spool back to the beginning of July and copied the birth announcements published at the end of every week, and then I did the same for June and August. When I was working through August, Mr

Parks pushed the book cart next to me and made a big deal out of straightening shelves and trying to pretend that he wasn't interested in what I was doing. I glanced up and caught him peeking over my shoulder. 'Yes?'

Mr Parks said, 'Heh heh,' then pushed the cart away. Embarrassed. They get bored in these small towns.

When I finished with August I had eighteen names. I put the little spools back into their box, turned off the microfiche, and returned the box to Mr Parks. He said, 'That didn't take very long.'

'Efficiency. Efficiency and focus are the keys to success.'

'I hear that.'

I said, 'Is there a phone book?'

'On the reference table next to the card catalog.'

I went over to the reference table and looked in the phone book for the names I had copied. I was on the fourth name when Mr Parks said, 'Seems to me you appear to be looking for someone.'

He was standing behind me again, peering over my shoulder.

I put my hand over the names. 'It's rather personal.'

He frowned. 'Personal?'

'Private.'

He peered at my hand as if he were trying to see through it. 'You're not from around here, are you?'

'No,' I said. 'I'm from the government. Central Intelligence.'

He looked offended. 'No reason to be rude.'

I spread my free hand.

He said, 'You were copying birth announcements. Now you're looking for those names in the phone book. I think you're trying to find someone. I think you're a private detective.' Great. The big-time Hollywood op gets made by the small-town librarian. He started away. 'Perhaps we should call the police.'

I caught his arm and made a big deal out of looking around. Making sure that the coast was clear. 'Thirty-six years ago, the person I'm working for was born in this area and given up for adoption. She has now contracted leukemia and requires a bone marrow transplant. Do you know what that means?'

He answered slowly. 'They need a blood relative for those transplants, don't they?'

I nodded. You toss it on the water and sometimes they take it, but sometimes they don't. He was a knowledgeable man. He'd know more than a little about marrow transplants. He could ask to speak with my client or my client's physician, and, if I were legitimate, they'd be more than happy to speak with him. He could ask me if the leukemia was acute or chronic, or he could ask me which type of white blood cells were affected. There were a hundred things he could ask me, and some of them I could scam but most of them could blow me out of the water.

He looked at my hand over the list of names, then he looked back at me and I saw his jaw work. He said, 'I saw some of your names there. I know some of those folks. This lady, the one you're working for, she gonna die?'

'Yes.'

He wet his lips, then pulled over a chair and sat down beside me. 'I think I can save you some time.'

Of the eighteen names on my list, Mr Albert Parks knew four, and we found another three listed in the phone book. The rest had either died or moved away.

I copied addresses and phone numbers for the seven still in the area, and Mr Parks gave me directions on how to find those people who lived in the outlying areas. He offered to phone the four that he knew to tell them that I'd be stopping around, and I said that that would be fine, but that he should ask them to respect my client's privacy. He said that he was certain that they would. He said that he hoped that I could find a donor for my client, and asked me to give her his very best wishes for a complete recovery. His wishes were heartfelt.

Mr Albert Parks worked with me for the better part of an hour, and then I walked out of the cool quiet of his library into the damp midday Louisiana heat feeling about three inches tall.

Lying sucks.

4

Of the seven names on the list, four lived in town and three lived in the outlying area. I decided to speak with the townies first, then work my way out. Mr Parks had recommended that I start with Mrs Claire Fontenot who, as the widowed owner of a little five and dime just across the square, was the closest. He said that she was one of God's Finest Women. I took that to mean that she was kind and caring and probably easy to manipulate. Sort of like Mr Albert Parks. As I walked over I thought that maybe I should just cut out this manipulation business and proclaim for all the world who I worked for and what I was after. If I did, I would probably feel much better about myself. Of course, Jodi Taylor probably wouldn't, but there you go. Her privacy would be violated and her confidence breached, but what's that when compared to feeling good about oneself? Elvis Cole, detective for the nineties, comforts his inner child.

Going into Fontenot's Five & Dime was like stepping backward in time. Cardboard cutout ads for things like Carter's Little Liver Pills and Brylcreem – a little dab'll do ya! – and Dr Tichnor's Antiseptic were taped and retaped to the door and the windows, filling the same spaces that they had filled when they were first put up forty years ago. Some of the cutouts were so faded that they were impossible to read.

An overweight girl in her late teens sat on a stool behind the counter reading a copy of *Allure*. She looked up when I entered.

'Hi. Is Mrs Fontenot in?'

The girl called out, 'Miss Claire,' and a stately woman in her early sixties appeared in the aisle, holding a box of Hallmark cards. I said, 'Mrs Fontenot, my name is Elvis Cole. I believe Mr Parks over at the library might've phoned.'

She looked me up and down as if she viewed me with caution. 'That's right.'

'May I have a few minutes?'

She viewed me some more, and then she put down the box of cards and led me to the rear of the store. She seemed rigid when she moved, as if her body were clenched. 'Mr Parks told me that you want to know something about a baby that was given up for adoption.' She arched an eyebrow when she said it, clearly suspicious of the practice and disapproving.

'That's right. Somewhere around the time that Max was born.' She had delivered a son, Max Andrew, sixteen days before Jodi Taylor's birth.

'I'm afraid I don't know anything about that. I kept all my children, believe you me.' Daring me to deny it. When she spoke, she kept both hands folded together between her breasts, as if she were praying. Maybe you did that when you were one of God's finest.

'Not one of your children, Mrs Fontenot. Another woman's child. Maybe you knew her, or maybe you just heard gossip.'

The eyebrow arched again. 'I don't gossip.'

I said, 'Ville Platte is a small town. Unwed pregnancies happen, but they would be rare, and babies given for adoption would be still more rare. Maybe one of your girlfriends at the time mentioned it. Maybe one of your aunts. Something like that.'

'Absolutely not. In my day, that type of thing wasn't tolerated the way it is now, and we would never have discussed it.' She clutched her hands tighter and raised both eyebrows, giving me All-knowing. 'Now, people don't care about this kind of thing. People do whatever they want. That's why we're in this fix.'

I said, 'Onward Christian soldiers.'

She frowned at me. 'What?'

I thanked her for her time and left. One up, one down. Six more to go.

Evelyn Maggio lived alone on the second floor of a duplex that she maintained six blocks south of the five and dime. Her duplex was a big white clapboard monster set high on brick piers in case of flood. Evelyn Maggio herself was a vital woman in her late fifties, twice married and twice divorced, with tiny teeth and too much makeup. She showed me the teeth when she let me in and latched onto my arm and said, 'My, but you're a good-lookin' fella.' Her words were long and drawn out, sort of like Elly May Clampett. She smelled of bourbon.

I was with her for almost forty minutes and in that time she called me 'sugar' eleven times and drank three cups of coffee. She drank it *royale*. She put out a little tray of Nabisco Sugar Wafers and told me that the very best way to eat them was to dip them in the coffee, but to watch because they could get too soggy and would fall apart. She put her hand on my arm and said, 'No one likes a limp sugar wafer, honey, especially not lil' ol' me.' She seemed disappointed that it wasn't what I wanted to hear, and, when it became clear that she knew nothing about a child being given to the state, she seemed even more disappointed when I left. I took two of the sugar wafers with me. I was disappointed, too.

I spent the next twenty-two minutes with Mrs C. Thomas Berteaux.

She was seventy-two years old, rail thin, and insisted upon calling me Jeffrey. She was quite certain that I had visited her home before, and when I told her that this was my first time in Ville Platte, she asked if I was sure. I said I was. She said she was certain that I had asked her about this adoption business before. I asked if she remembered her answer, and she said, 'Why, of course, Jeffrey, don't you? I didn't remember anything then, and I don't now.' She smiled pleasantly when she said it and I smiled pleasantly in return. I used her phone to call Mrs Francine Lyons, who said she'd be happy to see me, but that she was on her way out and could I call later. I said that I could, but then she volunteered that Mr Parks had mentioned something about a child given for adoption and that she just didn't know anything about that, though, as she'd said, she'd be happy to see me later in the day. I told her that that wouldn't be necessary and scratched her off my list. You either remember or you don't. Mrs C. Thomas Berteaux, watching from her chair, said, 'What's the matter, Jeffrey? You look disappointed.'

I said, 'Some days are more difficult than others, Mrs Berteaux.'

She nodded sagely. 'Yes, Jeffrey. I know that to be true. However, I might suggest that you speak with Mrs Martha Guidry.'

'Yes?' Martha Guidry wasn't on my list.

'Martha was a midwife at that time and, if I remember correctly, quite a well-known busybody. Martha may know.' Then she looked thoughtful. 'Of course, Martha may be dead.'

I let myself out.

Four up, four down, and nary a shred of evidence to show for it. I had three more women to see, and, if the results were the same, it was back to the drawing board. Not good. The key to all this seemed to be the sealed state documents. Maybe I should stop trying to investigate my way to Jodi Taylor's medical history and concentrate on unsealing those documents. I could shoulder my way into the appropriate state agency, pistol whip a couple of civil servants, and force them to hand over the documents. Of course, this method might get me shot or imprisoned, but wasn't that better than questioning women who called me Jeffrey? Of course, thirty-six-year-old documents would probably be buried under thirty-six years of more recent documents in an obscure state building long forgotten by any living person. You'd need Indiana Jones just to find the place.

I decided to think about it over lunch.

The Pig Stand was a white cinder-block building with handwritten signs telling you what they offered and a couple of windows to order the food. The people on the sidewalk were mostly thin guys with crêpey skin and women with pale skin and loose upper arms from eating too much deep-fried food. Everybody was drinking Dixie beer and eating off paper plates and laughing a lot. Guess if you stand around eating barbecued ribs in this kind of heat you had to have a sense of humor.

An enormously wide black woman with brilliant white teeth looked out of the order window at me and said, 'Take ya awdah, please?'

I said, 'Do you have *boudin*?' I had wanted to try *boudin* for years.

She grinned. 'Honey, we gots the best *boudin* in Evangeline Parish.'

'That's not what they say in Mamou.'

She laughed. 'Those fools in Mamou don' know nuthin' 'bout no *boudin*! Honey, you try some'a this, you won't be goin' back to no Mamou! This magic *boudin*! It be good for what ails you!'

'Okay. How about a couple of links of *boudin*, a beef rib with a little extra sauce, some dirty rice, and a Dixie.'

She nodded, pleased. 'That'll fix you up jes' fine.'

'What makes you think I need fixing?'

She leaned toward me and touched a couple of fingers beneath her eye. 'Dottie got the magic eye. Dottie *know*.' Her eyes were smiling when she shouted the order into the kitchen, and I smiled with her. It wasn't just the food around here that gave comfort.

Passing cars would beep their horns and diners would wave at the cars and the people in the cars would wave back, sort of like everybody knew everybody else. While I was waiting, a sparkling new white Mustang rag-top cruised past, top up, giving everybody the once-over and revving his engine. The Mustang circled the block, and when he came back around an older guy with a thick French accent yelled something I couldn't understand and the Mustang speeded up. Guess the older guy didn't like all the engine-revving.

A couple of minutes later, Dottie called me back to the window and handed out my order on a coarse paper plate with enough napkins to insulate a house. I carried the food to the street, sat the Dixie on the curb, then went to work on the food. The *boudin* were plump and juicy, and when you bit into them they were filled with rice and pork and cayenne and onions and celery. Even in the heat, steam came from the sausage and it burned the inside of my mouth. I had some of the dirty rice, and then some of the beef rib. The dirty rice was heavy and glutinous and rich with chicken livers. The rib was tender and the sauce chunky with onion and garlic. The tastes were strong and salty and wonderful, and pretty soon I was feeling eager to dive back into the case. Even if it meant being called Jeffrey.

The black woman looked out of her little window and asked, 'Whatchu say 'bout dat *boudin* now?'

I said, 'Tell me the truth, Dottie. This isn't really Ville Platte, is it? We're all dead and this is Heaven.'

She grinned wider and nodded, satisfied. 'Dottie say it'll fix you up. Dottie know.' She touched her cheek beneath her left eye and then she laughed and turned away.

At ten minutes after two, I used a pay phone at an Exxon station to call the last two women on my list. Virginia LaMert wasn't home, and Charleen Jorgenson said that she'd be happy to see me.

Charleen Jorgenson and her second husband, Lloyd, lived in a double trailer two miles outside of Ville Platte on Bayou des Cannes. The double trailer sat upon cement-block piers and looked sort of ratty and overgrown. A small flat-bottomed boat rested on a couple of saw horses in the back yard, and a blue tick hound slept in a tight knot in the shade thrown by the boat. They had a little drive made out of the crushed oyster shells, and when I pulled up, the oyster shells made a loud crunching sound and the blue tick hound charged at my car, barking and standing on its back legs to try to bite through the window. An old guy in his seventies came out on the step yelling, 'Heah naow! Heah naow!' and threw a pop bottle at the dog. That would be Lloyd. The bottle missed the dog and hit the Taurus's left front fender. Lloyd said, 'Uh-oh,' and looked chagrined. Good thing it was a rental.

Charleen Jorgenson told me that she wished she could help, but she just didn't remember anything like I was asking.

I said, 'Think hard, Mrs Jorgenson. Are you sure?'

She sipped her coffee and nodded. 'Oh, yes. I thought about it when that other fellow was here.'

'What other fellow?'

'Another young man was here a few months ago. He said he was trying to find his sister.'

I said, 'Do tell.'

'He wasn't very nice and he didn't stay long.'

'Were you able to help him find his sister?'

'I would've been happy to, but I just couldn't help him. He became very abusive. Lloyd like to threw a fit.' She nodded her head toward Lloyd, as if one of Lloyd's fits was quite a spectacle. Lloyd, sitting in a heavy chair that had been covered with a bedspread, had fallen asleep as we talked. She said, 'You're trying to find some kind of organ donor, aren't you?'

'Yes, ma'am. A marrow donor.'

She shook her head. 'That is so sad.'

'Mrs Jorgenson, this guy who was here, was his name Jeffrey?'

She had more of the coffee, thinking. 'Well, maybe. He had red hair, all piled up on his head and oily.' She made a sour face. 'I remember that.'

'Ah.'

'I've never been comfortable with a red-haired person.'

People say the damnedest things, don't they?

I left Charleen Jorgenson's home at twenty-five minutes after four that afternoon and stopped at a bait and tackle shop on the road leading back to town. They had a pay phone on the wall under a huge sign that said LIVE WORMS. I tried calling Mrs C. Thomas Berteaux to ask if Jeffrey's

234

hair had been red, but I got no answer. Probably out. I tried Virginia LaMert again, but also got no answer. Virginia LaMert was the last name on my list, and if she didn't come through it was drawing-board time. I called Information and asked them if they had a listing for Martha Guidry. They did. I dialed Martha Guidry's number and, as I listened to her phone ring, the same white Mustang I'd seen at the Pig Stand turned into the parking lot and disappeared behind the bait shop.

Martha Guidry answered on the sixth ring. 'Hello?'

I identified myself and told her that Mrs C. Thomas Berteaux had suggested I call. I said that I was trying to find someone who was born in the area thirty-six years ago, and I asked if I might pay a visit. She said that would be fine. She told me her address and gave me directions and said that, as old as she was, if I didn't hurry she might be dead before I arrived. I was going to like Martha Guidry just fine.

I hung up and stood at the phone, waiting. A blue Ford pickup pulled in and a young guy with a scraggly beard went into the bait shop. An older man came out of the shop with a brown bag and got into a Chevy Caprice. The young guy came out with a Budweiser Tall Boy and hopped back into his truck. The Mustang didn't return.

I climbed back into my car and followed the directions toward Martha Guidry's house. Maybe this business with the Mustang was my imagination, like the heat.

I had gone maybe three-quarters of a mile when the Mustang swung around a Kleinpeter Dairy milk truck and eased in behind me. He came up so close that I could see the driver in my rearview mirror. He had a scoop-cut pompadour maybe six inches high and long nasty sideburns carved down into points so sharp you could cut yourself.

And he had red hair.

5

The guy in the Mustang wouldn't let anyone get between us, as if he wanted to follow me and thought he had to stay close to do it. He was wearing a short-sleeved shirt with the sleeves rolled, and he drove with his left hand hanging down along the door. One of those.

I turned off the state road and headed back toward town, and the Mustang turned with me. I pulled into an Exxon station and topped off my tank and asked a kid in a grease-stained uniform about the local bass fishing. The Mustang drove past while the kid was telling me, but a couple of minutes later it pulled up to a stop sign a block away and sat waiting. Following me, all right.

I took it easy up through town, letting him follow, and twice managed to stop for traffic lights. Each time I stopped he eased up behind me, and each time he made a big deal out of staring off to the side. The ostrich technique. If I don't see you, you can't see me. I had to smile at this guy. He was something. At a four-way stop a kid in a red Isuzu pickup tried to turn in behind me, and the guy in the Mustang jumped the stop sign and blew his horn, cutting him off. Maybe he thought I wouldn't notice.

A set of railroad tracks ran through the center of town. The tracks were prominent and the road was old, so everybody was slowing to ease their cars across the tracks. On the other side of the tracks there were several businesses and a couple of cross streets and, still further down, a little bridge where the road crossed the bayou. Cars were waiting at most of the cross streets, people getting off work.

I eased the Taurus across the tracks, then punched it, putting enough distance between me and the Mustang for a woman in a light blue Acura to get between us. The Mustang came up to her fast, swerving into the oncoming lane, but there was too much traffic for him to pass. I swung to the right onto the shoulder, floored it past six or seven cars, then jerked it back into the traffic lane and then right again around a bread truck and into a Dairy Queen parking lot. He wouldn't have been able to see me turn past the bread truck. I pushed it around the back of the Dairy Queen, threw it into park, then jumped out and ran up the side past a

236

couple of kids sucking malts in a '69 VW Bug. The Mustang was still behind the woman in the Acura, blowing his horn and swerving from side to side, until finally she couldn't take it anymore and pulled to the side. He horsed it past her, giving the finger and screaming that she should get her head out her butt, and then he blasted away up the shoulder, spraying gravel and dust and little bits of oyster shell. I wrote down his license number, went back to my car, and turned again toward Martha Guidry's. I checked the rearview mirror from time to time, but the Mustang didn't reappear. You had to shake your head.

I drove up the center of Evangeline Parish through dense stands of hardwood trees and sweet potato fields, passing small frame houses set near the road, many with rusted cars and large propane gas tanks and chickens in their yards. Martha Guidry lived in such a house across the street from a strawberry stand. She was a small bony woman with skin like rumpled silk and cataract glasses that made her eyes look huge and protruding. She was wearing a thin housedress and socks and house slippers, and when she answered the door she was carrying a large, economy-sized can of Raid Ant & Roach Killer. She squinted out the thick glasses. 'You that Mr Cole?'

'Yes, ma'am. I appreciate your seeing me.'

She pushed open the screen door and told me to come in quick. She said if you don't come in quick all kinds of goddamned bugs come in with you. As soon as I was in she fogged the air around the door with the Raid. 'That'll get the little bastards!'

I moved across the room to get away from the cloud of Raid. 'I don't think you're supposed to breathe that stuff, Ms Guidry.'

She waved her hand. 'Oh, hell, I been breathin' it for years. You want a Pepsi-Cola?'

'No, ma'am. Thank you.'

She waved the Raid at the couch. 'You just sit right there. It won't take a moment.' I guess she was going to give me the Pepsi anyway. When she was in the kitchen there was a sharp *slap* and she said, 'Gotcha, you sonofabitch!' The thing about this job is that you meet such interesting people.

She came back with two plastic tumblers and a single can of Pepsi and the Raid. She put the glasses on her coffee table, then opened the Pepsi and poured most of it in one glass and a little bit in the other. She offered the full glass to me. 'Now, what is it you want to know?'

I lifted the glass but noticed something crusted down in the ice. I pretended to take a sip and put it down. 'Mrs Berteaux said that you're a midwife.'

She nodded, eyes scanning the upper reaches of the room for incoming bugs. 'Unh-hunh. Not in years, a'course, but I was.'

'Thirty-six years ago on July ninth a baby girl was born in this area and

237

given up for adoption. Chances are that the child was illegitimate, but maybe not. Chances are that the mother was underage, but maybe not.'

Her eyes narrowed behind the thick lenses. 'You think I birthed the child?'

'I don't know. If not, maybe you heard something.'

She looked thoughtful. 'That was a long time ago.'

'Yes, ma'am.' I waited, letting her think. Probably hard with all the nerve damage from the Raid.

Martha Guidry scratched at her head, working on it, and then seemed to notice something in the far corner of the room. She put down her Pepsi, picked up the Raid, then crept across the room to peer into the shadows behind the television. I got ready to hold my breath. She said, 'Goddamned ugly bugs,' but she held her fire. False alarm. She came back to the chair and sat. 'You know, I think I remember something about that.'

Well.

She said, 'There were some folks lived over here around the Nezpique.' She was nodding as she thought about it, fingering the Raid can. 'They had a little girl, I think. Yes, that's right. They gave her away.'

Well, well. 'You remember their names?' I was writing it down.

She pooched out her lips, then slowly shook her head, trying to put it together. 'I remember it was a big family. He was a fisherman or somethin', but they might've cropped a share. They lived over on the bayou. Right over here on the Nezpique. Wasn't no bastard, though. Just a big family with too many mouths to feed.'

'A name?'

She looked sad and shook her head. 'I'm sorry. It's right on the tip of my tongue and I just can't remember it. You get old, everything goes to hell. *There's one!*' She raced to a potted plant beneath the window and cut loose with the Raid. Clouds of gas fogged up around her and I walked over to the door, leaned out, and took deep breaths. When she was finished with the Raid I went back to the chair. Everything smelled of kerosene and chemicals.

I said, 'These bugs are something, aren't they?'

She nodded smugly. 'They'll run you out of house and home, let me tell you.'

I heard the crunch of a car pulling off the road. Not in her yard, but further away. I went back to the door. The white Mustang was sitting across the street by the strawberry stand. I said, 'Ms Guidry, has someone else approached you about this?'

She shook her head. 'Unh-unh.'

'A few months ago.'

She got the thoughtful look again. 'You know, I think a fella did come here.' She made a face like she'd bit into something sour. 'I didn't like his looks. I won't deal with anybody I don't like the way they look. No, siree. You can tell by a person's looks, and I didn't like that fella, at all. I ran 'm off.'

I looked back out the door. 'Is that the man?'

Martha Guidry came over next to me and squinted out through the screen. 'Well, my goodness. That's him. That's the little peckerwood, right over there!'

Martha Guidry charged through the screen door with her can of Raid as if she'd seen the world's largest bug. She screamed, 'Here, you! What are you doin' over there?!'

I said, 'Oh, God.'

She lurched down the steps and ran toward the highway, and I was wondering if maybe I should tackle her before she became roadkill. Then the Mustang fishtailed out onto the highway and roared back toward Ville Platte and Martha Guidry pulled up short, shaking her fist at him. I said, 'Martha, do you remember his name?'

Martha Guidry stalked back up the steps, breathing hard and blinking behind the thick glasses. I was hoping I wouldn't have to dial 911. 'Jerry. Jeffrey. Somegoddamnthing like that.'

'Aha.'

'That rotten sneak. Why do you think he was out here?'

'I don't know,' I said. 'But I'm going to find out.'

She took a deep breath, shook herself, then said, 'God *damn*, but I feel like a drink! You're not the kind of fool to let a lady drink alone, are you?'

'No, ma'am, I'm not.'

She threw open the door and gestured inside with the Raid. 'Then get yer ass in there and let's booze.'

6

At twenty minutes after six that evening I checked into a motel in Ville
Platte and phoned Lucille Chenier at her office in Baton Rouge. I only
had to wait eight or nine minutes for her to come on the line. She said,
'Yes?'

'Guess who?' Martha had been generous with the Old Crow.

'I'm very busy, Mr Cole. Is there some way I can help you?' Some
people just weren't around when they handed out laugh buttons.

'Can your office run a license plate check for me?'

'Of course.'

I gave her the Mustang's number and told her about the red-haired
man. She said, 'He was also asking about a child?'

'Yes.'

You could hear her fingernails clicking on her desk. Thinking. 'That's
odd. I wonder why he would be following you?'

'When he tells me, I'll pass it along.'

'It's very important that this not be associated with Jodi Taylor.' She
sounded concerned.

'I'm telling people that I'm searching for a marrow donor. In a case like
this, you have to ask questions. People talk. This kind of thing can be
exciting to folks, and they like to share their excitement.'

'And people with secrets want to protect them.'

'That's the point. But I've no reason to believe that anyone I've yet seen
has secrets.'

'Except, perhaps, for your red-haired man.'

'Well, there is that. Yes.'

She told me that she would have the information on the Mustang's
owner by ten the next morning, and then she hung up. I stared at the
phone and felt strangely incomplete now that the connection was broken,
but maybe that was just all the Raid I had breathed. Sure. You spend most
of the afternoon breathing Raid and drinking Old Crow, it heightens your
sense of dissociation. It also puts you to sleep.

At eighteen minutes after nine the next morning, the phone rang and

240

Lucy Chenier said, 'Your Mustang is registered to someone named Jimmie Ray Rebenack.' She read two addresses, both in Ville Platte.

'Okay.'

'Mr Rebenack lists his occupation as a private investigator. He was licensed two and a half years ago.'

I was grinning. 'If this guy's for real, he has to be the world's worst detective.'

'Prior to licensing, he was employed as a full-time auto mechanic at an Exxon station in Alexandria. His tax records indicate that he continues to derive the majority of his income from part-time mechanic work.'

'Wow. You guys work fast.'

'The firm is well positioned. You'll keep me informed?'

'Of course, Ms Chenier.' Elvis Cole, Professional Detective, discourses in a professional manner.

I located Rebenack's addresses on my map of Ville Platte, then went to find him. One was a business address, the other a residence. The residential address put Jimmie Ray Rebenack in a small frame duplex on the east side of town, four blocks north of a switching station for the Southern-Pacific Railroad. It was an older neighborhood, and it wasn't particularly proud, with small unkempt houses and spotty lawns and cars and trucks that were mostly Detroit gas guzzlers in need of paint. Jimmie's Mustang was not in evidence.

I cruised the block twice, then drove to Jimmie Ray Rebenack's office two blocks north of Main above a fresh-seafood market. The seafood market was set between a barber shop and a secondhand clothes store, and there was a little stairwell between the seafood and the clothes, and a black felt and glass directory for the offices up the stairs.

I circled the block, looking for the Mustang, but as with the house the Mustang was not there. I parked around the corner, then walked back to the little directory. There were five businesses listed, and Rebenack Investigations was the third. You had to shake your head. Jimmie Ray Rebenack in his brand-new Mustang, thinking he wouldn't be noticed as he followed me all over town.

I crossed the street to a little coffee shop opposite the fish market. There was a counter and a half-dozen Formica tables spread around the place sporting overweight men in thin cotton shirts drinking coffee and reading the newspapers. A napkin dispenser sat on each of the tables, alongside a bottle of Tabasco sauce. I sat at a table in the window, watching the fish market until a sturdy woman with about a million miles on her clock came over with a coffeepot. She poured without asking, and said, 'You wan' some breakfast, sugah?'

'How about a couple of hard poached eggs, toast, and grits?'

'Wheat or white?'

'Wheat.'

She walked away without writing anything and left me to sip at the coffee. It was heavy with flavor and about a million times stronger than the coffee people drink in the rest of the world, sort of like espresso that's been cooked down to a sludge. Mississippi mud. I tried to pretend that I enjoyed it, and I think I did a pretty good job. Maybe the Tabasco was on the tables for the coffee. I sneaked glances at the men with their papers. Okay. If they could drink it, I could drink it.

When the waitress brought the food, I said, 'Mm-mm, that coffee's some kinda strong!'

She said, 'Uh-huh.'

I smushed the eggs into the grits and mixed in a little butter and ate it between bites of the toast. The grits were warm and smooth and made the awful coffee easier to drink. I watched the fish market. People came and went, and a couple of times people climbed the stairs, but none of them was Jimmie Ray Rebenack. The front of the fish market was covered with hand-lettered signs saying CATFISH and LIVE CRABS and GASPERGOO $1.89. The people who patronized the fish market came out with brown paper bags that I took to be the catfish and the crabs, and, as I watched them, I wondered what a gaspergoo was and why someone might want to eat it. Another little sign had been painted on the door. WE HAVE GAR BALLS! These Cajuns know how to live, don't they?

I was halfway along my third cup of sludge when Jimmie Ray Rebenack's Mustang rumbled down the street and pulled into a metered spot outside the clothing store. Jimmie Ray fed some money into the meter, then trotted up the stairs. He was wearing blue jeans and a red western shirt and gray snakeskin boots. His pompadour looked a foot high and must've taken most of the morning to shellac into place.

I gave it a few minutes, then paid at the counter, left a hefty tip, and crossed the street to Jimmie Ray Rebenack's office.

The building was dingy and low class, with crummy linoleum floors and water-stained paint. The smell of fish was strong, and seemed a part of the fiber of the building. Three offices overlooked the front street, and three overlooked the alley behind the fish market. Rebenack had the middle office over the alley. I listened for a second, didn't hear anything, then let myself in.

Jimmie Ray Rebenack was sitting behind a plain wooden desk, feet up, staring at some papers when he heard the door. He saw me, then came out of the chair as if somebody had poured hot oatmeal into his lap. 'Hey.'

'Nice boots, Jimmie Ray. You going for that Joey Buttafucco look?'

'Who?' Out of the cultural loop, down here in Ville Platte. 'What do you want?' He slid the papers into his desk drawer. Surreptitious.

Jimmie Ray Rebenack had sharp features and pockmarks on his neck and the pink skin of a natural redhead. Maybe an inch shorter than me, but muscular in a rawboned kind of way. Grease from his part-time mechanic's job was embedded in the thick skin of his knuckles and fingers. He'd tried to wash it off, but the grease was in deep and probably a part of him. A lowboy gray metal file cabinet sat in one corner of the little room, and a couple of padded dinette chairs sat against the wall opposite his desk. Both of the chairs looked like they had been out in the rain, and the padding on one had been patched with duct tape. Classy. Everything in the place looked like it had been picked up at a yard sale, or maybe bought secondhand from the Louisiana public school system. There was a framed picture of Tom Selleck as Magnum sitting on top of the file cabinet.

I said, 'I want to know why you're following me, Jimmie Ray.'

'Man, what d' hell you talkin' 'bout? I ain't followin' you.' The accent was somewhere between Cajun and French Quarter New Orleans.

I crossed his office and looked out the window. He had a view of the dumpster behind the fish market and, beyond that, a backyard with a little tomato garden. A mayonnaise jar with a two-headed turtle floating in alcohol was on his windowsill. Keepsake, no doubt. I said, 'You're Jimmie Ray Rebenack. You drive this year's Mustang, license number 213X455, and you possess Louisiana State investigator's license number KAO154509.'

You could see him relax. I hadn't shot him or thrown a punch, so the surprise of my entry was wearing off and he was getting himself together. He put together a pretty good smile, sort of a Jack Nicholson number, part sneer and part smirk. He sat again, leaning back and trying to look expansive. 'You made me, huh? You must be pretty good.'

'Jimmie, a twelve-year-old could've made you. Why are you following me?'

'I heard you was in town and I wanted to find out why, you know? Like there might be some money in it, thas all.'

'Why were you talking to Martha Guidry and Claire Fontenot and Evelyn Maggio last year?'

He frowned and dug at the inside of his teeth with his tongue. Nervous. 'I don't know whatchu talkin' 'bout, man.'

'C'mon, Jeffrey.'

He stared at me like he was trying to think of something to say, but couldn't. I grinned at him. 'Gotcha.'

He frowned, not happy about it. 'They got me confused with somebody else.'

'With hair like that?'

He leaned forward. 'Hey, podnuh, this is my town. I ain't gotta tell you dick. I know your name is Elvis Cole, and you're from Los Angeles. I know you're stayin' at the motel over here.' He pointed his thumb at me and smirked. 'You see? I ain't no goddamned slouch in the detectin' department, either.'

'Wow. You think we could have a detect-off? You think we could duke it out for the world middleweight detective championships?' I looked at the picture of Tom Selleck. Jesus Christ.

He said, 'Maybe my business is knowing your business. Maybe I figured that since you was workin' in *my* town, I could cut myself in.' He leaned back again, grinning at me like I was supposed to believe it. 'These coonies won't open up to a stranger, and I know my way around. Figured that might be worth some cash. Whatchu think?'

'I think you're full of shit.'

Jimmie Ray shrugged like what I thought didn't matter, and then I heard steps coming up the linoleum stairs. The steps came closer and then the door opened and a guy in his mid-forties stepped in. Something large filled the hall behind him.

Jimmie Ray kept grinning at me and said, 'This my podnuh, LeRoy.' He nodded at the shape in the hall. 'That there's René, behind him.'

LeRoy's eyes narrowed and he looked at Jimmie Ray as if Jimmie was the world's largest turd. LeRoy was maybe five-eight, with dark weathered skin just beginning to loosen and eyes like a couple of hard black marbles. He was in a thin short-sleeved plaid shirt and worn denim pants, and there was a tattoo on his forearm so obscured by wiry hair that I couldn't make it out. Anchor, maybe. Or a bulldog. He looked surprised to see me, and not particularly happy about it. 'Who d'fuck dis?' He said it with a heavy Cajun accent.

Jimmie Ray's smile lost some of its confidence. 'Just some guy. He's leaving. Let'm pass, René.'

René moved into the room behind LeRoy, and when he did I stepped back the way you might when something large passes very close to you, say a mobile home, or some great African beast. René was only six-three or six-four, but his body possessed size in the way a dirigible possesses size, as if there were a quality to its bulk that could block out the sun. He had a tiny round head and thin, sandy hair and fingers as thick as my wrists. He wore humongously thick glasses that made his eyes seem tiny and far away, and the lenses were speckled with white flecks of matter. There were liver-colored blotches on his forearms and ears that looked like birthmarks, and a large misshapen lump riding the top of his right shoulder like a second head. His skin looked like tree bark. I said, 'Jesus Christ.'

Jimmie Ray said, 'That René is somethin', idin' he? Had him a job in a carnival down 'round Bossier City. Useta bill him d' Swamp Monster.' Jimmie Ray liked René the same way he liked the two-headed turtle. Something in a jar.

244

LeRoy still had the narrow eyes on Jimmie Ray. 'Jus' some guy? You callin' names wi' jus' some guy? How goddamn stupid you are?'

Jimmie Ray raised his hands like what's the big deal? 'It's nothin', man. Eve'body cool here.' The sharp smile fell away and you could see that Jimmie was scared.

LeRoy said something in French.

Jimmie Ray nodded. 'Hey, Cole, there's nothin' I can tell ya, all right? Now, I got business. Go on.'

LeRoy had put the narrow eyes on me. 'Whatchu lookin' at, podnuh?'

Rebenack came around the desk and took my arm. 'C'mon, Cole. Out. I gotta go.' Now he was trying to get me out of there and damned anxious to do it.

I said, 'Are you okay with this?'

Jimmie Ray Rebenack looked at me with wide, surprised eyes. 'Hey, yeah, no problem.'

LeRoy squinted at me, then at Rebenack. 'Who dis guy?' Then back at me. 'You his boyfrien', what?'

I said, 'If you're in trouble with these guys, Rebenack, don't go with them.'

Rebenack waved me toward the door, making a big deal out of showing me that everything was fine. 'Hey, these are just a couple of pals. It's not your business, man. Now, c'mon, I gotta lock up.'

I let myself get shown out, and then I went down the stairs and back across to the little coffee shop. In a couple of minutes, LeRoy and René and Jimmie Ray came down and climbed into a rusty, gold Polara double-parked at the curb. When René got in, the Polara groaned and settled on its springs. They eased away down the street, did a slow K-turn, then headed back to Main Street and swung left.

I ran hard around the corner to my car, jumped in, pushed it hard through the little alley behind the fish market to Main, then jumped out of the car, climbed onto the hood, and looked both ways to find them. The gold Polara was moving south, just winding a bend in the street maybe three blocks and a dozen cars away. I followed them.

Jimmie Ray might be a turd, but he was my turd.

7

They were easy to follow. I trailed them south of Ville Platte, staying four to six cars back. LeRoy drove slowly, and a train of cars piled up behind them, unable to pass because of the narrow road.

Six miles south of Ville Platte we crossed a little bayou, and the line of traffic slowed as LeRoy turned west. I didn't turn after him because no one else had, and the land was wide and flat and empty of trees. Sweet potato fields, maybe. I pulled onto the shoulder and waited until the Polara was out of sight, and only then did I turn. If Jimmie Ray was doing the following, he'd be tooling along a couple of car lengths behind, thinking he was invisible because he was playing the radio. Hmm. If I was the world's greatest detective and Jimmie Ray was the world's worst, maybe this was some kind of karmic coming together.

Maybe a mile off the main road another road branched away, this one going through a gate with a big sign that said ROSSIER'S CRAWFISH FARM, MILT ROSSIER, PROP. The farm was hidden from the road by a heavy windbreak of hardwood trees, and I couldn't see beyond the windbreak into the farm. I could see pretty far up the tarmac road, and the gold Polara wasn't visible. No dust trail, either. Hmm, again. I drove a hundred yards past the gate, pulled onto the shoulder, then trotted back into the trees.

The windbreak was maybe a hundred yards deep, with more fields beyond cut through by a regular crosswork of shell roads. The gold Polara was parked on the far side of a large rectangular pond about the size and shape of a football field. There was another pond of identical size and shape beyond it, and another one after that, and a couple of long, low cinder-block buildings. The Polara was parked beside a white Cadillac Brougham and an Evangeline Parish Sheriff's Department highway car. Jimmie Ray and LeRoy and René were standing at the edge of the pond with a guy in a tan sheriff's uniform. The sheriff was maybe in his fifties, and everybody seemed to be talking to a heavy guy with baggy trousers and a cheap white short-sleeved shirt and a straw field hat on his head. He looked about the same age as the sheriff, but he might have been older, and he carried himself with the unmistakable bearing of an overseer. He gestured out toward the pond, and everybody looked. He gestured in the opposite direction, and everybody looked there, too. Then he leaned against the Cadillac and crossed his arms. Milt Rossier, no doubt. Proprietor.

I watched for another few minutes, and then I made my way back through the trees, drove back to town, and let myself into Jimmie Ray Rebenack's office. It was as we had left it, quiet and smelling of raw shrimp, the sounds of the alley and backyards below drifting nicely through the open window. A lawnmower was growling a few houses away, and the rich smell of cut St Augustine grass mixed nicely with the shrimp. The two-headed turtle was milky in its jar on the sill, and Tom Selleck looked bored in his frame atop the file cabinet. I could see Jimmie Ray Rebenack, watching *Magnum* reruns, watching Tom Selleck drive the fast car and mug with the beautiful women. Jimmie sitting in his little duplex in Ville Platte, thinking, yeah, I could do that, then taking some mail-order course, *How to Be a Private Eye!*

I opened his desk to see what he had been reading, and suddenly the lawnmower sounds faded and the office was very quiet. Jodi Taylor smiled up at me from the cover of *Music* magazine. The cover and an accompanying article had been clipped from the magazine and stapled together. The *People* article was under it. I took a breath and let it out. Sonofagun. I went through the rest of the desk, but the rest of the desk was empty. I moved to the file cabinet. Two cans of Dr Pepper were hiding in the bottom drawer, and a single roll of prank toilet paper, the kind with Jerry Falwell's face printed on each of the sheets. Office-warming gift. The second drawer was empty, and the third was nicely outfitted with hanging file folders in various colors, only the folders were as empty and as clean as the day Jimmie Ray had installed them. There were eight hanging files in the top drawer. One of them held a Polaroid snapshot of a nude woman with a Winn-Dixie shopping bag over her head. A lot of blond hair peeked out beneath the bag, and she was cheap-looking, wearing rings on her third and fourth fingers. Girlfriend, no doubt. Another held a surveillance report that Jimmie Ray Rebenack had written for a Mrs Philip R. Cantera, who was convinced that her husband was playing around. Jimmie Ray's report said that he had observed Mr Cantera in intimate embrace on several different occasions with (a) a young woman who worked at Cal's Road House and (b) another young woman who sold beer at the Rebel Stock Car Oval. The next three files contained case notes from similar jobs, two of them involving suspected infidelity, and the remaining being a grocery store owner who suspected an employee of stealing houseware products. The fifth folder contained more pictures of Jodi Taylor clipped from magazines and newspapers and what looked like studio press release sources, only sandwiched in with the articles were the Xeroxed copies of the first two pages of a document relinquishing the care and trust of one Marla Sue Johnson, a baby girl, to the State of Louisiana from her natural parents, Pamela E. Johnson and Monroe Kyle Johnson, on 11 July, thirty-six years ago. The document was incomplete and bore no signatures. Jodi Taylor's birth certificate was paper-clipped to the document along with a second birth certificate, this one stating that Marla Sue Johnson had been born to Pamela E. Johnson and Monroe Kyle Johnson on 9 July. Jodi Taylor's birthday.

Jesus Christ.

An address had been written in pencil on the back of the birth certificate: 1146 Tecumseh Lane. I copied it.

I stared at the birth certificate and the relinquishment document for quite a while, and then I put Jimmie Ray's office back as I had found it, let myself out, and went back through the smell of wet shrimp to the little diner across the street. The same cook with the cratered nose was leaning on the counter. The same crinkled old man with the snap-brimmed hat was smoking at the little window table. Dignified. I said, 'Use your pay phone?' They have a pay phone on the wall by the restroom.

The cook nodded help yourself. Watching me gave him something to do.

I fed a quarter into the phone and dialed Martha Guidry, who answered on the second ring. I said, 'Martha, it's Elvis Cole.'

'*What?*' The Raid.

I had to yell. 'It's Elvis Cole. Remember?' The old man and the cook were both looking at me. I cupped the receiver. 'Her ears.' The cook nodded, saying it's hard when they get like that.

Martha Guidry yelled, 'Goddamn bugs!' You could hear the flyswatter whistle through the air and snap against the wall, Martha cackling and saying, 'Gotcha, you sonofabitch!'

'Martha?' Trying to get her back to the phone.

Something crashed, and she came back on the line, breathing harder from her exertion. 'You have a bowel movement yet? I know how it is when I travel. I cross the street, I don't go potty for a week.' A living doll, that Martha.

I said, 'The people you were trying to remember, were their names Johnson?'

'Johnson.'

'Pamela and Monroe Johnson.'

There was a sharp *slap*. 'You should see the size of this goddamned roach.'

'The Johnsons, Martha. Was the family named Johnson?'

She said, 'That sounds like them. White trash lived right over here. Oh, hell, Pam Johnson died *years* ago.'

I thanked Martha Guidry for her help, then hung up and stared at the address I had copied. 1146 Tecumseh Lane. I fed another quarter into the phone and dialed Information. A pleasant female voice said, 'And how are you today?' She sounded young.

'Do you have a listing for a Pamela or Monroe Johnson on Tecumseh Lane?'

She didn't say anything for a moment, and then she said, 'No, sir. We've got a bunch of other Johnsons, though.'

'Any of them on Tecumseh Lane?'

'I'm sorry, sir. I don't show Pamela or Monroe Johnson, and I don't show a Tecumseh Lane, either.'

I hung up.

The cook said, 'No luck?'

I shook my head.

The old guy at the window table said something in French.

'What'd he say?'

The cook said, 'He wants to know what you want.'

'I'm trying to find Monroe and Pamela Johnson. I think they live on Tecumseh Lane, but I'm not sure where that is.'

The cook said it in French, and the old man said something back at him and they talked back and forth like that for a while. Then the cook said, 'He doesn't know these Johnson people, but he says there's a Tecumseh Lane in Eunice.'

'Eunice?'

'Twenty miles south of here.' Ah.

I smiled at the old man. 'Thank him for me.'

The cook said, 'He understands you okay, he just don't speak English so good.'

I nodded at the old man. *'Merci.'*

The old man tipped his hat. Dignified. *'Il y a pas de quoi.'* You take your good fortune where you find it.

I went out to my car, looked up Eunice on the Triple-A map, and went there. Like Ville Platte, the landscape was flat and cross-cut with bayous and ponds and industrial waterways, mostly sweet potato fields and marshlands striped with oil company pipelines and vent stations. The town itself was bigger than Ville Platte, but not by a lot, and seemed like a neat, self-contained little community with a lot of churches and schools and quaint older buildings.

Tecumseh Lane was a pleasant street in an older residential area with small frame houses and neatly trimmed azalea bushes. 1146 was in the center of the block, with a tiny front lawn and an ancient two-strip cement drive and a big wooden porch. Like every other house in the area, it was set atop high brick pillars and, even though the land was flat, you had to climb three or four steps to enter the house.

I left the car at the curb and went up to the house and rapped at the door. An older black woman in what looked like a white nurse's uniform answered. 'May I help you?'

I gave her one of my nicer smiles. 'Mrs Johnson?'

'Oh, no.'

'I'm looking for Mr and Mrs Johnson. I was told they lived here.' The air behind her smelled of medicine and pine-scented air freshener.

She was shaking her head before I finished. 'You'll need to speak with Mrs Boudreaux. I work for her.'

'Who's Mrs Boudreaux?'

'She owns this house.' A wet, flapping sound came from deeper in the house, and a raspy old man's voice yelled something about his pears. The black woman took a half-step out onto the porch, pulling the door so I wouldn't hear. 'She doesn't live here, though. She only comes by in the morning and the evening.'

I let myself look confused. A relatively easy task. 'Did the Johnsons move?'

'Oh, Mr Johnson's her daddy. She used to rent this place out, but now she lets him live here.' She pulled the door tighter and lowered her voice, letting me in on the know. 'He can't live by himself, and they didn't want to put him in a home. Lord knows he couldn't live with them.' She raised her eyebrows. 'He's very ill.'

I said, 'Ah. So Mr Johnson does live here.'

She nodded, then sighed. 'He's eighty-seven, poor thing, and he takes spells. He's a devil when he takes a spell.' The voice in the house yelled again, something about the TV, something about Bob Barker and the goddamned pears.

I said, 'How is Mrs Johnson?'

'Oh, she died years ago.'

Score another for Martha Guidry. 'If I wanted to speak with Mrs Boudreaux, how could I do that?'

'She'll be here in a little while. She always comes around two. Or you could go by her shop. She has a very nice formal wear shop on Second Street by the square. They call it Edie's. Her first name is Edith, but she goes by Edie.'

'Of course.'

She glanced back toward the house. 'Twice a day she comes, and he don't even know it, most days. Poor thing.'

I thanked her for her time, told her I'd try to stop at the house again around two, then drove back to the square. Edith Boudreaux's boutique occupied a corner location next to a hair salon, across from a little square filled with magnolia trees. I parked on the square, then walked back and went inside. A young woman in her early twenties smiled at me from a rack of Anne Klein pants suits. 'May I help you, sir?'

I smiled back at her. 'Just sort of browsing for my wife.'

The smile deepened. Dimples. 'Well, if you have any questions, just ask.'

I told her I would. She finished racking the Anne Kleins, then went through a curtained doorway into the stockroom. As she went through the curtains, an attractive woman in her late forties came out with an armful of beige knit tops. She saw me and smiled. 'Have you been helped?'

The similarities to Jodi Taylor were amazing. The same broad shoulders, the good bone structure, the facial resemblance. They were, as the saying goes, enough alike to be sisters. We would have to unseal the sealed documents to be sure. We would have to compare the adoption papers from the Johnson family to the Taylor family to be positive, but Edith Boudreaux and Jodi Taylor were clearly related. Maybe Jimmie Ray Rebenack wasn't the world's worst detective, after all. I said, 'Are you Ms Boudreaux?'

'Why, yes. Have we met?'

I told her no. I said that her shop had been recommended and that I was browsing for something for my wife, but if I had any questions I would be sure to ask. She told me to take my time and she returned to her stock. I browsed around the store another few minutes, then let myself out, walked to a pay phone on the other side of the square, and dialed Lucy Chenier. I said, 'Well, I've done it again.'

'Tied your laces together and tripped?' Maybe she had a laugh button, after all.

I said, 'I have found a gentleman named Monroe Johnson. Thirty-six years ago on Jodi Taylor's birthday, his wife, Pamela Johnson, delivered a baby girl. They gave the child up for adoption. I saw his adult daughter, a woman named Edie Boudreaux, and she is Jodi's spitting image.'

Lucy said, 'You've done all this in two days?'

'It is not for nothing that I am the World's Greatest Detective.'

'Perhaps you are.' She sounded pleased.

'Also, Rebenack found them for me.' I told her what I had found in his office.

'Oh.' She didn't sound as happy about that.

I said, 'I still don't know what Rebenack's interest in all this might be, but if these people are, in fact, Jodi's biological family, Edie Boudreaux should be able to provide whatever medical information Jodi wants.' I gave her Bogart. 'So it's all yours, shweetheart.'

'Was that Humphrey Bogart?'

Some people are truly cold.

She said, 'The next step is to approach these people. Perhaps we can figure out a plan of action over dinner.'

I said, 'Is this an invitation, Ms Chenier?'

'It is, Mr Cole, and I advise you to accept. There may not be another.'

'Dinner sounds very nice, thank you.'

'Where are you?'

'Eunice. The family lives here.'

She said, 'Can you be back at the Riverfront and ready to be picked up by six-thirty?'

'I think I can manage.' If I grinned any wider I'd probably split my gums.

'Good. I'll see you then.' She paused, and then she said, 'Good work, Mr Cole.'

I hung up, went to my car, and sat there with the grin until a guy in a Toyota flatbed yelled, 'Hey, pumpkinhead! You're gonna catch bugs that way!'

Southern humor.

8

I went back to the motel in Ville Platte, showered, shaved, then drove back across the Atchafalaya Basin to Baton Rouge. It seemed a lot faster than when I had driven from Baton Rouge to Ville Platte, but maybe that was because I was looking forward to getting there. I am nothing if not goal oriented.

I checked into the Riverfront again and was nursing a Dixie beer in the lobby bar at six-thirty when Lucy Chenier walked in wearing a rose blazer over a clay-colored blouse and tight jeans. Two businessmen at a little round table watched her walk in. So did the bartender. She smiled when she saw me and her eyes seemed to fill the room. She offered her hand. 'Did you satisfy your urge for local cuisine, or are you still feeling adventurous?'

I said, 'Adventure is my middle name.'

She smiled wider, and her teeth and eyes sparkled, but maybe that was just me. 'Then you're in for a treat.'

Lucy waited while I paid the bar bill, then we went out to her car. She was driving a light blue Lexus 400 two-door coupe. The sport model. It was clean and sleek and had been freshly washed. There was an AT&T car phone, and the small backseat was littered with CDs, mostly k. d. lang and Reba McEntire. She looked good behind the wheel, as if she and the car were comfortable together. 'Nice,' I said.

She flashed the laugh lines, pleased. Lucy Chenier drove cleanly and with authority, very much the way I imagined she practiced law or played tennis, and pretty soon we turned into a great warehouse of a building with streams of people going in and coming out. Ralph & Kacoo's. She said, 'Let me warn you. The decor is kind of hokey, but the food is wonderful.'

'No problem,' I said. 'I go for that Barnacle Bill look.'

Ralph & Kacoo's made an airplane hangar look small. It was festooned with fishing nets and cork buoys and stuffed game fish and mutant crab shells the size of garbage can lids. There must have been seven hundred people in the place. A lot of families, but a great many couples, too. All it needed was Alan Hale in a yellow slicker greeting everyone with a hearty 'Ahoy, matey!' I said, 'Kind of?'

Lucy Chenier nodded. 'We're big on hoke down here.'

A young woman who looked like a college student seated us and asked if we'd care for a drink. I said, 'Shall we order a bottle of wine?'

'Never with Cajun food.' Lucy grinned, and now there was a glint of fun in her eyes. 'You're going to think it's hokey again.'

'What?'

She looked at the waitress. 'Could we have two Cajun Bloody Marys, please?'

I raised an eyebrow. 'Cajun Bloody Marys?'

'Don't laugh. They're made with cayenne and a hint of fish stock. You said you're adventurous.' She turned back to the waitress. 'And we'll have an appetizer of the alligator sausage.'

The waitress went away.

I said, 'First, it's dinner at Gilligan's Island, now it's alligator sausage. What could be next?'

Lucy looked at her menu. 'The best is yet to come.'

The waitress came back with Bloody Marys that were more brown than red, with a ring of lemon floating in them. I tasted. There was the hint of fish, and the flavors of Tabasco and pepper and cayenne were strong and tingly, and went well with the vodka.

Lucy said, 'Well?'

'This is good. This is really very good.'

Lucy smiled. 'You see?'

The waitress returned with the alligator sausage and asked if we were ready to order. I tried the sausage. It could have been chicken or pork, but the texture was interesting.

Lucy said, 'If you really want to taste Louisiana, I'd suggest any of the crab dishes, or the crawfish. The crab dishes tend to be fried; the crawfish boiled or made in a soup.'

'Sounds good.'

Lucy Chenier ordered the crawfish étouffée, and I ordered the crawfish platter. With the platter I would get a bowl of crawfish bisque, as well as boiled crawfish and fried crawfish tails. The fried tails were called Cajun popcorn. We finished the first Bloody Marys and ordered two more. The waitress brought our salads, and I watched Lucy eat as, in her office, I had watched her move. To watch her was a singular, enjoyable occupation. She said, 'To be honest with you, when Jodi told me that she was bringing in an investigator from California, I tried to discourage it. I didn't think you'd be as effective as a local investigator.'

'Reasonable.'

She tipped her glass toward me. 'Reasonable, but clearly misplaced. You're good.'

I tried to sit straighter in the chair. 'You're making me blush.'

She sipped the Bloody Mary. She didn't seem too interested in the salad. 'What did Mr Rebenack have to say for himself?'

I went through it for her. I told her that Jimmie Ray Rebenack had approached at least two of the women I interviewed and presented himself as someone seeking to find a sister, and that when I questioned him about this, he denied it, and also denied approaching the women. I told her that I had taken the opportunity to enter his office, and that when I did I discovered what appeared to be Louisiana State adoption papers and a birth certificate for a girl child born to Pamela and Monroe Johnson on the same day as the day of Jodi Taylor's birth. When I said that part of it, Lucy Chenier put down her Bloody Mary and held up a hand. No longer smiling. 'Let me stop you. You broke into this man's office?'

'Yes.'

She shook her head. 'Breaking and entering is a crime. I will not be a party to criminal behavior.'

I said, 'What office?'

She sighed, still not liking it.

I said, 'The state papers were standard stuff, showing that the Johnsons remanded all rights and claims on the child to the state. Someone had written the Johnsons' address on back of the birth certificate. It could be coincidence, but if it is, it's a big one.'

'Were the Taylors mentioned anywhere on the papers?'

'There was a copy of Jodi's birth certificate. That's all.'

'Do you think this man Rebenack is related to Jodi Taylor or to the Johnson family?'

'I have no way to know. He denied all knowledge, yet he had the file. He's interested in Jodi Taylor, and he's linked her to the Johnsons. He had Monroe Johnson's address, so he may have approached them, but I don't know that.'

Lucy Chenier stared into midspace, thinking. Now that we were on the serious stuff, she seemed intent and focused and on the verge of a frown. Her court face, I thought. A mix of the tennis and the law. I had more of the Bloody Mary and watched her think. Watching her think was as rewarding as watching her move, but maybe that was just the vodka. My mouth tingled pleasantly from the spices, and I wondered if hers was tingling, too.

She said, 'The documents you're describing are part of the files sealed by the state. The biological parents would've been given a copy, what you might call a receipt for the child, but there's no way Mr Rebenack should have a copy.'

'Only he has it.' I wondered what it would be like to kiss someone with a tingling mouth.

She said, 'Still, that document doesn't prove that Jodi Taylor is in fact the child given up by the Johnsons. We'll have to open the state files for that. We'll have to approach Edith Boudreaux to confirm that what you've found is correct. If her father is incapacitated and her mother is dead, then it falls to her to give the state permission to open the files. That's the only way to officially confirm that Jodi Taylor was born to Pamela Johnson.'

'And that we'll do tomorrow.'

She nodded. 'Yes. I think it's best if we approach her at the boutique. We'll make contact there, on ground where she's comfortable, and ask to speak with her in private. That should be me, because I've done it before and because women are less threatened by other women.'

'You mean, we don't just walk up and say, hey, babe, how'd ya like to meet your long lost sister?'

Lucy Chenier smiled, and had more of her drink. 'Perhaps in California.'

I said, 'Is your mouth tingling?'

She looked at me.

'From the spices.'

'Why, yes. It is.'

I nodded. 'Just wondering.'

The waitress took the salad plates away and came back with the étouffée for Lucy and the crawfish platter for me. A bowl of bisque was in the center of my plate, surrounded by a mound of boiled crawfish on one side and the fried crawfish tails on the other. The fried tails looked like tiny shrimp, curled tight and lightly breaded. I forked up several and ate them. They were hot and tender and tasted in a way like sautéed baby langostinos. 'Good.'

Lucy said, 'The bisque is like a soup that's been enriched with crawfish fat. The heads have been stuffed with a mixture of crawfish meat and bread crumbs and spices. You can pick it up, then use your spoon to lift out the stuffing.'

'Okay.' The bisque was a deep brown, and several stuffed crawfish shells bobbed in it. I did as she said and dug out the stuffing and tasted it. The stuffing tasted of thyme. 'This is terrific. Would you like one?'

'Please.'

I spooned out one of the stuffed shells and put it on her plate. She said, 'Here. Try the étouffée.'

The étouffée was a rich brown sauce chunky with diced green bell peppers and celery and crawfish tails over rice. She forked some onto one of the little bread plates, then passed it to me. I tasted it. These people have redefined the word *yummy*.

She said, 'Does the étouffée you get in California taste like this?'

'Not even close.'

Lucy Chenier picked up the stuffed shell I had given her and spooned out the filling. As she did, a brown drop of the gravy ran down along the heel of her hand toward her wrist. She turned up her hand without thinking about it and licked off the drip. I felt something swell in my chest and had to swallow and then had the rest of the Bloody Mary. I said, 'Would you like another?'

Nod. Smile. 'Maybe one more. I have to drive.'

I flagged at the waitress and showed her two fingers. *Two bags of ice and a cold shower, please.* Lucy said, 'You eat the boiled crawfish by breaking the tails out of the body, then pinching the tail so that the shell cracks and you can get out the meat.' She took one of my crawfish and demonstrated. 'You see?'

'Unh-hunh.' Maybe if I concentrated on the food. The food could save me.

'Then you put the head in your mouth and suck it.'

I blinked at her as she put the head in her mouth and sucked it. She smiled simply. 'Gets out the juice.'

I coughed and covered my mouth. I drank some water. Think about the food. The food. The waitress brought our drinks and I drank mine without stopping. Lucy looked concerned. 'What's wrong?'

'Nothing.' I shook my head. 'Not a thing.'

She sipped her new drink and ate some more of her étouffée. I noticed that most of my food was gone and most of hers was still on her plate. I hope she didn't think me a glutton. 'Are you from Baton Rouge?'

'That's right.'

'Your accent is softer than the others I hear.'

She smiled. 'I'm not the one with the accent, Mr Cole.'

I spread my hands. Busted.

'I went to LSU for prelaw, but I attended law school in Michigan. Living with Yankees can devastate your accent.'

'And you returned home to practice.'

'My boyfriend was here, working, and we wanted to be married. He was a lawyer, too. He still is.'

'How about that.'

'We were divorced four years ago.'

'That happens.' I tried not to beam.

'Yes, it does.' It seemed as if she was going to say more, but then she went back to the étouffée. 'Now tell me about you. Do you have a background in law enforcement?'

'Nope. I've been licensed for twelve years and, before that, I apprenticed with a man named George Fieder. George had about a million hours of experience and was maybe the best investigator who ever lived. Before that, I was in the army.'

'College?'

257

'University of Southeast Asia. The work-study program.'

She shook her head, smiling. 'You look too young for Vietnam.'

'I looked older then.'

'Of course.'

'May I ask you a personal question, Ms Chenier?'

She nodded, chewing.

'Have you sought out your birth parents?'

'No.' She shook her head, then used the back of her wrist to move her hair from her eyes. Fingers still sticky from the crawfish. 'The vast majority of adopted children don't. There may be a minor curiosity from time to time, but your mom and dad are your mom and dad.'

'The people who raise you.'

'That's it. A long time ago a woman gave birth to me, and gave me over to the state because she felt it best for both of us. She now has her life, I have mine, and my birth father his. I can appreciate on an intellectual level that they birthed me, but emotionally, my folks are Jack and Ann Kyle. Jack helped me ace algebra and Ann drove me to the court every day after school to practice tennis. Do you see?'

'Sure. They're your family.'

She smiled and nodded and ate more of the étouffée. 'Just like yours.'

'Yet you've devoted your career to this kind of work.'

'Not really. Most of my practice is in the area of divorce and custody disputes. But I don't have to want to recover my birth parents to appreciate that need in others. All of us should have access to our medical histories. Because I feel the weight of that, and because I'm in a position to help those with the need, I do.'

'You share a mutual experience with other adopted children and you feel a kinship. All brothers and sisters under the skin.'

She seemed pleased. 'That's exactly right.' Amazing how a little vodka can dull the senses, isn't it? She put down her fork and crossed her arms on the table. 'So, Mr Adventure, tell me what you think of our Louisiana crawfish. Is it the most incredible thing you've ever eaten?'

'I ate dog when I was in Vietnam.'

Lucy Chenier's smile vanished and she looked uncertain. 'How ... adventurous.'

I shrugged and finished off the crawfish tails.

She said, 'Arf.'

I looked up.

Lucy Chenier's face was red and her mouth was a dimpled tight line. She opened her mouth and breathed deep and blinked to clear her eyes. 'I'm sorry, but the idea of it.' She covered her face with her napkin. 'Was it a poodle?'

I put down my fork and folded my arms on the table. 'Oh, I get it. Humor.'

'I'm sorry. It's just so funny.'

'Not to the dog.'

Lucy laughed, then motioned to the waitress and said, 'I really do have to be going.'

'Would you like coffee?'

'I would, but I can't. I have another appointment with a very special gentleman.'

I looked at her. 'Oh.'

'My son. He's eight.'

'Ah.'

The waitress brought us Handi Wipes. Lucy paid, and then we drove back to the hotel. I suggested that we go together to Edith Boudreaux's shop the next morning, but Lucy had two early meetings and thought it better if we met there. I told her that that would be fine. We rode in silence most of the way with an air of expectancy in the car that felt more hopeful than uncomfortable, as if the night held a kind of static charge waiting to be released.

When we stopped at the Ho-Jo's front entrance, it was almost ten. She said, 'Well.'

'I had a very nice time tonight, Lucy. Thank you.'

'Me, too.'

We sat in the neon light another moment, looking at each other, and then I leaned across to kiss her. She put her hand on my chest and gently pushed, and I backed up. She looked uncomfortable. 'You're a neat guy, and I had a good time with you, but we're working together. Do you see?'

'Sure.' I swallowed and blinked, and then offered my hand. 'Thanks for dinner. I enjoyed myself.'

She took my hand, eyes never leaving mine. 'Please don't take this wrong.'

'Of course not.' I tried to smile.

We shook, and then I got out of Lucy Chenier's car and watched her drive away.

The night was balmy and pleasant, and I walked along the levee and up the little hill and along the nighttime Baton Rouge streets, drunk not from the vodka but with the joyful awareness that tomorrow I would see her again.

9

The next morning I left the hotel just before eight, drove across the Huey Long Bridge, and, one hour and five minutes later, parked in a diagonal spot beneath the Eunice town clock just across the square from Edith Boudreaux's clothing store. A CLOSED sign hung in the window, and the red and white store hours sign said that they opened at ten A.M. It was twelve minutes after nine.

I went into a coffee shop, bought two coffees to go, and brought them and a handful of sweetener and creamer packs out to my car. I sat there with the windows down, sipping the coffee and watching the store. At twenty-six minutes after nine Lucy Chenier's Lexus came around the square and parked four spaces down from me. I got out with the coffees, walked over, rapped on her fender, then opened her passenger-side door, slid in, and handed her a coffee. 'There's sweetener and creamer. I didn't know what you take.'

'This is so thoughtful. Thank you.'

'We're a full-service operation, ma'am.' She popped the plastic top off the Styrofoam cup, blew on the coffee, then sipped it black. Even watching her sip was an adventure.

She said, 'Is that the store?'

'Yes. Edie's. They open at ten.'

Lucy Chenier sipped more of the coffee and watched the store. When she sipped, the steam from the coffee brushed over her face like a child's fingers. The amber-green eyes seemed darker today, almost brown, and I wondered at their change. She was wearing a crushed linen jacket over a white blouse and baggy camel pants, and she smelled of buttermilk soap. If I stared at her any more I'd probably reveal myself to be the world's largest doogie. I forced myself to look at the store.

At fourteen minutes before ten, Edith Boudreaux walked around the corner and came down the block and let herself in through the shop's front door. I said, 'That's her.'

'My God, she does look like Jodi, doesn't she?'

'Yep.'

Lucy finished her coffee, then said, 'Let's go see her.'

We walked across the square and went in. The same little bell rang when we entered, and the air was as chill today as I remembered it. Edith Boudreaux looked up at us from the cash register where she was loading a fresh tape. She said, 'Sorry. We're not open yet.' She hadn't yet turned around the CLOSED sign.

Lucy smiled pleasantly and stepped into the store as if they were old friends. 'I know, but I was hoping we might spend a few minutes now. My name is Lucille Chenier. I'm an attorney from Baton Rouge.' Lucy crossed with her hand out and Edith Boudreaux took it without thinking. She seemed sort of puzzled, and then she recognized me.

'You were in yesterday.'

'That's right.'

She brightened and glanced at Lucy. 'You brought your wife this time.'

Lucy gave a friendly laugh. 'No. Mr Cole and I work together.' She patted Edith Boudreaux's hand, calming her, telling her that we were good people and there was nothing to be frightened of. Friendly people come to change your life. Lucy said, 'I know you need to ready for opening, but it's better that we're alone.'

'What are you talking about?' Looking at me. 'Why alone?'

Lucy said, 'I practice civil law, and part of my practice involves adoption recovery. It's a sensitive, private matter, and I treat everyone's confidence with the utmost respect.'

Edith Boudreaux's face darkened and she took a single step back. Jimmie Ray had been to see her, all right.

Lucy went on, 'Birth parents who want to find their children or adoptees who want to find their birth parents or learn something about their biological relatives employ me to help make those connections. I'm working for such a person now, and Mr Cole and I have come across something that we need to check.'

Edith Boudreaux glanced from Lucy to me and back to Lucy. Her mouth opened slightly, then closed, and her hands came together beneath her breasts. Lucy said, 'Mrs Boudreaux, I hope this won't come as a shock to you, but it may. This isn't bad news in any way. It is very, very good news. Were you aware that your mother gave birth to a child on 9 July, thirty-six years ago, and then gave that child up for adoption?'

The eyes flicked again. Me to Lucy. Lucy to me. 'Why did you come here? Who sent you here?' Jimmie Ray, all right.

The bell tinkled again and the young blond clerk came through the door. Edith Boudreaux clutched at Lucy and said, 'Please don't say anything.'

She went to the young woman and said something so softly that we could not hear. Lucy looked at me and lowered her voice. 'Why's she so scared?'

I shook my head. Edith Boudreaux returned and said, 'That's Sandy. Sandy helps out. We can go in back.' She hustled us through the curtained doorway and into the stockroom. Racks of plastic-covered clothes filled most of the floor space, and blue and white garment boxes were stacked against the walls and on cheap shelves. An Arrowhead water cooler stood outside what I guessed was a restroom. Edith pulled the curtain and wrung her hands. 'I don't know what you want of me.'

Lucy's voice was calm and measured and soothing, an FM disc jockey playing easy listening after midnight. She said, 'My client may be the child that your mother gave away. Your sister, Edith. She wants nothing of you, or anyone else in her biological family, except to learn her medical history.'

Nodding now. Squinting like all of this was going by very fast and it was difficult to contain. I wondered what Jimmie Ray had told her. I was wondering where he'd gotten the money to buy the Mustang. She said, 'I don't know.'

Lucy said, 'The only way we can be sure that my client is the child that your mother gave away is if both parties submit to the state's adoption registry search so we can see if there's a match. If there is a match, the state will unseal the records and confirm the identity.'

Edith Boudreaux was nodding, but I'm not sure the nods meant anything. She said, 'You think your client is that baby?'

'We believe she is, yes.'

'That's who sent you here? The baby?' She was so nervous she was rocking, swaying back and forth as if in time with a heartbeat.

'My client is thirty-six years old. She's a woman now.'

'That was all so long ago.'

'She doesn't want anything from you, Mrs Boudreaux. She simply wants to know the particulars of her medical heritage. Does breast or uterine cancer run in the family? Is the family long-lived? That kind of thing.'

'My mother's dead.'

'We know. And we know that your father is ill. That's why we came to you. Won't you help us?'

She was still making the little rocking moves, and then she said, 'I have to call my husband. I need to speak with him.'

She went out through the curtain without looking at us. Lucy blew out a loud sigh and took a cup of water from the cooler. 'What's wrong with this picture?'

'Somebody scared her. Probably Jimmie Ray.'

Lucy crumpled the cup, didn't see any place to toss it, put it in her pocket. 'With what? All we're talking about here is an adoption.'

It didn't take long for Edith Boudreaux to talk to her husband, and it didn't take long for him to arrive on the scene. We waited maybe eight or nine minutes, and then the outer bell tinkled and a tall, florid man about Edith's age came through the curtain ahead of her. He was thick across the shoulders and butt, with small eyes and a sun-reddened face and large hands that looked callused and rough. He was wearing a crisp khaki Evangeline Parish sheriff's uniform open at the collar, and he was the same cop I'd seen with Jimmie Ray Rebenack at the crawfish farm.

He said, 'My name's Jo-el Boudreaux. I'm the sheriff here in Evangeline Parish. Could I see some identification, please?' As he said it he looked over Lucy and then he looked over me. His eyes stayed with you without blinking. Cop eyes.

Lucy showed her driver's license and gave him a business card. When he looked at my investigator's license he said, 'California.'

I nodded.

'You carrying?'

I shook my head. 'Nope. Not licensed in Louisiana.'

'Why don't we see?'

He pointed at the wall and I assumed the position and he patted me down. Lucy Chenier looked surprised and then angry. She said, 'There's no need for that. I'm an attorney, this man is a licensed investigator. This is a legitimate inquiry.' She was breathing quickly, confused by his manner. Everything had suddenly risen to a level she wasn't used to.

I said, 'It's okay.'

The sheriff copied some information off the license into a little notepad. After that he flipped back the license, and he didn't much care if I caught it or not. He said, 'Yeah, well, we'll check on that. We'll see. Now that we know where we stand, why don't you tell me what you're after.' He squared himself off at us, the way he'd front a kid he'd stopped for driving too fast on a back road.

Lucy didn't like it, but she went through it again for Jo-el Boudreaux, telling him about the sealed state documents, about the possibility that our client was the child given away by Pamela Johnson, about our client's desire not to contact her long lost family but simply to establish her medical history.

Jo-el Boudreaux was shaking his head before she finished. 'You got any proof that this baby and your client are the same person?'

Lucy said, 'No, sir. But they were born on the same day, and they're both female, and they were both given up to the state. That's why we need the records opened.'

He was shaking his head again. 'Not interested. I want you people to leave my wife alone. Whatever you're selling, we don't want any.'

Edith Boudreaux looked like she wasn't as sure. She said, 'Jo-el, maybe we should—'

He cut her off. 'Edith, what's there to say? The past is the past, isn't it?'

Lucy said, 'Our client doesn't want anything from you, Mr Boudreaux.

She simply wants to know her medical history. You can understand that, can't you?'

He said, 'I understand that a lot of my wife's family's dirty laundry is going to be stirred up again. You people go around town spreading crap about my wife's family, it'll go hard on you.'

Lucy stiffened and the court face appeared. 'Is that a threat, Sheriff?'

'Yes, ma'am. I've just threatened legal action. As an attorney, I'm sure you understand that.' He handed back her card. 'We've got nothing to say to you.'

Lucy looked at Edith Boudreaux. She was small behind her husband. Her eyes looked hurt. 'Is this what you want?'

Edith repeated it. 'What's past is past. Let's not stir things up.' Nervous.

Lucy stared at the other woman for a time, then carefully put her business card on a stack of Anne Klein boxes. 'I can appreciate your confusion. If you change your mind, please call me at this number.'

Sheriff Jo-el Boudreaux said, 'There's no confusion, counselor. If you leave the card, I can cite you for littering.'

Lucy picked up the card, thanked Edith for her time, and walked out.

I said, 'A litter bust. That'd probably make your month.'

The cop eyes clicked my way. 'You wanna push for the prize, podnuh?'

I said, 'How'd a guy like Jimmie Ray Rebenack get you so scared?'

The big sheriff looked at me, and a single tic started beneath his left eye. The blocky hands flexed, and Edith Boudreaux touched her husband's arm, and it was suddenly still in the little room. Outside, the doorbell tinkled, and I wondered if it was Lucy leaving. Edith said, 'Jo-el?'

Boudreaux went to the curtained door and pulled the curtain aside and held it for me. 'You'd better leave now, podnuh. That'd be best for you. That'd be best for everyone.'

I wished Edith a good day and then I walked out past the blond clerk. She smiled brightly and told me to have a good day. I told her I'd try. When I got to the door I looked back, but the curtain was drawn again and Jo-el Boudreaux and his wife were still in the stockroom. I thought I heard a woman crying, but I could have imagined it.

It was supposed to be a simple case, but cases, like life, are rarely what they seem. I walked out of Edie's Fashion Boutique wondering at the pain I'd seen in their eyes.

10

Lucy was waiting on the sidewalk, her arms crossed and her face set. A couple of teenagers were behind her, looking at the sheriff's shotgun through the driver's side window of his highway car, the older of the two sneaking glances at Lucy's rear end. He cut it out when he saw me approach. Lucy said, 'I've been doing this for almost eight years and I've never had a reaction even close to that. Something's wrong.'

'They're scared. Him, maybe more than her.'

As we walked back to our cars, I told her about Jimmie Ray Rebenack and the two goons who'd come to his office. 'I followed them to a place called Rossier's Crawfish Farm. Boudreaux was there, and some older guy with a Panama hat who was probably Milt Rossier. Boudreaux didn't look thrilled to be there, but he and Rebenack are connected.'

'Do you think that Rebenack has seen these people about Jodi Taylor?'

'Looks that way.'

'Maybe he's working for them, just like we're working for Jodi.'

'Maybe.'

When we reached the cars, Lucy leaned against her Lexus and shook her head. 'I don't believe it, but even if he were, so what? All we're talking about is a child who was given away for adoption. It's a simple matter to unseal the files and confirm the biological link. It's done all the time.'

I looked at her. 'Maybe the problem is coming from an altogether different place.'

She squinted at Edith Boudreaux's dress shop, thinking about it. Frustrated. 'Well, it can't just end here. They say no, thanks, so that's the end of it. Jodi still has a right to find out about herself, and I'm still going to help her do that.'

'All right.'

Jo-el Boudreaux came out of his wife's store, got into his highway car, and roared away. He didn't look at us, but perhaps he didn't know that we were across the square. I said, 'Does Sonnier, Melancon practice criminal law?'

'Yes.'

'Have someone run a check on Rebenack and also on that guy LeRoy Bennett. I don't know René's last name, but he might be listed as a known associate if Bennett has a sheet. And run the paper on Milt Rossier, too.' I thought about it. 'And Edith Johnson.'

Lucy said, 'I guess you're serious.'

'While you're doing that, I'll look up Jimmie Ray again.'

She crossed her arms at me. 'What does that mean?'

'We were interrupted last time, and Jimmie didn't have a chance to answer my questions. Maybe I'll go see him again and see if he's more forthcoming.'

She held up a hand. 'If you do anything illegal I don't want to know about it.'

I grinned. 'You won't.'

Lucy made a big deal out of sighing, then got into her car and drove away.

The trip from Eunice to Jimmie Ray's office in Ville Platte took thirty-six minutes, but when I got there Jimmie Ray's Mustang was not in evidence and neither was Jimmie Ray. I double-parked behind the fish market and ran up to see, but the office was empty. I could have rifled his files again, but I didn't expect that there would be anything different in them from yesterday.

I drove to Jimmie Ray's duplex, circled the block, then eased to a stop. No Mustang here, either.

Jimmie's duplex was a shotgun with two doors coming off a common porch and the whole thing sandwiched on a long, narrow lot that was overgrown and kind of crummy beneath a dense oak canopy. I went to Jimmie Ray's door and pressed the bell. I pressed the bell again and knocked loudly, and again no one answered. No sounds came from the adjoining apartment. I went around the side of Jimmie Ray Rebenack's house as if I had been doing it every day for the past ten years and let myself in through his kitchen door. I called, 'Hey, Jimmie, what's going on, man?'

Silence. Just think of all the fun Lucy Chenier was missing. And I couldn't even tell her about it.

Jimmie Ray's home smelled of fried food and dust. The kitchen was small. There were dishes piled in the sink and on the tile counter, and the grout between the tiles looked like it hadn't been scrubbed since 1947. A Formica dinette set with mismatched chairs filled the dining area, and a monstrously large overstuffed couch took up most of the living room. The couch was upholstered in a kind of black and white cowhide fabric, and there was a single matching chair and a square glass coffee table. The couch and the chair and the coffee table were too big for the room and ended up jammed together. A Sony home entertainment unit was stacked in the corner, and there wasn't enough room for that, either. Everything

266

except the Sony looked low-end and cheesy, as if the local discount store had run a clearance sale: COMPLETE BACHELOR PAD – ON SALE NOW!!! 'Taste,' I said. 'You can't develop it; you have to be born with it.'

There were two rooms on the second floor, along with a bath and a linen closet. Jimmie Ray Rebenack was using the front room for his bedroom and the back room for a study. I went into the back room first. Two cardboard cartons sat against one wall, and a flimsy red card table with a single folding chair stood in the center of the room. A poster of the Bud Light models was pinned to the wall along with a couple of posters of bikinied women dressed up like commandos and holding machine guns. Ah, the bachelor life. One of the cardboard cartons held old copies of *Penthouse* and *Sports Illustrated* and a single VHS videotape called *Seymore Butts and The Love Swing*, but the other was where Jimmie Ray kept his bills and receipts. I lifted the stuff out, turned the stack upside down, and went through it back to front, returning the items to the box so that they'd be in their original order. I didn't think Jimmie Ray would be able to tell, but you never know. Guys like Jimmie Ray can surprise you.

There were Visa card bills going back eight months, and receipts for his office rent and the rent he paid on the duplex. The Visa charges were incidental. Most of the paperwork in the box had to do with buying the Mustang. He had purchased it used for $29,000 three months ago from an outfit called High Performance Motors in Alexandria, Louisiana. It had 8200 miles on the odometer at the time of purchase, and he had made the purchase for cash with a check drawn on his personal account. Three months ago, exactly two days before he bought the Mustang, he deposited $30,000 into his checking. Prior to that he held a balance of $416.12. Makes you wonder, doesn't it? Further on in the box there was warranty information and auto insurance papers and phone and utility bills. I didn't bother with the utilities. The phone bills went back five months, and during that time he had made seven phone calls to Los Angeles, California, at two different numbers. Two of the calls were lengthy.

I went out past the bathroom and into the front room and looked out at the street. Still clear. The front bedroom was as well appointed as the rest of the place, with an unmade oversized futon against the wall opposite a yard-sale dresser and a couple of lamps. Two thin pillows had been used as a backrest at the head of the futon, and a black sheet and a quilted spread were kicked to the side. The black sheet highlighted the hair and the lint and the crud in the bed nicely. That Jimmie Ray.

There was a closet beside the dresser, but I didn't have to go into the closet or look through the dresser or dig around under the futon to find what I was looking for. Jimmie Ray had what looked like the entirety of the sealed state files on the relinquishment of Marla Sue Johnson and the adoption of Judith Marie Taylor, and he had left them scattered on the bed. There were nine separate documents, at least two of which appeared to be originals, and all of the documents were complete. They were mixed with more articles and clippings about Jodi Taylor, and with yellow legal pages of what were probably Jimmie Ray Rebenack's handwritten notes. I whistled between my teeth and knew that I could not leave it here. Oh, Jimmie. How'd you get this stuff?

Maybe Jimmie Ray Rebenack wasn't the world's worst private investigator after all.

I gathered everything together, went back into the other room for the phone bills, then let myself out and drove back to the motel. Jimmie would know that someone had been in his house and he would probably know it was me, but if things played out the way I thought they might, Jimmie and I would be discussing these things soon enough.

I phoned Lucy Chenier at her office, but she wasn't back yet. I told Darlene to have her call me as soon as she returned, and Darlene said that she would. I hung up and went through what I'd found. As near as I could tell, everything was there. All of the documents were either original or were new clean copies of the originals. The original birth certificate showing Pamela Johnson as the mother of Marla Sue Johnson was attached to the complete original document showing that the Johnsons had relinquished all rights to the child to the state of Louisiana. A Louisiana State Department of Social Services document showed that Steven Edward Taylor and Cecelia Burke Taylor, lawfully wedded man and wife, were adopting the child known as one Marla Sue Johnson. A Louisiana juvenile-court document showed that Marla Sue Johnson's name was henceforth changed to Judith Marie Taylor. Each of the documents had a file and case number. The handwritten notes were mostly about Jodi Taylor and were probably culled from magazine articles: where she was born, her birth date, the name of her studio and agency and personal manager. Edith Boudreaux's name and address and phone were written on the back of one of the sheets. Jimmie Ray had been to see her, all right. On another sheet the name LEON WILLIAMS was written in big block letters and was the only name I didn't recognize. Six phone numbers were scrawled in no particular order on two of the sheets, two of them with Los Angeles area codes. The name 'Sandi' had been written a half-dozen times around the page. I checked the numbers against the numbers from the phone bill, and the numbers matched. I picked up the phone and dialed one of the Los Angeles numbers, thinking maybe I'd get someone named Sandi. A young man answered, 'Markowitz Management. May I help you?'

'Jesus Christ.'

'Pardon me, sir?'

'Is this Sid Markowitz's office?'

'It is, sir. May I help you?'

I didn't know what to say.

'Sir?'

'Does someone named Leon Williams work there?'

'No, sir.'

'How about someone named Sandi?'

'No, sir. Who's calling, please?'

I said, 'Tell Sid it's Elvis Cole, the Lied-to Detective.'

'Pardon me?'

I hung up and dialed the other L.A. number. A young woman's voice said, 'Jodi Taylor's office.'

I went through it again. No Leon Williams. No Sandi. I hung up.

In the past three months, Jimmie Ray Rebenack had made seven calls to Sid Markowitz, one of the calls lasting almost an hour and one of the calls lasting thirty-five minutes. They were lengthy calls implying meaningful conversation. The longest call was made just three days before Jimmie Ray Rebenack deposited $30,000 in his checking account. My, my.

I put down the phone and stretched out on the floor and thought about things. A large monetary payoff seemed to imply the 'B' word. But if Jodi Taylor was in fact being blackmailed, why not tell me that and hire me to find out who was doing it? Of course, since Sid had spent so much time on the phone with Jimmie Ray, it looked as if they already knew who was doing it and, besides that, what was there to blackmail her with? That she was adopted? That had already been in *People*. Jodi Taylor spoke of it publicly and often. Maybe they wanted me to get their money back. That seemed reasonable. Then again, it would seem even more reasonable if they had told me the score. I went back to the phone and called Sid Markowitz again. The same young man answered. I said, 'This is Elvis Cole. May I speak with Sid?'

'I'm sorry, Mr Cole, but he's not in.' Great.

'Would you have him call me, please?'

'Of course.'

I left the motel number and I called Jodi Taylor again, but she, too, was unavailable. I was getting angry at having been lied to and I wanted to know what was going on. I got up and paced around the room, and then I called Lucy's office again. Still not in. Nobody was in. Maybe I should leave and then I wouldn't be in, either. I looked up Jimmie Ray's office number, dialed, and hung up on the twenty-sixth ring. Another one. I decided to go back to Jimmie Ray's house and wait for him.

I gathered together the documents and the articles and hid them between the mattress and box spring. The Dan Wesson was too big to wear at my ankle, so I clipped the holster on the inside of my waistband

and pulled out my shirt to hang over it. Neatness counts, but bullets often count more.

I had locked my room and was getting into my car when LeRoy Bennett and his sidekick René drove up. LeRoy showed me a Colt Government .45. 'Get in,' he said. 'We goin' f' a little ride.'

I guess Jimmie Ray would have to wait.

11

I said, 'Well, well. Bill and Hillary.'

LeRoy lowered his gun. 'Knew we'd see you again, podnuh.' He tilted his head toward the backseat. 'C'mon. Don't make ol' René have to get out.'

René was in the backseat. His eyes were filmy and moved independently of each other, and I was struck again with the sense that maybe he was here with us, but maybe not. I said, 'What if I won't go?'

LeRoy laughed. 'Knock off da bullshit and le's go.'

I said, 'Tell me something, is René for real or did someone build him out of spare parts?'

René shifted and the Polara squeaked on its springs. He had to tip in at close to four hundred pounds. Maybe more. LeRoy said, 'Get in front wi' me. René, he won't fit up front. He ride in back.'

I got in and they brought me south through Ville Platte and down along the highway to Milt Rossier's Crawfish Farm. We drove slowly up between the ponds and along the oyster shell road past a couple of long low cinder-block buildings. The buildings had great sliding doors and the doors were open and you could see inside. Hispanic men driving little tractors towed open tanks alive with wiggling catfish into the near building. There, Hispanic women working at large flat tables scooped up the catfish, lopped off their heads, then gutted and skinned them with thin knives. Other men drove trucks filled with crawfish into the far building where women washed and sorted and bagged the crawfish in heavy burlap bags. With the windows down and no air conditioning, the crunching oyster shells were loud in the car and sounded like breaking bones. Jimmie Ray Rebenack's Mustang was parked on the far side of the processing sheds, and Jimmie Ray was standing with Milt Rossier at one of the ponds. LeRoy parked by the nearest building and said, 'Here we go.'

We got out and went over to them.

Milt Rossier was in his early sixties, with blotched crêpey skin and cheap clothes and a gut that hung well out over his belt. The short stub of a cigar was fixed in one side of his mouth, and his hands were pale and freckled with liver spots. He wore a long-sleeved shirt with the sleeves down and cuffed at his wrists, and he was wearing the Panama hat again. Sensitive to the sun, no doubt. Milt said, 'My name is Milt Rossier. They tell me you're some kinda private investigator.'

'Did they?' René walked past us to the edge of the pond and stared into the water.

'Mm-hmm.' The cigar shifted around in the side of his mouth. 'What you doin' heah?'

'LeRoy brought me.'

Rossier frowned. 'I don' mean heah, I mean in my town. You been makin' waves in my town, and I want it to stop. You got no bidniss heah.'

I said, 'Wrong, Milt. I do have business here.'

Jimmie Ray said, 'He was with some woman, Milt. Some kinda attorney.' I looked at Jimmie Ray and grinned. He couldn't have known that unless Sheriff Jo-el Boudreaux had told him.

I said, 'I've been trying to find you, Jimmie Ray. I've been in your house.'

Jimmie Ray looked at me as if I'd just shot him in the foot, but then he turned a very bright red. He said, 'Well, we'll see about that. That ain't why you're here.'

René suddenly dropped to his knees at the edge of the pond and reached into the water. He moved faster than I would have thought possible for such a large man. One moment out of the water, the next in. He lifted out something black and wiggling and bit it. The wiggling stopped.

LeRoy yelled, 'Goddammit, René. You stop that!'

René dropped what was left back into the pond.

'Spit it out.'

René spit something red and black and glistening into the grass. He walked a few feet away and sat down. LeRoy squinted after him, then hurried over for a closer look. 'Goddammit, he's sittin' in red ants. Get up, *fou!*' René lumbered to his feet, and LeRoy brushed at his pants. '*Fi de chien! Emplate!*'

Milt Rossier shook his head, then took out a handkerchief and wiped his brow. It had to be a hundred degrees in the sun, and the sweat seeped out but had nowhere to go with the humidity. He said, 'That boy is a trial.'

'I'll bet.'

He looked back at me. 'You know anythin' about me, son?'

'I can guess.'

'Don't let's guess. I got business interests all over this parish, and I have to protect those interests. It's the dollah, you see?'

'Sure.'

'Someone from outta town comes in, diggin' aroun', that can push things outta kilter.' He took out the cigar, examined it, then put it back in his mouth. 'Why you heah, son?'

'I'm here because you're blackmailing my client.'

He stared at me, and when he did I could tell that he didn't know. I looked at Jimmie Ray, who was squirming like something from one of the ponds. It wasn't Rossier; it was Jimmie Ray, all by his lonesome. I said, 'I'm here because this asshole is blackmailing a woman in California.'

Jimmie Ray shrieked, 'That's a goddamned lie!' He waved a hand at Milt Rossier. 'That's pure bullshit, Milt! He's makin' this shit up!'

'No,' I said. 'I'm not.' I looked at Jimmie Ray. 'Three hours ago I broke into your house and found documents there relating to the birth of my client. I also found evidence linking you to a series of conversations with my client, predating a thirty-thousand-dollar deposit into your checking account.' I glanced back at Milt Rossier. 'I don't know what this has to do with whatever you've got going, but I don't give a damn. All I care about is how it affects my client.'

Jimmie Ray said, 'Oh, man, what a bare-faced liar!' Laughing like he couldn't believe these lies.

Milt Rossier swiveled the Panama toward Jimmie Ray, his eyes hard black dots. 'I thought you were workin' for me, son. You out on your own?'

'This is bullshit, Milt. Who you gonna believe, me or this turd?'

Rossier squinted harder. 'You bring me something and I pay for it, it's mine.'

Jimmie Ray looked greasy and he kept shooting glances at René. 'Hell, yes, it's yours. This sumbitch is jus' tryin' to weasel!'

Rossier shook his head and sighed. 'Goddammit.'

'I swear, Milt. I'm tellin' you the truth.'

LeRoy came back and slapped Jimmie Ray on the back of his head, knocking the pompadour sideways. '*Emplate!*'

Jimmie said, 'Hey!'

Milt Rossier spit at the weeds, then headed for the near building. 'Y'all c'mon. Bring'm, LeRoy. René! You, too, now.'

We followed Rossier between the two buildings and out to a small circular pond surrounded by a low wire fence. LeRoy picked up a two-by-four as we walked. The banks of the pond were muddy and scummed with something green and slimy, probably runoff from the processing sheds. Rossier got there first and waited impatiently for the rest of us to catch up. He gestured at the pond with his cigar. 'René. You get Luther. Be careful, now.'

I said, 'Luther?'

Jimmie Ray shook his finger at me and laughed. 'Yo' ass is grass now, boy.'

René stepped over the fence, knelt at the edge of the little pool, and slapped the water. He slapped three or four times, and then something moved beneath the surface and the water swirled. René jumped in up to his knees and his hands plunged down and caught something that made him stagger. He found his balance and then his face went red with strain and he lifted out a snapping turtle that had to be three feet across and weigh almost two hundred pounds. It was dark and primordial with a shell like tank armor and a great horned head and a monstrous beak. The head twisted and snapped and tried to reach René, but couldn't. Its mouth was almost a foot across, and every time it snapped there was a sharp clicking sound, like a ruler rapping on a desk. René trudged up out of the water, stepped across the fence, and put Luther down. When he did, the turtle pulled its feet and head up under its shell. The head was so big it didn't fit and its snout was exposed. LeRoy was grinning like a jack-o'-lantern. He waved the two-by-four in front of the turtle. The big head flashed out and the big jaws snapped and the board splintered. LeRoy beamed. 'That Luther's somethin', huh?'

Jimmie Ray shook his finger at me some more. 'We'll see who's lyin' now.'

Milt Rossier said something in French, and René grabbed Jimmie Ray and jerked him toward the turtle. Jimmie Ray said, 'Hey!'

Jimmie Ray tried to pull away from René, but he didn't have any better luck than Luther. René carried him by the back of the neck and the belt, and pushed him down on the ground just outside of Luther's range. You could see the beady turtle eyes following the action from up under the shell. Jimmie was yelling, 'Goddamn, Milt, stop it! Please!' His eyes were big, and he had gone as white as typing paper.

René let go of Jimmie's belt and grabbed his right forearm and forced his right hand toward the turtle. Jimmie Ray screamed.

Milt said, 'Now you tell me true, son. You using my information to blackmail this gal?'

'I swear I ain't, Milt. I swear.'

'René.'

René forced the hand closer. Luther's eyes blinked, and the big jaws parted.

Milt said, 'Try again, son.'

I took a half-step forward. 'That's enough, old man. Make him stop.'

Milt said, 'LeRoy,' and LeRoy pointed the big .45 at me. LeRoy was grinning. Milt shook his finger at me. 'You jes' sit tight.' He stepped closer to Jimmie Ray and squatted beside him. 'Ol' Luther looks like he's anxious, boy. You better tell me.'

Jimmie Ray was babbling. 'I didn't see what it'd hurt. It didn't have nothing to do with you or us and I thought I could just make a little extra cash please Milt please make'm stop I never woulda done it if I thought you'd be mad I swear to Christ!'

'All right, René. He's done.' Jimmie Ray Rebenack had peed his pants.

René lifted Jimmie Ray out of harm's way. The wet stain spread across the seat of his pants and down his legs. Milt chewed on the cigar and stared toward the buildings. His eyes were small and hard and not a great deal different from the turtle's. He moved the cigar at me. 'The only reason you're heah is because of this blackmail thing?'

'That's it.'

Milt chewed on the cigar some more. 'René, put ol' Luther back.'

René put Luther back in the pond. Luther slipped beneath the water, and the water grew still. Milt said, 'We feed ol' Luther there catfish heads. Had a fella from LSU out here once said Luther might be better'n a century old.'

Jimmie Ray was on his knees with his face in his hands. I felt embarrassed and ashamed both for him and for me. Milt Rossier went over to Jimmie and patted his shoulder. 'You see what dishonesty gets fo' ya? You go behin' my back, now this fella's heah. You see where ya get?'

'I'm sorry, Milt. I swear to God I am.'

Milt Rossier looked over at me with the Luther eyes. He stared at me, thinking, until LeRoy said, 'He was with some woman, Milt.'

Milt spit. 'Yeah. I guess so.' Disappointed, as if he had come to a serious decision about something, only now to change his mind. He patted Jimmie Ray's shoulder again, then helped him up. 'C'mon, now, Jimmie Ray. Get up and stop blubberin'. You get yourself on outta heah.'

Jimmie Ray said, 'I didn't think I was doin' anythin' wrong, Milt. I swear to Christ.'

'We'll jus' forget about it. Go on, now.'

Jimmie Ray looked like a man who'd just won Lotto, like he couldn't believe that Milt Rossier was giving him a pass on this one. Milt Rossier said, 'Goddammit, get outta my sight.'

Jimmie Ray scrambled back to his Mustang, and the Mustang's rear end fishtailed hard as he drove away.

Milt shook his head, then turned back to me. 'You go on back where you come from and tell your woman everythin's over with. What we got down here, it don' have nothin' to do with her, and nothin' to do with you, either. You understand that?'

'Sure. You want me to go home. You want me to stop stirring things up.'

He nodded, looked at the cigar again, then tossed it in the pond. It floated for a second, sending out perfect circles, and then the water exploded and the cigar was gone.

Milt Rossier made a little dismissive gesture and walked away. 'LeRoy, you see this fella gets back real safe, you hear?'

LeRoy said that he would.

René and LeRoy brought me back to the motel in the gold Polara and let me out in the parking lot. I watched them leave, then went to my room and tried to let myself in, but I couldn't get the key in the lock. I tried as hard as I could, and then I sat on the sidewalk with my hands between my knees and pressed my knees together to try to make myself stop shaking. I pressed for a very long time, and finally the shaking stopped.

12

I double-locked the door and showered, letting the hot water beat into me until my skin was red and burning and I began to feel better about things.

I was out of the shower and getting dressed when Lucy Chenier returned my call. She said, 'Sorry it's taken so long. I was trying to find out about Milt Rossier.'

'I just came back from Milt's. Before that, I broke into Jimmie Ray Rebenack's home and found what I believe to be the entire state file on Jodi's adoption. I found other things, too, and I learned some things at Rossier's that we need to talk about.' Maybe there was something in my voice that the shower hadn't washed away. She didn't say anything about the break-in.

'Can you drive back to Baton Rouge this evening?'

'Yes.'

'I have to leave the office soon to be home for Ben, but you could meet me there and we could have dinner. Is that all right?'

'That would be fine.'

Lucy gave me directions to her home and then we hung up. I dressed, then got the papers together from under the mattress, and drove back to Baton Rouge. I brought flowers.

The late afternoon was clear and bright when I found my way through a gracious residential area east of Louisiana State University to Lucy's home. The streets were narrow, but the houses were large and set back on wide rolling lawns amid lush azaleas and oaks and magnolia trees, worthy digs for doctors and lawyers and tenured professors from LSU. I slowed several times for families on bicycles and young couples with strollers or elderly people enjoying a walk. Two girls and their dad were on one lawn, trying to launch a blue kite with no breeze; on another, an elderly man sat on a glider, gently swaying in the evening shade beneath an oak tree. Everything seemed relaxed and wonderful, the ideal environment in which to escape the realities of lying clients, enraged snapping turtles, and the loneliness of being far from home. Maybe I should move here.

Lucy Chenier lived in a brick colonial with a circular rock drive and a large pecan tree in the front yard. A knotted rope hung from the tree and, higher in the branches, several boards were nailed together into a small platform. Somebody's treehouse.

I crunched into the drive, got out with the flowers and the documents, and went to the front door. When I had stopped for the flowers I had picked up a folder in which to hide the documents. Can't very well be seen sneaking stolen documents into an attorney's home. Might get her disbarred. The door opened before I reached it and a boy with curly brown hair looked out. He said, 'Hey.'

'Hey. My name's Elvis. Are you Ben?' He was looking at the flowers.

'Yes, sir. My mom's on the phone, but she says you can come in.'

'Thanks.'

He opened the door wider and let me in. He was still with the flowers. Suspicious. 'Are those for my mom?'

'Unh-hunh. Think she'll like 'm?'

Shrug. 'I dunno.' Can't give stray guys too much encouragement, I guess.

From somewhere in the house Lucy called, 'I'm on with the office. I'll be off in a minute.'

I called back, 'Take your time.'

Ben stood straight and tall in cut-off jeans shorts and a gray LSU Athletic Department T-shirt. Every kid in Louisiana was probably issued an LSU T-shirt at birth. He led me through a spacious home that was neat and orderly, but still lived-in and comfortable and clearly feminine, with plenty of photographs in delicate frames and pastel colors and plants. The entry led into the family room and the kitchen. Everything was open and casual, with the family room flowing into the dining area, which looked out through French doors across a brick patio and a large backyard. Tennis trophies filled the shelves of a wall-sized entertainment center in the family room, but pictures of Ben and books and ceramic animals were crowding out the trophies. I liked that. Balance.

Ben leaned against the counter that separated the kitchen from the family room, watching me. I said, 'You play tennis like your mom?'

He nodded.

'She's pretty good, huh?'

He nodded again.

'Can you beat her?'

'Sometimes.' He cocked his head a little bit to the side and said, 'Are you a detective?'

'Doesn't it show?'

He shook his head.

'I left my trench coat at the motel.'

'What's a trench coat?'

278

Times change.

He said, 'Is it fun?'

'Most of the time it's fun, but not always. You thinking about becoming a detective?'

He shook his head. 'I want to be a lawyer like my dad.'

I nodded. 'That'd be good.'

'He practices corporate law in Shreveport. He really goes for the jugular.' I wondered where he'd heard that.

Lucy came through the family room and smiled at me. 'Hi.'

'Hi, yourself.' I held out the flowers. Mr Charming. 'I didn't want to come empty-handed.'

'Oh, they're lovely.' Her eyes crinkled nicely when she took the flowers, and I flushed with a kind of pleasure that made me return her smile. She was wearing khaki hiking shorts and a loose white cotton top and sandals, and she seemed relaxed and comfortable in her home. Looking at her made me feel relaxed, too. 'Let's put them in water.'

Ben said, 'Can I set the coals?'

'Not too many.'

Ben ran out the back, slamming through the French doors. Someone had set up a Weber grill on the patio, and he went to work with the coals. Lucy said, 'I picked up potato salad and coleslaw from the market. I thought we'd grill hamburgers since we're going to work. Something simple.'

'Hamburgers are great.'

'Would you like a glass of wine?'

'Please. That would be nice.'

She took an unopened bottle of Sonoma-Cutre chardonnay from her refrigerator, offered it to me with a corkscrew, and asked if I'd mind opening it. She put out two wineglasses, then used kitchen shears to trim the flowers before placing them in a simple glass vase. I poured the wine. When the flowers were finished, she said, 'They're absolutely lovely.'

'Drab. Drab and plain next to you.'

She laughed. 'Tell me, do all men from Los Angeles come on this strong?'

'Only those of us with an absolute confidence in our abilities.'

The laugh became a smile, then she put on the red reading glasses and motioned at the folder, jammed with the documents and handwritten notes and phone bills. 'Why don't you tell me what happened while I see what we have?'

I went through everything that had happened since I'd last seen her, up to where René and LeRoy brought me to Milt's farm. I had arranged the papers with the state documents on top, so she saw those first. As I spoke, a vertical frown line appeared between her eyebrows and she no longer

279

looked happy and relaxed. She said, 'These are real. These are court-sealed documents. How could he get these?'

'I don't know.'

'Illegally possessing these is a felony under state law. They're numbered and referenced, and I can have their authenticity checked, but these are real. These papers do in fact show that Jodi Taylor was born Marla Johnson. I can't believe he has these.'

'Had.'

Ben came in to tell us that the coals were ready to be fired and Lucy went outside to make sure he did it safely. I sat at the counter with my wine, watching them, and found myself smiling. Ben struck the big safety matches and tossed them on the coals while Lucy supervised. They looked comfortable and at ease with each other, and you could see Lucy in his features and in the confident way he carried himself. Reflections. When the flames were rising and the grill was in place, Lucy returned and smiled at me smiling at her. She said, 'What?'

'You guys look good together. Happy. I like that.'

She turned and looked at her son. He had left the grill and was climbing into a pecan tree. A knotted rope hung from the limbs, just like the tree in the front yard, but he didn't use the rope. She said, 'You seem to have passed the test.'

'What test?'

'He's leaving us alone. He's very protective of me.'

'Does he have to guard you often?'

She looked smug. 'Often enough, thank you.' She took two plates from the Sub-Zero, one with hamburger patties and the other with sliced onions and tomatoes and lettuce, both covered with Saran Wrap, and put them out to warm. She returned to the file, now skimming Rebenack's handwritten notes. 'Who's Leon Williams?'

'I don't know, but you can tell from what's written that these are the notes Rebenack made when he was digging into Jodi's past, so Williams might be significant.'

Lucy made a note on the legal pad. 'I've got a friend at the Baton Rouge Police Department. I'll see if they have anything.'

'Okay. Here's where it gets worse.' I showed her Jimmie Ray's phone bills. I pointed out the long-distance calls. 'Do you recognize these phone numbers?'

She shook her head. 'They're calls to Los Angeles.'

'This is Sid. This is Jodi. Rebenack had at least seven conversations with Sid Markowitz over the past five months.'

Lucy didn't move for a very long time, and then she left the kitchen. She came back a few minutes later with a leather date-book jammed with notes and papers and business cards. She opened it to a phone index and compared the numbers she found there with the numbers on the phone bill. She shook her head. 'Sid never mentioned this to me.'

'Nor to me.' I pointed out the longest call. 'Three days after this call Rebenack deposited thirty thousand dollars into a checking account. He used the money to buy a car.'

'Do you think he's blackmailing them?'

'He admitted it.' I told her about Jimmie Ray and Milt and Luther.

'But blackmail doesn't make sense. Jodi's never kept her adoption a secret, and even if she had, so what? What could he blackmail them with?'

I spread my hands. 'I guess that's what we still have to figure out, and it doesn't end with Jimmie Ray Rebenack. Milt has something going on, too, and I'm also guessing that it involves the Boudreauxs. That's why the sheriff was out at the crawfish farm. That's why the Boudreauxs are scared.'

Lucy brought her address book to the kitchen phone and stabbed in a number. She puffed out her cheeks and blew a hiss of breath while she waited. 'This is Lucille Chenier calling for Mr Markowitz. May I speak with him please?' She walked with the phone in a small circle. 'You must have him call me as soon as possible. It's urgent. Let me give you my home number.' She left the number, then hung up and went through it again with Jodi Taylor. No luck there, either.

I said, 'I phoned them too. They haven't gotten back to me.'

She shook her head. 'I can't believe they didn't tell us. We've got an Evangeline Parish sheriff involved with a convicted felon and possible blackmail, and no one tells us. Were we hired to uncover information that was already known?'

'Looks that way.'

She took off her glasses, rubbed at her eyes, then assembled the papers and put them aside. 'Enough work, Mr Cole. More wine.'

She held out her glass, and I poured.

When the coals were ready we brought out the burgers and put them on the grill. They hissed nicely, and soon the silky twilight air was filled with the smell of cooking meat. She had mixed ground sirloin with Worcestershire sauce, and it smelled wonderful. Somewhere a dog barked, and cicadas were making their buzz-saw racket. Ben was still in the tree, hanging upside-down. Lucy called, 'Ben, it won't be long. Wash your hands.'

Ben dropped out of the tree, but didn't go in. 'Can I have a cheeseburger?'

Lucy nodded. 'Sure. Elvis?'

'You bet.'

She handed me the spatula and went in for the cheese. When she was gone I looked at Ben and caught him grinning at me. I said, 'What?'

'She likes you.'

'She does?'

He nodded. 'I heard her talking to her friend, Marsha. She called you Studly Do-Right.' He giggled.

I looked in at his mother and then I looked back at the hamburgers. 'She probably wouldn't like it that you told me.'

'Why not?'

'Women tell other women things that they don't tell men. It's a law they have.'

He giggled some more.

Lucy came back and put cheese on the hamburgers, then covered the grill so that the cheese would melt. Ben and I stood with straight faces until Ben couldn't stand it anymore and giggled. I concentrated on the burgers, hoping that they wouldn't overcook. Ben giggled harder. Lucy said, 'What?'

I said, 'Nothing.' Ben giggled harder.

Lucy smiled. 'Hey! What were you guys saying?'

Ben giggled louder and I looked at Lucy. 'Studly?'

Lucy turned a deep rich red. '*Ben!*'

Ben howled. I said, 'It wasn't Ben. I am Elvis Cole, the World's Greatest Detective. I know all and see all, and there can be no secrets from the All-Seeing Eye.'

Lucy said, 'I hate you both.'

Ben put out his hand and I gave him a low-five. Masculine superiority strikes again.

Lucy said, 'Benjamin. *Wash.*'

Ben ran into the house, cackling, and Lucy shook her head. 'That little traitor.'

I said, 'Studly.'

She waved the spatula at me. 'I was just being cute. Don't get any ideas.'

'I won't.'

'Fine.'

'But what do I do with the ones I've got?'

She closed her eyes, maybe envisioning the line we shouldn't cross. 'You're really quite something, aren't you?'

'Most people think so.'

She opened her eyes and looked at the sky. 'Oh, God.'

'Well, no. But close.'

Lucy laughed, and I laughed, too.

When the cheese was melted we brought the burgers inside and ate them with the potato salad and coleslaw and the rest of the Sonoma-Cutre. Ben ate quickly, then asked to be excused and raced to the TV so that he could watch *Star Trek – The Next Generation*. Lucy called after him, 'Not too loud!'

I said, 'Won't bother me. I like *Star Trek*.'

Ben yelled, 'Cool!'

Lucy shook her head and rolled her eyes. 'Oh, Studly.' She tilted her glass toward me. 'Pour.'

So we watched *TNG*. It was the one where you follow the android, Data, through a twenty-four-hour period in his life, most of which is spent attempting to comprehend the vagaries of the humans around him. The fun comes in watching the logical, emotionless Data try to make sense of the human condition, which is akin to trying to make sense of the senseless. He never quite gets it, but he always keeps trying, writing endless programs for his android brain, trying to make the calculus of human behavior add up. When you think about it, that is not so different from what I do.

When *Star Trek* was over I said that I had better be going. I told Ben good night, and Lucy walked me out. I thought that she'd stop at the door, but she didn't. It was a clear night, and pleasant. She said, 'Will you drive back to Ville Platte tonight?'

'Yes. There are still plenty of questions and Jimmie Ray might be willing to answer them.'

She nodded. 'Okay. I'll call you there tomorrow as soon as I have something.'

'Great.' A man and a woman and an Akita walked past. The Akita was a big brindle pinto, and watched me suspiciously as his people nodded hello. I said, 'Good-looking dog.'

The man said, 'Thanks.'

Lucy and I stood silently until they were gone, vanishing gently in the humid dark.

We looked at each other. 'This is the second time you've fed me. Thanks again.'

'It's an ugly job, but somebody's gotta do it.'

We both grinned. I said, 'Oh, man. Dueling comedians.'

She looked at me carefully and said, 'I have a good time with you.'

I nodded. 'Me, too.'

Then she said, 'Oh, damn.' She leaned forward, kissed me, then pulled away. 'I've just kissed a man who ate dog. Yuck.'

She ran back into her house.

I guess there are lines, but sometimes lines bend.

13

The night canopy above the Atchafalaya Basin was velvet black as I drove through the sugarcane and the sweet potato fields and the living earth back to Ville Platte. A woman I had known for approximately four days had given me what was maybe the world's shortest kiss, and I could not stop smiling about it. A lawyer, no less.

I folded up the grin and put it away and rolled down the window and breathed. Come to your senses, Cole. The air was warm and rich and alive with the smells of water and loam soil and blossoming plants. The sky was a cascade of stars. I started singing. I stopped singing and glanced in the mirror. Smiling, again. I let the smile stay and drove on. To hell with senses.

When I got back to Ville Platte there was a message from Jimmie Ray on the motel's voice-mail system, his voice tight and sounding scared. 'This is Jimmie Ray Rebenack and you really put me in a world of hurt, podnuh.' You could hear him breathing into the phone. The breathing was strained. 'It's twenty after six right now, and I need to talk to ya. I'm at home.' He said the number and hung up.

It was now ten fifty-two, and there were no other messages in the voice mail.

I dialed his number and got a busy signal. I took off my shirt, then went into the bathroom to brush my teeth and wash my face. I dialed his number again and again got a busy signal. I dialed his office, got his answering machine, and hung up without leaving a message. I redialed his home. Busy. I called the operator. 'I need an emergency break-in.'

'Number, please?'

I gave her the number. She went away for a little bit and then she came back. 'I'm sorry, sir, but that number seems to be off the hook.'

'He's not on the line?'

'No, sir. The phone's probably just off the hook. It happens all the time.'

I put my shirt back on and drove once more to Jimmie Ray's house. A couple of houses on his street were still bright with life, but most of the

284

street was dark and still. Jimmie Ray's Mustang was parked at the curb in a dapple of moonshadows, and the front upstairs window of his duplex was lighted. The bedroom. Probably with a woman. They had probably been thrashing around and had knocked the phone out of its cradle. I left my car on the street, went to his front door, and rang the bell. I could hear the buzzer go off inside, but that was it. No giggles. No people scrambling for their clothes. I rang the bell twice more, then went around the side of the house and let myself in through the back exactly as I had twelve hours ago.

The ground floor was dark, and the kitchen still smelled of fried food, but now there was a sharp, ugly smell beneath it. I moved across the kitchen and stood in the darkness, listening. Light from the upstairs filtered down the stairwell and put a faint yellow glow in Jimmie Ray Rebenack's bachelor-pad living room. I said, 'Oh, Jimmie. You goof.'

The imitation zebra-skin couch was tipped over on its back and Jimmie Ray Rebenack was lying across it, head down and arms out, Joey Buttafucco boots pointing toward the ceiling. The living-room phone had been knocked off its hook when the couch went over. I took out the Dan Wesson, held it along my thigh, and went past Jimmie Ray to the stairs and listened again. Nothing. I went back to Jimmie Ray and looked without touching him. His neck was bent at a profound and unnatural angle, as if the vertebrae there had been separated by some tremendous force. His neck didn't get that way by tripping over the couch or by falling down the stairs. It took a car wreck to do that to a neck. Or a four-story fall. His face was dark with lividity, and the big, stiff pompadour was crushed and matted on one side, the way it might be if someone with large hands had grabbed his head and pushed very hard to make the neck fail. René.

I went upstairs and looked in the two rooms, but everything was pretty much as it had been twelve hours ago, the magazines and posters still in their places in the back room, the bed still rumpled in the front room. The pants he had worn at Rossier's crawfish farm were soaking in the upstairs lavatory. Getting out the pee stains. The front bedroom's light was on, and the room showed no evidence of a search or other invasion. No one had come to search. No one had come to steal. Whoever had been here had come only to murder Jimmie Ray Rebenack, and they had probably done it not so very long after he'd called me. Maybe Jimmie Ray had finally realized that he was in over his head and had called for help. That was possible. A lot of things are possible until you're dead.

The message counter on Jimmie Ray's answering machine showed three messages. The first was a young woman who did not identify herself and who said that she missed Jimmie Ray and wanted to speak with him. The second message was from a guy named Phil who wanted to know if Jimmie Ray would like to pick up a couple of days' mechanic work. Phil left a number and said he needed to hear by Friday. The third message was the young woman again, only this time she sounded irritated. She said she thought that Jimmie Ray was rotten for not calling her, but then her voice softened and said she really did wish he'd call because she really, really missed him. She whispered, 'I love you, Jimmie,' and then she hung up. There were no other messages. So long, Jimmie Ray.

I left the upstairs light on and the rooms as I'd found them and Jimmie Ray Rebenack's body in its frozen position across the overturned couch. I wiped the kitchen doorknob and the places on the jamb I might have touched, and then I let myself out and went around to the front porch and wiped the doorbell button. I called the police from a pay phone outside a Winn-Dixie supermarket. I gave them Jimmie Ray's address twice, then said that there was a body on the premises. I hung up, wiped the phone, and went back to the motel where I called Lucy Chenier. Two hours ago I'd been feeling pretty good about things.

Lucy answered on the second ring, her voice clear the way it might be if she were awake and working. I said, 'Rebenack's been murdered.'

'Oh, Jesus God. How?'

'I think it was Rossier, but I can't be sure. I think he paid off Jimmie for the double-dealing.'

She blew a loud breath. 'Did you call the police?'

'Yes, but I didn't identify myself.'

'They'll want to speak with you.'

'If I talk with them I'll bring in Jodi Taylor, and I don't want to do that. Do you see?'

She said, 'Oh, my God.'

'Do you see?'

It took her a few seconds to answer. 'I understand. What are you going to do?'

'Wait for you to find out about Leon Williams.'

She paused again. 'Are you all right, Elvis?'

'Sure.'

'You sound upset.'

'I'm fine.'

'If you want to talk, I'm here.'

'I know. Call me when you find out about Leon Williams.'

We hung up, and in that moment my little motel room there in Ville Platte, Louisiana, became more empty than any room I have ever known. There were the sounds of crickets and frogs and the rumble of a passing truck, but the sounds seemed to heighten the emptiness rather than fill it. The cheap motel furniture stood out in a kind of stark clarity, as if everything were magnified through some great invisible lens, and the emptiness became oppressive.

I turned off the light and went out into the parking lot and breathed the warm air. I had come two thousand miles believing that I had been hired to uncover a woman's medical history, and now a man was dead. He was a goof and an extortionist, but somewhere near his final moment a young woman had called and said that she loved him. I wondered if he had played back the message. Jimmie Ray Rebenack was just the kind of guy who would have missed the message, or, if he'd heard it, wouldn't have listened. Guys like Jimmie Ray never quite learn that love doesn't visit often, and that even when it comes, it can always change its mind and walk away. You never know.

I went back inside and double-locked the door and wedged one of the flimsy motel chairs under the knob. The locks and the chair wouldn't keep out a guy like René, but there was always the Dan Wesson.

I lay on the bed and tried to sleep, but sleep, like love, is not always there when you want it.

14

The phone in my room rang at 9:14 the next morning as I stepped out of the shower. I had been up early, eating breakfast at the diner across from what used to be Jimmie Ray's office and waiting for the morning paper. A couple of police cars had been outside the fish market, but when the paper came there was nothing in it about Jimmie Ray's murder. Not enough lead time, I guess. When I answered the phone, Lucy Chenier said, 'I spoke with my friend at BRPD.'

'Could he identify Leon Williams?' I toweled off as I listened.

'Yes. Leon Williams was killed by a single gunshot to the head on 12 May, thirty-six years ago, in Ville Platte.'

'Sonofagun.'

'There was an investigation by the Ville Platte police and the Evangeline Parish Sheriff's Department, but there were no suspects and no one was arrested for the crime. The case currently resides in the unsolved homicide file.'

'My first move in Ville Platte was to scan through the microfiche at the local library. The May films were missing.'

'Do you think it's connected?'

'Maybe. Maybe there's something in the local news coverage that someone didn't want us to see.'

She didn't say anything for a time. 'There's LSU. The School of Journalism keeps an extensive library of state papers. You might be able to find it there.'

'That sounds good. I'll check it out.'

She paused again. 'Have you heard anything about Mr Rebenack?'

I told her about the cops at his office and the local papers. I left out the part about wedging the chair against the door because I was scared.

She said, 'Is there any way they can connect you to him?'

'I move with the silence of a stalking leopard. I leave less evidence than a passing shadow. I am invisible as is the breeze.'

She sighed. 'Yes, well, we have an able staff of criminal attorneys should you need us.'

'Hey, the fragile male ego needs constant reinforcement, not cheap humor.'

'My rates are anything but cheap, Mr Cole, I assure you.' Then she said, 'I enjoyed myself last night, Elvis. I hope we can get together again.'

'I could probably be there in thirty minutes. Faster, if I run down the highway naked.'

She laughed. 'That would probably be worth seeing, but I think you should concentrate on Leon Williams.'

' "Probably"?'

'Ah, the male ego is indeed a fragile beast.'

Lucy hung up. I got the LSU School of Journalism's number from Information, called, and spoke with a woman who sounded to be in her fifties. I explained what I wanted and she told me that she'd have to connect me with the journalism library. A man came on the line. 'May I help you?'

'I'm looking for the Ville Platte *Gazette*.' I told him the year and the month. 'Would you guys have that on microfiche?'

'Can you hold while I check?'

'Sure.'

He came back on the line maybe thirty seconds later. Fast checker. 'We have it. Would you like me to put it aside?'

'Please.' I gave him my name and told him that I was coming from Ville Platte but that I would be there directly. He said fine. Maybe things were looking up. Maybe I was getting to the bottom of this and, once reaching the bottom, would bounce over the top. Of course, reaching the bottom can sometimes be painful, but we try not to think of that. Imagine an egg.

One hour and ten minutes later I drove through a wide gate that said Louisiana State University. A young guy in an information kiosk gave me a map of the university, pointed out the journalism building, then told me to park in a big lot by the football stadium. I left the car where he told me, then walked back between Tiger Stadium and the basketball arena where Pistol Pete Maravich used to rack up forty-four points a game. The House that Pete Built. It was a pretty campus with green lawns and curved walkways, and I remembered once hearing the radio broadcast of an LSU basketball game in which Maravich scored fifty-five points against Alabama. It was in 1970, and I was in the army at Fort Benning, Georgia. Ranger School. A guy in my platoon named James Munster was from Alabama and loved basketball. His parents had recorded the game and sent it to him and six of us listened to the tape on a Saturday night. Jimmy Munster loved the Crimson Tide and he hated LSU, but could only shake his head at the miracle that was Pistol Pete Maravich, saying, 'What can you do? That guy owns the basket. What can you do?' Seven months later Specialist Fourth Class James Munster died in a VC ambush while on a long-range reconnaissance patrol just south of the Cambodian highlands. He was eighteen years old. I still remember the score of that game. LSU 90, Alabama 83.

A clutch of coeds in biking shorts and T-shirts cut so that you could see their midriffs passed and smiled at me, and I smiled back. Southern belles. A little sign saying TENNIS STADIUM pointed past the arena, and I thought maybe it'd be fun to see where Lucy had played, but then I thought it might be more fun if she were with me to give me the tour. Have to ignore the coeds, though.

I walked up a little hill and past a couple of stately buildings and into Memorial Hall, also known as the School of Journalism. The kid in the kiosk had told me that the journalism library was in the basement, so I found the stairs, went down, and wandered around for twenty minutes before I located the right door. Professional detection at its finest.

A bald guy in his early thirties was sitting with a placard that said RESEARCH. He looked up from a textbook and said, 'May I help you?'

I told him that I had called a little while ago. I told him it was about the Ville Platte *Gazette.*

He said, 'Oh, yeah. I've got it right here.' He had a little box on his desk. 'You a student?'

'Nope.'

'I'll need your driver's license, and I'll need you to sign right here. You can use any of the cubicles down that aisle.'

I gave him my driver's license, signed where he wanted, then took the single spool of microfiche film to the first cubicle and threaded it into the projector. On 13 May, there was a short article on page 6 stating that a male Negro named Leon Cassius Williams, age 14, had been found floating at the south bank of Bayou Maurapaus by two kids fishing for mudcats. Sheriff Andrus Duplasus stated that the cause of death was a single .38 caliber gunshot wound to the head, and that there were no leads at present. The article ended by saying that Leon Cassius Williams was the son of Mr and Mrs Robert T. Williams, of Ville Platte, and that services were scheduled at the African Methodist Episcopal Zion Church. The entire article was four inches long, and set between an ad for Carter's Little Liver Pills and an article about a guy who'd caught an eight-pound large-mouthed bass in Bayou Nezpique.

On 17 May, another short article appeared on page 4, this one reporting that Leon Cassius Williams, 14, found murdered the week before, had been laid to rest. An obituary included within the article said that Leon was survived by his mother and father and three siblings, all of whom were listed, along with their ages. I copied the list. Sheriff Duplasus was quoted as saying that there were no new developments in the case. The last article relating to Leon Williams appeared on page 16 of the 28 May paper. Sheriff Duplasus reported that investigations within the Negro community had led him to believe that Leon Williams was murdered by a Negro transient seen earlier that day, and that the murder very likely resulted from a dispute over a gambling debt. Duplasus said that he was continuing to compile evidence, and had issued a description to state police authorities, but that the chances for an arrest were minimal. None of Leon Williams's survivors were referred to except for a single quote from Mrs Robert T. Williams, who said, 'I feel like they robbed my heart. I pray the good Lord watches after my baby.'

When I reached the end of the film I turned off the projector and thought about what I had found. Leon Williams, a fourteen-year-old African-American male, had been murdered, and the murder was unsolved. Nothing in the articles indicated a connection to the Johnson family, or to any other principal in my investigation. I had thought there might be, but there you go. *Nada*. Jimmie Ray Rebenack was very likely the guy who had stolen the May microfiche film from the Ville Platte Library. I didn't know that, and I hadn't found it at his home, but it made sense. Jimmie Ray had found some significance in Leon and had made note of him. Since Jimmie Ray had done all right with the other stuff, further investigation was in order.

I brought the film back to the bald guy, then went to a bank of pay phones at the side of the building. There were three names on the list of Leon Williams's siblings: Lawrence, 17; Robert, Jr, 15; and Chantel Louise, 10. Thirty-six years later, Lawrence would be fifty-two and Chantel Louise forty-six. Chantel Louise would very likely have a different last name. I called Ville Platte Information and asked for numbers and addresses for Lawrence Williams and Robert Williams, Jr. There was no listing for a Robert Williams, Jr, but they had Lawrence. I copied his number and address, thanked the operator, then dialed Lawrence Williams. On the third ring, a woman with a precise voice answered. I said, 'May I speak with Mr Lawrence Williams, please?'

There was a pause, and then she said, 'I'm sorry, but Mr Williams is deceased. May I help you?' Deceased.

'Is this Mrs Williams?'

'Yes, I am Mrs Lawrence Williams. Who is calling, please?'

I told her my name. 'Mrs Williams, did your husband have a younger brother named Leon?'

'Why, yes. Yes, he did. Leon died, though, when they were boys. He was murdered.' Maybe this was going to work out after all.

'That's why I'm calling, Mrs Williams. I'm a private investigator, and I'm looking into the murder. Did Mr Williams speak about it with you?'

'Mr Williams did not. I'm afraid I can't help you.'

'There was another brother and a sister.'

'Robert, Jr, died in 1968. Over in that war.'

'How about the sister? Do you know how I might reach her?'

Her voice became crisp. 'She's working right now. She works for a Jew in that damned sausage factory, and you shouldn't be calling her there. When you call, that Jew answers the phone and he doesn't like that. You'll get her in trouble.'

'Please, Mrs Williams. It's important.'

'Feeding her five children is important, too. That job is all she has, working for a Jew.' Oh, man.

'I promise I won't get her in trouble, Mrs Williams.' Like a kid, *cross my heart and hope to die.*

'How do I know you're who you say you are? You might be up to no good. I assure you that I am not to be trifled with.'

'There's an attorney in Baton Rouge named Lucille Chenier. I can give you her number and you could call her office and speak with her about me.'

That seemed to mollify her. 'Well, perhaps that won't be necessary. I take pride in knowing a sincere voice.'

'Yes, ma'am.'

'Chantel lives right over here in Blue Point. She has lunch soon. Why don't you see her at lunch. Her name is Chantel Michot now, and she always goes home for lunch. She has to put dinner on for those little ones.'

I looked at my watch. 'That's fine, Mrs Williams. I'm coming from Baton Rouge.' It was a quarter before eleven. I could get there by twelve-thirty.

'Well, then, I guess this must be important, all the way from Baton Rouge.'

'Yes, ma'am, it is.'

'We'll be expecting you.' We.

'Yes, ma'am, I'm sure you will.'

I copied the directions as she gave them, and then I went to see Chantel Michot, Leon Williams's younger sister.

15

Blue Point, Louisiana, was a wide spot in the road five miles south of Ville Platte at the tip of Bayou des Cannes. You had to go to Ville Platte first, then take a little state road that wound its way over narrow steel bridges and sluggish channels of water and sweet potato fields. It was rural country, with a lot of barbed-wire fences and great live oaks bearded with Spanish moss, and the air was heavy with pollen and bees and moisture.

Chantel Michot lived in a clapboard shotgun house at the edge of the road that backed upon a wide green pasture. The pasture was fenced and the fence ran behind her house as if a little square had been cut from the owner's pasture so that the Michot family might live there. The house looked old and poorly kept, with peeling paint and a green shingle roof that was missing tiles and a wooden front porch that was cracked and splintered. There was a screen door like every other house in Louisiana, but the screen was cruddy and stretched, and little wads of pink Kleenex had been stuck into holes to keep out the mosquitoes. Martha Guidry would have a field day. Tire ruts ran down from the road past the house and the rusted chassis of a very old Dodge and across the pasture. Maybe a dozen chickens pecked in the dirt around the chassis. Yard birds. A late-sixties Bel Air sedan was parked beneath an elm tree, and a newer Pontiac Sunbird was parked behind the Bel Air. I pulled in behind the Sunbird and got out. The engines of both the Bel Air and the Sunbird were still ticking. Couldn't have gotten here more than ten minutes ago.

The screen door opened and a little boy maybe four years old came out and looked at me from the lip of the porch. He was barefoot in shorts, with a little round belly and a runny nose and an ocher complexion. Hair more curly than nappy. His left index finger was stuffed up his nose to the first joint. I said, 'My name's Elvis. What's yours?'

He pushed the finger in deeper and didn't answer. I often have that effect on people.

The door opened again and a light-skinned woman in her forties came out, followed by an older, heavier woman with skin the color of burnished walnuts. The younger woman was wearing a thin cotton smock over faded Bermuda shorts and open-toed sandals. Her hair was piled on her head and held there with a broad purple band. It wasn't particularly neat, but she didn't have it like that for style; she had it like that for work. Keep the hair out of the sausage. The older woman was in a light green rayon suit with a little white hat and white gloves and a crocheted purse the size of a grocery bag. All dressed up to meet the detective. The older woman said, 'I am Mrs Lawrence Williams. Are you Mr. Cole?'

'Yes, ma'am. I appreciate you and Ms Michot agreeing to see me.'

Chantel Michot said, 'I got to see about these children and I got to get back.' Not exactly thrilled to meet the detective. She was holding a filter-tipped cigarette and kept one arm crossed beneath her breasts. I offered her a card, but Mrs Lawrence Williams took it. 'Ada say this about Leon.' Ada was Mrs Williams.

'That's right. I know you were only ten when he was killed, but I thought we might speak about it.'

'Why?'

'I'm working on something and Leon's name came up, and I don't know why. Maybe you can help me with the reason.'

Chantel Michot sucked on the cigarette and blew smoke. Trying to figure me. There were children's voices behind her in the house, and another little boy came to the door, this one maybe five. He pressed against the screen and looked out. She said, 'Anthony, get on in there and eat that lunch.' Anthony disappeared. 'Ada, would you make Lewis sit at that table, please?'

The little boy with his finger up his nose said, 'No.'

Mrs Lawrence Williams pulled the big purse in closer and raised her eyebrows. Not liking the idea of being inside with the children and left out of all the great stuff on the porch. 'Well, if I must.' Snooty. She took Lewis by the arm and brought him inside. Lewis yelled bah bah bah bah as loud as he could.

I said, 'They never caught Leon's killer. No arrest was made.'

'You the police?'

'No.'

'All these years, you gonna find the guy done it?'

'That's not what I'm after.'

'But maybe?' All these years, she was still hopeful.

'I don't know, Chantel. I found Leon's name in a place it doesn't fit and I want to find out why it was there. I don't want to lead you on. I know you've got to get back to work.'

'Least you ain't lyin' about it.' She stared at me a minute, motionless, a thin trail of smoke drifting from her cigarette, barely moving in the still air, and then she made up her mind. 'You want some lemonade? I put some up this morning.'

I smiled at her and she smiled back. 'That'd be fine. Thanks. If you've got the time.'

'I got a few minutes.'

We sat in the shade of the little porch on a sofa that was covered with crocheted bedspreads. Mrs Lawrence Williams came to the door every few minutes, still pissed about being inside, always with the big purse. She probably had something in there in case I decided to trifle with them. 'This is good lemonade.'

'I put honey in with the sugar. That's clover honey. A man down the bayou keeps a hive.'

I said, 'The newspaper reports said that the sheriff believed that Leon was killed by a transient over a gambling dispute.'

'Leon was fourteen. What he know about gamblin'?'

'What'd your parents think?'

'Said it was silly. Said it was just the sheriff's way of shinin' us on. A black man gets killed, they don' care.'

'Did your parents have an idea of what happened?'

She squinted out at the road. Trying to remember. A truck pulling a natural-gas tank rumbled past and made the thin glass in the windows rattle. 'Lord, it's been so long. Daddy died in seventy-two. Mama went, oh, I guess it was eighty-one, now.'

'How about Lawrence or Robert, Jr? Did they ever say anything?'

She thought harder. 'Lawrence didn't really have nothin' to do with Leon, but Leon and Junior were close. I remember Junior sayin' somethin' 'bout some gal. I guess there coulda been some gal mixed up in there.'

'Like maybe Leon got killed over a girl?'

'Well. I guess.' Chantel pulled deep on the cigarette, then flicked the butt out into the yard. A skinny Rhode Island Red hen picked it up, ran a few feet, then dropped it, squawking. The other chickens circled it, cocking their heads for a better look, then ignored it. Chantel said, 'The gals did flock around Leon, let me tell you. He was a beautiful boy, and, my, he could talk. Charmin'? I was just a baby and I remember that. Robert used to get *jealous*! Oo!' She crossed her arms and leaned forward on her knees, enjoying the memories. 'You know, I haven't thought about that in years. Here it is, sometimes I can't even remember Leon's face, but I remember that.'

Mrs Williams came to the door, still with the big purse, still with the pissy expression. 'You don't have time for all this, now, girl. You have to get back to work.'

Chantel nodded without looking.

'You late, that Jew'll get after you.'

Chantel closed her eyes. '*Ada!*'

'Well, he's a Jew, isn't he?'

295

'Ada. Please.'

Mrs Williams harumphed and stalked back into the house. Chantel Michot said, 'That woman is such a trial.'

I said, 'Think about Leon. Maybe you'll remember something else.'

She stood up. 'I may have something. You wait here.' She went into the house and came back a few minutes later with a King Edward cigar box and sat with it on her knees. 'This is mostly Robert's things, but there's some stuff from Leon in here, too. Lord, I haven't looked in here in years.'

She opened the box and stared down at the contents, as if the letters and snapshots and papers within were treasures awaiting discovery. 'You see Leon? Here's Leon right here. That's Lawrence and that's Junior and that's Daddy.'

She handed me a yellowed Kodak snapshot with a little date marker on the white border: 1956. An older man was standing in front of an enormous Chevrolet roadster with three boys. Mr. Williams and his sons. Lawrence and Junior and Leon. They were light-skinned men with delicate features. Leon was the smallest, with large expressive eyes and long lashes and an athlete's carriage. He would have been twelve. She said, 'We had some good-looking men in this family, but that Leon, he was plain pretty.'

'He's handsome, all right.'

She fingered through handwritten notes and birthday cards and a couple of elementary school report cards and tiny black-and-white snapshots of older black men and women, all neatly dressed and stiffly formal. 'My momma gave me these things. She said these were the little bits of us that she held dear. This is me. This is Robert and Lawrence. Oh, my God, look how young.' She smiled broadly and the smile made her seem younger and quite pretty, as if for a moment she was free of the weight of the five children and the crummy job at the sausage factory. 'Robert was killed in the army,' she said. 'He died in that Tet thing.' That Tet thing.

'Uh-huh.'

She lifted out a white government envelope, its edge ragged from being torn, now yellow and flat from the years in the box. *We regret to inform you . . .* There were spots on the envelope. I wondered if they were tears. 'They gave him a medal. I wonder where it is.'

I shook my head.

Mrs Williams reappeared at the door. 'You are going to be *late* now.'

'I am busy, Ada.' Sharp.

Ada shook her finger at me. 'You are going to get her in trouble with that Jew.'

'*Ada!*'

Mrs Williams stalked away.

296

She said, 'Oh, here's some of Leon's things.' She lifted out two brown newspaper clippings, the originals to the articles I'd read on the LSU microfiche, brittle and brown and very likely untouched since the day her mother had cut them from the Ville Platte *Gazette* and put them in the King Edward box. She took out more bits of paper and photographs and passed them to me. Leon sitting on a tractor that looked a million years old. Leon and a swaybacked mule. There were a couple of Mother's Day cards drawn in a child's hand and signed 'Leon', and a poem he had written. She handed me things as she found them, and she was still fingering through the box when I opened a piece of yellowed notebook paper filled with the doodles you make when you're bored in class. Most of the page was class notes about the Louisiana Purchase, but in the borders there were finely detailed pencil drawings of Sherman tanks and World War II fighter planes and the initials EJ EJ EJ. LW + EJ.

I was wondering about EJ when I saw a little heart at the bottom right-hand corner of the page. The kind kids draw when they have a crush on someone. And that's when I knew about EJ, and all the rest of it, too.

Inside the heart Leon Williams had printed I LOVE EDIE JOHNSON. Edie Johnson. Edie Boudreaux.

Edith Boudreaux wasn't Jodi Taylor's sister. She was Jodi Taylor's mother. And Jodi's father was Leon Williams.

16

I folded the paper and handed it back to her and twice she spoke and both times I had to ask her to repeat herself. *I love Edie Johnson.* When we had gone through the rest of the things, she said, 'Does any of this help?'

'Yes. I believe it does.'

She nodded, pleased that her effort was of value. 'You wanna take any of these things, you may.'

I smiled. 'No. These are your precious things. Keep them safe.'

She put the papers back in the King Edward box and closed it. 'I wonder if they'll ever catch that man who killed Leon.'

'I don't know.'

'It's been so long now. I can't imagine anyone would care.'

I patted her hand and then I stood. 'Somebody cares, Chantel. Somebody somewhere cares. I've always believed that.'

She gave me a nice smile and we finished our lemonade and then I left. I followed the back roads north to Ville Platte, checked out of the motel there, then stopped by the Pig Stand and bought a link of *boudin* for the road. I told Dottie that my business here was finished, and that this would be our last time together. She laughed and told me that I'd be back. She touched the place beneath her eye as she had done before and said she had the second sight. I wished that she would have used it earlier. Jimmie Ray might still be alive.

I ate the *boudin* as I drove back to Baton Rouge and listened to the same female radio evangelist screaming about plague-carriers from abroad and once more crossed the big Huey Long Bridge and arrived back at the Riverfront Ho-Jo at 1:40 that afternoon.

I didn't bother trying to call Sid Markowitz or Jodi Taylor. I booked the first available flight back to Los Angeles, checked out, then phoned Lucy Chenier's office from the lobby. Darlene said that Lucy was in and asked if I wished to speak with her, but I said no, that I was at the Riverfront and would walk over. Ten minutes later I rode the elevator to the Sonnier, Melancon, & Burke offices. Lucy's smile was wide and bright, and she seemed glad to see me. Something ached in my chest when I looked at her, and the ache increased when I took her hand. I said, 'I think I've come to the end of the line on this and there are some things we need to talk about. I'm going back to Los Angeles.'

She stopped smiling, and said, 'Oh.'

We sat on the flower-print couch and I showed her the copies I'd made of the articles reporting Leon Williams's murder, and as she read them I told her about Mrs Lawrence Williams and Leon's sister, Chantel Michot, and the little heart that said *I LOVE EDIE JOHNSON*. She finished reading before I finished talking, then sat quietly, watching me with sharp lawyer eyes until I was done with it. 'Jodi told me none of this.'

'I didn't think that she had.'

'And you believe she knew all of this? She knew that Leon Williams was her father.'

'I think that's how Jimmie Ray bought his Mustang. I think he went to them with the documentation, and they paid to have him sit on it.'

She placed both hands in her lap, one atop the other, then stood and went to the window, and then she came back around her desk and leaned against the front of it. 'This is silly. It's the nineties. What does she think will happen?'

I shrugged.

She waved her hand. Adamant. 'It isn't even compelling evidence. "Edie Johnson" is hardly an uncommon name. The possibility of coincidence is large.'

'Maybe she didn't see it that way.'

She shook her head again. 'But why hire us to find out something she already knew? Why lie to us about it? She had to believe that we'd find out.'

'I'm going to ask her.'

Lucy pursed her lips and stared at the floor. She took a breath, let it out, then looked up at me. 'So you're going back.'

'I don't think I was hired to learn anything about her medical history. They knew Jimmie Ray was blackmailing them, so they didn't hire me to uncover his identity. I think she just wanted to know if it was real.'

Lucy sighed again and stared out the window. Maybe she, too, was looking for Huck and Jim.

'Also, I don't like being lied to. I like it less because the lying may have had something to do with getting Jimmie Ray Rebenack killed.'

Lucy came over and sat beside me. 'I know you're angry, but may I offer something?'

'Always.'

'Adopted people often wonder at their histories, but there are more obvious traits by which we define ourselves. How tall we are. The color of our hair. I want you to consider that the entirety of Jodi Taylor's identity has been called into question. Not just her name, but what she sees when she looks in the mirror.' Lucy's face was softer now, and I wondered if she were putting herself in Jodi Taylor's place. 'She has a career and friends, and she is probably wondering if everyone in her life will see her differently. Do you understand?'

'You're making it hard to stay mad.'

She smiled, but it was sad. 'Mad is always easier, isn't it?'

I nodded. 'Are you going to call them?'

'Of course. I don't like being lied to, either, and if my employment is at an end, then we have to terminate the file.'

Termination. There didn't seem to be a whole lot left to say. 'I guess that's it.'

'I guess so.'

I nodded at her. 'I'm glad we had a chance to meet.'

She nodded back. 'Yes. I am, too.'

We stared at each other. The Lawyer and the Big Time Op, not knowing what to say. She stood and I stood with her. 'Well. I hope we stay in touch.'

'Christmas. We can do cards.'

'That would be nice.'

'I write very funny cards.'

'I'm sure you do.'

We stood like that for a time, and then she put out her hand and I took it. 'Tell Ben I said 'bye.'

'I will.'

'I'll see you, Lucy.'

'Good-bye, Elvis.'

Lucy went back to her desk and I rode the elevator down to my rental car, and four hours and twelve minutes later I was descending through the haze into midafternoon Los Angeles.

It was ten minutes after three, L.A. time, and I was home. There had been no significant earthquakes in my absence, and the temperature was a balmy eighty-four, the humidity twenty-nine percent, winds out of the northwest. Home. The freeways were jammed, the smog was a rusty shade of orange, and Lucy Chenier was two thousand miles away. On the other hand, we didn't have hundred-year-old snapping turtles and mutant Cajuns. Also, I wasn't very likely to get anyone else murdered in the foreseeable future. If I could keep myself from strangling Sid Markowitz, I might even be able to drink enough beer to stop seeing Jimmie Ray Rebenack's body. That's the great thing about L.A. – anything's possible. Portrait of the detective looking on the bright side of life.

I phoned Sid Markowitz's office from the terminal. His secretary said, 'I'm sorry, but Mr Markowitz is unavailable.'

'This is Elvis Cole. Do you know that I'm working for him?'

'Yes, sir. I do.'

'It's important that I speak with him.'

'I'll give him the message when he checks in, Mr Cole. He's at the studio now, with Ms Taylor.'

I hung up and dialed Jodi Taylor's number on the General-Everett lot. A man's voice answered. 'Ms Taylor's office.'

'This is Elvis Cole. Is Ms Taylor or Mr Markowitz available?'

'Oh, hi, Mr Cole. Jodi's on the set, now. May I take a message and have her get back to you?'

'Nope.'

I rode the escalator down to baggage claim where a representative of the airline informed me that my bag had been misrouted to Kansas. They said that they would be very happy to deliver it to my home upon its recovery, and they smiled when they said it. I said fine. I caught the airport shuttle to long-term parking to pick up my car. The shuttle bus was jammed with Shriners from Orange County, and I had to stand. No problemo. A fat guy with breath like a urinal stood in front of me. Every time the shuttle hit a bump he lost his balance and stepped on my toes. Every time he stepped on my toes he would excuse himself and burp into my face. Sour. We were on the shuttle bus for twenty-two minutes, and most of that time I was trying not to breathe. Looking on the bright side. When I got to my car, the top had been slashed and my CD player stolen. A Blaupunkt. I tried to file a report, but the parking attendant didn't speak English. Hey, that's L.A. It took forty-five minutes to get out of the airport and onto the freeway, only to find that the freeway was gridlocked. A bald guy in a deuce-and-a-half truck cut me off in a sprint to the exit ramp. He called me an asshole, but he was probably having a bad day. At the bottom of the ramp he squeaked through on the yellow, but I got caught by the red. No big deal. Look at the bright side. A homeless woman wearing a garbage bag spritzed oil on my windshield and told me Jesus was coming. She said that in the meantime she'd be happy to clean my windshield for a dime. I paid her, and said that if Jesus didn't get here soon I was going to stop looking on the bright side and kill somebody. Welcome home.

I sat at the light and thought about Christmas.

At Christmas, I could send Lucy Chenier a card.

17

Songbird kept its standing sets on Stage 12 at the rear of General-Everett
Studios. I parked at a Shell station across from the front gate, called a
friend of mine on the lot, and had them send down a pass.

Much of the time when you walk along the back streets of a movie
studio, you see Martians and Confederate soldiers and vehicles of strange
design and other magical things. I have visited the different studios
maybe a hundred times, and I have never grown tired of that little-boy
surprise at seeing the strange and unexpected. But not this time. This
time, the magic had been put away and the walk to Stage 12 seemed
somehow oppressive and unwelcome.

The little streets around Stage 12 were alive with activity. Big eighteen-
wheelers were wedged against the soundstage walls, belly to butt with
costume trailers and makeup trailers and a honeywagon. Econoline vans
and station wagons were parked between the larger vehicles, all of which
had little cards with the *Songbird* logo displayed in the windshields. Burly
men wearing ball caps sat in the station wagons reading newspapers or
Dean Koontz novels. Teamsters. Sid Markowitz's Jaguar XJS convertible
was parked behind a full-sized motor home near a door in the side of the
soundstage with a red light over it. The red light was on, and a couple of
people who looked like grips were watching it. I walked up like I had
business there, and we stared at the light together. When the light went
out, a loud buzzer rang inside the soundstage and we went in. I followed
the two guys along a stream of heavy electrical cables between false walls
and through dark sets: Jodi Taylor's bedroom in the series, her family's
kitchen, the big bedroom where all four of her tiny blond children lived.
Welcome to Oz, the Land of Make Believe where the nation's favorite
family drama comes to life.

I came out at the roadhouse set where Jodi Taylor sang every week in
Songbird, chasing her character's dream of becoming a star. Maybe forty
people were setting up for a shot: the camera crew positioning the camera
on its dolly and gaffers rigging lights and stand-ins and extras waiting for
their call to the set. A woman in an L.A. Raiders cap and baggy bush

pants was with Jodi and the actor who played Jodi's husband, framing a shot with her hands. She would be the director. A guy with a walkie-talkie and a guy with long gray hair were watching, the guy with the hair suggesting something every once in a while and whispering to the camera crew. The guy with the hair would be the director of photography. Sid Markowitz was talking to a woman in a business suit by a coffee machine in the shadows to the side of the set. I went over and said, 'Hi, Sid.'

Sid Markowitz's face turned the color of fresh clams. 'It's you.'

I held up two fingers. 'Two words, Sid. Leon Williams.'

The fresh clam color went fishbelly white and Sid Markowitz pulled me away from the woman in the business suit. 'Jesus Christ, keep your voice down. Whattaya doin' here, f'Christ's sake? All this is confidential.'

'That was before I found out you lied to me, Sid.'

I stepped away from him into Jodi Taylor's line of sight and crooked my finger at her. She looked at me as if she wasn't quite sure who I was, and then she recognized me and her face shut down into a grim chalk mask. Now you're smiling, now you're not. Sid hurried up behind me and took my arm again. 'C'mon, Cole, don't make a scene here, okay?'

I said, 'If you don't stop touching me, I'm going to break off your hand and stuff it up your ass.'

Jodi Taylor left the woman in the Raiders cap and came up to me as if we were the only two people in the soundstage, as if everyone else were only shadows flickering on the wall, cast by a tree through an unseen window. She said, 'Leon Williams is my father, isn't he?'

'Yes.'

Sid Markowitz had Jodi by the arm, now, trying to move her away from me. 'Jesus, would the two of you keep it down? Let's go outside.' Then he was back with me again. 'We had our reasons for not coming clean, all right? What's the big deal?'

'Jimmie Ray Rebenack is dead. A human being died, and now it's time to tell the truth because I have to decide what to tell the police.'

Neither Jodi Taylor nor Sid Markowitz said anything for several heartbeats, and then Sid Markowitz said, 'I'm gonna call Bel, kid. Bel needs to know.' Beldon Stone was the president of General-Everett Television.

I said, 'Other people know about this?'

'About *this*, but not about you. We hired you without telling anybody.'

We went out to the motor home, Jodi moving as if she were numb and Sid Markowitz fluttering like a moth around a Bug-Zapper. The motor home was the full-size luxury model, with a bedroom and a bath and a kitchenette with a dining table. Last week's Nielsen ratings had been push-pinned to a little corkboard in the kitchenette, along with a couple of clippings from the *Hollywood Reporter* and *Daily Variety*: HIT

SERIES!!, SONGBIRD SCORES AGAIN!. A teamster was sitting in the driver's seat, listening to the afternoon race report and reading the paper. Sid said, 'Eddie, we need a little privacy here, okay?'

The teamster left without a word. Jodi Taylor curled up on the motor home's couch, and folded her hands in her lap while Sid went to the phone. Jodi looked small and frightened.

A few minutes later a studio limo double-parked next to the motor home, and two men in suits and a woman in a short skirt got out. One of the men was in his fifties, and the other was in his thirties. The woman was in her twenties, but she looked older. Sid Markowitz saw them and said, 'Oh, Christ, Beldon's gonna be pissed.' He shook his head and chewed at his lip and went into the Bug-Zapper routine again. 'I told you, Jodi. Didn't I tell you?'

Jodi pulled herself tighter and nodded without looking at him. On TV, Jodi Taylor was strong and resilient and exuded confidence. But that was TV, and this was real. I guess they don't put you on the cover of *People* for being real.

They came into the motor home without knocking, Beldon Stone first and his two assistants in trail. Beldon Stone had a great hawk nose and tiny eyes, and he looked like he wanted to swoop down and eat someone. Sid plastered on a big smile and said, 'Hey! Bel!' and offered his hand, but Beldon Stone ignored him. Stone looked first at me, then at Jodi, and then at Sid, and you could tell that he read it before the first word was spoken. 'Well,' he said, 'it seems someone else is in on our little secret.'

Jodi said, 'I'm sorry, Bel.' A voice like a child.

I said, 'Okay, Markowitz, the gang's all here. Knock off the bullshit and tell me what's going on.'

Beldon Stone said, 'Yes, Sid.' His voice was resonant and smooth and filled with authority. 'Tell us how this gentleman comes to know our secret.' He said it to Sid Markowitz but his eyes never left me, as if I were a potential adversary and might attack him.

Sid identified me as a private investigator who had been recommended by Peter Alan Nelsen. He used Peter's name at least six times in the telling, as if that might take the edge off. He said, 'Jodi couldn't just let it hang there, Bel. She had to know if all this stuff Rebenack was saying was true. You can understand that, can't you? She hired this guy to find out if it was true.'

Everything was Jodi, even the business about not telling me the whole story. Putting the blame on her. When Markowitz was finished weaseling to Beldon Stone, he looked back at me. 'Rebenack was threatening to sell the stuff to the tabloids. Hey, all the guy wanted was thirty grand and thirty grand's nothing to keep the lid on something like this, so we paid him. Everybody agreed.' He glanced at Beldon Stone like he expected Stone to chime in with how much he agreed, but Stone was silent.

Markowitz said, 'I don't see what you're so pissed about, Cole. We were paying this guy, and we wanted to find out if what he had was really real.' Really real. 'We didn't wanna stir the water, so we didn't hip you to the whole deal. So sue us. We wanted you to go into this with a fresh eye. That makes sense, doesn't it? We wanted to see if you'd get to the same place as the goof with the hair. If he had bupkis, you didn't need to know. If it was emmis, then you'd confirm it and we'd know it's real. Okay, it's real. We know what we wanted to know and you got paid. Whattaya makin' a case for?'

'The goof with the hair was found murdered two days ago. He was probably murdered because I was in something that I should've known about but didn't.'

Sid Markowitz rolled his eyes. 'Oh, a fuckin' blackmailer was murdered! What a loss!'

I grabbed Sid Markowitz and pushed him against the table and the woman in the short skirt made *ee-ee* noises and the younger guy tripped over himself trying to get out of the way. Markowitz tried to back away from me, but there was no place to go. 'Lemme go! Lemme go! There's witnesses here!'

Everything seemed to slow and grow silent. My eyes felt large and dry, and my shoulders felt swollen. The woman in the short skirt kept making the noises, and I pressed Markowitz back into the table, but once he was there I didn't know what to do with him, as if he was suddenly beside the point. Jodi Taylor said, 'I'm sorry we lied to you. I didn't know what else to do and I'm sorry.'

I let go of Markowitz and stepped away from him. I was breathing hard and blinking, but my eyes still felt dry. I said, 'Maybe it hasn't dawned, genius, but when an extortionist turns up dead, they always suspect the extortee.'

Markowitz said, 'Hey, we didn't even know!'

Beldon Stone had not moved. I guess people at his level grab each other all the time. He said, 'The gentleman who was extorting Ms Taylor is dead?'

'Yes.'

'And his documents?'

'I have them.'

He nodded. 'And what do you want?'

'I don't know.' My head began to ache, and that made me even more angry. I thought I had known why I was coming back, but now I didn't. Maybe I was expecting to find some great evil, but instead there was only a frightened woman and the greedy men around her.

Beldon Stone settled onto the couch beside Jodi Taylor and patted her leg. Reassuring. Fatherly. He reached into his jacket and came out with a slender cigar, looked at it for a moment, then ran it beneath his nose. He neither put it in his mouth nor lit it, but the smell seemed to comfort him. 'I realize you're upset, Mr Cole, but would you do me the courtesy of telling me if Mr Rebenack's assertions were correct?'

'Yes.'

'And how do you know this?'

I blinked at him.

He made a small gesture with the cigar. 'You were paid for your services, were you not?'

Sid Markowitz said, 'Goddamn right he was. Three grand.'

Stone made the gesture again. 'Then please tell these people what you found.'

I didn't give them all of it, but I gave them enough. I told them about finding the woman whom I believed to be Jodi Taylor's birth mother, and I told them about Leon Williams. As I told it, Jodi Taylor watched me as if she were peering out from a cave. When I finished, she said, 'You found my birth mother?'

'Yes.'

Stone patted her knee again. He was larger and older, and his touch cut her off. He said, 'And no one else knows these things, or suspects?'

'The man responsible for Rebenack's death probably knows, but he's not interested in Jodi Taylor. He probably killed Rebenack because this business with the blackmail put some other crime he's got going in jeopardy.'

Jodi Taylor peered out from the cave again. 'Crime involving my birth mother?'

Beldon Stone patted her knee again, again cutting her off. *There, there, little girl.* 'The important thing is that the information is contained.' As if he couldn't care less what Jodi Taylor was feeling or what she wanted to know.

I said, 'Are you people crazy? Who cares if Leon Williams was Jodi Taylor's father?'

Beldon Stone looked at me with great empathy. 'Well, certainly none of us, Mr Cole. But perhaps not everyone is as generous as we.'

The younger guy said, '*Songbird*'s a solid hit. We're looking at a five-year run and a potential back-end profit exceeding two hundred million dollars.'

Sid Markowitz nodded. 'Fuckin' A.'

Stone said, 'Jodi Taylor has been given a gift that many dream of but few are granted. She's a star.' He patted her knee again, and she stared at the floor. 'Our audience sees her every week, mother to four adorable blond children, wife to a blond Nordic husband. Would that audience accept a person of color in the role?'

'Jesus Christ, Stone.'

'Our series has built its popularity on traditional family values. Our advertisers pay for that popularity and expect us to protect it. We have enemies, Mr Cole. Every left-wing, ultraliberal reviewer and special interest group has taken shots at this series since the beginning. They make fun of us. They criticize us. They condemn us for portraying a white, middle-class nuclear family in a fragmented multicultural world. Wouldn't they love to learn that our star is not only part African-American, but illegitimate?'

Jodi Taylor sat with her head down, as if she were shrinking away from what he was saying, as if she could just make herself small enough the words would pass by and be gone and her life would continue on its way.

Stone said, 'I regret that you were brought into this matter, Mr Cole, but considering the way things have worked out, I think some sort of bonus is in order.'

'I didn't come sucking around for a payoff.'

Stone raised an eyebrow. 'No?'

'I have information pertaining to a homicide, and by withholding that information I am violating the law. I don't like that.'

Sid Markowitz said, 'Jesus Christ, Cole, I'm sorry Rebenack died and I'm sorry you feel bad about it. You want an apology? I apologize. The guy was puttin' it to us, all right? He was trying to ruin Jodi Taylor. Who'd Jodi Taylor ever hurt? Huh? Answer me that?'

'Tuck in your shirt, Markowitz. Your ten percent is showing.'

Beldon Stone smiled the fatherly smile at me. 'It seems that everyone is sorry, Mr Cole. I am certainly sorry that you were brought into this, and I am also sorry that a man has died, even a man such as Mr Rebenack.'

'Sure.'

He patted Jodi again. 'But now it appears the ball is in your court. If you wish to go to the police, I suppose you can do that.' The pat again. 'We didn't want Jodi hurt.' Leaving it on me, saying do what you do and bring it down on Jodi Taylor. Elvis Cole, Bad Guy. My head was splitting, and it felt like a couple of steel rods had been jammed into my neck.

I said, 'Fuck you.'

Beldon Stone smiled and stood. It was over, and he knew it. I knew it, too. He paused at the door to the motor home and fixed the hawk eyes on Sid Markowitz. The warm, fatherly expression was gone. 'I'm disappointed that you went behind my back, Sid. We'll have to speak about this again.'

Sid Markowitz looked as if he'd just received a positive biopsy. 'You gotta understand, Bel. Hey, we hadda know.'

Beldon Stone stayed with the killer eyes another moment, and then he left, the younger guy and even younger woman after him.

It was quiet in the motor home except for the air conditioner and the generator and the sound of Jodi Taylor crying. They were small sounds, pained and somehow distant.

Sid Markowitz brightened, coming up with the big idea. 'Hey, how 'bout that bonus? You came through. You're playin' it straight. We'll give you a fat bonus. You deserve it.'

I said, 'Sid?'

'Yeah, a bonus. We'll treat ya right. Whaddaya say?'

I shook my head and then I walked out. If I had stayed any longer, I was afraid that I'd kill him.

18

It was twenty minutes after six when I left the General-Everett lot, picked up my car from the Shell station, and drove to the Lucky Market on Sunset. The traffic was heavy, with plenty of horn-blowing and fist-shaking, but I drove without a sense of personal involvement, as if I were somehow apart from the world around me. I parked in the Lucky's lot, went inside, and selected two baking potatoes, green onions, a very nice Porterhouse steak, and three six-packs of Falstaff beer. Nothing like a well-balanced meal after a hard day at the office.

I pushed my cart to the registers and stood in line behind an overweight woman with a cart filled with Dr Pepper, chicken parts, and jumbo family packs of Frosted Flakes and Cocoa Puffs. The Cocoa Puffs were open, and the woman was eating them dry. She would reach into the box and pluck out a handful and put them into her mouth and then repeat the process. The woman stared blankly into a huge display of Purina Dog Chow, and the process seemed without conscious thought or direction. Automatic eating. A little girl maybe two years old stood in the cart surrounded by the Frosted Flakes and the Cocoa Puffs, bouncing up and down and going *ga-ga-ga-ga*. The overweight woman ignored her. Maybe that's what I needed to do. Ignore what went on around me. Maybe I could become Elvis Cole, Zen Detective, and let the ugly realities of life flow around me without effect, like water passing over a stone. *A client hires you under false pretenses? No problem! Withholding evidence from the police during a homicide investigation? No big deal! A guy gets zapped because you shoot off your mouth? Those are the breaks!* The road to inner peace through Cocoa Puffs was sounding pretty good. Of course, you probably had to eat Cocoa Puffs to achieve this state of grace, and I didn't know if I was up to that.

When I got closer to the cashier there was a little four-pocket *TV Guide* rack above the Certs and the chewing gum, and Jodi Taylor was staring at me from the covers. She was sitting on one of the *Songbird* kitchen stools, surrounded by the guy who played her husband and the four kids who played her children, and everyone was smiling. The slug line on the top of the picture said 'America's Favorite Family'. Funny. I had just left Jodi Taylor, and she had looked small and frightened and nauseous. Amazing how pictures lie, isn't it? The overweight woman was already gone, else I would've asked to try the Cocoa Puffs.

I drove home and let myself into the kitchen. It was just before eight and the house was quiet. I opened a Falstaff, put the others in the refrigerator, and left the meat and the potatoes and the onions on the counter. I brought my suitcase upstairs, put the dirty things in the hamper and the clean things away, and then I changed out of the travel and client clothes and into something more suitable for a gentleman of leisure: sweatpants and a Bull-winkle T-shirt. No maiden to save, no dragon to slay, no client to serve. There would also be no money coming in, but what's that to a tough guy like me? Maybe Pike and I would go river kayaking in Colorado. Maybe we'd run with the bulls in Pamplona. Why not? When you're between jobs, you can do things like that.

Halfway through the sorting and changing I discovered that most of the Falstaff was gone. Leaky can. I went back downstairs, opened another Falstaff, then got KLSX on the radio for Jim Ladd, the best disc jockey in the universe. Jim was playing George Thorogood. What could be better than that? I went out onto the deck and stoked the Weber. The sun was down and the air was cool and smelling of mint and honeysuckle. George finished, and Jim put on Mick Jagger singing about his lack of satisfaction. I layered mesquite charcoal into the kettle, splashed on the starter fluid (EPA approved), and fired up. The flames rose tall and orange and a wave of heat rolled over me, and in that moment of warmth I wondered what Lucy Chenier was doing. I had more of the Falstaff and thought that it might be pretty nice if Lucy were out here on the deck with me. Maybe we'd spent the day at Disneyland, and now we were back and feeling good about it. We'd be a little bit sunburned and a little bit tired, but Lucy would be smiling. She'd stand at the rail and think the view was fine, only she'd find the desert nights chilly and I'd put my arms around her to ward off the cold. I had the rest of the Falstaff. Funny. Thought I'd just opened the can.

I washed the potatoes, slit the tops, and wrapped them in foil. I put them in the oven at five hundred degrees. They were small and wouldn't take long. I took the steak out of its package, stabbed it with a fork a zillion times on each side, then sprinkled it with pepper and garlic powder and soy sauce. I washed the green onions, chopped them, then mixed them with a container of non-fat yogurt. Everything was ready to cook. Your basic fast meal. Of course, since I was unemployed, fast wasn't a requirement. A nine-course Julia Child extravaganza would have been appropriate. Goose in aspic, perhaps. Or oyster-stuffed quail in chili poblano sauce. Maybe Pike and I should head down to Cabo San Lucas and go after billfish. Our friend Ellen Lang might like to go. So might my friend Cindy, the beauty-supplies distributor. I opened another Falstaff.

The cat came in while I was thinking about it, and hopped up onto the counter the way he does when he's hoping I won't notice. You could see his nostrils working, smelling the steak. I said, 'Bet you missed me, huh?'

He made a little cat nod.

I carved a piece of steak, then put the cat and the steak on the floor. He sniffed once, then went to work on the meat. I said, 'I missed you.'

I was sitting on my kitchen floor, drinking beer and petting the cat when the doorbell rang, and there was Jodi Taylor. She was wearing a gray sweatshirt over jeans, and no makeup. Her hands were in her pockets, and she looked closed and pensive, not unlike she had in the motor home. Awkward. I said, 'Well, well. The TV star.' It was only my fourth beer, wasn't it?

She said, 'I hope you don't mind.'

'Why should I mind? It beats getting lied to.' Maybe my fifth. I held up a hand, shook my head, and stepped back. 'Forgive me for saying that. I'm feeling sorry for myself, and I've been drinking. It's a boy thing.'

She nodded.

'Please come in.' I showed her in, only moderately embarrassed by the Falstaff and the Bullwinkle shirt. 'Have you eaten?'

She kept her hands in her pockets. 'I'm not hungry. I feel bad about what happened and I wanted to talk about it.'

'Okay. I was just about to put a steak on the grill. Do you mind talking while I eat?'

She said of course not and followed me to the kitchen. 'Oh. You have a cat.'

The cat looked up from his piece of steak, lowered his ears, and growled. 'Don't try to pet him. He doesn't care for people and he bites.'

She moved away. The cat stopped growling and went back to work on the meat. I said, 'Would you care for a drink?'

'That might be nice. Do you have Scotch?'

'I do.' I put ice in a short glass, then dug around for the Knockando.

'Do you live here alone?'

'Yep. Except for this cat.'

'You're not married?'

'No.'

She looked around at my home. 'This is very nice.' Like she wanted to talk but didn't know how to begin.

I held out the glass and she took her hands from her pockets to accept it. I went back into the kitchen, opened the oven, and squeezed the potatoes. They were soft. I put them on a wooden trivet on the counter, then removed the little bowl of yogurt and green onions from the fridge. I brought the steak and the steak tongs outside to the grill. Jodi Taylor watched me do these things and followed me out onto the deck without speaking. Her face was creased and intent and I hoped that she wasn't thinking me a drunk. She said, 'I love the way barbecues smell. Don't you?'

She held the glass with both hands, and I saw that the glass was already empty. Nope. She wouldn't be thinking me a drunk. I brought out the bottle of Knockando, refreshed her drink, then put the bottle on the deck rail. 'Your mission this evening, Ms Taylor, is the care and handling of this bottle. You are to replenish your drink at your discretion without asking for my permission or awaiting my action in same. Is this clear?'

She giggled. 'I can do that.'

I smiled back at her. 'Fine.'

I put the steak on the grill. The coals were a fierce, uniform red, and the meat seared nicely with a smell not unlike the hamburgers we'd cooked at Lucy Chenier's. *Put her out of your head, Elvis.*

Jodi said, 'I'm sorry about what happened.'

'Forget it.'

'I want to apologize.'

'Accepted, but forget it. It's over. It's time to move on.' Would Lucy like Cabo? *Stop that!*

The canyon was quiet except for a couple of coyotes beyond the ridge. Below us, a single car eased along the road, its headlights sweeping a path in the darkness. The sky was clear and black, and the summer triangle was prominent. Jodi said, 'This isn't easy for me.'

I turned the steak and prodded it with the tongs so the fat would flame on the coals.

'My dad died in 1985. My mom died two years after that. They were everything to me.'

'Uh-huh.'

'I know who my mom and dad were. My dad was Steve Taylor. My mom was Cecilia Taylor. Do you see?'

'Yes.'

'I loved them more than anything. I still do.'

Something dark flicked by overhead. An owl gliding along the ridge. Jodi Taylor had more of the Scotch and stared at the flames licking the meat. 'There are things about Louisiana I want to ask.' Her voice was soft, and her eyes never left the flames.

'All right.'

'Do I look like her?' We both knew who she meant. Jodi sighed when she said it, as if, in the saying, she had started down a path she had long avoided.

'Yes. You could be sisters.'

'And my birth father is dead?' Her eyes never left the flames, never once looked at me, as if, by refusing human connection, the questions were unreal and of no more substance than those questions you speak to yourself in the moments before sleep.

'Yes. I spoke with his younger sister.'

'My aunt.'

I nodded.

'Do I look like her?'

'No.' The steak was done but Jodi Taylor seemed poised upon some internal precipice between painful things, and I didn't want to upset her balance.

'But you saw a picture of my birth father?'

'You don't look like him. Your birth father's family is light-skinned, with fine features, but you look like your birth mother.'

I flipped the steak again. 'Are you sure you want to hear these things?' In the restaurant she had said no; in the restaurant she had been adamant.

Jodi Taylor blinked hard several times and had more of the Scotch. The cat crept out onto the deck and sat downwind, barely visible in the dark. Watching. I often consider, *Does he wonder at the human heart?* Jodi said, 'I feel like I'm being pulled apart. I feel guilty and ashamed, as if I'm betraying my mom and dad. I never so much as thought of my birth parents, and now I feel that if I can't find some peace with this it's going to get larger and larger until it's all that I am and I won't be me anymore. Do you understand that?'

I took the steak off the grill. I put it on a plate and stood in the night, looking at her.

She said, 'I didn't want to pay that man. I said it doesn't matter. I said no one will care about these things.' Her eyes were filling again.

'But Beldon and Sid convinced you.'

She nodded.

'They frightened you, and they made you ashamed.'

She blinked harder. 'God, I'm scared. I don't know what to do.'

'Sure, you do.'

She looked at me and took more of the Scotch.

I said, 'Why did you come here, Jodi?'

'I've got two days off before we start shooting the next episode. I want to hire you again. I want you to take me down there. I want to see where I come from, and see who I am. Will you do that for me?'

Lucy Chenier.

'Yes.'

She nodded, and neither of us spoke again.

We went inside with the steak. I guess Cabo San Lucas and the billfish would have to wait. The human heart bears greater urgency.

19

Jodi Taylor and I flew to Louisiana the next day, catching the seven A.M. flight through Dallas/Fort Worth and arriving in Baton Rouge just before noon. We rented a gray Ford Thunderbird in my name and drove to Lucy Chenier's office. Jodi wanted to apologize, and I didn't argue. I phoned Lucy's office from the airport and told her assistant that we were on our way. Darlene said, 'I didn't think we'd see you again.'

'Miracles happen.'

Darlene said, 'Unh-hunh.'

Lucy greeted us pleasantly at the door, offering her hand first to me, then Jodi. I was grinning as wide as a collie in a kibble factory, but Lucy seemed cool and somehow distant, and her handshake was professional. 'Hello, Mr Cole. Hello, Ms Taylor. Please come in.' Like that.

We sat, and Lucy told us that Sid had phoned and that they had discussed what had happened and why, and she said that she would certainly be happy to continue assisting Jodi in whatever way possible. She said it to Jodi and did not once look at or speak to me. I said, 'Hi, remember me?'

'Of course. It's nice to see you again.' Professional. Lawyerly. She refocused on Jodi.

Jodi said, 'I knew Sid was going to phone, but I wanted to personally apologize for what happened. I should've been honest with you, and feel ashamed of myself.'

Lucy stood and came around her desk. 'Please don't be. Are you going to introduce yourself to Edith Boudreaux?'

Jodi Taylor shook her head and also stood. It seemed as if we had just arrived. 'I don't want to meet these people, and I don't want to know them. I guess I just want to see them. Can you understand that?'

Lucy took her hand. 'Of course, I can. We all have that curiosity. Seeing her is a way of seeing a part of yourself, even if you have no wish to know her.'

Jodi said, 'Yes. That's it.'

Lucy said, 'If there is any way I can help you, even if you just want to talk, don't hesitate to call.'

'Thank you.'

I told Jodi that I would be along in a moment, and she left. Lucy was standing at the door, still not looking at me. I said, 'Is there something here that I'm missing?'

'I don't think so.'

'Would you join me for dinner tonight?'

'That's very nice, but I can't.'

'We could bring Ben.'

She shook her head.

'Are you angry?'

'Of course not. I think Jodi is waiting for you.'

'You sound angry.'

She raised her eyebrows. 'If Jodi requires my assistance she may call any time. She has the number.'

'I'll tell her. Thank you.'

I walked out of the office, and Jodi and I went down to the car. I got in behind the wheel and she climbed into the passenger seat, neither of us speaking. Jodi sat with her knees up and her hands clasped between her legs, staring out the window. She said, 'What's wrong with you?'

'Nothing. Nothing is wrong with me.'

She frowned at me and then she went back to staring out the window.

We crossed the Mississippi River, and pretty soon Baton Rouge was behind us. We made good time past Erwinville and Livonia and Lottie, and, at 1:36 that afternoon, we neared the exit for Eunice. I said, 'Edith Boudreaux lives here with her husband and her family. She's married to a man named Jo-el Boudreaux. He's the sheriff. She has a dress shop in the center of town. Her father lives here, too. Leon Williams's sister is a woman named Chantel Michot. She lives fourteen miles north of here. You were born in a private home thirty miles north of here, above Ville Platte. What do you want to see first?'

'I want to see the woman.' The woman. You knew she didn't mean Chantel Michot. You knew she meant Edith Boudreaux.

We left the highway, and Jodi put both hands on the dashboard and held herself with an expectancy that was a physical thing within the car.

I brought her to Edith Boudreaux's home first. Edith and her husband lived in a well-kept brick colonial ringed with azaleas bright with flowers and a large, neat yard. The street was quiet and slow; warm, with the smell of fresh-cut St Augustine grass and scores of great black and yellow bumblebees lumbering around the azaleas. A shirtless black teenager pushed a mower along the side of the street, and nodded at us when we passed. I let the Thunderbird slow, and we stopped at the mouth of the drive. Jodi twisted in the seat, eyes wide. Neither the sheriff's highway car nor Edie's Oldsmobile Eighty-eight was present. Jodi said, 'Is that where she lives?'

'Yes. She drives an Oldsmobile, and it's not here. She's not home.'

'She's married to the sheriff?' She already knew that.

'Yes. His name is Jo-el.' She already knew that, too.

'Does she have children?'

'She has three children, all in their twenties. I don't know if any of them live here.'

'What are their names?'

'I don't know.'

'Are they boys or girls?'

'I'm not sure.'

She stared at the house as we spoke, tracing its lines with her eyes as if she was trying to read some truth there. When she had enough of the house we drove first to the small home where Monroe Johnson was waiting to die, and then to Edith Boudreaux's dress shop. Edie's car was neither at her father's nor at the dress shop. Jodi seemed uninterested in the old man, but when we cruised the dress shop she asked me to see if Edie was inside. I parked along in the square and looked in the window but there was only a dark-haired woman I hadn't seen before. I went back to the car. 'What next?'

'The Michot woman.' Jodi was frowning and her eyes were hard.

I said, 'It's almost two. Would you like something to eat?'

'No.'

'Do you need a bathroom?'

'Show me the Michot woman.'

'She works. We won't be able to see her now.' I hadn't eaten since the airplane, and my head was throbbing.

'Then show me where she lives.'

I stopped at a 7-Eleven for two Slim Jims and a bag of peanut M&M's. Lunch. We took the old road north to Point Blue and Chantel Michot's shotgun house. Lewis and Robert were chasing each other around the Dodge, and an older girl was sitting on the porch, very near where I had sat, doing homework. I drove past, found a place in the road to turn around, then came back and pulled off onto the grass across from them. The older girl looked up from her homework and stared at us. I said, 'The little guy's name is Lewis. The other boy is Robert. I don't know the girl. Chantel is Leon Williams's baby sister.'

Jodi Taylor leaned forward in the seat again, eyes wide. 'These are her children?'

'Yes.'

'They're so poor.'

I nodded. The girl had gone back to her homework, but kept glancing up at us, unable to concentrate. A fat Rhode Island Red hen stepped out from beneath the house, pecking at the dirt. The rest of the chickens followed her. Jodi said, 'This is overwhelming. I can't believe this.'

I didn't answer.

'These people are related to me.'

I nodded. Robert ran in a circle around Lewis and Lewis tripped, bumping his head on the Dodge. He landed on his bottom and rubbed at his head, crying. Robert ran back to make sure his little brother was all right. The chickens scratched around them, undisturbed.

Jodi Taylor took a deep breath and let it out. The girl was staring at us again. She put her book aside and came to the edge of the porch and called to the little boys and all three of them went inside. An older boy maybe a year or two younger than the girl came to the door and looked out at us. Jodi said, 'I want to see the woman.' Edith, again.

'It's late, Jodi. We should head back to the city. We can come back tomorrow.'

'I didn't come here to sit in a goddamned hotel. I want to see that woman.' She was out at the edge, now, strung tight and fraying. Cheeks the color of milk.

I looked at her.

'Please.' Her face softened and she took my arm. 'Let's try her shop again. If she's not there, we'll go to the hotel.'

I took her back to Eunice.

We got there just before four, and again I had to get out and look in the window, and again Edith wasn't there. I went back to the car, and got in shaking my head. Jodi said, 'What do you have to do to get a break around here?'

We were just pulling away when Edith Boudreaux's metallic blue Oldsmobile passed us and parked at the curb and Edith got out. Jodi and I saw her at the same time. I said, 'That's her.'

Jodi came erect and stiff in the seat, her face almost to the windshield, both hands on the dash. Her lips parted, and there seemed a kind of electrical field flooding the car. I looked from Jodi Taylor to Edith Boudreaux and back again. Looking at Edith was liking looking at an older, softer version of Jodi.

It took Edith maybe fifteen seconds to move from her car to her shop and then she was gone.

I said, 'Are you okay?'

Jodi stared at the closed door. Her breasts rose and fell, and a pulse hammered in the smooth skin beneath her jaw.

I said, 'Jodi?'

Jodi blinked twice and looked at me, and then she shook her head. She said, 'I was wrong. I can't leave now. I have to go in there.'

20

The sun was high and bright, and the sky was a deep, rich blue, and maybe I hadn't heard her correctly. Maybe she wasn't talking about Edith Boudreaux. Maybe we had taken a wrong turn coming back to town and we weren't even in Eunice, Louisiana, anymore. Maybe we were in Mayberry, and she had seen Aunt Bea slip into this dress shop and she wanted to meet the old gal. Sure. That was it. I said, 'I thought you didn't want to meet her.'

'I've changed my mind.' She didn't look at me when she said it. She was looking past me, at the dress shop, as if Edith might suddenly make a break for it and disappear.

I said, 'Are you sure you want to do this?'

She shook her head.

'The smart thing is to bring in Lucy Chenier. Lucy knows about this.'

Jodi shook her head again. 'I might chicken out.'

'If you're not sure, maybe you should chicken out.'

'Why are you trying to talk me out of this?'

'Because you were adamant about not meeting her. Once you meet her you can't take it back, either for you or for her. I want you to be sure.'

She kept her eyes on the store, drumming her fingers on the dash.

I said, 'At the very least I should go in first and prepare her.'

She said, 'Let's just get this over with.' Jodi pushed out of the car the way you come off the high board, all at once so that you don't give yourself time to reconsider. The way you do when you're not sure you want to go, but you're going to go anyway.

I got out with her and we crossed the street and went into Edith's place of business, me in trail and Jodi ahead, plowing on come hell or high water. Two women in their sixties were browsing through a rack of summer frocks to our right, and the young blond sales clerk was talking with a red-haired woman who was looking at herself in one of those three-sided mirrors in the rear of the place. Edith was standing at the register, frowning at a sales receipt. She looked up when the little bell chimed and smiled automatically, and then she saw me and her smile froze with the abruptness of a stopping heart. Her eyes went to Jodi for a moment, held there, then came back to me. Jodi froze in the center of the store as if she'd been spiked to the floor. Up close is different than out in the car. I said, 'Hi, Mrs Boudreaux. I hope this is a good time.'

She wasn't liking it that I was back. 'Well, it isn't really.' She looked at Jodi again. She knew that this wasn't the same woman who was with me before. Jodi was still in the dark glasses and ball cap, with her hair pulled back and a shapeless cotton top and big dangly earrings and no makeup. She didn't look the way she did on television.

I went to the counter, trying to act as if this was the most mundane visit in the world. 'Mrs Boudreaux, could we speak with you in private?'

She glanced at Jodi again, and this time the look was curious. 'Why?'

'Because we want to discuss something personal, and it's better if we don't do it here.' I kept my voice low, so that only Edith could hear.

She shot another glance at Jodi, and now she looked nervous. 'My husband spoke quite clearly for us the last time. I don't have anything to say and I'd rather you leave.'

Jodi took off the sunglasses. Her eyes hadn't left Edith since we entered, and now Edith was staring back at her.

Edith said, 'You look familiar.'

Jodi opened her mouth to say something, then closed it. She came closer and stood next to me, so close that her shoulder was touching my arm. She didn't look full-steam-ahead now. Now, she looked the way you would look after you leaped off the board, and realized the pool was empty. She said, 'My name is Jodi Taylor.'

Edith seemed confused, then nodded and gave a little smile. 'You're on television. We see you all the time.'

Jodi moved toward Edith Boudreaux. 'Mrs Boudreaux, I believe that you and I are related. State records indicate that I was born to your mother, Pamela Johnson, thirty-six years ago. But I don't believe that. I believe that you gave birth to me. Is that true?'

The color drained from Edith Boudreaux's face, and her lips parted and she said, 'Oh my God.'

The two women in their sixties turned toward us, one of them holding a rust-colored dress that had to be four sizes too small. 'Edie, do you think this works for me?'

Edith didn't hear them. She took a half-step back and then stepped forward again, gripping the Formica counter to steady herself. I smiled at the two women. 'I'm sorry, but Mrs Boudreaux is busy, now.'

The woman with the rust dress made a face and said, 'I don't think anyone asked *you*.'

Edith blinked six or eight times, then said, 'Jill, will you help Maureen, please?' You could barely hear her.

319

The blond clerk went over to the two women, but Maureen wasn't happy about it.

Jodi said, 'There are some questions about myself that I'm hoping you will answer.' She said it without emotion or intimacy, as if she had no more stake in the answers than a census taker.

Edith reached out as if to touch Jodi, but Jodi took a half-step back, her hands at her side. I said, 'Why don't we go for a walk?'

Edith told the clerk that she had to go out for a while, and the three of us walked across to the square, me telling Edith what we knew and how we knew it. I thought she was going to deny it, but she didn't. I thought she might evade us, or start screaming for her husband, or make a big deal about how dare we invade her life like this, but she didn't do any of that. It was as if she had been waiting thirty-six years for Jodi to walk through the door, and now Jodi had and Edith couldn't stop looking at her. They walked on either side of me, keeping me between them, Jodi with her hands in her pockets, staring straight ahead, Edith anxious and staring at Jodi, as if Jodi might suddenly disappear and Edith wanted to have her committed to memory. When I finished, Edith said, 'I can't believe how much she looks like me. She looks more like me than the children I raised.' She said it to me, as if Jodi was a dream, and not really there.

I said, 'If the state papers Rebenack had were legitimate, then Jodi is the child that Pamela Johnson handed to the state welfare authorities. There aren't any papers that indicate that the child was born to you. Nor are there documents that establish fatherhood.'

She shook her head. 'No. No, there wouldn't be.'

Jodi said, 'Then you don't deny that you're my birth mother?'

Edith seemed surprised. 'No. No, of course not. Why would I?'

'You denied it thirty-six years ago.'

'Oh.'

I said, 'Well, now that we're all together, maybe I should wait in the yogurt shop and let you two talk.'

They both said, 'No!' and Jodi grabbed my hand. She said, 'I want you to stay. This won't take long.'

We walked past a couple of wrought-iron benches to a little gazebo in the square. An older man in coveralls and a red engineer's cap was on one of the benches, head back, mouth open, eyes closed. Sleeping. He had a tiny dog on a leash with him, the leash tied to the bench. The dog sat in the shade beneath the man and whined when we passed. The little dog was black and shaggy and its hair was matted. I thought it must be hot, with all the hair. We walked up the steps onto the gazebo and stood there in the shade. It was still hot, there in the shade.

Jodi stood well away from Edith, still holding my hand. She said, 'So.'

Edith uncrossed her arms, then recrossed them. She started to say

320

something, then stopped. The little dog crept out from under the bench and tried to follow us up onto the gazebo, but reached the end of its leash and cried. Both Edith and Jodi looked at it.

I said, 'Don't everybody talk at once.'

Jodi frowned. 'That's not funny.'

'Nope. I guess not.'

We stood there some more. The gazebo was sort of nestled in a stand of three mature magnolia trees, and the air was heavy with their scent. The big bumblebees zigged in and around the gazebo like police helicopters on patrol.

Edith said, 'I'm sorry. I don't know what to say. I always thought you might come back to me. I would think of you, sometimes, and try to imagine what this moment would be like, and now here we are.'

Jodi frowned, and her face pulled into a tight, uncomfortable knot. 'Mrs Boudreaux, I think I should make something clear.'

'All right.'

'I haven't come here to find my mother. I have a mother. She's the woman who raised me.'

Edith glanced at the little dog again. 'Of course.'

'Just so we understand.'

Edith nodded. 'Oh, yes.' She pooched out her lips, and then she added, 'I hope the people who got you were good to you.'

'They were. Very.'

Edith nodded again.

Jodi said, 'Was Leon Williams my father?' She said it abruptly, the same way she had gotten out of the car when she decided to go into Edith's store, like she had to do it that way or it wouldn't get done.

Edith's eyes flagged. Knew it was coming and here it was. 'Yes. Leon was your father.'

Jodi drew a slow breath, her mouth still the tight knot. 'All right,' she said. 'All right.'

Edith uncrossed her arms and cupped her right hand in her left at her breast. She looked at me, and then she looked back at Jodi. 'That is what you wanted to know, isn't it?'

Jodi nodded.

Edith again took a single step toward Jodi, and Jodi lifted her free hand, stopping her. She still held onto me. 'Please don't.'

'Does it bother you that your father was a black man?'

Jodi's face tightened even more. 'It seems to bother a great many people.'

'It always has,' Edith said. 'I was just a girl, and Leon wasn't much older. We were children, and we were friends, and it became more than that.' Her eyes grew wet and she blinked several times. 'I hope you don't hate me for all of this.'

321

Jodi stared at the little dog, and then she leaned against the gazebo rail. Even in the shade it was hot, and a single line of perspiration ran down the side of her face in front of her left ear. She didn't say anything for a while, maybe trying to put it in a kind of order. A couple of flies buzzed around the old man's face and he swatted at them without opening his eyes. She said, 'Of course, I don't hate you. Don't be silly.'

Edith was blinking harder. 'Someone was blackmailing you with this, weren't they?'

'That's right.'

Edith smiled softly, but there was no pleasure in it. Just a kind of acknowledgment of shared experience. 'Yes, well, I know about that, too. When they say getting in trouble, they really mean it, don't they? It looks like you get everybody in trouble.'

Jodi looked at me, embarrassed, as if she suddenly regretted being here and speaking with this woman and witnessing her pain.

Edith said, 'You've grown into quite a beautiful woman. I'm very proud of you.'

Jodi said. 'How did Leon Williams die?'

Edith drew breath and closed her eyes. 'My father murdered him.'

'Because he was black?'

Edith wet her lips and thought for a moment, and I found myself wishing that I were not present. I had no right to what was happening, and no place in it, and the sense of alienness made me feel large and intrusive, but Jodi still gripped my hand, and seemed to be holding on all the tighter. Edith said, 'I think he shot Leon because he couldn't bring himself to shoot me.'

Jodi said, 'Jesus Christ.'

Edith leaned back against the gazebo rail and told Jodi how Jodi came to be. Jodi hadn't asked that Edith tell her these things, but it seemed important to Edith, as if she needed to explain herself to Edith as much as to Jodi. She described an impoverished home dominated by rage and a brutal father who beat wife and children alike. She sketched herself as a shy, fearful girl who loved school, not so much for learning but simply because school allowed brief escape from the numbing despair of her home, and that after school she would buy yet more moments of peace by walking along the levees and the bayous, there to read or write in her journal, there to smell the air and enjoy the feeling of safety that being anyplace other than home allowed her. The Edith Boudreaux she described did not seem in any way like the person in the gazebo, but then, of course, she wasn't. She described a day on the bayou, her feet in the water, when Leon Williams had come upon her, an absolutely beautiful young man with a bright, friendly smile, who asked what she was reading (*Little Men*, she still remembered) and made her laugh (he asked how tall they were) and who, like Edith, dreamed of better things (he wanted to own an Esso station). When Edith spoke of Leon, her eyes closed and she smiled. She said that they had run into each other again the following week, very much by accident, and that Leon had again made her laugh and how, after that, the meetings were planned and no longer left to chance. As Edith went through it you could see the old emotions play across her face, and after a while it was like she wasn't with us anymore. She was with Leon, sitting in the warm shade, and she told us that it was she who had first kissed him, how she had thought about it for weeks and wanted him to do it but that all he did was talk until she finally realized that he wasn't going to cross that line, her being white and him not, and that she finally said, oh, to hell with it, and she took the bull by the horns, so to speak, and kissed him, and when she said it you knew that she was seeing his face as plain and clear before her as if it were happening now. She said the meetings became more frequent and frenzied and then she missed her period and then another, and she knew she was pregnant, thirteen and white and pregnant by Leon Williams, he of the African-American persuasion (no matter how watered-down that might be). She had been terrified to tell her mother and then she grew even more terrified not to, until finally she had, and then, of course, her parents demanded to know the identity of the father. Edith stopped abruptly, as if she realized that she wasn't Edith Johnson anymore, but was now Edith Boudreaux. She grew very quiet, and her face darkened. She said, 'My father wanted me to name the boy. He kept after me for weeks, and I wouldn't tell them, and then one night he was drunk and he was beating me, and my mother was screaming you're going to make her lose that baby, and I didn't want to tell him but I was so scared that I would lose you . . .' She shook her head and crossed her arms again and began to blink back tears.

I said, 'It's okay, Edith. You were a child. You were scared.'

She nodded, but she didn't look at us, and the tears came harder. 'He went out after Leon and he shot him. Just like that.' A whisper.

Jodi said, 'My God.'

Edith wiped at her eyes, smearing the tears and her mascara and the mucus running from her nose. She gave a weak smile. 'I must look like such a fool. I'm sorry.'

Jodi said, 'No.'

Edith was getting control of herself. 'Would you come back to my house? I could make coffee. There's so much more I'd like to tell you.'

Jodi looked uncomfortable. 'I really don't think I can.' She looked at me like she wanted me to say something, like maybe we had someplace to go and I should check my watch and get her away from there.

Edith's eyes grew panicky. 'You have three sisters, did you know that? I could show you their pictures.' Pleading.

Jodi said, 'I'm sorry. I have to get back to Los Angeles.'

Edith shook her head and her face seemed to close and grow fearful. She said, 'I didn't want to tell. I have cursed myself every day for it, but I just wasn't strong enough to save him.' She put her face in her hands. 'I want you to know that I would have kept you if I could. I want you to know that I've wondered about you, and prayed for you. God forgive me, I wasn't strong enough to save either one of you. Please forgive me for that. Please please please forgive me.' Her shoulders heaved and she turned away and put her hands on the rail and wept.

The old man on the bench opened his eyes and sat up and looked at us. He said, 'What in hell's going on over there?'

I leaned toward him. 'Shut up or I'll kick your ass.'

The old man untied the little dog and hurried away. I was blinking fast. Dust in the air. Damn dust is something.

Jodi said, 'Edith?'

Edith shook her head.

Jodi said, 'Edith, I forgive you.'

Edith shook her head again, and her body trembled.

Jodi looked at me, and I said, 'Whatever you want.'

Jodi pursed her lips and blew a stream of air and stared at the rough board deck of the gazebo. She said, 'Edith, I need to know one more thing. Did you love my father?'

Edith answered in a voice so small that we could barely hear her. Maybe we imagined it, hearing only what we wanted to hear. She said, 'Oh, God, yes. I loved him so. God, how I loved him.'

Jodi went to Edith and put her hands on her shoulders, and said, 'Maybe we could stay for a little while, after all.'

The two of them stood like that, Edith crying, Jodi patting her shoulder, together in the heat of the day.

21

We drove to Edith Boudreaux's house, parked in the drive, then went inside so that she could share her life with her long-lost daughter.

It was a nice house, furnished in Early American and smelling faintly of Pine-Sol. Everything was clean the way a home can be clean only after the children are older and have moved out. A grandfather clock stood in the entry, and a Yamaha piano was against the wall just inside the door. A cluster of family photographs sprouted on top of the Yamaha. Edith and Jodi moved together ahead of me, and there seemed a careful distance between them, each overly polite, each watchful and uncertain. Jodi said, 'You have a lovely home.'

'Thank you.'

'Have you lived here for very long?'

'Oh, yes. Almost fifteen years, now.' You see? Like that.

I sat in a wing chair at the end of the couch as they moved around the room examining the artifacts of Edith's life, as if we had stumbled upon a long-sealed chamber beneath the Great Pyramid. *This is my husband, Joel. This is when we were married. These are our daughters.* Pictures of the three grown daughters were spotted around the living room and hanging on the walls. Red-letter stuff: the graduation, the marriage. *That's Sissy, our oldest; she has two boys. That's Joana and Rick, they live in New Orleans. Barb's the baby, she's at LSU.* Jodi followed Edith from picture to picture with her hands clasped behind her back, unwilling to touch anything. She didn't seem particularly happy to be there, but maybe it was just me.

After a little bit of that, Edith said, 'Would you like coffee? Coffee won't take but a minute.' Nervous, and anxious to please.

Jodi looked at me, and I said, 'That would be very nice. Thank you.'

When Edith was gone, I lowered my voice. 'How are you doing?'

Jodi made a little shrug. 'It feels creepy.'

'We can leave whenever you want.'

She shook her head. 'I'm here. I might as well learn whatever I can learn.'

'Sure.'

'I won't be coming back.'

I spread my hands.

Jodi frowned. 'Well, I can't very well be rude.'

'Absolutely not.'

When Edith came back with the coffee, Jodi was looking at the pictures on the piano. Edith had bypassed the Yamaha before, and didn't seem thrilled when she saw Jodi over there. Jodi said, 'Are these your brothers and sisters?'

Edith poured the coffee, then handed me a small plate with three pecan pralines. I hadn't had pralines in years. She said, 'Some of them.' Not looking that way.

Jodi said, 'Show me who's who.'

Edith made a little frown as she joined Jodi at the pictures. 'This is my mother, standing with my aunt. That's Jo-el when he was a boy. And these are my brothers and sisters. That's me. I was sixteen.'

Jodi nodded and leaned closer to the pictures. 'Which one is your father?'

Edith seemed to pull herself in. 'I don't keep a picture of my father here.'

'Elvis says you take care of him.'

'Yes, that's true.'

Jodi stared at Edith for a moment, then looked back at the pictures. 'How do you and they live with it?'

Edith started to speak, stopped, then found some words. 'Families keep secrets. We've never once spoken of it in all this time. My brother Nick was closest to my age. He was twelve, but he's dead. Sara was ten, and the others even younger. I don't know if they know or not.'

Jodi made a whistling sound through her teeth. 'He murdered a child and he got away with it. Just like that.'

Edith crossed her arms again, as she had at the gazebo. 'A man named Duplasus was the sheriff back then. He came to the house, and my father told him exactly what happened and why.' She pulled her arms tighter, protection from the cold. 'I'm sure Mr Duplasus felt that my father's rage was justifiable, a white girl being ruined by a colored.'

Jodi said, 'Jesus Christ.'

Edith came back to the couch. 'Yes. Well. Things like this used to be called crimes of passion. Would you like more coffee, Mr Cole?'

'Yes, ma'am. That would be nice.'

Jodi turned away from the piano and stood in the center of Edith's living room. 'You could've said something. You still can.' She looked at me. 'There's no statute of limitation on murder, is there?'

'Nope.'

Edith said, 'My father is eighty-six years old. He's incontinent and he talks to himself, and much of the time he's incoherent. I care for him now in ways that he doesn't always like, but I'm the only one to do it.' She shook her head. 'I'm not as angry as I used to be. Leon's been gone a very long while.'

Jodi's jaw worked.

Edith made a little shrug, and seemed profoundly tired. 'It's just the way we feel about it. I guess that's why we have this trouble.'

I said, 'Milt.'

Edith looked at me. 'My, but you must be a good detective.'

Jodi said, 'Who's Milt?'

Edith looked at her. 'He didn't tell you what's going on?'

Jodi was frowning. 'What didn't you tell me?'

Edith said, 'Some of the same people who were blackmailing you are blackmailing us, too.'

Jodi looked at me. 'What?'

I said, 'I told you what was relevant to you. Edith's business is Edith's business.'

'Jesus Christ, but you're a tight-lipped sonofabitch.'

I shrugged. 'Privacy is my middle name.' Jodi wanted me to fill her in and Edith said it was all right with her. I said, 'Rebenack was working for a man named Milt Rossier. As near as I can figure it, Rebenack uncovered Leon Williams's murder and sold it to Rossier so that Rossier would have leverage over Edith's husband. Rebenack double-crossed Rossier by going behind his back to blackmail you. Rebenack thought he was being sharp, but that brought me into it and focused attention on Rossier.' I looked at Edith. 'You know Rebenack is dead.'

She looked confused. 'No. Jo-el hasn't said anything.'

Jodi said, 'Jesus Christ. Is everything in this family a secret?'

I said, 'After Lucy Chenier and I came to see you, Rossier's goon picked me up and brought me out to the crawfish farm. There's no way that Rossier would've known that I came to see you unless your husband told him. Rebenack was out there, too. Rossier wanted to know why I was digging around, and he became upset when I told him that Rebenack was putting the twist on Jodi. He didn't know that, and I suspect he killed Rebenack because of it.'

Edith shook her head. 'Jo-el wouldn't murder anyone. I don't believe that.'

I shrugged.

Edith put down her coffee cup and said, 'I told Jo-el that thirty-six years is enough lying. I said that I didn't want him to do anything wrong, and he said what was he supposed to do, go arrest my father?' She shook her head again and rubbed at her eyes. 'This is a nightmare.'

I looked at Jodi Taylor. 'Sound familiar?'

'What?'

'You didn't want to pay extortion, either.'

Jodi pursed her lips, then leaned toward Edith. 'Can't your husband do something?'

'He wants to, but he doesn't know what. This is killing him.' The skin around her eyes and mouth was tight, and showing the strain.

Jodi said, 'I think it's killing both of you.'

A car turned into the drive and Edith went to the door. 'That will be Jo-el. I want you to meet him.'

The front door opened and Sheriff Jo-el Boudreaux walked in, campaign hat in one hand, a rolled copy of *Sports Illustrated* in the other, looking the way you look when you're calling it quits after a long day. He stopped when he saw us, and said, 'What's going on here?' Calm and reasonable, like you walk in every day to see a detective and a TV star sitting in your living room. Only not. His eyes flicked to Jodi, then came to me, and the calm look was the kind guys get when their hearts are pounding, but they know they've got to cover. Every cop I ever knew could get that look.

Edith stood. 'Jo-el, this young lady is named Jodi Taylor.' She wet her lips. 'She's my daughter.'

Jodi stood and offered her hand. 'Hello, Mr Boudreaux.'

Edith said, 'She's the one on TV, Jo-el. She's the little girl I gave away.'

Jo-el Boudreaux took Jodi's hand without apparent feeling, shaking his head and making out as if all of this was sort of benignly confusing. 'I don't understand, hon. Your mother gave away a baby.' Like she had made a mistake recalling which day she'd gone to the market.

'We don't have to pretend, Jo-el.' Edith put a hand on his arm. 'They know. Those people were blackmailing her, too, just like they're doing to us.'

Jo-el's eyes got wide and he wet his lips and his eyes flicked nervous and frantic. One minute you're coming home to take it easy with the new *Sports Illustrated*, the next you're watching your life go down the toilet. 'No one's blackmailing us.'

I said, 'We're not going to hurt you, Jo-el. It's okay.'

Sheriff Jo-el Boudreaux waved the *Sports Illustrated* at me. 'I don't know what you think you've dug up, but we don't want any part of it.' He squared himself toward me, making himself large and threatening. Cop technique. 'I think you should leave.'

Edith jerked at his arm. 'You stop that! We need to talk about this. We need to start dealing with this.'

Jo-el was frantic now and didn't know what to do. He said, 'There's nothing to deal with, Edie. Do you understand me? There's nothing to talk about here, and they should leave.'

Edith's voice grew harder. Insistent. 'I want to know what's going on. I want to know if you're involved in a murder.'

Jo-el Boudreaux's left eye ticked twice, and he took a single step toward me and I stood. Edith was pulling at his arm, her face red. I said, 'I saw you with Milt Rossier. We know about Leon Williams and Edith's father. Rebenack was extorting Jodi and her studio, and Rossier is extorting you.'

Boudreaux's eye ticked again and he shook his head. 'No.'

Edith said, 'He says that Rossier killed that redheaded man. Do you know about that? Are you covering up for him?'

Boudreaux blinked hard, and he looked at his wife. 'You know better than that.' He squinted at me to stop the blinking. 'If I knew who murdered Jimmie Ray Rebenack I would make an arrest. Maybe you did it. Maybe I should take you in for questioning.'

I said, 'Sure. That would look good in the local papers.'

He shook his head again, and now the eye was ticking madly, like a moth caught in a jar. 'I don't know what Edie's been saying to you, but she's been confused. She's not making sense.'

Edith made a sudden, abrupt move and slapped her husband on the side of the face. There wasn't a lot on it, but the sound was sharp and clear, and Jo-el stepped back, surprised. Edith grabbed his arm and shook him. 'Don't you dare speak about me that way! We have been living in a way that makes me ashamed, and I want it to stop. I want it to stop, do you hear?'

Jo-el took his wife by her upper arms. You could barely hear him. 'You want me to go arrest your father? That's what will happen, and won't that be fine? You can even testify at his trial.'

Edith was crying.

Jodi said, 'We're on your side. Maybe we can help you. Maybe we can work together.'

Jo-el Boudreaux said, 'There's nothing to talk about. I don't know anything about this, so you take care of your business and let me worry about mine.'

Edith was crying harder. 'I want to stop lying. I want this to end.'

Jo-el said, 'Edie, goddammit. *There's nothing to talk about.*' Denying it to the end.

Edith pulled away from him and ran back through the house, and a door slammed. For a long moment no one moved, and then Boudreaux went to the front door and held it open. He was breathing hard, and it took him a minute to control it. He looked at me and said, 'Do you have a statement that you wish to make in the murder of Jimmie Ray Rebenack?'

'Let us help you, Jo-el.'

He looked at Jodi. 'I'm glad Edie had a chance to meet you, but there's just been a misunderstanding here. We don't know anything about Milt Rossier, or about the murder of Leon Williams.'

Jodi said, 'You're being a fool.'

Boudreaux nodded and looked back at me. 'Where's it go from here?'
I said, 'Jesus Christ, Boudreaux.'

He blinked hard once. 'I want to know.' I thought he was about to cry.

I took a deep breath. 'It starts here, it stops here. We won't give you up.'

Sheriff Jo-el Boudreaux stood at the door, the big hand holding it open, the soft sounds of the neighborhood drifting in with the moist scent of cut grass, and then he simply walked away, back across the living room and through a door and after his wife.

Jodi and I went out through the door, closed it behind us, and drove away. The late afternoon had given way to the evening, and the sky in the east was beginning to purple. Fireflies traced uneven paths in the twilight.

Jodi huddled on her side of the car, arms crossed, staring out the window and chewing her lip. The lip started bleeding so she stopped with the lip and chewed at a nail. We drove in silence.

I said, 'So say it.'

'They're good people. He thinks he's protecting her because he's a big dumb goober, but he's making it worse for both of them.'

'Uh-huh.'

She glanced at her watch and her right knee began bouncing. Nervous energy. 'I have to go back to L.A. to finish the show, but I can't just walk away. I want you to stay here and find out what's going on and see if you can help them.'

The air had cooled, and smelled sweet, but I didn't know from what. 'I have found that, in cases like this, the only way to escape the past is to confess it. They don't seem anxious to do that.'

'I want you to try. Will you?'

'What about you?'

She looked at me. 'What does that mean?'

'Who are you, Jodi? Do you want these people in your life?'

She stared at me for what seemed like years, and then she crossed her arms and settled back into the shadows. 'I don't know what I want. Just help them, okay?'

'Okay.'

22

We drove directly to the airport. Jodi bought the last remaining first-class seat on a flight readying to leave the gate. They held the plane. Can't just fly away and leave America's sweetheart holding her bag.

Jodi said, 'Call me whenever you want. The pickups should only take a few days, and then I'll come back.'

'Sure.'

She gave me a kiss, and then she was gone. A businessman with a receding hairline watched Jodi get on the plane. 'Say, podnuh, that who I think it is?'

'Who'd you think it was?'

'That one on TV. The singer.'

I shook my head. 'Nope.'

As I walked back through the terminal, I felt alone and at loose ends and overly aware that Lucy Chenier was only a short drive away. Of course, Lucy didn't seem particularly interested in my proximity, but that didn't make it any easier. I tried not thinking about her. I thought, instead, that perhaps I should do something exciting to clear my head. With a clear head, I could probably think of a way to help Edith Boudreaux, which was, of course, what I was being paid to do. Also, something exciting would probably make it easier not to think about Lucy.

It was twenty-three minutes after seven, and there were exactly six people in the terminal besides me. A man of action is ever resourceful, however, and one's options are limited only by one's imagination. Hmm. I could hike up to the levee and shoot rats, but that would be noisy and one probably needed a rat-shooting permit. Difficult to obtain. Okay, I could scale the outside of the state's thirty-two-story capitol building then paraglide onto the Huey Long Bridge, but where would I get the parasail? Rent-a-chute was probably closed, too. *Elvis Cole, this is your life!*

I drove to the Riverfront Ho-Jo, checked in yet again, then ordered a turkey sandwich from room service, and went up to my room. Twenty minutes later I was eating the sandwich when the phone rang. I said, 'Diminished expectations. Elvis Cole speaking.'

Lucy Chenier said, 'If that was a play on *Great Expectations*, it's too obscure.'

I said, 'Hi.' My heart speeded up and my palms went damp. We are often not as tough as we make out to be.

Lucy said, 'I want to apologize for the way I acted. I'd like a chance to explain.'

'It's not necessary.'

'Jodi phoned me from the plane. She told me a little of what's going on, and, as before, she asked me to assist you in any way possible.' She sounded mechanical, as if she were nervous.

'All right.'

Lucy didn't say anything for a moment, and I wondered if the line had gone dead. Then she said, 'I'm making dinner. If you'd like, you could join me and we could talk about these things.'

'That would be very nice. Thank you.'

'Do you remember the way?'

'Of course.'

There was another pause before she said, 'Then I'll see you soon.'

'Yes.'

'Good-bye.'

I hung up and stared at the phone. Well, well. I threw away what was left of the turkey, took a quick shower, then talked the bartender in the hotel bar into selling me a bottle of merlot and a bottle of chardonnay for three times what they were worth. I made it to Lucy's in fourteen minutes. Try getting across Los Angeles in fourteen minutes. You'd need a Klingon battle cruiser.

Lucy's neighborhood was quiet, and her home was well lit and inviting. The same man and woman were walking the pinto Akita. I parked in the drive behind Lucy's Lexus, and nodded at them. The woman said, 'It's such a lovely night.'

I said, 'Yes. It is, isn't it?'

Lucy answered the door in jeans and a soft red jersey top and dangling turquoise earrings, and I thought in that moment that I had never before been in the presence of a woman who looked so lovely. My heart pounded, hard and with great intensity. She said, 'I'm glad that you could come.'

I held up the bottles. 'I didn't know what we were having.'

She smiled and looked at the labels. 'Oh, these are wonderful. Thank you.'

She showed me into the kitchen. The kitchen was bright, but only a single light burned in the family room, and Janis Ian was on the stereo. Lucy and her home and the atmosphere within it seemed to have a kind of hyperreality, as if I had stepped into a photograph featured in *Better Homes & Gardens*, and I wondered how much of it was real and how much was just me. I said, 'It smells terrific.'

'I have rumaki in the oven for an appetizer, and I'm making roast duck with black cherry sauce for dinner. I hope that's okay.'

I said, 'Wow.'

'I was having a glass of wine. Would you join me?' A bottle of Johannesburg Riesling was on the counter near a mostly empty wineglass. The bottle was mostly empty, too.

'Please.'

'Why don't we save your wine for dinner and have the Riesling now.'

'Sounds good.' She seemed to be moving as carefully around me as I was around her.

I opened the merlot to let it breathe while she brought out another glass and poured. I said, 'Is there anything I can do to help?'

'Everything's done except for the cherry sauce. Why don't you sit at the counter and bring me up to date about Jodi while I do that.'

Lucy opened a can of black pitted cherries and poured them into a saucepan with lemon juice and port and a lot of sugar, and then put the pan over a low fire. I told her how I had given Jodi the tour of Eunice and Ville Platte and how Jodi had introduced herself to Edith Boudreaux and what had happened when they met. Lucy nodded every once in a while and frowned when I got to the part about Jodi steaming into Edith's dress shop while there were customers, but mostly she sipped at her wine and concentrated on her cherry sauce. Nervous, I thought. Distracted. She finished her glass of wine and refilled it and added a drop to mine. The Riesling bottle was empty, and I'd only had one glass. I wondered how long she'd been working at it. I said, 'I think the rumaki's burning.'

She said, 'Oh, damn,' and took the rumaki from the oven. The rumaki were little bits of water chestnut wrapped in bacon and held together with toothpicks. The toothpicks were black and smoking, and a couple of the rumaki were overdone, but mostly they were fine. She put them on the stove.

I said, 'I like them like that.'

She smiled lamely and had another belt of the wine.

I said, 'Are you okay?'

She put down the wineglass and looked at me. She'd been working at it, all right. 'I really like you.'

Something clutched in my stomach. 'I like you, too.'

She nodded and looked at the rumaki. She began taking them off the cooking pan and arranging them on a serving plate. I was breathing faster, and I tried to take it easy and slow the breathing. 'Lucy?'

She finished arranging the rumaki and put the little plate on the counter between us. She said, 'Would you please eat one of these things and tell me that it's wonderful.'

I ate one. 'They're wonderful.'

She did not look happy.

'They're great. I mean it.'

She drank more wine. I was breathing so fast that I thought my head might fill with blood and explode. I put my hand across the counter and she put her hand into mine. I said, 'It's okay.'

She shook her head.

I said, 'It's going to be fine.'

She took her hand back and walked across the big kitchen, and then she came back again. She put both hands flat on the counter and looked directly at me and said, 'I'm drunk.'

'Big secret.'

She frowned. 'Don't laugh at me.'

'If I don't laugh at something I'm going to have a stroke.'

She said, 'When you went back to Los Angeles I realized how much I was liking you. I don't want to be involved with a man who lives two thousand miles away. I was mad at you for going. I got mad at you for coming back. Why'd you have to come back?'

The blood seemed to be rushing through my head, and my ears were ringing and I was blinking.

She said, 'I have this rule. I don't get involved with people I work with. I'm feeling very confused and stupid and I don't like it.'

I got a handle on the breathing, but I couldn't do anything about the ears. I looked at the table in the dining area. Candles. Elegant seating for two. I said, 'Where's Ben?'

'I sent him to sleep over at a friend's.'

I stared at her and she stared back.

She said, 'Jesus Christ, what kind of lousy detective are you? Do I have to draw you a map?'

I looked at the table and then I looked at the wine and then I looked at the rumaki. I went around the counter and into the kitchen and I said, 'Help me detect some coffee.' I started opening cabinets.

She waved her arms. 'I just offered myself to you and you want coffee?'

I found a jar of Folger's Mountain Grown. I started looking for cups. 'We're going to have coffee. We're going to eat.' I found cups. I looked for a spoon so I could fix the goddamned coffee. 'I do not want you to go to bed with me if you have to get drunk to do it!' I stopped all the slamming around and looking and turned back to her. 'Do you understand that?'

Lucy opened her mouth, then closed it. She put one hand to the side of her head, then lowered it. She nodded, then thought for a moment, and then she shook her head, confused. 'Is this some kind of male power trip or something?'

'Of course. Isn't that why men do everything?' I think I was yelling. Lucy grew calm. 'Please don't yell.'

I felt the way I had when I'd lied to the Ville Platte librarian.

She crossed the kitchen and took my face in both her hands. She said, 'I think the coffee is a good idea. Thank you.'

I nodded. 'You are absolutely beautiful.'

She smiled.

'You are all that I think about. You have filled my heart.'

She closed her eyes, and then she put her head against my chest.

We had the coffee, and then we had the duck. We sat on the couch in the dim family room and we listened to Janis Ian and we held hands. At a quarter to ten she made a phone call and asked how Ben was doing and then she wished him a good night. When she hung up she came back into the family room and said, 'Watch this.'

She stood with her feet together, held out her arms, then closed her eyes and touched her nose with her right index finger. She giggled when she did it, then opened her eyes. 'Do I pass, Officer?'

I picked her up and carried her to her bedroom. I said, 'Ask me that in the morning.'

'Studly, you probably won't last until morning.'

23

I woke the next morning relaxed and warm and at peace, with Lucy snuggled beside me in her king-sized bed, small beneath light gray sheets and a comforter. Her breathing was even, and when I burrowed under the sheet and kissed her back, she said, 'Mrmph.'

I touched my tongue to her skin, and she said, 'Sleepin'.'

Her back was salty with sweat dried from the hours before. The bed and the room smelled of us and our lovemaking and the warmth of our bodies, and under it was the sweet smell of her fragrance and shampoo and soap. I lay there for a time, enjoying the warmth of her and the memories that the smells triggered, and after a while I could smell the food from the night before and the jessamine that grew around her home. Lucy's bedroom was large, her bed facing toward double French doors that opened toward the backyard. There were drapes, but the drapes were open so that I could see the used-brick patio and the Weber where we'd grilled the hamburgers. Three or four cardinals and maybe a half-dozen sparrows were clustered around the bird feeder, chirping and scratching at the seed. We had cardinals in L.A., but you rarely saw them. The patio and the yard beyond it were filled with bright light, and somewhere there was the two-cycle whine of a lawnmower. It seemed as if there was always the sound of a lawnmower in Louisiana. Maybe that was the nature of this place, that the land was so fertile that life grew and expanded so quickly that a never-ending maintenance was in order, and without it the people who lived here would be overcome. I wondered for an instant if it could be that way with love, too, but then the thought was gone.

I eased out of the bed, careful not to wake her, then pulled on my underwear and went into her bathroom. I brushed my teeth with my finger, then went out to the kitchen. We had probably burned twenty thousand calories last night, and it was either make breakfast or fall upon Lucy and end up arrested for cannibalism.

I washed the dishes from the night before, then searched through her cupboards and fridge until I found Bisquick and frozen blueberries and some low-fat cottage cheese. There was a pancake griddle in a tall drawer beside the dishwasher, but I found a large skillet instead. Old habits. I poured a cup of the blueberries into a little bowl and covered them with water, then found a larger bowl and made a batter with the Bisquick and the cottage cheese and some nonfat milk. I sprayed the pan with butter-flavored Pam, then put it on a medium fire. While it was heating I ran out into the garden, clipped a pink rose, then ran back inside. I drained the blueberries and was mixing them in the batter when Lucy Chenier squealed, 'Somebody help! There's a strange man in my house!'

She was standing on the other side of the counter, wrapped in a sheet. I gave her Groucho. 'Don't be scared, little girl. That's not a chain saw. I'm just happy to see you.'

'Ho, ho. Keep dreaming.'

I held out my hand, fingers spread. She laced her fingers between mine. Her fingers were warm and felt good. I said, 'Good morning.'

'Good morning.' We grinned at each other. She made a big deal out of looking around and shook her head. 'You cleaned up. You're making breakfast.'

I turned back to the berries. 'We're a full-service agency, ma'am.'

She let the sheet drop and came around the counter and snuggled against me. 'You can say that again, Trooper.' She looked out from under my arm at the batter. 'Pancakes. Yum. What can I do?'

'Find me a spatula?'

She did.

I gave her a kiss. 'Will you go in today?'

She snuggled against me again. 'Maybe after lunch. I can barely walk, you animal.'

I increased the heat under the pan, then spooned in four equal amounts of batter, making sure each pancake had a like number of berries. I made the batter dry so that the cakes would be thick and fluffy. I said, 'A woman of your advancing years needs regular workouts, else she gets out of shape.'

'Pig.' She dug her thumb between my ribs, then hugged me again and widened her eyes. 'Hmm. I could think of something to eat besides pancakes.'

I adjusted the heat down. When they're thick like that you have to be careful with the heat, hot at first to set the cake and keep it from spreading, then low so that it will cook through without burning. 'A man of my advancing years needs enormous sustenance to even pretend to keep up with a woman of your years.'

'I guess that's right. Female superiority.'

'Tell me about it.' I put down the spatula, touched the tip of her nose, then her lips. I said, 'You are devastatingly beautiful.'

She nodded. 'Um-hm.'

I ran my finger down between her breasts and along the flat plane of her belly. 'Perfect in all discernible ways.'

She made a purring sound. 'Ah.'

'And a pretty fair lay.' I turned back to the pancakes.

'That's not what you said last night, big guy.' She pressed her breasts into my back, and then she stepped back and touched the places on my lower back and side. 'What are these?'

'I caught some frag in Vietnam.'

I felt her fingers move from scar to scar. They're little scars. 'How did that happen?'

'I was trying to hide in the wrong place at the wrong time.'

She bent low and kissed one of the marks and then she touched the puckered scar high on the top of my left trapezius. 'What happened there?'

'A hood named Charlie DeLuca shot me.'

She ran her finger along the scar. It's a little crater shaped like an arrowhead. She said, 'Do you get shot often?'

'Only the once.'

She came around in front of me and pulled my face down and looked deep into my eyes, frowning. 'Do me a favor and don't get shot anymore, okay?'

'Aw, shucks. Not even a little bit?'

She shook her head. Slow. 'Uh-uh.'

When the pancakes were done we heaped them with sliced bananas and maple syrup, then sat at the counter with our knees touching. She said, 'These are wonderful.'

I nodded. 'Old family recipe. Ideal for restoring one's energy reserves and reinvigorating the libido.'

'Ah. Something to look forward to.'

I wiggled my eyebrows.

She said, 'So are you going to be able to help the Boudreauxs?'

'I don't know. Jo-el isn't going to cooperate, so I'll have to figure out what Milt has going and how to make him back away. I'll probably need help to do that, so I'll have my partner come in.'

'You have a partner?'

'An ex-police officer named Joe Pike. He owns the agency with me.'

She ate a piece of the pancake, then a slice of the banana. 'Do you have any leads?'

'Sandi.'

'The name in Jimmie Ray's papers?'

I nodded and kept eating. I was getting close to the end of the pancakes and was thinking I should make a couple more. 'I found two messages on his answering machine from a woman who implied some sort of romantic relationship. If that's Sandi, maybe Jimmie Ray told her what was going on.'

'And maybe she'll tell you.'

'Maybe.' I finished my plate and frowned at the batter. Enough for one more, maybe two.

Lucy split what was left on her plate and pushed the larger piece onto mine. Mind reader. 'I won't be able to finish.'

'Thanks.' I dug in.

She took a last bit of pancake, then set her fork onto her plate. 'How will you find her?'

'Shouldn't be hard. If they were close, they would've talked often. I'll go back through his phone bills and try the most frequently dialed local numbers. I'll dial them and hope that someone named Sandi answers.'

Lucy leaned forward on her elbows and grinned. 'You make it sound easy.'

'Private detecting has very little in common with multidimensional calculus, Lucille.' I finished the last of the pancake and touched my napkin to my lips. 'Also, it is only easy if the call from Jimmie Ray's to Sandi's was a toll call. If she lived across the street, her number won't show up on the bills and we're screwed.'

Lucy grinned wider and looked devilish. 'There's no way I'm going to work without knowing this.' She slid off the stool and came back with her briefcase and we went through the papers I had taken from Jimmie Ray Rebenack. It didn't take long. We had four phone bills stretching back five months, the two most recent, then a missing bill, and then the two earlier bills. We started with the earliest bill and found fourteen calls to the same number in Baton Rouge. This was during the same month in which he'd made the calls to Jodi and Sid. The next month showed twelve calls to that number, and the two most recent bills showed six calls and two calls respectively. Lucy said, 'Do you think it's her?'

I used Lucy's kitchen phone and dialed the number. It rang four times, and then a woman's voice said, 'Hi! I can't come to the phone right now, but please leave your message and I'll get back to you! Promise!' The voice was bright and cheery, and was exactly the same voice I'd heard on Jimmie Ray Rebenack's machine.

I hung up and spread my hands. '*Voilà*'.

Lucy said, 'You sonofagun.'

I tried to look modest. 'The kid's a pistol.'

Lucy wrote down the number and made a note beside it. 'I can run the number through our office and get a name and address. Would that help, oh great seer, or can you just sort of infer those things from the way her phone rang?'

'It's important for the little people to feel helpful. You can take care of it.'

She put the note and the papers into her briefcase, then put the briefcase aside and leaned close to me. 'The pancakes were wonderful, Elvis. Thank you.'

'Darlin', you ain't seen nothing yet.'

She slid off the stool and patted my arm. 'Perhaps I'll see it this evening. I've got a one o'clock that I can't miss and I smell. I'm going to take a shower.'

I watched her disappear into the rear of her home, put the dishes into the sink, and then I used her kitchen phone to call Joe Pike. He answered on the second ring and said, 'It's you.' That Pike is something, isn't he?

'How did you know it was me?'

He didn't answer.

I gave him the short version on Edith and Jo-el Boudreaux and Milt Rossier and what we wanted to do. I told him about Sandi. When I was done he said, 'I can come in tonight or tomorrow.'

I said, 'Tomorrow's fine. Tonight I have plans.'

He said, 'Uh.'

I said, 'Call Lucy Chenier's office with your arrival time. I'll pick you up.'

Joe hung up without another word. Some partner, huh?

I put the dishes in the sink, then walked back to Lucy's bedroom and into her bath. The water was running, and the steam from the water had fogged the mirror. I peeled off my underwear and let myself into the shower and ran my hands over her back and down along her sides and across her belly. She was slick and glistening, and her flesh was firm. Her hair was white with bubbles. She said, 'Well, I guess the old family recipe is working.' She turned and pressed into me. 'Let's not forget my one o'clock. I don't have very much time.'

'Efficiency,' I said. 'Efficiency is the key to all happiness.' I worked my fingers into her hair.

'Perhaps I could be ravished and cleaned at the same time. Do you think?'

I worked the soap down along her neck and shoulders. 'I think I'm up for the try.'

She smiled and sank down to her knees. 'You are,' she said. 'But not for long.'

24

The next morning, Lucy and I were in the Baton Rouge Airport at 11:40, waiting for Joe Pike. We had been together twenty-eight minutes and had done a fine job of keeping our clothes on. I was pleased with my self-control. I had cramps, but I was pleased.

When Pike's plane taxied in, she said, 'How will I recognize him?'

'He's six-one and he weighs right at one-ninety. He has short brown hair and large red arrows tattooed on the outside of each deltoid. He'll be wearing jeans and a gray sweatshirt with the sleeves cut off and dark glasses.'

'How do you know what he'll be wearing?'

'It's what he wears.'

'All the time?'

'If it's cold, he wears a Marine Corps parka.'

She smiled. 'And if the occasion were formal?'

'Think of it as consistency. Joe Pike is the most consistent person I know.'

'Hm.'

'And if he speaks, he will be direct. He won't say much. That's just his way.'

'It sounds like you're warning me.'

'Preparing. Preparing is a better word.'

Joe Pike materialized in the file of passengers as if he were there yet not there, as separate from them as one photograph superimposed upon another. He came to us, and we shook. I said, 'Lucy Chenier, this is Joe Pike. Joe, Lucy.'

Lucy put out her hand and said, 'It's a pleasure, Mr Pike.'

Pike's head swiveled toward her and he gave her the full focus of his attention. He is like that with people. You are either there to him, or you are not. If you are there, he gives you all of himself. He said, 'Joe.' He took her hand, held it for a moment, then kissed it. Gracious.

Lucy beamed. 'Why, thank you.'

'You're a couple.'

That pleased her, too. 'Is it that obvious?'

Joe nodded.

I said, 'You can let go of the hand, now, Joe.'

Joe's head swiveled my way, his eyes hidden and secret behind the black lenses of his glasses. His mouth twitched, and he let go of Lucy's hand. Joe will never smile, but his mouth will twitch, so you know he found this funny. He looked at Lucy again, then came back to me. The mouth twitched a second time. A riot, for Joe. Absolute insane hysteria. He said, 'I've got a bag.'

We collected an olive-green duffel bag from the claim area, then picked up the car, and drove cross town toward Lucy's office. Pike rode in the back and Lucy was in the front. She sat sideways so that she could see him. 'Have you been to Louisiana before, Joe?'

Pike said, 'Uh-huh.'

'When was that?'

'A while back.'

'Did you enjoy yourself?'

Pike didn't answer.

She twisted more in her seat to get a better look at him. 'Joe?'

Pike was staring out the window, the passing scenery racing across the dark lenses. Immobile.

Lucy looked at me and I patted her leg. You see?

As we drove I brought Joe up to speed on Milt Rossier and Jodi Taylor and what Jodi wanted us to do. I told him what I had uncovered about Leon Williams, and how Rossier was using it against the Boudreauxs, and I told him about Jimmie Ray Rebenack and Sandi. 'Lucy ran a DMV check on Sandi through her firm and got us a name and an address.'

Lucy said, 'Sandi's last name is Bergeron. She's twenty-eight years old, unmarried, and she works in the Social Services Department here in the capitol building.'

I said, 'A guy like Jimmie Ray couldn't get sealed state documents without help, so maybe that's Sandi.'

Pike said, 'Um.' It was the first sound he'd made in fifteen minutes. 'What about Rossier?'

Lucy took a 9 by 12 manila envelope from her briefcase and passed it to Pike. 'My friend in the attorney general's office gave me a printout of Rossier's file. Rossier ran prostitution and intimidation rackets through the sixties and seventies until he was convicted of supplying methamphetamines to a local motorcycle gang in nineteen seventy-three. He pulled twenty-four months in Angola, then went into the fish farm business. The fish farm is legitimate, but its primary purpose is to launder money. He was indicted as a co-conspirator in two drug-related murders, and suspected of involvement in six additional homicides.'

Pike looked through the file as they spoke. 'So how come this guy's walking around?'

'Action was dropped on the indictments when the state's witnesses disappeared. They don't think Rossier pulled the trigger, but they believe he ordered it. They think LeRoy Bennett did the shooting, or a man named René LaBorde.'

Pike offered the file back, but Lucy shook her head. 'You can keep it if you'd like. Just be careful with it. My friend could get in trouble if anyone found out he'd given it to me.'

I said, 'He?'

Pike tapped my shoulder. Getting my attention. 'You think Boudreaux is involved with Rossier in some kind of crime?'

'I don't think so. I think he's just looking the other way so that Rossier can do whatever he's doing.'

Pike said, 'But we don't know what that is.'

I shook my head. 'Not yet, but maybe Sandi Bergeron can tell us.'

Pike went back to staring out the window. 'Some great gig, helping people who don't want to be helped.'

Lucy twisted around to look at Pike again. 'Mrs Boudreaux wants the help. She'd like to put this behind her. Jodi Taylor hired us to do that.'

Pike said, 'Us.'

Lucy said, 'Do you have a problem with that?'

Pike's mouth twitched. 'Not at all.' He squeezed her arm. 'Thanks for the help.'

I frowned. 'What's your relationship to this guy in the A.G.?'

Lucy made a big sigh. 'I love a man with raging hormones.'

We dropped Lucy at the curb outside her office. She gathered her things and offered her hand to Joe Pike. 'It was a pleasure, Joe. You're an interesting man.'

Pike said, 'Yes.'

Lucy gave me a kiss, then let herself out and went into her building. I twisted around in the seat and looked at Joe. 'She says you're interesting and you say yes?'

Pike got out of the back and into the front. 'Did you want me to lie?'

We drove to the capitol building and parked in the shade of an enormous oak near the banks of a lake. The Louisiana State capitol building is thirty-four stories of art deco monolith rising above the Mississippi River, sort of like the Empire State Building in miniature. It's the largest state capitol building in the nation, and looks like the kind of place that Charles Foster Kane would call home. Huey Long was assassinated there.

A tour group of retired people from Wisconsin was filing through the lobby, and we filed with them, slipping past a couple of guards who were laughing about the New Orleans Saints, and taking an elevator to the

343

sixth floor. The Social Services Department was on the sixth floor. We could have phoned ahead and asked to speak with Sandi Bergeron, and Sandi might have been willing to talk with us, but you never know. Surprise is often your only recourse.

We went through a door marked SOCIAL SERVICES and up to an older African-American woman sitting behind a high counter. You had to pass her if you wanted access to the rest of the social services offices, and she didn't look like she'd be easy to pass. I said, 'I'd like to see Sandi Bergeron, please.' Lucy's DMV check said that Sandi was something called an associate claims monitor, and that she worked in this office.

The woman said, 'Is she expecting you?'

I gave her one of my nicer smiles. 'It's kind of a surprise. Tell her it's Jimmie Ray Rebenack.' She would either know he was dead, or she wouldn't. If she knew, she'd call security. If she didn't, she'd come out to see him.

The woman picked up her phone and punched some numbers. I said, 'We'll wait outside in the hall.'

The woman covered the receiver and said that that would be fine, and Pike and I went out into the hall.

We were there no more than thirty seconds when a woman in her late twenties hurried out. She had teased blond hair and thin shoulders and rings on both the third and fourth fingers of her right hand, just like the woman in the photograph I'd found at Rebenack's office. Sandi Bergeron, letting Jimmie Ray put a bag on her head and snap a nudie shot. She wore too much makeup, and her nails were the color of Bazooka bubble gum.

She glanced at me and Pike, then looked past us, first one way down the hall and then the other. Looking for Jimmie Ray. She frowned when she didn't see him and started back inside. I said, 'Ms Bergeron?'

She stopped. Confused. 'Are you here with Jimmie Ray?' She didn't know he was dead.

'I've got some bad news, Ms Bergeron. Is there someplace we can talk?'

She looked from me to Pike and back again. She looked nervous. 'Are you the police?'

I shook my head. 'No, ma'am.'

'Where's Jimmie? They said he was here.'

'He couldn't make it. Is there someplace we can talk?'

You could see the world slow down for her. You could see the ceiling lower and the end of the hall recede and the pounding of her pulse grow to mask all lesser sounds. She seemed to sway, the way a reed might in a soft breeze, and then she shook her head. 'I'm sorry. I don't know you, and I don't think I have anything to say to you.'

She turned back to her office. I took her arm and quietly said, 'Jimmie's dead. Milt Rossier had him murdered.'

In that instant she tried to pull away from me, but I held on, and, just as quickly, she stopped pulling. Tears welled and she blinked frantically, and pretty soon the tears were gone. People moved along the hall, in and out of offices, in and out of the elevators. I let go of her and stepped back.

I said, 'We're not the police, and we're not from Milt Rossier. We won't hurt you.'

She nodded.

'I'm a private investigator, and I'm not after you. I'm after Milt. He's the guy I want to hurt. Do you understand?'

She nodded again. Getting her breath under control. 'He killed Jimmie Ray?'

'I believe so. Yes.'

'It's about those files, isn't it?'

'We shouldn't talk in the hall.'

She brought us two flights down to an employees' cafeteria that smelled of hamburgers and lima beans. We sat at a table with a view across the city and drank coffee while Sandi Bergeron told us that she had met Jimmie Ray ten months ago when he had come to her office to ask for Jodi Taylor's adoption records. Just like that, he had walked in and asked if he could have a copy. They'd told him no, of course, and turned him away, but Jimmie Ray had hung around out in the hall by the Coca-Cola machine, stomping about and fuming and convinced that 'the Boss Bitch', as he'd called Mrs Washington, was just looking for a payoff. Sandi had gone out for a Dr Pepper and had met Jimmie there when he'd asked her if she had change of a dollar. She was surprised when he'd phoned a few days later, tracking her down by calling the Social Services Department and saying that he'd like to speak with 'the pretty blond girl.' They had connected him with two other women before they put on Sandi Bergeron, who was not pretty, and never would be, and would always feel bad about it.

Three weeks later, when they were lying in bed, he'd asked what was the big deal with these sealed documents, did they keep 'em in a goddamned vault or somethin'?

Two weeks after that, when they were lying in bed, he'd asked if she'd ever *seen* one of these sealed documents and, if she hadn't, how did she know they were really there?

One week after that, when they were lying in bed, he'd asked if she could get her hands on Jodi Taylor's adoption records, and, if she could, would she give it a quick read and tell him Jodi's bio-mama's name?

He hadn't asked her to steal the file, she said, but by the time she had it in her hands she was just so god-darned nervous that it was just easier to steal it than to stand there reading the thing. So she had.

I said, 'Did you know that Jimmie Ray was working for Milt Rossier?'

'Not then he wasn't. He was just lookin' for somethin' he could sell to the *National Enquirer* or one of those magazines. Only he found that thing about Leon Williams and that sheriff over there, and he took it to Milt Rossier.'

'You knew about the blackmail?'

She looked defensive. 'Jimmie Ray said Mr Rossier was gonna put him on retainer. He said he wouldn't have to work as a mechanic anymore. Jimmie didn't want to be a nobody all his life.'

Pike said, 'He doesn't have to worry about it anymore, does he?'

Sandi Bergeron stared at him, and then had some of her coffee.

I said, 'Did Jimmie Ray tell you why Milt was blackmailing the sheriff?'

She shook her head.

'Did he tell you anything about Rossier's business?'

'I'm sorry.'

'Please try to remember.'

She put down the coffee cup and picked at the table. The bubble-gum nails were long and French-tipped and probably false. She made a little shrug. 'Jimmie didn't know everything that old man had going, and Jimmie Ray had spent a lot of time trying to find out. He told me so himself. He said that Mr Rossier was so careful about all these things that he'd never get caught. He said he learned a lot from that old man.'

'Like what?'

You could see her work to try to remember. 'He said the old man never got involved himself. He had this other guy do that.'

'LeRoy Bennett.'

'Jimmie Ray called him a stooge. He said that if there was ever any trouble, it would all go back to the stooge.'

'What else?'

She chewed at her lips, thinking harder. 'He told me about this place called the Bayou Lounge.'

'Uh-huh.'

'Mr Rossier owns it. Jimmie Ray said that the old man bought it so he wouldn't have to bring any of his bad business home. Jimmie thought that was just the smartest thing. He said the old man's stooge would go to the Bayou Lounge to take care of business. That way they didn't have to bring it home. You see?'

I glanced at Pike, and Pike nodded. He said, 'If we're looking for something, maybe we should look there.'

Sandi Bergeron crossed her arms over her middle. She said, 'Am I going to get in trouble?'

I looked at her. 'Maybe, but not because of us. The cops are going to investigate Jimmie's murder, and they may find you the way we found you, but it won't be because we told them. We won't.'

She nodded and looked at her coffee. 'I know that what I did was wrong. I'm really sorry.'

'Sure.'

'I think I'm going home. I don't feel well.'

We walked to the elevator with her. She pressed the button for *up*. We pressed for *down*. The *up* elevator came first, but she didn't get on right away. She stopped in the door and said, 'I know what you're thinking, but it's not so. Jimmie Ray didn't use me. He loved me. We were goin' to get married.' She stood straight when she said it, as if she were challenging me to disagree.

I said, 'Sandi?'

She stared at me.

'I got to know Jimmie Ray a little bit before he died. You were all he talked about. He did want to marry you. He told me so.'

She blinked hard twice and her eyes filled. She stepped backward into the elevator, the doors closed, and she was gone.

We stood in silence for a moment, and then Pike said, 'Is that true?'

The *down* elevator came. We got aboard, and I did not answer.

25

We drove back to the Riverfront Ho-Jo, checked out, then called Lucy at her office and told her that we were on our way to Ville Platte. She said, 'Do you know what you're going to do when you get there?'

'Sit on the Bayou Lounge and establish a pattern for Rossier and his people. It could take a while.'

She didn't say anything for a moment. 'Yes. I guess it could.'

'I'm going to miss you.'

'Me, too, Studly. Try not to get shot.'

At a little bit before two o'clock that afternoon, Pike and I took the same room I had used before in Ville Platte and unloaded our things. I changed into waterproof Cabela boots and a black T-shirt. Pike stayed in the same clothes, but took a Colt .357 Python out of his duffel and put it under his sweatshirt. I put my Dan Wesson into a clip-on holster, put the clip-on on the inside of my waistband, and left the T-shirt out to cover it. My T-shirt didn't hide the Dan Wesson as well as Pike's sweatshirt hid the Python. People would probably think I was wearing a colostomy bag.

We went down to the Pig Stand for a couple of catfish poboys, then walked across to the little superette, bought a cheap Styrofoam ice chest, ice, and enough Diet Coke, Charmin, and sandwich stuff to last a couple of days. Pike went for the cheese and peanut butter, I went for the pressed chicken and Spam. Pike shook his head when he saw the Spam. He was shaking his head about the Spam even before he was a vegetarian. The woman at the register thought we must be going fishing, and we said sure. She said the *sac-à-lait* were biting real good. She said her husband went out just last night and got a couple dozen on the bayou just over there by Chataignier. We thanked her and said we'd give it a try. Walking out, Pike said, 'What's a *sac-à-lait*?'

'I think it's a kind of white perch. Like a crappie.'

Pike grunted.

I said, 'They eat gar balls down here, too.'

Pike gave me a look like, yeah, sure.

Lucy had provided us with a current address for LeRoy Bennett. We got the Bayou Lounge address from Information. Pike and I decided to split our time between LeRoy's and the crawfish farm during the day, then watch the lounge together at night. We went to LeRoy's first.

LeRoy Bennett lived on a narrow residential street on the west side of Ville Platte in a tiny clapboard house that was dusty and dirty and overgrown by weeds. All of the houses on the street were small, but most were well kept with neatly trimmed lawns and edged walkways. The St Augustine at LeRoy's place had to be a good eight inches tall, the crabgrass and weed sprouts even taller. Twin tire ruts were cut into the yard, with great black dead spots between them where LeRoy had parked the Polara and the engine had dripped. There was a drive, but why use the drive when you can park on the grass? I was hoping that LeRoy and his car would be there so that Pike could see them, but they weren't. Of course, maybe they were hidden behind all the foliage. I said, 'That's LeRoy's place.'

Pike shook his head. 'No self-esteem.'

I stopped at the mouth of LeRoy's drive. 'He drives a gold Polara with a lot of sun damage.' I looked up and down the street. Cars were parked along both sides of the street. 'Best place for a stake would be on the next block, under that oak.'

Pike looked and approved. Next door to LeRoy's, a man in his mid-sixties was working Bond-o into the side of a beige '64 Chevelle. His home and his lawn were immaculate, but the weeds from LeRoy's crappy yard hung over onto his property like shaggy hair curling over a collar. He looked at us, taking a break from the Bond-o, and we drove away.

We went to Milt Rossier's crawfish farm. I cruised the front gate to let Pike have a look, then parked the car on a little gravel road maybe a quarter-mile away. We worked our way through the trees to the edge of Milt's property and crouched by a fallen pine. We could see pretty much everything, from the ponds and the processing buildings on our left up to Milt's home on the little knoll to our right. When we were in position and looking, I said, 'Well, well. The gang's all here.'

LeRoy Bennett was talking to a heavyset woman by the processing buildings and Milt Rossier was driving a little golf cart between the ponds with one of his skinny foremen. LeRoy's Polara was parked up by the house, and René LaBorde was at the house, too, sitting in a white lawn chair, either sleeping or staring at his crotch. Pike squinted when he saw René. 'This is some operation.'

'Uh-huh.'

We watched as people waded into ponds, scattering what was probably crawfish food and pulling weeds and keeping the bottoms stirred. In other ponds, people used trucks with winches to seine out slick gray catfish or dark red crawfish, emptying filled nets into little trailers with open tops. Some of the people working the ponds were African-American

349

women, but most of them were short, blocky Hispanics. A couple of older, skinny white guys in wide-brimmed straw hats moved between the pools, telling everybody else what to do. Upper management. I said, 'Seen enough?'

Pike nodded.

We made our way back to the Thunderbird, then drove to the Bayou Lounge, just west of Ville Platte off the State 10 near Reddell. It was a small, white building set back from the road in a little clearing carved into the woods. An abandoned bait shop sat nearby, its windows boarded over, painted ground to roof with ICE and WORMS in ten-foot letters. Both buildings were surrounded by crushed oyster shells and little patches of grass and weeds, and felt sort of like LeRoy Bennett's place. Crummy. A rusted steel pole jutted up from the side of the bar with a sign that said SCHLITZ. The Bayou Lounge didn't look like a hotbed of criminal activity, but you never know.

We eased off the road past the bait shop, stopped, and looked back. It was thirty-six minutes after three. A blue Ford Ranger was parked on the side of the lounge and a Lone Star truck was parked out front. If there was a bayou around, you couldn't see it from the road. A guy in a blue-and-white Lone Star uniform pushed a hand truck out the door, followed by a woman with a clipboard. The woman with the clipboard had a lot of bright red Clairol hair piled atop her head and red nails and red lipstick. Thin in the shoulders and wide in the butt, with white denim pants that were ten years and fifteen pounds too tight. She talked with the guy as he loaded the dolly onto his truck, then watched him drive away before she went back inside. Pike said, 'I make it for her Ford. You want to check it, or me?'

'Me.'

We pulled around to the front of the lounge and parked by the Schlitz sign, and I went in. Six cases of Lone Star were stacked at the end of the bar, and the woman was frowning at a thin Hispanic guy as he lugged them one at a time behind the counter. Eight or nine small square tables were scattered around the place, all with upended chairs on top of them, and a Rockola jukebox was against the back wall beside a door that said RESTROOMS. An industrial wash bucket was by the jukebox, and the back door was open for the breeze. The woman looked over at me and said, 'Sorry, sugah. We closed.'

'I'm supposed to meet a guy here. What time you open?'

''Bout five, give or take. Who you lookin' by?' She gave me a loose smile. She was maybe forty-five, but looked older, with rubbery skin pulled tight by all the smiling. The Hispanic guy stopped working to look at us.

'Oh, just a friend.' Mr Mysterious.

'You keepin' it a big secret or what, sug? I'm here all the time.' When she said it she noticed the Hispanic guy and snapped at him. 'Don't just stand there, goddammit! Put that stuff away! *Endelay!*' The Hispanic guy spun back to his work with a vengeance. I wasn't sure if he understood what had been said to him, but he understood that she was pissed. The Clairol Queen flipped her hand at him, disgusted. 'These spics are somethin'. Gimme a good nigger any day.'

I said, 'A guy named LeRoy Bennett said I could find him here.'

She went back to the smiling and folded herself against the bar. It was probably a pose that played well with the older guys after a dozen or so beers. 'Oh, yeah. LeRoy's here all the time. I can take a message, you want.'

'Nah. I'm on my way to Biloxi. I'll catch him on the way back.'

I went back to the car and climbed in beside Pike. 'They open at five. LeRoy's here all the time.'

'Who could blame him?'

We drove up the road for a mile and a half, then turned around and went back. One hundred yards past the bait shop I eased onto the shoulder, and Pike got out with his duffel and moved into the trees. I drove on for maybe another four hundred yards until I found a gravel timber road running across a plank bridge, and pulled off. I locked the car, then trotted back to the bait shop. By the time I got back Pike was inside and set up, watching the bar through a clean spot he'd made on the dusty plate glass.

The Bayou Lounge might have opened at five, but no one showed up until six, and then it was mostly younger guys with deep tans and ball caps, looking like they had just gotten off work and wanted to have a couple of cold ones before heading home. Someone cranked up the Rockola at nine minutes before seven, and we could hear Doug Kershaw singing in French.

Pike and I made cold sandwiches and drank Diet Coke and watched the people come and go, but none of them were Milt Rossier or LeRoy Bennett or even René LaBorde. Crime might have been rampant, but if it was, we didn't see it.

The bait shop was an empty cinder-block shell containing the remnants of a counter and a couple of free-standing shelves and a cement floor. We sat on the floor, surrounded by the odd-cut piece of plywood and about a million rat pellets. Everything was covered with a thick layer of heretofore undisturbed dust, and everything smelled of mildew. 'Just think, Joe, some guys have to wear a tie and punch a time clock.'

Pike didn't answer.

At 8:15 that night, seven cars were parked in the oyster shell lot and maybe a dozen people were inside the Bayou Lounge, but Milt Rossier and LeRoy Bennett were not among them. Pike rarely spoke, and there wasn't a great deal to do in our watching, and I found myself thinking of

Lucy, wondering where she was and what she was doing, seeing her in her office, seeing her on the couch in her family room, seeing her snuggled with Ben watching *Star Trek*. After a while I got tired of all the thinking about it and tried to stop, but then I thought that maybe I could walk across to the Bayou and use the pay phone to call her. Of course, if I did, ol' Milt and LeRoy would probably amble in at exactly that time. It's one of those laws of nature. Pike said, 'You deserve someone.'

'What are you talking about?'

'Ms Chenier.'

I stared at him. Do you think he reads minds? 'We enjoy each other's company.'

He nodded.

'I like her and she likes me. It's nothing more or less than that.'

He nodded again.

By 9:15 we were down to two cars, and by ten the lot was empty except for the blue Ford Ranger. Pike said, 'This place is a gold mine.'

At twenty minutes before eleven, a beat-up Mercury station wagon bumped into the lot and sat with its engine running. The little Hispanic man and a Hispanic woman I had not seen came out, got in, and the wagon lurched away. The woman was carrying what looked like a brown paper grocery bag. Pike said, 'Latin guy driving.'

I squinted, but couldn't be sure. 'Joe? Do you find it odd that there are so many Latin people down here on the bayou?'

Pike shrugged.

At ten minutes after eleven, the Bayou Lounge went dark, and the woman who ran the place got into her Ford and drove away. Pike and I gathered our things, walked up the road to our car, then returned to the motel. I wanted to phone Lucy, but it was just before midnight, and I thought I might wake her or, if not her, Ben.

The last thing I remember that night was the sound of Lucy's laugh and the smell of her skin, and the deep, hollow feeling of her absence.

26

At eighteen minutes after five the next morning, Joe Pike slipped into the woods fronting Milt Rossier's crawfish farm. I went back to Ville Platte and parked beneath the oak tree one block down from LeRoy Bennett's house. The sky began to lighten at twenty minutes after six, and by 7:30 the old man who lived next to LeRoy was again working at the beige Chevelle with the Bond-o and the putty knife. A fluffy white cat strolled up to the old man, shoulder bumped against his legs, and the old man scratched at the cat's head. The old man and the cat seemed to be enjoying each other when LeRoy Bennett came out with a little green towel, hawked up a lugey, and let'r fly into the overgrown front lawn. The old man stopped with the cat and scowled at Bennett. Bennett had to see him but pretended he didn't, and neither of them spoke to the other. LeRoy wiped the dew off his front and back windshields, then tossed the wet towel up onto his front steps, climbed into the Polara, and drove away. The old man watched him drive off, then looked at the towel and at LeRoy's crummy yard. The towel looked like hell, just thrown there. The old man looked at his own immaculate yard and shook his head. Probably wondering why he should bother with all the yard work if LeRoy was going to let his place look like a shit hole, probably thinking that all the stuff you hear on the talk radio was right; America was going to hell in a handbasket and he was stuck with living proof of it.

The plan had been for me to stay on LeRoy until four, whereupon I would break contact and pick up Pike to return to the Bayou Lounge. We hoped that LeRoy would, in his capacity as Milt Rossier's right-hand man, have a variety of important errands to accomplish through the day, perhaps one or more of said errands providing a clue as to Milt Rossier's criminal operation. When LeRoy Bennett cleared the corner, I pulled a quick U-turn, took it easy going around the corner to make sure he wouldn't see me, then followed him directly to the Ville Platte Dunkin' Donuts. LeRoy stoked up on crullers with sprinkles, then bought four dollars of gas at the Sunoco self-serve and tooled directly to Rossier's place. By 8:36 that morning, LeRoy was sitting in the white lawn chairs outside Rossier's main house, flipping through a magazine, and I was crouching behind the fallen pine tree with Joe Pike. So much for clues. I said, 'Some operation.'

Pike was watching him through a fine pair of Zeiss binoculars. 'He's not reading. He's just looking at the pictures.'

I nodded. 'Geniuses rarely go into crime.'

We sat on plastic poncho liners amid the sumac and the small plants of the forest's floor and let the day unfold. The heat rose, and with the heat the air grew heavy and damp, and a thick gray buildup of rain clouds appeared overhead. The woods were alive with the sounds of bees and lizards and squirrels and swamp martins, and only occasionally did we catch the voices of the people before us, moving through their labors in the ponds and pools of the fish farm. It was ordinary business and none of it appeared illegal or suspicious, but maybe all of it was.

About midmorning Milt Rossier came out of his house, and he and Bennett strolled down past the ponds to the processing sheds. Milt stopped and spoke with each of the foremen, nodding as they spoke and once taking off his hat and mopping his brow, but that was probably not an actionable offense. René LaBorde came out of the processing shed and lurched his way over to them and followed them around, but no one spoke to him. I hadn't seen him arrive, and Pike hadn't mentioned him, so maybe he had been in the processing shed all along. Maybe he lived there.

The guy who bossed the processing shed came out when Rossier and Bennett got down there, and the three of them spoke. René stood outside their circle for a time, then walked to the turtle pond and waded in up to his knees. The straw boss saw him first, and everybody got excited as LeRoy ran over to the edge of the pool, yelling, 'Goddammit, René, get outta there! C'mon, 'fore Luther bites you!' René came back to the shore but stared down at the murky water, his shoes and pants muddy and dripping. He didn't seem to know what he had done or to understand why he'd been made to stop. Pike shook his head. 'Man.'

After a while, Rossier and LeRoy started back to the main house and everyone went back to work. René continued staring down at the water, his large body giving the occasional lurch as if his synapses had misfired. Halfway up to the house, Rossier saw that René wasn't following, slapped at LeRoy, and LeRoy trotted back for René. René followed LeRoy back to the main house, and the two of them sat in the white chairs, passing the day, the water and mud drying on René's pants, LeRoy looking at the pictures in his magazine.

The clouds continued to build, and by three o'clock the sky was dark. Lightning arced somewhere in the trees behind us, producing a deep-throated rumble, and it rained, slowly at first but with increasing intensity. LeRoy and René went into the main house and, one by one, the people working the ponds sought shelter in the processing sheds. Pike and I pulled on ponchos and made our way out to the car. We were leaving earlier than we had planned, but with everyone hiding from the rain the possibility of crime seemed remote. We stopped at an AM/PM Minimart on the state road to Reddell, and I used a pay phone to call Lucy at her office. She was with a client, and Darlene asked if I wanted to leave a message. I said to tell her that I had called and would call her again when I had the chance. Darlene said that that wasn't much of a message, considering. I said considering what? Darlene laughed and hung up. Do women always tell each other everything?

The sky was the color of sun-bright tarmac, and forks of lightning were dancing along the horizon when Pike and I again moved into the bait shop across from the Bayou Lounge. The rain hammered down in a steady, thunderous assault, and leaked in tap-water streams through the roof, but it was better than standing in the woods. By seven that night, the only people in the place were a couple of old codgers who'd come in a white Bronco. By eight they were gone, and by nine the same green wagon once more came around for the Hispanic couple. By 9:30 the Bayou Lounge was closed. Maybe the rain had kept people away. Maybe if it rained all year round, the crime rate would be zero.

Pike and I went through it again the next day and the day after, with no great variety of pattern. Every morning I would wait for LeRoy Bennett outside his house, and every morning he would beeline first to the Dunkin' Donuts and then to the crawfish farm where he would sit and wait and page through his magazines. Working off the sugar high, no doubt. Once Milt Rossier came out at midday and said something to LeRoy, and LeRoy hopped into his Polara and brodied away. I ran back through the woods to the car in time to see LeRoy hauling ass up the road toward town. I followed him directly to the Ville Platte McDonald's where he loaded up on a couple of bags' worth of stuff, then hauled ass back to Rossier's. I guess even criminals like Big Macs.

If the days were bad, the nights were worse. We would sit in the dust on the bait shop floor, watching the cars come and go, and noting the people within them, but the people within them were never LeRoy Bennett or Milt Rossier, nor did anything happen to point to or indicate illegal activity. Once, a fat man in a cheap suit and a thin woman with Dolly Parton hair had sex in the backseat of a Buick Regal, and two nights later the same woman had sex with a skinny guy with a straw Stetson in the back of an Isuzu Trooper, but you probably couldn't indict Milt Rossier for that. Another time, three guys staggered out of the bar, laughing and hooting, while a fourth guy in a white ball cap stumbled out into the center of the road, dropped his pants, and took a dump. He lost his balance about midway through and fell in it, and the other three guys laughed louder and threw a beer can at him. Nothing like a night out with the boys.

Over the next three days I had exactly two opportunities to call Lucy, and missed her both times, once leaving a message on her home answering machine and once again speaking with her assistant. Darlene said that Lucy very much wanted to speak with me and asked if couldn't we prearrange a time when I might call. I told her that that would be impossible, and Darlene said, 'Oh, you poor thing.' Maybe Darlene wasn't so bad after all.

We had two dry days and then another day of rain, and all the watching without getting anywhere was making me cranky and depressed. Maybe we were wasting our time. Maybe the only illegal stuff was the stuff behind closed doors, and we could sit in the woods and the bait shop until the bayous froze and we'd never quite make the link. Pike and I took turns exercising.

At 8:22 on the fourth night in the bait shop, the rain was tapping the roof and I was doing yoga when Pike said, 'Here we go.'

LeRoy Bennett and René LaBorde pulled in and parked next to the blue Ford. Six cars were already in the lot, four of them regulars and none of them suspicious. LeRoy climbed out of the Polara and swaggered into the bar. René stayed in the car. Pike said, 'I'll get the car.'

He slipped out into the rain.

At 8:28, a dark gray Cadillac Eldorado with New Orleans plates pulled in beside the Polara. A Hispanic man in a silver raincoat got out and went into the bar. At 8:31, Pike reappeared beside me, hair wet with sweat and rain. Maybe two minutes later, the Hispanic man came out again with LeRoy Bennett. The Hispanic man got into his Eldo and LeRoy got into his Polara, and then the Polara moved out with the Eldo following.

Pike and I hustled out to our car and then eased onto the road after them. As I drove, Pike unscrewed the bulb in the ceiling lamp. Be prepared.

No one went fast and no one made a big deal out of where they were going, as if they had made the drive before and were comfortable with it, just a couple of guys going about their business. Traffic was nonexistent, and it would have been better if we'd had a car or two between us, but the steady rain made the following easier. We drove without lights, and twice oncoming cars flicked their headlights, trying to warn us, the second time some cowboy going crazy with it and calling us assholes as he roared by. If the guy in the Eldo was watching the rear he might have seen all the headlight switching and wondered about it, but if he was he gave no sign. Why watch the rear when you own the cops and you know they're not looking for you?

We turned onto the highway leading to Milt Rossier's crawfish farm, and I thought that was where we were going, only we came to the gate and passed it, continuing on. I dropped further back, and Pike leaned forward in his seat, squinting against the rain and the windshield wipers to keep the red lights in sight. Maybe a mile past Rossier's gate, the Eldo's taillights flared and Pike said, 'They're turning.'

The Polara grew bright in the Eldorado's headlights as it turned onto a gravel feeder road forking off into the marsh through a heavy thatch of wild sugarcane and bramble. We waited until their lights disappeared, then closed the distance and turned across a cow bridge. An overgrown cement culvert thrust up from the earth by the cow bridge, ringed by chain link to protect pipes and fittings and what looked in the darkness to be pressure gauges. Abandoned oil company gear. I said, 'If this was anymore nowhere, we'd be on the dark side of the moon.'

The little road narrowed and followed the top of a berm across the marsh, moving in and out of cane thickets and sawgrass and cattails, occasionally crossing other little gravel roads even more overgrown. We had gone maybe half a mile when a wide waterway appeared on the left, its banks overgrown but precise and straight and clearly manmade. I said, 'Looks like an industrial canal.'

Pike said, 'They turn and head back on us, we've got a problem.'

'Yeah.' When we came to the next crossing road, we stopped and backed off the main road, far enough under the sawgrass to hide the car, then went on at a jog. Once we were out of the car we could hear the rain slapping the grass and the water with the steady sound of frying bacon. We followed the little road for maybe another quarter-mile and then an enormous, corrugated-tin building bathed in light rose up from the swamp like some incredible lost city. It stood on the edge of the canal, a huge metal shed, maybe three stories tall, lit with industrial floodlamps powered by a diesel generator. Rusted pipes ran in and out of the building, and some of the corrugated-metal panels were hanging askew. The isolation and the technology lent a creepy air to the place, as if we had stumbled upon an abandoned government installation, once forbidden and now best forgotten.

The Polara and the Cadillac were at the foot of the building, along with a couple of two-and-a-half-ton trucks. Both of the trucks were idling, their exhausts breathing white plumes into the damp air like waiting beasts. Pike and I slipped off the road and into the sawgrass. I said, 'Pod people.'

Pike looked at me.

'It's like the nursery Kevin McCarthy discovers in *Invasion of the Body Snatchers*. The one where the pod people are growing more pods and loading them onto trucks to be shipped all over the country.'

Pike shook his head and turned back to the building. 'You're something.'

A huge, hangarlike door was set into the side of the building. Three guys in rain parkas climbed out of the trucks, opened it, then climbed back into the trucks, and drove them inside. A couple of minutes later, the steady burping of a diesel grew out of the rain and a towboat came up the canal, running without lights and pushing a small barge. It reduced speed maybe a hundred meters from the mouth of the big shed, and the Hispanic guy walked to the water's edge and waved a red lantern. The towboat revved its engines, then came forward under power and slipped inside the building. LeRoy and René and the guy from the Cadillac hurried in after it. Pike and I skirted the edge of the lighted area until we could see through the truck door. I had thought that we'd see people loading bales of marijuana onto the barge or maybe fork-lifting huge bricks of cocaine off the barge, but we didn't. Inside, maybe three dozen people were climbing off the towboat and into the trucks. Many of them looked scruffy, but not all. Many of them were well dressed, but not all. Most of them were Hispanic, but two were black, three were white, and maybe half a dozen were Asian. All of them looked tired and ill and frightened, and all of them were carrying suitcases and duffel bags and things of a personal nature. Pike said, 'Sonofabitch. It's people.'

When the trucks were full, the guys in the parkas pulled down canvas flaps to hide their cargo, climbed back into the cabs, pulled out of the building, and drove away into the rain. When the trucks were gone, a couple of hard-looking guys came up out of the barge dragging a skinny old man and carrying something that looked like a rag doll. The old man was crying and pulling at the hard guys, but they didn't pay a lot of attention to him. The old guy went over to the guy from the Eldorado with a lot of hand-waving, and then fell to the ground, pulling at the Eldorado's legs. The guy from the Eldorado kicked at the old man, then pulled out a small revolver, put it to the old man's head, and we heard a single, small *pop*.

My breath caught and I felt Pike tense.

The guy from the Eldo kicked the old man's body away, then said something to LeRoy Bennett, and Bennett nodded. The guys from the towboat climbed back aboard, and LeRoy and the guy with the gun walked out to the Eldo. The shooter opened the Eldo's trunk, took out a small handbag, and gave it to LeRoy. LeRoy brought it to his Polara. The towboat's engines revved, it backed from the shed, spun slowly into the canal, then eased back the way it had come, still without lights, the low gurgle of its engines fading into the mist. The shooter got into his Eldo and followed after the trucks. Now there were only four of us. Pike said, 'Too late for the old man. What do you want to do?'

'Let's see what happens.'

LeRoy took a shovel from the Polara, then he and René dragged the old man and the rag doll along a little trail into the weeds. Pike and I crept after them, moving closer. René dug a small depression in the wet earth, dumped in the bodies, covered them, then went back to their car. LeRoy turned off the generator, and the swamp was suddenly dark. He and René got into their car, and then they, too, were gone.

I said, 'Okay.'

Pike and I moved to the shallow grave and pushed the mud away with our hands and found the old man and a little girl. The girl was maybe five. She was small and thin, and perhaps she might have been ill, but maybe not. Her face was dark with the rich earth, but as the rain kissed her skin the dirt washed away. I stroked her hair and felt my breath slow and the muscles along my neck and back and across my ribs tighten. She might have been the old man's granddaughter, but maybe not. Maybe she was alone, and he had befriended her. Maybe he just cared, and in the caring expressed his outrage at her death, and for his outrage he'd been killed. We went through his pockets hoping for some sort of identification, but there was none. There was only a small photograph, bent and water-stained, of the man and a group of people who may have been his family. The man was smiling. I put the photograph in my pocket. I said, 'Let's get them out of here.'

Pike touched my arm. 'We can't, Elvis.'

I looked at him.

'If we move them, Rossier will know. We have to wait. We have to know more before we help them.'

I breathed deep in the wet air, and then I nodded. I didn't like it, but there you are.

We sat in the rain with the old man and the little girl, and after a while we left.

27

We returned to the motel at a little before two the next morning, driving slowly along roads that were glassy with rain, through a town so still that it seemed as lifeless and empty as the bodies we'd left in the mud and the sawgrass. We were all that moved in Ville Platte, Joe and I, neither of us speaking, lit only by flashing yellow signal lights that whispered *caution*.

We showered and changed, Joe going first, and when we were done and the lights were out, I said, 'Joe?'

I heard him move on the floor, but it took him several seconds to answer. 'Yes.'

'Oh, Jesus, Joe.'

Pike might have slept, but I did not. I was in the dry room, yet not. I was with the old man and the girl, yet not. I crouched in the sawgrass beside them, the night air dank and muggy, the rain running out of my hair and down my back, the great fat drops falling on the faces below me, washing circles of perfect clarity on the muddy skin, but a clarity that did not maintain and soon faded, obscured by more drops, as if every new truth clouded an old.

The rain stopped falling a few minutes after four, and at 7:05 we called Lucy at her home and told her what we had seen. She said, 'Do you think these people were illegal aliens?'

'We counted thirty-five people climbing onto the trucks, but there could've been more. A few Asians, a few whites and blacks, but the majority were Hispanics.' I told her about the old man and the girl.

Lucy said, 'Oh, my God.'

'We left them in place. Rossier wasn't at the scene, and I'm not certain we can tie this to him. We'd get Bennett and LaBorde for sure, but maybe not Rossier.'

She said, 'Did you get the Cadillac's license number?'

I gave it to her.

Lucy said, 'Stay where you are. I'll call you as soon as I have something.'

'Thanks, Luce.'

She said, 'I miss you, Studly.'

'I miss you, too, Luce.'

One hour and thirteen minutes later Lucy called back. 'The Eldorado is registered to someone named Donaldo Prima from New Orleans. He's thirty-four years old, originally from Nicaragua, with three felony convictions, two for dealing stolen goods and one firearms violation. There's nothing in his record to link him to illegal immigration, but the feds are out of the loop on most of this stuff. I've got a friend here in Baton Rouge you can talk to. She works for an alternative weekly called the *Bayou State Sentinel*, and she's done some pretty good work covering the immigration scene. She might be willing to help.'

'Might.'

'You'll see.' Lucy gave me directions, hung up, then Pike and I drove to Baton Rouge.

The *Sentinel* had their offices in a little clapboard house on a street just off the LSU campus that was mostly rental houses for students and people who enjoyed the student lifestyle. Some of the houses had been converted to businesses, but the businesses were all places like used-CD stores and grunge shops and a place that sold joss sticks and papier mâché alligators. Alternative. A couple of mountain bikes and a Triumph motorcycle were chained to a bikestand in front of a house with a little sign that said BAYOU STATE SENTINEL – THE LAST BASTION OF TRUTH IN AMERICA. I guess being a bastion of truth didn't prevent people from stealing your bicycles.

Pike and I parked at a meter, and Pike said, 'I'll wait in the car.' Pike's not big on alternative.

I went up a little cement walk and in through the front door to what had probably been the living room when people were living here instead of working here. Now, five desks were wedged into the place, along with a coffee machine and a water cooler and a lot of posters of Kurt Cobain and Hillary Clinton and framed *Sentinel* covers. The covers had headlines like LIFE SUX and FIVE REASONS TO KILL YOURSELF NOW. Alternative. A couple of African-American women in their late twenties were working at Macintosh computers further back in the room, one of them on the phone as she typed, and an athletic white guy with short red hair was at a desk just inside the door. A parrot sat on a perch in the waiting area, copies of the *New York Times* and the New Orleans *Times-Picayune* spread on the floor beneath it. The parrot flapped its wings when it saw me, then lifted its tail feathers and squirted a load of parrot shit onto the *New York Times*. I said, 'Man, this parrot is something.'

The red-haired guy smiled over at me. 'That's Bubba, and that's what we think of the mainstream press. What can I do for you?'

I gave him one of my cards. 'Elvis Cole to see Sela Henried. Lucille Chenier called her about me.'

He looked at the card and stood. 'I'll go see. You want some coffee or something?'

'No. Thanks.'

He disappeared into a little hall, then came back a couple of minutes later with a tall woman who didn't look thrilled to see me. She said, 'You're the guy Lucy called about?'

I said, 'Is it that disappointing?'

She frowned when I said it, then went to the windows and peered out at the street, like maybe there would be a horde of FBI agents in my wake. 'Lucy said there were two of you.'

'He's waiting in the car.'

She looked back at me, and her eyes narrowed as if it were somehow suspicious that Pike would wait in the car. 'Well. Okay. Come back to my office.'

Sela Henried had a long face and short blond hair that had been bleached white and cut into spikes, and a row of nine piercings running up along the edge of her left ear. A small blue cross had been tattooed on the back of her right hand between the thumb and forefinger, and she was wearing cheap silver rings on most of her fingers. I made her for her mid-thirties, but she could have been older. Her office had once been a bedroom at the front of the house. She went to the windows, looked out at Joe Pike again, then put her hands on her hips. 'I don't like him sitting out there.'

'Why not?'

'He looks like a cop. So do you.' She turned back to me and crossed her arms. 'Perhaps you are.' Suspicious, all right.

I said, 'Ms Henried, did Lucy explain to you what this is about?' Maybe I should turn on the old charm. The old charm might be just the ticket.

'Yes, or I wouldn't be seeing you. I've known Lucy Chenier for a very long time, Mr Cole. We played tennis together at LSU, but this is a very controversial newspaper. Our phones have been tapped, our offices have been searched, and there is a damn long list of agencies that would like to see us out of business.' She sat and stared at me. 'This interview will not take place unless you agree to be searched.'

'Searched?' Maybe the old charm wasn't going to do much good, after all.

'I trust Lucy, but for all I know you've duped her to take advantage of me.'

I spread my hands. 'Are we talking a strip search or just your basic frisk job?'

She yelled, 'Tommy!' The red-haired guy came in. 'Would you see if he's wearing a wire, please?'

Tommy smiled shyly at me. 'Sorry.'

'No problem.'

362

Tommy patted me down, moving his hands up under my arms and down the hollow of my back and around my waist. Professional. Like he'd done it before, and like he'd had it done to him. When he reached the Dan Wesson he looked up, surprised. 'Hey, he's got a gun.'

She frowned at me. One of the posters over her desk showed a pistol with a big red slash across it and the words STOP THE HANDGUN MADNESS. She said, 'May we see your wallet?'

'Sure.' I took out my wallet and gave it to Tommy. He looked through everything the way a kid might, sort of curious but without any real involvement. 'It says he's a private investigator from California. There's a license for the gun.'

'All right, Tommy. Thanks.'

Tommy handed my wallet back and left. Polite. Another day at the truth factory.

Sela Henried went around behind her desk, and sat. She leaned back and put a foot up on the edge of her desk. Doc Martens. 'Lucy says you have questions about the immigration scene in Louisiana.'

'That's right. We're trying to find out about a guy named Donaldo Prima. We think he's running illegal aliens, but there's no record of it.'

'She mentioned Prima.' Sela Henried picked up a plastic pencil and tapped it against her knee. 'I looked through my notes and I can't find Prima mentioned, but that doesn't mean anything. We have what the mainstream press likes to call an "immigration problem" down here. New Orleans is a main entry port for people entering the country through the Gulf, and dozens of coyotes work the coast.'

'If you can't help us, maybe you know someone who can.'

She shook her head. 'I'm sorry.' She knew something, she just didn't want to talk about it.

'It's important, Ms Henried.'

She jabbed the pencil at me. 'I've covered the victimization of those trying to enter our country for years. The *Sentinel* supports the concept of open borders and the activities of those who circumvent our country's racist and exclusionary immigration policies.'

'Ms Henried, I work for some people who are being victimized in a pretty big way themselves. If I can find out about Donaldo Prima, I may be able to stop their own little slice of the victimization. It ain't saving the world, but it's what I can do.'

She said nothing.

'At a little bit after midnight last night, I saw Donaldo Prima shoot an old man in the head with a .32 caliber revolver. I think he shot the old man because the old man was making a stink about a little girl who died in the hold of the barge bringing them into this country. I saw both bodies. I touched them. Is that the kind of activity you support?'

She hissed out a little breath, then dropped her foot from the desk and leaned forward. 'Is that bullshit?'

'It's the truth.'

'Will you show me the bodies?'

'No.'

'Why not?'

'Because to do so might compromise my clients.'

'Maybe this issue is larger than your clients.'

'Then I'll have to live with it.'

She frowned at me some more, then got up, and went to the window to see if Pike was still there. She came back to her desk. 'Maybe I know someone. His name is Ramon del Reyo, and he could probably help you out. He wouldn't speak over the phone, though. He's helped a lot of people into the country and the feds just about live up his ass.'

'Okay.'

She let out another long breath. 'I want you to know how much I'm putting at risk, here. I believe in what Ramon's doing. He's a tough little sonofabitch, and everybody's after him, all the way from the feds to the goddamned hoods down in Nicaragua, and I'd hate like hell for anything to happen to him. Do you understand that?'

'I just want Prima, Ms Henried. Will your guy speak with me?'

She said, 'I have to make a call, and I won't do it from here. You can wait, or you can come along.' She stood again. 'Which is it?'

We walked up the street to a pay phone outside of a Subway Sandwich shop, and Sela Henried placed one call, using her body to block the phone so that I could not see the number she dialed. She spoke for maybe two minutes, then she hung up, keeping her hand on the receiver. 'Someone will call back.'

I nodded.

Nine minutes later the pay phone rang, and Sela Henried picked up before the first ring had finished. She spoke for a few minutes, this time writing something in a small reporter's notepad. When she hung up she gave me what she had written. 'This is in New Orleans, okay? It's a storefront. You have to be there at one o'clock, but you've got plenty of time.'

'Thanks, Sela. I appreciate it.'

She put the pad in her pocket, then looked at Pike. You could see him sitting in the car down the block, but you couldn't tell where he was looking or what he was thinking. She said, 'Ramon will be there, and he'll be with people who can protect him. Do you understand what I'm telling you?'

'Sure. Don't do anything stupid.'

She nodded. 'I wouldn't bring the gun. It will only make them nervous, and they will probably take it away from you, anyway.'

'Okay.'

She nodded again, then looked in my eyes the way you do when you want to make sure the person you're talking to doesn't just understand you, but actually gets it. She said, 'I'm trusting you with a very great deal, Mr Cole. Ramon is a good man, but these are dangerous people with a very great deal to lose. If they think you pose a threat to them, they will kill you. If they think that I set them up, they very well might kill me. I hope that matters to you.'

I looked at the pay phone, and then I looked back at the offices of the *Bayou State Sentinel.* 'If the feds want you enough to tap the phones in your office, they'll tap all of the nearby pay phones, too.'

She nodded, and now she looked tired, as if all the years of paranoia and fear were getting to be a little too heavy to bear. 'Like you, we do the best we can. I hope this helps, Mr Cole.'

Sela Henried walked back to the *Sentinel,* and Joe Pike and I drove to New Orleans. The drive took a little less than an hour and a half, through forests and swamps so thick they looked like jungle. As we drove I told Pike what Sela Henried had said about Ramon del Reyo and the people around him. Pike listened quietly, then said, 'I know guys from down south. They're dangerous people, Elvis. They've grown up with war. To them, war is a way of life.'

'Maybe we should split up. Maybe I should meet Ramon, and you should hang back and walk slack for me.' Slack was having someone there to pull your ass out of the fire if things went bad. Joe Pike was the best slack man in the business.

Pike nodded. 'Sounds good.'

The freeway rose the last twenty miles or so, elevated above swamp and cypress trees and hunched men in flat-bottomed boats. Lake Pontchartrain appeared on our left like a great inland sea, and then the swamps fell behind us and we were driving through a dense collar of bedroom communities, and then we were in New Orleans. We took the I-10 through the heart of the city past the Louisiana Superdome, which looked, from the freeway, like some kind of Michael Rennie *The Day the Earth Stood Still* spaceship plunked down amid the high-rises. We exited at Canal Street and drove south toward the river and the Vieux Carré.

At twenty minutes before one, we parked the car in a public garage on Chartres Street and split up, Pike leaving first. I put the Dan Wesson under the front seat, waited ten minutes, and then I followed.

I walked west on Magazine into an area of seedy, rundown storefronts well away from Bourbon Street and Jackson Square and the tour buses. The buildings were crummy and old, with cheesy shops and Nearly-Nu stores and the kinds of things that tourists chose to avoid. I found the address I'd been given, but it was empty and locked. A FOR LEASE sign was in the door, and the door was streaked with grime as if nobody had been in the place for the past couple of centuries. I said, 'Well, well.'

I knocked and waited, but no one answered. I looked both ways along the street, but I couldn't see Joe Pike. I was knocking for the second time when a pale gray Acura pulled to the curb and a thin Hispanic guy wearing Ray-Bans stared out at me. A black guy was sitting in the passenger seat beside him. The black guy looked Haitian. I said, 'Ramon?'

The Hispanic guy made a little head move indicating the backseat. 'Get in.'

I looked up and down the street again, and again I saw no one. I took a step back from the Acura. 'Sorry, guys. I'm waiting for someone else.'

The Haitian pointed a fully automatic Tec-9 machine pistol at me across the driver. 'Get in, mon, or I'll stitch you up good.'

I got in, and we drove away. Maybe splitting up hadn't been so smart, after all.

28

We drove four blocks to the big World Trade Center at the levee, then swung around to Decatur and the southern edge of the French Quarter. We parked across from the old Jackson Brewing Company, then walked east toward Jackson Square past souvenir shops and restaurants and a street musician working his way through 'St Vitus Day March'. He was wearing a top hat, and I pretended to look at him to try to find Joe Pike. Pike might have seen our turn; he might have cut the short blocks over and seen us creeping through the French Quarter traffic as we looked for a place to park. The Haitian pulled my arm, 'Le's go, mon.'

The air was hot and salty with the smell of oysters on half shell and Zatarain's Crab Boil. We walked beneath the covered *banquette* of a three-story building ringed with lacy ironwork, passing souvenir shops and seafood restaurants with huge outdoor boilers, wire nets of bright red crawfish draining for the tourists. Midday during the week, and people jammed the walk and the streets and the great square around the statue of Andrew Jackson. Sketch artists worked in the lazy shade of magnolia trees and mules pulled old-fashioned carriages along narrow streets. It looked like Disneyland on a Sunday afternoon, but hotter, and more than a few of the tourists looked flushed from the heat and shot glances at the bars and restaurants, working up fantasies about escaping into the AC to sip cold Dixie.

I followed the guy with the Ray-Bans and the Haitian across the Washington Artillery Park to a long cement promenade overlooking the river, and then to a wide circular fountain where another Hispanic guy waited by a Popsicle cart. He had a rugged bantamweight's face, and he was slurping at a grape Popsicle. I said, 'You Ramon?'

He shook his head once, smiling. 'Not yet, podnuh.' No accent. 'You carrying anything?'

'Nope.'

'We gonna have to check.' First the red-haired guy, now this.

'Sure.'

'Just do what I tell you, and everything'll be fine. Ramon's nearby.'

'I'm Mr Cooperation.'

'Piece a' cake, then.' He sounded like he was from Brooklyn.

He told me to stand there like we were having a grand little time, and I did. Ray-Ban and the Haitian laughed it up and patted me on the shoulders like we were sharing a laugh, their fingers dancing lightly beneath my arms and down along my ribs. The new guy yukked it up, too, but while he was yukking he dropped his Popsicle, then felt my calves and ankles as he picked it up. Like the red-haired guy, they had done it before. He tossed the Popsicle away and smiled. 'Okay. We're fine. Let's see the man.'

We walked to the other side of the fountain where Ramon del Reyo sat on a little bench beside a couple of sculpted azalea bushes. The azaleas were in profuse bloom, their hot pink flowers so dense and pure that they glowed in the blinding sun and cast a pink light. Ramon stood as we approached and offered his hand. He was about my height, but thin and scholarly, with little round spectacles and neat hair. Academic. He was smoking, and his thin cotton shirt was damp with sweat. He said, 'My name is Ramon del Reyo, Mr Cole. Let's walk along, shall we?'

He started off and I went with him, the others following alongside, some closer, some farther, and everybody keeping an eye out. I had seen presidential Secret Service bodyguards work public places, but I'd never seen anyone work a place better than these guys. You'd think we were in the middle of the cold war someplace, but then, maybe we were. Del Reyo said, 'Sela Henried is my friend and so I will speak with you, but I want you to know that there is a man near here with a rifle in the seven millimeter Magnum. He is very good with this thing, you see? He can hit the running deer cleanly at five hundred meters.'

I nodded. 'How far away is he now?'

'Less than two hundred.' Del Reyo looked at me with a studied air. 'If anything happens to me, you will be dead in that instant.'

'Nothing's going to happen, Mr del Reyo.'

He nodded. 'Please look here. On your chest.'

He gestured to the center of my chest, and I looked. A red dot floated there, hard and brilliant even in the bright sun. It flickered, then was gone. I looked up, but could not find the rifleman. I said, 'Laser sight.'

'Just so you know.' He made a dismissive wave. 'Please call me Ramon.' A guy tells you you're a trigger pull from dead, then says please call me Ramon.

'Who is Donaldo Prima?'

Ramon took a deep pull on the cigarette, then let the smoke curl out of his mouth and nostrils. 'He is dog shit.'

'Seriously, Ramon. Tell me what you really think.'

Ramon del Reyo smiled gently and ticked ash from the cigarette with his thumb. A couple of beat cops strolled by, grinning at some college girls from Ole Miss. The cops were wearing shorts like the tourists, and short-sleeved shirts with epaulets and knee socks like they were on safari. Del Reyo said, 'He is trying to be the big gangster, you see? *El coyote.* Someone to whom people go when they wish to enter our country.'

'Like you.'

Ramon del Reyo stopped smiling and looked at me the way he'd look at a disappointing student. 'Donaldo Prima is a smuggler. Automobiles, cocaine, farm equipment, people is all the same, to be bought and sold, you see? To be taken advantage of if possible. I am a political activist. What I do I do for free, because I care about these immigrants and their struggle to reach our country.'

'Sorry.'

He shrugged, letting it go. 'It is a nasty business. He is having problems.'

'What kind of problems?'

'He used to work for a man named Frank Escobar. You know Escobar?'

I shook my head. 'I don't know any of this, Ramon. That's why I'm talking to you.'

'Escobar is the big criminal, the one who controls most of what is smuggled into and out of the port of New Orleans. *El coyote grande.* He, too, is very bad. From the military in El Salvador. The truth squads.'

Great.

'A nut.'

Del Reyo smiled slightly. 'Yes. A killer, you see? He make much money sending stolen American automobiles to Central America when the boat go south, then bringing drugs and refugees here for even more money when the boat comes north. You see?'

'How much profit can there be in smuggling poor people across the border?'

'It is not just the poor who wish to come here, Mr Cole. The poor crawl under the fence at Brownsville and work as day laborers picking vegetables. The upper classes and the educated wish to come here, also, and they wish to bring their lives and professions with them. That is much more difficult than crawling under a fence.'

'They want to buy an identity.'

'*Si.* Yes. The coyote, he tells them that they are buying citizenship, you see? They will be given birth certificates, a driver's license, the social security card, all in their own names and usually with their actual birth dates. This is what they pay for, and they pay a very great deal. With these things they can bring the medical degree, the engineering degree, like that.'

'And do they get what they pay for?'

'Almost never.' We walked to the edge of the promenade. The river was below us, cutting a great brown swath through the city, flat and wide and somehow alive. The river's edge was prickly with loading cranes and wharfs and warehouses. He glanced at the Haitian and lowered his voice. 'Four months after he came, seven members of his family also bought passage through Frank Escobar. They were put in a barge out in the Gulf, fifty-four people put into a little space ten feet by eight feet, with no food and water, and the barge was set adrift. It was an old barge, and Escobar never intended to bring them ashore. He already have his money, you see, paid in full? A tanker reported the abandoned barge, and the Coast Guard investigated. All fifty-four men, women, and children had died. It got very hot in the hold of the barge with no openings for the ventilation and no water to drink. The hatch had been dogged shut, you see?' The Haitian's skin was a deep coal black, greasy with sweat. 'His father was a dentist. He wishes to be a dentist, also, but we see.' He let the thought trail away and looked back at me. 'That is the way it is with men like Escobar and Prima, you see? They get the money, then *fft*. Life means nothing. This is why I have so much protection, you see? I try to stop these men. I try to stop their murder.'

Neither of us spoke for a time. 'So what about Prima?'

'I hear that he has gone into business for himself, undercutting Escobar's price.'

I said, 'Ah.'

Del Reyo nodded.

I said, 'If Prima has set up a competing business, Escobar can't like it.'

He sucked on the cigarette. '*Si*. There is trouble between them. There is always trouble between men like this.' The smoke drifted up over his eyes, making him squint. 'You say you know nothing about the coyotes, yet you ask about Donaldo Prima. You say you know that he is a bad man. How do you know these things?'

'I saw his people bring a dead child off a barge sometime around eleven-thirty last night. There were other people, but only the child was dead. An old man was making a deal about it, and I saw Prima shoot the old man in the head.'

Ramon del Reyo did not move. 'You saw this thing?'

I nodded.

'You have proof?'

'May I reach into my pocket?'

'Yes.'

I showed him the old man's picture. He held it carefully, then took a deep breath, dropped the cigarette, and stepped on it. 'May I keep this?'

'The cops might need it for the identification.'

He stared at it another moment, then slipped the picture into his pocket. 'I will return it to you, Mr Cole. You have my word.'

I didn't say anything.

'I tell you something, and if you are smart you will listen. These men come from places of war where life has no value. They have executed hundreds, perhaps thousands. This man Frank Escobar, he has murdered many and he murders more every day. Prima himself is such a man.' He seemed to have to think about how to say it. 'There is so much murder in the air it is what we breathe. The taking of life has lost all meaning.' He shook his head. 'The gun.' He shook his head again, as if in saying those two words he had summed up all he was about, or ever could be about.

I said, 'What about the feds?'

Ramon del Reyo rubbed his thumb across his fingertips and said nothing.

I said, 'If I wanted to take down Donaldo Prima, how could I do it?'

He looked at me with steady, soft brown eyes, then made a little shrug. 'I think that by asking these things, you are looking to do good, but you will not find good here, Mr Cole. This is a Godless place.'

'I don't think you are without God, Mr Del Reyo.'

'I am afraid I will not know that until the afterlife, no?' We reached the little bench by the azaleas. Ramon del Reyo sat, and I sat with him. 'We have talked enough, now. I will leave, and you will sit here for exactly ten minutes. If you leave before then, it will be taken the wrong way and you will be killed. I am sorry to be rude in this way, but there we are.'

'Of course.' I imagined the man with the rifle. I imagined him watching for the sign, and I wondered what the sign might've been. A yawn, perhaps. Perhaps wiping the brow. The sign, the trigger, history.

Ramon del Reyo said, 'If the man who is with you approaches, have him sit beside you and he will not be harmed.'

I said, 'What man?'

Ramon del Reyo laughed, then patted my leg and moved away, del Reyo and the guy with the Ray-Bans, then the others, and finally the Haitian. The Haitian made a pistol of his right hand, pointed it at me, and dropped the hammer. Then he smiled and disappeared into the crowd. What a way to live.

I sat on the lip of the bench in the damp heat and waited. My shirt was wet and clinging, and my skin felt hot and beginning to burn. Joe Pike came through the crowd and sat beside me. He said, 'Look across the square, corner building, third floor, third window in.'

I didn't bother looking. 'Guy with a rifle.'

'Not now, but was. Did you make him?'

'They told me. They made you, Joe. They knew you were there.'

Pike didn't move for a while, but you could tell he didn't like it, or didn't believe it. Finally he made a little shrug. 'Did we learn anything?'

'I think.'

'Is there a way out for the Boudreauxs?'

I stared off at the river, at the steady brown water flowing toward the Gulf, at the great ships headed north, up into the heart of America. I said,

'Yes. Yes, I think there is. They won't like it, but I think there is.' I thought about it for a time, and then I looked back at Joe Pike. 'These are dangerous people, Joe. These are very dangerous people.'

Pike nodded and watched the river with me. 'Yes,' he said. 'But so are we.'

29

A hot wind blew in off Lake Pontchartrain. The last of the clouds had vanished, leaving the sky a great azure dome above us, the afternoon sun a disk of white and undeniable heat. We drove with the windows down, the hot air roaring over and around us, smelling not unlike an aquarium that has been too long uncleaned. We reached Baton Rouge, but we did not stop; we crested the bridge and continued west toward the Evangeline Parish sheriff's substation in Eunice, and Jo-el Boudreaux. He wouldn't be happy to see us, but I wasn't so happy about seeing him, either.

It was late afternoon when Pike and I parked in the dappled shade of a black-trunked oak and walked into the substation. A thin African-American woman with very red lips and too much rouge sat at a desk and, behind her, a tall rawboned cop with leathery skin stood at a coffee machine. The cop looked over when we walked in and watched us cross to the receptionist. Staring. I gave the receptionist one of my business cards. 'We'd like to see Sheriff Boudreaux, please. He knows what it's about.'

She looked at the card. 'Do you have an appointment?'

'No, ma'am. But he'll see us.'

The rawboned cop came closer, first looking at Pike and then looking at me, as if we had put in a couple of job applications and he was about to turn us down. 'The sheriff's a busy man. You got a problem, you can talk to me.' His nametag said WILLETS.

'Thanks, but it's business for the sheriff.'

Willets didn't let it go. 'If you're talkin' crime, it's my business, too.' He squinted. 'You boys aren't local, are you?'

Pike said, 'Does it matter?'

Willets clicked the cop eyes on Pike. 'You look familiar. I ever lock you down?'

The receptionist said, 'Oh, relax, Tommy,' and took the card down a short hall.

Willets stood there with his fists on his hips, staring at us. The receptionist came back with Jo-el Boudreaux and returned to her desk. Boudreaux looked nervous. 'I thought you were gone.'

'There's something we need to talk about.'

Willets said, 'They wouldn't talk with me, Jo-el.'

Boudreaux said, 'I've got it now, Tommy. Thanks.'

Willets went back to the coffee machine, but he wasn't happy about it. Boudreaux was holding my business card and bending it back and forth. He looked at Joe. 'Who's that?'

'Joe Pike. He works with me.'

Boudreaux bent the card some more, then came closer and lowered his voice. 'That woman is back and she's been calling my wife. I don't like it.'

'Who?'

He mouthed the words. 'That woman. Jodi Taylor.' He glanced at Willets to make sure he hadn't heard.

'Sheriff, that's just too damn bad. You want to talk out here?'

Willets was still staring at us from the coffee machine. He couldn't hear us, but he didn't like all the talking. He called out, 'Hey, Jo-el, you want me to take care of that?'

'I've got it, Tommy. Thanks.'

Boudreaux took us to his office. Like him, it was simple and functional. Uncluttered desk. Uncluttered cabinet with a little TV. A nice-looking largemouth bass mounted on the wall. Boudreaux was big and his face was red. A hundred years ago he would have looked like the town blacksmith. Now, he looked awkward in his short-sleeved uniform and Sam Browne. He said, 'I want you to know I don't appreciate your coming here like this. I don't like that woman calling my wife. I told you I'd handle my troubles on my own, in my own way, and there's nothing we got to say to each other.'

'I want to report a crime. I can report it to you, or to the clown outside.'

He rocked back when I said it. He was a large-boned, strong man and he'd probably fronted down his share of oilfield drunks, but now he was scared and wondering what to do. I wasn't supposed to be here. I was supposed to have gone away and stayed away. 'What do you mean, "crime"? What are you talkin' about?'

'I know what Rossier's doing, Sheriff. You're going to have to put a stop to it.'

He put his hand on the doorknob like he was going to show us out. 'I said I'll take care of this.'

'You've been hiding from it for long enough, and now it's gotten larger than you and your wife and your father-in-law.'

He said, 'No,' waving his hand.

'I'm showing you a courtesy here, Boudreaux. Neither your wife nor Jodi Taylor knows about this, though I will tell them. I'm giving it to you first, so that we can do this in private, where you want to keep your fat-ass troubles, or we can do it in front of your duty cops.'

Pike said, 'Fuckin' A.' Pike really knows how to add to a conversation.

Boudreaux stopped the waving.

I said, 'At eleven-thirty last night we saw a man named Donaldo Prima shoot an old man in the head at an abandoned pumping station a mile south of Milt Rossier's crawfish farm. They were bringing in illegal immigrants. Rossier's goons were there when it happened.'

Jo-el Boudreaux stopped all the twitching and waving as completely as if he had thrown a switch. His eyes narrowed briefly, and then he put his palms flat on his desk and wet his lips again. When he spoke I could barely hear him. 'You're reporting a homicide?'

'It's not the first, Jo-el. It's been going on, and it will keep going on until it's stopped.'

'Rossier was there?'

'Prima met LeRoy Bennett at Rossier's bar, the Bayou Lounge. Bennett and LaBorde were at the pumping station, but Rossier's the guy who's in business with Prima.'

His fingers kneaded the way a cat will knead its paws, only without satisfaction. 'Can you prove that?'

'They buried the old man and a little girl. Let's go see them.'

He came around the desk and put on his hat. 'God help you if you're lyin'.'

Tommy Willets was gone when we walked out through the substation and climbed into Jo-el's car.

The sheriff drove. I spoke only to give directions, and a little less than twenty minutes later we turned across the cattle bridge and moved into the marsh and the cane fields. The rain had left the road pocked with puddles, but the ruts from the big trucks were still cut and clear. Everything looked different during the day, brighter and somehow magnified. Egrets with blindingly white feathers took dainty steps near thickets of cattails, and BB-eyed black birds perched atop swaying cane tips.

We parked alongside the pumping station. The sun was cooking off the rain, and, when we left the car, it was like stepping into a cloud of live steam. We moved north along the edge of the waterway for maybe eighty yards until we came to the little grave. The rain had washed away some of the soil, and part of the old man's arm was visible. There was a musty smell like sour milk mixed with fish food, but maybe that was just the swamp.

Jo-el Boudreaux said, 'Oh, my Lord.'

Boudreaux bent down, but did not touch the earth or what was obscured by it. He stood and turned and looked out across the waterway, shaking his head. 'Jesus, ain't this a mess.'

I said, 'It isn't just you and your wife anymore, Boudreaux. Rossier isn't just selling meth to crackers. He's in business with animals, and people are getting hurt. You can't ignore that.'

He wiped at his forehead with a handkerchief. 'Oh, holy Jesus. I didn't know about any of this. I never knew what he was doing. That was the deal, see? I just stayed away. That's all there was to it. I just let him go about his business. I never knew what he was doing out here.'

'This thing is going to end, now, Jo-el. You're going to shut Rossier down.'

He looked confused. 'What do you mean?'

'I mean that I can't walk away and let it go on. If you don't stop it, I'll give you up.'

He blinked hard and looked from me to Joe Pike, then back to me. His face was bright pink in the sun, and slicked with sweat. 'You think I'd let someone get away with this? You think I'd just turn away?'

I pointed at the grave. 'That old man and that little girl are dead because you turned away.'

The pink face went red, and in that moment he wasn't the scared blacksmith; he was the leather-tough farmer he'd had to be when he was fronting down Saturday-night drunks waving broken Budweiser bottles. He said, 'I've got a wife to protect. I had to look out for her goddamned daddy.'

Pike moved to the side, and I stepped into Jo-el Boudreaux's face and said very softly, 'It was almost forty years ago. Edith was a child, forty years ago. You went along because you didn't want anyone to know she'd been with a black man. It's the race thing, isn't it?'

Jo-el Boudreaux threw a fist the size of a canned ham at me with everything he had. It floated down through the thick air and I slapped it past, stepping to the outside. He threw the other hand, this time crossing his body and making a big grunt with the effort. I slapped it past the same way and stepped under. He was big and heavy and out of shape. Two punches and he was breathing hard. Pike shook his head and looked away. Boudreaux lunged forward, trying to wrap me up with the big arms, and I stepped to the side and swept his feet out from under him. He rolled sideways in the air, flaying at nothing, and hit the muddy ground. He stayed there, crying, hurting for himself but maybe hurting for the old man and the little girl, too. I thought Jodi Taylor was right. I thought that he was a good man, just stupid and scared, the way good men sometimes are. Somewhere nearby a fish jumped, and tiny gnats swarmed around us in great rolling clouds. Boudreaux got control of himself and climbed to his feet. He said, 'I'm sorry about that.'

I nodded. 'Forget it.'

He looked down at his pants. 'Jesus, I look like I wet myself.'

Pike handed Boudreaux a handkerchief.

Boudreaux wiped at his hands and his face, then blew his nose. 'I ain't cried like that since I was a kid. I'm ashamed of myself.'

I said, 'You ready to talk about this?'

He offered the handkerchief back to Pike but Pike shook his head. Boudreaux shrugged. 'Jesus, I don't know what to do. If I knew what to do, I wouldn't be in this fix.' He blew his nose into the handkerchief again, then put it into his pocket. 'I gotta talk with Edie.'

'Your choices are limited, Jo-el. The one choice you do not have is inaction. Inaction has led to this, and I will not allow this to continue.'

He nodded and looked at the water. It was muddy and still and probably didn't offer much in the way of advice to him. He said, 'Man, isn't this a mess. Isn't this a goddamned mess.' He looked at the shallow grave and what was in it. 'Shit.'

Pike said, 'There's a way to survive this.'

When he said it something cold washed down my spine. I said, 'Joe.'

Jo-el Boudreaux squinted at Pike, his eyes curious and hopeful. 'What?'

Pike said, 'Prima's at war with another coyote named Frank Escobar. Escobar's been trying to take out Prima because Prima's cutting into his trade. If he knew that Rossier was in business with Prima, and he knew how to get to them, he might take them out.'

Jo-el Boudreaux's left eye began ticking. He stared at Pike, and then he looked at me. 'That's murder.'

I said, 'I don't know if this is helping, Joe.'

Pike said, 'We could make it happen. Rossier's gone. Prima's gone. You bust Escobar.' He cocked his head, and the hot Louisiana sun gleamed off his glasses. 'No one ever has to know what Rossier knows.' He cocked his head the other way. 'You see?' The world according to Pike.

Jo-el Boudreaux wet his lips and looked shaken. 'Jesus Christ, I don't know.'

I said, 'There are a couple of ways to go with this, but what you can't do is nothing. Doing nothing is why those people died.' I pointed at the little grave. 'If Jodi Taylor's back, I'll have to see her. I have to see Lucy Chenier. You have until tomorrow, Jo-el. Talk about all of this with Edith and decide. We'll call you tomorrow.'

He was nodding again. 'Okay. Yeah. Sure. Tomorrow.' He wet his lips again, then looked again at the little grave and shook his head. He said, 'Those poor folks. Those poor folks.' He started back toward the highway car.

'Where are you going?'

He answered without looking back at me. 'Gotta get the coroner's people out here and recover these bodies. Can't just let these folks stay like that.'

He vanished behind the emerald-green cane and the sawgrass.

Pike said, 'What do you think he'll do?'

I shook my head. 'I don't know, but I hope he does something.'

We waited beside the little grave, the two of us staring down at the old man's arm, reaching up out of the earth, reaching as if he was trying to find his way back from darkness.

———

30

Two Evangeline Parish sheriff's cars and a gray van from the parish coroner's office came out to disinter the bodies. A powder-blue Buick sedan arrived a few minutes later, driven by a man named Deets Boedicker. Boedicker owned a Dodge-Chrysler dealership and had been elected coroner, a job that mostly consisted of overseeing the technicians from Able Brothers Mortuary to make sure they didn't screw up any evidence until the police had finished with the scene. Able Brothers had a contract with the parish. When the police had finished with their photographs and measurements, Boedicker asked how the bodies were discovered, and Sheriff Boudreaux said that a couple of kids fishing for channel cats in a *bateau* had found them and phoned it in. Boedicker said, 'Looks like a couple of Mexes to me. Ain't that just the thing? Sure been a lot of Mexes around here lately.' I guess that was the extent of his expertise.

Sheriff Boudreaux told a young black deputy named Berry to finish up with the mortuary people, and then he drove us back to the Eunice substation. None of the cops or coroner's people had asked who we were or why we were on the scene. I guess they had grown used to not asking questions, and the thought of that bothered me, but perhaps it should have bothered me more.

We reached the hotel in Baton Rouge at eight minutes after seven and went to our rooms to shower and change. I asked the front desk people if Jodi Taylor had checked in, and they said she had, but when I called her room she wasn't there. I called Lucy at home, and asked if Jodi was with her.

'Yes, she is. She flew in yesterday.'

'Good. I found out what's going on. I spoke with Boudreaux, and I should tell Jodi about it. Things are going to happen, and they'll probably happen quickly, and she might be affected.'

'We've already eaten, but you and Joe could come over for dessert and we can discuss it.'

I told her that that would be fine, and then I showered and changed and rapped on Joe Pike's door. He didn't answer, so I let myself in, thinking he might be in the shower. He wasn't. There was a haze of fog on the bathroom mirror, but all water had been wiped from the tub and the damp towels had been folded and rehung on their racks. The room was immaculate, the bedspread military tight, the magazines squared on the table by the window, the chairs undimpled by the weight of a reclining body. The only sign that he was here or ever had been was the olive-green duffel on the closet floor. It was zipped shut and locked with a tempered-steel Master Lock. Now you see him, now you don't. Off doing Pike things, no doubt.

At ten minutes before eight, Lucy let me into her home with a smile that was as warm as the sun glittering off dew-covered grass. I said, 'Hi.'

She said hi back. The master and mistress of restraint.

Jodi Taylor was standing behind her in the entry with a glass of red wine, clearly expectant. But where it was easy to look at Lucy, it was hard for me to look at Jodi. It would be harder still to tell her the things I would tell her. Jodi said, 'Did you find out what's going on?'

'Yes. We need to talk about it.'

Lucy led us to the kitchen. The lights in the backyard were on, and Ben and another boy were using the rope to climb into the pecan tree. A black-and-white dog ran in frantic circles around the base of the tree, its rear end high and happy.

Lucy said, 'I have a key lime pie. Would you like coffee?'

'How about a beer?'

She took a bottle of Dixie from the Sub-Zero and opened it for me. I drank some. The key lime pie was sitting on the counter beside a little stack of glass dessert plates and forks and cloth napkins. Two pieces of the pie were missing, and I deduced that the two boys in the yard had probably already had their dessert. I am a powerhouse of deduction. A veritable master of the art.

Jodi said, 'What's wrong? Why aren't you saying anything?'

I had more of the beer and watched Lucy cut equal slices of the pie and put the pie on the plates.

Jodi pulled at my arm. 'Why do I think that something's wrong?'

'Because something is. Rossier and a guy named Donaldo Prima bring in illegal aliens, and sometimes it works out but sometimes it doesn't, and they don't much care.' I went through everything. There was a kind of comfort in the telling, as if with each telling the memory of it would become less clear, the sharp lines of the old man and the young girl less distinct.

When I told the part about Donaldo Prima killing the old man, Jodi said, 'Waitaminute. This man *murdered* someone?'

'Yes.'

'You actually saw a *murder*?'

I said yes again.

Jodi looked at her wineglass. Lucy caught the look, and refilled the glass. Jodi said, 'I can't believe this. I'm an actress. I sing, for God's sake.' She shook her head and looked at the two boys. Outside, Ben was hanging upside-down on the rope, and the other boy was pushing him. Moths and June bugs swarmed around the patio lights. The black-and-white dog danced happily. Inside, the adults were discussing murder and human degradation. Just another day in middle-class America.

Lucy said, 'Did you find a way to help the Boudreauxs?'

I shook my head. 'No.'

Jodi looked back at me. 'What do you mean no?'

'I had hoped to find a way to force Rossier out of the Boudreauxs' lives so that they could keep their secret, but there doesn't seem a way to do that. Rossier has no family and no known associates other than Donaldo Prima, and their association seems one of convenience. Like all criminal activities, it is a cash business, and Rossier has carefully laundered all the money through his crawfish farm. Milt Rossier answers to and depends on no one. He's safe.'

Jodi said, 'Well, there must be something.'

'We can kill him or arrest him.'

She flipped her hand. 'Oh, that's silly.'

'Prima used to work for another coyote named Frank Escobar. Prima wanted to go into business for himself, but needed a safe and reliable way to move people up from the coast. That's Rossier. Without Rossier, Prima's out of business. Escobar would very much like Prima to be out of business, also. If Escobar knew how to get to Rossier and Prima, he might take care of our problem.'

Lucy was not moving. Her hands were on the counter. 'You're talking about arranging a murder.'

'I am talking about sharing information with Frank Escobar, then letting nature take its course.'

Jodi crossed her arms, then uncrossed them. 'Are you serious?'

Ben and the other boy came in through the French doors, slick with sweat. Ben was barefoot, and his knees were grass-stained and dirty. The other boy was wearing a Wolverine T-shirt. Ben said, 'MomI'mgonnago-overtoGary'sokay? Hi, Elvis.'

'Hi, Ben.' I guess the other boy was Gary.

Lucy glanced at the clock on the wall above her sink. 'I want you home by nine.'

Both boys sprinted away before she finished. 'Thanks, Mom.'

After the front door crashed, the house was silent. Lucy went to the sink, ran a glass of water, and drank it. Jodi shook her head. 'Well, that killing thing is silly. You can't just kill someone. And the Boudreauxs can't arrest him. If they arrest him, he'll tell.'

'The sheriff has no choice. I am not going to allow things to continue.'

Jodi put her hands on her hips. 'What does that mean?'

Lucy turned back from the sink.

I said, 'An old man got shot in the head because Jo-el Boudreaux is scared of something that happened thirty-six years ago. This is not acceptable.' My neck felt tight. 'If things continue as they have, more old men will be shot and more little girls will die of heatstroke, and that is also not acceptable.' The tight neck spread to my scalp, and my voice felt hard and far away. 'I have told Jo-el these things, and now he must do something, even if it means giving up his secret, because I will not allow any more old men or little girls to die. I will act if he doesn't.' My temples were pounding.

Jodi's eyes flicked to Lucy, then came back to me. 'What does that mean? What will you do?'

'I'll go to the Justice Department and give them the case against Rossier and Prima.'

Her eyes flicked to Lucy again. 'But Rossier will tell on the Boudreauxs.' *Tell on the Boudreauxs.* Like he might *tattle.*

'I know.'

Jodi took one step closer to me, her eyes wide. 'But then they'll know about *me.*'

'I know that, too. I'm sorry.'

Jodi walked out of the kitchen and into the dining area. She raked her fingers through her hair and looked at herself in the window overlooking Lucy's backyard. It was now dark out, and the glass was a mirror to the room. We weren't talking about the Boudreauxs anymore; we were talking about her. She said, 'What happened to confidential? What happened to protecting my interests? You promised me, remember?'

I didn't answer. Her eyes were red-rimmed and filling. I wanted to comfort her and tell her that everything would be fine, but I could not lie to her.

I said, 'I saw Boudreaux earlier today. He's going to talk about all of this with Edie tonight, and we'll see how they want to play it tomorrow. I'm sorry, Jodi.'

Jodi Taylor walked out. Lucy went after her, and I heard them at the front door, but I could not make out their words. I put my palms on the counter and stared between them. The Corian was flat and gray and seemed of great depth. It was a lovely surface, and I pressed against it and wondered how much pressure it could take. I thought about hot frying pans being placed upon it, and I wondered how often the pans might be placed and how hot they might be before the Corian would be forever changed.

Lucy was gone for a long while, and then there were footsteps and she was standing beside me again, leaning with her back to the counter, her arms crossed. She said, 'You look like hell, Studly.'

'Thanks.'

Lucy took a deep breath, then said, 'I know you were in Vietnam, but I have to ask this. Have you killed men in the course of your job?'

'Yes.'

'Have you committed murder?'

'No. Each time, I was threatened. Each time, I was trying to help an innocent person whose life was in imminent danger.'

'Have you acted to create those moments?'

I thought about it. There have been so many moments. Freckles on the arm of a man who works in the sun. 'When you involve yourself in these things, you assume a measure of risk. There always comes a point when you can turn it over to the police, but at that point the risk expands. Will the police blow it? Will the client be helped or harmed? Will justice be served? There are always questions. The answers are not always clear, and are often unknown even after the fact.'

She let the breath out. 'In a given moment you opt to trust yourself.'

'Yes,' I said. 'Always.'

She said nothing for several moments, then she turned sideways and reached up to touch my hair. 'Well. At least you're honest.'

'As the day is long.' I tried to smile, but it wasn't much.

'I'm having trouble with this.'

'I know.'

'The framework of the law is how we define and protect justice. If everyone were to define justice subjectively, order and law would cease and there would be no justice. There would be only anarchy.'

'Easy for you to say.'

She frowned. Humor often fails when we need it most.

'But you're right. Of course.'

She said, 'You don't have to do this. You could just walk away, or you could act unilaterally and go directly to the Justice Department to give them Rossier, but you haven't. You're still in it, even though it troubles you.'

I looked at her and tried to frame how I felt. 'I help people. I work with their problems and try to stay within the parameters that they set and bring them to a conclusion that is just. Their confidence is sacrosanct to me. Do you see?'

'You define yourself through your service to your clients.'

'In a way.'

'And you've never breached that confidence, or that service.'

I shook my head.

'And now you might, for a justice that you see as greater than your client.'

'Yes.' My voice was phlegmy.

Lucy pulled me around to face her. She gripped each of my biceps and looked up at me. I watched her look at the different parts of my face and head and ears and hair. Her eyes drifted lower, glancing at my chest, maybe the buttons there, maybe the folds of my shirt, as if whatever answers she sought might be in the fabric. She closed her eyes and snuggled into me. 'You're a good man, Elvis. You're a very good man.'

She went to the kitchen phone, pressed a speed-dial button, then asked someone if Ben could stay over. She said that she would be happy to drive car pool in the morning if he could. The someone must have agreed. Lucy said thank you, hung up, then came back to me and took my hand. She gave me one of the gentlest smiles that I have ever seen. She said, 'Did you hear?'

'Yes.'

'Will you come to the bedroom with me?'

'Can I think about it?'

Her smile got wider and she squeezed my hand.

'Well. Okay.'

She hooked her arm in mine and walked me to her bedroom, but this night we made a different kind of love. We lay upon her bed, still in our clothes, and held each other until dawn.

31

Lucy was driving car pool the next morning when her office called, telling her phone machine that Jo-el Boudreaux had phoned, looking for me. I picked up the phone midmessage and Darlene said, 'Well, well. Fancy meeting you there.'

'You'll probably be a riot in the unemployment line, too.'

'Oh, we're testy in the morning.' These assistants are something, aren't they? 'May I speak with Ms Chenier?'

'She's unavailable. What did Boudreaux want?'

'There were two messages on the machine and he sounded anxious. He left a number.' She gave it to me and then she hung up.

I called the number, got the Evangeline Parish sheriff's office, Eunice substation, and then I got Boudreaux. He said, 'I can't just murder somebody. Jesus Christ. I can't do anything like that.'

'All right. But doing nothing is no longer an option. So what are you going to do?'

You could hear background noise and the squeaks a chair makes when someone large shifts position.

I said, 'Talk to me, Jo-el.'

'Edie says you're right. She says it's time to stop hidin' from yesterday. She said that from the beginning, but I guess I was too scared to listen.' He was working his way through the guilt, and not just the guilt about his wife. He'd probably seen the old man and the little girl a thousand times last night. He said, 'I'm gonna arrest the sonofabitch. I should've arrested him six months ago. I should've arrested him when he came to my house with this stuff and started his blackmail.'

I said, 'It's the right thing, Jo-el.'

'It's not just that old man. It's the whole operation. Prima. The poor bastards they been sneaking in through my parish. I can't get that little girl out of my head.'

I said, 'You want it to stop.'

'Yes. Hell, yes. I don't want any more little girls like that. Oh, hell, yes.'

His voice sounded thick when he said it. 'Jesus Christ, I'm just a hick cop. I don't know how to do this stuff.'

'Jo-el, have you spoken with the parish prosecutor about this?'

'Unh-unh. Edie and I want to talk to the kids. We want to let'm know about us and their grandfather before they hear it in the news. I pop Rossier and he'll be screaming.'

'Maybe there's a way to put this together, Jo-el.'

'You mean get 'em all?'

'Maybe. Let me talk to Lucy about it. We'll need to know the legal end because we'll want to avoid entrapment, but maybe there's a way.'

I hung up, then showered and dressed and was standing on the patio with the black-and-white dog when Lucy returned from car pool. She was carrying a wax-paper bag and two large containers of coffee. She offered one of the coffees. 'Good morning again.'

'Darlene called with a message from Jo-el Boudreaux. I'm afraid I've compromised our liaison.'

'Oh, don't worry. She's used to it.' These dames.

I told her about the call to Jo-el and asked her opinion. Lucy took a single plain donut from the bag and held it for me to take a bite. I did. Tender and light and still warm from the frying. Not too sugary. She took a bite after me and shook her head. 'I have no experience in criminal law, Studly, but there are several ex-prosecutors at the firm.'

'Think we could round one up for a quick trip to Eunice?'

She had more of the coffee and fed a small piece of the donut to the dog. 'It's possible. After this donut, I'll make some calls.'

'Great.'

She sipped the coffee and ate a bit of the donut and stared at the camelia bushes that separated her backyard from her neighbor's. The bright morning sun painted their leaves with an emerald glow. She said, 'You should tell Jodi. If it's going to come out, you should give her as much warning as possible.'

'Of course.'

She held out the donut again for me, but I shook my head no. She gave the remainder to the dog. 'It won't be easy for you, will it?'

'You helped last night, Lucy. Thank you.'

She smiled and patted my arm. 'Let me make those calls.'

It took about twenty minutes. A senior partner named Merhlie Comeaux agreed to drive to Eunice with Lucy and give an opinion based on his experiences both as a criminal defense attorney and the sixteen years he'd spent as an East Baton Rouge Parish prosecutor. Lucy would pick him up, and the two of them would meet Pike and me at Jo-el Boudreaux's office. I called Jo-el to see if this was agreeable, and he said that it was. He sounded nervous, but he also sounded relieved that someone who knew what they were doing was willing to advise him.

386

When I hung up, I called Jodi Taylor at the hotel. She answered on the sixth ring, her voice puffy with sleep.

I said, 'I spoke with Jo-el this morning, and I'm going to drive over there. He's going to arrest Milt Rossier.'

She didn't say anything.

'I thought you should know. You want to talk about any of this?'

She said, 'I wouldn't know what to say.' Her voice sounded hollow, and I didn't know what to say either. She hung up. Another satisfied customer.

I called Joe Pike, told him the plan, then picked him up at the hotel and we went to Eunice.

The drive across the Atchafalaya Basin went quickly, the waterways and sugarcane fields and great industrial spiderworks now familiar. Men and women worked the fields and fished the waterways and sold burlap sacks of live crawfish for fifteen cents per pound. Some of their faces seemed familiar, but maybe that was my imagination. I tuned in to the radio evangelist to learn the topic of the day, and this morning it was the liberal plot to destroy America by breaking down the nuclear family. She said that the liberals had already accomplished this in the Negro community, but that the Negroes were getting wise, which explained the rise in popularity of the black 'Musluns'. She concluded, inevitably, with warnings of the coming race war, which was not part of the liberal plot but which was clear proof that the liberals were not as smart as they thought they were, since the liberals thought they could use the 'blacks' to distract Christian America from their 'true plan'. Pike said, 'Turn it off.'

'Aren't you interested in learning about the "true plan"?'

'No.'

I turned it off, wondering how many of the people in the fields and on the water and in the houses were listening to this. Maybe none. Maybe Pike and I had been the only ones because everyone else had long since turned her off. Maybe, now that we had turned her off, too, she was broadcasting into dead air, just another noodle-brain with an eight-thousand-watt transmitter and nothing much to do all day except smoke cigarettes and rail into the microphone about how crummy things were, a voice alone in the dark, her signal spreading like silent ripples in a pond, unheard on the earth but traveling ever outward into space, past the moon and Mars, past the asteroids and Pluto, on into eternity. I hoped the people on Alpha Centauri were smart enough to turn her off, too.

Twenty minutes later we parked next to Lucy's Lexus outside the Eunice substation. The same woman was at the same desk, and the same pristine magnolia was in its little jar. She smiled when she saw me and said, 'They're in with the sheriff. They're expecting you.'

Lucy and Jo-el were sitting with a great, broad African-American man with white hair and a gut the size of a fifty-five-gallon oil drum. Merhlie

Comeaux. Lucy made the introductions, then looked back at Jo-el. 'Sheriff, before we begin this we need to establish the ground rules. Merhlie is a former EBR prosecutor, but he is now a partner in the firm of Sonnier, Melancon, & Burke, for private hire. As such, anything said by you in this room is subject to the attorney–client privilege. Is that understood?'

Jo-el looked confused. 'But I didn't hire you.'

'We are under agreement with Jodi Taylor to work in your best interests. If you are so informed and agree to that arrangement, then we are, de facto, your attorneys.'

Jo-el looked at me. 'Do I need lawyers?'

I said, 'Just listen to her, Jo-el.'

He frowned and nodded and looked back at her. Lucy said, 'We are about to discuss your awareness of and involvement in activities that may, in the future, result in criminal charges being filed against you. We don't want anything said by you today to prejudice your case at that time.'

Jo-el looked embarrassed. 'I'm not going to try to get out of anything.'

Lucy spread her hands. 'That is your choice, of course. You may feel differently at some later date. Also, we may discuss issues of a personal and potentially criminal nature as regards other members of your family. By accepting the attorney–client privilege with us, you also serve to protect them. Do you understand that?'

Jo-el nodded. 'Protect them.'

'Do you accept this arrangement?'

Jo-el said, 'Yes.'

Lucy nodded, then glanced at Merhlie Comeaux. 'We have prior consent from Jodi Taylor to discuss her affairs openly with the Elvis Cole Detective Agency.' She looked back at Jo-el. 'As we discussed, Mr Comeaux is here in an advisory capacity in the criminal apprehension of Milt Rossier. He can't speak for the state, but he can provide his opinion and guidance in the building of such a case. Do you understand that, too, Sheriff?'

'Yes. I need all the help I can get.'

Merhlie Comeaux said, 'Why don't you gentlemen give me what you have?'

Jo-el raised his eyebrows at me, and I told Comeaux everything that I knew. I started at the head of it with Jimmie Ray Rebenack and what happened at Rossier's crawfish farm, and I brought it up through the meeting between Rossier and Donaldo Prima at the Bayou Lounge and what I had seen at the pumping station. When I told him about the old man's murder and the bodies we recovered from the grave, Comeaux asked for the police report. Jo-el showed him the file and Comeaux stared at the pictures. He said, 'Did you get an ID?'

'Not yet. We're running it through New Orleans.'

Comeaux shook his head and sighed. 'You got any coffee around here?'

Jo-el asked the receptionist to bring in coffee. After she had, I went through the rest of it, describing my meeting with del Reyo and what I had learned about Donaldo Prima and Frank Escobar and how Prima was using Rossier to move illegals up through the Gulf Coast waterways. When I was finished with it, Merhlie Comeaux nodded like he was thinking, then looked at the sheriff. 'Do you have anything to add to that?'

Jo-el said, 'Unh-unh. No, sir.'

Merhlie looked back at me and laced his fingers across his ample belly. He had clear, hard eyes, and the eyes made me think he had been an aggressive prosecutor. 'Let's go back to what happened at the pumping station. You saw this Prima pull the trigger?'

'Yes.'

He looked at Joe Pike. 'You saw it, too?'

Pike nodded.

'Where was Rossier?'

'He wasn't there.'

'How about those two boys who work for him?'

'Bennett and LaBorde were inside with Prima.'

'You get IDs on any of the illegals who came in?'

'No.'

'Can you produce any of these people?'

'No.'

Merhlie Comeaux pursed his lips and sipped at the coffee. When he lifted the cup his little finger stuck out at an angle.

Lucy said, 'What do you think, Merhlie?'

Comeaux made a shrug, like he would do the best he could with what he had to work with. 'It's not a lot, Lucille. You have Mr Prima all right, but you don't have a thing on this Rossier.'

Boudreaux said, 'Well, hell.'

Comeaux spread his hands. 'He holds a lease on the land, maybe the state could file on an accessory, but it's junk. You want him, you gotta get him at the scene.'

I said, 'What about on the illegals?'

'*What* illegals? If you can't produce them, you cannot, in fact, prove that these people are aliens.'

Lucy said, 'Oh, come on, Merhlie.'

He spread his hands again. 'That's my opinion. If you think you can get more, go to the state and see what they say.'

Jo-el said, 'If we go in now that sonofabitch will know we're onto him.' He chewed at his lip, then went to the window before turning back and staring at the largemouth on his wall. He stared at it, but I'm not sure he was seeing it. 'Goddammit, me and my family are gonna do something

389

pretty goddamn hard here. Maybe we shoulda done it a year ago, but if we're gonna do it now I want that sonofabitch to pay for his pleasure. I want him in jail. I don't want any more little girls like that.' He jerked an angry gesture toward the case file. The one with the pictures.

I said, 'So you'll have to bust him in the act.'

They looked at me.

I said, 'That wasn't the first time Prima brought up a load of people. We just have to be there the next time. And we have to make sure that Rossier is there to take delivery.'

Comeaux was shaking his head. 'Go easy with that, son. If he's entrapped, you've got nothing.'

I was thinking about Ramon del Reyo. 'All we have to do is give him a strong enough reason to be there. It won't be easy, but it might be possible.'

Comeaux said, 'Tell me what you have in mind.'

I did. It didn't take very long, and then he got up and Lucy got up with him. The last thing he said was, 'It's your neck, podnuh. Go with God.'

A frown line had appeared between Lucy's eyebrows. 'Can you pull something like that off?'

I looked at Pike. 'Can we pull this off, she asks.'

Pike was frowning, too. I guess he had his doubts.

I used Jo-el's phone to make some calls, and when I was finished Lucy and Merhlie were gone. Jo-el stood in his office window, passing his palm across his hair and staring down along the street of his town. Maybe at the rows of buildings, maybe at the cars and the people walking on the sidewalks. He said, 'I should've done this six months ago. When that bastard came to my house and started all this, I should've dropped the hammer on him then and goddamned there.'

'You were caught off guard, and you were scared. People get scared, they don't think straight.'

'Yeah.' He didn't look convinced. He glanced at the floor, and then he looked up at me. 'I appreciate this. So will Edie.'

Pike said, 'Buy us a beer if we live through it.'

That Joe. He's a riot, isn't he?

We went out to our car and drove to New Orleans.

32

The Haitian was waiting for us at a beignet shop on South Rampart Street along the northern edge of the French Quarter. He hung there just long enough to make eye contact, then started walking without waiting for us. We went west to Canal, then south, and after a couple of blocks, Pike said, 'Across the street and half a block behind.'

I glanced back and saw the guy with the Ray-Bans. I nodded. 'Security conscious.'

Pike said, 'Creepy.'

Ramon del Reyo was waiting in the front passenger seat of a Yellow Cab a little bit down from Carondelet, where the old green streetcars make their turnaround from St Charles and the Garden District. The cab's OFF DUTY light was on. The Haitian opened the back door for us, then got in behind the wheel. He didn't start the engine. Ramon smiled at Pike. 'So. You are with us this time, señor.'

'With you last time, too.' Pike tilted his head. 'Guy with the glasses across the street. Another guy to our left by the horse carriage. I haven't made the rifle.'

Ramon made a little shrug. 'But you know he's there. The man with the rifle is always there, you see?'

Pike's mouth twitched.

I said, 'I can take Donaldo Prima and Frank Escobar off the board. How badly do you want it to happen?'

The Haitian twisted in his seat to look at me, but Ramon del Reyo did not move.

I said, 'I know how and where Prima gets people into the country, and I've got a parish sheriff who is willing to make the case.'

Del Reyo wet his lips. 'It is a Justice Department case.'

'My guy will make the bust and collect the evidence. Justice comes in after the fact, everything laid out and undeniable.' I leaned toward him. 'It's solid. My guy just wants to clean up his place of business.'

The Haitian looked at del Reyo. Del Reyo said, 'There is more than that, my friend.'

I said, 'Yes, but I'm not going to tell you.'

Del Reyo said nothing.

'All you need to know is that if we can set it up well, both Escobar and Prima are over.'

The Haitian said something in Spanish, but del Reyo did not respond. The Haitian said it again, and this time del Reyo snapped something angrily. He frowned at me. 'What is it you want?'

'I need Escobar to make the case. That means I need to learn about the coyote business. I need to know how much it costs and how much people get paid and how Escobar works and how Prima works. I want to make Escobar think I'm in the business, and that I'm trying to cut a deal with him, so I have to know what I'm talking about. If I don't have Escobar, I can't make it happen.'

Ramon del Reyo laughed. 'You're a fool.'

'I think you've got someone inside with Escobar. I think that's how you keep tabs on him. Help me inside, Ramon. Come on.'

The Haitian said something else, and this time Ramon nodded. He didn't seem to be liking it a whole lot, but he was going along with it. He said, 'Why would Frank Escobar want to see you?'

'Because he hates Prima, and I can give him Prima. And if he wants Prima dead, I can give him that, too.'

Ramon smiled at me.

'We haven't identified the old man, Ramon. I want the picture.'

Ramon smiled some more and shook his head. He got out of the cab and walked south on Canal. He was gone for the larger part of an hour, and when he returned there was a middle-aged Asian guy with him. The Asian guy was slight and dark and looked Cambodian. The Cambodian leaned in to look at me and Pike, then he and del Reyo stepped away from the cab to talk. After maybe ten minutes the Cambodian walked away, and Ramon came back to the cab. He spent a little less than thirty minutes with us, first describing Escobar's setup, and then Prima's. He told us how much a guy like Escobar charged to sneak someone into the country and how much a guy like Prima paid to use Milt Rossier's pumping station. Everything was related to some sort of by-the-head payment. Escobar charged so much per head to get people in. Prima paid so much per head to use Rossier's waterway. Like we were talking about cattle. Something less than human.

Del Reyo gave me a slip of paper with a phone number. 'We have a man on very good terms with Escobar. He is arranging the meeting. Should anyone need a reference, have them call this number.'

I put it away without looking at it.

'I will leave you now. Jesus will take you there.' I guess the Haitian was Jesus. 'He will drop you off and leave, and you will be alone. If something happens, we will not be there to help. Do you understand this?'

'Sure.'

Ramon del Reyo walked away without another word and without looking back. No 'I'll be seeing you.' No 'Good luck.' No 'Win one for the gipper.' Maybe he knew something we didn't.

We drove north across the city toward Lake Pontchartrain, and soon we were out of the business district and driving along narrow residential streets with high curbs and plenty of oak and magnolia and banana trees, and old people in rockers on front verandas. We seemed just to sort of drive around, turning here and there, taking our time without any clear destination. Killing time. The air was warm and moist and oily like air that was vented from a low-class kitchen, and the cab smelled of sweat and body odor. Maybe the cab smelled like fear, too, but I was trying not to think of that part of it. Elvis Cole, Fearless Detective. I glanced over at Pike and he appeared to be sleeping. Passed out from fear, no doubt.

Pretty soon the neighborhoods became nicer, and we were driving along a beautiful emerald golf course and a sculpted canal, and then we were at the lake. The levee was lush and well maintained, and Jesus wound through streets now lined with mansions, some behind walls and gates but most not. We turned into a cul-de-sac fronting the levee and stopped at an enormous two-story brick home with oak trees in the front and along the sides. A couple of Japanese mountain bikes were lying on the lawn, and a Big Wheel was in the drive. You could look down the drive and see a four-car garage in the back, along with a pool house and a pool, but it seemed pretty quiet. Jesus stopped the car and said, 'Just go to the door and knock. It's set up.'

'Thanks, Jesus.'

Jesus said, 'You got a gun this time?'

'Yeah.'

He nodded. 'Good.'

Pike and I got out of the cab, and Jesus drove away. Amazing how alone you can feel in somebody's front yard. I looked at the bikes and the Big Wheel. 'Helluva house for a hood.'

Pike grunted.

The door opened before we reached it, and an attractive dark-haired woman smiled at us. She was wearing a tasteful one-piece swimming suit with a towel wrapped around her hips like a skirt. She was barefoot, and her hair was wet as if she'd just gotten out of the pool. She said, 'Are you Mr Cole?'

'Yes, ma'am.'

Beaming, she offered her hand. 'I'm Holly Escobar. Please come in. Frank's in back.'

Pike offered his hand and introduced himself. Holly Escobar said that she was happy to meet us. A little boy maybe five years old raced out between us, hopped aboard the Big Wheel, and roared around the cul-de-sac, blurrping his lips to make engine noises. He was as brown as a walnut, and wearing only baggy red swimming trunks. Holly Escobar closed the door. 'He's all right out there. We don't have any traffic.'

She brought us through a house that looked like anyone else's house, past family photographs and a very fine collection of riding trophies (which I took to be hers) and two older boys planted in front of a television and into a bright, homey island kitchen where a man in baggy plaid shorts was stacking sandwiches on a plastic tray. He was about my height, but younger, with heavy muscles and slicked hair and blunt fingers. He looked at us when we walked in and Holly Escobar said, 'Ronnie, these are the men Frank's expecting. Why don't you take them out and I'll finish here.' She smiled back at us. 'Everybody's in back.'

Ronnie led us out through a couple of French doors. Three men were sitting at a round table by the pool, drinking, and a woman was on a chaise longue, sunning herself. Like Holly Escobar, she wore a one-piece, and she looked like somebody's wife. No bimbos at the house. Two of the men were wearing baggy shirts over their shorts, probably to cover weapons, but one of the men was shirtless. Ronnie said, 'Frank?'

Frank Escobar was shirtless. He was short and wide and maybe in his early fifties, with a powerful, thick-bodied build. The hair on his head was streaked with gray, but his chest hair had already gone over, a thick gray thatch. He looked over at his name, and stood up when he saw us. 'Oh, yeah, hey, let's go in the pool house for this.' There was a slight accent, but he'd been trying to lose it. He held up a short glass. 'We're doing gin and tonics. You guys want one?' The gang lord as host.

'No. Thanks.'

He said, 'C'mon. We'll have some privacy in here.'

He staggered when he got up, and one of the shirted guys had to catch him. Middle of the day and he was zorched. The gang lord as lush.

We filed into the pool house. Pool table. Bar. Couple of slot machines and video games. A life-sized portrait of Frank Escobar from the old days, wearing an officer's uniform in some Central American jungle, close-cropped hair and bandito mustache. The real Frank Escobar slumped into a tall chair and waved his hand at Ronnie. 'Check these guys, huh? See what they got.'

I held my arms out. 'It's on my right hip.'

Ronnie took it, then gave me a quick pat. When he was done with me he moved to Pike, but Pike said, 'No.'

Frank Escobar frowned and said, 'What do you mean no?'

Pike held his hand palm out toward Ronnie. 'You want me to wait outside, fine. But he's not going to touch me, and I'm not going to give up my gun.'

Escobar rubbed at his eyes. 'What the fuck.' He finished the rubbing. 'You wanna keep your gun, tha's fine. We'll do it another way.' Frank

Escobar reached under one of the shirts and came out with a little Beretta .380 and pointed it at my head. He said, 'Keep your fuckin' gun, you want. We'll do it like this.' He waved at the shirt. 'Leon, hold on this guy, okay, this other asshole wants to keep his gun.' Leon took the .380 and held on me, and Frank Escobar glared at Pike. 'There. You happy now, you with your gun?'

Pike nodded. Some friend.

Escobar looked back at me. 'Okay. What do you have for me?'

'Donaldo Prima.'

Escobar's left eye narrowed, and he didn't seem drunk anymore. Now, he seemed as dangerous as the man in the life-sized picture. 'What do you know about Prima?'

'I know how he's getting his people in, Frank. He's working with a friend of mine. My friend provides the transportation and the secure location, but the money's not there.'

'Who's your friend?'

'A guy named Rossier. He's got the land and the water. A very secure location for delivering goods. Prima approached him and set up the deal, but now we're dissatisfied. You know what I mean?'

Escobar said, 'How much he gettin'?'

'Grand a head.'

Escobar laughed. 'That's shit.' Exactly what del Reyo had said.

'We think so.'

'Why doesn't your friend just go into business for himself?'

'Prima has the goods, Frank. Like you. Two grand a head and Prima's out. We've got people coming in now, and we'd like to increase our take.'

'Just like that? It's that easy?'

'Whatever you want.'

Frank Escobar wet his lips, thinking. He had some of the gin and tonic. A drop of it ran down from the corner of his mouth to his chin. He said, 'Prima.'

'That's it, Frank. You want to think about it and ask around, fine. We've been in business with Prima maybe six months. He brings up the money personally with every shipment. Like that.' Giving him Prima. Saying, here, take him.

Frank Escobar nodded at me.

I said, 'Think about it, Frank. You want to get me, I'm staying at the Riverfront in Baton Rouge. You want to give me a number I can call you, that's fine, too.' I spread my hands. 'Whatever you want. What *we* want is two grand a pop.'

Holly Escobar stepped in out of the sun with the tray of sandwiches, smiling the pretty smile, saying, 'Would you guys like a sandwich?' She froze in the door when she saw the guy in the baggy shirt pointing the gun at me, and the smile fell away. 'Frank?' The guy lowered the .380.

Frank Escobar lost the grip on his drink, and it fell. His face went as purple as overcooked liver and he came off the chair. 'Didn't I tell you never walk in on me?'

She took a single step back, trying to rebuild the smile, but the smile was clouded with fear. 'I'm sorry, Frank. I'll wait outside.'

The guy with the shirt whispered, 'Oh, shit.'

Frank Escobar rushed at his wife and yanked her back into the pool house. The big plastic plate and the sandwiches spun up and over and sandwiches rained down on the pool table and out onto the patio. Holly shrieked at the pain of his grip, saying, 'That hurts!' and then he slapped her twice, first with the palm of his left hand and then the back of his right. She fell over sideways, through the door and out onto the patio. The man and the woman at the pool stood.

I felt Pike move beside me, but it was over. As quick as it had come, it was gone. Escobar pulled his crying wife to her feet, saying, 'You gotta listen to me, Holly. You gotta mind what I say. All right? Don't never walk in like that.' He brushed at her hair and wiped at her face, but all he did was smear the blood. He said, 'Jesus, look at what you made me do. Go get your face, will you?'

Holly Escobar ran toward her house, and Frank wiped blood from his right hand onto his shorts. 'Go with her, Ronnie. Make sure she's okay.'

Ronnie set off after Mrs Frank Escobar.

The guy with the shirt said, 'You all right, Frank?' Like it was Frank doing the bleeding.

'I'm fine. Fine.' Escobar picked up his glass and seemed almost embarrassed. 'Jesus. Fuckin' stupid women.' Then he looked over at us and must've seen something in Pike's face. Or maybe in mine. He said, 'What?' Hard, again. A flush of the purple, again.

Pike's mouth twitched.

Escobar stared at Joe Pike another few seconds, and then he waved his hand to dismiss us. He said, 'I'll think about it, okay? I know where to reach you.' He motioned toward the guy in the shirt. 'Call these guys a car, huh? Jesus, I gotta get another drink.'

He walked out and went back to the little round table and picked up someone's glass and drank. Nothing like a gin and tonic to take off the edge after tossing a fit, nosireebob. I stared at him.

The guy in the shirt said that he'd call a cab, and we could wait out front. He said the cabs never took long, Frank had a deal. He said we could take a sandwich, if we wanted. Joe Pike told him to fuck himself.

We walked out past the pool and down the drive and into the street. The little boy was riding the Big Wheel round and round in circles, looping up into one driveway then along the sidewalk and then down the next drive and into the street again. He looked like a happy and energetic child.

Pike and I stood watching him, and Pike said, 'Be a shame to drop the hammer on his old man.'

I didn't answer.

'But it wouldn't be so bad, either.'

33

We were stopped for speeding outside St Gabriel, Louisiana, and again outside Livonia, but we passed under Milt Rossier's sign at just after five that evening as the air was beginning to lose the worst of the day's heat. The people who worked the ponds were trudging their way toward the processing sheds and the women who worked the sheds were walking out to their cars. Quitting time. Everybody moved with a sort of listless shuffle, as if their lot was to break their backs for Milt Rossier all day, then go home and break their backs some more. It wasn't the way you walk when your body has failed you; it was the way you walk when you've run out of heart, when the day-to-day has worn away the hope and left you with nothing but another tomorrow that will be exactly like today. It would be the way Holly Escobar would walk in another few years.

We drove up past the processing sheds like we owned the place and headed toward the house. The women on their way home didn't look, or, if they looked, didn't care. It's not like we had a big sign painted on the car, THE ENEMY. Pike said, 'This is easy.'

'What'd you expect, pill boxes?'

We could see the main house from between the processing sheds, and the little figure of Milt Rossier, sitting out on his lawn furniture, still wearing the sun hat. René LaBorde was standing out between the ponds, staring at their flat surfaces, and didn't seem to notice us, but LeRoy Bennett was coming out of the processing shed with one of the skinny foremen when we passed. He yelled something, then started running after us. He'd have a pretty long run. His Polara was parked at the house.

We drove the quarter-mile or so up to the house and left our car on the drive by LeRoy's Polara. The house looked pretty much deserted except for a heavyset black woman we saw in the living room and Milt Rossier back on the patio. We were going around the side of the house when Milt met us, coming to see who we were. He was in overalls and the wide hat, and he was carrying a glass of iced tea. I said, 'Hi, Milt, remember me?'

Milt Rossier pulled up short, surprised. He knew me, but he'd never seen Pike before, and when Pike took out his .357 and let Rossier see it, the old man said, 'Well, goddamn.'

Pike said, 'Let's go back to the patio. Comfortable there.'

Rossier looked back at me. 'We ran you outta here. I thought you left.'

I said, 'Everybody always thinks that, Milt, and everybody's usually wrong.'

Pike said, 'The patio.' Down below us, LeRoy Bennett was yelling for René to get his ass up to the house. René looked our way, but you couldn't be sure what he saw or what he was thinking.

Rossier frowned at Pike's gun and then we went back to the patio. I said, 'Sit down, Milt. We've got a business proposition.'

Milt Rossier eased his bulk down into one of the white lawn chairs, and Pike lowered the gun. Rossier said, 'Somebody got to old Jimmie Ray. I told you he'd stop messin' with that little gal, and he has. I thought we were shut of that.' He tried looking at me, but he kept glancing at Pike and the gun. Nervous.

I smiled. 'Not that kind of business, Milt.' LeRoy Bennett was a white midget down between the ponds, arms and legs pumping as he ran toward us. René LaBorde was finally headed our way, walking with a stiff-legged lumbering gait like Frankenstein's monster. I said, 'Milt, here's the word. You're gettin' screwed by Donaldo Prima, and we can double your money.'

When I said Donaldo Prima the old man's face tightened and he tried to put down the iced tea, but he missed the little table and it shattered on the patio. Just like Frank Escobar. Maybe poor hand–eye went with a life of crime. He said, 'I don't know what you're talking about.'

I looked at Joe Pike. 'Man, these guys come up with the good lines, don't they, Joe?'

Pike didn't move. LeRoy was closer, and Pike was watching him. René was still down between the ponds, but he was getting up a head of steam. I guess Pike was thinking about having to shoot them.

I said, 'You and Donaldo are moving illegal aliens upriver through bayous upon which you hold the leases. Donaldo deals with the people down south and contracts with the illegals, and you provide intercoastal transportation and a secure location through which they can enter the country.'

Rossier was waving his hands, feeling panicked and trying to push up out of the chair. 'I don't know any of that. I don't know what in hell you're talking about.' Pike leaned forward and shoved him back. Rossier swatted at Pike's hand the way you would swat at an aggravating gnat, and Pike palmed him hard once on the top of the head. Milt stopped the swatting. 'I don't know any Prima or illegal alien nonsense or anything else. You'd better get out of here right goddamn now 'fore I call the law!' Giving us an old man's outrage.

I held up two fingers. 'Two words, Milt. Frank Escobar.'

He stopped sputtering, and his eyes focused on me.

'Escobar controls the coyote scene through the port of New Orleans and the intercoastal region. We left him a couple of hours ago. Prima used to work for Escobar, but now he's gone into business for himself with you, and Escobar doesn't like it that Prima's taking his business. Prima's getting the business because he's cutting prices, and Escobar likes that even less. You following me with this, Milt?'

Milt was squinting at me big time now.

'And because Prima's charging less, *you* are getting less. Do you see? You're getting, what, a grand a head for your end?'

Now Milt wasn't bothering with the denials. We were with the money, and when you're with the money you have their attention.

'Frank will give you two grand apiece, Milt. Double your money. If you're getting one load of illegals a week, thirty people on average, that's thirty thousand a week, one hundred twenty thousand a month from Mr Prima. But Frank doubles it. The thirty becomes sixty. The one-twenty becomes two hundred forty thousand per month, every month, just for using Escobar and cutting out Prima. Are we talking about the same thing, now, Milt?'

LeRoy Bennett chugged up to the patio, winded and barely able to keep his feet. He saw the gun in Pike's hand and clawed under his shirt, trying for his own piece. Pike punched him once in the side of the face. Bennett dropped. Pike bent over and disarmed him. Pike said, 'Some muscle.'

Rossier stared at LeRoy thoughtfully and said, 'I am surrounded by dunces.'

I made a little shrug.

Rossier shook his head and settled back into the lawn furniture. 'Well, I guess you're the new Jimmie Ray Rebenack, aren't you? He thought he tripped over Easy Street, too. Look where he is.'

'Milt, Jimmie Ray and I aren't even from the same planet. Don't forget that and we'll be okay.'

René lumbered up and stopped at LeRoy, and then he looked at Joe Pike, and the big body gave a shudder. His eyes focused, and he stepped across LeRoy and Pike brought up the Python. 'I'll kill him.'

Milt Rossier screamed, 'René! Goddamn it, you stop right there, René.' The old man's face was mottled, and he looked close to apoplexy.

René looked confused. LeRoy moaned, then rolled over and saw René staring down at him. 'Don't just stand there, you dumb fuck, help me up.'

René picked up LeRoy as if he were made of air. LeRoy hobbled to one of the lawn chairs, holding his side. 'Got a goddamned stitch from d' run.'

Pike said, 'Exercise.'

Bennett scowled. 'You fuck. We'll see 'bout it, sometime, heh?'

Pike said, 'Unh-hunh.'

Rossier said, 'Forget all that right now. We're talkin' business.' He looked back at me. 'What do you get out of this?'

'We get what Escobar pays you for the first delivery. Call it sixty thousand.' Big lies are always easier.

'Bullshit.'

'What's the bullshit, Milt? I'm brokering the deal. You would've kept going with Prima because you don't know any better, with him laughing behind your back. I've figured it out for you, and I've set it up. Your money doubles right away, and for this service, Joe and myself get exactly one week's take. After that it's all yours. You recoup in two weeks over what you were making from Prima.' I gestured to Joe Pike. 'Seems fair to me, Joe. How about you?'

Pike nodded. 'Fair.'

You could see Milt Rossier working it through, thinking about all that free money just for giving the spics a place to dock their boats. Convincing himself. That's the way the best cons work, they convince themselves. He said, 'Frank Escobar, huh?'

I said, 'Let me give you a couple of pointers, Milt. Two a head is top end, so don't start thinking you can get Prima to pay more. Frank is looking for what we call exclusivity here, and he will want to make sure that Donaldo is permanently out of the picture. Do we understand each other?'

'Unh-hunh.'

'Frank wants you to let Prima bring in another load, only this time we'll all be out there at the pumping station together. Prima won't know about Frank and Frank's people, of course, because if he did, he wouldn't show. When he shows, Frank wants to pay him back personally, you see?'

Milt Rossier was shaking his head. 'He don't need me there for that.'

'Yeah, Milt, he does. Frank figures that if you'll sell out Prima, you'll sell out him, too, so you guys are going to have to make a marriage out there. No marriage, no two grand per. Two hundred forty thou every month, Milt. Prima won't be going home, but everybody else lives happily ever after.'

Milt Rossier was thinking about it.

I gave him the phone number that Ramon del Reyo had given me. 'I'm giving you a number to call. Call it if you want, or not. Up to you. It's not Escobar, but it's his people. If you're interested, check out if the deal is real. If not, blow it off. Your choice.'

He took the little slip and looked at it. 'What's to keep me from cutting you out?'

'Milt, you don't live in a fortress. You cut us out, you're over.'

Pike twitched the .357.

LeRoy Bennett said, 'Oh. Yeah.'

Milt Rossier stared at Pike for a time, then glanced over at LeRoy. LeRoy was feeling a little better, but his eye was swelling where Pike had hit him. It probably didn't inspire confidence. Rossier said, 'I've gotta think on it. How can I let you know?'

I told him where we were staying in Baton Rouge, and then Pike and I started back around the house. Milt Rossier called after us. 'Hey.'

We turned back.

Rossier said, 'Podnuh, if either of you ever pull a gun on me again, you'd best use it.'

I smiled at him. 'Milt, if we pull a gun on you again, we will.'

34

When we got back to Baton Rouge I called Jodi Taylor's room from the lobby and got no answer. The desk clerk told me that she had checked out sometime in the early afternoon and that she had left neither note nor message. He said that she seemed distraught. Hearing that she had gone created an empty feeling in my chest, as if I had somehow left a job unfinished and, because of it, had performed beneath myself. I said, 'Well, damn.'

Pike said, 'It's a good night. Clear. I'm going for a run.' The lobby was empty except for Pike and myself and the clerk. Desultory voices leaked from the bar. 'Come with me.'

'Give me a chance to make some calls.'

He nodded. 'Meet you out front.'

We rode up to our rooms, and I changed into shorts and running shoes and then called Lucy. I told her what had happened with Escobar and Rossier and that there was nothing left to do except wait and see if Rossier would go for it. I asked her if she'd heard from Jodi Taylor. Lucy said, 'Yes. And from Sid Markowitz. Sid is saying that they'll sue. I'm not so sure that Jodi wants that, but she sounds upset and confused.'

'Did she say anything about Edith Boudreaux?'

'No.'

Neither of us spoke for a time, and then Lucy said, 'Studly?'

'Yes, ma'am?'

'Ben's going to bed at ten. You could come over and we could neck in the car.'

'Pike and I are going for a run. It's been a helluva day.'

She sighed. 'Just so you know.'

'I knew there was a reason I called you.'

We hung up and I phoned Jo-el Boudreaux next. I told him exactly what I had told Lucy, and when I was done he said, 'Did they go for it?'

'We'll see. Rossier will dig around to see if we're legit, and when he finds out we have something working with Escobar, he'll decide.'

'Okay. Then what?'

403

'He'll call me here. When he calls, I call Escobar. We won't have much time, so you have to be ready.'

'I can get my guys in five minutes. Bet your ass on that one, podnuh.'

'Whatever.'

Pike was waiting out on the cement drive at the hotel's entry, stretching his hamstrings. I joined him, bending deep from the hips until my face was buried between my knees, then sitting with my legs in a great wide V and bending forward until my chest was on the cement. After a day spent mostly driving, and with the tension of dealing with criminal subhumans, it felt good to work my muscles. Maybe I wasn't down about Jodi Taylor after all. Maybe I had merely grown loggy from a lack of proper exercise and was in serious need of oxygenation. Sure. That was it. What's bailing out on a client compared to proper physical conditioning?

Pike did a hundred pushups, then flipped over and lay with his legs straight up against the wall and did a hundred situps. I did the same. The kid from the front desk came out and watched, standing in the door so he could keep an eye on the desk. He said, 'Man, you guys are flexible. Goin' for a run?'

'That's right.'

'Gotta be careful where you run. We got some bad areas.'

I said, 'Thanks.'

'I'm not kidding. The downtown isn't great. Any direction you go, you're gonna run into the blacks.'

Pike said, 'I think I hear your phone.'

The kid ducked inside, then reappeared shaking his head. 'Nah. Must've been something else.'

As my muscles warmed, the tension began to loosen and fall away like ice calving from a glacier and falling into the sea.

The kid said, 'They say we're one of the top ten most dangerous cities in the country.' He seemed proud of it.

I said, 'We'll be careful.'

Pike said, 'Let's get going before I hit this twerp.'

We ran south along the street that paralleled the levee, then up the little rise past the old state capitol building and then east, away from the river. The night air was warm, and the humidity let the sweat come easily. I concentrated on my breath and the rhythms of the run and the commitment needed to match Pike's pace. The run became consuming in its effort, and the focus needed to endure it was liberating. The downtown business area quickly gave way to a mix of businesses and small, single-family homes. Black. We ran along a major thoroughfare and the traffic was heavy, so we stayed on a narrow sidewalk as much as possible. The blocks were short and the cross-streets were numbered, and each time we crossed one you could get a glimpse of the lives in the little neighborhoods. We passed African-American kids on skateboards and bicycles, and other African-American kids playing pepper in the streets or tackle football on empty lots. They stopped as we passed and watched us without comment, two pale men trekking swiftly along the edge of their world, and I wondered if these were the areas the desk clerk had been talking about. As we ran, Pike said, 'You did your best for her.'

I took steady breaths. 'I know.'

'But you're not happy with yourself.'

'I let her down. In a way, I've abandoned her.' I thought about it. 'It's not the first time she's been abandoned.'

A lone running black man turned onto the street across from us and matched our pace. He was about our age, with a receding hairline and ebony skin and the slight, lean torso of a serious runner. Like us, he was shirtless, clothed only in shorts and running shoes, his chest and back slicked with sweat and shining the way highly polished obsidian might shine. I glanced over at him, but he ran eyes forward, as if we were not opposite him, and pretty soon I found that my eyes were forward, too, though I could see him in the periphery. I said, 'She hired me to do one thing, and now I'm doing another. She hired me with every expectation that I would protect her interests, but now I'm taking this in a direction in which her interests are secondary.'

We ran past a high school and shopping centers, Pike and me on our side of the street and the black runner on his, our strides matching. Pike said nothing for several minutes, and I found comfort in the loud silence. The sounds of our breathing. Our shoes striking the pavement. A metronome rhythm. Pike said, 'You didn't fail her. You gave her an opportunity for love.'

I glanced over at him.

'You can't put something into her heart that isn't there, Elvis. Love is not so plentiful that any of us can afford to reject it when it's offered. That's her failing. Not yours.'

'It's not easy for her, Joe. For a lot of very good reasons.'

'Maybe.'

The black runner picked up his pace and moved ahead of us. Pike and I glanced at him in the same moment, and we picked up our pace, too. We caught him, matched him, and then we pulled ahead. Our lead lasted for a few hundred meters before he once again came abreast of us. I pushed harder, Pike pushing as one with me, and the runner across from us pushed harder still. My breath was coming in great, quick gasps, the oxygen-rich Louisiana air somehow energizing, the sweat dripping out of my hair and into my eyes, and we ran ever harder, sprinting now, we on our side of the street, he on his, and then we came to a busy intersection and slowed for the light and I turned to the other runner, smiling and intending to wave, but the black runner was gone. He had turned away from us with the cross-street, I guess, and I tried to find him but he was no longer there. We jogged in place, waiting for the light, and I found myself wishing I had called to him earlier. Now, of course, it was too late.

The light changed. Pike and I pushed on, and the miles crept behind us and the night grew late. We came to a park of soccer fields and softball diamonds, and we turned north, running along the western edge of the fields, and then west again, heading back to the river and the hotel. We had been running for almost an hour. We would run an hour still. Pike said, 'Are you still thinking about her?'

'Yes.'

'Then think about this. You've taken her as far as is right. Wherever she's going, she has to get the rest of the way on her own. That's not only the way it is. That's the way it should be.'

'Sure, Joe. Thanks.'

He grunted. Philosophy-R-Us. 'Now stop thinking about her and start to think about Rossier. If you don't get your head out your ass, Rossier will kill you.'

'You always know how to end the moment on an upbeat note, don't you?'

'That's why I get the big bucks.'

35

Milt Rossier called at fourteen minutes after nine the next morning. First thing out of his mouth was, 'I'll go along for twenty-five hunnerd a head.'

'Forget it.'

'Twenty-two five, then, goddammit, or I'll just leave things the way they are.'

I hung up on him. If I had a strong hand, I'd play it. If I didn't, he'd know I was shooting blanks.

Six minutes later the phone again rang and he said, 'Twenty-one hunnerd, you sonofabitch. You know goddamn well there's some give. Be reasonable.'

I thought my heart was going to come through my nose. 'There's more, Milt, but I'm taking it. It's a one-shot, then I'm back home and out of it. After that, if you can screwdriver Escobar out of the extra cash, go for it.'

Milt Rossier said, 'You sonofabitch,' but now he was laughing. One slimebag to another. Just a couple of good ol' boys ripping off each other. 'Prima's bringing a load up tonight. That too soon for you boys?'

'Nope. What time?'

'The boat comes in around ten. Prima meets my boy LeRoy at a place called the Bayou Lounge. You know it?'

'Not tonight, Milt. Have Prima meet us at the boat. Escobar and I will meet you at your place at eight. Escobar wants to go in early.' If I could get Escobar. If he'd go for it.

Milt said, 'Escobar gonna bring the money?'

'Sure.'

'Well, good.'

I said, 'You didn't tip Donaldo, did you, Milt?'

'Hell, no.'

'Frank wants him, Milt. That's the deal.'

'I said I didn't, goddamn it. If Frank wants to be in business with me he can have Prima's ass in a goddamned croaker sack. I'll gut him and skin him, he wants.'

'Good enough. He's looking forward to meeting you, Milt. He's thinking he can run in three loads a week.'

Milt Rossier said, 'Holy jumpin' Jesus.' There were probably dollar signs in his eyes.

'Happy days, Milt.'

He said, 'One thing, podnuh.'

'What's that?'

'You be at the Bayou waitin'. You ain't there, I'll back away from this thing like a mud bug divin' down his hole.' Ah, that southern color.

'Wouldn't miss it, podnuh.' Now I was doing it.

'Ol' Frank don't show, you gonna wish you had. Milt Rossier don't take shit from any man on this God's earth. You hear where I'm coming from?'

'Loud and clear, Milt.'

I hung up and called Frank Escobar. I said, 'Donaldo Prima is bringing in a boat of people tonight at ten P.M. Rossier says you can have him. Are you in?'

Escobar said, 'Yes.'

'He wants to meet at a place called the Bayou Lounge. We'll meet him there, then go to the boat. You have to have the money.'

'Don't worry about it.'

I hung up and called Jo-el Boudreaux at his home. He answered on the second ring, and his voice was shaky. He said, 'Did they go for it?'

'We're on for tonight. Can you get your people together?'

He said, 'Oh, Christ.'

'Can you get it together?'

'Yeah. Of course, I can.' He sounded strained.

'Calm down, Jo-el. The boat will come at ten, but I have to meet him at his bar at eight, and that means your people have to be in position by seven. Are you going to be able to arrange that?'

'Yeah. Yeah, sure. I'll get my guys and have them come over to the house around four, and we'll set everything up.'

'I'll be there.'

'Hey, Cole.'

'What?'

'I appreciate this.'

'Sure.'

I hung up and phoned Lucy at her office and told her we were on. She said, 'Do you think Jo-el can pull it off?'

'There's nothing to it, Luce. When the bad guys are all together with the money and the illegals, all he has to do is arrest them. The trick was in getting everybody together. There's nothing fancy in the bust.'

'I guess not.' She didn't sound convinced.

I told her that we would be putting it together at the Boudreauxs' house at four, and she said that she'd call Merhlie Comeaux and that they would meet us there. We hung up, and then I went next door for Pike. I said, 'We're on.'

He went to his closet and got the duffel. When he picked it up you could hear the clunk of padded metal. He said, 'I've been ready for years.'

At three o'clock that afternoon, we went down to the car and drove across the bridge to Eunice.

Three Evangeline Parish Sheriff's Department highway cars were parked on the grass in front of Jo-el Boudreaux's house, and Lucy's Lexus was in the drive. I wondered if the neighbors might think it odd, so many cars, but maybe not. Just a little midweek barbecue for the boys. Pike and I went to the door, and Edith Boudreaux let us in. She smiled when she greeted us, but the smile seemed strained.

Lucy and Merhlie Comeaux were in the wing chairs, and three parish cops were on the sofa. The young black cop named Berry was there, along with the cop named Tommy Willets. The third cop was was a guy named Dave Champagne, who looked like the Pillsbury Doughboy with a pink downy face. Willets frowned when he saw us, then looked away, shaking his head. Still with the attitude. Champagne and Berry were younger than Willets. Boudreaux introduced everybody, and I stayed with the group while Pike went off by himself and stood against the wall. Both Berry and Champagne kept glancing at him. A little tray of Fig Newtons and sugar cookies was on the coffee table, and Edith Boudreaux offered us coffee in fragile china cups. She seemed anxious that we accept, and she hovered at the edges of the room, as flighty as a mayfly trapped behind glass. I thought that, in a way, this might be harder on her than on anyone else. Jo-el said, 'I've told everybody that we're goin' after Milt Rossier tonight. I told'm about the illegals and Donaldo Prima and Frank Escobar and what we're tryin' to do. You wanna tell'm what you saw out there?'

I went through it about the towboat and the pumping station and the old man and the little girl, and then I told them about backtracking on Prima to uncover the scam. When I was in the middle of it Willets sat forward on the couch and stopped me. He said, 'You saw a damned murder you shoulda come in right away.'

Jo-el said, 'He had his reasons, Tommy.'

Tommy Willets was staring at the sheriff. 'Not reportin' a crime is against the law, Jo-el. Jesus Christ, who made this guy the goddamned sheriff?' He shot a glance at Edith. 'Sorry, Edie.'

Jo-el Boudreaux was looking embarrassed when Dave Champagne said, 'Oh, put a sock in it, Tommy. We're gonna finally take down ol' Milt Rossier. Ain't that a hoot?' He was grinning so wide his face looked like a fuzzy pink pumpkin. I looked at Pike, and Pike shook his head. We were making this bust with a Boy Scout troop.

Lucy said, 'How is this thing going to be staged?'

I said, 'I'm going to meet Milt Rossier and Frank Escobar at the Bayou Lounge at eight, and then we're going to the pumping station to meet the boat. The boat's due in at ten. Prima is supposed to arrive with the boat.'

Jo-el looked at Merhlie Comeaux. 'How we doin' with this? We clear on entrapment?'

Merhlie nodded. 'I don't see a problem, Sheriff. It looks clean. We give the state a clean bust with Rossier in possession of cash and a truck full of illegal aliens, and they'll put his name on a double occupancy suite in Angola. I guarantee.' He said it *gah-rawn-tee*. Cajun.

I said, 'Rossier may not actually take possession of the cash. It could go to Bennett. That's what happened last time.'

'Same thing,' Merhlie said. 'Bennett works for Rossier, and Rossier holds the lease on the land.' He looked back at Boudreaux. 'I'll wait by the phone. Just lemme know when it's done and I'll call Jack Fochet at State and we'll have ol' Milt arraigned by tomorrow noon. Jack Fochet is a good boy.'

Berry was looking concerned. 'I know the old Hyfield Oil station. How are we supposed to see any of this if it happens inside there?'

'Prima flags the towboat in from the shore, then they bring the trucks into the building through a couple of barn doors,' I said. 'They leave the doors open. You won't have any problem. That's how we saw the old man killed.'

Jo-el said, 'We're gonna be in the weeds, so we may not be able to see what's going on. Maybe we oughta have a sign or somethin'.'

Merhlie frowned. 'Well, hell, Jo-el, what do you want him to do, wave a red bandanna? Those sonsofbitches have guns and they like to use them.'

When he said it, Lucy sat forward in her chair. 'You're going to be with them when the arrests are made?'

'Yes.'

She looked at Pike, and then back to me. 'Is that necessary?'

'I'm what holds it together. I'm putting Rossier and Escobar together, and they're going to want me with them all the way. Rossier's nervous, and Escobar's only going along because he thinks he's going to kill Prima.' I looked at Boudreaux. 'Prima isn't expecting Escobar, so when these guys see each other all hell's going to break loose. You'll have to move fast.'

Jo-el nodded. 'Sure. You bet.' He was pale and he kept rubbing at his jaw.

Willets hooked a thumb at Pike. 'Where are you going to be, podnuh?'

Pike said, 'Watching.'

Willets didn't like that. 'What in hell does that mean?'

Jo-el said, 'Don't worry about it, Tommy. He'll be there.'

Willets stayed with it. 'We should know where everyone is. There might be shooting. Be a shame if somebody got shot accidental-like.'

Pike said, 'Don't worry about it, Willets.'

Willets frowned, but he let it go.

Berry said, 'Where we gonna be?'

Boudreaux said, 'We'll set up in the cane with a view through the doors. We'll have to hide the cars off the main road, then hike in. I want you fellas to go home and get your waders. You're gonna need'm.'

Willets said, 'How much time do we have? I got things I need to do.'

Boudreaux checked his watch. 'We got about an hour before we have to get in place. That about right?' He looked at me, asking. I nodded, and Willets snorted, disgusted that Boudreaux would ask. Boudreaux ignored him and went on. 'I want you boys to change into old clothes, cause we're gonna get wet, but I want everybody in a Sheriff's Department shell parka. I wanna know who's who out there.' Boudreaux had brought it to the end, and now he looked at me. 'I think maybe we oughta get going. You got anything you wanna say?'

'Yeah. Nobody shoot me.'

Berry and Champagne laughed, and everybody stood, moving toward the door. The sheriff went to Merhlie Comeaux, and Lucy pulled me aside. Her mouth was still in the tight line, and she pulled me as far from the others as she could. She said, 'Do you really have to be out there?'

'I've done things like this before. Trust me.'

Her nostrils flared, and she stared across the room, frowning. 'Well, isn't that just great. And what do I get to do, wait here with the womenfolk?'

'If you ask him nice, Pike might loan you a rifle.'

She said, 'Oh, right,' and stalked away to Comeaux.

Pike looked at me from across the room and cocked his head toward the door. I met him there. He said, 'You okay with these guys?'

'They're what we have.'

He glanced at Willets. 'I don't like the dip with the attitude.'

'See you on the other side, Joe.'

Pike nodded, and I went out to my car and left for the Bayou Lounge.

Years ago, a friend and I booked a package cruise from Tahiti to Hawaii, sailing north. The passage took five days, crossing waters so remote that we were beyond all radio contact with land. As we sailed, the sea grew deeper until, three days out of Papeete, the crew told us that the sonar could no longer ping the bottom. The charts said that the bottom was seventeen thousand feet beneath the hull, but, for all purposes, the ocean was bottomless. No way to know what's down there, they said. No way to call home for help, they said. Here there be monsters.

Great dense clouds grew on the western horizon, towering anvil thunderheads that rolled steadily toward me, filling the sky with the slate-steel color of deep ocean water, water with no bottom.

36

A light rain fell as I parked on the oyster shell lot next to the Bayou Lounge. The heavy cloud layer brought an early twilight that filled the air with an expectancy of wind and lightning. Four or five American sedans were lined up on the oyster shells and, inside, half a dozen guys hawked the bar, scarfing poboys and Dixie beer. The woman with the hair smiled when she saw me and said, 'Sugah, I didn't think you'd pass this way again.'

'Small world, isn't it?'

'Oh,' she said. 'It's a lot bigger than we think.' A guy with a grease-stained Evinrude cap laughed when she said it.

I ordered a club soda and took it to one of the little tables by the door. The door was wedged open and it was cooler there, but it was a damp cool that made my skin clammy. The Dan Wesson would be picking up a lot of moisture, and I would have to clean it before it began to pit. Of course, if things didn't go well tonight, I wouldn't have to worry about it.

A couple of minutes later LeRoy Bennett's Polara pulled past the door and LeRoy Bennett came in, shaking his hat to get rid of the rain. He was wearing an Australian drover's coat, and he looked not unlike the Marlboro man. Cancer on the hoof. The woman with the hair squealed, 'Hey, LeRoy,' and leaned across the bar to plant one on his cheek. His face split with a smile and he pawed at her breasts, but she pushed him away like she didn't really mean it. A couple of the good ol' boys at the bar nodded at him, and he shook one man's hand. Old home week with the barfly regulars. He got a long-necked Dixie for himself, then came over and dropped into the chair across from me. His eye was still dark from where Joe Pike had hit him. He said, 'Where're your spics?'

I said, 'I'm here early.'

He had some of the Dixie, shooting a wink at the woman with the hair. 'Yeah? Well, your spics better show or you in deep dodo.'

I said, 'LeRoy?'

He was sucking at his teeth.

'Do yourself a favor and don't call them spics.'

LeRoy frowned like I was a turd. 'That's what they are, ain't they?'

I shook my head. Some people never learn. Some people you just can't talk to.

I said, 'Where's Milt?'

'He'll be here.'

'I thought he might come with you.'

LeRoy pulled on the Dixie. 'You jus' worry about your spics.' He lipped a Tarryton 100 and lit it with a big steel Zippo. The first two fingers on his right hand were yellow with smoke stains. His fingernails were grimed. He grinned at me and let the smoke leak out between his teeth. Probably hadn't brushed in a year.

LeRoy got up and put money in the jukebox. He finished the first Dixie and got himself a second. While he was at the bar the woman with the hair whispered something in his ear, and he whispered something back. She laughed. It's odd what appeals to people, isn't it? The guy with the Evinrude cap and a heavier guy who walked with a limp went home. I wished I could go with them. The rain came harder, filling ruts and depressions in the shell lot and hammering on the bar's roof, and little by little the remains of day were lost to the night. The parking lot filled with white light two quick times, followed almost instantly by twin booms of thunder, and the guys at the bar applauded. The thunder was so loud and so near that the little building shook, rattling glasses and making the jukebox skip. And they talk about earthquakes.

At two minutes before eight, headlights swung across the door, a baby-blue BMW crunched onto the lot, and Frank Escobar came in, the guy with the pocked face holding an umbrella the size of a parachute canopy. LeRoy said, 'Well, it's about goddamned time.' He was working on his third Dixie and he said it too loud.

They came to the table and sat, Escobar shaking off his coat. 'You pick a shit time to do business. Is Rossier here?'

'Not yet.'

LeRoy stuck out his hand. 'Mr Escobar, my name is LeRoy Bennett. It's a pleasure, sir, yes it is.'

Escobar looked at me without acknowledging the hand or the person. 'Who is this?'

'Rossier's stooge.'

LeRoy said, 'Hey, what the fuck?'

Escobar hit LeRoy with the back of his right hand so hard that LeRoy almost went out of the chair. It was exactly the same move he'd used on his wife. Two of the guys at the bar looked over and the woman gave a little gasp. Escobar grabbed LeRoy by the face and dug a thumb under his jaw. 'You see me sitting here?'

LeRoy tried to get away from the thumb, but couldn't. 'Hey, yeah. Whatchu doin', bro?'

'If I'm here, where's your goddamned boss? You think I got time to waste?'

Even as he said it more lights swept the open door and you could hear the crunch, even over the jukebox and the rain. LeRoy stood away from the thumb, saying, 'That's gotta be Milt right now,' just as Milt Rossier walked in.

The woman behind the bar said, 'Hey, Milt,' but Milt didn't acknowledge her. He saw us at the little table and came over, offering his hand to Frank Escobar. 'Frank, I'm Milt Rossier. Lemme apologize if I've kept you, but this rain is a bitch.'

Escobar said, 'Hey, forget about it. You shoulda seen the drive up from Metairie.' He held Milt Rossier's hand longer than he needed to hold it. 'I'm looking forward to a fruitful partnership, Milt, but let's get first things first. Where's Prima?'

'Oh, he'll be at the pumping station. You bet.'

Escobar glanced at me, then put it back on Milt Rossier. He still had the old man's hand. 'I wanna make money with you, Milt, but you have to understand it's personal here, me and Prima. We ain't goin' forward with this until I get this bastard.'

Milt was nodding and trying to get his hand away. Escobar's eyes were dark splinters and Milt Rossier seemed afraid of him. 'Frank,' he said, 'I'm gonna bring you right to him.' He finally got the hand away. 'You ready to do some business or you wanna little snoot before we go? This is my place. It's on the house.' Like a guy worth millions wouldn't pass up the chance at a free belt.

Escobar shook his head and stood. He snapped his fingers, and the pocked guy stood with him. 'Prima.' Talk about one track. You could see his hands flexing, already pulling the trigger. His coat flared when he stood, and you could see a glint in the darkness.

Milt smiled. 'Well, hell, let's go do it.'

We stepped out into the rain. Milt wanted everybody to go together in LeRoy's Polara, but there were five of us and it would be crowded, so Milt asked if Escobar would mind following us in his own car. Escobar said that that would be fine, and he and his goon hurried to their BMW, anxious to get out of the rain. Lightning crackled again, filling the parking lot with light. Escobar and his thug opened the Beamer's doors, the BMW's interior lights came on, and then two men stepped out from behind the Bayou Lounge. Balls of lightning flashed from their hands, and there was the sharp snapping of autoloading pistols muffled by the rain, and Escobar and his goon fell against their car. The pistols were still snapping when LeRoy Bennett slammed the side of my head with something hard and cold. I went down into the mud and Bennett was over me, hitting me twice more and saying, 'Who's a stooge now? Who's

415

a fuckin' stooge?' and then Rossier pushed him away, saying, 'Stop that, goddammit, we ain't got time for that! Get'm up.'

René LaBorde stepped out of nowhere and pulled me to my feet. Bennett, grinning like his face was split, took my gun and hit me again.

The rain fell harder and no one stirred from the Bayou Lounge.

The two men finished their killing and came to us. One of the men was Donaldo Prima. The other was Evangeline Parish Deputy Sheriff Tommy Willets. Willets looked scared. Donaldo Prima said, 'We got that fawkuh good!' I knew then that the good guys were alone at the pumping station. All of the bad guys were here.

I said, 'Jesus Christ, Willets.'

Willets hit me on the forehead with the butt of his pistol and knocked me into the side of Bennett's Polara. Then Milt said, 'Hurry up, goddammit, and get'm in the car. We got a lot of people to kill.'

37

Willets put his cuffs on me, then got René to help put me in the backseat of Bennett's Polara. Willets breathed hard as he did it, a torrent of rain running off the brim of his campaign hat, his Evangeline Parish sheriff's poncho molten in the lightning flashes. The lounge's wooden front door was closed, and I thought maybe Bennett had closed it as we'd left. Maybe.

Across the lot, Bennett and a short guy with a heavy mustache loaded the bodies into Escobar's trunk, the short guy Donaldo Prima's thug. Donaldo Prima came over to the Polara and waved his gun at me. 'This fawkuh set me up?' His eyes were blood simple from the kill.

Rossier said, 'We might need the sonofabitch! *Put it away!*'

Prima pushed past Milt, screaming, 'I gonna kill his ass!' When Prima touched Milt, René's snake-fast hands shot out, grabbing and lifting and twisting the gun away. Prima hissed something in Spanish, then said, 'Make him let go!'

Rossier made René put him down, and then Prima and Rossier went to Escobar's car with Bennett and the mustache. Willets got into the backseat of the Polara with me, and René stood in the rain. René was wearing a raincoat, but it was unbuttoned and looked as if someone had put it on for him. There was no hood, and the rain beat at his head and plastered his hair. Willets sat with his service revolver in his hand, still with the breathing, staring wide-eyed through the rear window at the group of men in the rain as if I weren't there. The glass around us began to fog. I said, 'How much does it cost for a guy like you to sell out, Willets?'

'Shut up.'

'I know he paid you enough to keep tabs on the sheriff, but is it enough to buy a night's sleep?'

'Shut up.'

'Willets, if you sold your balls by the pound, you didn't get enough to feed a parking meter.'

Willets looked over at me, blinked twice, then backhanded me with his

417

revolver. The barrel and the cylinder caught me above the left eye, snapping my head back and opening the skin. There was an instant of blackness, then a field of gold sparkles, and then only sharp pain above the eye. I could feel blood run down across the outside corner of my eye. I grinned. 'You didn't think it'd come to this when you sold them, did you? Guys like you never think that far ahead. Only now it's here and happening fast and you're scared shitless. You're in the deep water, Willets, and you oughta be scared.'

He wet his lips and looked again at the men in the rain. Scared, all right. 'I'm not the guy who has to worry about it.'

'Were you in on Rebenack?'

He still didn't look at me.

'That's perfect, Willets. Perfect.'

LeRoy and Milt came back to the Polara. Prima went behind the lounge, alone, and LaBorde and the mustache climbed into Escobar's Beamer. The Beamer pulled away, and Willets's highway car came from behind the lounge. We pulled out, and the highway car fell in behind us. No one had stirred in the Bayou Lounge, and no one had come out to look. All of it had been covered by the rain and the thunder.

I said, 'I can't believe you didn't go for it, Milt. Two thousand a head is a lot of money.'

Rossier turned in the front passenger seat and grinned at me. His old man's face looked cracked and splintered, and he was holding Bennett's government .45. He said, 'Goddamned right it is. You almost had me, you sonofabitch. I woulda swallowed the whole damn hook if Willets here hadn't tipped me.'

'Willets isn't the only cop who knows. A lot of people are in it, and Jo-el Boudreaux is going to take you down. The blackmail won't work anymore.'

Willets licked his lips. 'He's right, Milt. We oughta not play it this way.'

Milt said, 'Who else knows?'

Willets was licking his lips again. 'The guys out at the station, Jo-el's wife and that lawyer from Baton Rouge, and Merhlie Comeaux. Comeaux went home, and the two women are at the Boudreauxs'.'

Milt Rossier nodded and grinned still wider. 'We'll just round 'm up and kill 'm and that's that.' He said it the way you'd tell someone you wanted pickles on your potted meat sandwich.

I said, 'You're out of your mind.'

Willets said, 'Jesus Christ, that's crazy.'

Milt nodded. 'We'll see.'

Willets said, 'You can't just kill all these people.'

Milt nodded and asked Bennett if he knew how to get there, and Bennett said yes. Willets was licking his lips every few seconds, now. He said, 'Hey, Milt, you don't mean that, do you? You can't just murder these people?'

Milt cocked his head and looked at Willets as you might a slow child. 'Son, simple plans are best. What else can I do?'

Willets squirmed in his seat, holding the service revolver limply in his lap. I wondered if I could move fast enough to snake it from him before Milt shot me. Willets said, 'But that's three officers. That's Jo-el's wife. How we gonna explain all that? Jesus Christ.'

I said, 'Hey, Willets, how do you think he's going to explain you being the only one left alive?'

Milt Rossier said, 'Oh, that one's easy.' Then he pointed LeRoy Bennett's .45 at Deputy Sheriff Thomas Willets and pulled the trigger. The sound was enormous, and the heat and muzzle blast flashed across my face, and Tommy Willets's head snapped back into the seat and then jerked forward, and a spray of red splattered on the vinyl and the door and the windows and me. When Willets's head came forward he slumped to the side and was still.

LeRoy said, 'Man, dat was loud as a pork fart, yeah.'

Milt reached back and took Willets's revolver and had Bennett pull over. Bennett put the body in the trunk and we went on. I said, 'You really mean it. You're going to kill everybody, aren't you?'

Milt said, 'Uh-hunh.'

We drove to Jo-el Boudreaux's house and turned into the drive, Prima pulling the highway car in behind us. I said, 'If you hurt them, Rossier, I swear to God I'll kill you.'

LeRoy said, 'Save the big talk, asshole. You gonna need it later.'

Milt got out of the car and met Prima and the mustache, and together they went to the front door. Around us, the street was quiet and well lit and masked by the rain. Just another dreary southern evening in paradise.

Milt rang the bell, and Edith Boudreaux answered. The mustache pushed past her into the house, and as quickly as that they were bringing Lucy and Edith across the lawn to the highway car. Lucy was struggling, and the mustache had to keep a hand over her mouth. You never expect the bad guys will come to the door. You never expect that they'll ring the bell. When Rossier climbed back into the car, he was smiling. 'We'll see what ol' Jo-el does, now. Yes, I guess we will, won't we?' I'm not sure he was saying it to me or to Bennett. Maybe just to himself.

They brought us to the crawfish farm, driving through sequined curtains of rain, and put us in the processing shed. Escobar's BMW was already there, René standing in the rain and mud like some great oblivious golem. When Milt Rossier saw him, he shook his head and made a *tsk*ing sound. I guess you never get used to it. They taped Lucy's and Edie's wrists with duct tape and made the three of us sit on the floor beneath the gutting tables. Rain hammered in through the big, open front of the processing shed, but we were well back and protected. The rear of the place was open, too, and more rain dripped there. Milt and Prima and Bennett gathered together, then Bennett got back into his Polara and drove away. Going to give the news to Jo-el Boudreaux. Edith looked pale and drawn, and Lucy looked scared. After Prima and the mustache finished with the taping and left us alone, I said, 'Fancy meeting you here.'

Lucy didn't smile. The beautiful tanned skin was mottled, and her nostrils were white. Her eyes moved from Rossier to the mustache to LaBorde to Prima, like something might happen at any moment and in that instant she must be ready or it would be forever lost.

I said, 'It's not over. There's Pike, and there's me. I'll get you out of this.'

She nodded without looking at me.

'Did I tell you that I'm an irresistible force?'

A smile flickered at the edges of her mouth, and her eyes came to me. She said, 'You really know how to show a girl a good time, don't you?'

'Irresistible,' I said. 'Unstoppable. Able to leap tall buildings in a single bound.'

She relaxed the tiniest bit and nodded.

I said, 'A moment will come. When it does, I want you to move back under these tables. You, too, Edith. Did you hear me?'

Edith was as waxy as a mannequin, and I couldn't be sure that she heard me. Then Rossier came over and kicked me hard in the leg, twice. 'Shut up that talk!' He tore off strips of the duct tape and covered our mouths.

We sat on the damp cement floor and watched Rossier and Prima and the mustache move around the processing shed, making their plans. René followed Rossier like a dog after its master. Rossier went up to the main house and came back with a couple of pump shotguns and a thin, weathered man with mocha skin. Another thug. He gave one of the shotguns to the mustache and the other to Donaldo Prima. They talked for a while in the doorway, Rossier pointing and gesturing, and then the black man and the mustache went out into the rain. Setting up a field of fire. I worked at the duct tape with my tongue and rubbed it against my shoulder and the gutting table's leg, and it began to peel away.

Milt stayed in the sliding doors, looking out, and in a little bit lights appeared and LeRoy Bennett's Polara came toward the sheds. It wasn't alone. Jo-el's highway car was behind it, but he wasn't coming in with sirens wailing and light bar flashing. He came slow and easy, like he was trying not to make things worse than they were. LeRoy put his Polara on the side of the processing shed, then came inside. He was soaked, but he looked excited. He said, 'I got'm. I told'm what you said and they came just like you said they would, goddammit! I got their goddamned guns. I busted their goddamned radio.' He was smiling a crazy grin, like we were kids and all of this was some kind of summer-camp game. Blood simple.

Edith straightened to see, and so did I. From where we sat you could see through the wide opening and out to the highway car. Parked in the killing field. Jo-el got out of the near side of his car and stood in the rain, and Berry and Dave Champagne climbed out the other side. I thought I saw a shadow slip from the rear of the car when Berry got out, but I couldn't be sure. Milt Rossier said, 'Where's the other one?'

Bennett said, 'Who?'

'The one knocked you on your ass, goddammit!' Pike wasn't with them.

Bennett squinted out into the rain. 'We couldn't find him, Milt. He's still out in the swamp.'

Rossier swatted at Bennett, his face etched hard. 'You dumb sonofabitch! I said *everybody!*'

'We couldn't find him, Milt!' Whining. 'Hell, we'll get him come light.'

Milt Rossier said, 'Shit!' then went to the big door and yelled, 'Come on in here, Jo-el, and let's talk this thing out!'

Out in the rain, Jo-el yelled back, 'Like hell, you bastard. You come out here. You're under arrest!' Boudreaux stayed where he was.

I heard something at the rear of the shed, out where they wash the blood and the scales. Pike, maybe. I worked my feet under me and rubbed harder at the tape, thinking that if things didn't work out I would try to put myself over Lucy.

Rossier yelled, 'I got your wife, goddammit. Now get in here and let's talk about this.'

Jo-el came forward and stepped inside the door. His side holster was empty. He saw me first, and then he looked at his wife and Lucy. He seemed older and tired, like a man who had run a very long race and had not been in shape for it. He said, 'You okay, Edie?'

She nodded.

No one was looking at me. I got to one knee, the other foot beneath me.

Jo-el said, 'How we gonna work this out, Milt?'

Rossier said, 'Like this,' and then he raised Tommy Willets's service revolver. I lunged forward just as Joe Pike stepped in through the back and shot Milt Rossier high in the left shoulder, spinning him around and spraying blood like polka dots across Jo-el. Edith made a wailing sound deep in her throat and came off the floor and into Milt Rossier as if she'd been fired from a cannon. Even with her hands and mouth taped she battered at him with her head and face, her eyes wild and rolling. Rossier dropped his gun and grabbed at his wound, making a high whining sound. René went for Joe Pike, and Pike shot him square in the chest two times, the .357 Magnum loads putting René down on his knees. René tried to get to his feet, and Pike shot him in the center of the forehead. Rossier tried to shove past Edith for his pistol, but I hit him low in the back. Prima fired his little revolver at Pike, but Pike dived to the side. The people outside were yelling. LeRoy screamed, 'I'll get the sonofabitch,' and stood up from behind one of the gutting tables where he'd run for cover. He aimed his .45 at me, his tongue stuck in the corner of his mouth like a kid trying to color between the lines, and then a tiny red dot appeared on his chest. He looked down at the flicker and said, 'Huh?' just before his back blew out and something kicked him across the room in a spray of blood and bone and the heavy crack of a high-powered rifle rocked through the rain.

Donaldo Prima lowered his gun and looked confused. 'The fuck?'

Pike rolled to me and used his .357 to bust the chain on my handcuffs. 'Del Reyo.' When my hands were free I ripped off the tape.

The red dot flickered on Prima's face like a firefly searching for a place to light. He swatted at it, and then his head blew apart and again there was the distant *BOOM*.

Pike said, 'Flash in the treeline. Gotta be two hundred meters.'

I said, 'Rossier has people outside.'

Pike shook his head. 'Not for long.' His mouth twitched.

There were more booms.

I drove into Edith, pushing her down, and yelled for Lucy to stay under the table. Berry was yelling, too, saying, 'Somebody's shooting at us!' Pike shouted for him to crawl under the car.

Rossier climbed to his feet, still clutching his arm, and the dot found him. I pushed him aside just as something hot snapped past and slammed into the wall. Rossier picked up LeRoy's .45, scrambled to his feet again, and lurched out through the rear of the processing sheds, firing as he went. I went after him.

There was one more boom from the treeline, and then the rifle was silent. Behind the sheds, we were hidden. Rossier tripped and fell into the mud and got up and ran on, still making the whining noise. He shot at me, but with all the slipping and falling and the hurt shoulder, the shots went wild.

I yelled, 'It's done, Milt. C'mon.'

He fired twice more, and the slide locked back and he was out of bullets. He threw the gun at me and ran again, straight into the low wire fence that encircled the turtle pond. In the dark and the rain he hadn't seen it. He went over the wire sideways, hit the mud on his bad shoulder, and slid headfirst into the water. It was a flat silver surface in the rain until he hit it, and then the surface rocked. He sat up, gasping for air, and I stepped across the wire and held out my hand. 'C'mon, Milt. Let's go.'

Pike and Jo-el came up behind me.

Milt Rossier flopped and splashed, stumbling farther out into the pond. 'He'p me! You gotta he'p me!'

Jo-el said, 'You're not drowning, you fat sonofabitch. Just stand up!'

His eyes wide and crazed. 'He'p me! Please, Christ, get me out!'

The water swelled at the far side of the pond, and I remembered Luther.

I stepped into the water to my ankles. 'Get up, dammit. Take my hand!'

Rossier tried to stand but lost his balance and fell backwards, farther out in the pond. I went in up to my knees. 'Take my hand, Milt.'

Something large moved fast beneath the surface, making a wake without breaking the rain-dimpled plane of the water. Pike said, 'Jesus,' and fired at the head of the wake. Jo-el Boudreaux fired, too.

I said, '*Take my hand!*'

Rossier made it to his feet, struggled toward me, and grabbed my hand. His grip was wet and slippery and I pulled as hard as I could, but then his left leg was yanked out from beneath him and he was pulled down into the water.

The screaming and the thrashing went on for several minutes, and maybe I screamed as loudly as Milt Rossier, but probably not.

38

Jo-el Boudreaux called in the State, and the State brought its prosecutors and the crime-scene people, and by noon the next morning there were over three dozen parish, state, and federal officials up to their ankles in mud. The rain kept coming, and did not slacken.

After the bodies were cleaned up and the statements taken, Jo-el removed his badge and told the young cop, Berry, to place him under arrest on a charge of obstruction of justice for failing to act against Milt Rossier.

Berry looked at the badge as if it were radioactive and said, 'Like hell I will!'

One of the prosecutors from New Orleans shouldered his way in and said he'd be happy to accept the badge. He was a guy in his forties with tight skin and short hair, and he had spent a lot of time walking the area and shaking his head. When he tried to get the badge, Berry knocked him on his ass. A state cop from Baton Rouge tried to put Berry in a restraint hold, but Joe Pike moved between them and whispered something in the state cop's ear and the state cop walked away. After that, the prosecutor spent a lot of time sitting in his car.

Lucy spoke quietly to Jo-el for over an hour, pleading with him not to do or say anything until he spoke with Merhlie Comeaux. Edith said, 'Listen to her, Jo-el. You must *please* listen to her.'

Jo-el finally agreed, though he didn't seem to like it much. He sat in the front seat of his highway car with his face in his hands and wept. Jo-el Boudreaux was in pain, and ashamed, and I think he wanted to suffer for his sins. Men of conscience often do.

Joe Pike returned to Los Angeles the following day.

I stayed in Louisiana for a week after the events at Milt Rossier's crawfish farm, and much of that time I spent with Lucy. She spoke on a daily basis with Edith, and twice we went to visit.

With Milt and LeRoy Bennett out of the picture, the Boudreauxs could have kept their secret, but that wasn't the way they played it. They phoned their three children, saying that it was important that they see them, and the three daughters dutifully returned home. Jo-el and Edith sat them down in the living room and told them about Leon Williams and Edith's pregnancy and the murder that had happened thirty-six years ago. Much to the Boudreauxs' surprise, their children were not shocked or scandalized, but instead expressed relief that they had not been summoned home to be informed that one or both of their parents had an incurable disease. All three adult children thought the fact of the murder ugly and sad, but had to admit that they found the story adventurous. After all, these things had happened thirty-six years ago.

Edith's youngest daughter, Barbara, the one who was attending LSU, grinned a lot, and the grinning made Edith angry. Sissy, the oldest daughter, the one with two children, was fascinated with the idea that she had a half-sister and asked many questions. Neither Edith nor Jo-el revealed that the child she'd had was now the actress known as Jodi Taylor. Edith no longer wanted to keep secrets about herself, but other people's secrets were a different matter.

Truths were coming out, and the world was making its adjustments.

On the fourth day after the events at Milt Rossier's crawfish farm, I was waiting for Lucy in the Riverfront Ho-Jo's lobby when the day clerk gave me an envelope. He said that it had been left at the front desk, but he didn't know by whom. It was a plain white envelope, the kind you could buy in any drugstore, and 'Mr E. Cole' was typed on the front.

I sat in one of the lobby chairs and opened it. Inside was a typed note:

Mr Cole,

I regret that I am unable to return the photograph as promised. An associate identified the gentleman, and, as you know, we have acted accordingly. I hope you do not think me small for exceeding the parameters of our association. As I told Mr Pike, the man with the rifle is always there. Regrettably, the child remains unknown, but perhaps now there will be fewer such children.

There was no signature, but there didn't need to be.

I folded the letter and put it away as Lucy crossed the lobby. The Ho-Jo door was flooded with a noonday light so bright that Lucy seemed to emerge from a liquid sun. She said, 'Hi.'

'Hi.'

'You ready?'

'Always.'

We went out to her Lexus and drove to the airport. It was hot, but the sky was a deep blue and vividly clear except for a single puff of white to the east. Lucy held my hand. She released me to steer through a turn, then immediately took my hand again. I said, 'I'm going to miss you, Lucy.'

'Oh, me, too, Studly.'

'Ben, too.'

She glanced at me and smiled. 'Please let's not talk about the leaving. We still have time.'

I kissed her hand.

We turned into airport parking and went into the terminal, still holding hands, walking as close as two people can walk, as if the most important thing in the world was to occupy the same space and share the same moment. We checked the flight information. I said, 'The plane's here.'

We walked to the concourse, and I didn't like it much. In a few days we'd make this drive and walk again, only then I would be leaving. I tried not to think about it.

We met Jodi Taylor as she came off the plane. She was wearing jeans and a satin vest over a red top, and she was clearly Jodi Taylor. Not hiding now. The pilot was falling all over himself to walk with her, and a guy in a charcoal suit was trying to cut in on the pilot. She looked nervous.

I said, 'Pardon us, gentlemen,' and led her away from them.

Lucy said, 'How're you doing?'

Jodi nodded. 'I'm okay.' She didn't look okay. She looked the way you might look if you'd spent the past couple of days with an upset stomach.

A little girl in a Brownie uniform approached. She was holding what looked like a napkin and a ballpoint pen. Her mother had encouraged her. The little girl said, 'Miss Taylor, may I have your autograph?'

'Sure, honey.' Jodi signed the napkin and tried to smile, but the smile looked weak. Nervous, all right.

When the little girl was gone, I took Jodi's hand. 'You sure you want this?'

'Yes,' she said. 'Yes, I'm sure.'

'What about Sid and Beldon?'

Jodi's face grew hard. 'I know what I want.'

Lucy took Jodi's other hand, and we walked out of the airport.

We brought Jodi to pick up Edith, and then the four of us went to visit Chantel Michot. I had called in advance and Chantel was waiting. There was a lot they wanted to talk about.

Sunset Express

AN ELVIS COLE NOVEL

For Leonard Isaacs,
who opened the door,
and
for Kate Wilhelm and Damon Knight,
who invited me in.

Acknowledgments

The author would like to thank Bruce J. Kelton, former Assistant United States Attorney and a managing director of the investigative firm Kroll Associates, for sharing his knowledge of the law and the criminal justice system. Additional thanks go to Det. John Petievich, whose counsel on matters relating to the Los Angeles Police Department in this novel and others has been invaluable. Any errors contained herein are solely the responsibility of the author.

Special thanks go to the world's greatest editor, Leslie Wells.

The author would also like to thank Patricia Crais, Lauren Crais, Robert Miller, Lisa Kitei, Carol Perfumo, Samantha Miller, Brian De Fiore, Marcy Goot, Chris Murphy, Kim Dower, and Jennifer Lang for their support, superior talents, and great efforts on the author's behalf.

Sunset Express

Prologue

The sky above the San Fernando Valley that Saturday morning was a deep blue, washed clean of the dirt and chemical particulates that typically color L.A. air by a breeze that burbled out of the San Gabriel Mountains and over the flat valley floor and across the high ridge of the Santa Monica Mountains. Mulholland Drive snakes along the crest of the Santa Monicas, and, if you were walking along Mulholland as Sandra Bernson and her father were doing that morning, you would have been able to look south almost forty miles across the Los Angeles basin to the tip of the Long Beach Peninsula or north some thirty-five miles across the San Fernando Valley and through the Newhall Pass to the deep purples of the Santa Susana mountains and the peaks surrounding Lake Castaic. It was a day of unusual clarity, the far horizons magnified as if by some rare trick of optical law that might even allow you to see into the lives of the sleeping millions in the valleys below. Sandra Bernson later said that as she watched the small private airplanes floating into and out of Van Nuys Airport in the center of the valley that morning, she imagined them to be flying carpets. On mornings like these, she later said, it was easy to believe in magic.

Sandra was a fifteen-year-old honor student at the prestigious Harvard-Westlake School, and her father, Dave Bernson, was a television writer and producer of moderate success, then working as the supervising producer of a popular series on the Fox Television network. The Bernsons lived in a contemporary home on a small private road off Mulholland Drive in Sherman Oaks, approximately one mile west of Beverly Glen, and they left their home at exactly 6:42 that morning. Both Sandra and Dave were able to tell investigators their exact departure time because it was Dave's habit to call out when their walks began so that they could time themselves. They intended to walk east along Mulholland to Warren Beatty's home approximately one mile east of Beverly Glen, where they planned to reverse course and return. Their typical walk would cover four miles round-trip and take almost exactly fifty minutes.

435

On this particular Saturday, however, they never made it to Beatty's and they didn't complete the walk.

On this Saturday, Sandra Bernson saw the deer.

They proceeded east from their home, climbing one of Mulholland's steeper grades to a high, flat stretch of road abreast Stone Canyon Reservoir. That was Sandra's favorite part of the walk because she could see the valley to the north and the reservoir to the south, and just before they came to Beverly Glen Canyon they would reach the Stone Canyon overlook. The overlook is built into the top of a little knoll there beside Mulholland, with manicured walks and observation points and benches if you want to sit and admire what realtors like to call a 360-degree jetliner view. Sandra remembers that as she and her father reached the top of the overlook she saw the deer creeping up from the valley side of Mulholland, sniffing and listening, and she whispered to her father, 'Look, Dad!'

'Mule deer. See the size of his ears? It's a buck, but he's already shed his horns. See the knobs above his eyes?'

The deer heard them. It looked in their direction, its huge ears cocked forward, and then it bounded across Mulholland and the overlook's little parking lot and disappeared. Sandra said, 'I wanna see where he goes!'

She slid across the overlook's low wall and ran to the edge of the knoll just as the buck vanished near a cut in the slope that had caught a lot of dead brush and beer cans and newspapers and brown plastic garbage bags. Dave arrived at her side a moment later. Everything caught by the cut looked old and dusty and weathered as if it had been there for a very long time, except for the garbage bags. They looked shiny and new, and Sandra was using them as a landmark to point out to Dave where she had last seen the mule deer when she saw the hand sticking out of the bags. The nail polish was very red and seemed to gleam in the breathtakingly clear morning sun.

It never entered Dave's mind that the hand might be a movie prop or belong to a mannequin; the moment he saw it he knew it was real. It looked real, and it also looked dead. Dave recalls that he considered working his way down to the body, but then says that he remembered things like clues and evidence, and so he led his daughter back to Mulholland where they flagged down a passing Westec private security car. The security cop, a twenty-eight-year-old ex-Marine named Chris Bell, parked his unit and went to see for himself, then returned to his car and reported the find to the Westec offices. In less than eight minutes, two LAPD patrol units arrived on the scene. The uniforms observed the hand protruding from the plastic, but, as had Dave Bernson, decided not to venture down the slope. The uniforms relayed their observations in code by radio, then secured the area to await the arrival of the detectives.

Dave Bernson offered to wait also, but by that time Sandra had to pee really bad, so one of the uniforms drove them home. Forty minutes after

Sandra Bernson and her father were returned to their home, and thirty-nine minutes after Sandra began calling her friends just as quickly as she could to tell them about this incredibly gross thing that had just happened, the first detective unit arrived on the scene.

Detective Sergeant Dan 'Tommy' Tomsic and Detective-two Angela Rossi were in the first car. Tomsic was a powerfully built man who'd spent a dozen years on the street before making the transfer to detectives. He had almost thirty years on the job, and he viewed the world through suspicious, unblinking eyes. Angela Rossi was thirty-four years old, with twelve years on the job, and had been Tomsic's partner for only five weeks. Rossi spoke her mind, was entirely too confrontational, and, because of this, she had trouble keeping partners. So far Tomsic didn't seem bothered, but that was probably because he ignored her.

Eleven minutes after the first car, the senior detectives arrived on the scene. Detective Sergeant Lincoln Gibbs was a tall, thin African-American with mocha-colored skin, a profoundly receding hairline, and tortoise-shell spectacles. He looked like a college professor, which was a look he cultivated. He had twenty-eight years on the job, less than Tomsic, but more time in grade as a detective sergeant, so Linc Gibbs would be in charge. He arrived with Detective-three Pete Bishop, a twenty-two-year veteran with an M.A. in psychology and five divorces. Bishop rarely spoke, but was known to make copious notes, which he referred to often. He had a measured IQ of 178 and a drinking problem. He was currently in twelve-step.

The four detectives got the story from the uniforms and the Westec cop, then went to the edge of the overlook and stared down at the hand. Gibbs said, 'Anybody been down there?'

One of the uniforms said, 'No, sir. It's undisturbed.'

The detectives searched the ground for anything that might present itself as evidence – scuff marks, drops of blood, footprints, that kind of thing. There were none. They could see the path that the body had followed as it slid down the slope. Scuffs on the soil, broken and bent plants, dislodged rocks. Linc followed the trail with his eyes and figured that the body had been dumped from a point just at the rear of the parking lot. The body was between twelve and fifteen yards down a damned steep slope. Someone would have to go down, and that presented certain problems. You wouldn't want to follow the same path as the body because that might disturb evidence. That meant they'd have to find another route, only everything else was steeper and the drop-off more pronounced. Linc was thinking that it might take mountaineering gear when Angela Rossi said, 'I can get down there.'

The three male detectives looked at her.

'I've done some rock climbing in Chatsworth and I work terrain like

437

this all the time when I'm backpacking.' She pointed out her route. 'I can work my way down the slide over there, then traverse back and come up under the body. No sweat.'

Dan Tomsic said, 'That goddamned soil is like sand. It won't hold your weight.'

'It's no sweat, Dan. Really.'

Rossi looked like the athletic type, and Gibbs knew that she had run in the last two L.A. marathons. Tomsic sucked down three packs a day and Bishop had the muscle tone of Jell-O. Rossi was also fifteen years younger than the rest of them, and she wanted to go. Gibbs gave his permission, told her to take the camera, and Angela Rossi went back to the car to trade her Max Avante pumps for a busted-out pair of New Balance running shoes. She reappeared a minute later, and Gibbs, Tomsic, and the others watched as she worked her way down to the body. Tomsic frowned as he watched, but Gibbs nodded in approval – Rossi seemed graceful and confident in her movements. Tomsic was praying that she wouldn't lose her balance and break her damned neck – one slip and she'd flop ass over teapot another sixty or eighty yards down the slope.

Down below, Rossi never once entertained the notion that she might fall. She was feeling absolutely confident and more than a little jazzed that it was she who had taken the lead in recovering the body. If you took the lead you got the promotions, and Rossi made no secret that she wanted to become LAPD's first female chief of detectives. It was a goal she had aggressively pursued since her days at the academy and, though there had been what she called her Big Setback, she still hoped that she could get her career back on track and pull it off.

When Rossi reached the body, she could smell it. The sun was rising and the dark plastic was heating quickly and holding the heat. As water evaporated from the body it collected on the plastic's inner surface, and, Rossi knew, it would be humid and damp inside the bag. The victim's abdomen would swell and the gases of decay would vent. Decomposition had begun.

Linc called down to her, 'Try not to move the body. Just take the snaps and peel back the bags.'

Rossi used the Polaroid to fix the body's position for the record, then pulled on rubber surgical gloves and touched the wrist, checking for a pulse. She knew that there would be none, but she had to check anyway. The skin was pliant but the muscles beneath were stiff. Rigor.

Rossi couldn't see much, as yet, but the body appeared intact and double-bagged in two dark brown plastic garbage bags. The bags were secured around the body with silver duct tape, but the job appeared to have been done hastily. The bags had parted and the hand had plopped out. Angela Rossi peeled the bags apart to expose the shoulder and head of a blonde Caucasian woman who appeared to be in her early thirties.

438

The woman was clothed in what looked like a pale blue Banana Republic T-shirt that was splattered with blood. The woman's left eye was open but her right eye was closed, and the tip of her tongue protruded between small, perfect teeth. The hair on the back and right side of her head was ropey and matted with blood. Much of the blood was dried, but there was a shiny, wet quality to much of it, also. The skull at that portion of the hair appeared depressed and dark, and brain matter and ridges of white skull were obvious. The woman's nose was straight and her features rectangular and contoured. In life, she would've been pretty. Angela Rossi had an immediate sense that the woman looked familiar.

Tomsic yelled down, 'Don't pitch a goddamned tent down there. What's the deal?'

Rossi hated it when he spoke to her that way, but she clenched her jaw and took it. She'd been taking it more and smarting off less since the Big Setback. Anything to resurrect the career. She called back without looking at them. 'Caucasian female. Early thirties. Blunt force trauma to the back of the head.' She pushed the garbage bag back farther, exposing the victim's head and shoulders. She saw no additional injuries and wanted to peel back the bags even farther, but was concerned that the body would dislodge and tumble down the slope, possibly taking her with it. She took more pictures, then said, 'The blood around the wound appears to be tacky, and it's wet in some spots. She hasn't been here long.'

Bishop said, 'Lividity?'

'A little, but it could be bruising.'

Above her, Linc Gibbs was growing impatient with all the conversation. He didn't like Rossi perched on such a steep slope, and he wanted to call in the criminalist. He said, 'What about a weapon?' Murderers almost always dumped the murder weapon with the body.

He watched Rossi lean across the body and feel around the bags. She moved out of sight twice, and each time he tasted acid because he thought she'd fallen. Another Tagamet day. He remembers that he was just getting ready to ask her what in hell was taking so long when she said, 'Don't see anything, but it could be under the body or in the bag.'

Gibbs nodded. 'Leave it for the criminalist. Take some more pix and get back up here.'

Rossi took the remainder of the roll, then worked her way back up the slope. When she reached the top, the others crowded around to see the pictures. All of the male detectives pulled out reading glasses except for Gibbs, who wore bifocals.

One of the uniformed cops said, 'Hey. She looks like somebody.'

Rossi said, 'I thought so, too.'

She didn't look like anyone to Gibbs. 'You guys recognize her?'

Bishop was turning the pictures round and round, as if seeing the victim from every possible view was important. All the turning was making Tomsic nauseated. Bishop said, 'Her name is Susan Martin.'

The Westec cop said, 'Holy Christ, you're right. Teddy Martin's wife.' All four detectives looked at him.

The Westec cop said, 'They live right over here in Benedict Canyon. It's on my route.' Benedict Canyon was less than one mile from the overlook.

Gibbs said, 'I'll be damned.'

The four detectives later testified that they thought pretty much the same thing at the same time. Teddy Martin meant money and, more important than money, political power, and that meant the case would require special handling. Dan Tomsic remembers thinking that he wished he had called in sick that day so some other asshole would've answered the call. Special cases always meant special trouble, and investigating officers almost always caught the short end of the deal. Teddy Martin was a rich boy who'd made himself even richer; a successful restaurateur and businessman who used his wealth to cultivate friends and social position and notoriety. He was always having dinner with city councilmen and movie stars, and he was always in the newspaper for giving millions of dollars to all the right causes. Tomsic knew the name because Teddy Martin had opened a new theme restaurant with a couple of movie star partners that his wife had been nagging him to take her to. He'd been foot-dragging because he knew it'd cost sixty bucks for a couple of pieces of fish just so the wife could eyeball some second-rate movie props and maybe some closet-fag actor. Tomsic hated guys like Teddy Martin, but he kept it to himself. Guys like Teddy Martin were headline grabbers and almost always phonies, but a phony with the right connections could end your career.

Pete Bishop said, 'It's gonna be a headliner. We'd better call the boss.'

Gibbs said, 'Use your cell phone. You put it on the radio, we'll have media all over us. Tommy, see if there's anything on the wire.'

Angela Rossi walked with Tomsic and Bishop back to their units. Fine soil and foxtails had worked down into her running shoes and between her toes, so she sat in the backseat of her radio car and cleaned her feet with a Handiwipe before changing back into her Max Avantes. While she sat in the car, Tomsic and Bishop stood apart from each other in the overlook's parking lot, each talking into their respective cell phones.

By the time Rossi finished cleaning her feet and had rejoined Gibbs at the top of the slope, both Tomsic and Bishop were off their phones. Tomsic said, 'Nothing on the board about a Susan Martin.'

Bishop said, 'I called the boss and notified the coroner. Criminalists are on the way, and the boss is coming out.' The boss was the detective captain who oversaw the Westside detectives. When he reached the scene, everyone knew he'd decide whether Gibbs would keep the case or it would be reassigned to someone else. Gibbs knew that because of Mr

Martin's stature, the case would almost certainly be assigned to one of the elite robbery-homicide units downtown. He had no problem with that.

Gibbs said, 'Okay, we'd better notify Mr Martin and see what he says.' He looked at the Westec guy. 'You know where they live?'

'Sure. I'll take you over, you want.'

Gibbs started for his car. 'Okay. Let's go.'

Bishop was shaking his head. 'We'd better stick around for the boss, Linc.'

Tomsic said, 'Angie and I'll go.'

Angela Rossi later said that if she'd known where it was going to lead, she would have shot Tomsic right there.

Dan Tomsic and Angela Rossi followed the Westec guy east along Mulholland to Benedict, then south down through the canyon into a lush winding world of million-dollar homes and Mercedes convertibles. Most of the homes were new and modern, but the Westec guy pulled off the road in front of a Mediterranean mansion that could have been a hundred years old. A big mortar wall with an ornate iron gate protected the mansion from the street, the wall laced by delicate ivy with tiny, blood-red leaves. The wall was cracked and crumbling beneath the ivy, but you could see the cracks only if you took your time and looked between the vines. A gate phone stood to the left of the drive so you could identify yourself before being buzzed in. Tomsic figured the grounds for four or five acres, and the house beyond for maybe twenty thousand square feet. Tomsic and his wife and four children were squeezed into a twenty-two-hundred-square-foot cracker box in Simi Valley, but those were the breaks. Anyone could be a cop, but it took real talent to serve bad food in an overpriced restaurant.

They were getting out of the car when Angie said, 'The gate's open.'

The big wrought-iron gate was open maybe nine or ten inches. You didn't live behind walls and gates and security cops, then leave the front gate open so that any stray goofball or passing psycho could come inside and make himself at home. Tomsic remembers that his first thought on seeing the open gate was that they would find a body inside.

They went to the gate and pressed the button on the call box twice, but they got no answers. Angie said, 'We don't need to wait for a warrant, do we?'

Tomsic said, 'Shit.' He pushed at the gate and went through.

The Westec guy said, 'We can't just walk in, can we?' He looked nervous. 'I'll call the office and they can ring the house.'

Tomsic ignored him, and Rossi followed Tomsic toward the house.

The drive was hand-laid Mexican pavers and had probably cost more than Tomsic's house, his two cars, and the quarter interest he owned in a Big Bear Lake cabin combined. The mansion itself was built of mortar and rough-hewn wooden beams and was finished with an ancient Spanish tile roof. A healthy growth of ivy covered the ground along the east side of the drive, nestling up to a couple of monstrous podocarpus trees before continuing around a four-car-garage. Each car had its own door, and the whole effect was more that of a stable than a garage. A large fountain sat just off the front entry, trickling water.

Tomsic thought that it looked like the kind of house that Errol Flynn might've owned. His wife would love the place, but Tomsic knew that most of the old stars, just like most of the new stars, were perverts and scumbags, and if you knew the things that went on in places like this you wouldn't be so thrilled with being here. Normal people didn't go into the movie business. Movie people were shitbirds with serious emotional problems who kept their secret lives hidden. Just like most lawyers and all politicians. Tomsic completely believed this, probably because everything he'd seen in almost thirty years on the job confirmed it. Of course, Tomsic had never in his thirty years shared what he knew with his wife because he didn't want to rain on her parade. It was easier to let her think he was a grump.

Nothing seemed amiss. No bodies were floating in the fountain and no cars were parked crazily on the front lawn. The massive front door was closed and appeared undamaged. A large ornate knocker hung in the center of the door, but there was also a bell. Tomsic pressed the button, then used the knocker. Loud. The Westec guy came running up behind them. 'Hey, take it easy. You're gonna break it.' His face was white.

Angie said, 'Stay back, okay? We don't know what we have here.'

Tomsic glanced at Angie and shook his head. Fuckin' Westec geek, worried about losin' the account. Angie rolled her eyes.

Tomsic slammed at the door two more times without getting an answer and was starting back to the car when the door opened and Theodore 'Teddy' Martin blinked out. Martin was a medium-sized man, a little shorter than average, with pale, delicate skin. He was unshaven and drawn with hollow, red-rimmed eyes. Tomsic says that he would've bet that the guy had spent most of the night blasted on coke or crystal meth. 'Mr Martin?'

Martin nodded, his head snapping up and down. He was wearing baggy gray sweatpants and no shirt. His torso was soft and undeveloped and covered with a thick growth of fine hair. He squinted against the bright morning sun. 'Yeah, sure. What do you want?'

Both Tomsic and Angela Rossi later testified that Tomsic badged him and identified himself as a detective with the Los Angeles Police Department. Angela Rossi noted that Teddy Martin never looked at the badge. He kept his eyes on Tomsic and blinked harder as if something were in his eyes. Angela Rossi thought at the time that he might have allergies. Tomsic said, 'Mr Martin, does a woman named Susan Martin live here with you?'

When Tomsic asked the question, Angela Rossi says that Teddy Martin took a single sharp breath and said, 'Oh, my Christ, they killed her, didn't they?'

People say the damnedest things.

Tomsic took Rossi aside, gave her his cell phone, and told her to call Gibbs and tell him to get over here. Rossi walked out to the drive and made the call. When she returned to the house, Tomsic and Teddy Martin and the Westec geek were inside, Tomsic and Martin sitting on an antique bench in the entry. Teddy Martin was blubbering like a baby. 'I did everything they said. I did everything, and they said they'd let her go. Jesus Christ. Oh, Jesus, tell me this isn't happening.'

Tomsic was sitting very close to Martin and his voice was soft. He could make it soft whenever he wanted to calm people. 'You're saying she was kidnapped?'

Martin sucked great gulps of air as if he couldn't breathe. 'Christ, yes, of course she was kidnapped.' He put his face in his hands and wailed. 'I did everything they said. I gave them every nickel. They said they'd let her go.'

Angela Rossi said, 'You gave someone money?'

Martin waved his hands, like a jumble of words were floating around him and he had to grab hold of the ones he wanted to use. 'Half a million dollars. Just like they said. I did everything exactly the way they said. They promised they'd let her go. They *promised*.'

Tomsic gently took Teddy's wrists and pushed his hands down. He said, 'Tell me what happened, Mr Martin. You want to tell me what happened? Can you do that?'

Martin seemed to regain control of himself and rubbed at his eyes. He said, 'I came home Thursday night and she was gone. Then this guy calls and says he's got Susan and he puts her on. I think it was around eight o'clock.'

Rossi distinctly remembers asking, 'You spoke with her?'

'She was crying. She said she couldn't see anything and then the guy came back and he told me that if I didn't give them the five hundred thousand they'd kill her. I could hear her screaming. I could hear her crying.'

Tomsic said, 'Did you recognize this man's voice?'

'No. No, I asked him who he was and he said I should call him James X.'

Tomsic glanced at Rossi and raised his eyebrows. 'James X?'

'He said they were watching the house. He said they if I called the police and they would kill her. Oh, Jesus, I was so scared.' Teddy Martin stood, taking deep breaths and rubbing his stomach as if it hurt. 'He said

I should get the money and he would call tomorrow and tell me what to do with it.'

Angie said, 'Tomorrow was yesterday?'

Martin nodded. 'That's right. Friday. I got the money just like he said. All in hundreds. He wanted hundreds. Then I came back here and waited for his call.'

Tomsic said, 'You just walked into the bank and got five hundred thousand dollars?'

Teddy Martin snapped him an angry look. 'Of course not. My business manager arranged it. He cashed bonds. Something like that. He wanted to know why I wanted the money and I told him not to ask.'

Rossi saw Tomsic frown. Tomsic prompted Martin to continue. 'Okay. So you got the money, then came back here to wait.'

Martin nodded again. 'I guess it was around four, something like that, when he called. He told me to put the money in a garbage bag and bring it to a parking lot just off Mulholland at the four-o-five. They have a little lot there for people who carpool. He told me that there was a dumpster, and I should put the money into the dumpster, then go home. He said they would give me exactly twelve minutes to get there, and if I was late they'd know I was working with the police and they'd kill Susan. They said I should just drop the money and leave, and that after I was gone they'd pick up the money and count it and if everything was okay they'd let Susan go. They said it probably wouldn't be until nine or ten with the counting.' He sat again and started rocking. 'I did everything just like they said and I've been waiting all night. I never heard from them again. I never heard from Susan. When you rang the bell I thought you were her.' Teddy Martin put his face in his hands and sobbed. 'I made it in the twelve minutes. I swear to God I made it. I was driving like a maniac.'

Tomsic told Angie to take the cell phone again, call Gibbs, and this time tell him to have someone check the dumpster. She left, and Tomsic stayed with Martin and the Westec guy. Rossi was gone for only four or five minutes, but when she returned she looked burned around the edges. He said, 'You get Gibbs?'

She didn't answer the question. Instead, she said, 'Dan, may I see you, please?'

Tomsic followed her outside to the ivy alongside the expensive Mexican drive. She took out her pen, pushed aside some leaves, and exposed a ball peen hammer clotted with blond hair and bits of pink matter. Tomsic said, 'I'll be damned.'

Rossi said, 'I was just looking around when I saw it. The handle was sticking up out of the ivy.'

Tomsic stared at the hammer for several seconds, noticing that a single black ant was crawling in the pink matter. Tomsic made the same

444

whistling sound that he'd made at the Stone Canyon overlook when he'd seen the body. Angela Rossi then said, 'He killed her, didn't he, Dan?'

Lincoln Gibbs and Pete Bishop turned into the drive as she said it. Dan Tomsic, who had a million years on the job and whose opinion as a professional cynic almost everyone valued, glanced at the mansion and said, 'The sonofabitch killed her, all right, but now we have to convict him.'

'Hey, we've *got* this guy, Dan! He's *ours!*'

Dan Tomsic stared at her with the disdain he reserved for shitbirds, defense attorneys, and card-carrying members of the ACLU. He said, 'It's easier to cut off your own goddamned leg than convict a rich man in this state, detective. Haven't you been around long enough to know that?'

It was the last thing that Dan Tomsic said to her that day.

Susan Martin's murder made the evening news, as did the events that followed.

I was able, months later, to piece together the events of that Saturday morning from police reports, participant interviews, court testimony, and newspaper articles, but I couldn't tell you what I was doing when I heard, or where I was or who I was with. It didn't seem important.

I did not think, nor did I have reason to believe, that Susan Martin's murder and everything that grew from it would have such a profound and permanent impact upon my life.

1

Jonathan Green came to my office on a hazy June morning with an entourage of three attorneys, a videographer, and an intense young woman lugging eight hundred pounds of sound recording equipment. The videographer shoved past the attorneys and swung his camera around my office, saying, 'This is just what we need, Jonathan! It's real, it's colorful, it's *L.A.!*' He aimed his camera at me past the Mickey Mouse phone and began taping. 'Pretend I'm not here.'

I frowned at him, and he waved toward the lawyers. 'Don't look at me. At *them*. Look at *them*.'

I looked at *them*. 'What is this?' I was expecting Green and an attorney named Elliot Truly, but not the others. Truly had arranged the meeting.

A man in his mid-forties wearing an immaculately tailored blue Armani suit said, 'Mr Cole? I'm Elliot Truly. This is Jonathan Green. Thanks for seeing us.'

I shook hands with Truly first, then Green. Green looked exactly the way he had the two times I'd seen him on *60 Minutes*, once when he defended an abortion rights activist accused of murder in Texas and once when he defended a wealthy textile manufacturer accused of murder in Iowa. The Texas case was popular and the Iowa case wasn't, but both were victories for the defense.

The videographer scrambled backward across the office to fit us into his frame, the woman with the sound gear hustling to stay behind the camera as they captured the moment of our first meeting. Armstrong steps onto the moon; the Arabs and the Israelis sign a peace accord; Jonathan Green meets the private detective. The woman with the sound equipment bumped into my desk and the videographer slammed against the file cabinet. The little figures of Jiminy Cricket on the cabinet fell over and the framed photo of Lucy Chenier tottered. I frowned at him again. 'Be careful.'

The videographer waved some more. 'Don't look at me! *Not at me!* You'll ruin the shot!'

I said, 'If you break anything, I'll ruin more than the shot.'

Green seemed embarrassed. 'This is tiresome, Elliot. We have business here, and I'm afraid we're making a bad impression on Mr Cole.'

Truly touched my arm, trying to mitigate the bad impression. 'They're from *Inside News*. They're doing a six-part documentary on Jonathan's involvement in the case.'

The woman with the sound equipment nodded. 'The inner workings of the Big Green Defense Machine.'

I said, 'Big Green Defense Machine?'

The videographer stopped taping and looked me up and down as if he found me lacking but wasn't quite sure how. Then it hit him. 'Don't you have a gun?' He glanced around the office as if there might be one hanging on a wall hook.

'A gun?'

He looked at Truly. 'He should be wearing a gun. One of those things under the arm.' He was a small man with furry arms.

Truly frowned. 'A shoulder holster?'

The woman nodded. 'A hat would be nice. Hats are romantic.'

I said, 'Truly.'

Jonathan Green's face clouded. 'I apologize, Mr Cole. They've been with us for the past week and it's becoming offensive. If it bothers you, I'll ask them to leave.'

The videographer grew frantic. 'Hey, forget the gun. I was just trying to make it a little more entertaining, that's all.' He crouched beside the water cooler and lifted his camera. 'You won't even know we're here. I promise.'

Truly pursed his lips at me. My call.

I made a little shrug. 'The people who come to me usually don't want a record of what we discuss.'

Jonathan Green chuckled. 'It may come to that, but let's hope not.' He went to the French doors that open onto the little balcony, then looked at the picture of Lucy Chenier. 'Very pretty. Your wife?'

'A friend.'

He nodded, approving. When he nodded, the two lesser attorneys nodded, too. No one had bothered to introduce them, but they didn't seem to mind.

Jonathan Green sat in one of the leather director's chairs across from my desk and the two lesser attorneys went to the couch. Truly stayed on his feet. The videographer noticed the Pinocchio clock on the wall, then hustled around to the opposite side of my desk so that he could get both me and the clock in frame. The Pinocchio clock has eyes that move side to side as it tocks. Photogenic. Like Green.

Jonathan Green had a firm handshake, clear eyes, and a jawline not dissimilar to Dudley Do-Right's. He was in his early sixties, with graying hair, a beach-club tan, and a voice that was rich and comforting. A minister's voice. He wasn't a handsome man, but there was a sincerity in his eyes that put you at ease. Jonathan Green was reputed to be one of the top five criminal defense attorneys in America, with a success rate in high-profile criminal defense cases of one hundred percent. Like Elliot Truly, Jonathan Green was wearing an impeccably tailored blue Armani suit. So were the lesser attorneys. Maybe they got a bulk discount. I was wearing impeccably tailored black Gap jeans, a linen aloha shirt, and white Reebok sneakers. Green said, 'Did Elliot explain why we wanted to see you?'

'You represent Theodore Martin. You need investigators to help in the defense effort.' Theodore 'Teddy' Martin had been arrested for Susan Martin's murder and was awaiting trial. He had gone through two prior defense attorneys, hadn't been happy with them, and had recently hired Jonathan Green. All the hirings and firings had been covered big time by the local media.

Green nodded. 'That's right. Mr Cole, I've spoken at length with Teddy and I believe that he's innocent. I want your help in proving it.'

I smiled. '*Moi?*'

The videographer edged in closer. I raised a finger at him. Unh-unh-unnh. He edged back.

Truly said, 'We've talked to people, Mr Cole. You've an outstanding reputation for diligence, and your integrity is above reproach.'

'How about that.' I glanced at the camera and wiggled my eyebrows. The videographer frowned and lowered the lens.

Jonathan Green leaned toward me, all business. 'What do you know about the case?'

'I know what everybody knows. I watch the news.' You couldn't read the *Times* or watch local television without knowing the business about James X and the five hundred thousand dollars and the dumpster. I'd heard Theodore Martin's sound-bite version of it ten thousand times, but I'd also heard the DA's sound-bite version, too, that Teddy and Susan weren't getting along, that Susan had secretly consulted a divorce attorney and told a friend that she was planning a divorce, and that Teddy had offed her to keep her from walking away with half of his estimated one-hundred-twenty-million-dollar fortune. I said, 'From what I hear, the police have a pretty good case.'

'They believe they have, yes. But I don't think all the facts are in.' Green smiled and laced his fingers across a knee. It was a warm smile, tired and knowing. 'Did you know that Teddy and Susan loved to cook?'

I shook my head. That one had slipped right by me.

'Teddy arrived home early that night, and they had no engagements, so the two of them decided to cook something elaborate and fun. They spent the next couple of hours making a pepper-roasted pork tenderloin with wild cherry sauce. Teddy makes the sauce with fresh cherries, only they didn't have any, so he ran out to get some.'

Truly took a step toward me and licked points off his fingers. 'We have the receipt and the cashier whom Teddy paid. That's where he was when Susan was kidnapped.'

Green spread his hands. 'And then there's the question of the money. What happened to the money?'

Truly ticked more fingers. 'We have the bank transactions and the business manager. The manager says that Teddy was visibly shaken when he came for the money that Friday morning. He says Teddy was white as a sheet and his hands were shaking.'

Green nodded. 'Yet the cashier remembers that Teddy was relaxed and happy a dozen hours earlier.' Green stood and went back to the balcony. The videographer followed him. At the French doors he turned back to me and spread his hands again. I wondered if he thought he was in court. 'And then we have the murder weapon and the crime scene evidence.'

Truly ticked more fingers. He had used up one hand and was starting on the next. 'There were fingerprints on the hammer, but none of them match Teddy. There were also fingerprints on the garbage bags that Susan was in, but those don't match Teddy, either.'

I said, 'You think he's innocent because of that?'

Green came back to the director's chair, but this time he didn't sit. He stood behind it, resting his hands on the wooden posts that hold the back. 'Mr Cole, I don't win the number of cases that I do because I'm good. I turn down ten cases every day, cases that would bill millions of dollars, because I will not represent people I believe to be guilty.'

The videographer went down to the floor for a low-angle shot, the woman with the sound equipment with him, and I heard him mumble, 'Oh, man, this is great.'

Green said, 'I don't represent drug dealers or child molesters. I only take cases that I believe in, so that every time I walk into court I have the moral high ground.'

I leaned back and put my foot on the edge of my desk. 'And you believe that Teddy is innocent.'

'Yes. Yes, I do.' He came around to the front of the chair and tapped his chest. 'In here I know he's innocent.'

The videographer muttered, 'This is fabulous,' and scrambled around to keep Jonathan Green in the shot.

Green sat and leaned toward me, elbows on knees. 'I don't yet know all the facts. I need people like you to help me with that. But I do know that we've received several calls that are disturbing.'

Elliot Truly said, 'Have you heard of our tip line?'

'I've seen the ads.' Green's office was running television, radio, and print ads offering a reward of one hundred thousand dollars for anything leading to the capture, arrest, and conviction of James X. There was a number you could call.

Green said, 'We've received over twenty-six hundred calls and there are more every day. We try to weed out the cranks as quickly as possible, but the workload is enormous.'

I cleared my throat and tried to look professional. 'Okay. You need help running these things down.'

Green raised his eyebrows. 'Yes, but there's more to it than that. Several of the callers have indicated that one of the arresting officers has a history of fabricating cases.'

I stared at him. The videographer scrambled back across the office, again running into the cabinet, but this time I did not look. 'Which officer?'

Truly said, 'The detective who claims to have found the hammer. Angela Rossi.'

I looked at Truly. 'Claims?'

Jonathan Green, Elliot Truly, and the camera stared at me. No one spoke.

I looked back at Green. 'Do you believe that Angela Rossi planted evidence against Teddy Martin?'

Green shifted in the chair and the camera swung back toward him. He looked uncomfortable, as if the subject bothered him. 'I don't want to say that, not yet, but I believe that the possibility exists. She was the first to go down to Susan's body, and she went alone.'

Truly said, 'She had the opportunity to recover the murder weapon and secrete it on her person.'

'A full-size ball peen hammer.'

Truly smiled. 'Where there's a will.'

I shook my head. 'Why would she take the chance?'

Green said, 'Elliot.'

Truly leaned toward me, serious. 'Rossi was on a fast track up the promotion ladder until she blew a homicide investigation two years ago. She failed to Mirandize a suspect who subsequently confessed, and the suspect walked. She might feel she needs a headline case to resurrect her career, and if she tampered with evidence to make this case, it may not be the first time she's done so.' Truly made a little hand move at one of the lesser attorneys, and the lesser attorney slipped a manila envelope from his Gucci case and brought it to me. Truly said, 'Rossi arrested a man named LeCedrick Earle five years ago for possessing counterfeit money and attempting to bribe an officer. He's currently serving a six-year sentence at Terminal Island.' Terminal Island is the federal facility down in San Pedro. 'Earle phoned six days ago and told us that Rossi planted the money.' He gestured at the envelope. 'He's been saying that he was set up since day one, and sent us a copy of his case file and the various letters of complaint to prove it.'

I opened the envelope and fingered through the arrest reports, legal correspondence, and letters of complaint. Terminal Island return address, all right. I said, 'All perps claim they're innocent and every cop I know has had charges brought against him. It goes with the job.'

Green nodded, reasonably. 'Of course, but Mr Earle's claim seems to have a bit more merit than the others.'

Truly said, 'A former LAPD officer named Raymond Haig told us about the Earle case, also. Haig was Rossi's partner.'

I said, 'Haig was her partner at that time?'

'Yes.'

'And he said that she planted the goods?'

Truly smiled again. 'He wouldn't say that, but he says that he knew her and that she would do anything to further her career. He suggested that we look into it.'

I said, 'If Earle made the allegation, there would've been an internal police investigation.'

The smaller lesser attorney said, 'There was, but no charges were filed.'

Green said, 'Mr Haig indicated that Detective Rossi has a history of excessive behavior.'

I put the envelope down and tapped at the edge of my desk. The videographer crept back to the water cooler and focused on me. I said, 'Mr Green, you should know that my partner, Joe Pike, is a former LAPD officer.'

'We're familiar with Mr Pike.'

'I work with LAPD often, and I have many friends there, and in the district attorney's office.'

He leaned toward me again, very serious now, sincere. 'I'm not looking for a stooge. I have plenty of those, believe me.' He tried not to glance at the lesser attorneys but couldn't help himself. 'I'm looking for an honest detective who won't just tell me what I want to hear. I want the truth. Without the truth, I have nothing. Do you see?'

I nodded. Maybe I could see why he was one of the world's greatest defense attorneys after all.

Truly said, 'What we're discussing with you is only a small part of the larger picture. We have sixteen investigators working with us now, and we'll probably have as many as thirty, but you'll be the only investigator working on this aspect of the case.'

The larger lesser attorney said, 'We have fourteen attorneys on board, in addition to the investigators.'

The smaller lesser attorney's head bobbed. 'Not to mention eight forensic specialists and three criminalists.' He seemed proud when he said it. Peace through superior firepower.

I made a whistling sound. 'The best defense money can buy.'

Jonathan Green stayed serious. 'As I said, there's plenty of work to go around, and more work every day. Will you help us, Mr Cole?'

I leaned back, thinking about it, and then I held up the envelope. 'And what if I find out that Rossi's okay?'

'Then that's what you find. I owe it to myself and my client to exhaust every possibility. Do you see?'

I said, 'Wherever it leads.'

'That's exactly right.'

'The moral high ground.'

'My reputation rests on it.'

I watched the Pinocchio clock. I looked at the picture of Lucy Chenier. I nodded. 'If Rossi's clean, that's what I'll report.'

'I wouldn't have it any other way.'

Jonathan Green put out his hand and we shook.

2

We worked out my fee, Elliot Truly cut me a check, and the Big Green Defense Machine left me to get on with it. I stood in the door as they walked to the elevator, watching the videographer record every moment of the departure. Cindy, the woman who runs the beauty supply distribution office next door, came out of the elevator as they were getting on and saw Jonathan. She stared at him until the doors closed, and then she smiled at me. Incredulous. 'Isn't he that guy? The lawyer?'

'Jonathan Green.'

'I saw him on *Geraldo*. He's famous.'

I held out crossed fingers. 'We're like this.'

Cindy opened her door, then cocked an eyebrow at me. 'I always did think you were cute.'

'Big time. I am nothing if not big time.'

She laughed and disappeared into her office. That's Cindy.

I went back into my office, closed the door, and looked at the picture of Lucy Chenier. She was sitting in her backyard wearing shorts and hiking boots and an LSU T-shirt. I had had the picture in my office since Lucy sent it to me a little over three months ago, and I looked at it a lot. Lucy was a lawyer, too, but she hadn't been on *Geraldo*. His loss. I stared at the picture. Something about it wasn't right and, being an astute detective, I deduced that this was because the videographer had bumped the cabinet. It was not too late to rush down the stairs and shoot him, but that would probably be overreacting. Besides, he was part of the Big Green Defense Machine, and teammates shouldn't shoot each other. Jonathan Green might think me small.

I adjusted the picture, then went back to my desk and dialed Lucy's office in Baton Rouge, Louisiana. If Cindy was impressed with Jonathan Green, so might be Lucy Chenier. I am also nothing if not a show-off.

A warm southern voice said, 'Ms Chenier's office.' Lucy's assistant, Mrs Darlene Thomas.

'It's me.' I'd phoned quite often in the three months since I'd been in Louisiana, and the calls were becoming more frequent.

'Hello, Mr Cole. How are we today?'

'We're fine, Darlene. And yourself?' Small talk.

'Very well, thank you. I'm sorry, but she's in court today.'

'Oh.' Dejected.

Darlene said, 'She'll call for her messages, though. I'll tell her that you phoned.'

'Tell her that I'm lonely, Darlene.'

Darlene laughed. 'I'll tell her that Mr Cole says he's lonely.'

'Tell her that I miss her, Darlene. That the longing grows with every passing moment and has become a weight impossible for me to bear.'

Darlene gasped. 'Oh *my*, but you do go on!'

I was grinning. Darlene did that to me. 'Darlene, have I ever said that you've got a very sexy voice?'

'Get on with you, now! You stop this nonsense before I tell Ms Chenier!'

We said our good-byes and I called Joe Pike to tell him that we were once more employed. His answering machine picked up on the first ring and beeped. He used to have a one-word message that just said, 'Speak,' but I guess he felt it was long-winded. Now, there was just the beep. When I asked him how people were supposed to know who they had gotten or what to do, he'd said, 'Intelligence test.' That Pike is something, isn't he?

I said, 'This is the Lone Ranger, calling to inform you that someone has once again been foolish enough to give us money. We're working for Jonathan Green.' I hung up. It might be days before I heard from him.

The envelope that Truly left contained a copy of LeCedrick Earle's arrest report as well as a formal letter of complaint written by a public defender on Earle's behalf. The arrest report was written by Officer Angela Rossi and stated that Rossi had arrested Mr Earle at his home after Mr Earle attempted to bribe his way out of a traffic code violation with eight hundred dollars in counterfeit one-hundred-dollar bills. The letter of complaint alleged that Rossi had planted the counterfeit money on Mr Earle and that Mr Earle was innocent of all wrongdoing. The arrest report said little, and the letter of complaint said even less. She said, he said. A single sheet bearing both Angela Rossi's home address and Raymond Haig's business address and phone number was the last entry in the file. A newspaper photograph of Rossi was clipped to the sheet. It was an old photo that showed an attractive woman with a lean, rectangular face and intelligent eyes. She looked determined.

I put everything back into the envelope, then called my friend Eddie Ditko at the *Examiner*. Eddie has been a reporter for about ten million years, and he answered with a voice that was maybe three weeks away from throat cancer. 'Ditko.'

'Is this Eddie Ditko, the world's finest reporter?'

He made a hacking sound like a cat gakking up a hairball. 'Yeah, sure, it says that right here on my Pulitzer. Hold on a minute while I wipe my ass with it.' That Eddie. Always with just the right thing to say.

'A guy named LeCedrick Earle was busted on a funny money beef five years ago. He claimed it was a setup by the arresting officer.'

'They all claim that. It's a natural law.' You see?

'The arresting officer was Angela Rossi.'

'I'm hearing Notre Dame.' Bells.

'Rossi put the cuffs on Teddy Martin. She found the hammer.'

Eddie made the gakking sound again. 'You're shitting me.'

'Nope.'

He wasn't saying anything. Thinking. Sniffing the words and smelling a story. 'What's this to you?'

I didn't say anything.

He gave the big sigh, like I was asking for an organ donation. 'What do you want?'

'Whatever you've got on the Earle arrest, and anything in your files about Rossi.' Ever since the Christopher Commission the *Examiner* kept a database on LAPD officers. The Fourth Estate's version of Big Brother.

'What's this have to do with Teddy Martin?'

I didn't say anything some more.

'Yeah, right. I'll get back to you.' Then he said, 'You really give me ass cramps.'

He hung up without another word. Always the pleasant conversationalist.

I put everything back in the envelope, then locked the office and drove up through Hollywood and the Cahuenga Pass and into the San Fernando Valley. I left the Hollywood Freeway at Barham and drove east along the foot of the Verdugo hills through Burbank into Glendale. Raymond Haig owned a Mr Rubber Discount Tire franchise in an area of gas stations and falafel stands and flat single-story buildings with shops that sold secondhand clothes and wholesale electronics. A weathered Hispanic guy in a broken straw hat had set up a little *churro* cart outside the tire store, the *churros* hanging in ropes inside the glass cart. The Hispanic guy was decked out in cowboy boots and jeans and a wide leather belt with a gleaming silver buckle inlaid with the image of a Brahma bull. A *vaquero*. A couple of kids with skateboards were holding fistfuls of wax paper and long brown *churros*, and a black dog with a bandana around its neck was sitting between them, looking first at one, then the other. Hopeful.

I parked on the street in front of the *churro* cart, then went into the store. A young Hispanic woman with tired eyes and too much makeup was sitting behind the counter, staring at a little television. I handed her a card. 'I need to see Mr Haig. If you tell him that Elliot Truly sent me, he'll know what it's about.'

She took the card and disappeared through a door leading to the service bay, and a couple of minutes later she came back with a tall guy in his late forties. Haig. He was wearing a plaid shirt and a maroon knit tie, and he had a pencil caddy in his shirt pocket. The caddy's plastic flap said *Beamis Shocks*. He came over. 'You Cole?'

'That's right. Elliot Truly said that someone from his office spoke to you, and that you'd be willing to answer a few questions about Angela Rossi.'

His face split with a sleek smile and he put out his hand. 'You bet. Let's go in back and I'll tell you everything you need to know about that rotten bitch Rossi.' Nothing like an unbiased opinion.

He led me to a small office cluttered with parts catalogs and product manuals and posters of bikinied young women posing on lug wrench displays. Enlightened. A couple of padded chairs sat opposite his desk for customers, and a Mr Coffee with a tower of Styrofoam cups sat on a table next to the glass door. 'You want a little coffee?'

'No, thanks.'

Haig poured a cup for himself and brought it to his desk. There was a picture of a younger Haig in an LAPD uniform on the desk.

I said, 'How long were you on the job?'

'Fifteen bullshit years.' Unbiased, all right. 'Best move I ever made was getting out and going into business for myself. Yes, sir.' He settled in behind the desk, then picked up an unlit cigar and popped it into the side of his mouth. I took out a little pad and a Uniball pen to take notes. He said, 'Rossi's the reason I left the goddamned force.'

'How so?'

'I didn't want to ride with a woman.'

I smiled at him. 'You left because you didn't want to ride with a woman.'

He pulled the cigar from his mouth and made a move with it. 'Hey, you get these women in a car, they're either scared shitless and not worth a damn when things get hairy, or they're out of their minds aggressive and you never know what they're gonna do.'

'And Rossi was aggressive?'

'Christ, yes. Always tryin' to be more man than a man.' He had some of the coffee, then sucked at the cigar again.

I said, 'You were partners when she made the LeCedrick Earle arrest?'

'Yep. That's the bust got her into plainclothes. She got a big promotion off that bust.' He leaned back, and I noticed that small brown flecks of matter were scattered over the catalogs and desk and floor. I squinted at them and wondered what they were.

I said, 'LeCedrick Earle claims that she planted the money, and Truly says that you agree.' I felt something gritty on the arms of the chair and looked. More flecks. Sort of like brown dandruff.

Haig chewed at the cigar, then took it out and examined it. The end was soggy and frayed, and while he looked he absently spit little pieces of tobacco off his tongue. I saw a piece land on an air filter catalog. I saw another piece land on the framed photo of young LAPD Haig. Haig didn't seem to notice, or didn't care. I lifted my elbows from the chair and brushed at my arms. Yuck. Haig shook his head. 'Nope. I didn't say that. I said that I wouldn't put it past the bitch.'

'But you don't know?'

He shrugged and spit more tobacco. 'If you read the arrest report you know I wasn't listed as an arresting officer. Rossi went back later without me. That way only one name gets credit for the collar. You see how she was?'

'She cut you out.'

Another shrug. 'Just her way. When it came to wearin' a uniform she was just passin' through and she made no secret of it. All she used to talk about was gettin' ahead, gettin' that gold shield. She told me she'd do anything to get that gold shield, and that's what I told Truly. I had to listen to that every goddamned day like a goddamned matrah.'

'Mantra.'

'Whatever.'

The Hispanic woman rapped at the glass then stepped into Haig's office. She was holding a clipboard. 'Warren wan's you to sign these estimates.'

Haig grinned and made a little c'mere gesture. 'Lemme see what you've got.'

She kept her eyes down when she crossed to him, probably because Haig was making a big deal out of looking at her. A gold wedding band and a large, ornate engagement ring were on her left hand, the stone square and flat and enormous, and probably zircon. The polished gold of the rings looked warm against her brown skin. She said, 'Warren says a truck is here with the new tires. He says he needs you to come see.' Warren was probably Haig's assistant.

'Yeah. I'll be out in a minute.'

Haig took the clipboard and flipped through a couple of pages without really looking at them. He used one hand to flip the pages and the other to feel her right hip. He scratched his name and handed back the board, still with the big grin. '*Gracias*, babe. Lookin' good.'

'Warren says he needs you about the new tires.' Like Warren had been making a thing and she didn't want to mention it, but felt obligated.

Haig's grin turned brittle. 'Tell Warren to hold his water. I'll come when I come. *Comprende?*' He patted her hip again, letting his hand linger.

She took the board and walked out, Haig watching her go. He spit more tobacco, and I thought that if any of the flecks landed on me I might shoot him. Haig glanced at his watch and frowned. Warren.

I said, 'Okay, Rossi was ambitious. But did she ever do anything illegal to your knowledge?'

'Not to my knowledge.'

'Ever rig an arrest?'

Haig shook his head.

'Plant evidence?'

'Not with me around.' Offended.

'You told Truly that you thought Rossi was capable of falsifying evidence. You said that your statement was based upon your experience as her partner. Do you really know anything, Haig, or are you just blowing smoke?'

Haig frowned. 'Look, Rossi used to skirt the line all the time. She'd do anything to make a case, go through a window, pop a trunk, jump a fence. I used to say, hey, you ever heard of the search and seizure laws? You ever heard of a warrant?'

'And what would she do when you said that?'

'Look at me like I'm an asshole.' He chewed at the cigar some more, then suddenly seemed to realize what he was doing and dropped it into the trash. 'Christ, she made me crazy in the car, always running plates, always looking for the collar.'

'Sounds like good police work.'

'Try livin' with it every day.' He glanced at his watch again. 'I gotta get going.'

'One more thing. You weren't with her when she made the Miranda violation.'

'Nah. That was later. I was already off the job and she was a detective-one. Rossi the hot shot, bustin' balls like always.'

'Then how do you know about it?'

'I saw her after. Bobby Driskoll's retirement up at the Revolver and Athletic Club.' The Revolver and Athletic Club is the Police Academy's bar. 'She was goin' on about it, sayin' how rotten it was, sayin' that she was going to do whatever it took to get her career back on track.'

'Were there other people around?'

'Hell, yes. Rossi never made a secret about her ambition. "They can't keep me down." That's the way she talked. "All it takes is one big bust and I'm on top again." Like that.'

'But you have no personal knowledge of her having done anything illegal?'

Haig frowned at me. 'Any bitch that in-your-face is up to something.'

I closed the pad and put it away. Jonathan Green probably wasn't going to like what I had to say about Haig. 'Tell me something, Haig. Are you an asshole by choice?'

Haig gave me the hard cop eyes, and then the slick grin came back and he stood. 'Yeah, I guess it sounds that way, but there's more to it than her attitude. You see where she lives?'

I didn't know what he meant. 'No.'

'Go see where she lives.'

We walked out to the little showroom together. A guy who was probably Warren was standing with a black guy in a Goodyear shirt, and together they were reading what was probably a delivery manifest. They looked up when we came out and Warren said, 'We got those tires.'

Haig ignored him. He slipped behind the counter and I went to the door, and neither of us said anything to the other.

The Hispanic woman was behind the counter. Haig moved against her and mumbled something that the rest of us couldn't hear. She didn't look at him, and didn't respond. She stared at the TV, as if by staring hard enough it wouldn't be happening.

I went out into the sun, thinking that maybe I should have shot him anyway.

3

The two kids with their skateboards were gone, but the dog was still sitting by the *churro* cart, watching the *vaquero*. The *vaquero* was still waving his *churro* at the passing cars and looking sad. All the way up from Zacatecas to stand on a corner and sell something that no one except a couple of kids and a dog wanted. A man who had worked with the Brahmas, no less.

I climbed into my car and opened Truly's envelope and looked at Angela Rossi's address, wondering what Haig had meant about seeing where she lived. 724 Clarion Way. I looked up Clarion Way in the Thomas Brothers Guide, found it in Marina del Rey, and thought, 'Well, hell.'

The Marina wraps around the ocean on a stretch of sand just south of Santa Monica. It's home to sitcom writers and music producers and people who own Carpeteria franchises, maybe, but not cops. The cheapest house in the Marina maybe goes for six hundred thousand, and even the smallest apartments would set you back fifteen hundred a month before utilities. Condos had to start at three hundred grand. Raymond Haig was probably just a raging sexist who had been shown up on the job and was working out on the person who had shown him up, but how did that explain a cop living in the Marina? Of course, there were probably ten million explanations for how Rossi might live there, but I probably wouldn't ferret them out sitting in front of a tire store in Glendale.

The *churro* salesman caught me staring at him and gestured with the *churro*, his eyes somehow embarrassed in their sadness. I climbed out of my car and paid him thirty-five cents for ten inches of fried dough that had been dusted with powdered sugar and cinammon. He thanked me profusely, but he still seemed sad. I guess there's only so much you can do.

I went back to my car and worked my way across the valley floor, then up onto the San Diego Freeway and down through the westside of Los Angeles to the Marina. It was sunny and bright, with the sun still riding a couple of hours above the horizon. The air smelled of the sea and crisp white gulls floated and circled overhead, eyeing McDonald's and Taco Bell parking lots for fast-food leftovers. Women with ponytails raced along the wide boulevards on Rollerblades and shirtless young men pedaled hard on two-thousand-dollar mountain bikes, and everybody had great tans. Aging *vaqueros* selling rubber-hose *churros* weren't in evidence, but maybe I hadn't looked close enough.

I turned down Admiralty Way with its wide green traffic island and drove along the Silver Strand to a short cul-de-sac lined with low-density condominiums partially hidden behind tropical plantings. Clarion Way. Seven twenty-four was part of a four-unit building at the front of the curve, and even from the street I could see that the units were large and spacious and expensive. Definitely not cop digs. A gated drive led down beneath the building, and a gated walk led along the front of the units. A mail drop was built into the front gate, along with a security phone so that you could call inside to let the residents know you'd come to visit. I circled the cul-de-sac, parked across the street at the curb, and walked back to the mail drop to see if Angela Rossi's name matched the address. No names. I guess the postman was expected to know who lived where.

A thin man with thick glasses and a bulging forehead squinted out at me from behind the gate. 'May I help you?'

I gave him one of my better smiles and tried to look reasonable. 'Do you know if Keith's home?'

He frowned at me. 'Keith?'

I nodded. 'That's right. Keith Adams in seven two four. He said he'd wait for me, but no one answers.'

He shook his head. 'You must have the wrong address. There are only four of us in the building, and no one by that name lives here.'

I dug out my wallet, drew a cash receipt from Hughes Market, and frowned at it. 'It says seven twenty-four Clarion.'

He was shaking his head before I finished. 'Maybe there's another Clarion. I know the woman in seven twenty-four. I don't think she's home now.' The woman.

'You don't think we could be talking about Keith's wife, do you?' I peered through the gate. A boy's red bike was leaning against a planter in the entry to seven two four. A plastic hamper filled with Nerfballs stood behind the bike.

He put his hands on his hips, still shaking the head. 'Oh, no. It's just Angie and her kids.' Angie. You see how it adds up?

I put my wallet away and scratched my head. Klem Kadiddlehopper comes to the big city. 'Has she lived here long? Maybe Keith moved.' Trying to find out how a cop could afford to live here. Trying to find out if she rented or stayed with a friend or had won the place in a lottery.

'Not long. She moved in two years ago.'

'She own it, or does she rent?'

Now he was frowning. Suspicious. 'Why don't you leave your number. Maybe the lady knows something about your friend and will call you.' The detective presses his luck a tad too hard.

'That's okay. I'm pretty sure I've got Keith's number back at the office.'

I thanked him for his time, went back to my car, then drove to a pay phone in a little shopping center at the mouth of the Marina where I called a realtor friend who works in Pacific Palisades. A bright woman's voice said, 'Westside Realty, how may I help you?'

I tried to sound like a G-man. 'Adrienne Carter, please.'

'May I tell her who's calling?'

'Richard Tracy.'

'Please hold.'

Maybe twenty seconds later another woman's voice came on. 'This is Adrienne Carter.'

'I'd like to buy the Hearst Castle. Wanna handle the deal?'

Adrienne Carter laughed. 'Dick Tracy. Oh, *please.*'

I gave her Angela Rossi's address and asked if she could run an owner-of-record check for me. I told her it was a matter of utmost urgency and the security of the nation depended on her. She said, 'I'll bet, *Dick.*' I think I had started something that I was going to regret.

Forty minutes later I made the slow pull up Laurel Canyon into the mountains above Hollywood and the rustic A-frame I have there. It's woodsy where I live, and though I have neighbors, our homes are separated by mature eucalyptus and olive trees that give us shade and lend stability to the steep slopes upon which we live. I bought the place many years ago when it was in disrepair and, over time, have rebuilt and refinished it both alone and with the help of friends.

I parked in the carport, let myself in through the kitchen, and was looking in the refrigerator for something to eat when the cat-door squeaked and the cat who lives with me walked in. I said, 'Hey.'

The cat is large and black and one ear sits kind of cocked to the side from when he was head-shot with a .22. The flat top of his head is laced with scars and his ears are shredded and lumpy. When he was younger he would often bring me bits of squirrel and bird to share, but he's older now and the gifts are not as frequent. Perhaps he's slowing, or perhaps he's just less generous. He snicked across the floor and sat by his bowl. 'Naow.'

'I'm hungry, too. Hang on.'

I took out leftover chicken that I'd baked with garlic and rosemary, and a half can of tuna. I turned the oven to 350, wrapped the chicken and canned new potatoes together in foil, then set it in the oven to heat. I forked the tuna into the cat's bowl, then set the can next to it so he could lick the juice. He prefers the chicken, but the garlic gives him gas, so I've had to draw the line. He doesn't like me for it, but there you go.

It was eighteen minutes after seven, and I was getting ready to take a shower when the phone rang. Adrienne. I said, 'Hi, Adrienne.' Elvis Cole, Too Hip Detective, pretends he can read minds.

Lucy Chenier said, 'Adrienne?' The Too Hip Detective steps in deep doo-doo.

'A realtor friend,' I said. 'I'm expecting her to call with some information I need.'

'Do tell. Well, heaven forbid I should tie up your line.'

I gave her Groucho. 'Can't think of anyone I'd rather have tie me up, heh heh.'

'Oh, you.' I love it when she says 'oh, you.' And then she said, 'Hi, Studly.'

I felt the smile start deep in my chest and grow large like an expanding bubble, and then I was standing in my kitchen with the phone and Lucy Chenier's presence seemed to fill the house with warmth and light. I said, 'I miss you, Luce.'

'I miss you, too.'

'Hmm.'

'Hmm-mm.' We often have conversations like this.

I had met Lucy Chenier three months earlier when I was working in Louisiana for an actress named Jodi Taylor. Lucy was Jodi Taylor's lawyer and I was Jodi Taylor's detective, and the attraction, as they say, was immediate. We had called each other regularly since then, and two months ago I had flown back to Louisiana to spend a long weekend with Lucy and her eight-year-old son, Ben. Three weeks after that, Lucy and I had met in Cancun for four days of snorkeling and grilled shrimp and sunburns, and it was harder still to say good-byes when she boarded her plane and I boarded mine. Thereafter, the phoning grew more frequent, and the conversation less necessary, and soon we were in a kind of comfortable/uncomfortable place where the occasional murmur on the other end of the line was enough, but not nearly enough. Over the weeks an increasing part of my day has become the anticipation of the evening's call, when I would sit in my home and Lucy would sit in hers and we would share a few minutes together linked by two thousand miles of fiber-optic satellite relays. It wasn't as nice as actually being with her, but if romance were easy, everyone would do it. I said, 'You may be interested in why I am waiting for Adrienne to call.'

'I'm sure I don't want to know.'

'Do I detect coolness?'

'You detect indifference. They are not the same.'

I said, 'Ha. We'll see if you feel the same after you hear my news.'

She said, 'Let me guess. You've changed your name to Jerry Lee Lewis Cole?' You see what passes for humor in Louisiana?

'I'm working with Jonathan Green.'

There was a moment's silence, and then Lucy Chenier said, 'Is that true, or is this more of the famous Elvis Cole wit?' Not joking, now.

'Hired me today for the Big Green Defense Machine.'

Lucy Chenier made a soft whistling sound, then said, 'Oh, Elvis. That's wonderful.' You see? Impressed. Lucy being impressed made me want to thump my hind leg on the floor and roll over so that she could scratch my belly. She said, 'We used to study his cases in law school.'

'How about that.'

'It must be very exciting.'

'He's just another client.'

She said, 'I have news, too.' She sounded happy, like maybe she was smiling when she said it.

'Okay.'

'The firm has business to take care of in Long Beach, and they're sending me out. Ben's out of school, so how would you like a couple of freeloading house guests?'

The background noise of the TV and the CNN newscasters was suddenly a million miles away. I said, 'I could handle that.'

'What?' I guess she hadn't heard me. I guess my voice had come out hoarse and small.

'Hold on a minute and let me check my calendar.'

'You rat.'

I was smiling. I was smiling so wide that my face felt tight and brittle, as if I smiled any farther my cheeks would crack. 'Yes. Yes, I think that would be fine. Are you kidding? That's great.'

'I thought so, too.'

I said, 'I'll be at the airport in an hour.'

She laughed. 'You can be there in an hour, but Ben and I won't be there until the day after tomorrow. I'm sorry to spring this on you, but I didn't know for sure until this afternoon.'

I was too busy smiling to answer.

'I'll call tomorrow and give you the flight information.'

'Hey, Luce.'

'Hm?'

'I'm really happy about this.'

'Me, too, Studly. Oh, you don't know.'

We talked for another hour, mostly about where we would go and what we would do and how excited we were that we would see each other again. When my food was warm I sat on the kitchen floor, eating as we talked, and the cat came over and stared at me. Purring. Lucy asked about Green and the Teddy Martin case, and as I told her I listened to the soft country sounds of k.d. lang behind her, and the passing voices of Ben and his best friend as they tumbled through her home. The sounds of Lucy Chenier's life. I told her about the videographer and that Green was

464

shorter and thinner than he looked on television, though still imposing, but after a while our conversation drifted back to us, and to how our tans from Cancun were fading and how much fun we'd had drinking blue iced cocktails and eating the fresh *ceviche* that the hotel chefs would make at the beach, and then after a while the conversation was over.

Lucy blew me a kiss and hung up and I lay back on the kitchen floor with the phone on my stomach, grinning at the ceiling. The cat stopped purring, and came closer to stare into my face. He looked concerned. Maybe he didn't know I was grinning. Maybe he thought I was dying of some sort of hideous facial stricture. Is that possible? Death by grinning. I said, 'She's coming to see us.'

He hopped up onto my chest and sniffed at my chin and began to buzz again. The certainty of love.

Later, I washed the dishes and shut the lights and went up to bed. I lay there for a very long time, but sleep wouldn't come. I could only think of Lucy, and of seeing her, and as I thought the grin seemed to grow. Perhaps the grin would grow so wide that it would crash through the sides of the house and slop down across the mountain and just keep expanding until it became The Grin That Ate L.A. Of course, if that happened, the grin would eat LAX and Lucy couldn't land. Then where would I be?

At a little after two that morning, I went downstairs to the guest room and stripped the bed and put on fresh linen and then dusted and vacuumed and cleaned the guest bath. I figured I could borrow a camper's cot from Joe Pike; Ben could use the cot and Lucy could have the bed.

At sixteen minutes before four, I went out onto the deck and stared down at the lights in the canyon below. A family of coyotes who live around Franklin Reservoir were singing, and a great desert owl who lived in the eucalyptus trees made his hooting call. I breathed the cool night air and listened to the coyotes and the owl, and I thought how fine it was that so much of my being could have so suddenly become focused on an airplane's time of arrival.

I did not sleep, but I did not mind.

4

By nine o'clock the next morning I had gained some measure of control over the sappy grin and was once more feeling focused, productive, and ready to swing into investigative action. Sappy grins are fine in your personal life but somehow seem less than professional when one is representing the Big Green Defense Machine. Credibility, as they say, is everything.

By eight-forty I had shaved, showered, and phoned Terminal Island to arrange an interview with LeCedrick Earle. I was eating a breakfast of nonfat yogurt and sliced bananas when Eddie Ditko called and said, 'Hold on a sec while I fire up a smoke.' First thing out of his mouth.

'Top of the morning to you, too, Edward.'

There was the sound of the strike and a little pause like maybe Eddie was sucking up half of the earth's pollutant supply, and then a burst of coughing that sounded wet and phlegmy. He said, 'Christ, I'm passing blood.'

So much for breakfast. I pushed the bowl away and said, 'Are you all right?'

'Think I'm gonna drop a goddamned lung.' He croaked it out between coughs.

'You want to call back?'

The coughs settled to a phlegmy wheezing. 'Nah, nah, I'm fine.' When he got his breathing under control, he said, 'Whadda they make these things outta nowadays, fiberglass? Ya gotta rip the filters off to get any taste.'

'Jesus Christ, Eddie.'

Eddie Ditko said, 'Listen, I made a few calls and got some stuff for you.'

'Okay.'

'Rossi looks like a pretty sharp gal.' Gal. 'Divorced. Got a couple of little boys. Her ex is some kind of middle manager at Water and Power.'

'All right.' I was making notes. I had been thinking that she might've married well and gotten the expensive house in the divorce, but middle managers at Water and Power aren't known for their bank accounts.

'She was top of her class at the academy and moved right up the promotion ladder once she got into uniform. She responded to more calls, worked more hours, and made more arrests than all but three other officers with her time in grade. That's probably where the marriage went.'

I was still writing.

'The LeCedrick Earle bust is what led to the gold shield, and everybody kind of figured that Rossi had a shot at being the first female chief of detectives until the Miranda thing. You blow a murder-one case because you failed to Mirandize a suspect, and that's it for you. She lost a grade in rank and received a letter of censure. That pretty much killed her career.'

I was nodding as I wrote. Everything he said was confirming both Haig and Truly. 'What happened with the Miranda?'

'Two idiots armed with machetes robbed a Burito King in Silverlake and hacked three people to death. Rossi spotted a car matching the getaway vehicle and collared one of the suspects after a high-speed chase. She was jazzed from the pursuit and forgot to give the guy his warning before he confessed and implicated his accomplice. They hadda let both idiots walk, and Rossi took the heat for it. You see?'

'Man. Did she dispute the Miranda?'

'Nope. She blew it and she admitted it. How about that?' Like he was surprised that someone would take responsibility for their actions. 'I can fax you this stuff, you want.'

'Thanks, Eddie. What about Earle?'

'Another genius. Rossi tags the guy for a taillight violation and he slides across a C-note with his license, which he saw some moron do in a Dirty Harry movie. Rossi recognizes the Franklin's a fake and tells him it'll cost him a lot more than that, so he brings her back to his house where he pulls out a stash and says she can have all she wants. She says thank you very much and let's go to jail.'

'That's her side of it.'

Eddie laughed. 'Yeah, sure. Your man LeCedrick is what we call a career-type criminal. Prior to the funny-money arrest, he'd been in and out of the system half a dozen times, mostly dope and burglary charges, including two prior associations with a guy named Waylon Mustapha. Mustapha makes his living by selling down funny money for points.' Selling for points is when you discount the face value of the counterfeit money to sell it in quantity. Sort of like being a broker. 'My guy at the PD says that the bills they recovered when Rossi made the collar matched up with the goods Mustapha handles.'

I tapped the pen against the pad, frowning. 'Just because LeCedrick was a creep most times doesn't mean he was a creep *that* time.'

Eddie laughed harder. 'Keep dreaming.'

I said, 'You hear anything that would indicate she might be willing to fudge a case?'

'You talk to his mother?'

'Whose mother?'

'Earle's mother was in the house when Rossi made the collar. She saw the whole thing.'

'Anything in the file?'

'*Nada*. IA would've talked to her, though. 'Course, whether they listened is a different matter.'

'Do you have her address, Eddie?'

He did, and he gave it to me. It was the same address in Olympic Park as that listed on LeCedrick Earle's arrest report. I hung up, then phoned information for Louise Earle's number and called her. I still needed to see LeCedrick, but maybe I could see her first. Maybe she had something to offer that might bolster his version of events, or clarify it. I let the phone ring ten times but got no answer. Guess I'd have to see LeCedrick *sans* clarity.

I hung up again, washed the dishes, then climbed into my car and made the long drive south to see LeCedrick Earle.

The harbor town of San Pedro lies on the water at the southeast point of the Palos Verdes peninsula, sixty miles south of Los Angeles. It's pretty much a straight shot down the San Diego Freeway across a rolling flat fuzz of low buildings and single-family homes, past Inglewood and Hawthorne and Gardena to Torrance, and then yet farther south on the Harbor Freeway to the water. The Port of Los Angeles is down there, with the gleaming white cruise ships that come and go and the great *Queen Mary* that forever stays and the U. S. Federal Correctional Facility at Terminal Island.

Terminal Island is on the western side of the harbor, and the facility itself is on the outermost end of the island. The *Queen Mary* is next door, as are the berths for the cruise ships, but neither can be seen from the prison. From the prison, you could only see open water, and the water looked very much like iron. Sort of like the bars of the cells.

I crossed a land bridge to the island and followed the signs to the prison, and pretty soon I passed through a high chain-link gate and parked at the administration building. A tall link fence topped by concertina wire surrounded the prison, which was new and modern and clean. A guard tower overlooked the grounds, but it was new and modern and clean, too. No gun ports. No swivel-mounted machine guns. No snarling guard dogs or barrel-chested yard-bulls sapping prisoners into line. All of the guards wore blue blazers and ties, and none of them carried guns. They carried walkie-talkies, instead. Modern justice.

I went inside to the reception desk, identified myself, and told the guard that I had an appointment to see LeCedrick Earle. The guard was a clean-cut guy in his early thirties. He found my name in his log, then turned it around for me. 'Sign here, please. Are you armed?'

'Nope.'

He flipped through a large loose-leaf book until he found Earle's name, then used his phone to tell someone that he wanted prisoner number E2847 brought out. When he was finished he smiled at me and said, 'Someone will be right out for you. Wait by the sally port.'

A couple of minutes later a second guard brought me through the sally port to a glass-walled interview room. A neat new table sat in the middle of the floor with four comfortable chairs around it. A second glass door was behind the table, and there was a nice gray berber carpet. The air smelled of Airwick. If it weren't for the guards peering in at you and the wire in the glass, you'd never know you were in a prison. Portrait of the Big House as corporate America.

Thirty seconds later the same guard opened the rear door and an African-American guy in his late twenties came in and squinted at me. 'You that guy come about Rossi?'

The guard said, 'Buzz me when you're done and I'll come get him.' The guard had bored eyes and spoke to me as if Earle wasn't there and hadn't said anything.

'Sure. Thanks.'

The guard left, locking the door.

LeCedrick Earle was maybe an inch shorter than me, with dark glossy skin and a shaved head. He was wearing a prison-issue orange jumpsuit and Keds. I said, 'That's right. I work for an attorney named Jonathan Green.'

'You a lawyer?'

'Nope. I'm a private investigator.'

Earle shrugged. 'I saw that ad in the paper and called. I talked to some guy say he was a lawyer.'

'The ad was about information leading to the arrest of James X for the murder of Susan Martin.' Truly had filled me in before he'd left the office. 'You know anything about that?'

He dropped into the near chair, put his feet on the table, and crossed his arms. Showing smug. 'Don't give a damn about that. I know about Rossi. I read in the paper she one of the cops arrest Teddy Martin. She put the fuck on me, I figure she maybe put the fuck on him, too.'

'You don't care about the reward?'

'Fuck the reward.' Giving me righteous. Giving me can-you-believe-this? 'Can't a brother just wanna do his civic duty?'

'I read your arrest report, and I read the letter of complaint your lawyer filed against her. What happened with that?'

'Shit, what you think happened? They didn't do a goddamned thing. Say it's my word against hers.'

469

'Your mother was there.'

All the show and the exaggeration flicked away. His eyes darkened and his face seemed to knot. 'Yes, well, she don't know nothing. Just a crazy old lady scared of the police.'

I said, 'Okay, so the arrest report is wrong and Rossi is lying.'

'Goddamned right. Bitch set me up.'

'She says that you tried to buy your way out of a traffic violation with a fake C-note.'

'Bullshit. That money was real.'

'You really tried to buy your way out with a C?'

'Man, I had so many outstanding warrants. I was scared she was gonna run me in. *That's* what I was tryin' to avoid.'

'So what happened?'

He uncrossed his arms and leaned forward. 'I pass her the note and she laughs. She says she don't come that cheap and I say it's all I got. She says I guess we gonna get locked down, then won't we? I'm gettin' the Hershey squirts cause of all the warrants, so I say I got a few hundred stashed at the house. She says let's see it, and that's when we go home.'

'She followed you to your house to get more money.'

'Oh, yeah. That part's true.'

'Okay.'

'So we get there and go inside and I got the money back in my room, not much, a few hundred, but it's real. I worked for that cash.'

'Okay.'

'We go back to my room to get the money and the next thing I know the gun's coming out and she's screamin' at me to get on the floor an' I'm squirtin' for real 'cause I think the crazy bitch gonna shoot me and so I go down and she snaps on the cuffs and then she takes this little bag of cash from under her jacket and that's the shit.'

'The funny money?'

He was nodding. 'I say, what's that? I say, whatchu think you doin'? She say shut the fuck up. Oh, man, next thing I know more cars are pullin' up and she's tellin' them other cops that the flash cash is mine and now I'm in here. How you like that shit?'

I stared at LeCedrick Earle and LeCedrick Earle stared back. His eyes did not waver. He said, 'Well?'

'Well what?'

'Just thinking.'

'Thinkin' what?'

'Wondering about you and Waylon Mustapha.'

He waved his hand. 'That's just bullshit bad luck.' He waved the hand some more. 'Waylon grow up down the street from me. Waylon and me know each other since kindergarten and blow a little smoke together,

470

that's all. I can't help it I know Waylon. I know guys who killed people, an' I ain't no murderer.'

'The money Rossi booked into evidence matched with paper that Waylon deals.'

LeCedrick crossed his arms and grinned. 'Half the funny money on the street come from Waylon. She probably got it from the goddamned evidence room. She mighta even bought it from Waylon his own damn self.'

'Okay.' I stared at him some more.

LeCedrick Earle started to fidget. 'Now what you lookin' at? You don't believe me, jus' say so, callin' me a liar.' He got up and walked in a little circle.

I said, 'I'm going to write down everything you've said. I'm going to check it out. I'm going to pass it along to Jonathan Green. You sure you don't want a piece of the money?'

'Fuck the money. I just wanna get out of here.'

I nodded.

He jabbed a finger at me. 'I'm tellin' you and God and everyone else that bitch set me up. You check it out, you see. Bet she set up this Teddy Martin, too.'

I said, 'Something about what you're saying bothers me, LeCedrick. You want to help me with something?'

His eyes narrowed. Suspicious. 'What?'

'If she wanted to set you up, she didn't need to go to your house. All she had to do is bust you on the street and say she found the money under the front seat.'

'Damn bitch is crazy! Who know how a goddamn crazy bitch think?' He threw up both hands, then came back to the table and slapped the buzzer for the guards. 'Shit on this. I shoulda known you asshole muthuhfuckuhs wouldn't believe me. Fuck you and fuck her, too. I guess a brother just has to rot in here.'

The guard came and took LeCedrick Earle back to his cell.

5

As I tooled north back to Los Angeles I tried to keep an open mind. Just because someone looks like a liar and acts like a liar doesn't mean that he is a liar. It doesn't even mean he's a liar when his story is full of holes. Even the truth has been known to have holes. Of course, when his story doesn't make sense it becomes a little more difficult to swallow. I could see Angela Rossi's side of it, but not LeCedrick Earle's. Rossi's report said that she followed Earle to his house because he only had the single hundred-dollar bill on his person and she knew that he could plead innocent to a knowledge of its being counterfeit; she reasoned that if he had more at home as he stated, he couldn't reasonably deny knowledge and the intent to defraud, and the arrest would stick. LeCedrick Earle said that she followed him to his home where she produced a hidden amount of counterfeit money and made the arrest. He opined that she might've done this so that there would be no witnesses, yet Mrs Louise Earle had been there and Rossi apparently consummated the arrest. Rossi's version made sense and LeCedrick Earle's didn't.

Still, people sometimes do strange things for strange reasons, and I decided to see what Mrs Louise Earle had to offer. I expected that she would support her son's claims, but in the doing perhaps she would add something to give them greater credence.

I opened Truly's envelope, shook out my notes, and looked up her address. It would be polite to pull off the freeway and call again to see if she was at home, but when people know you're coming they often find reasons to leave. I decided to risk it.

Forty-five minutes later I dropped off the Harbor Freeway onto Martin Luther King Boulevard, and five minutes after that I found my way to Olympic Park.

Olympic Park is a downscale residential area just north of USC and Exposition Park and the Natural History Museum, not far from downtown L.A. The Coliseum is nearby, along with the L.A. Sports Arena, and on game nights the surrounding residential streets are

472

jammed belly to butt with parked cars and pushcarts and hawkers selling souvenirs and iced drinks.

Louise Earle lived in a stucco bungalow on Twenty-fifth Street, four blocks south of the freeway, within walking distance of USC. The houses and the yards are small and the drives are narrow, but the properties are neat and clean, and the Earle home was painted a happy yellow with about a million multicolored flowers blooming on her porch in about a million clay pots and wooden planters. Flowers hung from the eaves and filled the porch and two large wrought-iron baker's racks. There were so many flowers on the porch that you had to walk along a narrow path to make your way to the door. It probably took her two hours a day just to water the things.

A six-year-old Buick Skylark was parked in the drive and an air conditioner was humming in a side window. I parked at the curb opposite her house, then went up the drive past the Buick and through the jungle of flowers to her door. The Buick's engine was still ticking. Recent arrival. A little metal plaque under the doorbell said WELCOME. I rang the bell.

The door opened and a thin woman in her early sixties looked at me. She was wearing a simple print dress in a flowered pattern and comfortable canvas shoes and her gray hair had been pulled into a bun. Neat. I said, 'Mrs Earle?'

She smiled at me. 'Yes?'

I gave her my card. 'Mrs Earle, my name is Elvis Cole. I'm an investigator looking into your son's arrest. May I ask you a few questions?'

She frowned, but she might've been squinting at the sun. 'Are you from the police?'

'No, ma'am. I'm private.' I told her that I was working for an attorney named Jonathan Green, and though Green did not represent LeCedrick, the events of his arrest might have a bearing on another case.

She shifted in the door, uncomfortable and unsure about what I might want. 'LeCedrick is at Terminal Island.'

'I know. I understand that you witnessed his arrest, and I have some questions about that.' Something moved in the house behind her.

'Well, I guess it would be all right.' Reluctant. She glanced back into the house, then stepped aside and opened the door. 'Why don't you come in so we don't let all the cool air out.'

I stepped in and she closed the door.

A short, slight gentleman was standing in the living room. He had wavy marcelled hair and he was wearing a brown summer-weight suit that had probably been new twenty years ago. His hair was more gray than not, and his skin was the color of fine cocoa parchment. He was holding a

473

small bouquet of zinnias. I made him for his late sixties, but I could've been off five years either way.

Louise Earle said, 'This is my friend, Walter Lawrence. He just dropped in, and now he'll have to be leaving. Won't you, Mr Lawrence?' She said it more to Mr Lawrence than to me, and he didn't seem to like it very much.

Mr Lawrence frowned, clearly disappointed. 'I suppose I could come back later.'

Louise Earle said, 'And I suppose you could just phone later and see whether or not a person is busy before you drop around, now couldn't you?'

Mr Lawrence ground about four inches of enamel off his teeth, but he managed a grim smile anyway. He wasn't liking this one bit. 'I suppose.'

She nodded approvingly, then took the flowers. 'Now you just let me get these lovely flowers in some water and we'll speak later.' She cradled the flowers and encouraged him toward the door.

Mr Lawrence stood very straight when he walked, trying to get as much height as he could. He mumbled something to her that I couldn't hear, frowned at me as he passed, and then Louise Earle shut the door. A couple of heartbeats later the Skylark backed out of the drive. I said, 'Ah, romance.'

Louise Earle laughed, and the laugh made her fifteen years younger. 'May I offer you coffee, Mr Cole, or something cool to drink?'

'Coffee would be fine, Mrs Earle. Thank you.'

She took the flowers back to her kitchen, calling over her shoulder. 'Please make yourself comfortable.'

I sat on a well-worn cloth couch with a handmade slipcover and needlepoint throw pillows. An overstuffed chair made an L with the couch and the couch and the chair were angled around an inexpensive coffee table, and all of it looked across the room at a cherry wood armoire. The armoire was open and its shelves were lined with tiny vases and knickknacks and family photographs, some of which were of LeCedrick. LeCedrick as a teenager. LeCedrick as a child. LeCedrick before choosing a life of crime. He seemed like a happy child with a bright smile. Her home was neat and cared for and smelled of the flowers.

Mrs Earle appeared a few moments later with two cups of coffee, walking carefully so as not to slosh. She said, 'That business with LeCedrick was several years ago. Why are you interested in that now?'

'I'm investigating the officer who arrested him.'

'Oh, yes. I remember her.' She put the cups on the table, then offered one to me. 'Would you care for milk or sugar?'

'No, ma'am. Then you were present during the arrest?'

She nodded again. 'Oh, yes. The police came to see me about that. They came back three or four times. Those affairs people.'

'Internal Affairs?'

'Mm-hm.' She sipped at her coffee. It was so hot that swirls of steam followed the contours of her face and fogged her glasses.

'You know LeCedrick is disputing the arrest.'

'Of course, I know.'

'LeCedrick claimed at the time of his arrest, and still claims, that Officer Rossi planted counterfeit bills in order to make the arrest.'

Mrs Earle nodded, but it was noncommittal, like she was waiting to hear more.

'Is that what you told the Internal Affairs people?'

Mrs Louise Earle gave a deep sigh and the mask of noncommittal detachment melted away into eyes that were tired and pained. 'I know he says that, and I'll tell you just what I told those affairs people.'

I leaned toward her.

'You can't believe a thing that child says.'

I blinked at her.

She put down the coffee and waved toward the armoire. 'I was standing right there when LeCedrick and that officer came in. I saw every little thing that happened.' Louise Earle closed her tired eyes, as if by closing them she could see it all again, just like she'd told the affairs people. 'The officer stood right there, holding her hat and telling me about her day. I remember that she was holding her hat because I thought how polite that was, to hold her hat like that. I didn't know she'd come to arrest him.'

'She didn't go back to his room?' LeCedrick had said that Rossi had gone back to his room.

'Oh, no. She just came in and stood there, talking with me the whole time. I was certainly angry when she arrested the boy, but she was very nice about it.' Very nice about it. I could see Jonathan Green when I related this. I could see his color drain, his eyes bulge. I wondered if he would pass out and Truly and I would have to administer CPR.

'LeCedrick claims that she accompanied him to his room. He says that she had a bag under her jacket containing the counterfeit bills.'

'It was summer. What would anyone be doing with a jacket in summer?' Louise Earle shook her head, and now there was a sadness to her. She crossed her hands in her lap. 'Mr Cole, you listen to LeCedrick and you'd think he was just the most innocent thing, but that just isn't the way it is. LeCedrick will lie at the drop of a hat, and always has.'

I sighed. So much for LeCedrick Earle.

Louise Earle said, 'Make no mistake about it. I love that child and it grieves me no end he's in jail, but he's said exactly the same thing every other time he's been arrested. It's always somebody else's fault. It's always the police out to get him. Like that.'

I nodded. 'Yes, ma'am.'

'If you're lookin' for me to say that boy is innocent, I can't. If you're lookin' for me to speak against that lady officer, I can't do that, either.' She looked stern when she said it.

'No, ma'am. I'm not looking for that.'

'He wanted me to lie for him back then, and I wouldn't. He wanted me to cover for him, and make excuses, and I said no. I said, LeCedrick, you have to learn to stop makin' excuses, you have to learn to be a man.' Her voice wavered and she stopped. She picked up the coffee, sipped, then said, 'It's cost me greatly, but it's for him. Something has to shock some sense into that boy.'

'Yes, ma'am.'

'He hasn't spoken to me since the trial. He said he'd never speak to me again.'

'I'm sorry, Mrs Earle.' I didn't know what else to say. I felt awkward and ashamed that I'd come into her life and driven off Mr Lawrence and made her relive something that was clearly so painful.

'I tried to raise that boy right. I loved that boy as much as any mother could, and tried to show a good example, but he just went wrong.' Her eyes grew pink and a single tear worked its way down her cheek. 'Maybe that was where I went wrong. Maybe I held him too close and excused too little. Is it possible to love someone too much?'

I looked at her, and then I looked at the furniture and the pictures, and then back at her weary eyes and the weight they carried. 'I don't think there can ever be too much love, Mrs Earle.'

She seemed to consider that, and then she put her coffee down again. 'Has this helped you?'

'Yes, ma'am. It has.' Jonathan Green wouldn't think so, but there you go.

She stood, and it was clear that she wanted me to leave. 'If you don't mind, then, I should clip those zinnias and get them in water.'

'Yes, ma'am. I'm sorry I interrupted you and Mr Lawrence.'

The tiny smile came back, though it wasn't as strong as before. 'Yes, well, it'll take more than a little interruption to discourage that man.'

'Men are like that, Mrs Earle. We find something worthwhile, we stay with it.'

The tired eyes crinkled and suddenly the younger self was there again. 'Oh, you get on with you, now.'

She walked me to the door and I went out into the sun and got on with me.

6

The early afternoon heat shimmered off the sidewalks and cars and surrounding roofs in a kind of urban illusion of life's silver lining. It was just before two on the second day of my investigation into Angela Rossi and the doors of investigative possibility were rapidly closing, and with every closed door Angela Rossi looked better and the people making claims against her looked worse. Louise Earle was credible, cogent, in full command of her faculties, and did not seem to be a person who would miss seeing a cop carrying a bag of funny money through her living room. Of course, maybe Angela Rossi was a master of misdirection and had secreted the money behind her back. She might've shouted, 'Look over there!' and run to LeCedrick's room and planted the cash when Louise turned to look. Perhaps my investigative task for the afternoon should be finding out whether or not Angela Rossi was an amateur magician.

Or maybe not. Three teenaged girls with long skinny legs and halter tops came out of the house across the street and went to an ancient Volkswagen Beetle parked in their drive. They were lugging beach towels and bottles of Evian water, and everybody wore thongs. Off to the beach. Maybe I should offer to go with them and protect them from the thugs at the beach. Maybe we could discuss my findings. On the other hand, Lucy Chenier was arriving tomorrow, and maybe I should snap out of it before I found myself in really deep doo-doo. *C'est la vie.*

When I reached the sidewalk a tall, muscular black guy appeared beside my car. As he reached the car a heavy white guy in his early fifties climbed out of a blue sedan parked across the street and started toward me. The black guy was in impeccably pressed designer jeans and a tight knit shirt that showed his muscles, and the white guy was in a rumpled light gray winter-weight suit. A million degrees, and he's wearing winter weight. Cops. A woman's voice said, 'Excuse me, sir. May I have a word with you?' Polite, and kind of cheery.

The cheery woman was coming toward me from the adjoining yard as if she had been standing at the corner of the house there, waiting. She was maybe five-eight, and dark the way you're dark when you spend a lot of time in the sun running and working out and playing sports. I made her for her early- to mid-thirties, but the lines around her eyes and mouth were deep. Probably from all the sun. She was wearing designer jeans like the black guy and Reebok court shoes and a loose linen top that she would probably cover with a linen sport coat if it weren't so hot. Stylish and attractive, even with the Browning 9mm clipped to her right hip. She badged me with an LAPD detective shield as she approached, still cheery with the smile, and I recognized her just before she said, 'Mr Cole, my name is Angela Rossi. The detective in the gray suit would like to ask you a few questions.'

She glanced at the guy in the bad suit and I followed her look just as she knew I would, and when I did she stepped close and threw an overhand with a black leather sap, trying for the side of my head. Sucker shot. I picked up her move and tried to twist out of the way, but she was good and fast and I caught most of the sap on my right cheek with a blossom of pain. The guy in the suit yelled, 'Hey!' and the black guy grunted, 'Shit!' like they were surprised, too. Rossi followed the sap with a hard knee, but it caught me in the thigh instead of the groin, and then the older guy was there, wedging himself between us, forcing her away and saying, 'Dammit, Rossi, you want another beef in your file? Is that what you want?'

I wobbled, but kept my feet and let the older guy move her back.

The black guy hustled up behind me and his hands went to my wrists, pulling my arms behind me. The three girls ran up onto their porch and watched from the door, one of them with her hand to her mouth. My right cheek felt like someone had popped a firecracker under the skin and my eyes were watering. I didn't want to double over, but I couldn't exactly stand up straight either. It's hard to look tough when you're thinking that maybe you'll vomit. Especially when you've been suckered with an eye-fake. Maybe Rossi was a master of misdirection after all.

Angela Rossi jabbed her finger at me, saying, 'This shitbird came to my *home!* What were you doing at my *home*, you creep?' She wasn't smiling, now. Her face was etched and drawn, and she looked as if she wanted to rip out my eyes.

The older guy pushed her hand down and shoved her further away. 'Dammit, Rossi. Step back.'

The black guy locked my right arm above the elbow, walked me to a white Cressida, and pushed me down across the trunk. The skin of the car was so hot from the sun it felt like a branding iron. I said, 'Are you guys really cops or is this *America's Funniest Home Videos?*'

The black guy ignored me. He went through my pockets and down my pants, and then he said, 'He's clean, Tommy.'

Rossi stopped all the squirming and trying to get at me. The older guy came over and badged me, too. 'I'm Detective Tomsic, and you're being investigated for stalking a Los Angeles police officer. Do you understand that?'

The teenage girl with her hand to her mouth disappeared inside the house. The other two stayed on the porch, watching. A couple of faces appeared in the windows, and I said, 'Hey, look, Tomsic. I think they've got a video camera.'

Tomsic said, 'Good. Let'm watch.'

'Maybe they got the sap on tape. You think?' Saps are classified as dangerous weapons. They are illegal to carry, sort of like rocket launchers and samurai swords.

Rossi said, 'What were you doing at my home?' She was breathing hard, but she was well back on the sidewalk and she probably wasn't going to hit me again.

'ID and license are in my wallet. I'm a private investigator.' The black guy tossed my wallet to Tomsic.

Rossi said, 'We know who you are, shitbird. Tell me why you came to my house.'

'I was investigating a lead that you were living beyond your means.'

'Why?'

'It's what I do. Investigate.'

The third girl returned from her house to join her two friends, but Tomsic didn't seem overly concerned. He was going through the wallet like he had all the time in the world. 'He's our boy, all right. California PI license. Elvis Cole.' He looked at me. 'You've got a license to carry here. Where's the piece?'

'Under the seat.'

The black guy laughed. 'You left it under the seat?'

'I was talking to a woman in her sixties. Who would I shoot?'

The black guy said, 'I hear you.' He went to my Corvette without having to ask which car was mine. They'd probably followed me. Rossi's neighbor had probably copied my tag number and they'd run the plates and picked me up at my house or maybe even on the way to Terminal Island.

Rossi frowned at Louise Earle's place. 'You investigating the Le Cedrick Earle thing?'

'Earle claims you planted the cash.'

'That's bullshit.'

I nodded. 'I had to check it out.'

She put her right hand on her right hip, just above the Browning. 'Who are you working for?'

'Jonathan Green. In the matter of Teddy Martin.'

Tomsic said, 'Well, fuck me.'

The black guy stood out of the Corvette, grinning. 'You on the Martin defense? Whadda they call it, the Big Green Defense Machine?' Like he wanted to laugh.

I looked back at Rossi. 'People are making accusations that may be relevant to the defense effort, and I'm checking them out. So far you look pretty good.'

She looked surprised. 'What accusations? Teddy Martin killed that woman.'

I made a little shrug. 'If you planted evidence once, the theory is that you'd plant it again. Some people called Green and told him that you've got a history of doing anything it takes to jump your career. Green hired me to see if there's anything to it.'

Angela Rossi squared herself and took a step toward me. Tomsic shook his head. 'Angie.'

Rossi took another step closer and the black guy came back to stand with Tomsic between us. Like the two of them were scared of what she might do. She said, 'Green's a shithog and so are you.'

Tomsic said, 'Take it easy, Angie.'

Rossi shoved at Tomsic. 'Hey, I don't have to take this shit! Assholes coming into my life and trying to put this on me!'

I said, 'No one's trying to put anything on you. I just want the facts. No one's looking to axe you.'

Rossi jabbed her finger at me, but spoke to Tomsic. 'This guy's in *my life*, Dan!'

Tomsic said, 'Chill out, will you? This stuff happens. I've been investigated nine thousand times.'

I said, 'Look, Rossi, it's like I said. I've been through most of it and you're looking good. This is a legal investigation, and if you check out clean I'll report that to Green and that'll be the end of it.'

Tomsic said, 'You hear that? Clean.' Like we were both on the same team, now, trying to keep her calm. Maybe Haig had been right about her being a nutcase. Tomsic was acting as if he was scared what might happen if she lost control of herself. He turned back to me. 'You understand why we dropped on you, right? Your nosing around her house.'

'No problem.' My cheek was throbbing and the skin around my eye was starting to stretch, but there was no problem. Sure.

A black and white LAPD radio car turned onto the block and came at us with its light bar flashing, probably responding to a call from the three girls. The radio car roared in to a sliding stop with a couple of uniforms unloading even before the car stopped rocking. An Asian guy in his mid-forties was driving with an Hispanic guy in his late-twenties along for the ride. Tomsic said, 'Fuckin' great. A cheering section.' He nodded toward the black guy, then the uniforms. 'Robert, chill out these guys, okay?'

Robert badged the uniforms and trotted over. The Asian guy had a couple of stripes on his sleeve and was built like he'd spent the last twenty years in the LAPD's weight room. His name tag read SAMURA. Robert met Samura first and spoke to him in low tones as they walked back to us. When Samura heard my name he looked at me. 'You're Cole?'

'Unh-hunh.'

He looked at Tomsic. 'This guy works with Joe Pike.'

Robert and Tomsic stared at me. So did Rossi. Robert said, 'No shit?'

I spread my hands. 'Somebody has to.'

Tomsic's face went red and he wasn't so friendly any more, like he and I were no longer on the same team. '*The Joe Pike?*'

'How many you know?'

His jaw worked, and he said, 'The Joe Pike I know can kiss my goddamned ass.' When Joe left the PD it hadn't gone well.

I smiled at him. 'I'll give you his number. You can tell him yourself.'

A little tick started in Tomsic's left eye. 'Maybe we should march your butt in, after all. Dig around and see if you're in violation of your license.'

I rolled my eyes. 'Oh, please, Tomsic. Spare me.'

The tick fluttered into a rapid-fire blink, but then he stepped back and looked embarrassed. Samura pretended not to notice. 'We got a robbery in progress call. What's the deal?'

Tomsic filled him in, telling him about my nosing around Rossi's home, telling him about Teddy Martin and Jonathan Green and Rossi's role in the Martin arrest. Samura listened, but didn't seem particularly interested. You spend enough years on the street, you're not even interested if a nuke goes off.

When Tomsic was finished, Samura said, 'Cole has a good rep. I know guys who've worked with him.' He squinted at me, then took off his hat and wiped his face. It had to be a million degrees, standing in the sun. 'You remember a guy named Terry Ito?'

'Sure.' I'd worked with Ito four or five years back.

Samura put his hat back on and looked at Tomsic. 'You don't have to sweat it. Ito thinks that this guy's the cat's ass.'

I said, 'Terry has a way with words, all right.'

Robert said, 'We didn't know who the guy was and he was poking around an officer. You know how it is.'

'Sure.' Samura squared his hat, then nodded toward his radio car. His partner drifted away. Samura started after him, then turned back and looked me over. 'I'd never heard Terry Ito say a good thing about anybody. Terry know you work with Joe Pike?'

'Yes.'

Samura cracked the world's smallest grin, then went back to his car and drove away. The three girls were still gaggled at their front door, but most of the other faces had disappeared from the windows. You've seen one crime scene, you've seen'm all.

Tomsic looked at Rossi. 'Okay. We know who this guy is and what he's doing. You okay with it?'

She made a grudging shrug.

Tomsic looked back to me. 'How about you? You gonna file a beef because of the sap?'

'Barely touched me.'

Robert laughed. 'Yeah. Look at you.'

Tomsic said, 'Okay, then. Everybody knows where it stands.' He nudged Rossi. 'We don't have to like it, we just have to know where it stands.'

Rossi said, 'One thing.'

I looked at her.

'You're doing a job, and I can live with that. Investigate all you want, but stay the hell away from my home. If you come around my home again, I'll break you down. If you even look at my kids, I'll kill you on the spot.'

Tomsic said, 'Jesus Christ, Angie, knock that shit off. Sayin' shit like that is what gets you in deep.'

She raised a neutral hand. 'Just laying it out.'

I said, 'You're looking good, Rossi. Don't sweat it.'

'Yeah, sure.' She stared at me for another couple of seconds, but she didn't look relaxed and she didn't look as if she believed it was over. She was breathing hard, and the crinkled skin around her eyes was jumping and fluttering as if tiny butterflies were trapped there, trying to get out. Then something that looked like it might've been a smile flickered at the corners of her mouth and she said, 'Tell Joe that Rossi says hi.'

Angela Rossi turned away without another word, crossed the street, and slid into the passenger side of Tomsic's dark blue G-ride. Tomsic joined her, and Robert got into a tan Explorer. In a couple of minutes they were gone. Even the three girls were gone, vanished in their Volkswagen for a belated trip to the beach.

I stood there for a time, alone except for the dull ache in the side of my face, and then I got into my car and drove to my office.

7

I stopped at a 7-Eleven to buy ice for my eye. A Pakistani gentleman was behind the counter, watching a miniature TV. He was watching an episode of *COPS*, and he viewed me with suspicion as I paid.

I told him what the ice was for and asked if I could use the bathroom to look at myself, but he said that the bathroom was for employees only. I asked if he had a little mirror that I could borrow, but he said no again. He sneaked a look toward the door as if he wanted me to leave, as if whatever wraith of urban violence had assaulted me might suddenly be visited upon him and his store. Guess I couldn't blame the guy. You look at enough episodes of *COPS*, and pretty soon you're thinking that life is a war zone.

I thanked him for the ice, then went out to the car and looked at my eye in the rearview mirror. A neat little mouse was riding high on my right cheek and was already starting to color. Great. I wrapped a handful of ice in my handkerchief and drove back to my office with one hand. Nothing like bucking rush-hour traffic with a faceful of ice.

It was just after five when I reached my building and turned down the ramp into the building's garage. A line of cars was on its way out, but most of the garage was already empty. Cindy's Mazda was missing, and so were the cars belonging to the people who worked at the insurance company across the hall from my office. I left my car in its spot, walked up to the lobby, then took the elevator to my floor. Lights off, doors locked, empty. Empty was good. Maybe if Los Angeles had been empty I would've been able to spot two carloads of cops tailing me around half the city.

I let myself into my office, popped on the lights, and found Joe Pike sitting at my desk. I said, 'You could've turned on the lights, Joe. We're not broke.'

Pike cocked his head to the side, looking at my eye. 'Is that a pimple?'

'Ha-ha.' That Pike is a riot. A real comedian, that guy.

Joe Pike is six foot one, with long ropey muscles, dark hair cut short, and bright red arrows tattooed on the outside of each deltoid. He got the tattoos in a faraway place long before it was stylish for rock stars and TV actors and Gen X rave queens to flash skin art. The arrows point forward, and are not a fashion statement. They are a statement of being. Pike was wearing a gray sweatshirt with the sleeves cut off and Levi's and dark pilot's glasses. Even at night he wears the glasses. For all I know he sleeps in them.

I went to a little mirror I have on the wall and looked at the eye. The side of my face hurt like hell, but the ice was working; the swelling had stopped. 'Your friend Angela Rossi hit me with a six-ounce sap. Suckered me with an eye move.'

'I know.'

I looked at him. 'How do you know?'

He got up, took two Falstaffs from the little fridge, and handed one to me. If you listened as hard as you could, you still wouldn't hear him move. 'Angie called and told me. She wanted to know what we were doing.'

'She called you.'

He popped the tab on his Falstaff and had some. 'I've been here a while. Lucy called. I didn't know she was coming out.'

'Tomorrow.'

'I left her flight information on your desk.' Pike took his beer to the couch. 'Why are we working for Theodore Martin?'

'We're not. We're working for Jonathan Green.' I told him about Haig and his allegations that Rossi would fabricate evidence to boost her career. I told him about LeCedrick Earle and his allegations that Rossi had done just that. 'Green hired us to look into the allegations. I told him that we would report what we found, even if it hurt his case. He said okay.'

'Lawyers are lizard people.' Life is simple for Pike.

'Lucy's a lawyer.'

Pike's head shifted a quarter of an inch. 'Not Lucy.'

I said again, 'Angela Rossi called you.'

He stared at me with impenetrable black lenses. Two months before I'd had canvas Roman shades installed on the French doors to cut the western exposure in the afternoon, and when the shades were down the office filled with a beautiful gold light. They were down now, and Pike was bathed in the light. It made his dark glasses glow. 'We worked Rampart Division together. She was coming on when I was going out.' Pike had spent three years riding in a radio car for LAPD. 'I knew Haig. Haig was an asshole. I knew Rossi, too. I didn't ride in a car with her, but she seemed like a straight shooter.'

'Okay.'

'That what you find?'

I took my ice and my Falstaff and went to my desk. I saw the notepaper with Lucy's flight information. Pike's printing was meticulously neat, but so small it was almost impossible to read. 'She's aggressive, ambitious, and no one likes her much, but there's no evidence that she dumped LeCedrick Earle or anyone else. Haig comes across like a crank, and Earle's own mother said that her son is a liar.'

Pike nodded.

'The only thing that doesn't fit is her house. Two years ago she bought a condo in the Marina that had to go for four hundred thousand dollars. I've got a call in to Adrienne Martin.'

'Forget the house. Her mother left her an apartment building in Long Beach. When Rossi sold it she had to roll the cash into another property or get hit with the capital gains.'

I stared at him.

'We were close.'

'I see.'

'Very close.' Still hidden behind the black lenses.

I stared at him some more, and then I nodded. 'I guess that's it, then. No crime, no graft, no corruption. Jonathan won't like it, but there it is.' There hadn't been much to check and it hadn't taken long, but it rarely does when everything is above board.

'She's a sharp cop, Elvis. It's a tough game for a woman, tougher still if the woman is better than the boys and lets them know it.'

I smiled at him. 'She doesn't seem like the retiring type.'

He canted his head a couple of degrees. 'She had a real shot at being the first female chief of detectives. She still might, even with the Miranda beef.'

'High praise coming from you.'

Pike shrugged.

I said, 'Joe, are you soft on this woman?'

Pike finished his beer, then got up and placed the empty carefully into the wastebasket. 'I admire her, Elvis. In much the same way I admire you.'

I didn't know what to say to that, so I said, 'Since you admire me so much, I've got a favor to ask.'

He waited.

'Lucy and Ben are coming, and I've got the two-seater. Can I borrow your Jeep to pick them up?'

Pike stood motionless. The Jeep was in immaculate condition, and Pike kept it flawless. You could shave in the fender. You could eat off the engine block.

I said, 'I'll wash it before I give it back. If someone dents it I'll shoot them.'

Pike's head swiveled one-half a degree. I think he was stricken. 'Why don't I come with you to pick them up?'

'Joe.' It was like pulling teeth.

485

He still wasn't happy about it, but he finally nodded. Once.

I said, 'I'll draft the report on Rossi tonight. I'll call Truly and tell him that I'm going to turn it in tomorrow, and he'll probably want to see me. You want to go along?'

Pike said, 'No.' Lizard people.

'Just thought I'd ask.'

Pike went to the door, then looked back at me, and gestured to his right eye. 'That's going to look nice for Lucy.'

'Thanks, Joe.'

'Good to see Angie hasn't lost her touch.' His mouth twitched a single time and he left. Pike never smiles or laughs, but sometimes you'll get the twitch. Mr Hilarity.

I had the rest of my beer, then phoned Elliot Truly. When Truly came on the line, I said, 'I've concluded the investigation into Angela Rossi. I'm going to write the report tonight.'

He didn't say anything for a second. 'So soon?'

'I'm fast, Truly. Cases solved in no time flat or your money back.'

Truly said, 'Well, hell.' Like he was disappointed it hadn't taken longer, like he was maybe thinking that I had given the job short shrift. 'What did you find?'

'She's clean. Earle is a liar and Haig is a crank with a grudge. There's absolutely no evidence that Rossi's ever been anything other than a good cop.'

Another silence. 'You'd better come in. Jonathan will want to talk about it.' You see?

'I have guests coming in from out of town at five tomorrow evening.' I could hear him fumbling with something. 'We're going to have a staff meeting here tomorrow morning at nine. Can you make that?'

'I'll be there.'

It took less than twenty minutes to write the report, and then I drove home listening to k. d. lang. k. d. lang was Lucy's favorite, and as I drove I found that I was thinking less about Jonathan Green and Angela Rossi, and more about Lucy Chenier. I thought that I might clean the house and make a shopping list. The house was already clean and it was too late to shop, but that didn't matter. My work was done and Lucy was coming, and what could be better than that? Anticipation is everything.

When I got home, Pike's Jeep was waiting in the drive, freshly washed, immaculate and gleaming. I found a note under the windshield that said, *Give my love to Lucy, and please drive carefully.*

That Pike is something, isn't he?

8

At twenty minutes before nine the next morning I worked my way down the mountain along Laurel Canyon to Sunset, then turned west toward Jonathan Green's office.

Most prominent attorneys in Los Angeles will blackjack their mothers to find office space in Beverly Hills or Century City, both of which are considered prestige addresses for the legal community. Jonathan Green's office was on Sunset Boulevard in an ornate four-story Spanish office building across from the Mondrian Hotel. I guess if you're Jonathan Green, any place you happen to be is a prestige address.

The building was older, with an established landscape of royal palms and bougainvillea, and state-of-the-art security equipment discreetly hidden from public view. A tasteful sign built into the front of the building simply said THE LAW OFFICES OF JONATHAN GREEN. The parking garage was gated, and the gate wouldn't open until a gentleman wearing a red blazer strolled out to my car and asked my name. He was exceedingly polite, and possessed of a bulge in the line of his jacket beneath his left arm. The bulge, like the sign and the security equipment, was also discreet.

I left my car in the garage, then followed the guard's directions past a Spanish tile fountain in the lobby to the elevators, and then to the top floor. Another blazered gentleman smiled at me in the lobby, and a third just happened to be on the elevator. Both were polite and both, like the guard in the parking garage, had the corded necks of men who spent a lot of their time honing confrontational skills. Corded necks are a dead give-away.

When the elevator opened, Elliot Truly was waiting for me. I guess the parking guard must've called. I said, 'Some security.'

He stared at my eye.

'Cut myself shaving.'

Truly realized he was staring and looked away. 'Yes, well, I guess that happens.'

I followed him past the floor receptionist and along a glass hall. 'Why all the spooks?'

'Many of Jonathan's cases are unpopular, as you might imagine. You'd be surprised at the number of people who don't believe that defendants are entitled to the best possible defense.'

'No kidding.'

Men and women in business suits hurried in both directions, some carrying files, others long yellow legal pads, still others small Styrofoam cups of what I took to be coffee. Nine in the morning, and everyone looked tense. I guess tension is a way of life when you're trying to give people the best possible defense. Especially at five hundred dollars an hour.

I said, 'Are all of these people working for Teddy Martin?'

'Oh, no. The firm is involved in over two hundred active cases.'

'Mm.'

'Jonathan only involves himself in the more, ah, trying cases.' He gave me a sly smile.

I nodded.

He looked at me. '"Trying."'

'I got it.'

Truly looked disappointed. 'Oh.' Lawyer humor.

We turned down another hall and then into a conference room about the size of Rhode Island. A breakfast buffet had been set up at one end of the room with coffee and mineral water and enough lox and bagels to sink the *Lexington*. Six men and three women were crowded around the buffet, talking in soft whispers. Everyone had coffee, but no one was eating. Probably too tense. Truly said, 'Would you like something to eat?'

'Just coffee.' Elvis Cole, at one with the team.

'Let me introduce you. Jonathan will be along in a moment.'

We got the coffee, and Elliot Truly introduced me. Everyone in the room was an attorney except me. While the introductions were under way, yet more attorneys arrived. I stopped counting at fourteen. The large lesser attorney came in, followed by the small lesser attorney, both of whom were wearing beige linen Armani suits. So was Elliot Truly. I said, 'Beige.'

Truly said, 'Pardon me?'

'Nothing.' Jonathan Green would be wearing beige, too. You could bet your house on it.

Thirty seconds later Jonathan Green came in wearing a beige linen Armani. You see? I said, 'Shucks.'

Truly glanced at me and whispered, 'What?' Now that Jonathan was here I guess we would whisper.

'No videographer. I was hoping for more air time.'

Truly blinked at me, then seemed to get it. 'Oh, right. Ha-ha.' Ha-ha. We're just a riot at nine A.M.

Another man came in behind Jonathan. He was a little shorter than me, but his arms were as long as backhoe shovels and his shoulders so wide they looked like they had been built of steel frame girders. The arms and the shoulders didn't go with the rest of him, as if they had once belonged to King Kong or Mighty Joe Young or some other large mammal, and now this guy was using them. He was carrying a manila envelope.

Green smiled when he saw me and offered his hand. 'Thank you for coming. This is Stan Kerris, our chief of security. Stan, this is Mr Cole.' Stan Kerris was the guy with the shoulders. He had a monstrously high forehead, sort of like a Klingon's, and eyes that looked at you but gave you nothing, like windows to an empty room.

Truly said, 'Let's get started.'

Jonathan Green took his seat at the head of the table with Stan Kerris sitting next to him. The two lesser attorneys elbowed each other to sit nearby. Like the lesser attorneys, everyone else tried to jockey as close to Jonathan Green as possible. Truly sat next to me. When everyone was down, Green crossed his legs, and smiled at me. 'So. Elliot tells me that you've found no corroborating evidence to Mr Earle's claims.'

'That's right.'

'And the same for Mr Haig?' He raised his eyebrows in a question.

'That's right. I spoke with Haig and with Earle, then with Earle's mother. I did a cursory background check on Earle, and reviewed the Internal Affairs investigation into the funny money bust. IA found that Rossi made a quality bust.'

Truly was shaking his head. 'What does that mean? Of course, they would say that.'

'No, Mr Truly. They wouldn't. LAPD takes these things seriously.' I looked at Green. 'I concur.'

Green laced his fingers across a knee and settled back. 'Please tell us why.'

At least seven of the assembled attorneys copied what I said. I started with Raymond Haig and worked my way through Eddie Ditko and Rossi's condo and my interviews with both LeCedrick Earle and Louise Earle. I told them about LeCedrick's past record, including his close association with Waylon Mustapha, and I described in detail how Louise Earle's version of events matched with Rossi's police report. I spoke for close to twenty minutes, and for twenty minutes pens scratched on legal pads and Jonathan Green sat unmoving. His eyes narrowed a couple of times, but mostly he watched me as if he could absorb the details without effort and assimilate them. Or maybe he was just bored.

When I finished Kerris said, 'Anything we can use in the Miranda?'

'What do you mean, use?'

Truly smiled. 'Was there anything in her action indicative of malice aforethought or a willingness to commit an illegal act?'

I took the reports that Eddie Ditko had faxed me from my file and passed them to Truly. I told them about the guys with the machetes. I described what had happened at the Burrito King. 'They let both these guys walk and Rossi took the heat for it. I don't think there was much forethought to blowing out her career at the end of a high-speed chase because of an adrenaline rush.'

Truly smiled again and shrugged at Kerris. 'Guess not.'

Jonathan Green said, 'You're sure about these things?'

'Yes, sir. There is no evidence that this woman has ever done anything illegal or even improper other than the Miranda beef, and she stood up for that one. She wouldn't have had to set up LeCedrick Earle. He's a career criminal.'

Green nodded. 'Then you don't believe that she could've planted the hammer on Theodore's property?'

'No, sir.'

'We should abandon this as a legal theory?'

'That would be my opinion, yes, sir.'

Jonathan Green nodded again, then stared at the far wall for what seemed like several minutes. No one moved, and no one spoke. All of the other attorneys stared at Jonathan as if he might suddenly utter some dictum and they would have to act on it. Apprehensive.

I looked at my watch. It was nine forty-two, and the staring continued. Maybe Jonathan Green had lapsed into a trance and no one knew it. Maybe he would continue to stare all day and I'd still be sitting here when Lucy and Ben landed at LAX. I drummed my fingers on the table and Elliot Truly looked horrified. I guess it just wasn't done.

Jonathan Green suddenly spread his hands, then placed them on the table and leaned forward. 'Well, that's that. Better to know now than embarrass ourselves in court. You've done an outstanding job, Mr Cole. Thank you.'

The other attorneys breathed as one and broke into large smiles, saying what an outstanding job I'd done.

Green swiveled toward Truly and said, 'It was one theory, and there's still plenty of ground to cover. We'll just have to roll up our sleeves and try harder.' Green swiveled back to me and leaned forward again, absolutely serious. 'I remain convinced of Teddy's innocence, and I'm determined to work all the harder to prove it.'

The fourteen other attorneys around the big table nodded, and I guess I could understand why. Green seemed to bring it out in you. I wanted to nod, too.

Jonathan Green said, 'Mr Cole, I know you were hired for this specific

490

part of our investigation, but it's very important to me that people of your caliber work with the team.'

Elliot Truly said, 'Here, here.' Really.

Green gestured toward Kerris. 'We've been absolutely overwhelmed with people calling our hotline, haven't we, Stan?'

Kerris nodded, but the nod conveyed nothing, sort of like his eyes. 'We've gotten several hundred calls from people claiming to have information about the kidnapping. We can dismiss some based on the phone interview, but most have to be checked. We're dividing these things up among our investigators.'

Green said, 'Stan, give him the envelope, please.'

Kerris pushed the envelope down along the table to me. I opened it. Twenty single-sheet interview forms were inside.

Jonathan said, 'Each sheet contains the name, phone number, and address of a person claiming to have information about Susan Martin's murder. If you could see your way clear to staying with us on this and checking these people out, we would appreciate it.'

I looked at the sheets. I slipped them back into the envelope. 'I have guests coming into town.'

Truly shrugged. 'There isn't a rush with this, Cole. Sure, sooner is better than later, but you know the justice system.'

'Okay.'

Green broke into a wide smile. 'Well, that's just great. That's fabulous.'

The assembled attorneys told me how great it was.

I glanced at my watch, thinking I could knock off three or four interviews before Lucy's plane. The more I finished before Lucy's plane, the more time I'd have for her.

Truly said, 'We don't know anything about these people. As Stan said, our screeners were able to rule out the obvious cranks, but you never know. We want you to use your best judgment to determine if they have anything of merit to offer.'

'Judgment. Okay.' I looked at my watch again. 'I've got it.'

Truly spread his hands. 'And when you're done with those, of course, there's more.'

The lesser attorneys chuckled and someone said, 'A *lot* more.' Even Jonathan Green chuckled at that one.

Green stood and everyone stood with him, and I was hoping I hadn't been too obvious with all the watch-glancing. Jonathan came around the table and offered his hand again, and this time when we shook he held it. He said, 'I want you to know that I appreciate the good, fast work you've done, Mr Cole. It's important to me, and it's important to Teddy, also. I spoke with him yesterday and told him that you're on the team. You're going to like Teddy, Mr Cole. Everyone does.'

'I'll look forward.'

'Good hunting.' He tried to let go of my hand, but this time I held onto him, not realizing that I had. In that instant he smiled warmly and I let go.

Jonathan Green swept out in a wave, Kerris beside him and the lesser attorneys in his wake, jostling each other to better their positions.

9

It was a little before ten when I followed the trail of security men down to my car, then zipped to the Virgin Megastore, bought the new k.d. lang and a collection of Louisiana hits called *Cajun Party*, then sat in the Megastore's parking structure and went through the envelope of hotline tipsters. I had almost seven hours until Lucy's plane; plenty of time for the world's fastest detective to do his marketing and work his way through a significant number of interviews, especially if he attacked his investigatorial responsibilities in a methodical and professional manner.

I organized the twenty statement forms by location and decided to start with those people who were closest and work outward.

I went back into the Virgin, got change from a pretty young woman with a pin through her nose, then found a pay phone on Sunset Boulevard to arrange the interviews. A homeless man with a shopping cart filled with neatly folded cardboard squares was seated beneath the phone, but he graciously moved aside when I told him I needed to make some calls. He said, 'Please feel free. It is, after all, a public instrument.' He was wearing spats.

I fed in a quarter and dialed Mr C. Bertrand Rujillio, who lived less than five minutes away. A man with a soft, raspy voice answered on the fourth ring and said, 'Who is this?'

'My name is Cole, for the law firm of Jonathan Green. I'm calling for Mr C. Bertrand Rujillio, please.'

There was a pause, and then the rasp came back. 'Do you have the money?'

'Is this Mr Rujillio?'

Another pause, softer. 'The money?'

'If you mean the reward, that won't be paid unless the information you provide leads to the arrest and conviction of Ms Martin's murderer.' Truly said that the phone bank operators had explained all this. Truly said I wouldn't have to worry about it. 'I need to take your statement, Mr Rujillio. Can we arrange that?'

The pause again, and this time the line went dead. I stared at the phone for a couple of seconds, then hung up and scratched C. Bertrand Rujillio's name off the list.

The homeless man said, 'No luck?'

I shook my head.

Of the next three calls, two reached answering machines and one went unanswered. Nobody home. I said, 'Damn.'

The homeless man said, 'Four out of four is poor luck.'

'It can't last forever.'

'Will you have many more calls?'

'A couple.'

He sighed and looked away.

Two more calls and two more answering machines and all the nearby people were done. So much for efficiency. So much for my plan of starting in close and working out. I said, 'Well, hell.'

The homeless man said, 'Tell me about it.'

I looked at him. 'I had a plan, but no one's home.'

He made a sympathetic shrug, then spread his hands. 'Flexibility, my friend. Flexibility is the key to all happiness. Remember that.'

I told him that I would and shuffled through the witness forms and decided to hell with starting close. I called Floyd M. Thomas in Chatsworth. Chatsworth was a good forty minutes away. Floyd M. Thomas answered on the third ring in a fast, nervous voice and told me that he had been expecting my call and that he would be happy to see me. I hung up. The homeless man said, 'You see? When we force events we corrupt them. Your flexibility allowed events to unfold in a way that pleases you. We know this as synchronicity.'

'You're a very wise man. Thank you.'

He spread his hands. 'To possess great wisdom obliges one to share it. Enjoy.'

I drove to Chatsworth.

Floyd Thomas lived in a studio apartment on the second floor of a ten-unit garden apartment just off Nordhoff. Scaffolding was rigged around the front and sides of the place, and Hispanic men in baggy pants were chipping away cracked stucco. Earthquake repairs. Thomas himself was a thin, hunched man in his early fifties who opened his door only wide enough to peer out at me with one eye. When he opened the door a cloud of moist heat oozed out around him like a fog. I slipped in a card. 'Elvis Cole. I called you about the Martin murder.'

He looked at the card without taking it. 'Oh, yes. Floyd Thomas saw that. Floyd Thomas saw exactly what happened.' Floyd Thomas. Don't you love it when they speak of themselves in the third person.

'That's great, Mr Thomas. I'll need to take your statement.'

He unlocked four chains and opened the door just wide enough for me to enter. If it was in the high nineties outside, Thomas's apartment

494

must've been a hundred ten with at least three industrial-strength humidifiers pumping out jets of water vapor. Stacks of newspapers and magazines and periodicals sprouted around the room like some out-of-control toadstool jungle, and everything smelled of mildew and body odor. I said, 'Hot in here.'

'Floyd Thomas chills easily.' Sweat leaked down out of his scalp and along the contours of his face and made his thin shirt cling to his skin. Thirty seconds inside his apartment, and I was beginning to sweat, too.

'So what did you see, Mr Thomas?' I dug out the form and prepared to take notes.

He said, 'We were over the Encino Reservoir. They were in a long black convertible. A Mercury, I think.'

I looked at him without writing. 'Over the Encino Reservoir?'

He nodded. 'That's right. I saw them with a woman in their car, and I'm sure it was her. She was struggling.' His eyes shifted side to side as he spoke.

I put down the pen. 'How were you over the reservoir?'

His eyes narrowed and he looked suspicious. 'They'd taken me up in the orb to adjust the chips.'

'The orb?' I said. 'The chips?'

He pulled back his upper lips so that his gums were exposed. 'They force chips into my gums that no one can see. They won't even show up on X-rays.' He made a tiny laugh. Hee-hee. Like that.

I said, 'You believe you saw Susan Martin in a black Mercury convertible when you were up in the orb.'

He nodded again. 'There were three men in black and they had the woman. Black suits, black ties, black hats, dark glasses. She had seen the orb and the men in black had to make sure she was silenced. They work for the government, don't you know.'

'Of course.'

'When will I get the reward?'

'We'll let you know, Mr Thomas.'

I thanked Floyd Thomas for his time, then drove to a nearby 7-Eleven and made five more calls, which resulted in three more interviews. Mr Walter S. Warren of Van Nuys was a retired general contractor who was convinced that his younger brother, Phil, was behind the kidnapping. He revealed that Phil had once eaten in Teddy Martin's Santa Monica restaurant, had cracked a tooth while enjoying the steak tartare, and had promised to 'get that prick' for what had happened to his tooth. Ms Victoria Bonell, also of Van Nuys, was an extremely thin woman who shared her ranch-style home with seven pug dogs and nine million fleas. Ms Bonell described an elaborate scenario in which 'lipstick lesbians' and 'power dykes' were behind Susan Martin's murder, information she had overheard while having her hair colored at a place called Rosa's. I dutifully noted these things, then went to see Mrs Lewis P. Reese of Sherman Oaks, who offered me tea and finger cakes, and who clearly knew nothing of Teddy Martin, Susan Martin, or the kidnapping. She was elderly and lonely, and I stayed twenty minutes longer than necessary, chatting about her dead husband. The detective does his good turn.

I left Mrs Reese at twenty minutes after two, bloated on tea cakes, itching from fleas, and smelling of Floyd C. Thomas's pod-person environment. I thought that if I was going to make any more calls maybe they should be to Jonathan. Maybe I should ask him if he really wanted to spend his money having me interview these people?

I stopped at a Ralph's market, bought Tide, Downy Fabric Softener, two Long Island ducklings, enough salad ingredients for a family of nine, and was home by ten minutes after three. The airline told me that Lucy's flight was expected to arrive on time. I put the ducks into a large pot, covered them with water to thaw, and put the pot in the refrigerator. I showered, shaved, put on fresh clothes, and made a last-minute check of the house. Spotless. Pristine. Free from embarrassing dust bunnies.

I took Pike's Jeep, pushed back down the hill and made my way to LAX, arriving at the gate twenty-eight minutes early. I took a seat across from an older woman with brittle white hair and pleasant eyes. I nodded hello and she nodded back. She said, 'I'll bet she's very pretty.'

'Who?'

'The one you're waiting for. You should see the smile on your face.' Know-it-all.

The gate grew crowded and, with the growing crowd, I began to feel anxious and goofy. Then the plane was down and my heart was hammering and it was hard to breath. I said, 'Snap out of it, dummy. Try to get a grip.'

The older woman laughed, and a man holding a two-year-old moved away.

I saw Lucy first, emerging from the jetway behind three elderly gentlemen, and I wanted to yell, 'Hey, Luce!' and jump up and down.

Lucy Chenier is five feet five, with amber green eyes and auburn hair rich with golden highlights from all the time she spends in the sun. She was wearing black shorts and a white long-sleeved shirt with the sleeves rolled and white Reebok tennis shoes, and she was carrying a gray canvas shoulder bag that probably weighed nine thousand pounds and her Gucci briefcase. When she saw me she tried to wave but her hands were full with the bags. Ben yelled, 'Hey, there's Elvis!' and then I shouldered past two Marines and Lucy was hugging me and I was hugging her back, and then she stepped away and said, 'Oh, your poor eye!'

'You look so good, Luce. You don't know.'

We gave each other a long kiss, and then I hugged Ben, too. Ben

Chenier had grown maybe four inches in the three months since I'd last seen him. 'You're taller.'

He beamed. 'Four six and a quarter. I'm getting close to five feet.'

'Wow.'

I took the shoulder bag and we moved with the flow of arrivals down to baggage claim, Lucy and I holding hands and Ben ranging ahead of us, burning off eight-year-old-boy energy. Lucy's hand felt dry and warm and natural in mine, and as we moved along the white tiled corridors they told me about their flight (uneventful) and how Ben was spending his summer (a week at Camp Avondale with his Cub Scout pack) and about Lucy's business in Long Beach (amicably renegotiating a six-year-old divorce settlement involving complex corporate holdings). As we talked there was a growing feeling that these were not just two people with whom I would spend time, but two people I was allowing into my life. It was a thought that made me smile, and Lucy said, 'What?'

'Just thinking how glad I am that you guys are here.'

She squeezed my hand.

When their luggage arrived we loaded it into the Jeep and followed LaTijera out of the airport northeast up through the city. It was rush hour, and the going was slow, but going slow didn't seem to matter. Ben said, 'We're going to your house?'

'That's right. I live in the hills above West Hollywood.'

'Where are we gonna sleep?'

Lucy and I traded a smile. 'I've got a guest room. There's a bed for your mom, and a camper's cot for you.'

'What's your house like?'

Lucy said, 'You'll see when we get there, Ben.'

I smiled at him in the rearview. 'It's perched on the side of a mountain and it's surrounded by trees. A friend said that it reminds her of a tree house.'

Ben said, 'Cool.'

Lucy raised an eyebrow and looked at me. 'What friend?'

I said, 'That was years ago.'

'Mm-hmm.'

We made great time through the Slauson Pass, then climbed north through the Fairfax District past CBS and finally up Laurel Canyon and into the mountains, and then we were home. The summer sun was still high in the west as we turned into the carport and got out, and Lucy said, 'Oh, this is just wonderful!' You could smell the eucalyptus and the pine and, high above us, the two red-tailed hawks who lived in the canyon floated on rising thermals. I said, 'You guys hungry?'

Ben said, 'Yeah!'

Lucy said, 'Starving, but I want to take a bath first.'

I showed them in through the kitchen and led them past the entry and across the living room and, as we walked, I watched Lucy's eyes flick over the kitchen counters and the refrigerator with its Spider-Man magnets and the bar built into the dining room wall and the stone hearth in the living room and the bookcases and pictures; trying to take in as much of my life in those few seconds as she could. She caught me watching her and gave me a smile of approval. 'I like.'

I showed them their room and bath, then brought them out onto the deck. Ben said, 'Oh, wow,' and raced around the handrail, looking down. It's about a twenty-foot drop.

Lucy said, 'Elvis, it's beautiful.'

'This canyon merges with Nichols Canyon, which opens out into the basin. The little bit of city you see is part of Hollywood. Tomorrow morning we'll take the road below us down to the Budget Rent-a-Car.'

She turned back to the house and lowered her voice. 'And where does the master sleep?'

I grinned and pulled her close. 'The stairs off the living room lead to the master's quarters.'

She pushed away, then leaned against the rail and crossed her arms. It was a pretty good pose. 'Perhaps a bit later I'll get a chance to inspect the premises.'

I shrugged, but even pretending to be disinterested was somehow impossible. My voice came out hoarse and broken. 'If you're good, perhaps I'll let you.'

She let a smile curl out from under the world's longest eyelashes and lowered her voice still more and let the southern accent come thick. 'Oh, Studly, Ah intend to be very, very bad.'

The air seemed to spark with a kind of electric heat and then Ben raced back from the side of the house. 'Elvis, can I go down the hill?'

'Up to your mom, pal.'

Lucy looked over the rail. 'Is it safe?'

'Sure. It's a gentle slope. The people who live over there have a couple of boys, and they play all along the ridges.'

Lucy didn't look convinced, but you could tell she was going to give in. 'Well, okay, but stay close to the house.'

Ben ran around the side of the house again, and this time we could hear him crashing down through the dried grass and into the trees. Lucy looked at me and I looked back, but now she was giving me serious. 'So. Are you going to tell me about the eye, or do I have to keep wondering?'

'A police officer named Angela Rossi popped me with a sap.'

Lucy sighed and shook her head. 'Other women date doctors or businessmen. I have to fall for someone who gets into street fights.'

'It wasn't much of a fight. She suckered me.' I told her about what Green had hired me to do, and how I had done it, and how I had come to get the eye.

Lucy listened, interested more in the parts about Jonathan Green, and frowning when I told her how Rossi had eye-faked me. 'She caught you off guard. You underestimated her because she was a woman.'

'If I said that it would be taking something away from her. I didn't underestimate her; she was just good enough to sucker me with an eye-fake.'

Lucy gave me one of her gentle smiles, then touched the mouse. 'You're such a sweetie.'

I nodded.

She came close and went up on her toes and kissed it. 'I need to make some calls about tomorrow, and I want to take that bath. May I use your phone?'

'Sure.' I brushed at her hair, then stroked her upper arms. 'You don't have to ask, okay? Whatever you want to do while you're here, just do it. Ben, too.'

She went up on her toes and kissed me again. 'Keep an eye on Ben?'

'The good eye or the bad eye?'

'Funny.'

While Lucy was making her calls I fired the grill, then split the ducks and rubbed them with lemon juice and garlic and pepper. Lucy phoned two attorneys to arrange her next day's meeting, and then she called Jodi Taylor. Jodi was filming her series, *Songbird*, and had invited Ben to spend the day with her on the set. When Lucy was off the phone and in the bath I checked on Ben and, when the coals were right, put the four duck halves on the grill and covered them. I was back in the kitchen working on tarragon rice and salad when the cat door clacked and the cat walked in. He froze in the center of the kitchen floor and growled.

I said, 'Knock that off.'

He moved through the kitchen, stopping every couple of steps, his cat nose working and the growl soft in his chest. I said, 'We're going to have guests for a few days, and if you bite or scratch either one of them it will go hard for you.'

His eyes narrowed and he looked at me. I said, 'I mean it.'

He sprinted back through his door. There are some things you just can't talk to him about.

I checked on Ben again, then finished with the salad and set the table and put on the new k.d. lang. Lucy reappeared in fresh shorts and wet, slicked-back hair, wrapping her arms around me from behind and sharing her warmth. She said, 'Everything is just perfect.'

'Not yet,' I said. 'But soon.'

We called in Ben and ate, and little by little we moved through the evening, talking about and planning our coming days, Lucy and I gently touching as we talked, each touch a way of sharing something larger than a simple tactile experience, and after a while even the excitement of the adventure couldn't keep Ben going and Lucy finally whispered, 'He's sleeping.'

'Need help getting him to bed?'

'No. I'll get him on his feet and he'll walk.'

When their door was closed I shut all the lights save one, then went upstairs and took off my clothes. The house was still, and I thought that I could smell her the way, I supposed, the cat had. But maybe that was my imagination.

I lay in the dark for what seemed forever, and then I heard the door below open and the sound of her on the stairs, and I thought how very lucky I was that she had come, and that I was the one whom she had come to see.

10

The sun was bright and hot on the sheets, and I woke smelling coffee and hearing *Bewitched* on the television, Elizabeth Montgomery saying, 'But Darren is a wonderful man, Mother,' and Agnes Moorehead saying, 'That's the problem, dear. He's a *man*, and you deserve so much more.'

When I went downstairs, Lucy and Ben were up and dressed, Ben on the couch watching television, and Lucy at the dining room table, sipping coffee. She was wearing a pale yellow pants suit and her Gucci briefcase was open, with papers spread on the table beside her. Preparing for business. I said, 'Hey. There are people in my house.'

Lucy smiled. 'We tried to be quiet.'

'You were. I didn't hear a thing.' She held out her hand, fingers spread, and I laced my fingers through hers.

She said, 'Mm.'

I wiggled my eyebrows, then made a shifty look back toward the stairs. 'Mm-mm.'

Lucy took back her hand. 'No time, my dear. Jodi's going to pick up Ben on her way in to the studio, then you have to take me to the Budget office. She should be here soon.'

'Great.' We were grinning at each other with great loopy grins that probably looked silly. 'Did you sleep all right?'

Lucy managed a straight face. 'Very well, thank you. And yourself?'

I pretended to stifle a yawn. 'A little restless. I feel drained this morning.'

Lucy raised her eyebrows. 'Imagine that. Perhaps you need more rest.'

Ben looked at us from the couch, confused. 'You don't look tired to me.'

Lucy and I grinned, and Ben looked even more confused. 'What did I say?'

Lucy said, 'I got directions to my meeting, so all we need to do is pick up the car. You shower and dress, and I'll make breakfast. Deal?'

'Deal.'

I did and she did, and we were finishing coffee and toasted banana bread and scrambled eggs when Jodi Taylor's black-on-black Beemer tooled up and stopped across the drive. I pushed open the kitchen door and gave her a kiss as she entered. 'What, no limo for the star?'

Jodi Taylor tugged at my shirt and said, 'I'll buy a stretch if you'll come for a ride, handsome.' Then she winked at Lucy and said, 'Oops, sorry. I see he's already taken.'

I gave her the eyebrows. 'Taken, yes, but perhaps available for rent.'

Lucy said, 'In that case she should buy a hearse. Better to lay out the body.'

Jodi laughed. 'Grr-owl. These southern belles are *very* territorial.'

'Possessive,' Lucy said. 'The word is possessive.'

Lucy and Jodi hugged, and Ben ran in from the living room. Like Lucy, Jodi Taylor was from Louisiana, though, unlike Lucy, you couldn't hear it in her voice. She was maybe an inch taller than Lucy, with hazel eyes and dusky red hair and a kind of natural beauty that made her accessible and real to thirty million people every week. Supermarket beauty, they called it. The kind and quality of beauty that let you believe that you might bump into her in the market, buying Pampers or Diet Coke. *Songbird* had been renewed for a second full season, and Jodi Taylor had just begun production on the new episodes. She was happy and confident in returning to work, and was at ease with herself in a way that she hadn't been three months ago. Lucy said, 'Jodi, you look wonderful.'

Jodi smiled shyly. 'Thanks to you two.'

I had seen Jodi from time to time in the three months since I'd helped her, but Lucy hadn't, and they chatted and worked out the details of Ben's day while I cleared the table, loaded the dishwasher, then went upstairs to gather together my file of tipsters. I considered bringing along a can of bug repellent for the day's assignment, but decided against it. Too hard to force the can into my holster.

When I went back downstairs, Jodi and Lucy were standing together, grinning. Jodi said, 'You're working for Jonathan Green? My, my.' Impressed.

I spread my hands. 'He's just another client, ladies.' Mr Modest.

Lucy put her hands on her hips. 'No, he's not. He's Jonathan Green.'

I spread my hands again. They're carrying on like this, and I'm battling fleas and talking to people who think they've got chips in their gums.

Lucy made her voice low and breathy. 'He positively *dominates* a court room. And his presence is so *commanding.*'

Jodi Taylor slinked over to me and toyed with my collar. 'Could you arrange a personal introduction?'

Lucy said, 'Would he autograph my law school diploma? Would he do that for lil' ol' me?'

Jodi purred, 'I've got something else he could autograph.'

Girl humor.

Jodi and Ben finally left for the studio, and then I brought Lucy down to the Budget office, working our way along the back canyon road in silence. Lucy was staring out of the car, and I thought that she might be watching the alien scenery and the strange mountain houses, but she wasn't. She said, 'What I said about possessive. I was joking.' Her voice was soft, and when she said it she didn't look at me.

'Sure.'

Her hands were in her lap and her briefcase was on the floor beneath her legs. She said, 'Elvis?'

'Hm?'

Another pause. Longer. 'Do you see anyone else?'

I looked at her, but she still wasn't looking at me. I went back to the road.

Lucy said, 'I mean, it's none of my business. We've never talked about other people.'

I nodded. I looked at her again, but she still was focused outside. 'I went out twice in the month after I came back from Louisiana. Once with a woman I'd seen several times before, and once with a waitress I met in the Valley, and both times went poorly.'

'Oh.' She didn't sound disappointed.

'I was with them, but I was thinking of you. Then you and I started talking about going to Cancun. I haven't been out with anyone since then. I don't want to go out with anyone else.' I was looking more at her than the road, which isn't smart in the hills.

Lucy Chenier looked at me, then nodded once and turned back to the window.

I said, 'Have you been seeing anyone?'

She shook her head. 'No.'

I thought about it and what it meant. 'Good.'

Without looking at me, she put out her hand. I took it. We drove like that the rest of the way to the Budget office, where I dropped her off and began another exciting day in the employ of the Big Green Defense Machine.

11

After I dropped Lucy off I stopped at a diner on Hollywood Boulevard and made more calls. Of the remaining names on my list, two were in El Monte, one in San Marino, and one was in Pasadena, all of which were on the eastern rim of the Los Angeles sprawl.

I called a Mr James Lester first. A woman answered, sounding young and whiny, and told me that he was sleeping. She said that he didn't have to go in until noon, so he always slept late. I told her that I would be in their area later, and how about I call back then. She said, 'Mister, I don't give a rat's ass what you do.' Nothing like starting off your work day with a bang.

No one was home on my next call, and then I phoned Ms Mary Mason of San Marino. A woman with a low, breathy voice answered on the third ring. She identified herself as Mistress Maggie Mason and told me that Mary was her sister. When I told her why I was calling she said that Mary would be available shortly and gave me directions to their home. One for three.

Mary Mason lived on Winston Drive in a stately well-kept home set back from the street. It was an older place, built of heavy stone and stucco. I rang the bell three times, knocked twice, and was just getting ready to leave when the door opened and a tall, statuesque woman in a black leather teddy, net stockings, and six-inch platform shoes stepped out. A twined cobra was tattooed on her right thigh. She said, 'May I help you?' She had long black hair pulled back tight against her head.

'Are you Mary Mason?'

She smiled nicely. It was a friendly smile, relaxed and personable. 'No, I'm her sister, Maggie. I spoke with you earlier.'

'Ah.'

'Come in and I'll get Mary.'

The living room was tastefully decorated with minimalist Italian furniture, a spherical saltwater aquarium, and custom bookshelves lining three walls. The bookshelves were African teak and must've cost a fortune. Maggie Mason said, 'Wait right here and I'll get her.' She was bright and cheery, not unlike a Girl Scout troop leader from Nebraska.

I waited. The house was so quiet that I could hear neither street noise nor passing cars nor the sound of Maggie Mason getting her sister. I looked at the books. Short fiction by Raymond Carver and Joan Didion. Asian philosophy by T'sun T'su and Koji Toyoda. Crime novels by James Ellroy and Jim Thompson. Science fiction by Olaf Stapledon and Jack Finney. Eclectic and impressive. I had finished reading the titles on one wall and was starting on a second when Mary and Maggie Mason returned. Twins. Both were tall, but where Maggie was dressed in the teddy and the fishnet, Mary wore a smartly tailored business suit and conservative low-heeled pumps. Her face was very white and her lips were liquid red and her black hair was cropped short and oiled to severe perfection. I said, 'Mary Mason?'

Mary Mason sat next to the aquarium, crossed one gleaming leg over the other, and said, 'Four payments. I want the first payment now, another when there's an arrest, the third on arraignment, and the final on the first day of the trial. That's the only way I'll do business.'

I said, 'Business?'

Her sister smiled politely. 'If you'll excuse me, I have something to take care of.' She left without waiting for either of us to respond.

Mary Mason leaned toward me. 'I hear things.' She arched her eyebrows, which, like the rest of her, were perfect. 'I know the identity of James X. I can help Teddy Martin.'

I gave her the same news that I'd given Floyd Thomas, that there would be no money until a conviction.

Mary Mason said, 'Bullshit.' When she said it, a muffled *crack* came from the back of the house.

I looked past her. 'What was that?'

Mary Mason leaned closer and put her hand on my knee. 'Pay something as a sign of good faith. Five thousand dollars, and I'll give you a physical description. How about that?' There was another dull *crack* and then a whimpering sound.

I looked past her again. 'I can't do that, Ms Mason.'

She squeezed the knee. 'Three thousand, then. Teddy Martin can afford it.' She ran her tongue along glistening lips, and then a man in the rear of the house moaned something about being called a dog. The voice was muffled and far away, and I thought that maybe I'd heard him wrong. Then the man howled.

'Thanks for your time, Ms Mason.' I walked out, wondering if it were too late to change professions.

It was twenty-eight minutes after ten when I left the Mason twins and dropped south out of San Marino to San Gabriel. I pulled into a strip mall, made two more calls, and on each of the calls got an answering machine. That meant I was back to James Lester, who may or may not be awake. I called his number again anyway, and this time a man answered. I said, 'Mr Lester?'

A woman was shouting in the background. Lester shouted back at her, 'Just shut the fuck up, goddammit,' and then he came on the line. 'Yeah?'

'Mr James Lester?'

'Who wants to know?' One of those.

I told him who I was and what I wanted.

'You're the guy from the lawyer, right?'

'That's right.'

'Okay, sure. C'mon over.'

I went over.

El Monte, California, is a mostly industrial area north of the Puente Hills and south of Santa Anita, with small working-class neighborhoods to the south and west. James and Jonna Lester lived in a poorly kept bungalow on a narrow street just west of the San Gabriel River in an area of postwar low-income housing. The lawn was patchy and yellow from lack of water, as if the Lesters had given up against the desert and the desert was reclaiming their yard. Everything looked dusty and old, as if there were no future here, only a past.

I left my car on the street, walked up across the dead yard, and a guy I took to be James Lester opened the door. He was average-sized in dark gray cotton work pants, dirty white socks, and a dingy undershirt. His hair was cut short on the sides and on top, but had been left long and shaggy in back, and he looked at me with a squint. He was thin, with knobby, grease-embedded hands and pale skin sporting Bic-pen tattoos on his arms and shoulders and chest. Work farm stuff. I made him for thirty, but he could've been younger. He said, 'You're the guy called. You're from the lawyer, right?' A quarter to eleven in the morning and he smelled of beer.

'That's right.'

I followed him into a poorly furnished living room that wasn't in any better shape than the yard. Stacks of magazines and newspapers and comic books were piled around on the furniture, and no one had dusted since 1942. A tattered poster of the Silver Surfer was thumb-tacked to the wall, four darts growing out of the Silver Surfer's chest. Lester dropped into a battered, overstuffed chair and pulled on a workboot. An open can of Hamm's was on the floor by the boots. 'I gotta get ready for work. You wanna brewscalero?'

'Pass.'

'Your loss, dude. I can't get going without it.'

A barefoot woman with a swollen, discolored lip came out of the kitchen carrying a sandwich in a paper towel. She was wearing baggy shorts and a loose top and her skin was very white, as if she didn't get out in the sun much. She dropped the sandwich on a little table next to the chair as if she didn't give a damn whether he ate it or not. She looked sixteen, but she was probably older.

I smiled and said, 'I believe we spoke earlier.'

She said, 'Well, whoop-de-doo.'

James Lester pulled hard at his bootlaces. 'I need another brewscalero, Jonna. Go get it.'

Jonna Lester shot a hard look at her husband's back, then stomped back into the kitchen. Pouty.

James said, 'She don't do nothing but run around with her friends all day while I'm bustin' my ass. That's why it's such a sty in here. That's why it's a goddamned shithole.' They didn't have air conditioning. A couple of ancient electric fans blew hot air around the room, one of the fans making a slow, monotonous *chinging* sound. Jonna Lester came back with a fresh Hamm's, put it down next to the sandwich, then stomped out again. I hadn't been in their house for thirty seconds and already my neck was starting to ache.

I said, 'I'm here to follow up the call you made about Susan Martin's kidnapping and murder.'

Lester finished tying the first boot, then started on the second. 'Sure. That guy I spoke to on the phone, he said someone would come talk to me about it. That's you, I guess.'

'I guess.' Mr Lucky.

He looked over and grinned when he saw my eye. 'Hey, you and Jonna kinda match, doncha?' He laughed after he said it, huh-yuk, huh-yuk, huh-yuk. Like Jughead.

I stared at him.

James Lester killed what was left of the first Hamm's, then popped the tab on the second. 'I think I met the guys who did it.'

'Okay.'

He took another pull on the Hamm's, then had some of the sandwich. When he bit into the sandwich he jumped up and opened the sandwich as if he'd just bitten into a turd. 'Goddammit, Jonna, what in hell is this?'

'That's your potted meat!' Yelling from the kitchen.

'Where's the fuckin' mayonnaise?'

'We're out. I gotta get some.'

'Where's the *little pickles*?' Now he was whining worse than her.

'I'm gonna go get some, all right?' Screaming, now. '*Do you think I'm your fuckin' slave?*'

His face went sullen and his breathing grew loud. He had more of the Hamm's. He had more of the Hamm's again. My neck was hurting so bad I thought it would go into spasm.

'Tell me what you know, James.'

He stayed with the loud breathing a little longer, then closed the sandwich and took another bite. You'd think it was killing him, having to eat his sandwich without the mayonnaise and the little pickles.

I said, 'James.'

He went on with his mouth full. 'A week before it's on the news about her gettin' killed I stop in this place for a couple of brewscaleros. There's these two guys, one of the guys, he was wearing a Shell station shirt had the name "Steve" sewn over the pocket.'

'Okay.' I wrote *Shell station* on my notepad. I wrote *Steve*.

'We were talkin' about how shitty it was, havin' to work for a livin', and this guy, he gives me the big wink and says he's got her whipped. I'm all, whaddaya mean you got'r whipped? He goes, hey, a guy with the 'nads could snatch one of these rich Beverly Hills bitches and score enough fast cash to retire in style.'

I said, 'Steve said that?'

'Unh-hunh.' He stuffed the rest of the sandwich in his mouth and washed it down. 'I tell'm that sounds like a fast track to the gas chamber to me, but he goes, all you need is a layout of the house and a slick way in and out, stuff like that.' He swallowed hard and let out a gassy belch.

'The other guy say anything?'

'Nope. Just sat there drinkin'.'

'What'd they look like?'

'Steve was kinda tall and skinny, with light hair. I'm not sure about the other guy. Shorter. Darker.'

A phone rang in the kitchen and we could hear Jonna Lester answer. James's face clouded and he yelled, 'That better not be one'a your cunt friends!'

She yelled back, 'Fuck you!'

I said, 'James.'

He turned the cloud my way.

'"Cunt" is an ugly word.'

He squinted at me as if he wasn't sure what I'd said, and then he shook his head. 'All she does is yack with her friends. All she does is run around the mall while I'm bustin' my ass.' Like that should explain it.

I said, 'Steve and the dark guy say anything else?'

He sucked at his teeth, getting rid of the last bits of the sandwich. 'I hadda pee so I went to the head. When I come back they was gone.'

I stared at him, thinking about it. Seven interviews so far, and his was the only one that seemed to be worth checking out. It would probably add up to nothing, but you never know until you know. 'You remember the bar?'

'Sure. It was a place called the Hangar over on Mission Boulevard. I go there sometimes.'

I wrote it down. *The Hangar.*

'Last thing the guy says before I go to the head, he says he knows just who to grab, too. He says she's a one-way ticket to Easy Street.'

'Steve said that?'

'Yeah. Steve.'

'He say a name?'

'Unh-unh.'

Jonna Lester reappeared wearing strap sandles and carrying a small purse. She'd made her face, but the lip still looked puffy. He said, 'Where the fuck do you think you're going?'

She pouted the lips at him, giving him attitude. 'I gotta go to the store. I got things to buy.'

'You think you're gonna run around with your cunt friends while I'm bustin' my ass? You think you're gonna spend my dough in some fuckin' mall?'

'*We're outta mayonnaise. We're outta those little pickles.*'

He jumped up and grabbed her right arm. 'You're gonna stay here and clean this fuckin' rathole, that's what you're gonna do!'

I stood.

She tried to twist away from him, screaming, 'You piece of shit! I'm not your fuckin' slave!' She pounded at him with her left fist, pretty good shots that nailed him on the head and face and chest until he was able to grab her left arm, too.

'James.' The ache in my neck had moved up to my scalp. Never a good sign.

She said, 'You're hurtin' me, you asshole!'

'James. Leave go of her.'

James Lester said, 'Fuck you. This is my house. This is my wife. She's gonna do what I say or I'll give'r a fat lip!'

I held up my right index finger. 'Watch the finger, James. I want to show you something.'

His eyes went to the finger, like maybe it was a trick, only he couldn't figure out what the trick might be.

'Are you watching my finger?'

'Suck my ass.' She was watching my right finger, too.

I hit him flush on the nose with a left.

He yelled, 'Ow!' and grabbed at his face with both hands. He stumbled back and tripped over the little side table. Jonna Lester leaned over him, wiggled her butt, and yelled, 'Ha-ha, *asshole!*' Some wife.

James Lester was on his back, eyes watering, blinking at me. He said, 'You piece of shit. You wait'll I get up!'

I put my notes in the manila envelope, then went to the door. Lucy was probably in the midst of her negotiation right now. Ben was probably watching Jodi Taylor shoot a scene right now. The world was turning on its axis right now.

I said, 'Thanks for the statement, James. If anything comes of it we'll be in touch about the reward.'

'You better not jew me out of that reward! I'm gonna call the cops, you hear? I'm gonna have you *arrested!*'

I left them to their lives and walked out into the sun. You want to do the right thing, but sometimes there is no right thing to be done.

Another day, another moron. And to think, some people have to work for a living.

12

The Hangar was a small, bright hole-in-the-fence-type bar wedged between a place that sold balsa-wood rocket kits and another place that repaired appliances. They were doing a pretty good lunch business when I got there, selling chili tacos and grilled sausages to people swilling down schooners of beer. Both of the bartenders were women in their fifties, and neither of them knew a blond guy named Steve who worked for Shell. I didn't expect that they would, but you never know. The older of the two women called me 'sweetie.' The younger of the two didn't like it very much. Jealous.

I bought a grilled sausage with kraut, a schooner of Miller, and asked if they'd mind letting me use their phone book. The older one didn't, but the younger one warned me not to walk out with it. I assured them that I wouldn't. The younger one told me to be careful not to spill anything on it. The older one asked the younger one why she always had to make such a big thing, and the younger one said what if I ruined it? I assured them that I'd buy them a new phone book if I ruined the loaner. The older one said, 'Oh, don't you give it another thought, sweetie,' and the younger one went down to the far end of the bar and sulked.

Half the schooner later I had addresses for the nine Shell service stations located in the El Monte/Baldwin Park/West Covina area. I finished the sausage, thanked the older one for her help, and made the round of the Shell stations. At each stop I spoke to the manager or assistant manager, identified myself, and asked if a tall blond guy named Steve had worked there anytime in the past six months. At the first four stations I visited, the answer was no, but at the fifth station the manager said, 'You mean Pritzik?'

'Who's Pritzik?'

'We had a fellow named Steve Pritzik.' The manager was a Persian gentleman named Mr Pavlavi. He was short and round and stood in the shade of his maintenance center with his arms crossed. His maintenance center, like the rest of his service station, was polished and gleaming.

I said, 'Was he tall?'

'Oh, yes. Very tall.'

'Was he blond?'

'Oh, yes. Very blond.'

I said, 'Mr Pavlavi, is he employed here now?' Just because a tall blond guy named Steve worked here didn't mean it was the *same* tall blond Steve. Maybe it was just a coincidence.

Pavlavi frowned. 'Not in a very long while. He quit, you know. One day here, the next day not, never to return.' He sighed as if such things are the stuff of life, to be expected and therefore no great cause for anxiety or resentment.

'About how long ago was that?'

'Well,' he said. 'Let us see.'

He led me into the air-conditioned office and took a ledger from his desk. The ledger was filled with page after page of handwriting that, like the service station, was immaculate. 'Pritzik was last here exactly one hundred two days ago.'

'Hm.' Steve Pritzik had last been in four days before Susan Martin's murder.

'I owe him forty-eight dollars and sixteen cents, but he has not been in to collect. I will keep it for exactly one year, then give it to charity.'

'Mr Pavlavi, would you have an address on Pritzik?'

He did, and he gave it to me.

Steve Pritzik lived in one of a cluster of six small duplex cottages in an older neighborhood at the base of the Puente Hills, not far from the Pomona Freeway. The duplexes were single-story stucco and clap-board buildings stepping up the side of the hill and overgrown with original planting fruit trees and ivy and climbing roses.

I parked at the curb, then made my way up broken cement steps, looking for Pritzik's address. The steps were narrow, and the heavy growth of ivy and roses made them feel still more narrow. Pritzik's apartment was the western half of the third duplex up from the street. Each side of the cottage had its own little porch, separated by a couple of ancient orange trees and a trellis of roses. The eastern porch was neat and clean and decorated by a small cactus garden. Pritzik's porch was dirty and unadorned, and his mailbox was heavy with letters and flyers. I rang the bell and could hear it inside, but no one answered. I listened harder. Nothing. I went to the mailbox and fingered through gas and phone and electric bills. They weren't addressed to Steve Pritzik; they were addressed to a Mr Elton Richards. Hmm. I walked around the orange trees and up onto the adjoining porch and rang the bell. You could hear music inside. Alanis Morissette.

A woman in her late twenties opened the door. 'Yes?' She had long dark hair and great floppy bangs and she was wearing cutoff jeans under an oversized man's T-shirt. The T-shirt was blotched with small smears of color. So were her hands.

I gave her the card and introduced myself. 'I'm trying to find a guy named Steve Pritzik. I think he lives or used to live next door.'

She read the card and grinned. 'Are you really a private eye?'

'Pretty amazing, huh?'

She grinned wider and nodded. 'Cool.'

'You know Pritzik?'

She offered the card back, but I raised a hand, telling her to keep it. 'I don't think so. Elton lives next door.'

'Is Elton tall and blond?'

'Oh, no. He's short and kinda dark.' Ah. She rolled her eyes. 'He's such a creep. He's always hitting on me, so I try to avoid him.'

'I was just over there, and it looks like Elton hasn't been around.' I told her about the mail.

She pushed her hands in her pockets. 'You know, now that I think about it, I haven't seen him in a while. I haven't heard his TV or anything.'

'You think he might've moved?'

'I don't know.'

'Can you give me a guess how long he's been gone?'

She scrunched her face, thinking. 'Couple of months, maybe.'

'Between three and four months?'

She waffled her hand. 'He's just such a creep I try to duck him. Sorry.'

I said, 'You ever see a tall blond guy hanging around with him?'

She frowned.

'Maybe four months ago.'

She was swaying with Alanis, then she kind of cocked her head. 'You know, I think maybe there was a guy like that. Elton had such scuzzy friends.' She nodded, then, starting to see it. 'Yeah. There was this blond guy.' She nodded harder, the image pulling into focus. 'Oh, yuck, what an asshole. He sees me on the street and follows me up the walk one day. He asks me if I want to go inside and fuck, just like that. Oh, yuck. I think he worked at a gas station or something.'

I nodded.

'All of Elton's friends were like that. Real lowlifes.' She suddenly put out her hand. 'I'm Tyler, by the way.'

'Hi, Tyler.' We shook, and I gave her the big smile. 'Can I ask you something?'

'Sure.' She smiled back, anxious to hear what I was going to ask. Alanis was really tearing it up inside.

'I'm thinking about popping Elton's door and sneaking in to look around. You wouldn't call the police if I did that, would you?'

Her smiled grew wider as I said it. 'No way! Could I come, too?'

I shook my head. 'Then if we're caught, we're both in trouble, you see?'

She looked disappointed. Behind her, Alanis stopped singing and Tyler pulled a hand out of her pocket long enough to brush at the bangs. They were pretty incredible. 'You really know how to pick locks and stuff?'

'I'm a full-service professional, Tyler.'

She stared at me for a few seconds and then she crossed her arms. She looked out from under her bangs at me. 'And just what kind of service do you provide?'

'I've got a girlfriend. Sorry.'

Tyler stared at me from under the bangs for another couple of seconds, then uncrossed her arms and looked at my card again. 'Yeah, well. If I ever need anything detected, maybe I'll call.'

'How about the cops?'

Tyler made a zipping move across her lips.

I gave her the big smile again, then went next door, slipped the lock, and let myself into Elton Richards's half of the house. It was dim from the drawn shades, and I flipped the light switch but the lights stayed dark. I guess the power company had killed the juice. I said, 'Mr Richards?'

No answer. Next door, I could hear Alanis start again, faint and far away.

The house smelled musty. A ratty couch was against the wall under a Green Day poster, fronted by a coffee table made of a couple of 2 by 10 planks lying on cinderblocks and cornered by someone's secondhand lawn chair. A black streamline phone waited on the planks. A pretty good Hitachi electronics stack was against the opposite wall, and a beat-up Zenith television with a coat hanger antenna was on the floor, and everything was covered with a light patina of undisturbed dust.

I crossed into the kitchen and turned on the tap. No water. I went back to the living room, used my handkerchief, and lifted the phone. No tone. I guess Elton Richards had ignored his bills long enough for the power and water and phone companies to turn everything off. Say, about four months.

I stood in the living room by the phone and thought about it. James Lester had met a short dark man and a tall blond man named Steve in a bar about a week before Susan Martin's kidnapping and murder. Steve speaks of snatching a rich woman as a means of attaining the better things in life, and maybe the two are connected, but maybe not. Four months after the fact, I identify a possible Steve and trace him to this address which, in fact, is apparently owned by a shorter, darker man named Elton Richards. Maybe they are the same two men, but maybe not. Maybe tall blond guys named Steve just naturally have short dark friends.

Two small bedrooms bracketed the bath. I searched each thoroughly, looking for receipts or ticket stubs or anything else that might provide a clue as to when and where Elton Richards and Steve Pritzik went. There was nothing. I went into the bathroom and checked behind and beneath the toilet and in the water tank. I pulled the medicine cabinet out of the wall. I checked in the little wooden cabinet beneath the lavatory. *Nada.* I went back into the living room and pulled the cushions off the couch and found a single 9 by 12 manila envelope. It was the kind of envelope you get in the mail from those sweepstakes companies declaring that you've just won ten million dollars, and it was addressed to Mr Elton Richards. The end of the envelope had been scissored open, then retaped. I pushed my car keys under the tape, opened the envelope, and looked inside. Then I sat down.

I took deep rhythmic breaths, flooding my blood with oxygen and forcing myself to calm. Pranayamic breathing, they call it.

I looked in the envelope again, then tilted it so that the contents spilled out onto the couch. Inside there were seven separate photographs of Susan Martin and Teddy Martin, and two hand-drawn maps. One map was the floorplan of a very large house. The other was a street map showing the layout of someone's neighborhood and a house on Benedict Canyon Road. It was Teddy Martin's neighborhood, and it was Teddy Martin's house.

13

I went to my car for the new Canon Auto Focus I keep in the glove box. I made sure I had film and that the flash worked, and then I took a pair of disposable plastic gloves and went back into the house. I put on the gloves, then photographed everything as I had found it, making sure I had clear shots of the hand-drawn maps as well as the photos. When I was done, I left everything lying on the couch, then went next door and asked Tyler if I could use her phone.

I called Truly first, who listened quietly until I was finished, then said, 'I'll notify Jonathan and we'll get there as quickly as we can. Don't let anyone else in the residence.' He cupped the phone, and I could hear muffled voices. Then he came back. 'We'll notifiy the police, too. Cooperate with them when they arrive, but keep an eye on them. Watch that they don't destroy the evidence.'

'Truly, they won't do anything like that.'

He said, 'Ha.'

When I hung up, Tyler was leaning against the back of her couch, arms crossed, a long paintbrush in one hand. Her home smelled of fresh jasmine tea and acrylic paint, and was decorated with oversized sunflower sculptures that she'd made from cardboard and wire. 'You really think that this creep next door had something to do with Susan Martin's murder?'

'Maybe.'

'I thought her husband did it. That restaurant guy.'

'You never know.'

'They said on TV that he did.'

'That's TV.'

She shook her head. 'L.A. is so perverted.'

The first black and white arrived eighteen minutes later. The senior officer was a guy named Hernandez, and his partner was a younger African-American woman named Flutey. I went out to meet them carrying a glass of Tyler's jasmine iced tea. Hernandez said, 'You Cole?'

'Yep.' I told him what we had.

He nodded. 'Okay. Flutey, get the tape from the car and let's seal it, okay? I'll check inside and around back.'

Flutey went for the tape, and Hernandez looked at me. 'Where you gonna be?'

'I'll hang around out here unless you want company.'

Tyler called from the porch. 'Would you and the other officer like some iced tea?'

Hernandez smiled at her. 'That'd be real nice, miss. Thank you.' Tyler ducked back inside. Hernandez stared after her. Portrait of the crime scene as a social occasion.

Two detectives from the L.A. County Sheriff's Office arrived, followed almost immediately by a criminalist van. The lead detective was a heavyset guy with thinning hair named Don Phillips. A DA's car came next, off-loading a thin woman named Sherman, a bald guy named Stu Miller, and an intense African-American guy in dark glasses named Warren Bidwell. Sherman was the Assistant Deputy DA charged with prosecuting the Teddy Martin case. Miller and Bidwell worked for her.

All three of them slipped under the tape and went into Richards' duplex, then Miller and Sherman slipped out again and came over to me. Tyler gave them a bright smile and pushed aside her bangs. 'Would either of you like iced tea?'

Sherman said, 'No.' She squinted at me. 'I'm Anna Sherman from the district attorney's office and this is Stu Miller. Would you come inside, please?'

'Sure.'

Tyler said, 'Can I come, too?'

Anna Sherman said, 'No.'

I shrugged at Tyler and followed them.

Inside, Sherman said, 'Okay. Walk me through what happened.'

I told them about getting the address from Pavlavi and finding the duplex deserted and popping the lock to let myself in. I told them about finding the envelope under the couch cushions and opening the envelope. Sherman stopped me. 'You touched the envelope?'

'That's right.'

The criminalist said, 'What about the contents?'

I shook my head. 'Edges only. When I saw what I had I slid the stuff out onto the couch. I used my knuckles to separate the pages first time through. When I photographed the material I was wearing gloves.'

Bidwell was glowering so hard his body was making little jerks and lurches and I wondered if he knew he was doing it. He said, 'I want those photographs.'

I shook my head. 'I don't think so.'

Bidwell lurched harder. 'You don't? Are you a sworn officer? You have a search warrant or any authority to break into a private residence?'

I looked at Sherman. 'You want me to continue or should I call my lawyer?'

Sherman closed her eyes and shook her head. 'Not now, Warren.'

The yard and the walk outside grew crowded with cops and media people and rubberneckers from the neighborhood drawn by gathering news vans. Between questions I watched the on-air television talent fan out among the cops. A woman I'd seen a thousand times on the local NBC affiliate was talking with her camera operator when the camera operator saw me standing in the window and pointed me out. The reporter said something and the operator trained his camera on me. The reporter ducked past Flutey and hurried over to the window. She was all frosted hair and intelligent eyes. 'Are you the detective who found the kidnappers?'

I gave her Bill Dana. 'My name José Jimenez.'

She waved her camera operator closer. 'Look, we know that two men named Elton Richards and Steve Pritzik lived here and we'd like an on-camera statement.' The camera operator held the camera over his head, trying to scan the room.

Don Phillips saw the camera coming through the window and said, 'Jesus Christ!' He pushed in front of me, then leaned out the window and yelled at a uniformed sergeant. 'Clear the area, for Christ's sake. Seal it off from the street back.' The sergeant hustled away, and Phillips looked at me. 'Are you trying to be cute?'

I spread my hands. 'Trying has nothing to do with it.'

The uniforms were pushing the press and gawkers along the walk when a ripple spread up from the street and across the crowd as if someone had amped a jolt of electricity through the air. Heads turned and voices rose, and the TV people surged toward the street. Phillips said, 'Now what?'

Jonathan Green and Elliot Truly and the videographer from *Inside News* were working their way through the crowd. The videographer's sound tech was trying her best to move people out of their way, but it was hard going until Hernandez and Flutey and a couple of other uniforms lent a hand. Anna Sherman came to the window, then gathered Bidwell and Miller for a whispered conference. When Green and the others pushed their way through the front door past the uniformed sergeant, Phillips said, 'Where in hell do you think you're going?'

Anna Sherman came over and smiled tightly. 'Let them pass, detective.' She offered her hand. 'Hello, Mr Green.'

'Ms Sherman.' Jonathan Green smiled at me. 'Congratulations, son. I think you've made my day.' The videographer bumped into Phillips as he tried to get the shot, and Phillips shoved him away. Hard. The videographer said, 'Hey.'

Anna Sherman said, 'Detective Phillips, this is Jonathan Green. Mr Green represents Theodore Martin.'

Phillips said, 'How about that.'

Jonathan and Truly went to the couch and leaned over the papers without touching them. Phillips said, 'Don't touch anything. We haven't printed them yet.'

Truly was grinning wildly and shaking his head. 'This is wonderful. Would you look at this? This is absolutely fabulous.' He grinned at me and then he grinned at Sherman, only Sherman didn't return it.

Green said, 'Mr Cole, are these the same documents you found when you entered this residence?' He said it loudly so that everyone in the room could hear.

'Yes.'

Green motioned to videographer. 'Would you get a close up of this, please?'

The videographer almost tripped over himself getting there. Bidwell said, 'Who *is* this dork?'

Truly said, 'They're from *Inside News*. They're doing a documentary on Jonathan.'

Bidwell said, 'Oh, for God's sake,' and shook his head.

As the videographer panned the evidence, Jonathan looked back at me. 'There are no new documents, and none of the documents you found are now missing?'

'Of course not.'

The videographer panned up to Jonathan, and Jonathan said, 'Mr Cole photographed the documents found in this envelope before the police were summoned. That photographic record constitutes an accurate accounting of exactly what was here before the police took possession of the evidence. We intend to compare those photographs with these to see if the evidence has been tampered with.'

Phillips went red. 'Hey, what the fuck?'

Anna Sherman told him to shut up. She said that if Phillips couldn't control himself he should go outside.

Phillips said, 'I know what he's saying and I don't like it. I run a clean house, goddammit.' He was purple.

Sherman said something to Bidwell and Bidwell led Phillips out.

They had me go through it again, Jonathan Green and Elliot Truly asking questions and the videographer and the sound tech recording me. Anna Sherman listened with her arms crossed, occasionally digging her heel into the floor and rocking her foot, and, like Green and Truly, occasionally asking more questions. Bidwell and Phillips came back, but this time Phillips kept his mouth shut and glowered at us from the corner. When I was done, Jonathan Green looked at Sherman again and said, 'We'll want these documents preserved, and we'll want to examine them as soon as practicable. We'll want the results of your fingerprint analysis, and then, of course, we'll want to do our own.'

Anna Sherman's jaw was tight. 'Of course.'

'Do you have anything more for Mr Cole?'

The criminalist said, 'I asked Cole for permission to take his prints. He said okay.'

Green nodded. 'Please do it now in our presence.' The criminalist broke out his fingerprint kit and had me sit on one of the dinette chairs. He took my prints quickly and professionally, then gave me a Handiwipe to clean off the ink. The videographer recorded every moment. I said, 'Don't you ever run out of tape?'

The sound tech laughed.

Green walked back to the couch, again examined the papers without touching them, then looked back at Sherman. 'You realize what we have here, don't you, Anna?' The patient father.

Anna Sherman did not respond. The pouty daughter.

Jonathan Green smiled. 'If you don't, Ms Sherman, I'm sure the district attorney will. Tell him I'll expect his call soon, if you would.'

Her jaw flexed.

Green said, 'I think we can go, Elliot. Mr Cole's had a long and fruitful day. I expect he wants to go home.'

Phillips coughed loudly from his corner of the room, but the cough soundly suspiciously like, 'Fuck you.'

I followed them out. The street at the end of the walk was jammed with media people and broadcast vans and uniformed cops trying to clear a path. Hernandez and Flutey flanked Jonathan and we crossed under the tape, and the media people surged around us, pushing their cameras and microphones at Jonathan and shouting their questions. There were so many broadcast vans that it looked as if we were in a forest of transmitters, each spindly stack pointing at the same invisible satellite 22,500 miles above in geosynchronous orbit, like so many coyotes crying at the moon. I said, 'This is nuts.'

Truly yelled in my ear so that I could hear him. 'It hasn't even begun.'

The woman with the frosted hair jammed her microphone past Hernandez and shouted, 'Jonathan, can you tell us what was found?'

'I'm sorry. That information should come from the district attorney's office.'

She yelled, 'Is it true that a plan of Teddy Martin's house was found?'

'I'm sorry.' We were working our way toward Jonathan Green's Rolls-Royce.

A short man who himself had been an attorney before becoming a broadcast journalist shouted, 'Jonathan? Is it true that evidence found in the house exculpates Theodore Martin in the murder of his wife?'

Jonathan smiled benignly. 'I've seen the evidence that Mr Cole found, and I'll be in consultation with the district attorney's office sometime in the next few days. Now, if you'll excuse me.'

More questions exploded at us from a dozen directions, and they were all about Mr Cole.

I didn't think Jonathan was going to answer, but he stopped and put his hand on my shoulder and said, 'This is Mr Elvis Cole of the Elvis Cole Detective Agency, and I believe that his discovery is going to be the breakthrough that we need. I can't tell you how proud I am of this young man, and how impressed I am with the caliber of his work.'

I said, 'Gee.'

The microphones shifted toward me as one and the questions came so fast and loud that the words blended into white noise. I was pretty sure that no one heard me say, 'Gee.' I may have said it twice.

Green said, 'All we can say at this time is that we received a tip through our hotline, and Mr Cole followed it to this conclusion.' He squeezed my shoulder again as if I were his son and I'd just made Eagle Scout. 'What we have here is the result of good, solid detective work, and I suspect that when all is said and done Mr Cole will be the hero of this little drama.'

Truly added, 'And Teddy Martin the victim.'

Jonathan slid into his Rolls-Royce, and then Truly and the two uniforms walked me to my car. The press stayed with us, jostling and shoving and keeping up with the questions. We had to push a fat guy and two women away from my car to get the door open. Flutey lost her hat. Truly said, 'Screen your calls. If anyone gets through to you, refer them to our office. Jonathan is the only one who deals with the press. Do you have a problem with that?'

'No.'

'It should die down in a few days.'

'And if it doesn't?'

Truly shrugged. 'Enjoy the idolatry. You earned it, my friend. You really came through for us.'

A tall thin guy from one of the national networks yelled, 'Hey, Sherlock Holmes! Are you really that good or did you just get lucky?'

I said, 'Some idol.'

Truly laughed and I climbed into my car and drove away. Slowly. I almost ran over a cameraman.

14

I pulled into the carport at two minutes after six that evening. The TV
was on, and Lucy and Ben were at the dining table, Lucy still in her
business suit and Ben wearing a *Songbird* T-shirt. The cat was nowhere to
be found, but that was probably just as well. If he'd been home, Lucy and
Ben would probably need stitches.

Lucy smiled when she saw me and said, 'It's the world's greatest
detective. Congratulations, Sherlock.'

Ben jumped up and clapped. 'We saw you on television!'

I said, 'How do you know it was me? Maybe it was an imposter.'

Lucy crossed her arms and considered me. 'Now that you mention it,
the man on television was devastatingly handsome and darkly mysterious.'

I said, 'Oh. That was me.'

Lucy was beaming. 'We just turned on the news and there you were.
You and Jonathan Green. Was it exciting?'

'Being with Jonathan?'

'No, silly! They said you made some kind of breakthrough that might
turn the case around. Jonathan said that you were the finest investigator
he's ever worked with.'

I tried to look blasé and stifled a yawn. 'Oh, that.'

She punched me in the arm. 'Be serious.'

I gave her a kiss. 'There were so many reporters I thought I'd have to
shoot my way out.' I gave her a second kiss and then a nuzzle. 'Enough
about me. How was your day?'

'It was good. We'll meet again the day after tomorrow, then perhaps
once more, so there's plenty of time to play.' She was surrounded by
tourist brochures and tour books with Post-Its and a list of things to see
and do.

I looked at her list. They wanted to see my office and visit both
Disneyland and Universal Studios and take in a Dodgers game and eat a
hot dog at Pink's on LaBrea in Hollywood. They wanted to ride the roller
coasters at Magic Mountain and go to Malibu and spend a day at the

beach. They wanted to see the Venice boardwalk and Beverly Hills and Rodeo Drive. They wanted to see Griffith Observatory, where James Dean had his famous knife fight in *Rebel Without a Cause*, and the Hollywood sign. They wanted to see Ronald Colman's house. I said, 'Ronald Colman?'

Lucy said, 'Of course, silly. We can't miss that.' She was marking yet more things as I watched. She would finger through the tour books and refer to notes and frown as she juggled alternatives and weighed options and planned the Great L.A. Adventure. She glanced at me, then went back to the Frommer's, then came back to me again. She said, 'What are you smiling at?'

'How I Spent My Summer Vacation.'

She closed the Frommer's on a finger and looked miserable. 'There's so much.'

'Too much. You're never going to do all that in the few days that you have.'

She put down the Frommer's. 'What are your suggestions?'

'Visit more often.'

She smiled and patted my hand. 'What are your suggestions for *now?*'

'For now, how about dinner at Spago? For tomorrow, how about the Universal tour with lunch at the Universal City Walk, then either Beverly Hills and Rodeo Drive or Malibu and dinner at the beach?'

She looked longingly at the Frommer's. 'Couldn't we squeeze in Ronald Colman?'

I leaned close and lowered my voice so that Ben couldn't hear. 'We could, but that would fill the forty-five minutes I've alloted for lovemaking.' I stepped back and spread my hands. 'Your call.'

She frowned and drummed the table. 'We didn't need forty-five minutes last time.' Everyone's a comedian.

She shrugged and frowned like it was the trade-off of the century. 'Okay. Forget Ronald Colman.'

Ben said, 'Hey! You're on TV again!'

Lucy grabbed my hand. 'Oh, look!'

I looked as the local anchor said that there had been a 'surprise development today' in the Theodore Martin murder investigation that might 'derail the prosecution's case.' They cut to a clip of Elton Richards's duplex and the frosty-haired remote reporter took over. You could see me talking with Hernandez and Flutey in the background. Ben and Lucy both yelled, '*There you are!*'

The reporter told us that a private investigator working for the Big Green Defense Machine had followed a tip to evidence that implicated two El Monte men in the kidnapping/murder of Susan Martin. She referred to notes and said, 'We've learned that the two men are Stephen Pritzik and Elton Richards, both of whom have lengthy criminal records.'

The image shifted to grainy mugshots of Pritzik and Richards. Pritzik looked narrow and mean; Richards looked stupid. Lucy said, 'Oh, those guys are choice.'

The reporter said, 'Sources close to the investigation tell us that the evidence found here today provides a direct link between these men and Susan Martin's kidnapping.' They cut to a clip of me and Jonathan Green standing by Jonathan's Rolls-Royce, Jonathan with his hand on my shoulder, saying that I had found the breakthrough that the defense has needed. Both Lucy and Ben cheered again when Jonathan said it, and Lucy hooked her finger in my belt loop. I thought that I looked like a turnip head.

The anchor reappeared, said that the two men were being sought for questioning, then shifted to a story about sweatshops in East L.A.

I said, 'Shucks. He didn't put in the part where Jonathan said I would be the hero of the case.'

Lucy tugged at my belt loop. 'So what did you find?'

I told her about the map and the pictures. Lucy wasn't smiling now. She looked grave, and then she shook her head. 'Wow.'

I nodded.

'Do you think you'll be able to come out and play with us tomorrow?'

'I'll call Jonathan in the morning. I'll have to follow up on Pritzik and Richards, but it shouldn't take all day. Maybe just half a day.'

We stared at each other.

She held out her hand, and I took it. She said, 'It's okay, Studly. I understand.'

'I'll grab a shower and we'll eat.'

I phoned Spago for a reservation, then showered, changed, and when I came back down she was grinning. I said, 'What?'

Grinning wider. 'Nothing.'

'What?'

'Just a little surprise. Let's go.'

It was almost eight by the time we made it down the mountain, and the sky was deep purple edging into darkness. The Sunset Strip was alive with middle-aged hipsters driving Porsches to show off for women twenty years younger and goateed Val Dudes chasing the Christian Slater look and young women sporting navel rings set fire by the neon. The sidewalks outside of clubs like the Viper Room and the House of Blues and the Roxy were jammed with people, some of whom wanted to get in but most of whom were content to make the concrete scene out front, laughing and goofing and tossing back test-tube shooters of red dye number six vodka. Ben said, 'Mom, look! There's a man with a bone through his nose.'

I said, 'Welcome to Planet Los Angeles.'

Lucy shook her head and smiled. 'Well, it isn't Baton Rouge, is it?'

'Wait'll you see Melrose.'

'It's fun, though. Sort of like Mardi Gras three hundred sixty-five nights a year.'

'Yeah,' I said. 'L.A. is okay that way.'

She turned back to me. Serious. 'Do you like living here?'

'If I didn't, I wouldn't.'

She stared at me for a moment, then she nodded and turned back toward the window. 'Yes, I guess you wouldn't.'

We pulled into Spago and let the valet have the car. Lucy suggested that I wear my Groucho Marx nose as a disguise to prevent adoring fans from mobbing me, but I pointed out that then everyone might think I was Groucho Marx and I would be mobbed anyway. I decided to risk going as myself.

We went upstairs for very nice Caesar salads and duck sausage pizza and a pretty good merlot. Johnny Depp was there with several friends, and so were three of the cast members of *Beverly Hills 90210*. No one stared at me and no one asked for my autograph and no one took my picture. Everyone was looking at Johnny Depp. Even the *90210* people. Disappointing, but maybe the people who go to Spago don't watch the news.

Lucy said, 'Perhaps you should've worn the Groucho after all.'

'Perhaps.'

She patted my arm. 'Don't feel bad, sweetie. They would recognize you if all these *faux* celebrities weren't here.'

'Yeah.' I sneered. 'Johnny Depp.'

Throughout the meal Lucy would grin with the knowledge of her secret, and I would ask, 'What?' and she would say, 'You'll see.' Then everyone stopped looking at Johnny Depp and turned toward the door. Lucy grinned wider, and I looked, too.

Joe came over, gliding across the floor as the room parted for him. Tall men in sleeveless sweatshirts and dark glasses and brilliant red tattoos tend to stand out in Spago. Even Johnny Depp was looking.

Lucy stood to greet him. 'Hi, Joseph.'

Joe kissed Lucy's cheek, hugged her, then shook Ben's hand. 'You ready, sport?'

'Yeah!'

I said, 'What's going on?'

Joe swiveled my way, and you could tell he was amused. You could see that he was positively dying, even though his face showed nothing. 'Peter Nelsen's down in the car. Peter and I are taking Big Ben to a screening of Peter's new movie.' Peter Alan Nelsen is the third most successful movie director in the world. Once he was a client, but now he's a friend.

I looked at Lucy.

Joe said, 'We won't be back until late.'

I looked back at Joe.

'Very late.'

Lucy gave Ben a hug. 'You guys have fun.'

Joe's mouth gave the twitch, and then he and Ben were gone.

I looked back at Lucy, and she said, 'Alone time is very important.'

'You called him while I was in the shower?'

'Uh-huh.'

'I knew there was something I liked about you.'

She sipped her wine. 'I think that there's something you like very much about me.'

We enjoyed a slow, noisy dessert with Lucy and I playing footsie under the table. We spoke in greater detail about her day and mine, and I told her about the Mason twins and the Pug Woman and the man who claimed to have seen Susan Martin's kidnapping from the orb. I didn't often speak of my work, but it seemed natural with Lucy, and as we talked we laughed and goofed about orb people and stroked each other's hands and arms and fingers. The time passed with the slow, warm feel of dripping honey, and finally Lucy wrapped my feet with hers and said, 'Maybe we should go.'

We left Spago at 10:35, and when we got home Lucy went into her room and I put Janis Ian on the CD player, then poured a merlot that would go nicely with the one we'd had at Spago.

When Lucy came out she had changed into shorts and a cropped T-shirt that said *Tank Girl* and silver evening slippers with four-inch heels. The lights were low and Janis was singing. Lucy did a slow pirouette. 'Is the world's greatest detective tired after his long and successful day?'

I watched the pirouette. I watched the way the warm light caught her back and hair and the long, smooth line of her legs and the sexy counterpoint of the formal evening slippers to the shorts and T-shirt. 'He was, but now he feels a growing revitalization.'

'Ah. Is that what's growing?'

'One way to look at it.' I held out the merlot and Lucy took a sip. I said, 'Nice shoes.'

Lucy brushed against me, swaying to the music. The merlot left a sweet, rich taste in my mouth that I liked a lot. She said, 'You'll probably be on the news again at eleven. Shall we turn on the TV and see?'

I shook my head. 'Seeing me once is plenty. Besides, something else is already turned on.'

'Ah.'

'I think I'm ready for the rest of my surprise.'

She took my hand and tugged me toward the big glass doors. Outside, the sky was clear, and would be filled with stars.

I said, 'The deck?'

She let her hair fall across one eye. 'I thought your middle name was Adventure.'

'So it is.'

I followed her out, and what I found there tasted better than any wine, and was more beautiful than the stars.

15

Lucy and Ben woke giggling and excited and filled with plans. As they readied for their day, I phoned Elliot Truly at his office. 'It's Cole. Has there been word on Pritzik or Richards?'

'Not yet, but there'll be something soon.' He sounded distracted.

'I was thinking that I'd go back to Richards's place and talk to some of the neighbors, but the police will be there and they won't like it. Maybe Jonathan could talk to Sherman and smooth the way in the spirit of cooperation.'

Truly didn't say anything for a moment. 'Why do you want to go back there?'

'To try to get a lead on Pritzik and Richards.'

'Forget it. We're talking with the cops. We've got Kerris on it. Take the day off and relax.' I could hear voices behind him.

'It's a cold trail already, Elliot. We shouldn't let it get any colder.'

'Look, you just said that the entire area will be swarming with cops. We've got a staff meeting here in a couple of minutes to try to figure out what to do next. Jonathan's trying to get a meeting with the DA.'

'What does that have to do with finding Pritzik and Richards?'

'Take the day off, enjoy yourself, and I'll get back to you.'

'You want me to do nothing.'

'Yeah. What could be better than that?' He hung up, and I stared at the phone.

Lucy said, 'What's wrong?'

I looked at the phone some more and then I put it down. 'Not a thing. I get to spend the day with you. What could be better than that?'

Their excitement was contagious. We made a fast breakfast of sliced fruit and cottage cheese and toast, and then we dressed in shorts and light shirts and baseball caps for the always popular Ralph Cramden look. I considered bringing my Dan Wesson .38 caliber revolver, but thought it unsightly strapped over my flowered shirt. Besides, blue steel wheel guns aren't exactly requisite tourist attire in southern California. Florida maybe, but not yet California.

It was early, so we decided to see my office first, then head for the Universal tour. We took Lucy's rented Taurus down Laurel Canyon, then along Sunset toward the office. The sky was free of haze and smog, and more blue than white because of it. A great V of gulls floated above West Hollywood, heading toward the sea, and the streets were busy with cars sporting out-of-state license plates and people with camcorders and young Middle Eastern guys selling maps to the stars' homes. Summer had come to the City of Angels.

When we turned onto Santa Monica one block up from my office, we saw two television news vans parked at the curb in front of my building. I said, 'Uh-oh.'

Lucy said, 'Do you think they're here for you?'

'I don't know.' Maybe they were here for Cindy. Maybe they wanted to do a story about hot new beauty supply products.

'You don't want to speak to them?'

Jonathan's the only person on the team who talks to the press.'

I pulled past the vans. A very attractive young Asian-American woman was on the sidewalk talking to a guy holding a Minicam, and a guy who looked like a surfer in a sport coat was smoking with a scruffy woman in a work shirt. I pulled to the curb on the next block, asked Lucy for her cell phone, and called Cindy's office. Cindy answered on the first ring and said, 'Wow, are you ever the big deal.'

'Have they been upstairs?'

'All morning. They knock on your door and when you don't answer they come to me or the insurance people and ask about your hours.' The insurance people had the office across the hall. 'That was a great picture in the paper.'

'I'm in the paper?'

'You haven't seen it?'

'Uh-uh.' Mr With-it. Mr Hip L.A. Private Eye with his fingers on the pulse.

'Oh, man, you look so cool. And I saw you on TV, too. I saw you *twice.*' Even Cindy was excited.

'Is anyone upstairs now?'

'Yeah. There's a guy sitting in the hall. I think he's from a radio station.'

I thanked her and handed back Lucy's phone. Lucy was looking at me. 'They're upstairs?'

I nodded. 'You mind if we don't go up? I'll show you guys my office another time.'

She patted my leg and put away her phone. 'Another time is fine, Studly. I want to see my man in the paper.'

We stopped at a Sav-on drugstore where we bought the *Times,* the *Examiner,* and the *Daily News,* then stood in the parking lot, reading.

Elton Richards, Steve Pritzik, and the discovery I'd made in Richards's duplex were front-page news in all three papers. A picture of me with Jonathan Green was on page one of both the *Examiner* and the *Daily News* and on page three of the *Times*. Guess the people at the *Times* had higher standards. Lucy said, 'Oh, Elvis. This is so exciting.'

I said, 'Um.'

'Aren't you proud?'

'It's kinda neat, I guess.' I held up the paper next to my face and frowned. 'Do I look like Moe Howard?'

Lucy compared me to the picture, then nodded. 'Yes. Yes, I think you do.'

A round man with thick glasses and a nervous tic walked past, staring. He went to a brown Cressida, still staring, then called out, 'Hey, are you that guy?'

I folded the paper and tossed it in the car.

'I read about what you did. I saw you on the news. That was good work.'

I gave a little wave. 'Thanks.'

He said, 'These cops here in L.A. suck, don't they?'

I frowned at him. 'Some of my best friends are cops.'

He made a nasal, braying laugh, then climbed into his car and drove away.

I opened the door for Lucy and we drove east across West Hollywood and Hollywood, and then up through the Cahuenga Pass to Universal Studios. We parked in one of the big parking structures with about twelve million other tourists, then followed along with what seemed an endless stream of people to the ticket kiosks and then into yet more lines that led to the trams. It made me feel like a lemming.

We rode the trams around the Universal back lot and took goofy pictures of ourselves posing with giant toothpaste tubes and rode little cars past screeching dinosaurs and gargantuan gorillas, and then Lucy said, 'I feel the urge to spend.'

I looked at her. 'Spend?'

Ben made as if he was horrified. 'Not that, Mom! Not that! Try to control it!'

Lucy's eyes narrowed in concentration and her gaze went blank. 'The shopping gene is beyond all control. Souvenirs. *I must have souvenirs!*'

It was horrible to behold. Lucy bought; I carried. Three T-shirts, two sweatshirts, and a snow-shaker paperweight later, we had exhausted the selection in the upper park and trekked down to CityWalk in search of more booty. The CityWalk is a large, open-air mall with shops, bookstores, restaurants, and other fine places to spend your money. Some people have described the CityWalk as an urban version of Disney's Main

Street U.S.A., but I've always thought of it as a G-rated take on *Blade Runner*. Only without the rain.

It was just before noon when we got there, and, like the park above, the CityWalk was thick with tour groups from Asia and visitors from around the country. We walked the length of the CityWalk, browsing in the shops and watching the people, Lucy and I holding hands while Ben ranged around us. It felt good to be not working and good to be with Lucy. I said, 'Do you think you can rein in your spending spree long enough to eat?'

She looked at me the way the cat does when I take his bowl before he's finished.

'I may not be able to carry this stuff much longer without an infusion of calories.'

'You'll manage.'

'We may have to hire porters.'

'It's only money.'

'We may have to stop spending.'

She made a big sigh and rolled her eyes. 'Modern men are such wimps.'

I leaned close to her ear. 'That's not what you said last night on the deck.'

Lucy laughed and hugged my arm tight, biting my shoulder through the shirt. 'O.K., Studly, your wish is my command. Where would you like to eat?'

'You said that last night, too.'

She dug her thumb in my ribs and said, 'Shh! Ben!'

'He didn't hear. C'mon. There's a Puck's ahead. We can eat there.'

'Puck's! Oh, goody!'

We went to Wolfgang Puck's and stood in line for a table. Everyone around us was from Iowa or Canada or Japan, and no one seemed to have seen the news or read the paper or, if they had, didn't care. There was plenty of outdoor seating, and the people at the tables were enjoying salads and sandwiches.

We worked our way up the line to a pretty blonde hostess who told us that it would be just another minute when I caught an overweight guy staring at me. He was sitting at one of the tables, eating shredded chicken salad and reading a *Times*. He looked from me to the paper, then back to me. He stopped a passing waitress, showed her the paper, then they both looked at me. I turned so that I was facing the opposite direction. Lucy said, 'Those people are looking at you.'

'Great.'

'I think they recognize you.'

'I know.'

'He's pointing at you.'

The Korean couple behind us looked at me, too. I guess they saw the pointing. I smiled and nodded at them, and they smiled back.

Lucy said, 'Ohmigod, he's showing the paper to the people at the next table.'

I touched the hostess's arm. 'Do you think you could find us a table, please. Inside or out. First available.'

'Let me check.' She disappeared into the restaurant.

Lucy said, 'Maybe we should run for it.'

'Very funny.'

'We could leave. I don't mind.'

'No. You want Puck's, we're going to eat at Puck's.'

An older couple behind the Korean people craned around to see what all the looking and pointing was about. The woman looked from me to the people with the newspaper, then back to me. She said something to her husband and he shrugged. I turned the other way, and now the heavy man with the newspaper was locked in conversation with a table of six people, all of whom were twisted around in their seats to see me. I said, 'This is nuts.'

Lucy was smiling.

I said, 'This isn't funny.'

The woman behind the Korean couple said, 'Excuse me. Are you somebody?'

I said, 'No.'

She smiled at me. 'You're an actor, aren't you? You're on that show.'

Lucy began one of those silent laughs where your face goes red and you're trying not to but can't help yourself.

I said, 'I'm not. Really.'

'Then why is everybody looking at you?'

'It's a long story.'

The woman gave me huffy. 'Well, it's not very friendly of you, if you ask me, snubbing your public like this.'

Lucy leaned toward the woman. 'He can be just horrible, can't he? I talk to him about it all the time.'

I stared at her.

The woman said, 'Well, you should. It's so unkind.'

Lucy gave me a little push. 'Why don't you give her an autograph.'

I stared harder. 'You're some kind of riot, you know that?'

Lucy nodded. Brightly.

The woman said, 'Oh, that would be just so nice.' She gestured to her husband. 'Merle, we have a pen, don't we?' She shoved a pen and a souvenir napkin from Jodi Maroni's sausage kitchen at me to sign. The Korean couple were talking in Korean to each other, the man searching frantically through a shoulder bag.

532

I took the napkin and leaned close to Lucy. 'I'm going to get you for this.'

She turned away so no one could see her breaking up. 'Oh, I really, really hope you do.'

Ben said, 'Mom? Why are these people looking at Elvis?'

The older woman's eyes grew large. 'You're *Elvis?*'

The Korean woman held out an autograph book and the Korean man began taking pictures. Two teenaged girls who were seated behind the party of six saw me signing the Jodi Maroni napkin and came over, and then two younger guys from the table of six followed. A tall, thin man across the restaurant stood up at his table and aimed his video camera at me. His wife stood with him. An Hispanic couple passing on the CityWalk stopped to see what was going on, and then three young women who looked like they'd come up to the CityWalk on their lunch hour stopped, too. A woman with very loose upper arms pointed at me and told her friend, 'Oh, I just love his movies, don't you?' She said it loudly.

The heavy man with the newspaper who had started it got up and walked away. Lucy and Ben were walking away, too. Quickly. Off to ruin someone else's life, no doubt.

The crowd grew. I signed twenty-two autographs in four minutes, and they were the longest four minutes of my life. I finally begged off by announcing that as much as I enjoyed meeting them, the President required my counsel and so I must leave. When I said it the woman with the loose arms said, 'I didn't know he was in politics, too!'

When I finally found Lucy and Ben they were well along the CityWalk, grinning and walking fast away from me.

I said, 'Lucille Chenier, you can run but you can't hide.' I said it loud enough for them to hear.

Lucy and Ben laughed, and then they ran.

16

After another $182.64 in souvenirs, postcards, and gifts, Lucy called Baton Rouge to check her messages. I was hoping that there might be word on Pritzik or Richards, so I phoned my office, also. Sixteen messages were waiting for me. Of the sixteen, seven were from newspeople asking for interviews and five were from friends who had seen me on the news. Of the remaining four calls, two were hang-ups and two were from Elliot Truly. On the first hang-up a woman's voice said, 'Oh, shit,' and on the second the same voice said, 'Just eat me!' The voice was muffled and irritated. Truly's secretary left the first message from his office, asking me to return the call. Truly himself left the second message, saying, 'Cole? Cole, if you're there, pick up. This is important.' I guess Truly was irritated, too. Maybe I bring it out in people.

I returned Truly's call. When he came on the line he said, 'Thank Christ! I've been trying to reach you all day. Where have you been?' He sounded frantic.

'You told me to take the day off, remember?'

'Yeah, well, we don't want you to do that anymore. Channel Eight wants to interview you on the evening news and Jonathan thinks it would be a good idea.'

I said, 'Go on television?'

'It's maybe three minutes on the four o'clock newscast, and Jonathan wants you to do it.'

'Truly, I made plans. I've got guests from out of town.'

'Look, the team talked about this today and we want the press to have access to you. Either we're going to control the media or the district attorney's office will, and we'd rather it be us. Openness is important. Honesty is everything. That's all we have going for us.'

I was sorry that I had returned his call.

'They want to know how some guy all by himself beat the entire LAPD at their own game.'

'I didn't beat anybody. I followed a tip and got lucky.' Lucy had finished her call and was looking at me.

'Right. That's why you scored the breakthrough while eight thousand blue suits were sopping up coffee and donuts.'

'I didn't beat anyone, Truly.' He was getting on my nerves with that.

'All you have to do is sit there and be likable. People like you; you're a likable guy. That's all they care about. It's TV.'

I cupped the receiver and told Lucy, 'They want me to give a television interview this afternoon, and it'll interfere with going to Beverly Hills.'

Lucy smiled and rubbed my arm. 'If you have to you have to. We'll do Beverly Hills after.'

'It'll cut into your shopping time. Are you sure?'

She smiled again. 'We'll come watch you get interviewed. It'll be fun.'

Truly said, 'What did you say?'

'Relax, Elliot. I'll do it.'

Truly said, 'It's almost three now and they want you at Channel Eight by four-thirty. Grab a pencil and let me tell you where to go.'

Truly gave me the directions. Lucy, Ben, and I drove home, changed, then made our way back down the mountain to Channel Eight's broadcast studio just east of Western in Hollywood. KROK-TV. *Personal News from Us to You – We take it personally!*

We parked in the lot beside the building, then walked in the front entrance to a receptionist seated in a bulletproof glass booth. The lobby was walled off from the rest of the building with more heavy glass, and there was a big door next to the receptionist that she would have to buzz open to let you enter. I wondered if anyone had ever tried to shoot their way in. *Put me on the news or die!* You never know.

I told her who I was and why I was there, and a few minutes later a woman in her early forties appeared and opened the door from the inside. She said, 'Hi. I'm Kara Sykes, the news director. Are you Mr Cole?'

'That's right. This is Lucy Chenier and her son, Ben. They're with me.' I was holding Lucy's hand.

Kara Sykes held the door. 'That's fine. You'll go on in a few minutes, so we don't have much time. Please come this way.'

We followed her down a long hall, then through a newsroom filled with desks and production people and onto the news set. A man and a woman were seated at the anchor desk, facing cameras fitted with TelePrompTers. A floor director was standing between the cameras with his hand touching the TelePrompTer that the man was reading from. There were places at the anchor desk for a sportscaster and a weatherperson, but those seats were empty. The set was built so that the anchors were seated with their backs to the newsroom so the audience could see that the Channel Eight news team was bringing them personal news personally. Kara whispered, 'Lyle Stodge and Marcy Bernside are the five o'clock anchors. Lyle is going to interview you.'

'Okay.' Lyle Stodge was a rugged-looking guy in his early fifties, just going gray at the temples. Marcy Bernside was a profoundly attractive woman in her late thirties with dark hair, expressive eyes, and a wholesome, girl-next-door smile.

Kara said, 'Have you done a live interview before?'

'No.'

'It's no big deal. Just speak directly to Lyle. Don't look at the camera.'

'Okay.'

'I spoke with Jonathan, so I know how important this is. Everyone here is on your side.'

'My side?'

'Just relax and enjoy it. You're the man of the hour.'

Lucy squeezed my hand and whispered, 'I guess they heard how you were mobbed at Universal.'

Lucy's a riot, isn't she?

Lyle finished reading a story about illegal Taiwanese aliens found working in a sweatshop in Gardena, and Marcy began reading a story about Pritzik and Richards. She said that the police and the FBI had expanded their search into seven states, and that there was a growing though unofficial belief that Pritzik was, in fact, James X.

The floor director raised his hand, made a circling gesture, and Marcy Bernside said that Channel Eight's Personal News Team would return in just one minute. The director raised both hands, then announced, 'In commercial. We're clear.'

Marcy Bernside shouted, '*Fuck!* Who blew the feed to my *fucking* ear phone?' She twisted around to glare at the newsroom. 'Come on, Stuart. What're you assholes doing back there? Jesus *Christ!*' So much for wholesome.

Kara pulled my arm and said, 'Showtime.'

She hustled me to the anchor desk and had me sit in the sportscaster's vacant seat while the camera operators repositioned for a two-shot of me and Lyle. I could see Lyle's lines frozen on the TelePrompTer, waiting for the commercial to end. The floor director clipped a tiny microphone inside the lapel of my sport coat, then ran the wire under my jacket and plugged it into a larger cable that had been lying on the floor. Kara introduced me to Lyle Stodge who said, 'I'm glad that you could join us. You're quite a guy.'

I said, 'Will anyone notice if I make faces at the camera?'

Lyle Stodge shuffled loose yellow legal sheets. 'Don't worry about anything. I've done this ten thousand times, and I can make anyone look good. Even you.' I looked at Lucy and Lucy laughed. I looked back at Lyle Stodge and he winked. Another comedian.

A makeup person was adjusting Marcy Bernside's hair. Marcy was singing to herself and moving to the song as if she were alone in her home. She was singing the Z.Z. Topp song *Legs*. Nervous energy.

536

The floor director said, 'Ten seconds.' He raised his hand above Lyle's camera. Lyle straightened his jacket and leaned toward the camera. The makeup person left the set. Lyle said, 'Would you stop with the goddamned singing, for Christ's sake?'

Marcy Bernside gave him the finger and kept singing.

'Three, two, one –' The floor director touched the TelePrompTer and Lyle's script scrolled upward. Lyle made his patented crinkly-eyed smile at the camera. 'As we reported at the top of the hour, a private investigator working for the Big Green Defense Machine has made a startling discovery that may shed new light on the Theodore Martin murder investigation. He joins us now in a Channel Eight Personal News exclusive, bringing *you* the people who *make the news.*' Lyle turned the pleased smile toward me. 'Mr Elvis Cole, thank you for joining us in a Channel Eight Personal News exclusive.'

'Thanks, Lyle. It's good to be here.' Mr Sincerity.

Lyle laced his fingers and leaned toward me, getting down to serious journalistic business. 'How is it that one man working alone was able to uncover these things when the entire Los Angeles police department working for three months couldn't?'

'I followed a tip that Jonathan Green's office received on the hotline. If LAPD would've gotten the tip, they would've made the same discoveries, and probably sooner.'

Lyle chuckled good-naturedly. 'Sounds like you're being modest to me.' The chuckle vanished and Lyle turned serious again, cocking an eyebrow to let everyone know just how serious he was. 'Tell us, was it dangerous?'

'It's just meeting people and asking questions, Lyle. It's no more dangerous than crossing the street.'

Lyle made the chuckle again, then twisted around to smile at Marcy Bernside. 'Marce, I'll tell you, I've never met the real McCoy who liked to blow his own horn, have you?'

Marcy Bernside said, 'Never, Lyle. Real men let their deeds speak for themselves.'

Lyle twisted back to me. 'Theodore Martin has proclaimed his innocence from the beginning. Many people are now saying that your discovery proves him right.'

'It's another piece of the puzzle.'

Lyle leaned toward me, serious and professional. 'Many people are also saying that the LAPD botched this investigation, and now they're unwilling to admit their mistake.'

'LAPD is the finest police force in the nation, Lyle.'

Lyle nodded as if I'd just laid out the Unified Field Theory. 'Well, sir, we've checked into *your* background and learned that *you* certainly have

537

an excellent reputation, even among members of the police department and the district attorney's office.'

'Those guys. Did they really say that?'

Lyle nodded gravely. 'Personal News Eight is told that this isn't your first high-profile case. Apparently, you've worked in a confidential capacity for some very high-profile celebrities.'

'I never discuss my clients, Lyle. That's why it's called "confidential."'

Lyle squinted approvingly. 'A man of integrity.' He gave an encouraging smile. 'Most of us see private eyes on television or in movies but never get a chance to meet the real thing. Tell me, is it as exciting as it seems?'

'No.'

Lyle laughed. They paid him seven hundred thousand dollars a year for that laugh, and I wondered if he practiced it. 'Looks like you're a truthful man, as well. How does it feel to be compared to that famous, fictional Los Angeles detective, Raymond Marlowe?'

Marcy said, 'Philip Marlowe.'

Lyle looked confused and twisted to look at her again. I guess she'd said her bit and he hadn't expected her to speak again. 'What was that, Marce?'

'Raymond *Chandler* created *Philip* Marlowe.'

Lyle laughed again, but this time the laugh was strained. Guess you weren't supposed to correct the anchor while you were on the air. He twisted back to the camera and said, 'Well, it looks as if Los Angeles has found its very own Sherlock Homes, and, unfortunately, that's all the time we have for this segment.' Lyle Stodge offered his hand to me, and we shook as if he had just awarded me the Congressional Medal of Honor. 'Mr Cole, it's been my privilege to meet you. Congratulations, and thank you for taking the time to talk with us.'

'Thanks, Lyle. It's been personal.'

The floor director raised both hands. 'In promo. We're clear.'

Lyle Stodge glared at Marcy Bernside. 'You fucking cunt! Don't you ever do that to me again on air!'

Marcy Bernside gave him the finger again. 'It's Holmes, moron. Sherlock *Holmes*. With an *L*.'

'Oh, yeah, right. Sure.'

Kara Sykes unclipped my lapel mike and helped me off the set. No one gave me a second glance.

We followed Kara Sykes back to the lobby, then left the building and walked to the car. Lucy hugged my arm. 'That was almost as much fun as Beverly Hills.'

'Un.'

She stepped back and looked at me. She cocked her head. 'Are you okay, Studly?'

I said, 'Luce?'

'Mm?'

'If Truly wants me to do another of these, I'm going to shoot him to death. Will you represent me?'

She smiled sweetly. 'Oh, you know that I will, hon. You shoot him all you like.'

'Thanks, Luce.'

17

Lucy, Ben, and I spent the next two days seeing Disneyland and Malibu and the Griffith Observatory. We saw Ronald Colman's house. We shopped in Beverly Hills. I called Jonathan's office twice each day, asking to speak with either Jonathan or Truly, but neither was ever available. Busy, they said. In meetings. No one returned my calls.

I stayed away from my office because of the press. The answering machine was flooded with so many interview requests that I deleted them without playing them. The eat-me lady called back twice.

Elliot Truly's assistant phoned to arrange three more television interviews and two appearances on local talk radio. It's important to Jonathan, she said. We need our side of it known, she said. I asked her about Pritzik and Richards. I said that I wanted to know what was going on. She said that she would talk to Jonathan and get back to me. She didn't.

News reports questioning LAPD's investigative techniques appeared with greater frequency. A summer marine layer moved in, filling the morning sky with an oppressive layer of dark clouds. Sometimes they burned off by noon, but not always.

On the morning of the third day, Peter Alan Nelsen took Ben to spend the day on the set of his new movie and Lucy was dressing for her second meeting when the phone rang and Elliot Truly said, 'We're meeting with Teddy Martin at ten this morning in the Men's Central Jail. Teddy wants to meet you, and Jonathan would like you there. Can you make it?'

I said, 'What in hell is going on, Truly? How come no one returns my calls?'

'You're not the only investigator we have on this, Cole. We've been swamped. Jonathan's working sixteen hours a day.'

'I'm an investigator. I investigate. If you don't want me to investigate anymore, fine.' I was feeling sullen and petulant. Mr Maturity.

Truly said, 'Look, talk about it with Jonathan at the jail. One other thing. Jonathan's having a get-together at his home tonight, people who've been behind Teddy through this thing, some press people, like

540

that. Jonathan personally asked me to invite you. You can bring a date if you want.'

I cupped the phone and looked at Lucy. She was standing in the kitchen, dressed and Guccied and ready for business, eating peach yogurt. 'Would you like to go to a party at Jonathan Green's house tonight?'

Lucy blinked at me and the spoon froze between cup and mouth. 'Are you serious?'

'Truly just asked.'

She shook her head, the spoon forgotten. 'I don't have anything to wear to meet Jonathan Green.'

I uncupped the phone. 'Forget it, Truly. We can't make it.'

The yogurt cup hit the floor and Lucy grabbed my arm. 'I didn't say that! I'll get something!'

'My mistake, Truly. We'll be there.'

Truly said, 'Great. I'll see you at the jail. Ten o'clock.'

I smiled at Lucy. 'How about that? You'll get to meet Jonathan.'

Her eyes were glazed and distant. 'Ohmigod, what am I going to wear?'

'Wear what you have on. You look great.'

She shook her head. 'You don't understand. I'm going to meet Jonathan Green.'

I said, 'You've got time. Go to your meeting, then go into Beverly Hills. You'll find something.'

Lucy looked miserable. 'I wouldn't know where to go. It could take *days.*'

'Call Jodi. Jodi can tell you.'

Lucy's eyes widened and she latched onto my arm again. 'That's right. Jodi can save me!' I guess these things are relative.

Lucy set about arranging her salvation, and I drove down to my office. I hadn't been there in three days and wanted to check my mail and return calls. There weren't any news vans parked at the curb. Maybe my fifteen minutes of fame was over. Live in hope.

I locked the door in the outer office, then answered mail. Most of the mail was bills, but even World Famous Private Eyes have to pay their Visa charges. When the bills were done I was getting ready to return calls when the phone rang and I answered, 'Elvis Cole Detective Agency. Please leave a message at the sound of the beep. Beep.' The detective as Natural Born Wit.

There was a pause, and then a muffled woman's voice said, 'You're not a machine.' The eat-me lady.

'Who is this?'

'That weevil-dicked fuck James Lester is fulla shit. You find out about Stuart Langolier in Santa Barbara.' She was speaking through cloth, but I'd heard the voice before.

'El-ay-gee-oh . . .' Spelling it. 'No, wait . . . Capital el-ay-*en*-gee-oh-el-eye-ee-are.'

I said, 'Jonna?'

There was another pause, and then Jonna Lester hung up. I listened to the dial tone for several seconds, then called an investigator friend of mine named Toni Abatemarco who works at a large agency in Santa Barbara. Toni had worked as an investigator since the day she was old enough to get the license, and had hammered out twelve-hour days for years, building her small agency into one of Santa Barbara's finest. Then she met a guy, fell head over heels, and decided that she wanted a small herd of children. She sold the small agency to a larger outfit, had four little girls, and now worked three days a week for the organization that had bought her. She loved investigating, she loved being a mom, and the little girls often accompanied her to the office. They would probably grow up to be investigators, also.

I gave Toni the name, asked her to see what she could find, and then I went to jail.

The Men's Central Jail is an anonymous building behind Central Station, less than ten minutes from the Criminal Courts Building in downtown L.A. I parked in a neat, modern underground parking structure, then walked up steps to a very nice plaza. Nicely dressed people were sipping *lattes* and strolling about the plaza, and no one seemed to mind that the plaza adjoined a place housing felons and gangbangers and the wild men of an otherwise civil society. Perhaps because this is L.A. and the jail is so nice. There's a fountain in the plaza, and it's very nice, too.

Truly was waiting for me in the jail lobby. 'Jonathan and the others are in with Teddy. Come on. I've checked us in.'

'I'm carrying a gun.'

'Okay. Sure.' Like Terminal Island, you can't bring guns into the interview room or the holding areas.

We crossed the lobby past the deputies at the information desk to the gun locker, then went through the metal detector and flashed our IDs at the security gate. The guard there sits behind bulletproof glass and controls the metal doors that let you into or out of the interview area. He's the last guard that you'll see in the jail who has guns. He has shotguns, pistols, tasers, and CS gas. Preparation is everything.

The guard threw switches and the metal door crawled to the side. We stepped through into a room like a gray airlock, and then the door closed. When the door behind us was closed, the door in front of us opened and we stepped through into a large room sporting two long tables lined by metal stools. The tables were narrow and dark, sort of like public-school cafeteria tables, only with low vertical partitions running lengthwise down their centers. Inmates in orange jumpsuits sat on stools along the inside

542

of each table, staring across at the attorneys who sat opposite them. The vertical partition was supposed to make it hard for illegal contraband or weapons to be passed from one to another. Sometimes it worked. Another deputy sat behind glass in the far corner, keeping track of who came and who left and making sure that no one was stabbed to death. Sometimes that worked, too.

Everyday dirtbags had to sit in the big room at the long tables and talk about their cases with no privacy, but high-profile defendants like Teddy Martin rated a private interview room. I followed Truly along a short hall, then into a room that was not dissimilar to the one in which I had seen LeCedrick Earle at Terminal Island, only older and uglier and smelling of urine.

Jonathan Green said, 'Here he is now.'

The interview room was small and crowded. Stan Kerris, Green's chief of security, was leaning against the glass with his Fred Munster arms crossed. Jonathan Green was seated at a work table with one of the lesser attorneys and Teddy Martin. I had never met Teddy Martin before, but I knew him from his picture. Teddy Martin had a round, boyish face, a steeply receding hairline, and pale, soft skin. Theodore Martin looked like someone's younger brother grown older; a kind of nonguy who just happened to have built six family-owned hot dog stands into an empire. Truly said, 'Elvis Cole, this is Teddy Martin. Teddy, the man.'

Teddy Martin came around the table and offered his hand. He said, 'I don't know what to say except thank you.' His eyes were wide and kind of frantic. 'I did not kill my wife. I loved her, Cole. I tried to save her, do you see? They're blaming this thing on me, and it feels like you're the first one who's done anything to help me.'

'I'm glad we could finally meet.' He gripped my hand with both of his and pumped hard, as if hanging onto me was the most important thing in his life.

Green said, 'Theodore.'

Teddy Martin seemed to realize what he was doing and flushed. 'Sorry.' He let go and went back to the table.

I said, 'Why did you have me come down here?'

Green patted Teddy on the shoulder, much the way that he had patted me. 'Twofold. Teddy very much wanted to meet you, and I've arranged a press conference to take place in the plaza. The core of the team will be there, and I'd like you to be there, too.'

I looked at Kerris. The empty eyes were unimpressed. 'Press conferences are fine, Jonathan, but what about the investigation? I've called you guys five times, and nobody returns my calls.'

Jonathan Green's face stiffened ever so slightly, as if he wasn't used to being questioned and didn't like it.

Truly said, 'We're swamped. I told you.'

Jonathan waved his hand, cutting off Truly. 'What would you like to do?'

'Follow up Pritzik and Richards. Run down more hotline tips.'

Kerris shifted against the glass. 'I've got other people on Pritzik and Richards. I can give you all the hotline tips you want.'

Jonathan made the hand wave again. 'Let's not waste Mr Cole's time with that.' He left Teddy and sat on the edge of the table.

I said, 'The police and the feds are looking for Pritzik and Richards. We can launch a collaborative effort with them. The cops aren't our enemy.'

Jonathan spread his hands. 'If you want to work with the police, fine. If it helps us free Teddy any sooner, that's all to the good.'

I looked from Jonathan to Kerris to Truly. They were staring at me. The lesser attorney was staring at me, too. I said, 'There's something else. A woman I believe to be Jonna Lester called me. She said that James Lester was lying. She said that I should check into someone named Stuart Langolier.'

Jonathan nodded. 'By all means.' He looked at his watch. 'We really should be going now. Can't keep our friends in the press waiting.'

We said our good-byes to Theodore Martin, and walked out. Jonathan walked beside me. When we were out the door and down the hall, Jonathan said, 'A proper criminal defense effort is an enormous managerial task, akin to staging the Normandy invasion or launching the Gulf War. All the pieces will come together. Trust me on that.'

I nodded.

'Elliot tells me you'll be joining our little soiree this evening.'

'That's right. Thanks for inviting me.'

'I understand you have a lady friend.'

'She's an attorney, also. She's excited about meeting you.'

'Well, who can blame her?' Jonathan made a little laugh. 'Ha-ha.' I glanced at Truly and Truly was nodding. Serious.

Jonathan said, 'We'll discuss the team's progress and direction. I want you to be a part of that meeting. I don't want you to feel left out.'

I said, 'You don't have to handle me, Jonathan.'

'I know that, son. I respect you.'

I recovered my gun, then we stepped out into the plaza and a wall of people and cameras and microphones surged forward and enveloped us. I thought that maybe this wasn't the jail anymore and maybe I wasn't me. Maybe I'd stepped through Calvin and Hobb's transmogrifier and I was no longer a detective and Green was no longer a lawyer. Maybe we had just discovered life on Titan. Maybe we had found the cure for AIDS and were about to tell the world. Why else would so many people be here shouting questions?

Jonathan went to the microphones. 'We're not here to answer

questions, but I want to make a short statement.' He spoke in his normal voice, and the crowd shushed itself to hear him.

Jonathan's expression turned somber, and then he looked at me and again rested his hand on my shoulder. He said, 'As you all know, three days ago Mr Cole found important evidence that both the police department and the district attorney's office failed to uncover, evidence that we believe supports our client's claim of innocence. Both the police department and the district attorney's office promised to evaluate this evidence, and act on it, but they have not.' He let go of my shoulder, and the somber expression turned fierce. 'We demand that the police stop their footdragging and issue immediate arrest warrants for Stephen Pritzik and Elton Richards. Concurrently with this, and in consideration of the state's weakened case, I hereby request that the district attorney stop this injustice, admit the failure of his investigation, and dismiss all charges against Theodore Martin. In lieu of that, we have filed a motion with the bench to set bail so that Mr Martin might be released.'

Reporters in the back were tossing out questions as the reporters in front pushed their microphones even closer.

Jonathan's voice grew, and the fierce expression became outraged. He grabbed my shoulder again, and all the grabbing was making me uncomfortable. 'The tyranny of evil men cannot be hidden from the light of truth! We have not only uncovered evidence of a specific crime, but also of gross incompetence, negligence, and a police department all too willing to obfuscate the truth in an attempt to hide their own shortcomings.' Still cameras were clicking and videocameras were panning, and they seemed to be panning toward me.

I said, 'What's he talking about?'

Truly nudged me. 'Jonathan knows what he's doing.'

Green bellowed, 'We do not rest. We continue to investigate. And, ladies and gentlemen, we are about to blow the lid off the evil and the desire for personal gain that underlies this tragic and wrongful prosecution!'

Jonathan abruptly turned away from the microphones, and a wall of sound came from the press. They surged around us and shouted their questions, and just as abruptly Kerris and maybe a dozen of his security guys appeared from nowhere and surrounded us in a kind of flying wedge. Truly was smiling. I grabbed his jacket and shouted to make myself heard. 'What's he talking about, Truly? What just happened here?'

Truly laughed. 'The truth happened, Cole. Don't worry about it. We'll see you at the party.'

Kerris's people worked us across the plaza and down to the parking structure. I moved with the crush of bodies the way a leaf is carried by the wind, a part of an unseen world, yet not.

18

I drove back to the house feeling hollow and uncertain, and spent the rest of the afternoon waiting for Lucy to return from her shopping excursion with Jodi Taylor.

Darlene called at ten minutes after three and said, 'Good afternoon, Mr Cole. How are we today?'

'We're fine, Darlene. And yourself?' I wondered if she had seen the press conference.

'Would Ms Chenier be about?' I guess not.

'I expect her return shortly, Darlene. May I take a message?'

Darlene hesitated, and seemed confused. I have never known Darlene to sound confused. 'Oh, no message. Please ask her to call.'

'I don't expect her for another hour or so, Darlene, and it's already after five, your time. Is tomorrow okay?' Baton Rouge was two hours ahead of us.

'She could call me at home.'

'Is everything all right, Darlene?'

'Everything is fine, Mr Cole. Please have a good evening.'

We hung up, and maybe five minutes later the cat door clacked and I heard him in the kitchen. I got up from the couch and found him standing just inside his door, motionless, tiny nose twitching as he tested the air. I said, 'It's just us.'

He stared at me for maybe forty seconds, then crept to the living room and tested the air again. I said, 'How about some tuna?' He hadn't been home in almost four days, and I had missed him.

I opened a small can of Bumble Bee Fancy White, sat on the floor, and put it down beside me. He loves Bumble Bee Fancy White. It's his most favorite thing. That and field mice. 'Well?'

You could see him catch the scent. You could see his eyes widen and his nose shift gears and his ears perk. He looked at the can, took two steps toward me, then squinted back toward the living room. He made his little growl.

'Lucy and Ben aren't here, but they will be. You'd best get used to it and get over this attitude you have.'

He stopped the growling and came over but did not touch the tuna. I stroked his back, but he did not purr. 'I know, buddy. I feel a little bit disrupted, too.'

He head-bumped me, then trotted out of the kitchen and up the stairs, heading for the safety of my loft, moving fast in case Lucy or Ben was lying in wait. I had to shake my head, but at least he was home. You take your progress where you find it.

I checked my office messages at 3:45. Thirteen more interview requests were jamming the machine, but there was also a message from Toni Abatemarco, saying she had something on Stuart Langolier. I called her back and said, 'What's the word, Toni?'

'I'm showing seven arrests over a five-year period, starting when he was sixteen for grand theft, auto. We've got a couple more GTAs, one count of fencing stolen auto parts, and an armed robbery. Real working-class doofball stuff.'

'That's it?' I was thinking about Jonna Lester. I was wondering what Stuart Langolier had to do with James Lester.

'His most recent arrest was eight years ago. Nothing after that. I can fax this stuff to you if you want.'

'Sure.' I gave her the number. 'Is there a James Lester listed as an accomplice or a known associate?'

'Hang on and lemme see.' I waited. 'Nope. I don't see one.'

I thought about it some more. 'How about a phone number or address listed for Langolier?' I thought I might call him. I thought I might ask him why Jonna Lester had brought him into this.

'There is, but it's eight years old, so I double-checked with information. There is no Stuart Langolier listed or unlisted in Santa Barbara, or anywhere in Ventura county.'

'How about an attorney?' His docket sheet would list his attorney of record. I could call the attorney and see if they had a current address.

She said, 'Sure. He had a public defender named Elliot Truly.'

I was poised to write it down, but I didn't. I said, 'Stuart Langolier was represented by a public defender named Elliot Truly.'

'That's right. You want his number?'

'No, babe. I think I have it.' I thanked Toni for the good work, told her to say hi to her husband, Frank, and then I hung up.

I stood in my kitchen, staring at the canyon through the glass doors for a time, and then I dialed Truly's number. 'Mr Truly's office.'

'This is Elvis Cole. Is Truly in?'

'I'm sorry. Could I take a message?'

'How about Jonathan?'

'I'm afraid they can't be disturbed.'

I hung up again.

I showered and changed and was just getting ready to run down to my office when Lucy got back. I wanted to check the fax. I wanted to have the facts with me when I confronted Truly at the party and asked him what in hell was going on. Lucy came in flushed and excited and beaming, carrying a shopping bag with shoes and a long plastic dress bag. She said, 'I want to show you! It's absolutely gorgeous and they took up the hem right there while we waited and it's just perfect!'

Her smile made me smile. 'You would look perfect in anything.'

'Yes, but I'll look even better in this.'

I reached to peek into the bag, but she held it away. 'Don't peek. I want you to see me with it on.'

'How about I see you without it on, then with it on, so I can decide which way I like you better. Sort of like before and after.'

She smiled. 'If you're as smart as I think you are, you'll rave about me both ways.'

I pulled her close. 'I'll rave, but smart has nothing to do with it.'

She kissed my nose. 'I'm having such fun.'

'Me, too, Luce. I'm glad you guys are here.'

We kissed again, and then I told her that Darlene had called and said that Lucy should phone her at home.

Lucy frowned. 'She said to call her at home?'

'Unh-hunh. I asked if there was a problem, but she said no.'

Now Lucy wasn't smiling. She seemed somehow distant and distracted. 'Lucy?'

She smiled again, but now it was forced. She stepped back. 'I'd better call Darlene and see. Why don't you go along to the office and I'll show you the dress when you get back?'

'You sure?'

She was already moving toward her room. 'I'm sure it's business and it could take a while. I'll model the dress when you get back.'

She disappeared into the guest room and closed the door.

I said, 'Okay.'

The marine layer had burned off but it was bright and hot as I drove down to my office. We get these inversion layers, and the air stops moving and grows milky from the exhaust of five million cars. A thin haze was forming to the east. I was surprised that Jonathan Green would allow an inversion layer on a day when he was going to have a party. Might cast a pall on the entire affair.

I parked in my spot, walked up the four flights to my floor, and saw that my door was open. I stepped in and found Dan Tomsic sitting on the couch. He looked large and heavy, and his eyes were closed. I glanced at the fax. Something had printed out in its basket. I looked back at Tomsic. 'I could've sworn that I locked the door.'

Tomsic opened his eyes but didn't move. His arms were spread along the back of the couch, and he appeared neither surprised nor concerned. 'You did, but what's that to a couple of guys like us?'

I stared at him.

'I'm trying to figure you out, Cole. I ask around and everyone says that you're solid, but now there's this shit with Pritzik and Richards, and the double-dealing with Rossi.'

I shook my head. 'What are you talking about?'

'The press conference. You and Green looked real sweet standing out there on the plaza. A couple of liars.'

'I don't know what you're talking about, and I don't know what Jonathan was talking about, either. All I know is that no one seems to be doing very much about Pritzik and Richards.'

Tomsic frowned, like maybe he was confused, and then the frown became a nasty smile. 'You don't know, do you?'

'Know what, Tomsic?'

'Pritzik and Richards are dead. They died together in an auto accident three weeks ago in Tempe, Arizona.'

'So what's the big secret? All you had to do was let us know.'

Now the smile dropped away like a gold-digger's interest. 'We didn't find out until last night. We called Green's office and notified him at five minutes after nine this morning.'

I stared at him. I opened my mouth, then closed it.

Tomsic stood and walked past me to the door. 'That's some asshole you're working for. He knew that they were dead even when he was making a big speech about how we weren't doing enough to find them. Foot-dragging, he said. Covering up.'

I said, 'Were either Pritzik or Richards ever represented by Elliot Truly?'

Tomsic squinted at me. 'How in hell should I know?'

I glanced at the fax again.

Tomsic came very close to me. 'Shitting on the department is one thing, but Rossi's personal. You said she was clear. You said she was out of it.'

'She is, Dan.'

'That's not what Green's saying on the news. They're saying she planted the hammer. They're saying she set him up and that they've got proof. You call that being out of it?'

I didn't know what to say.

Tomsic turned back to the door, then raised a single finger, like a teacher instructing a pupil. 'My first name is for my friends. You don't rate.' He lowered the finger. 'Jonathan Green is willing to destroy a good detective's life to save a piece of shit murderer. That makes him a piece of shit, and you're a piece of shit, too.'

'Don't mince words, Dan. Tell me what you really think.'

Dan Tomsic kept the flat cop eyes on me for another lifetime, and then he left.

My heart was hammering and my head felt swollen. I collected the pages from the fax, then turned on the little Sony TV and found the four o'clock news. The frosty-haired reporter was saying that Pritzik and Richards had plowed into a culvert, saying that they had been drinking, saying we might never know if Pritzik had in fact been James X.

The chiseled male anchor came on, and they cut to a live shot of Jonathan on the sidewalk outside his office. Jonathan and Truly and the lesser attorneys were accusing Angela Rossi of planting the murder weapon, and they were demanding a full investigation, not only of Rossi but of the LAPD command that was protecting her. Jonathan said that his team had uncovered proof that Rossi had tampered with evidence on other occasions, and then Stan Kerris brought out Mrs Louise Earle. When I saw Mrs Earle I leaned forward and the swollen feeling spread to my neck and my shoulders. Jonathan introduced her, saying that she had come forward through the efforts of Elvis Cole. He reminded everyone that Elvis Cole was the fine young detective who had made the breakthrough about Pritzik and Richards. He said that what Mrs Earle was about to say was even more shocking. The camera closed on Mrs Louise Earle, and she said that Detective Angela Rossi had planted counterfeit money on her son, LeCedrick, and then arrested him. She said that Rossi had threatened to have him killed in prison if she said anything. Mrs Earle was crying when she said it, and Jonathan Green put his arm around her shoulders to comfort her.

I watched the news for another ten minutes and then I turned off the television. I said, 'What in hell is going on here?'

No one answered.

I took a deep breath, let it out, then leaned back in my chair and wondered if I could feel any more out of the loop. I could, and in about twelve seconds I did.

I paged through the faxes until I came to Stuart Langolier's D-55 booking page from the Ventura County Sheriff's office. The booking page showed Stuart Paul Langolier's fingerprints in two rows of five along the bottom of the page, and his front- and side-view mug shots above the prints. The fax quality was poor and the prints had come through mostly as black smudges, but the mug shots were clear enough.

It was eight years ago and the hairstyle was different, but Stuart Langolier wasn't just Stuart Langolier. He was also James Lester, one-time client of Elliot Truly.

I gathered together the faxes, locked my office, and went home to pick up Lucy.

It was going to be a hell of a party.

19

It was just after six when I got back to the house. I let myself in through the kitchen and saw Lucy on the deck. She was standing at the rail, and she was wearing a white silk slip dress with spaghetti straps that left her shoulders and back bare. The silk was without embroidery or detail, and seemed to glow in the lowering sun.

I said, 'Simple. Elegant. Utterly devastating.'

She turned and smiled, but the smile seemed strained. 'Ben called. Peter's going to bring him home after dinner.'

'Great.'

'You were gone a long time.'

'Angela Rossi's partner was waiting for me. Have you seen the news?'

'No.'

I turned on the local station, but now they were talking about a fruit fly infestation in Orange County. I changed channels twice, but other things were happening in the world. 'They've got a woman I interviewed saying that Rossi framed her son.'

'Congratulations.' She didn't understand.

'That isn't what she told me. Rossi didn't frame anyone. I cleared her, and that's what I reported to Jonathan.'

'I'm sure it's just a misunderstanding. These things happen.' She said it, but it was as if she wasn't really there.

I turned off the television and looked at her. 'Is everything okay with Darlene?'

'Of course.' She glanced away, then made a little shrug. 'Just something at the office.'

I looked closer. 'You sure?'

Lucy stiffened ever so slightly. 'Shouldn't you get ready, or are we not going?'

'Luce, he made it sound like I uncovered this woman. He made it sound like I turned up something that implicates Angela Rossi.' I said it carefully.

'Perhaps you're just being sensitive.' Cool.

I took a step back and went upstairs and put on a jacket and tie. The cat watched me from the closet. Hiding. I said, 'Don't say a word.'

He didn't.

I folded the fax from Santa Barbara and put it into my inside jacket pocket, and then we went out to the car. I said, 'Would you like the top up or down?' Thinking of her hair.

'It doesn't matter.'

I left the top down.

I said, 'If there's a problem, I wish we could talk about it.'

She looked out the window. 'Please don't start one of those conversations.'

I nodded.

Lucy relaxed as we moved along Mulholland and down Coldwater, and by the time we gave the car to a valet she was smiling again and holding my hand. She said, 'There're so many people.'

Jonathan Green lived in an expensive home on a corner lot just north of Sunset in Coldwater Canyon. It was an older, established area of great red pines and curving drives and ranch-style estates that looked not unlike the Ponderosa. A small army of valets was trotting along the walks, and the curbs were already lined with cars and limousines and an awful lot of people who looked as if they'd just stepped out of the Academy Players Directory.

Jonathan's front entry was open, and, as we approached, we could see that his home was crowded. I said, 'Prepare to be stared at.'

She glanced at me. 'Why?'

'You'll be the most beautiful woman there.'

She hooked her arm through mine.

'In the most beautiful dress.'

She squeezed my arm. I'm such a charmer.

A news crew from Channel Eight had lights set up on Jonathan's front lawn and was interviewing a well-known figure who had starred in a hit television series in the early seventies, and who now ran a major studio. Lucy said, 'Isn't he somebody?'

'Yep.' He was well known for his efforts as an active fund raiser for private social programs and had received humanitarian-of-the-year awards twice, in large part because Teddy Martin had contributed heavily to his causes. He was less well known for the violent, hair-trigger temper that he has frequently shown toward the young men whom he supplies with heroin.

As we passed, he was telling the reporter, 'I've known from the beginning that Teddy is innocent, and this proves it. Teddy has been a force for good in our community for years. He's stood by us, and now it's our turn to stand by him. I can't understand why the district attorney has this vendetta.' Other reporters were spread through the crowd, interviewing other supporters.

The entry was wide and long and opened onto a great room that flowed outside through a line of French doors. The floors were Spanish tile and the decor was western, with plenty of rich woods and bookshelves and oil paintings of cattle and horses. An original Russell hung over a great stone fireplace. Behind the French doors were a pool and a pool house and, still farther back, a tennis court. Maybe a half-dozen of Kerris's security people were standing around, trying to be unobtrusive and not having a lot of luck at it. The grounds were lush and dramatically lit, and waiters and waitresses moved through the crowd, offering wine and canapés. Maybe three hundred people were drifting through the house and around the pool. Lucy said, 'This is beautiful.'

I nodded. 'Crime pays.'

'Oh. There's Jonathan.'

Green was near the fireplace, talking with a couple of men in dark suits and a together-looking woman in her late fifties. One of the men was tall and thin, with little round spectacles and a great forehead and bulging Adam's apple. Intense. As we approached, he said, 'LAPD has an entrenched white male racist attitude that is impervious to change. I'm telling you that the time is right to simply abolish them.'

The together woman said, 'That's a non-issue, Willis. Angela Rossi is a white female.'

Willis jabbed the air. Agitated. 'And as such must subjugate herself to the dominant white male racist attitudes that surround her. Don't you see that?'

The together woman said, 'But LAPD is over fifty percent women and minority now, and the percentage is inceasing.'

Willis's eyes bulged. 'But is it increasing fast enough to save us? My God, we're living in a virtual police state! If it could happen to Teddy, it could happen to any of us!'

Jonathan saw me and offered his hand, looking not altogether unhappy to shut Willis off. 'Everyone, I'd like to introduce Elvis Cole, an integral member of the team.'

Willis's eyes lit up and he grabbed my hand. 'Great to meet you. You're the one who nailed that fascist bitch.'

The together woman drew a deep breath and Lucy said, 'Please don't refer to any women by that word in my presence.' She said it politely.

Willis stepped back and held up his hands. 'Oh, hey, I apologize. Really. But these cops have just gone over the line, and I'm so frustrated.'

The together woman said, 'You're such a hog.'

Jonathan introduced us. The woman was Tracy Mannos, the station manager from Channel Eight. Willis was a writer for a local alternative weekly, the *L.A. Freak*.

When Green was finished introducing me, I introduced Lucy. She said, 'It's a pleasure, Mr Green.'

He smiled warmly and took her hand. 'Please call me Jonathan. I understand that you're an attorney.'

She nodded. 'I practice civil law, but your cases have been inspirational. Especially the Williams case in nineteen seventy-two.' He was still holding her hand.

'That's a lovely accent. Where are you from?' He patted her hand. 'Louisiana.'

'Well, perhaps we'll have the pleasure of working together some time.'

He patted her hand again, and I said, 'Jonathan, I'd like to see you.'

As I said it, Kerris appeared behind Jonathan and whispered something. Jonathan stared at me as Kerris spoke, and then Jonathan nodded at me. 'I have to see the others for a moment. Why don't you come along?'

I left Lucy with Tracy Mannos and followed Jonathan through his house to an office that was the size of my living room. Elliot Truly was there, along with the larger of the lesser attorneys and two men who looked vaguely familiar. One of them was tall and hard and African-American. When Kerris closed the door, I said, 'Jonathan, I saw the statement you made this afternoon. What's going on with Louise Earle?'

Jonathan spread his hands. 'I'm sorry. I don't know what you mean.'

'She's changed her story. She didn't implicate Rossi when I talked to her.'

Kerris said, 'Guess you got it wrong.' He had drifted to the wall behind Jonathan so he could lean. Every time I saw him he was leaning. Guess it wore the guy out carrying all those shoulders and arms.

'I cleared Rossi, and now you're attacking her. You made it sound like I'm behind it.'

No one said anything for a moment, and then Jonathan spread his hands. 'Angela Rossi found the murder weapon when she went down the slope to Susan's body. She hid it on her person, then planted it on Teddy's property in order to frame him for Susan's murder. She was hoping that if she was credited with solving such a high-profile case, her career would be resuscitated.' He smiled at me. 'It's as simple as that.'

I looked at Truly and Kerris and the two other guys. 'That's nuts.'

Kerris crossed the arms. He was so wide that maybe he was twins who didn't quite separate. 'What's your problem? Everyone thinks you're a hero.'

I stared at him. 'What's going on?'

Jonathan shook his head.

'How'd you get Mrs Earle to change her story?'

Jonathan smiled the way you smile when you're incredulous. 'Excuse me. Are you accusing me of tampering with evidence?'

Kerris said, 'Good thing for us that I double-checked your work. Here everyone thinks that you're some kind of top-dog investigator, and the truth is you suck.'

Jonathan frowned. 'Please, Stan. There's no need to be insulting.'

Kerris kept the empty eyes my way. 'He sucks. I'm with the woman five minutes and she breaks down, telling me she's terrified, telling me she's wanted someone to help her for damn near six years because those cops framed her son, then threatened her into keeping her mouth shut.'

Everyone was so still that they might have been a fresco. Elliot Truly had a kind of idiot half-grin. He glanced away when I looked at him. I said, 'James Lester is a fraud.'

Truly was shaking his head before I finished. 'That's not true. I should've said something about him when you mentioned Langolier at the jail, but I didn't know how Jonathan wanted to handle it.'

Jonathan glared at him.

I took the fax from my pocket and tossed it at Jonathan. 'James Lester is an alias. James Lester is a convicted felon named Stuart Langolier. Truly knew him.'

Jonathan didn't touch the fax. 'This is my fault. You're used to working on small cases and this is a large case, and I should've briefed you on our meetings. Then you wouldn't think we're keeping things from you.'

Truly shrugged and looked apologetic. 'Look, I didn't realize that Lester was Langolier until I saw his picture in the paper, okay? As soon as I knew I notified Jonathan. We called the district attorney's office and filed a brief about it this afternoon.'

Kerris said, 'There's a reason they call it "coincidence."'

I said, 'No secrets?'

Jonathan shook his head. 'I'm sorry that I've left you out of the loop. An effort like this is such a large undertaking.'

'Like the Gulf War.'

'That's right. There are no secrets here.'

I said, 'What about the lies here? You knew Pritzik and Richards were dead when you attacked the police this morning.'

Jonathan frowned as if I were a child he had once thought backward but now stubborn. 'I'm disappointed, Elvis. Clearly, you don't understand a team effort, or my obligations as a defense attorney.'

Truly shook his head. 'What a spoilsport. This case has made you a celebrity.'

I said, 'Spoilsport?'

Kerris said, 'How about "prick?"'

I looked at him, and Kerris shifted away from the wall. Jonathan said, 'No, Stan.'

I smiled at him. 'Kerris, anytime you want to go for it, I'm available.'

Jonathan said, 'No, Stan.'

Kerris settled against the wall again, and still the empty eyes did not move. The black guy was grinning at me. So was the other idiot.

I looked back at Jonathan Green. 'You're right, Jonathan. I don't appreciate it. I quit.'

Jonathan said, 'I'm sorry to hear that, but under the circumstances I understand.'

Kerris said, 'You want I should walk him out?'

I said, 'Kerris, if you walk me out you won't make it to the door.'

Kerris said, 'Oo.'

I walked out of the office and slammed the door and stood in the crowded living room until my pulse slowed and my ears stopped ringing. The room was so crowded and so noisy that no one heard the door slam. Foiled again. I wandered around for twenty minutes before I found Lucy and Tracy Mannos talking by the pool. Willis and the other guy were nowhere in sight. Just as well for Willis. I said, 'Excuse me.' My face felt tight, and obvious. 'Luce, could I see you please?'

Tracy Mannos handed Lucy a card. 'It's been fun, Ms Chenier. Call me when you get the chance.'

Lucy smiled at her, then Tracy Mannos walked away. Lucy said, 'Interesting woman.'

'I'm glad you're having a good time.'

She looked at me. 'What's wrong?'

'I am no longer a member of the Big Green Defense Machine. It would probably be appropriate for us to leave.'

Lucy stared at me. 'What happened?'

'I quit.'

We got the car from the valets and found our way back to Coldwater and climbed the mountain to Mulholland. 'I'm sorry that we have to leave this way. I know you were excited about meeting Jonathan.'

'I don't care about Jonathan. Are you all right?'

I told her about Truly and Lester. I told her again about Mrs Earle, and about Jonathan making the misleading statement about Pritzik and Richards. I said, 'I don't get it. The guy's Jonathan Green. He's an All-World attorney. What does he think he's doing, behaving in this manner?'

She looked at me. 'He probably thinks he's doing his job.'

I shook my head.

'It's his job to attack the prosecution's case. That's how he creates reasonable doubt.'

'Is it his job to lie?'

'No, but you're assuming it's a lie. Reasonable people can disagree and have opposing interpretations of the facts. It's Jonathan's job to present an interpretation that's favorable to his client. It would be malpractice for him to do otherwise.' When she said it she was stiff and testy, and it felt like we were having a confrontation.

I said, 'What's wrong?'

'Nothing's wrong.'

'Are you mad that we had to leave the party?'

'Why are you staying with this? I told you that nothing is wrong.'

'Fine.'

'Fine.'

I turned on k. d. lang. k. d. sang, but I'm not sure either Lucy or I listened. Neither of us spoke.

Peter Alan Nelsen's black Range Rover was parked off the road across from my house, waiting. I said, 'Looks like they're home.'

Lucy still didn't speak.

We parked and went inside. Peter and Ben were on the couch watching a laser disc of *When Worlds Collide*. The house smelled of popcorn. Peter yelled, 'Hide the babes, Ben! It's the police!' Peter always yells things like that.

Ben said, 'Hi, Mom. You shoulda seen the neat stuff on Peter's set!'

'You can tell me in the morning, sweetie.'

Lucy walked across the living room and into the guest room and shut the door. Ben and Peter looked at me. I said, 'I guess she's tired.'

Peter said, 'Oh, yeah. Looks that way to me.'

I frowned at him, and then I stalked up to the loft.

Another fun evening in Tinsel City.

20

Sometime before sunrise the cat's door made its sound, then, a few minutes later, made its sound again. Come and gone.

When the eastern sky was lit gold and the great glass steeple opposite my loft with filled with copper I pulled on gym shorts and slipped down the stairs. The door to the guest room was closed. I went out onto the deck and breathed the cool morning air and did twelve sun salutes from the hatha yoga as the finches and the sparrows and two mockingbirds watched. The canyon was still and quiet and just beginning to fill with light. I did one hundred push-ups and one hundred sit-ups, enjoying the rhythm of the count and the feeling of accomplishment that came with the exertion and the sweat.

The cat climbed onto the deck and watched me from the corner of the house. He didn't look happy.

I worked through the stronger asanas, starting with the half locust, then the full, and then the scorpion and the peacock. The air warmed and the sweat began to flow more freely, and then I saw Ben standing in the glass doors, his face thoughtful. I said, 'You're up early.'

He nodded. Upset about last night, maybe.

'Come on out.'

Ben came out. He was wearing baggy pajama bottoms and a white T-shirt. When he came out the cat lowered his ears and growled. Ben said, 'He doesn't like me.'

'It's not you. He doesn't like anyone.'

'He likes you.'

I nodded. 'Yeah. He likes me and Joe, pretty much, but he doesn't care for other people. I've never known why.'

The low gutter of his growl spiraled up into his war cry and I grew worried he might charge. I'd seen him charge, and it wasn't pretty. I said, 'Knock it off.' Loud.

The growling stopped.

'That's better.'

His ears stayed down, but at least he didn't leave.

Ben crossed the deck to the rail, keeping one eye on the cat, and looked out at the canyon. He put his weight on the rail, then leaned out. He said, 'Hawks.'

Two redtail hawks were gliding low over the canyon. 'They're redtails. They nest up the canyon.'

He bounced on the rail. 'I think I heard coyotes last night. Was that coyotes?'

'Yep. A family lives by the reservoir.'

He bounced faster, then edged along the rail and bounced more. Nervous. I guess he hadn't come out just to look at the hawks. 'Your mom and I are going to work things out, Ben. It's okay.'

The bouncing stopped and he gave me the same eyes that he'd given me when we'd first met, eight-going-on-nine and taking care of his mom. 'She was crying.'

I drew a deep breath. I squinted at the canyon, then looked back at him. 'Is she crying now?'

He shook his head. 'I think she's sleeping.'

'She's upset about something, but I'm not sure what.'

The bouncing was over, but he still looked uncomfortable.

'She say anything?'

He looked down at the deck, and seemed even more uncomfortable.

'She seemed okay until Darlene called.' I watched him. 'After Darlene, she seemed kind of upset.'

Ben looked at the cat. The cat's ears were up now, and he seemed calm. Ben said, 'She's fighting with my dad.' Fighting.

'Ah.'

'My dad didn't want us staying here. He said we should be in a hotel.'

'I see.' The hawks reappeared, higher now, following the air back toward their nest. The female had something in her talons. 'Are you okay with this, Ben?'

He shrugged without looking at me.

I went to the rail and leaned next to him. 'It's tough when your parents are fighting. You get caught in the middle and no matter what you do, you always feel like you're letting one of them down.'

Ben said, 'She really likes you.'

'I really like her. I like you, too. I'm glad you guys are here.'

He didn't seem moved by that, but there you go.

I took a breath and went to the center of the deck and worked through a simple *kata* from the *tae kwon do* called the Crane. You do a lot of bending and your arms pinwheel a lot and you spin, but it isn't difficult. Ben watched me. I did the Crane slowly, moving from one end of the deck to the other, and taking great care in my movements, sort of like with the *tai chi*. When I reached the end of the deck, I turned and did it again, back to the other side, only much faster, moving at three-quarter speed. Ben said, 'What's that?'

'Ballet.'

Ben grinned. 'Nunh-unh.' He stopped leaning over the rail and crossed his arms. 'Is that karate?'

'Korean karate. It's called *tae kwon do*.' I went through it again. Left to right, right to left.

He said, 'They do that on *Power Rangers*. They beat up monsters.'

'Well, it's a fighting skill, but only if you look at it that way. That's a choice you make. You could also choose to look at it as a way to make yourself stronger and more flexible and healthy. It's also fun.' I did it again and watched him watch me. 'Want me to show you how?'

He came over and I showed him. I modeled the postures and adjusted his position and walked him through the moves. 'Don't try to hurry. Slow is better.'

'Okay.'

We did the Crane. After the Crane I showed him the Tiger. Ben took off his T-shirt and tossed it aside. Sweating. We worked through the *katas* together as the sun floated up from the eastern ridge and the air warmed, and then I saw Lucy watching us from the door. I smiled. 'Morning.'

'Hi.'

Ben said, 'Look at this, Mom! This is called the Crane. It's a *tae kwon do kata*. Watch.'

Ben worked his way through, and as he did, Lucy put her hand to the glass, fingers spread, and I put my hand to hers. She said, 'Joe's on the phone.'

Ben said, 'Mom, you're not watching!'

I went in and found the phone on the counter. 'Now what?'

Pike said, 'Put on Channel Five.'

I put it on and went back to the phone. The morning anchor was recapping yesterday's report on Green's accusations, and again ran the clip where Green made it look like I had been the one who turned up Mrs LeCedrick Earle. I said, 'We quit last night. We're no longer working for the Big Green Defense Machine.'

Pike grunted. 'Keep watching.'

The anchor said that LAPD had announced a full investigation into Angela Rossi. The anchor said that Rossi had been suspended pending the outcome. I felt a dropaway feeling in my stomach and said, 'Oh, man.'

Pike said, 'I tried calling her, but the phone's off the hook.'

'How about I pick you up?'

He hung up without answering. Lucy had come inside, and Ben was still on the deck. I said, 'We've got to go see about Rossi.'

Lucy nodded. 'I thought you might. I've got the meeting later in Long Beach. I'll take Ben.'

'Sure.'

She started away, then turned back. 'I liked seeing you together with him.'

I smiled, but I didn't say anything. I wanted to ask what was going on with her former husband, but I didn't want to press her. I wanted to be supportive, but sometimes support can be oppressive. Maybe it would work itself out. Maybe, too, it was none of my business. I decided to give her some room. Giving them room is often the better part of valor, especially when you're trying not to make things worse.

I showered and dressed, and then I drove down to Culver City and found Joe waiting at the curb. Pike slid into the right front seat and closed the door without a word. He buckled the seat belt and still didn't say anything. I guess he was angry, too.

It was a few minutes after nine when we drove to the beach, then turned south to the Marina and slowed at the mouth of Angela Rossi's cul-de-sac. We would've turned onto her street, but we couldn't because of the news vans jamming the cul-de-sac and spilling out onto Admiralty Way. Knots of reporters and camera people were clustered on the sidewalks and in the street, and a couple of women who were probably Rossi's neighbors were arguing with a short, stocky guy in a sport coat. Apparently, his van was blocking their drive. Apparently, they wanted the reporters to lay off Rossi and get out of their neighborhood. Pike said, 'Look at this crap.'

We parked across Admiralty and walked back. A beefy reporter sitting in a Blazer did a double-take when we passed, then hurried after us, asking if he could have a word. He reached Pike first and Pike seemed to give a lurch, and then the reporter sat down on the street hard, going 'Omph!'

Pike didn't lose a step. 'No comment.'

I guess some interviews are harder than others.

We walked past the reporters to the front gate. The thin man with the glasses and an older woman were telling an attractive red-haired reporter that they weren't going to let her in, when the thin man recognized me and shook his finger at me. 'It's you. You lied to me when you were here. You weren't looking for anyone named Keith!'

I said, 'Would you please tell Detective Rossi that Joe Pike and I would like to see her?'

The red-haired reporter turned and yelled for her camera operator to hurry up. She yelled that she wanted a shot of this.

The thin man kept shaking his finger. 'You're a prick. You should be ashamed of yourself.'

Joe Pike stepped to the gate and murmured something that I couldn't hear. Pike didn't seem threatening now. He seemed gentle and calming.

The woman went to Rossi's front door. I guess she was the thin man's wife.

The red-haired reporter's camera operator hustled up behind us and began taping. The reporter asked if I had any additional information implicating or incriminating Angela Rossi. She asked if I was here to get a statement from Rossi or to follow up a line of inquiry. I kept my back to her. I stared at the hamper filled with Nerf balls. I stared at the red bike.

The thin man's wife came back and let us through the gate. The red-haired reporter tried to push through, but the wife shoved her back, yelling, 'Don't you dare!' The thin man wasn't happy that I was coming in.

Joe Pike rapped at the door once, then opened it, and we stepped through into Angela Rossi's life.

It was a nice place, roomy and spacious, though the furnishings weren't expensive, just a sofa and love seat arranged in an L, and a BarcaLounger. I guess she'd put all of the money into buying the place and hadn't had a lot left over for furniture. A woman and a man were standing behind the love seat, and another woman was sitting on the couch, and two little boys were sitting on the floor, the smaller sitting in the larger's lap. I guess the boys belonged to Rossi. I guess the adults were friends or family come to lend support. Off-duty cops, maybe, but maybe not. Everyone in the room was looking at me. Even the boys.

Angela Rossi was standing by the sofa with her arms crossed. Her cheeks looked hollow and her eyes were dark and haunted. I said, 'I wanted to tell you that I didn't have anything to do with this. I told Green that you were clean. He told me that he bought it. I don't know what happened.'

'Okay. Thanks.' Like she was numb.

Joe said, 'Angie.'

She shook her head. 'I didn't do those things. I didn't frame that guy.'

Joe said, 'I know.'

Angela Rossi looked confused. 'I don't know why she's lying. She seemed like such a nice woman.'

I said, 'We'll talk to her. We'll get this straightened out.'

Angela Rossi said, 'It won't matter. I'm done with the job.'

Joe stiffened and shook his head once. 'Don't say that, Angela. You're not.'

'So what kind of career will I have when it's over?' She walked past us to the window and peeked out. 'I can't believe that all these people have nothing better to do.' She looked back. 'Can you?'

All of them kept staring. I wanted to say something, but I didn't know what to say. My eye still hurt where she'd hit me, and I was thinking that maybe she ought to hit me again. 'I'm sorry.'

'Forget it.' She shrugged, no big deal.

Joe said, 'We'll help you fight it.'

'Nothing to help. I've decided to resign.'

Joe leaned forward. His dark lenses seemed to blaze. 'Don't resign. You're too good to resign.'

She said, 'Oh, Joe.'

Pike was leaning so far forward he seemed to sway.

'They've taken everything away, but that's okay. I just have to survive this, and I know I can.' She smiled when she said it, as if she were at peace with all of this.

Joe said, 'What's wrong with you?' His voice was so soft I could barely hear him.

Angela Rossi's left eye began to flutter, then grew wet, and I had the sense that if she were fine china there would be a webwork of spider-silk cracks spreading beneath her surface. She held up her right hand and said, 'Please go now.'

Pike nodded, and I started to say something else, but then she turned the hand to me, and I nodded, too.

21

We left Angela Rossi's and walked out to the car. The whiny reporter who had once been a lawyer saw us first and ran toward us, shouting, 'They've come out! They've come out!' The rest of the reporters stayed back, shifting their feet and keeping their distance. Pike raised a palm at the whiny reporter, and he stopped, too. I guess word had spread, or maybe it was in our faces.

We drove slowly, neither of us speaking, and worked our way out of the Marina, up through Venice, and along the beach. It was automatic driving, going through the motions without conscious thought or direction, movement without destination or design. Pike hunkered low in the passenger's seat, his face dark in the bright sun, his dark lenses somehow molten and angry. It is not good to see Joe Pike angry. Better to see a male lion charge at close quarters. Better to hear someone scream, 'Incoming!' I said, 'Where do you want to go?'

His head swiveled sideways maybe half an inch.

'How about we just drive?'

His head moved up, then down. Maybe half an inch.

'Okay. We'll drive.'

We followed Ocean Avenue up through Venice and along the bluff above the beach, Pike as still as an undisturbed lake. We stopped for a light on Ocean Park, and I watched the joggers and bikers and smiling young women with deep tans who dotted the bike paths along the bluff. Everyone was smiling. Happy people having a great time on a beautiful day. What could be better than that? Of course, they could be happy because they hadn't just come from Angela Rossi's house. It's always easy to smile when you haven't helped destroy an innocent person's life.

The light turned green, and a red Toyota pickup filled with surfers and surf boards blew their horn behind us. The driver yelled for us to get out of the way, and Joe Pike floated up out of his seat and twisted around, and when he did the honking stopped and the Toyota jammed into reverse and sped away at high speed. Backwards.

I said, 'Well. I guess we'd better talk about this before we kill somebody.'

Pike frowned. His arms were knotted and tight, and the veins in his forearms were large. His dark glasses caught the bright sun, looking hot enough to sear flesh. The red arrow tattoos on his deltoids were as bright as arterial blood. I wondered if the idiots in the Toyota knew how close they'd come.

I said, 'It isn't just Angela Rossi, is it?'

Pike's head moved from side to side one time.

'You don't like the cops we know thinking that we're part of this. You don't like people thinking that you and I believe this garbage or had a part in destroying an innocent woman's life.'

Pike's head moved again. Just a bit. Just the smallest of moves.

'But that's the way it looks.'

Pike's jaw rippled with tension.

We went to a Thai place a few blocks up from the beach. It was still shy of noon when we parked at the curb and went in. Early. It's a tiny place with beat-up Formica tables, and it was empty except for two women sitting at the single window table. The young guy who greeted us said we could sit where we liked. An older woman who was probably his grandmother was sitting at the table nearest the kitchen, snapping the stems off an enormous pile of snow peas and watching a miniature Hitachi television. She smiled and nodded, and I smiled back. I have never been in their restaurant when she was not snapping peas. We took a table near her, ordered two Thai beers, squid pad thai, vegetable fried rice, and seafood curry. The little woman was watching the midday news as she worked. Something about the Middle East.

The beer came and I said, 'Joe, I'm thinking that there is something larger here than an attorney's zealous defense of his client.' The master of understatement.

Pike cocked his head toward me.

I told him about the connection between James Lester and Elliot Truly, and about Lester's record. 'Lester could be for real, and his tie to Truly could be a coincidence, but maybe it isn't. Pritzik and Richards were killed before Lester called the hotline.'

'Are you thinking he knew that?'

'Say he knew them better than he let on. Say he knew that they had gone to Arizona and were dead, and figured that they would be the perfect crash-test dummies to take the heat for Susan Martin's murder. Lester may have done a little homework and planted the evidence himself to take a shot at the reward.'

'Or Truly might have helped him.'

I nodded. 'Just thinking out loud.'

'Because you have no proof.' The veins in his arms weren't as prominent, and his tattoos had lost their glow. The danger of thermo-nuclear meltdown was passing.

I shook my head. 'No. Lester could be on the level, even though he's a creep.'

'What about the woman?'

'Louise Earle is different. Kerris went to see her, and now she's changed her story. I don't buy that she was lying to me, and I don't buy that Rossi held a gun to her head and made her lie six years ago. Rossi wouldn't have done that, and Louise Earle wouldn't have lied about it.'

'If she wasn't lying then, she's lying now.'

'Yes. But why?' The waiter brought our food, and the smells of mint and garlic and curry were strong. He set out the dishes and said, 'We make spicy. Like always.'

'Great.'

When the waiter was gone, Pike said, 'Because the law is war, and to defeat the prosecution Green must do two things. He must float a viable theory for what happened to Susan Martin, and he must discredit the prosecution's theory.'

'Okay.'

'Lester gives him the alternative theory. The business with Rossi gives him a way to discredit the prosecution's evidence.'

'If Rossi framed LeCedrick Earle, she's also framing Teddy Martin.'

Pike nodded. 'Yes.' Pike twisted toward the Hitachi and said, 'Listen.'

Jonathan Green was on the noon news. The lead story was Elliot Truly's connection to James Lester, also known as Stuart Langolier. Green was announcing that James Lester had revealed to a defense investigator that he had once been known as Stuart Langolier and, under that name, had once been represented by Elliot Truly. Green said that it was his understanding that Mr. Truly had no recollection of Mr. Lester as a client and added that the defense team had immediately notified the district attorney's office to mitigate the appearance of a conflict and to allow them the opportunity for a complete investigation. I said, 'He's doing just what he said.'

Pike grunted. 'Covering his ass.'

The little woman noticed that we were watching the TV and turned the Hitachi so that it would be easier for us to see.

The news anchor shifted the story to the charges against Angela Rossi and cut to the same tape of Louise Earle that I'd seen last night, Mrs Earle crying as she charged that Angela Rossi had framed her son, saying that the police had made her lie before, saying that they had threatened her. The tears looked real. Her pain looked real. Jonathan Green was standing next to her. Elliot Truly was standing behind them. Everyone looked oh-so-concerned.

Pike turned away. 'I can't look at this.'

566

I stared at the Hitachi. I watched Green and I watched Louise Earle, and it just didn't make sense. 'If what we're thinking about Lester and Louise Earle is true, why would a guy like Jonathan Green risk who he is and what he does?'

'Because he's an asshole.' The world according to Pike.

I said, 'Lizard people.'

Pike's glasses gleamed. 'We can talk about this forever, but the only way we're going to find out what's going on with these people is to ask them.'

The young waiter was watching us. He didn't like it that we hadn't touched the food, and he looked concerned. He said something to the little woman. She frowned at us and seemed to share his concern.

The waiter came over and wanted to know if anything was wrong. Pike looked at him and stood. 'Probably. But if there is we'll fix it.'

We picked up the Santa Monica Freeway and drove to Louise Earle's home in Olympic Park. We knocked twice, and rang the bell three times, but she didn't answer. Pike said, 'I'll look in back.'

Pike disappeared around the side of the house. The day was bright, and the same three girls were across the street, whiling away their summer on their porch. I waved and they waved back. Getting to be old friends. Pike reappeared from the opposite side. 'She's not home.'

'Then let's see Lester.'

We climbed back onto the freeway and worked our way east past Pasadena to La Puente and James Lester's house.

Lester's home was unchanged from the last time I was there. The yard was still dead, the Fairlane was still rusted, and everything was still covered with fine gray sand. We parked at the curb and walked across the gray soil to the house. The front door was open, and music was coming from the house. The George Baker Selection doing 'Little Green Bag.' When we got closer, Pike said, 'Smell it?'

'Yep.' The sweet rope smell of hashish was coming from the house.

When we reached the door we didn't have to knock. Jonna Lester was sitting on the couch, sucking hard on a glass pipe, the little electric fans arcing back and forth as they scattered her hash smoke. She was wearing a Michigan State University T-shirt and short-shorts and the clear plastic clogs. Her left eye was red and blue and swollen almost closed, and the bottoms of the clogs were crudded with something dark, as if she'd stepped through mud. She smiled stupidly when she saw me and waved the pipe at her eye. 'Helps with the pain. You wanna smoke a bowl?'

I opened the screen door and we went in. There was another smell in the room, just beneath the dope. I tilted her face to better see the eye. 'James do this?'

She pulled away from me and waved the pipe again. 'It'll be the last time, yessireebob.' She took another pull on the pipe.

'We need to see him.'

Jonna Lester giggled. 'He's in the bathroom. It's his favorite room in the house. He always said that.' She giggled again.

'Would you tell him we want to see him, please?' The other smell felt wet and old, like melons that had gone soft with age.

Jonna Lester sank back on the couch. 'This is such a cool song.'

Joe Pike walked over to the radio and turned it off. Jonna Lester screwed up her face and said, 'Hey!'

I called, 'James?'

Jonna Lester pushed to her feet and angrily waved toward the back of the house. 'He's back there, you wanna see the sonofabitch so bad. C'mon, I'll show ya.'

Pike and I looked at each other, and then Pike took out his .357 Python and held it down along his leg. We followed her out of the living room and across a square little hall to the bathroom. It was an old bathroom, built sometime back in the fifties, with a buckled linoleum floor and corroded fixtures and a brittle glass shower door, the kind that can hurt you bad if you fall through it. Jonna Lester stopped in the door and waved the hash pipe. 'Here he is. Talk to the sonofabitch all you want.'

I said, 'Oh, man.'

James Lester was lying through the broken shower door, half in the tub and half out, impaled on half a dozen jagged glass spikes. His head was almost severed, and the walls and the tub and the buckled linoleum were sprayed with gouts of dark red blood that looked not unlike wings raised toward heaven.

We had wanted to ask James Lester about Pritzik and Richards and the fabrication of evidence, but now he wasn't around to answer our questions. Neither were Pritzik and Richards.

Funny how that works. Isn't it?

22

I got as close to the body as I could without stepping in blood. Jonna Lester's footprints were already on the linoleum from an earlier visit, but there didn't seem to be any other marks or tracks or signs of passage. There was a single small window at the far end of the bathroom above the toilet, open for the air. The window's screen was dirty and torn, but was hooked from the inside and appeared undisturbed. Metallic black flies bumped against the screen, drawn by the blood. I said, 'Did you touch anything?'

She said, 'Yee-uck! I ain't touchin' that mess.'

'Your footprints are on the floor. There's dried blood on your shoes.'

Jonna Lester took another pull on the hash pipe. The hash nut must've gone out, because she frowned at the pipe and poked the bowl. 'I hadda turn off the water.' One of the black flies worked its way through the screen and droned low across the slick floor. You could see its reflection in the blood.

'The water in the sink was running?'

'Yeah.'

James Lester was wearing pants and the work boots, but no shirt. Both legs and one arm were crumpled in a kind of K on the floor, with the other arm and the upper half of his body hanging through the glass into the tub. There was water on the linoleum around the base of the sink where it had spilled over and mixed with James's blood. A bar of soap and a Bic razor and a can of Edge shaving cream were on the sink, which was splashed with water, like maybe he had been getting ready for work and turned and slipped and gone head first through the glass. I said, 'What happened, Jonna?'

She shook her head. 'I spent the night with my friend Dorrie, and he was like this when I came home. I guess he fell.' She made a big deal out of showing me her eye. 'The prick did this to me yesterday. You see what he did?' She shook her head and her lips went *wubba-wubba-wubba* like a cartoon character. 'Oh, man, doesn't that smell just make you wanna vomit?'

She went back into the living room, and we followed her. She tried stoking the pipe again, and I pulled it away from her. 'Hey, whatcha doin'?!'

'He's dead, Jonna. A material witness in a murder case who stands to collect a hundred thousand dollar reward doesn't just fall through a shower door.'

Jonna Lester slapped at me and tried to push me away. 'We had this big fight yesterday and I hadda get outta here! I don't know what happened!'

'Was he expecting anyone?'

'I don't know!'

'Did he mention anyone to you, like maybe he was concerned?'

She put her hands over her ears. 'I don't know I don't know I don't know!' Shouting.

I stepped back, breathing hard, and let her calm. I looked at Pike and Pike shrugged. I took a breath, let it out, then sat next to her. I said, 'Okay, Jonna, what did you guys fight about?' Calm.

'We fought because he's an asshole!'

'Was it because you blew the whistle to me about James being Stuart Langolier?'

She froze for a moment, and then she squinted at me. Suspicious. 'I don't know what you're talking about.'

'C'mon, Jonna. I recognized your voice. Why'd you tip me about James's real name?'

She slumped back on the couch and stuck out her lower lip. Sulking. 'James Lester was his real name. He changed it legally to get a fresh start when he gave up his life of crime.'

I said, 'Jonna.'

'I did it to fuck him.' Her voice was soft and petulant.

'Why?'

''Cause he was gonna cut me out. I know it.'

'How do you know it?'

''Cause he said that when he got the big payday he was gonna blow me off and get a Bud Lite girl.' Her eyes were welling in a delicate balance at the edge of tears. The point of her chin trembled.

Pike walked away. He has little tolerance for the vagaries of the human condition.

I said, 'Jonna? What else do you know?'

'What do you mean?' She rubbed at her eyes. When she touched the bruised eye she winced.

'He may not have been telling the truth. He might have made up the story about meeting Pritzik in a bar. I think maybe he planted the things I found in order to collect the reward, or someone else planted them and James was in on it.'

She shrugged, even more sulky. 'I dunno.'

'Did he know Pritzik and Richards? Did he tell you how he was going to set this up?'

She suddenly sat up, loud and animated. 'Hey, I'm still gonna get the reward money, ain't I? I mean, I get it now that he's dead, right?'

Pike said, 'Forget the reward. You'll be lucky if you don't go to jail.' Pike, the Intimidator.

Jonna Lester's eyes filled again and this time the tears leaked down her cheeks. 'Well, that's no fair.' No fair.

I said, 'Tell me about Pritzik and Richards.'

She shook her head. 'I don't think he knew them. I mean, he *coulda*, but I don't think so.'

'Why not?'

Shrug. ''Cause he didn't have any friends. Just this guy from the video store and Clarence at the transmission shop. Clarence is a Mexican.'

I glanced at Pike, but Pike was staring out the front door. Intimidating the neighborhood. I said, 'Maybe he mentioned a buddy who worked at a Shell Station or an ex-con he would have drinks with.'

She shook her head. 'He just went out with Clarence. I know 'cause I followed him.'

'You followed him.' The detective using advanced interrogation techniques.

She made the kind-of shrug again. 'When he started all that talk about gettin' a Bud Lite girl I got worried he might be doin' more than drinkin' when he went out.'

'And all he ever did was go out with Clarence?'

Her head bobbed. 'Uh-huh.'

'How many times did you follow him?'

'Eight or nine.' She thought about it. 'Maybe ten.'

I described Pritzik and Richards. 'You ever see him with guys like that?'

Another head shake. 'Nuh-uh. James and Clarence would just sit there and drink, and sometimes play video games.' Another big fly cruised through the room, this time passing between us before heading toward the bathroom. Jonna Lester watched it, realized where it was going, and made a face. 'Oh, yuck.'

Pike followed the fly, and closed the bathroom.

I walked over to the front door, stared out at the hot earth, then went back to James Lester's chair and sat. Maybe James hadn't known Pritzik and Richards. It was still possible that he had, but if he hadn't then he wouldn't have been able to fake the evidence. He wouldn't have known they were dead. He wouldn't have known where to plant it. Maybe James had been telling the truth. Of course, maybe his dive through the shower glass was an accident, too.

Jonna Lester got the hey-waitaminute-! look again, then frowned as if she was trying to see shadows within shadows and not having a lot of luck with it. She wiggled her finger in the air and said, 'I take it back! There was another guy I saw him with.'

I stared at her.

'This time that I followed him, he went to the Mayfair Market over here and talked to this guy.'

Pike crossed his arms and looked at me. Well, well.

'A guy in the Mayfair?'

'A guy in the parking lot. I thought he was going to the store, but he just parked there in the lot and went over to this other car. James just kinda squatted by the driver and talked through the window, and then this guy gives him a bag and James left.'

'The man in the car gave him a bag?'

'Mm-mm. Like a Mayfair bag. Brown paper.'

'When did this happen?'

Her lips made a tight line. Her eyebrows jumped up and down. Time sense distorted by all the hash. 'A long time ago. Two or three weeks.'

I looked at Pike again, and Pike's mouth twitched. It could've been after Pritzik and Richards were killed and before James Lester phoned the hotline. Maybe we were getting somewhere.

I said, 'What did the guy look like, Jonna?'

'Like a guy. I was behind them and he didn't get out.'

Pike said, 'What kind of car was it?'

'I don't know anything about cars. It was little.'

'What color?'

She frowned. 'Dark blue. No, waitaminute. I think it was black. A little black car.' She was nodding like she could see it.

I said, 'Did James ever mention someone named Elliot Truly to you?'

She shook her head. 'Who's that?'

'Truly was James's lawyer in San Diego.'

She shook her head again. 'Nuh-uh.'

I looked around their living room. I dug through the comic books and monster truck magazines, and looked under the couch. I finally found four days' worth of the *Los Angeles Times* at the bottom of a plastic trash can in the kitchen. I found the one with my picture and brought it out to her. You could see Elliot Truly clearly behind me and Jonathan Green. I pointed at Truly. 'Was this the man in the car?'

Jonna Lester shook her head. 'Oh, no. He didn't look anything like that.'

I pointed at Green. 'Him?'

'Oh, no. Not him, either.'

I glanced at Pike and Pike shrugged. He said, 'Could've been anybody about anything. Doesn't have to relate to this. Maybe he was buying the hash.'

572

Jonna Lester's pout had come back, and now it was rimmed with petulance. 'Look, I've been trying to help, haven't I? All those news people said it looked like we were gonna get the reward, and I think we still should. I mean, even though he's dead he's still due the reward, and that means I should have it, right?'

I stared at her.

'Well, it's only right. You're only guessing that he made it up, and even if he did you can't prove it. I don't think he made it up at all. I think he was telling the truth, even if he was a lyin' no good sonofabitch.'

I said, 'Jonna, in about two minutes you're going to call the police. Do yourself a favor and don't tell them how much you should get the cash.'

The pout edged over into full-blown petulance. 'Well, why not?'

Pike said, 'Because with all the remorse you're showing, they'll think you killed him for the money. You don't want them to think that, do you?'

Jonna Lester slapped hard at the couch, then threw the glass pipe to the floor. She stamped both feet. Mad. 'Life really sucks.'

'That's true,' I said. 'But think of it this way.'

She squinted at me, and I glanced toward the bathroom.

'Death sucks worse.'

23

Jonna Lester dialed 911, identified herself, and told them that she'd found her husband dead of an apparent bathtub accident. Jonna related the facts as I outlined them, and the operator said that the paramedics were on their way.

I made Jonna dump her hash down the disposal and spray Lysol to kill the smell. Flushing it down the toilet would've been better, but I didn't want anyone in the bathroom. Evidence. I had her wash her mouth with bourbon; if she acted goofy or giggly, they'd smell the booze and figure her for a drunk. The paramedics arrived first, then the police. A uniformed sergeant named Belflower shook his head when we told him who James Lester was and said, 'Hell of a thing, ain't it? Guy stands to collect a hundred grand and he gets his neck slit from slipping on a bar of Ivory.'

I said, 'You think?'

He frowned at me. 'You don't?'

We stared at each other until he went out to his squad car and called the detectives. Pike and I stayed until the police were satisfied that Jonna Lester had found the body on her own and that we had stumbled in later, and then they said we could go.

We stopped at an Arco station two blocks away where I used the pay phone to call a friend of mine who works at the Medical Examiner's office. I told him that James might've had help falling through the glass, and I asked if he might share his findings after the autopsy. He said that such a thing might be possible if I was able to share four first-base-side tickets to a Dodgers game. I said, 'I don't have first-base-side tickets to the Dodgers.'

My friend didn't say anything.

'But maybe I can find some.'

My friend hung up, promising to call.

I dropped Pike off, and it was twenty minutes before seven when I arrived home.

Lucy's rental was wedged on the far left side of the carport, silent and cool in the deepening air. The far ridge was rimmed with copper and bronze, and honeysuckle was just beginning to lace in and around the musky scent of the eucalyptus. I stood at the edge of the carport and breathed deep. I could smell the grease and the oil and the road scents of my Stingray mixing with the smells of the mountain. I could feel the heat of its engine, and hear the dings and pops of the cooling metal. The house was quiet. A horned owl glided across the road and down along the slope, disappearing past the edge of my home. Insects swirled over the canyon, erased by the dark blur of bats. I stood there, enjoying the cooling air and the night creatures just beginning to stir and twilight in the mountains. Home is the detective, home for the night. Sandbagged, unemployed, and feeling more than a little suspicious.

I let myself in through the kitchen. Lucy was on the couch in the living room, reading *Los Angeles Magazine*. Ben was on the deck, sitting crosslegged in one of the deck chairs, reading Robert A. Heinlein's *Have Spacesuit, Will Travel*. There wasn't much light, and he would have to come in soon. I said, 'Another strange day in Oz, Lucille.'

Lucy closed the magazine on a finger and smiled, but the smile was small and uncertain. 'We got back around four.'

'Sorry I'm so late.'

'It's okay.' She made a little shrug, and in that moment I wondered how much of the tension from last night was still with us.

'Are you two starving?'

Lucy made the uncertain smile again as if she recognized the tension and was trying to soften it. 'I made Ben a snack a little while ago, but we could eat.'

'How about I make spaghetti?'

'Oh, that would be nice.'

I went into the kitchen, popped open a Falstaff, and took a package of venison sausage from the freezer. I filled a large pot with enough water for the spaghetti, dropped in the sausage, then put on the heat. I heard the glass doors slide open and Ben yelled hi. I yelled hi back. I heard Lucy tell Ben that dinner would be ready soon and that he should take a bath. I heard the guest room door close and water run. The sounds of other people in my house.

I drank most of the Falstaff, then examined the cat's tray. Crumbs of dry food speckled the paper towel around his food bowl and a hair floated in his water. He'd probably slipped down the stairs during the day when no one was home, eaten, then made his escape. I tossed the old food and water, put out fresh, and wished that he was here.

I finished the Falstaff, then opened a bottle of pinot grigio, poured two glasses, and brought one to Lucy. She was still reading the magazine, so I put the wine on the table near her. I said, 'I meant to get home sooner, but Rossi's in pretty bad shape, and the day just sort of grew from there.'

I didn't tell her about James Lester. Lester would bring us back to Green, and I didn't want to go there. 'I was hoping that we'd have more time together.'

Lucy's face grew sad and she covered my hand with hers. 'Oh, Studly, I know you can't be with us every moment. It's okay.'

'It doesn't seem okay.'

Lucy stared past me and the sadness grew deeper. She wet the corner of her mouth as if she were going to say something, then shook her head as if changing her mind. 'There's a lot going on right now, Elvis, but it doesn't have anything to do with us.'

'Can we talk about it?'

She wet the corner of her mouth again, but she still didn't look back at me. She was staring at a point in midspace as if there was a third presence in the room, floating in space and demanding the weight of her attention. 'I'd really rather not. Not now.'

I nodded. 'Okay. Up to you.'

She looked back at me and made the little smile again, and now it was clearly forced. 'Let me help you cook. Would that be okay?'

'Sure.'

We went into the kitchen and collected things for the spaghetti sauce and talked about her day. We chopped mushrooms and onions and green peppers, and opened cans of tomatoes and jars of oregano and basil, and talked as we did it, but the talking was empty and forced, the way it might be if there was a distance between us and we had to shout to make ourselves heard. I asked how her meetings had gone and she said fine. I asked if she was finished with the negotiation, and she said that a final meeting tomorrow would do it. Ben came in and parked on one of the counter stools, but he seemed to sense the tension and said little. After a time, he went into the living room and turned on my Macintosh and went on-line.

We had just put the spaghetti in boiling water and were setting the table when the doorbell rang. I said, 'If it's a reporter, I'm going to shoot him.'

It was Joe Pike and Angela Rossi. Rossi looked ragged and uncertain, and there were great hollow smudges beneath her eyes. Lucy stared soundlessly from the kitchen, and Rossi glanced from her to me. 'I hope you don't mind.'

'Of course not.' I introduced them.

Angela Rossi glanced at Lucy again, and in that moment there was something very female in the room, as if Rossi somehow sensed the tension and felt that she was not so much invading my space but Lucy's. She said, 'I'm sorry.' To Lucy, not to me.

Lucy said, 'We were going to eat soon. Would you like to join us?' She was holding the sauce spoon over the pan, frozen in mid-stir.

Rossi said, 'No. Thank you. I can't stay very long.' She smiled at Ben. 'I have children.'

'Of course.' Lucy put the sauce spoon on the counter, then excused herself and took Ben out onto the deck.

We watched the glass doors slide shut, and Rossi looked even more uncomfortable. 'Looks like I've come at a bad time.'

'Forget it.'

Pike moved behind her. He hadn't yet spoken, and probably wouldn't.

Angela Rossi looked at the floor, then looked at me, as if her energy reserves were so depleted she had to conserve what little remained. She said, 'Joe told me about Lester. He told me what you've been trying to do.'

I nodded.

'I lost it this morning and I want to apologize. You're caught in this, too, just like me.'

'Yes, but it's worse for you.'

'Maybe.' She looked at the floor again, then looked back. 'I want you to know that I didn't lie to you. I want you to know that everything I told you was the truth. LeCedrick Earle is lying, and so is his mother. I didn't do those things.'

'I believe you, detective.'

When I said it her breath gave and her eyes filled and her face collapsed, but in that same instant she caught herself and rebuilt the calm cop exterior: her breathing steadied, her eyes dried, her face calmed. It wasn't easy to recreate herself that way, but I imagined that she'd had plenty of practice over the years and that, as with every other professional police officer that I'd known, it had become a necessary survival skill. She had allowed a window to her heart to open, then had slammed it shut the way you take a covered pan off the fire when it begins to boil over, removing the heat so that you don't lose the contents. 'I'm suspended. I've been ordered to stay away from all official police business or activities pending an IA investigation. The district attorney's office is also investigating me.'

'I know.'

'The people I work with, there's only so much they can do.'

I knew that, too. If Tomsic or the others did anything to find out what was going on, they'd be pounded for obstructing justice and probably accused of trying to cover up Rossi's alleged crimes.

She looked at Joe. 'You guys offered to help. Joe said that the offer still stands.'

'Of course.' I glanced at Lucy on the deck. She and Ben were at the rail. Ben was pointing at something far down the canyon and yakking, but Lucy seemed neither to hear him nor to see. As if the other presence were out there, too, and drawing her attention. I felt my own eyes fill, but, like

Angela Rossi, I also knew the tricks of survival. 'We're not going to walk away, Angie. We're not going to leave you hanging.'

Angela Rossi looked at me for a time, first in one eye and then the other, and then she glanced again at Lucy and Ben. 'I'm sorry I intruded.'

'Don't worry about it.'

She put out her hand. We shook, and then Angela Rossi left my home.

Joe Pike stood in the entry, staring out onto the deck, as if he, too, could somehow sense the tension. Maybe I should just put up a huge sign: DOMESTIC PROBLEM. I said, 'What?'

Pike stared a moment longer, then turned and followed Angela Rossi, leaving me in the shadows.

I went back into the kitchen, stirred the sauce, then turned off the heat. The spaghetti was limp and swollen. I poured it in the colander, rinsed it, and let it drain.

I could see Lucy and Ben in the light at the rail, haloed by a swirl of flying insects, Lucy still there but not there, Ben now quiet. The cat door made its *clack-clack* behind me, and the cat crept in. He moved cautiously, pausing between steps, sniffing the air. I smiled at him. 'It's okay, bud. They're outside.'

He blinked at me, but you could tell he was suspicious. He crept to the dining area, still testing the air, then came back and stood by my feet. I broke off a piece of the venison sausage, sucked off the tomato sauce, then blew on it until it was cool. I offered it to him, and as he ate it I stroked him. His fur was flecked with dust and bits of plant matter, and felt cool from the night air. White hairs were beginning to show through the black, and I wondered how old he was. We had been together a long time.

When he was finished he looked up at me, and I smiled. I picked him up and held him close, and after a time he purred. I said, 'Life is complicated, isn't it?'

He licked my cheek, then bit my jaw, but he didn't bite hard.

After a time he hopped down and made his way through the house. He moved slowly, staring toward the deck for a very long time before finally bolting up the stairs and into my bedroom.

I told Lucy and Ben that dinner was ready. We ate, and not long after that we doused the lights and went to bed.

Since Lucy did not come upstairs that night, the cat slept well.

24

The next day Lucy and Ben planned to spend the morning in Beverly Hills, then make the drive to Long Beach for what Lucy hoped would be the final meeting of her negotiation. They were leaving the day after tomorrow.

We made banana pancakes and eggs and coffee, and ate together, but Lucy still seemed pained and distracted as she readied to leave. I found that I was thinking more about her and less about me, but neither of us seemed to be making much progress toward a resolution. Of course, maybe this was because we had so far successfully avoided talking, and maybe the time for talk-avoidance had passed. The ducking of communication rarely leads to a resolution. I said, 'What time do you guys expect to be home?'

'Sixish.' Lucy was replacing her files in her briefcase. 'I don't expect that anything will hang us up in Long Beach.'

'Good. I'm going to take us someplace special for dinner.'

She smiled at me. The soft smile. 'Where?'

'Surprise.'

We held each other's gaze for the first time that morning, and then Lucy put out her hand. Her skin was warm and soft, and touching her made me tingle. 'A surprise would be nice.'

'Leave everything to me.' Elvis Cole, Master of the Universe, turns on the ol' charm.

They left the house at ten minutes before nine, and then I phoned my friend at the coroner's office. The autopsy of James Lester had been completed, and when I asked after the cause of death, he said, 'The guy took a header through the glass, and he was still alive when he made the fall. You want to know just what was severed and how?'

'Not necessary. Was there an indication that he might've had help going through the glass?'

'You mean, like, did someone beat the hell out of him first, then push him through?'

'That's one way to put it.' I could hear papers rustling in the background, and laughter. Someone sharing a big joke to start the day at the morgue.

'Nah. No sign of blunt-force trauma. No bruising, cuts, or scrapes that would indicate a physical altercation.'

'Hm.' So maybe it wasn't murder. Maybe James Lester was just clumsy.

'But we did find one thing that was odd.' Maybe James Lester wasn't just clumsy after all. 'There's a pattern of subcutaneous capillary rupture over the carotid area on his neck.'

'That sounds like bruising.'

'It's not the kind of bruising you'd ever see, and it wasn't caused by impact trauma.'

'So no one hit him.'

'You see stuff like this when someone vomits or has a coughing fit. Coughing can do stuff like that. You'd be surprised what coughing can do.' These medical examiners.

I was thinking about the carotid artery, and I was trying to imagine a type of force that might rupture microcapillaries without creating an impact bruise. 'Are you saying that he was strangled?'

'Nah. Bruising would be severe.'

'Could he have been strangled in a way to avoid the bruising?'

He thought about it. 'I guess he could've been strangled with something soft, like a towel, or maybe choked out, like with a police choke hold. That might show a rupture pattern like this.'

'So he could've been choked out, then tossed through the glass.'

'Hey, you're saying it, I'm not. We're just speculating.'

'But it's possible.'

'It's possible the guy swallowed wrong, started coughing, then lost his balance and went through the glass.'

I didn't say anything.

'But, yeah, he could've been choked out, too.'

I hung up, then called Mrs Louise Earle. Her answering machine answered, and I said, 'Mrs Earle, this is Elvis Cole. If you're there, would you pick up, please? We need to talk.' I was hoping to catch her before she started her day. I was hoping to convince her to see me.

No one picked up.

'Mrs Earle, if Angela Rossi or any other police officer threatened you, I wish you would've told me. I'd sure like to hear about it, now.'

Still no answer.

I hung up, then once more made the drive to Olympic Park. If I couldn't get her on the phone, I would try to see her in person. If she wasn't home, I would wait. What better way for an unemployed detective to fill his day?

The streets were still heavy with morning traffic, and the day was bright and hot, but a marine cloud cover had rolled across the basin that made the light seem sourceless and somehow disorienting and had charged the air with a kind of vague dampness. It was as if the sun had vanished and the landscape was lit by a weird kind of indirect lighting that made Los Angeles take on a 1950s tract-home fluorescent reality.

I parked two houses down from Louise Earle's, walked back, and rang her bell exactly as I had done yesterday. Still no answer. I stepped through the dozens of plants and peeked through the gap between the curtains of the same front window. What I could see of the room appeared unchanged from yesterday. Hmm. It was twenty-five minutes after nine, and I stood at the edge of Louise Earle's porch and wondered what I should do. The neighborhood looked calm and ordinary; maybe Louise Earle had simply run to the market and would soon be back. Of course, even it she wasn't back soon, it didn't matter a whole hell of a lot. Such are the joys of unemployment.

I went out to my car, put up the roof to cut the sun, and waited. It was hot, and, as the sun rose, it grew hotter. Sweat leaked out of my hairline, and my shirt stuck to my chest and back. A couple of Hispanic kids pedaled by on mountain bikes, both kids sucking on Big Gulps. A thin brown dog trotted behind them, the dog's tongue hanging from its mouth. The dog looked hot, too, and was probably wishing one of the kids would drop his drink. A Carrier Air Conditioning van pulled into a drive on the next block. Probably making an emergency call. An elderly man came down the sidewalk a few minutes later, covering his head with a *Daily News* the way you would if it was raining and you were trying to stay dry.

Two of the three girls showed up in their Volkswagen Beetle, pulled into their friend's drive, and honked. Guess it was too hot to go to the door. The third girl came out with her bag and an orange beach towel and jumped into the Beetle. As they drove away, they waved, and I waved back. Guess the third girl had noticed me when she was watching for her friends. People came and went, and when they did they raced between air-conditioned cars and air-conditioned homes at a dead run. No one stayed in the heat any longer than they had to, except, of course, for displaced private eyes working on a slow case of dehydration.

Louise Earle still had not returned two hours and twenty-one minutes later, when a very thin white woman wearing an enormous sun hat emerged from the house next door and crossed her yard to Louise Earle's porch. I made her for her late seventies, but she might've been older. She rang the bell, then peered through Louise Earle's window just as I had done. She tromped around to the side of the house, came back with a watering can, and began watering the plants. I got out of the car and went up to her. 'Pardon me, ma'am, but Mrs Earle doesn't wish to be disturbed.' The detective resorts to subterfuge.

She stopped the watering and squinted at me. 'And who are you?'

I showed her my license. You show them a license and everything looks official. 'The news people were bothering her, so I've been hired to keep them away.'

She made a little sniff and continued with the watering. Guess she didn't give too much of a damn whether I was official or not. 'Well, my name is Mrs Eleanor Harris and I can assure you that Louise Earle does not consider me a bother. We've been friends for forty years.'

I nodded, trying to seem understanding. 'Then you must've seen how awful the news people were.'

The stern look softened and she resumed the watering. 'Aren't they always, though. You watch the way these people on television act and you wonder how they can live with themselves. All that smug attitude.' She made a little shiver. 'That Geraldo Rivera. That horrible little man on Channel Two. Ugh.' She shook her head in disgust and the stern look came back. 'You should've been here yesterday. Yesterday is when people were trying to bother her.'

'They were?'

She squinted harder. 'You know, one of them looked an awful lot like you.'

'I came by yesterday to introduce myself, but she wasn't home. I came with my partner, a tall man with dark glasses.'

The squint relaxed, and she nodded. 'Well, you and your partner weren't the only ones. There were others. One of them even tried to get into her house.'

I looked at her. 'Who tried to get into her house, Mrs Harris?'

'Some man.' Great. 'I remember him because he came three different times. You and your friend came the once. All the different press people came the once.'

'What did he look like?'

She made a waving motion. 'He was pretty big. You'd better watch out.'

'Big.' I put my hand a couple of inches above my head. 'Like this?'

'Well, not tall, so much. But wide. Much wider than you.' She gave me a just-between-you-and-me look. 'His arms were so long he looked like a monkey.' Kerris.

'And he was here three times.'

She was nodding. 'The first time was before you and your friend, then he came back in the afternoon and once more at dusk. When he was here in the afternoon he tried the door and he went around back. He was back there for quite a while, and for all I know he got in. For all I know he did all manner of horrible things in there.' She made the little shudder again, equating all manner of horrible things with Geraldo Rivera and the little man on Channel Two. 'It's a good thing Louise went away.'

'No one told me that she'd gone away.'

Mrs Harris continued with the watering. 'Well, no one told me, either, and that is highly unusual. We've been friends for forty years and I always water her plants when she's away. We watch out for each other. Older people have to.'

I looked more closely at the plants. Some of the leaves were wilting and the soil was dry and beginning to crack. 'Do you know where I can find her?'

Mrs Harris continued with the watering and did not answer.

I said, 'Mrs Harris, I can't keep people away from her if I'm here and she's somewhere else. Do you see?'

The water can wavered, and then Mrs Harris looked around at the drying plants and seemed lost. She shook her head. 'She always calls when she goes away. Why wouldn't she call?'

I waited.

Mrs Harris said, 'I saw her leave and it just wasn't like her, let me tell you. It was the day before yesterday, the evening after all those horrible people were here, and she just walked away.'

I thought about it. 'Could she have gone to visit Mr Lawrence?'

'Not walking. Mr Lawrence would always come in the car.'

'Do you know where Mr Lawrence lives?' I thought I might drive over.

'I'm afraid I don't. I saw her from the window, dressed very nicely and carrying her bag, walking right up this street, and in all this heat, too.' She made her lips into a thin, wrinkled line. She was holding the can with both hands, and both hands were twisting on the handle. 'I came out and called after her. I said, "Louise, it's too hot for all of that, you'll catch a stroke," but I guess she didn't hear.' The thin lips were pressing together. Worried. 'People our age are very sensitive to this heat.'

'Yes, ma'am. And she didn't call.'

Mrs Harris looked at me with wet, frightened eyes. 'You don't think she's mad at me, do you? We've been friends for forty years, and I just don't know what I'd do if she was mad at me.'

'No, ma'am. I don't think she's mad.' I was wondering why she might be in such a hurry that she would just walk away.

'But why wouldn't she call? I always water her plants.'

'I don't know, Mrs Harris. Maybe she was just trying to get away from the press. You know how horrible they are.'

Her eyes brightened a bit, drawing a little hope. 'Yes. Yes, I'm sure that must be it.'

'I'm sure she'll be back soon.'

The ancient eyes finally smiled, and she turned back to the plants. 'When you find her, you'll keep them away from her, won't you? It must be awful, having people like that around.'

'Yes, ma'am. I'll take good care.'

I helped Mrs Harris water the remainder of Louise Earle's plants, and then I went back to my car, wondering why Kerris had come three times, and wondering if his coming around had had anything to do with her going away. If he had come here three times, that meant he very much wanted to see Louise Earle. Three times was a pattern, and if the pattern maintained, he might return again today. Of course, he might not, but I still didn't have a whole lot else to do.

I went back to my car, drove four blocks to a 7-Eleven, bought two large bottles of chilled Evian water, then drove back to Louise Earle's, parked on the next block behind the Carrier van so that Eleanor Harris couldn't watch me, and continued to wait.

Exactly twelve minutes after I pulled up behind the van and turned off my car, Stan Kerris returned, but did not stop. He was driving a Mercedes SL300, and this time he slowly cruised the block, peering at Louise Earle's house, maybe hoping to see if she was home. I copied his tag number, then pulled out the little Canon and took four quick snaps just as he turned the corner.

The Mercedes was small and black, and I was hoping that Jonna Lester would recognize it.

25

I drove south to a Fast-Foto in a minimall on Jefferson Boulevard about six blocks west of USC. A Persian kid was alone in the place, working at the photo processing machine. He said, 'I'll be with you in a moment.'

'I don't have a moment. I'll pay you twenty bucks if you stop what you're doing and take care of me now.'

He eyed me like maybe I was pulling his leg, but he got up and came to the counter. I put the film on the counter between us. 'There are only four exposures on the roll. I've got to make a call. If they're done when I get back, you get the twenty.'

He wet his lips. 'What size?'

'Whatever's fastest.'

I used a pay phone in the parking lot to call Angela Rossi at home. She didn't answer her phone; her machine got it. Screening. 'Detective Rossi, it's Elvis Cole. I think I might have something.'

She picked up before I finished saying it. She sounded tired, but then she probably hadn't slept last night.

I told her where I was and what I was doing and what I had seen. I said, 'Do you want a piece of it?'

'Yes.' She said it without hesitation and without fear, the way someone would say it when they were still in the game.

'I have to show the pictures to Jonna Lester, first. Call Joe. Have Tomsic call Anna Sherman in the DA's office. If this is going where I think, everything will begin to happen very quickly.'

'I'll be ready.'

'I'll bet you will.'

I hung up, then called Jonna Lester. She answered on the second ring, and I told her that I was on my way to see her.

She said, 'But me and Dorrie was just goin' to the mall!'

'Go to the mall after. This is important, Jonna. *Please.*' The detective stoops to begging.

'Oh, all right.' Long and drawn out and whiny. 'Dorrie wants to meet you. I told her you were really cute.' Then she giggled.

I hung up and closed my eyes, thinking that only twenty-four hours ago she'd found her husband impaled on glass. Man. I called the information operator last, and asked if they had a listing for Mr Walter Lawrence. They did not.

The Persian kid was waiting at the counter when I went back inside. He had the four shots waiting, too. Fast-Foto, all right. He said, 'That's all you wanted?' You could see the Mercedes clearly in three of the four pictures. You could see Kerris clearly enough to recognize him.

'That's all.'

I paid him for the developing, gave him the extra twenty, then drove hard to the freeway and made my way across town to Jonna Lester. She and her friend, Dorrie, were waiting for me in a cloud of hash smoke so thick that I tried not to breathe. Jonna Lester giggled. 'Y'see. I tol' you he was cute.'

Dorrie giggled, too.

Dorrie looked so much like Jonna that they might've been clones. Same shorts, same top, same clear plastic clogs and dark blue nail polish. Same gum. Dorrie sat on the couch and grinned at me with wide, vacant eyes while I showed the pictures to Jonna. I said, 'Have you ever seen this car?'

She nodded and popped her gum. 'Oh, yeah. That's the guy James went to see.' She didn't even have to think about it.

'The man at the Mayfair?'

'Uh-huh.'

'The man who gave James a large paper bag?'

'Yup.'

Dorrie said, 'You wanna get high an' fuck?'

I went to the phone without asking and called Angela Rossi, who answered on the first ring. 'A man named Stan Kerris met with James Lester twenty-three days ago, eight days before Lester phoned the hotline. Stan Kerris works for Jonathan Green. I think we can build a case that these guys have fabricated evidence and set you up.'

Angela Rossi said, 'That sonofabitch.'

'Yes.'

26

We agreed to meet on the second floor of Greenblatt's Delicatessen at the eastern end of the Sunset Strip at three that afternoon.

Angela Rossi was pacing in the parking lot behind Greenblatt's when I pulled up at two minutes before three. Rossi was wearing black Levi's and a blue cotton T-shirt and metallic blue Persol sunglasses. She was pacing with her arms crossed and her head down, and when she stopped to wait for me, she scuffed at the fine gravel on the tarmac with her shoes. I said, 'Didn't you think I'd show?'

Rossi shook her head. 'Too wired to sit. I think I'm going to vomit.'

'Is Sherman here?'

'Yeah. She's not happy about it, and she's not happy about me being here.'

I followed Rossi in past the deli counter and up the stairs to the dining room. This late in the afternoon Greenblatt's was mostly empty. Earlier, the upstairs dining room had probably been filled with wannabe television writers and ninety-year-old regulars and Sunset Strip habitués, but not now. Now, the only civilians were a couple of young guys with mushroom cuts and an African-American woman sitting alone with *People* magazine. Everybody else was cops.

Linc Gibbs, Pete Bishop, Dan Tomsic, and Anna Sherman were sitting at a table as far from everyone else as possible. Gibbs had coffee, and Bishop and Tomsic had iced tea. Anna Sherman didn't have anything, and she was seated with her back to the restaurant, probably because she was concerned about being recognized. Tomsic said, 'Here they are.'

Gibbs and Bishop turned, but Anna Sherman didn't. I hadn't met Gibbs and Bishop before. Tomsic introduced us, but before he was finished, Anna Sherman said, 'I want to make it clear that the only reason I'm here is because Linc and I have a history, and he's asked me to listen. I make no claims that anything said here is off the record. Is that clear?'

Tomsic scowled. 'It's great you're on the right side in this.'

Linc said, 'Dan.'

Tomsic crossed his arms and leaned back, his mouth a hard slash. Nothing like having everyone work to the same end.

Linc Gibbs hooked a thumb toward me. 'As I understand it, we're here to discuss possible criminal wrongdoing on the part of the attorneys involved in Teddy Martin's defense. Is that it?'

'Yes. I believe that Jonathan Green or agents working on his behalf fabricated the James Lester evidence. I believe that Lester was in on it. I suspect that they also coerced Louise Earle into changing her story, but that's only a suspicion. I haven't been able to locate Mrs Earle to ask her about it.'

Anna Sherman pooched her lips into a knot. She was leaning forward on her elbows, arms crossed.

Gibbs said, 'I thought you were working for these people.'

'I quit yesterday.'

Anna Sherman raised her eyebrows, saying let's hear it.

I said, 'James Lester's real name was Stuart Langolier. Eight years ago, he was represented on a grand theft beef in Santa Barbara by Elliot Truly. That's prior association.'

Sherman looked impatient. 'Green's office notified us about that. It's even been on the news.'

'James Lester's original call to Green's hotline was logged eleven days ago. Eighteen days ago, Jonna Lester followed James to a Mayfair Market where she saw him meet this man.' I handed her the three snapshots that I'd taken of the black Mercedes. She looked at them. Linc Gibbs frowned. 'Looks familiar.'

'Stan Kerris. He's the chief investigator for Green's office. She saw Kerris and Lester speak, then Kerris passed a shopping bag to Lester, who drove away.'

Tomsic said, 'Man.'

Anna Sherman glanced at me, and Pete Bishop made a tiny smile. Gibbs held out a hand, and Sherman passed him the first of the three pictures, then the second. She stared at the third. 'Jonna Lester identified him?'

'Yes. Green hired me to check out the allegations against Detective Rossi, then run down a series of tips he'd received via the reward hotline, one of which was from James Lester. I checked out Louise Earle and the allegations, and Rossi came up clean. I reported that to Jonathan Green, and he seemed to accept it.'

Sherman chewed at the inside of her cheek as if she was thinking about leaving.

I tapped the photo she was still holding. 'I took these photographs this morning outside Louise Earle's home. A neighbor saw Kerris visit Louise Earle's home three times yesterday, and I saw him there today. When I spoke with Mrs Earle a week ago, everything she told me confirmed

Rossi's version of her son's arrest and the subsequent LAPD investigation. Now she's suddenly changed her story and Kerris is living on her porch. First Lester, now Louise Earle. I think there's a connection.'

Sherman passed the final photograph to Lincoln Gibbs and began ticking her right index fingernail on the table. 'All right. What else do you have?'

'When the James Lester story hit the news, I wanted to stay after Pritzik and Richards, which would've been the natural thing to do, but Green had me work a dog and pony with the press. I now believe that it was a media manipulation to make Louise Earle's changing her story more credible to the public.'

Bishop said, 'I thought you were the guy who got her to change her story.'

I shook my head. 'That's part of the big lie. I saw her one time, and at that time everything she said confirmed Rossi's story. Three days later Stan Kerris pays her a visit and everything changes, and the next thing I know Green holds a press conference and says that I've turned up evidence to prove Rossi rotten. The wonder boy who showed up the cops and found James Lester now ferrets out the truth from the intimidated mother. You see?'

Anna Sherman continued ticking the nail. She stared at the table and made her mouth the small knot again. Then she looked up and shook her head. 'All of you must be out of your minds.'

Tomsic threw up his hands. 'What does *that* mean?'

The two kids with the mushroom cuts and the African-American woman looked over, and Lincoln Gibbs zapped Tomsic with a look that must've come from the days before he started affecting the professor image, flashing street eyes, mess-with-me-and-I'll-choke-your-eyes-out.

Tomsic settled back.

Sherman said, 'It means that if my office or the LAPD launched an investigation into Jonathan Green at this time based on this kind of bullshit evidence it would be a public relations nightmare.'

Gibbs said, 'This is worth something, Anna. You know it is. You can't just ignore it.'

She leaned toward him, ticking off the points. 'I spoke with Jonna Lester and I know her to be a hash head. Jonna Lester doesn't know if it was eighteen days ago or twenty-eight or just eight, which is exactly what Stan Kerris would say *if* he admitted to having met James Lester, which he almost certainly won't.' She ticked another point. 'Then, if he did admit to such a meeting, he would say that it was a preliminary interview conducted prior to Mr Cole's being assigned the follow-up, and, in case you've forgotten, Mr Lester isn't around to dispute that statement.'

I said, 'Did you review Lester's autopsy report?'

'There was no sign of foul play.'

'That isn't quite correct. Someone who was good could've choked out Lester, then put him through the glass.'

Sherman's nostrils flared and she closed her eyes. 'Could have.'

'I know you can't go to court with that one, Sherman, but it fits with the theory. You really think Lester just happened to cut his own throat?'

Tomsic said, 'Subpoena Lester's phone records, and pull Green's records, too. See who was calling who and when they were talking.'

Sherman made a hissing sound.

Angela Rossi said, 'No one's forgotten about Pritzik and Richards, either.'

Anna Sherman shook her head. 'You people are talking about accusing an attorney of Jonathan Green's stature of fabricating evidence without any substantive proof to back it up. With even less proof, you want me to accuse him of murder. Ask yourself this: why would Jonathan Green risk his career and his reputation and his freedom to falsify evidence for one client? The press is going to ask that, and you don't have an answer because it doesn't make sense.' She glanced from cop to cop, finally coming back to me. It was exactly what I had asked Pike. 'All you have are some unseemly coincidences and the testimony of a hash head. Jonathan Green will charge us with harassment, and he will bring us before the state bar, and I, for one, am tired of getting my ass handed to me in the *L. A. Times* every day.'

I said, 'Is that it?'

She nodded.

I looked at Rossi. I looked back at Anna Sherman. I said, 'Getting our asses kicked in the press is how we define truth in the American legal system?'

Anna Sherman stood. 'My boss is being pressured to drop the charges against Teddy Martin. I've been fighting him on it because I want to see this through, but I don't think he has the balls. I think he'll give in because he has arrived at his own personal definition of justice. He defines it as political survival.' Anna Sherman didn't say anything more for a time, then she looked directly at Rossi. 'I'm sorry, but this meeting is now over.' She tucked her purse under her arm and walked out.

Tomsic slapped the formica hard, and Bishop made a soft whistling sound through his teeth. Angela Rossi had pushed her fists between her legs onto her chair and gently rocked. Finally, Bishop said, 'So where are we, Linc?'

Lincoln Gibbs took a breath. 'You heard her. The district attorney's office is not interested in pursuing this investigation.'

Tomsic said, 'That's bullshit.' He jabbed the finger at me. 'Cole's onto something! These bastards are over the line!'

Gibbs made his voice harder. 'They will not pursue this line, Sergeant. That's the end of it.'

Tomsic wasn't letting it go. Now he was waving both hands. 'So Green can do whatever? He can murder people? He can rob banks? We just say, oh, we'll look bad if we do something?'

Lincoln Gibbs's nostrils were wide and hard and you could hear him breathe. But then the breathing calmed and he looked at Rossi. Sad. 'Sometimes we have the worst job in the world. High-priced, sleazebag shysters make millions getting off murderers and dope dealers and the dregs of this society, but they are wrong, and we are right. And if we have to take some bullets along the way, then we take'm.' He reached across the table and squeezed Angie's arm. 'Goes with the job.'

Tomsic said, 'That's bullshit.'

Linc Gibbs nodded. 'Of course it's bullshit, Sergeant, but it's where we are.' He looked at me. 'Thanks, Cole. It didn't pan out, but we owe you for the effort.'

Bishop got up, then Gibbs. Gibbs told Tomsic to come with them, and he told Angela Rossi he thought she should probably go home. He told her not to worry. He said that they weren't going to let it go, and that they would keep digging into the LeCedrick Earle thing and that they wouldn't abandon her. She nodded and got up and went with them, but she looked abandoned to me. Of course, maybe it was just my imagination.

I sat alone at the empty table for another three minutes, wondering what to do next and having no great surges of inspiration. I think I was feeling abandoned, too, but I probably wasn't feeling as abandoned as Angela Rossi.

I went down the stairs and out the back of Greenblatt's to my car. Anna Sherman was sitting in the passenger seat, waiting for me. A bead of sweat worked its way down along her temple and her cheek. She said, 'It's hotter than hell out here.'

I stared at her. 'Yes. It is.'

She ran her fingers along the dash. She tapped the shift lever. 'This is a classic, isn't it?'

'Yeah.'

'It's a Corvette?'

'Yeah. A Stingray.' I looked where she was looking. I touched where she was touching. 'I wanted one when I was a kid, and a few years ago I had the opportunity to buy this one, so I did. I couldn't afford it, but I bought it anyway.'

She nodded. 'I should do something like that. Something crazy.' She ran her fingers along the console. 'When was it made?'

'Nineteen sixty-six.'

'God. I was ten years old.' She looked older.

I wanted to start the engine and turn on the air conditioner, but I didn't.

Anna Sherman said, 'Three months ago an attorney named Lucas Worley was arrested in a drug sting in Santa Monica. He wasn't the target. He just happened to be there.' She tapped my glove box. 'I put his address in here.'

I waited.

'Worley has a heroin problem. He'll buy a kilo every now and then, then cut it and sell it to his friends to cover his costs. Worley was a junior litigator in Green's office.'

I smiled. 'Was.'

'Green had the case handled to minimize bad publicity for his firm, so Worley was able to cop a first offense probation plea.'

'Is Worley still with the firm?'

She shook her head. 'Resigned. I guess that was part of the deal.' She finally looked at me. It was the first time she'd looked at me since I got into the car. 'Worley was a tort litigator. That means he worked in Green's contract department. He would've had access to retainer agreements and to the contracts that Green had with his clients.'

'Is he employed?'

She made a little dismissive shrug. 'Probably dealing full time, but I don't know.'

'So you think there's something to this.'

She touched the dash again, watching her fingers move along the gentle lines. 'You always follow the money.' She shook her head and made a little smile. 'I've been doing this for twelve years. I've prosecuted hundreds of cases, and I have learned that people do crime for only two reasons: sex and money. There are no other motives.'

'What about power and revenge?'

'That's just sex and money under aliases.' The tiny smile again. 'If you're right, and if Jonathan Green is willing to break the law, then he's doing it for sex or money.'

I was starting to like Anna Sherman. I was starting to like her just fine. 'Do you think Worley will cooperate?'

She shrugged. 'Lucas Worley is a piece of shit. He sells dope because he likes it. He likes the people, he likes the scene. He says that it's a step up from practicing law.' She looked tired. 'Maybe he's right.'

I said, 'Hey.'

She looked at me.

'I'll tell you what I told Rossi. Don't give up. The good part of the system outweighs the bad. We just have to fix the bad.'

Anna Sherman got out of the car, closed the door, then looked in at me. She said, 'This conversation never happened. If you say it did, and if you say I gave you Worley, I'll deny it and sue you for slander. Is that clear?'

'Clear.'

She walked away without another word. I opened the glove box and found a plain white sheet of notepaper with Lucas Worley's address written in anonymous block letters.

27

I stopped for roses. I bought a dozen red long-stems, plus a single daisy, then went to a wine shop I know for a bottle of Dom Perignon and an ounce of Beluga caviar. While the clerk was bagging the champagne I used their phone to make a reservation at Musso & Frank for eight o'clock. When I was off the phone, the clerk grinned at me. 'Special date?'

'Very special.'

He laughed. 'Are there any other kind?' Cynic.

I drove home hard, hoping that I would get there before Lucy and Ben. I did. I put the flowers in the refrigerator and the Dom Perignon and three flute glasses in the freezer. The Dom Perignon was cold, but I wanted it colder. I hard-boiled an egg, minced an onion, then minced the egg. I put the egg, the onion, and some capers in three little Japanese serving plates, covered them with Saran Wrap, then arranged the plates on a matching tray with the caviar and put the tray in the refrigerator next to the flowers. I put out Carr's Table Water Crackers, then phoned Joe Pike and told him about Lucas Worley. Pike said, 'You think he might know something?'

'I think he might, or, if he doesn't, he might be able to help us find someone who does.'

'How do you want to play it?'

I told him.

Joe was silent for a time, then said, 'How about we bring in Ray Depente? Ray would be effective on a guy like Worley.'

'You think?'

'Ray could get a corpse to talk.'

I told him that would be fine. I told him that I would meet them outside Worley's place early tomorrow, and when I was done, Joe said, 'Is it going any better with Lucy?'

'Not yet, but soon. I'm about to turn on the charm.'

'Why don't you try working it out, instead.' Mr Sensitive.

I hung up, then ran upstairs to finish getting ready. I shaved, showered, put on a jacket and tie, then ran downstairs and took the Dom Perignon out of the freezer. I wanted it cold, not frozen.

When Lucy and Ben pulled into the carport I was waiting at the door when they came through with shopping bags from Saks and Bottega Veneta and Giorgio and Pierre Deux. Lucy looked tired until she saw me, and then she looked surprised. I held out the flowers. 'My God, you're beautiful.'

Ben smiled so wide I thought his face would turn inside out.

Lucy looked at the flowers. She glanced at me and then the flowers again, and then back to me. Her hands were still full of shopping bags. 'Oh, a daisy.'

I put the shopping bags on the dining room table, then opened the Dom Perignon. I poured apple juice for Ben. 'We have champagne. We have caviar. Then we will have dinner at Musso & Frank.'

She said, 'The restaurant in Hollywood?'

'Dashiell Hammett fell in love with Lillian Hellman there.' I gave her a glass of the Dom Perignon. 'It was a love that changed their lives, and endured for as long as they lived.'

Lucy seemed embarrassed. 'You're being so nice.'

I said, 'Ben. Would you give your mother and me a moment alone, please?'

Ben giggled. 'You want me to amscray?'

'Yes, Ben, I want you to amscray.'

Ben amscrayed into the living room. When the TV came on and Agent Mulder started talking about something that ate five human livers every thirty years, I took the flowers from Lucy and put them aside. I put aside her champagne glass, too, and held her upper arms and looked into her eyes. 'You have two more nights in Los Angeles. I want those nights to be easy for you. It's okay with me if you'd like to move to a hotel.'

Lucy stared at me for ten heartbeats, then shook her head. 'I'm exactly where I want to be.'

'I know that you're having trouble with your ex-husband. I know that he has a problem with you and Ben staying here. I want you to know that I'll support you in anything you want to do.'

Lucy sighed, and glanced toward the living room. 'Ben.'

'Don't blame Ben. I am a detective, Lucille. I know all and see all.'

'Darlene.'

'Does it matter?'

She sighed again, then leaned forward to rest her forehead against my chest. 'Oh, Studly, there is so much going on right now. I'm sorry.'

I put my arms around her and held her. 'You don't have anything to be sorry for.'

She looked up and her eyes were rimmed red and wet. 'I feel like I've ruined our time together.'

'You haven't.'

'I've let him intrude, and that's not fair to you or to me. I didn't tell you, and that is not the quality of honesty that I want in our relationship.'

'You were trying to protect me.'

She stepped back and looked into my eyes as if she were searching for something faraway and hard to see, something that she feared might change even as she saw it. 'There's so much going on right now. You just don't know.' She took a breath, then let it out. 'I really need to talk about this.'

'Then let's talk.'

She took my hand and led me out onto the deck into the cooling night air, with the last breath of day fading in the west. She held my right hand in both of hers and said, 'There are things you need to know.'

'I don't need to know anything about you, Lucille.'

'I'm not going to tell you deep dark secrets about myself. I don't *have* any secrets.'

'Shucks.' Trying to lighten the moment with a little humor.

Lucy frowned and looked away. 'These are things I need to say as much to help me get them straight as for you to be aware of what's going on. Do you see that?'

'Okay.'

She looked back. 'There are things happening between me and my ex-husband that I should've told you about, but didn't.'

I nodded, letting her talk.

'Not because they're secret or because I wanted to keep anything from you, but because I resent the intrusion and did not want these things to impact upon our time together. I did not want *him* to share this time with us.' The other presence. 'But I let him get to me, and he has intruded and that is not fair to either me or to you and I apologize.'

I started to tell her that she didn't have to apologize, but she raised a hand, stopping me.

I sighed. 'Okay. I accept.'

'I'm not asking for advice. I'm an adult, I'm an attorney, and I will handle this. Okay?'

I nodded.

'I mean, God, I'm paid to advise other people, am I not?'

I nodded again. Getting a lot of nod practice tonight.

She said, 'Richard has moved back to Baton Rouge.' Richard was her ex-husband. He'd been living in Shreveport for the past three years, and, in the time that I'd known Lucy, she'd mentioned him exactly twice. He, too, was an attorney. 'I've encouraged Ben to develop a relationship with his father, but Richard has taken it beyond that. He phones me at my office; he drops around my house unannounced; he invites himself to outings that I've planned with Ben; he's resurrected his friendship with a lot of the people at my firm. He has systematically reinserted himself into my life, and I do not like it.'

'You feel invaded.'

She made a brief, flickering smile. 'Studly, I feel like Normandy Beach.'

I said, 'Joe likes you. Joe would probably fly down and have a talk with him.'

The smile flickered again and, for just a moment, Lucy laughed. The tension was easing. 'Perhaps it will come to that.' The laugh and the smile faded then, and she said, 'When he found out that Ben and I were going to stay here, with you, instead of a hotel, he became abusive. He criticized my judgment and told me that I was setting a bad example for Ben and demanded that I leave Ben with him.'

I said, 'Luce?'

She looked at me.

I opened my mouth but did not speak. My mouth felt dry and there was a kind of faraway ringing and my fingers and legs suddenly went cold. There are those times when intellect fails us. There are those moments when the modern man fades to a shadow and something from the brain stem reasserts itself, and in that moment the joking is gone and we frighten ourselves with our dark potential. I said, quite normally, quite conversationally, 'What do you mean, abusive? Did he touch you?'

She shook her head, and then she placed both palms on my chest. 'Oh, no. No, Elvis. And if he had I promise you fully that I would've had him arrested so fast he would've had whiplash.'

I nodded again, but now the nods weren't funny. My fingers and legs began to tingle with returning blood.

She said, 'I thought it was past, but it isn't. That's why Darlene called. He's been phoning the office and leaving messages on my machine at home, and then I got upset even more that I had let him get me upset in the first place. Do you see?'

My breathing had evened out and the ringing was gone. I nodded. 'He pushed your buttons.'

'Yes.'

'He exerted a kind of power over you that you thought was behind you.'

She said, 'I'm so sorry you thought it was you, or that you had something to do with this. Oh, sweetie, it wasn't you at all. It was me.'

'It's okay, Luce. It's really okay.'

She rubbed my chest again and stared up at me because there was more. 'Everything is complicated because I haven't been happy at the firm or with where I am in my life, and I don't know what I'm going to do about it.'

I looked at her, and my heart began to thud.

'It started before I met you. It started even before Richard moved back.'

I looked at her some more, and the night air was suddenly sparkling with a kind of expectant electricity.

'I don't know if I want to stay at the firm. I don't even know if I want to stay in Baton Rouge.' She shook her head, glancing past me at Ben, glancing out at the warm house lights in the canyon. She finally looked back at me. 'Do you know what I'm saying?'

'Would you consider coming out here?' My heart was thudding so loudly I wondered if the people across the canyon could hear it.

'I don't know.' She took a deep breath and rubbed my chest again. 'I guess I just needed to tell you that I don't know.' She tried to make a joke. 'Damn, and I thought I was too young for menopause.'

I nodded.

'I'm feeling kind of stupid right now. It just seemed important to tell you.'

I touched her lips. I kissed her, with the center of my heart. 'I love you, Lucille. Rotten ex-husband or no. Long-distance relationship or no. Do you know that?'

Her eyes grew wet again, and she ran her hand along the line of my shoulder. She touched my tie. 'You look so nice.'

I smiled.

'You went to so much trouble with the champagne and caviar.'

I said, 'Would you like to go eat? We still have time.' They would hold the reservation. I was sure I could talk them into holding the reservation.

She took a breath, then let it out and carefully looked up at me. 'What I would like to do is stay home with my two guys. What I would like is to order a pizza and drink your wonderful champagne and play Clue.'

I grinned. 'You want to play Clue?'

She was suddenly very serious. 'I just want to be with you, Elvis. I just want to relax and enjoy being here. Do you know?'

I kissed her fingers. 'I know.'

I took off my jacket and tie, and we ordered Domino's pizza. We made a large Italian salad with pepperocinis and garbanzo beans and fresh garlic while we waited for the pie. When the pizza came, we drank the Dom Perignon and ate the pizza between bites of Beluga caviar mixed with capers and minced onion, and played Clue until very late that night. There was a smile on Lucy's face that did not leave, and made the room feel light and warm and explosive with energy. Ben laughed so hard that he blew soda through his nose.

It was as if the other presence was no longer with us, as if by exposing the other it vanished the way a shadow will when exposed to light.

We played until very late, and when Ben went to bed, Lucy and I finished the last of the champagne, and then she followed me upstairs into a night filled with warmth and love and laughter.

28

The next morning I left the house as the eastern sky bloomed with the onrushing sun and drove to Lucas Worley's condominium on a one-way street just off Gretna Green Way in Brentwood. Gretna Green is a connecting street between Sunset Boulevard and San Vicente, lined with apartment houses and condominium complexes and some very nice single-family homes, but in the dim time just before sunrise the traffic was sparse and the neighborhood still. It was a wonderful time of the day for lurking.

Worley's condo was set between the street and a service alley in a lush green setting. They were nice condos, large and airy and stylishly ideal for former on-the-rise young attorneys turned dope dealers. I slow-cruised the street first, then turned down the alley and idled past the rear. Each condominium had a double carport at its back protected by an overhead wrought-iron door, and Worley's was filled with a gunmetal blue Porsche 911 sporting a vanity plate. The vanity plate read EZLIVN. Guess the loss of his day job hadn't inhibited his lifestyle.

When I reached the end of the alley, Joe Pike and Ray Depente materialized out of the murk and drifted silently to my car. Ray was wearing a black suit over a white shirt with a thin black bow tie. I said, 'When did you go Muslim?'

Ray looked at himself and smiled. 'Joe said you wanted scary. You tell me anything a white boy's more scared of than a Muslim with a hardon?'

Ray Depente was an inch taller than Joe, but slimmer, with mocha skin and gray-flecked hair and the ramrod-straight bearing of a career Marine, which he had been. For the better part of twenty-two years Ray Depente had taught unarmed combat at Camp Pendleton, in Oceanside, California, before retiring to open a karate school in South Central Los Angeles. Now, he taught children the art of self-respect for ten cents a lesson, and instructed Hollywood actors how to look tough on screen for five hundred dollars an hour. The one paid for the other.

Ray extended his hand and we shook as he said, 'Haven't seen you in a while, my friend. Better get your butt down to my place before you get out of shape.'

'Too many tough guys down there, Ray. Some actor might beat me up.'

Ray smiled wider. 'Way I hear things been going for you, I guess it could happen.' The smile fell away. 'We got a plan for Mr Dope Dealer, or are we just gonna stand around in the dark waitin' to be discovered?' The eastern sky was cooling from pink to violet to blue. Traffic was picking up out on Gretna, and we could hear garbage trucks and cars pulling out of driveways as people left for work. Pretty soon housekeepers would be trudging past to their day work.

Joe tilted his head toward the Porsche. 'Worley's been inside since eight-thirty last night.'

'Is he alone?'

'Yes.'

I said, 'He's got to leave sooner or later. When he leaves we'll go in the house and find his stash. We find the stash, we'll have some leverage.'

Ray said, 'What if he doesn't have a stash?'

I shrugged. 'Then we'll live with him until he scores.'

Ray stared at the Porsche. 'Joe said this guy was a lawyer.'

'Yep. Until he got caught with the dope.'

Ray looked at the nice car and the nice condo and shook his head. 'Asshole.'

Joe and Ray vanished back into the thinning shadows, and I pulled out of the alley and down the little street to Gretna Green. I parked beneath a Moroccan gumball tree with an easy eyes-forward view of Lucas Worley's street and waited while the air slowly filled with a mist of brightening light and early morning commuter traffic increased and the city began its day.

At twelve minutes after nine that morning the 911 nosed out onto Gretna and turned south, heading for San Vicente. Worley was a pudgy guy with tight curly hair cut short and close-set eyes and a stud in his left ear. He was wearing a tattered dark gray sweatshirt with no sleeves, and his arms were thin and hairy. Probably just running out for coffee.

I left the Corvette, trotted across Gretna and down along the little street to Worley's condo, where Pike and Ray were waiting at the front door. Pike already had the door open.

Lucas Worley's condominium was all high-angled ceilings and stark white walls and rented furniture of the too low, too wide, and too ugly variety. A fabric and plastic ficus sat in the L of two full-sized sofas, and a big-screen TV filled one wall. A stack of stereo equipment ran along the adjoining wall with what looked to be a couple of thousand CDs scattered over the floor and the furniture and on top of the big screen. I guess neatness wasn't one of Lucas Worley's strengths. Framed movie posters from *Easy Rider* and *To Live and Die in L.A.* hung above the fireplace opposite mediocre lithographs of Jimi Hendrix and Madonna, and the effect was sort of like a nebbish's fantasy of how a high-end life-in-the-fast-lane hipster would live. He even had a lava lamp. Ray said, 'Would you look at this?'

A framed Harvard Law School diploma was leaning against the lava lamp.

Ray was shaking his head. Incredulous. 'The kids I work with down in South Central bust their asses just to get a high-school diploma so they can get away from this shit, and here this fool is with a goddamned ticket from Harvard Law.'

I said, 'He won't be gone long, Ray. We've got to find the stash.'

Ray moved away from the diploma. He glanced back at it twice and sighed as if he'd seen something so incomprehensible that understanding would forever be denied.

I started for the stairs. 'I'll take the second floor. You guys search down here.'

Pike said, 'Don't bother. It's in the tree.' Pike was circling the ficus.

I stopped at the base of the stairs. 'What do you mean, it's in the tree? How would you know that?'

'Because it's where a lightweight would put it.' Pike grabbed the ficus and yanked it up hard. The ficus came out of its pot, and there was the dope stash. Like Pike had sensed it.

Ray and I stared at each other. We stared at Pike. Ray said, 'Nawwww.'

Pike made a little shrug.

Ray said, 'You're pulling our legs. You saw him foolin' in there through the window last night.'

Pike angled the flat lenses at Ray. 'You think?'

You never know with Pike.

The ficus had covered two Baggies of white powder, one Baggie of brown powder, a metric scale, and assorted drug sales paraphernalia. I told Joe and Ray what I wanted them to do, and when, and then they left. I stayed. I took the dope out of the planter and put it in a neat pile on the coffee table, then replaced the ficus, looked through the scattered CDs until I found something that I liked, put it in the changer, turned on the music, and sat on the couch to wait. The Police. *Reggatta De Blanc.*

Forty-two minutes later, keys worked the lock, the door swung open, and Lucas Worley came halfway through the door before seeing me. He was carrying a newspaper and a Starbucks cup. He looked surprised, but he hadn't yet seen the dope on the table. 'What the fuck is this? Who are you?'

'Come inside and close the door, Luke. Can I call you Luke? Or is it Lucas? Lucas seems pretentious.' He was a little bit taller than he had looked in the car. His eyes were bright and sharp, and he spoke quickly. You could tell he was used to talking. You could tell he was used to saying bright things and having them appreciated, and you could tell that he thought he was brighter than he really was. Probably where the smugness came from.

He said, 'Maybe I'm confused. Isn't this my house? Isn't that my sofa? The only thing that doesn't seem to belong here is you.' Showing attitude.

'Look at me, Luke. Do you recognize me?'

'Sure. On television. You're the detective who's working with Jonathan.' He closed the door. He was moving slowly. Wary, but trying to be oh-so-cool about it. 'How's Jonathan?'

I smiled at him. 'Funny you should ask, Luke. Jonathan is why I'm here.'

That's when he saw the Baggies. He stared at them for most of an eternity, and then he said, 'What's that?' Like he'd never seen them before.

'Here's the deal, Luke. You used to work in Jonathan's contracts department, and I want to know everything there is to know about Jonathan and his relationship to Teddy Martin. You're going to tell me what you know, and then you're going to get me into his office so that I can see for myself. Are we on the same page with that?'

He shook his head as if I'd spoken Somali. 'Are you high? I don't know you. Get out of here.'

I leaned back and spread my arms along the back of the couch so that my jacket would open and he could see the Dan Wesson.

'Look, I'm not doing anything for you. I'm going to call Jonathan right now. I'm going to tell him what's going on.'

'Oh, you'll go along, Luke. Trust me.' I pointed at the Baggies with my foot. 'You've been a bad boy.'

He smiled like he'd decided exactly how he was going to play it out and he knew he could beat me because he was smarter than me. 'Is this how you're going to get me to do what you want? You're going to call the police? You figure you can have me bounced for violating probation?'

I shook my head. 'No way, Luke. We don't need the police.'

He smiled wider and moved past me, going to the phone. 'Tell you what. I'll call them for you.' He picked up the phone and waved it, showing me just how in control he thought he was. 'Because when they get here and pull us in, I promise you that I can beat this nine ways from Monday in court.' Waving the phone at the dope. 'That's not mine. You're here, you planted it, and you're trying to extort me to screw Jonathan because of the Martin case. Man, Jonathan will have a field day with that one. I can see it now.'

I looked disappointed. 'You didn't listen, Luke. I'm not going to call the cops. I've already made my call.'

Worley frowned and looked uncertain. 'Who'd you call?'

Someone knocked at the door.

Lucas Worley suddenly didn't look so sure of himself.

'Don't you think you should get that?'

He didn't look at the door. 'Who is it?'

Someone knocked again.

I said, 'I kinda figured that you wouldn't cooperate, and that if I tried setting you up with the police that you'd find a way to beat it, so I called a guy I know named Gerald DiVega. You know DiVega?'

His mouth formed into a little O, like the name was ringing a bell but he couldn't quite be sure of it.

I went to the door. 'Gerald DiVega sells drugs to westside hipsters like yourself. For many years he sold drugs on the streets, like so many other gentlemen of free enterprise, but in the past few years he's chosen to cultivate a more upscale clientele: movie and TV people, music people, lawyers and doctors, the very same people you're selling to with your little pissant business.' I opened the door and Ray and Joe stepped in. They were both wearing sunglasses and looking somber. Ray reached under his jacket and drew out a Colt .45 Government model. Joe Pike took out his Python. I said, 'This is Mr X and this is Mr Y. Mr D sent them because he doesn't like you cutting in on his clientele.'

Ray Depente said, 'This the muthuhfuckuh?' He took a black tube from his jacket pocket and screwed it onto the muzzle of the .45 as he said it.

'That's him.'

Lucas Worley's eyes went wide, and he took one step back. 'Hey. What is this? What's going on?' Smug was gone. Arrogance had vanished.

Ray and Joe crossed the room like two large, sinuous sharks gliding toward a blood spoor. Ray moved between Worley and the stairs, and Joe moved in from the other side and grabbed Worley's throat hard and rode him down on the couch. When Joe grabbed him, Lucas made a gurgling sound. I said, 'I guess you should've called the cops when you had the chance, Luke.'

Ray waved the .45 at me. 'You can split now, you want. Mr DiVega says thanks.'

'Can't I stay?'

Ray shrugged like it was nothing to him. 'Either way.'

Lucas Worley's eyes were bulging and his face changed from red to purple. He was clawing at Joe's one hand with both of his, but it was like a child trying to bend steel bars.

Ray jacked a round into the .45, then put the muzzle of the suppressor against Worley's cheek and held out his other hand to shield himself from the blood-splatter that would surely follow and Lucas Worley thrashed and moaned and his bowels and bladder went loose at the same time. Guess the real world wasn't seeming like *Easy Rider* anymore. Guess it wasn't like a movie or a television program. Not much glamor in messing your shorts.

I said, 'You guys don't shoot him, yet.'

Lucas Worley's eyes rolled toward me.

I walked over and squatted by him to look into the rolling eyes. I said, 'I helped Mr DiVega out a couple of years back, and he owes me. He knows that I want something from you, and he's willing to play this however I want. You see?'

Lucas Worley was trying to shake his head, trying to say he wasn't trying to cut in on anyone's trade and wouldn't do it anymore if only they'd let him live. Of course, since Joe was strangling him, we couldn't quite make out the words.

'These gentlemen have orders to kill you unless I tell them not to.'

Ray said, 'Kill yo' ass dead.' I frowned at Ray over the top of Worley's head, and Ray shrugged. Overacting.

I said, 'So what's it going to be, Luke? You going to help me out with Jonathan Green, or do I walk out the door and make these guys happy?'

Lucas Worley gurgled some more.

I said, 'I didn't understand you, Luke.'

Joe released some of the pressure, and Lucas Worley croaked, 'Anything. I'll do anything.'

Ray Depente pressed the gun in harder and looked angry. 'Shit. You mean we don't get to kill the little muthuhfuckuh?'

'Not yet. But maybe later.'

Ray squinted down at the rolling eyes, then withdrew the gun and stepped back. Joe let Worley go and also stepped away. Ray said, 'You got a pass this time, dipshit. But Mr DiVega be on your ass now, you understand?'

Lucas Worley was frozen on the couch like a squirrel in front of an onrushing car.

Ray said, 'You just retired from the dope dealin' business, didn't you?'

Worley nodded.

Ray said, 'You're giving Mr DiVega your word, and you know what will happen if you break your word, don't you?'

Worley nodded again. I think he was too terrified to speak.

Ray looked at the framed Harvard Law School diploma and shook his head. 'Dumb muthuhfuckuh. You oughta be ashamed of yourself.'

He put away the .45, then he and Joe Pike walked over to the bar and made themselves a drink.

I said, 'I told you that you'd see it my way, Luke. Now go wash off and change your clothes. We've got some work to do.'

29

When Lucas Worley was in the shower I looked at Ray Depente. '"Kill yo' ass dead"?'

'I thought it was very effective.'

Joe Pike shook his head. 'Samuel L. Jackson.'

Ray frowned. 'Since when did you become Sir Laurence Olivier?'

Pike's mouth twitched, and he went over to browse through Worley's CDs.

By the time we got Worley out of the shower and dressed and sitting in the living room, it was two-forty that afternoon. Joe and Ray were back in character, Joe standing behind the couch like an ominous shadow, Ray watching ESPN on the big-screen. I said, 'Luke, do you have a gun here in your house?'

He was sitting on the couch with his hands in his lap and his hair wet and spikey. He still looked scared, but now he wasn't looking panicked. 'Yeah. Up in the nightstand.'

Joe drifted up the stairs.

'That the only one, Luke? You wouldn't have any surprises tucked away, would you?'

He shook his head, eyes jumping with the certain knowledge that surprises would get him killed. 'That's all. I swear.'

'Are you expecting anyone?'

'No.'

'No one dropping around to pick up a little smack? No girlfriends? No repairmen?'

'No. Honest.' A dope-dealing ex-attorney saying *honest*.

'Okay. I am now going to tell you exactly what I want, and you're going to tell me how to do it. Okay?'

He looked worried. 'If I can.'

Ray whirled away from the big-screen, loud and angry and snapping, 'What did you say?'

Lucas Worley jumped as if he'd been slapped. 'I'll tell you how. Sure. Whatever you want.'

Ray's eyes narrowed, and he turned back to the big-screen, mumbling.

Joe Pike came back down the stairs with a pistol. 'Glock nine.'

'Anything else?'

'Nope.' He sat by Ray.

I said, 'Okay, Luke. Here's my problem. I suspect that your mentor, Mr Green, is suborning testimony. I think he may even be involved in murder, only I can't figure out why a man in his position and of his stature would risk his ass by so doing. Do you understand that?'

Worley wasn't just looking at me; he was watching my lips move, careful to get every word. He blinked when he realized that I'd quit speaking, then shook his head. 'Of course, he wouldn't. That's dumb.'

'That's what everyone says.'

'It's true. If he's caught he'd be throwing away his career.'

I smiled at him. 'Sort of like you.'

Lucas Worley swallowed, then shrugged. Like he was embarrassed. 'Yeah, but I was just a lawyer, and I never liked it much. He's Jonathan Green. He *loves* it.'

'Well, you're going to help me find out if it's dumb or not. Would Jonathan enter into a verbal agreement with a client?'

Worley grinned. 'You've got to be kidding.'

'Okay, so everything would be written.'

'Absolutely. But no one is going to admit to a crime on paper. You're not going to find a paper that says "I will do murder for X dollars."' He was smiling at the thought of it. 'Such a contract isn't enforceable, anyway. You couldn't sue somebody because they didn't perform an illegal act. You'd be incriminating yourself in conspiracy.'

'So Jonathan wouldn't put anything in writing that he couldn't support in a civil action.'

'Not a chance. No lawyer would.' He spread his hands. 'Look, you're not going to find anything incriminating there. I promise you. Jonathan isn't that stupid.'

'That's not your concern. Your job is to get me access to all the contracts between Teddy and Jonathan. That is the sum total of your value to me.' I nodded toward Joe and Ray. 'You know that much, don't you?'

The worried look came back. 'Hey, I said that I would. We can't just walk in there in the middle of the day. There're people.'

'When do the people go home?'

'The office closes at six, but some of them stay late. Christ, we used to work until ten, eleven at night. Sometimes later.'

Joe said, 'How many people?'

'A few. It's a big office.'

I said, 'But most of the people go at six?'

'Yeah. There shouldn't be more than eight or nine there later than that.'

'You have a card key to get in?'

'Oh, yeah. I kept it.'

'How about the elevator to Jonathan's floor?'

'The card key accesses the parking garage, the elevator, everything.'

I thought about it. 'How long would it take you to get into the files?'

Lucas Worley stared at me about six seconds too long. 'I dunno. It could take a while.'

Ray Depente pushed up from his seat and drew out the .45 and stalked over like he'd just hit the red line on the biggest bunch of bullshit he'd ever heard. 'I'm killin' this fuckwad right goddamned now! Weasely muthuhfuckin' bullshit, take a while my ass!'

Worley threw himself to the side and covered his head, screaming, '*Twominutes! Icandoitintwominutes, sweartochrist! It'sallondiskandIcanget-everycontractinthegoddamnedoffice!*'

Ray stood over him, breathing hard and pointing the big .45. Across the room I could see Pike shake his head as he flipped through a magazine. *Modern Living*. Ray smirked and went back to his seat.

I said, 'That's better, Luke. I think you and I are going to work this out just fine.'

We had Worley describe the layout of the contracts department, and how we could get in and get out, and then we settled in for the afternoon. Pike left for a time, then returned with a small blue gym bag.

We listened to Lucas Worley's CD collection until five forty-five that evening, and then the four of us wedged into Worley's Porsche and drove to Green's building on Sunset. We bypassed the public parking entrance and used Worley's card key to access tenant parking. It was fourteen minutes after six when we worked our way beneath the building, and Worley said, 'You see all these cars? There're still plenty of people working.'

We found an empty spot as far in the back as possible, pulled in, cut the engine, and waited. Secretaries and office workers and blue-coated security people and attorneys of one stripe or another trickled out of the elevators and, little by little, the offices above us emptied. By seven-forty the trickle had dried and there were only six cars left, every one of which Worley recognized. He said, 'The 420 belongs to Deke Kelly and the white Jag belongs to Sharon Lewis. They both work in Contracts. The little Stanza over there works in Contracts, also; I forget the kid's name. He was new. Sharon's assistant.'

Pike said, 'Contracts is on the third floor.'

'That's right. Just like I said.' We'd had him describe it five times. He'd even drawn a little map.

I said, 'And Jonathan is on the fourth.'

608

Worley nodded. 'Yeah, but we won't have to go up there. All we have to do is go to Contracts. They have everything in their computers.'

'What if Jonathan wanted something kept secret?'

Worley shook his head. 'We can still access it from Contracts. The whole office is on the same computer net. Jesus, I should know. I helped design the system.'

I looked at Pike and Pike shrugged. 'Whenever.'

Worley looked worried. 'But what about the people up there?'

'What about them?'

Worley was looking even more worried. 'You aren't going to kill them, are you?'

Ray glared at him. 'That up to you. You get outta line, we be killin' people now till next Tuesday.'

Pike looked at me and I rolled my eyes. Jesus, what a ham.

I pushed Worley out of the car and we walked in a tight group to the elevator, Pike with the gym bag, Ray with a hand on Worley's shoulder. Our footsteps were loud and gritty. 'You said two minutes, and that's all you're going to have, Luke. Don't mess up.'

Lucas Worley didn't answer. His eyes were blinking fast, and he kept wetting and rewetting his lips. Fear.

We got into the elevator and rode up to the third floor. If the doors opened and someone we recognized got on, I planned to say that I had come to see Truly and Jonathan and brazen it out, but when the doors opened on the third floor, the reception area was empty. The cleaning crews wouldn't be in until nine. The door to Contracts was on the left side of reception, opposite a pair of rest rooms. Joe checked the men's room and Ray the women's. They both reappeared, shaking their heads. Clear. Pike opened the gym bag and pulled out a single gray cylinder. Worley said, 'What's that?'

I pushed him toward Ray without answering. 'Okay, Luke. Here we go.' Ray pulled him to the men's room.

I pulled the fire alarm at the same time that Joe Pike used Worley's card key to open the door to Contracts, then yanked the fuse on the smoke canister and tossed it through the door. He held the door long enough to yell, 'We have a fire in the building! Please use the main stairs and go to the street!' The main stairs fed into the ground floor lobby and were off the reception area. There were utility stairs in the rear of the Contracts department that would lead down to parking. That's how we planned to get out.

Joe let the door close, and then he and I followed Ray and Worley into the bathroom and pressed against the door. We heard voices and curses and a woman's nervous laughter, and then I said, 'That's it, Luke. Showtime.'

I dragged Worley out, and we used the card key to open the door again as Pike turned off the alarm. I pushed Worley through white smoke and said, 'That's a minute, forty-five. The clock is running.'

Joe and Ray scrambled in behind us, Joe taking a dousing blanket from the gym bag and pulling on heavy gloves to recover the smoke canister. Leave no evidence. They stayed at the door and Worley led me into an office. He said, 'This used to be mine. Sharon must've taken it.' A Macintosh computer was up and running on the desk, as if she'd been in the middle of something when we pulled the alarm. I said, 'Ninety seconds. They'll be asking each other what happened. They'll be wondering why the alarm stopped and wondering if they should come take a look.'

Worley closed the files that were on-screen and opened others. A case log heading that read MARTIN, THEODORE appeared on the screen along with a list of topics. He grinned and slapped the desk. 'Y'see. Fuckin' magic. It's all right here.' Like we were on the same team, now. Like he'd forgotten that we'd had to put a gun to his head.

'Print it and open Green's personal file.'

Worley frowned. 'Whaddaya mean, personal file?'

'Letters, bills, work product, anything that has his name on it.' I went to the door and looked at Pike. The canister was out, but a heavy mist of white was spreading through the office as the smoke settled. I said, 'C'mon, Luke. Sixty seconds.'

Worley frowned harder. 'Faster if I disk it.' He could tell I didn't know what he was talking about. 'I'll just dupe it onto a disk. It's faster than printing.'

'Do it.'

Ray stepped into the door. 'We've got voices on the other side of the door.'

Worley slapped in a disk. He punched buttons.

I said, 'You'd better not be screwing with me, Luke.'

'Jesus Christ, I'm almost done.' His eyes were big again. 'Okay, now! We've got it! That's everything!'

He ejected the disk, and we hurried through the smoke in the outer office to the rear stairs and took them down to the parking level. I was sweating hard, thinking we might meet a blue coat or a maintenance man taking the back way up, but we didn't. Luck.

We crossed the parking garage and got into the Porsche and drove back to Lucas Worley's condominium. It was dark when we got there. No one had thrown up a road block to stop us, and a phalanx of police cars hadn't chased us in hot pursuit. I'd never seen a phalanx before, but I was happy to avoid the experience. I said, 'You did okay, Luke, but there's one other thing.'

He looked at me. The four of us were still in the Porsche, sitting there in his carport.

I said, 'You're going to keep your mouth shut about this. You're not going to tell your buddies. You're not going to brag to your girlfriend. We clear on that?' I was pretty sure that he would, eventually, but I wanted some time.

Ray said, 'DiVega still wants this fuckuh dead.'

I ignored Ray. 'We together on this, Luke?'

Lucas Worley's head bobbed. 'I won't breathe a word. I swear to Christ.'

I held up the disk. 'I'm going to check this stuff, and if it isn't complete, or if I figure you've screwed me, I'm going to call DiVega. We together on that, too?'

Luke flicked from Ray to Joe to Ray again. Ray was glaring at him. 'Man, I copied *everything*. If it was there, you've got it. I *swear*.'

Ray said, 'DiVega said we should do what you say, but I know he don't like it.'

I looked at him, making a big deal out of the look so that Worley would see. 'Tell Mr DiVega that we're even now. Tell him I said thanks.'

Ray turned back to Luke and punched him once in the forehead, lightly.

Worley said, '*Ow!*'

Ray said, 'You ever buy any more dope, we'll hear about it. You ever sell dope again, we'll be back. What happened here won't matter a damn. You understand, Mr Harvard Law?'

Worley's head snapped up and down like it was on a spring. 'Hey, I'm retired. You tell Mr DiVega. I swear.'

Ray and Joe and I climbed out of the Porsche, left Lucas Worley sitting in his carport, and walked out to the street and back to our cars. Ray said, 'Is this guy DiVega for real?'

'Nope. I made it up.'

Ray nodded. 'I was trying to scare the little dip. Maybe wake him up.'

'I know.'

'That little sonofabitch will be dealing again inside the month.'

'You can bet on it.'

Ray thought about it. 'If this fool goes back to dealing he's gonna meet a real Mr DiVega sooner or later.'

'They always do.' We stopped at my car and shook hands. 'Thanks, Ray. I appreciate the help.'

Ray was staring back toward Worley's condominium, looking more than a little sad. 'Think of the waste. Goddamned Harvard.'

'Yep.'

Ray Depente took a deep breath, let it out, and then walked on to his car. I guess he just couldn't understand how someone could turn his back on so much opportunity. I guess he'd be thinking about it most of the night.

Pike and I watched him leave, and then we drove back to my house.

30

We drove directly to my home, me in my car, Joe following in his Jeep, anxious to see if we had anything that Anna Sherman could use. It was eight-twenty when we arrived, and Lucy and Ben were snuggled together on my couch, watching what looked to be a Discovery Channel program about African plains game. The cat was watching the TV, too, but from the edge of the loft. He still didn't like Lucy and Ben much, but at least he wasn't growling.

Ben said, 'They're home! Hi, Joe.'

Joe said, 'Hey, bud. You want to show me how to boot up this Macintosh?'

'Sure.' Ben jumped up and the two of them went to the Mac. The cat stopped watching the television and started watching Joe. He began kneading his paws, but he still did not come down.

Lucy held up her hand, and I took it. She said, 'I'm still not going to ask where you've been or what you've been doing.'

I kissed her nose. 'Damnedest thing. Joe and I found a computer disk on the street. We suspect that it contains contracts and business agreements between Jonathan Green and Theodore Martin.' I held it up and showed her.

Lucy closed her eyes and slumped back miserably on the couch. 'God. For sure I don't want to know.'

'Of course, we won't know where it leads until we review what's here, and it would probably help to have an attorney decipher the stuff.'

Lucy buried her face in her hands. 'I'll be disbarred. I'll go to jail.'

Joe said, 'We're ready.'

I went over to the Mac. 'Yeah, you're right, Luce. Better stay over there out of the way.'

Lucy jumped up and hurried around the couch to join us. 'Oh, hell. It won't hurt to peek over your shoulder.'

We fed the disk into the computer and opened the files. The list of available documents pertaining to Teddy Martin's representation was lengthy. Lucy leaned past me and tapped her nail on the screen. She had put on her reading glasses. 'Most of this probably has to do with billing. You want the retainer agreement.'

I looked at Lucy. 'I thought you wanted no part in this.'

She took a half-step back and showed her palms. 'You're right. Forget I said anything.'

I turned back to the screen.

Lucy said, 'But you still want the retainer agreement.'

Ben went back to the couch. We found the retainer agreement files and opened them. There were three documents, the original agreement plus two amendments. The original agreement called for a flat fee of five hundred thousand dollars for Green to represent Teddy from the date of the agreement through final appeal, plus all expenses and costs related to the defense. The five hundred thousand was to be deposited into an escrow account of Jonathan Green's choosing and dispensed in equal parts between signing, pretrial hearing start date, pretrial finish date, main trial start date, and main trial finish date, with the ongoing balance payable on demand should the case be dismissed for any reason. I looked at Lucy and she shrugged. 'Looks pretty ordinary.'

Pike's face was dark. 'Five hundred grand. Ordinary.'

I said, 'Yeah. But these guys work for it.'

Lucy knuckled me in the ribs, and then we opened the amendments. Lucy made a soft, whistling sound, and said, 'I guess the price of justice went up.'

The first amendment transferred the functional ownership of the entirety of Theodore Martin's business holdings, known corporately as Teddy Jay Enterprises, Inc., as well as Theodore Martin's personal property, into twenty-six different escrow accounts under the control of the Law Offices of Jonathan Green. The list of property and assets went on for pages and included fourteen specific restaurants, the real property associated with same, Teddy's Benedict Canyon mansion, plus homes, apartment buildings, and commercial property in Palm Springs, Honolulu, Denver, and Dallas. Approximate values had been given to each holding, and the total valuation was listed as one hundred twenty million dollars. I said, 'Is this legal?'

Lucy scrolled through the document, lips parted, the screen reflected in her glasses. 'Free enterprise, Studly. It looks like the parties renegotiated Green's fee for services, and who cares if it's akin to hyenas feeding on the bones of the dead?'

I looked back at the screen and shook my head. There were retirement accounts and bonds and stock portfolios. 'Jesus Christ, Green's getting *everything.*'

She continued scrolling. 'Appears so.' Then her breath caught and the scrolling stopped. 'This is odd.'

'What?'

She touched the final paragraph of the amendment. 'These things are in escrow, but they're payable to Green only in the event that the charges against Teddy are dropped, or that he is acquitted.' She shook her head. 'This just isn't done. No attorney would predicate payment on the outcome of a case.'

Pike said, 'This one did.'

I nodded. 'Sex and money. A hundred twenty million is an awful lot of motivation.'

Pike leaned back, and the left corner of his mouth twitched. 'Enough to use James Lester to plant phony evidence, and enough to convince Louise Earle to change her story so that the press and the public doubt Angela Rossi's honesty.'

I frowned. 'I can see it with Lester, but you're not going to buy Mrs Earle. They had to threaten her in some way, and I'm wondering if maybe they've increased the threat.'

Lucy stepped away from the Mac and took off her glasses. 'I agree that you could argue motivation now, but there is nothing illegal about this agreement. It's simply unusual. It could also be argued that Jonathan is willing to take the chance on an outcome-based payment because the funds are so large. The very thing that makes it unusual also makes it reasonable.'

'You don't think Anna Sherman would be interested?'

Lucy spread her hands. 'I'm sure that she would be interested, but what could she do? The California Bar certainly has no grounds for an investigation, and, unless there were some corroborating grounds for an investigation, neither does she.' She gestured at the Mac. 'Besides, she couldn't show this to anyone. It was illegally obtained.'

I said, 'Hey, we found it.'

Lucy put on her glasses again and leaned past me to the keyboard. 'Let's see the final amendment.'

The final amendment was less than a page. It simply deleted four personal accounts and a vacation home in Brazil from the second amendment and contained an order releasing the accounts and home from escrow, returning them to Teddy Martin's control. Lucy said, 'Mm.'

'What?'

She shook her head and took off her glasses again. I guess, 'Mm,' meant nothing.

She said, 'I'm sorry. It's still a stretch.'

I looked at Pike, but Pike only shrugged.

I scrolled back through the original contract, then through the amendments. I considered the dates. 'Okay, how about this. The first agreement is legitimate. Teddy hires the best lawyer he can, and that's Green. He's thinking that if anyone can get him off, it's Jonathan.'

Lucy pulled over one of the kitchen stools and sat. 'Okay.'

'But as the blood evidence comes in from the police and FBI laboratories, and the investigation proceeds, things aren't looking so good. Maybe Jonathan goes to him and says that they should negotiate a plea. Teddy freaks. He's a spoiled, arrogant, egomaniac and he can't imagine not beating this thing. I don't know who mentions it first, maybe Jonathan, maybe Teddy, but someone floats the notion that there has to be a way to beat this thing, and if such a way were found it would be worth everything that Teddy Martin owns. One of them says it, and the other thinks about it, and then they agree. Maybe the actual plan is never discussed. Maybe the words are never spoken, but they both know what they're talking about and the amendment is drawn, and then things begin to happen. Truly suggests James Lester; Kerris contacts Lester; Lester calls the tip line; I get put on the job. You see?'

Joe shifted in his seat. 'Reality begins changing.'

Lucy crossed her arms and leaned forward. 'Are you saying that Jonathan stays away from it?'

'Sure. He's got Truly. He's got Kerris. He's hidden by layers of people. Jonathan Green's experience is that he has the ability to face twelve people and persuade them to accept the facts as he describes them. More often than not, the reality he constructs is false, but his entire experience is that he is able to convince a jury that this false interpretation is real.'

Lucy sighed. 'That's what makes a great defense attorney.'

'And Jonathan Green is one of the best. He's very good at it, he's very careful, and he leaves no direct evidence to link him to any crime.'

Lucy was nodding. 'But if what you're saying is true, and he created Lester as a witness, why would he have him killed? Lester was the one link who tied Pritzik and Richards to Susan's kidnapping, and could testify to that end.'

Joe said, 'Green knew that we'd begun to suspect him of manufacturing evidence. Maybe he decided to eliminate Lester because he was scared that Lester would give him up.'

I shrugged. 'Or maybe Lester realized what he had. Maybe he went back to Green and threatened to spill the beans. Maybe that's what he was talking about when he told Jonna about a big payoff coming in. Maybe he wasn't talking about the hundred thousand dollar reward, maybe he was talking about whatever he could get by extorting Jonathan Green, only when he made the move and tried to put a gun to Jonathan's head, Jonathan took care of the problem.'

Lucy didn't look convinced. 'Or maybe he just slipped on a bar of soap.' She frowned at the look that I gave her. 'Hey, bad luck happens.'

I stared at her some more, and then I looked back at the Macintosh. Nothing on the screen had changed. Nothing had presented itself that irrefutably linked Jonathan Green to any wrongdoing. 'That's what makes this guy so good, I guess. Everything can be explained. None of it leads anywhere else.'

Joe said, 'No. It all leads back to the money, and Green doesn't get the money unless Teddy beats the rap.'

Lucy was staring at the computer again, the temple of her glasses against her teeth. She said, 'Unless they aren't planning to get to trial.'

I shook my head. 'There's no way that the district attorney will drop these charges.'

Lucy reopened the final amendment, the one that released accounts and property back to Teddy, and put on the glasses again. 'A house in Brazil. A little less than ten million dollars in various holdings.' She stepped back and took off the glasses. 'We have no extradition with Brazil. Why would Green release the money and the house? Teddy had already agreed to them as part of his fee.'

Pike said, 'Bail. They're pushing hard for bail.'

Lucy was nodding, clicking at her teeth again with her glasses. 'I'll bet he's going to run. If he was willing to give up everything he owns to beat the charge, he's willing to leave it behind. Do you see?'

'Sure.' Maybe I should just sit with Ben and watch television. Let Lucy and Joe figure it out.

Lucy said, 'Maybe they've amended their agreement again, only this time not on paper. Maybe now it's payable on bail.'

I was nodding, too. Mr Getting-on-Board. Mr Getting-with-the-Program. 'Why wouldn't it be on paper?'

Pike said, 'Because payment on bail would indicate a foreknowledge of flight.'

I stared at him.

Lucy said, 'Joe's right. You two are in the picture and you're making trouble. Lester was a problem, and that's more trouble. Maybe Teddy and Jonathan are getting so pressed that they're willing to take the chance on each other.'

I was grinning. 'So once Teddy has the money, he arranges a funds transfer to Brazil while he's still in jail. Jonathan doesn't have anything to do with it. Then, if he's granted bail, he jumps. Teddy will have his freedom, and Green can deny any knowledge of Teddy's proposed flight.'

Lucy nodded. 'That would work. Plus, any communication between the two is privileged and not admissible in court.'

Pike said, 'Ain't justice grand.'

I said, 'Sonofagun,' and held up my hand and Lucy gave me a high five. It felt like we'd done something.

But then Joe said, 'And there's nothing we can do about it.'

I blinked at him. 'Man, are you ever Mr Wet Blanket.'

Joe watched me for a moment, then stood and went to Lucy. He towered over her. 'You're going tomorrow.'

'That's right. In the morning.'

Pike looked at me, but he spoke to Lucy. 'He's going to miss you. He's done nothing but pine since he got back from Louisiana.'

I said, 'Pine?'

Lucy smiled. 'I like pining.'

Joe frowned at me. 'You must be out of your mind, talking about this stuff when it's her last night.' He turned back to Lucy. 'I'm going to miss you, too.'

Lucy stood on her toes and gave him a quick kiss on the lips. 'Joe, thank you.'

Joe said, 'Hey, Ben.'

Ben rolled over the back of the couch and grinned at him. 'Bye, Joe. I hope you come visit.'

Joe pointed at him, then glanced again at Lucy and walked to the door. The cat saw that Joe was leaving, hurried down the stairs, and slipped out with him. Soulmates.

When Joe was gone Lucy wrapped her arms around me. 'He's so nice.'

'Nice isn't a word often used to describe him.'

'He cares a very great deal for you.'

'Joe's okay.'

She said, 'I care about you, too.'

'I know.' I put my arms around her then and hugged her. I lifted her off the floor and my heart filled, and in a strange moment I felt as if I were fading into a shadow and if I did not hang onto her tight enough I would disappear. I said, 'Want to do something wild?' I think I whispered it.

'Yes.'

'Want to do something crazy?' I said it louder.

'Oh, God, I can't wait.'

Ben said, 'Hey, can I do it, too?'

And I said, 'You bet, bud.'

I put her down, and then the three of us made hot cocoa and sat in the cool night air on my deck and talked about our time together as the coyotes sang.

We talked until very late, and then Lucy put Ben to bed, and she and I sat up still longer, no longer talking, now simply holding each other in the safety of my home, pretending that tomorrow would not come.

31

I brought Lucy and Ben to LAX at just after nine the next morning. We returned her car to the rental agency, then sat together at the departure gate until the plane boarded, and then I stood with them in line until they entered the jetway and I could go no farther. I watched them until an efficent young woman in a neat airline uniform told me that I was blocking the door and asked me to move. I went to the great glass windows and watched the plane, hoping to see Lucy or Ben in one of the ports, but didn't. I guess they were seated on the other side. We had spent the morning speaking of innocuous things: *It's certainly cloudy this morning, isn't it? Yes, but it will burn off by ten. Oh, darn, I forgot to phone the airline and order the fruit plate.* I guess it was a way of minimizing our separation. I guess it was a way of somehow pretending that her getting on an airplane and both of us going back to our lives wasn't somehow painful and confusing.

When the little tractor pushed the airplane away from the dock and out to the taxiway, I said, 'Damn.'

An older gentleman was standing next to me. He was stooped and balding, with a thin cotton shirt and baggy old-man pants pulled too high and a walking stick. He said, 'It's never easy.'

I nodded.

He said, 'Your wife and son?'

'My friends.'

'With me, it was my grandkids.' He shook his head. 'They come out twice a year from Cleveland. I put them on the plane, I always think that this could be the last time. The plane could crash. I could drop dead.'

I stared at him.

'I'm not a young man anymore. Death is everywhere.'

I walked away. Too bad you couldn't get a restraining order against negativity.

Joe picked me up outside the terminal and we drove directly to Louise Earle's. We parked at the mouth of her drive, again went up to her door, and once more rang the bell and knocked. If we knocked much more we'd probably wear a groove in the wood. I was hoping that she might've returned home, but the drapes were still pulled and the house was still dark, and there was no sign that she had come back, then left again. While we were standing there, Mrs Harris came out of her house and made a nervous wave at us. Pike said, 'Looks worried.'

'Yeah.'

We walked over to her. I could see that her face was pinched and frightened, and that she was cupping one hand with the other, over and over. She said, 'That man came back this morning. I thought it was the milkman, they came so early.'

'They.'

'There were three men. They were walking all around Louise's house. They walked around the side. They went in the back.'

Pike looked at me, and I showed her the photograph of Kerris. 'Was this one of them?'

She squinted at the picture and then she nodded. 'Oh, yes. That's the one who was here before.' She bustled to the edge of the porch, wringing her hands, flustered by the dark thoughts. 'They were in her house. The lights came on and I could see them moving.'

'Did you see them leave?'

She nodded.

'Did Mrs Earle leave with them?'

She looked at me with large, frightened eyes. 'What do you mean by that? What are you saying to me?'

'Did she leave with them?'

Mrs Eleanor Harris shook her head. Just once. Imperceptibly.

I said, 'Had Mrs Earle come home?'

She was looking at her friend's house, wringing the hands, shifting in a kind of encompassing agitation.

'Was Mrs Earle at home?'

She looked back at me with big eyes. 'I don't know. I don't think so, but she may have.'

Pike and I trotted around the side of Louise Earle's house and into her backyard. I felt washed in a cold air, the hair along the back and sides of my head prickling, and scared of what we might find. Pike said, 'The door.'

Louise Earle's back door had been forced. We slipped out our guns and went in and moved through the house. It was a small home, just the kitchen and the dining room and the living room and two small bedrooms and a single bath. Papers had been pulled from drawers and furniture shoved out of place and closet doors left open, as if someone had searched the place more out of frustration than with a specific goal. I was worried that we might find Mrs Earle, and that she might be dead, but there was nothing. I guess she hadn't come home, after all. Pike said, 'First Lester, now her. Green's tying off the loose ends to protect himself.'

'If she got scared, then she ran. If she ran, she might've bought tickets and they might show up on her credit cards. Also, she might've called a guy named Walter Lawrence.'

Pike said, 'I'll take the bedroom. You start in the kitchen.'

We went through her house quickly and without speaking. She had two phones, one in her kitchen and one in her bedroom. The kitchen phone was an older dial-operated wall mount with a little corkboard next to it filled with notes and clippings and Prayers-for-the-Day and messages that she'd written to herself and probably not needed for years. I looked through them all, then checked the Post-its on her refrigerator door, and then I went through the papers that Kerris's people had left on the floor. I was looking for a personal phone book or notes or anything that might help me find Walter Lawrence or point to where she might've gone, but if there had been anything like that Kerris and his people had taken it. When I finished in the kitchen I went back through into the bedroom. Pike was working in the closet. He said, 'Credit card bills by the phone.'

I sat on the edge of the bed by the phone and looked at what he'd found. There were five past Visa and MasterCard bills, three Visas and two MasterCards. Charges were minimal, and nothing on the bills gave any indication of where Louise Earle might've gone, but then I didn't expect them to. Tickets purchased within the past few days would not yet have been billed to her, but I didn't expect that, either. I picked up her phone, called the toll free number on back of the Visa bill, and said, 'Hi. I'm calling for my mom, Mrs Louise Earle.' I gave them the credit card number that showed on the bill and the billing address. 'She charged a plane ticket yesterday, and we need to cancel, please.'

The Visa woman said, 'Let me punch up her account.' She was very pleasant when she said it.

'Thanks. That'd be great.'

Maybe three seconds later, she said, 'I'm sorry, sir, but we're not showing an airline charge.'

'Gosh, she told me she'd bought the tickets. She always flies United.'

'I'm sorry, sir.'

I said, 'You know, maybe it wasn't an airline. Are you showing a bus or a train?'

'No, sir. I'm not.'

I made a big deal out of sighing. 'I'm terribly sorry. She told me about this trip and I got concerned. She's a bit older, now.' I let it trail off.

The Visa woman said, 'I know how that is.' Understanding.

I thanked her for her time, and then I called MasterCard and went through it again, and again I learned that Louise Earle had bought no tickets. Of course, she might've paid cash, but since I couldn't know that, it wasn't worth worrying about. Like most other things in life.

When I hung up from MasterCard, Pike was waiting. 'Looks to be some missing clothes. No toothbrush.'

'Great.'

'She has to be somewhere.'

I picked up the phone again, called my friend at Pacific Bell, gave her Louise Earle's phone number, and asked for every call that Louise Earle had made in the past five days. Her records would show only toll calls, so if she'd phoned someone the next street over I'd never know it. But, like paying cash for airline tickets, it wasn't worth worrying about.

My friend read off twelve numbers that I dutifully copied, nine of which were in local area codes (310, 213, or 818), and three of which were long distance. The long-distance calls were all to the same number, the first two of which were collect calls that she'd accepted the charges on. The third time she'd dialed the number direct. I thanked her for the help, then hung up and started dialing. Minimum-wage detective work.

I called each number and got two answers out of the first five calls, one from a pharmacy and one from an elderly woman. I hung up on the pharmacy and asked the elderly woman if she knew where I could find Mrs Earle. She didn't. The sixth number was long distance. The phone rang twice, and a male voice said, 'Federal Correctional Facility, Terminal Island.'

I didn't speak.

The voice said, 'Hello?'

I told him I was sorry, then hung up and looked at Pike. 'LeCedrick.'

Pike said, 'She probably didn't go to stay with him.' Everyone's a comedian.

'She didn't call LeCedrick. LeCedrick called her. LeCedrick calls, and she changes her story. She wouldn't do it six years ago, but she does it now. What do you think he told her?'

Pike shrugged.

I tapped the phone, thinking about it, and then I called Angela Rossi at her home. Her machine answered, but again she picked up when she heard that it was me. I said, 'At six this morning, Kerris and two other guys broke into Louise Earle's house, looking for her. They searched the place, and I don't know if they got a line on her or not.'

'Why are you telling me this?'

'Because LeCedrick Earle might know where she's gone. When I spoke with Louise she told me that she hadn't spoken to LeCedrick since he was sent up. She said he wouldn't speak to her. But four days ago he called her twice. Three days ago she changed her story. She called him the day before yesterday. That's the day she disappeared. He might know where she's gone. Do you see?'

622

Angela Rossi didn't say anything.

'I saw him before, but the last time he agreed to see me. I'm pretty sure he won't this time, and I need a badge to get in without his permission. Maybe you could talk to Tomsic. Maybe he could get me in.'

Angela Rossi said, 'Pick me up.'

'You're suspended, Rossi. You don't have a badge.'

'I'll get one, goddammit. Pick me up and we'll go see him. I'll get it set up before you get here.'

She hung up before I could say anything else.

32

Angela Rossi was waiting at the mouth of her cul-de-sac, looking professional in a dark blue business suit that'd she'd probably worn to work every other week for the past three years. She swayed back and forth the way cops do when they're anxious. It's an unconscious habit they pick up in their uniform days when they have to stand in a place for long hours with nothing to occupy themselves except their baton. It's called the nightstick rock.

We stopped at the curb, and she climbed into the back seat. She said, 'It's set up. The guards think we're coming to interview him about a past association. That's what he thinks, too.'

Pike said, 'Did you get a badge?'

'Don't worry about it.' Protecting someone, saying if you don't know you can't tell.

Pike pulled back in traffic without waiting for her to buckle in. I said, 'You could give us the badge, then you wouldn't have to come in. Less chance of anyone finding out that you're violating your suspension.'

She neither answered nor looked at me. Her mouth was set and her eyes empty. Cop eyes. Just another day on the job walking the razor's edge.

We picked up the San Diego Freeway and headed south, and once more I was passing Inglewood and Hawthorne and Gardena and Torrance. Angela Rossi sat behind me in silence, hands in her lap, gazing out the window without seeing, dressed in her cop clothes, carrying a cop's badge, going on a cop's mission. She had given her all to it for a great long while, and I wondered if she was thinking that it might now be at an end. I wondered if she was thinking that the dream of being the first female chief of detectives had been a silly one. I wondered if she had regrets.

Forty minutes later we crossed the land bridge onto Terminal Island and passed through the gate, and then we were at the administration building. We parked, took off our guns, and then Angela Rossi and I went in. I said, 'You okay?'

Rossi said, 'Keep your mouth shut and try to look like an officer. I'll do the talking.'

Yes, ma'am.

We went through the front door and up to the reception desk. I was worried that the reception guard would be the same guy, but he wasn't. This guy was paging through *Saltwater Fisherman* magazine, but looked up when we approached. He said, 'May I help you?' He was a young guy, tall and athletic and looking as if he'd just mustered out of the military. He was wearing the blue blazer and tie.

Rossi showed the badge. 'West L.A. robbery/homicide. I called to see an inmate named LeCedrick Earle.'

The receptionist jotted down the badge number, then said, 'Sure. Hold on.' He flipped through the loose-leaf book until he found Earle's name, then told someone on the phone that he wanted prisoner number E2847 in the interview room. When he hung up he said, 'Guns?'

Rossi said, 'Left'm in the car.'

'Great. Someone will be right out for you. Wait by the sally port.'

Rossi said, 'Would it be a problem to check your logs for the visitors that Mr Earle has had over the past two weeks?'

'No sweat.' He turned to a computer and typed something. 'We enter the log into the computer at the end of each day for the record. You want a hard copy?'

'Yes.'

It took maybe sixteen seconds, and then a laser printer spit out a single sheet. Modern crime fighting at its finest. He said, 'Here you go.'

Rossi took it and we looked at it as we went to the sally port. The only visitors that LeCedrick Earle had had in the past two weeks were Elliot Truly and Stan Kerris. How about that?

A second guy in a blue blazer opened the sally port for us and said, 'This way, please.'

We followed him through and turned right. He was a couple of years younger than Rossi and he looked her over. 'You guys down from L.A.?'

Rossi said, 'That's right.'

'What kind of case?' Rossi was trying to ignore him, but the guard was giving her the grin.

'Don't know yet.'

The guard grinned wider. 'How long are you going to be down here? Maybe we could get together for a drink.'

Rossi never looked at him. 'Do yourself a favor, sport. I just tested positive for chlamydia.'

The guard's grin faltered and he moved a half-step away. Talk about a conversation stopper.

He brought us to the same interview room that I had used before and opened the door. He stood kind of bent to the side so that Rossi wouldn't brush against him when she went by. 'I've got to lock you in. Your guy will be here in a minute.'

Rossi said, 'Thanks.'

He locked the door behind us and we were alone. I nodded at her. 'Chlamydia. Nice.'

Rossi shrugged. I guess it was something she'd had to do ten thousand times.

We had been there less than thirty seconds when the rear door opened and a third guard led in LeCedrick Earle. His eyes widened when he recognized us, and he shook his head at the guard. 'Forget this shit. I don't wanna see'm.'

The guard shoved LeCedrick toward the table without acknowledging him and said, 'Just punch the buzzer when you're finished.'

LeCedrick Earle said, 'Hey, fuck this shit. Take me back to my cell.'

Rossi said, 'Thanks, officer.'

The guard closed the door and locked it, and Rossi smiled. 'It's my favorite perp. How're you doing, LeCedrick?'

LeCedrick Earle glowered at us and stood with his back to the door, as far from us as possible. He said, 'I don't have anything to say to you.' He wiggled a finger at me. 'I said everything I had to say to you before. I ain't gotta see you without my lawyer.'

I said, 'Stan Kerris is trying to kill your mother.'

He blinked twice, and then he laughed. 'Oh, that's right. You drove all the way down here for that?' He laughed some more.

Rossi said, 'Jonathan Green's scam is falling apart, LeCedrick. He's falsified evidence and suborned testimony, and now he's scared that it's coming out. We believe that he ordered the death of a man named James Lester, and we believe that he's after your mother, too. If he is, then he'll probably come after you as well.'

'Bullshit. You just talkin' trash.' He wiggled the finger at Rossi. 'You just worried cause your ass is in a crack. You know I'm gonna get your ass for puttin' me in here.' He went to the near chair, plopped down, and put up his feet. 'I ain't sayin' nothing without my lawyer.'

'You want Mr Green?'

LeCedrick smiled wide. 'I think you'll find that he represents me in all matters criminal and civil. Especially in the civil case where we whack your ass for every nickel in your pension fund for planting bullshit evidence on me.'

I stepped past Rossi and slapped LeCedrick's feet from the table. He said, 'Hey!'

I said, 'We've got to get past that right now, LeCedrick.' He tried to get up but I dug my thumb under his jawline beneath his right ear. He said, 'Ow!' and tried to wiggle away, but I stayed with him.

Rossi pulled at me from behind. 'Stop it. We can't do that.'

I didn't stop it. I said, 'You didn't call the hotline about this, they called you. That's the way it started, isn't it?'

He grabbed at my hand, but he couldn't pry it away.

Rossi said, 'Stop it, dammit. That's over the line.'

'Kerris and Truly came to see you and convinced you to speak with your mother, didn't they?'

He was finally listening.

'What did they say, LeCedrick? You hadn't spoken to the woman in years, but you called her and convinced her to change her story. They offer you money? They say they could get you an early release?'

He stopped trying to pull at my hand, and I relaxed the pressure. Rossi said, 'Jesus Christ, they could arrest us for this.'

I said, 'Think about it, LeCedrick. Jonathan and Truly and all those guys went to see her and probably told her what to say and how to say it, and that means she could testify against them.'

Now he was squinting at me, hearing the truth of it, even though it was masked by his suspicions.

'I uncovered a connection between Lester and Green, and two days later Lester went through his shower door and damn near cut off his head. You see that in the papers?'

He nodded.

'The day after that I went to your mother's house to ask why she changed her story, and she was missing. You know Mrs Harris next door? Mrs Harris told me that Kerris had cruised your mother's house three times, that he'd walked around the place and tried to get in.'

He said, 'Mrs Harris?'

'At six this morning Kerris and two other guys went back to her house and turned the place upside down. Why would they do that, LeCedrick?'

Now he was shaking his head. 'This all bullshit.'

'Would Mrs Eleanor Harris bullshit you? You grew up next door to her. Would she bullshit you?'

He made a little headshake. One so tiny that it was hard to see. 'Lady 'bout raised me. Like a second mama.'

Rossi pushed the buzzer, and when the guard came she asked if we could have a phone. He said no problem, brought one, and when he was gone again I turned it toward LeCedrick Earle and said, 'Call her. I've got the number, if you need it.'

He stared at the phone.

'We have to find your mother, LeCedrick. If we don't find her before Kerris, he'll kill her. Do you see?'

He wet his lips.

Rossi said, 'Goddammit, you piece of shit, call the woman.'

LeCedrick Earle snatched up the phone and punched the number without asking for it, and spoke with Mrs Eleanor Harris. When she answered his manner changed, and he hunched over the phone and spoke in a voice that was surprisingly young and considerate. I guess the lessons we learn when we're small stay with us, even as we harden with the years. They spoke for several minutes, and then LeCedrick Earle put down the phone and kept his eyes on it, as if the phone had taken on an importance that dwarfed everything else in the room. He crossed his arms and started rocking. He said, 'Why they do that? Why they go there so early?'

Rossi said, 'They want to kill her. And after they kill her, they will almost certainly arrange to have you killed, and then no one can implicate them in the manufacture of false evidence. Do you see that?'

He didn't say anything.

I said, 'She left the house with a bag. She has a gentleman friend named Mr Lawrence.'

LeCedrick Earle nodded dumbly. 'That old man been chasin' her for years.'

'Would she go there?'

'Sure, she'd go there. She ain't got nobody else.'

I felt something loosen in my chest. I felt like I could breathe again. 'Okay, LeCedrick. That's great. Just great. Do you know where he lives?'

LeCedrick Earle slumped back in the chair with an emptiness that made him seem lost and forever alone. His eyes filled with tears, and the tears spilled down across his cheeks and dripped on his shirt. He said, 'I can't believe this shit. I just can't believe it.'

Rossi said, 'What?'

He rubbed at the tears, then blew his nose. 'I must be the stupidest muthuhfuckuh ever been born. That woman ain't never done nuthin' but what she try to do right, and this what she gets for it. A fool for a son. A goddamned stupid fool.' He was sobbing.

Rossi said, 'Goddammit, LeCedrick, what?'

LeCedrick Earle blinked through the tears at us. 'Your man Kerris called me 'bout an hour ago and asked about old Mr Lawrence, too. He say they need to get her story straight. He say they want her to do a news conference, and I told him where she was. I told him how to get there and now they gonna kill my momma. Ain't I a fool? Ain't I God's own stupid muthuhfuckin' fool?'

I was pressing the buzzer even before he was finished, and Angela Rossi was shaking him until he told us the address, and then we were running out to the Jeep. It was almost certain that Louise Earle was dead, but neither of us was yet willing to give up on her.

Maybe we were God's own fools, too.

33

Pike pushed the Jeep hard out of the parking lot and through the gate and across the land bridge. Angela Rossi used her cell phone to call Tomsic as we were climbing back onto the freeway. She told him about Kerris, and that Louise Earle was probably staying with a Mr Walter Lawrence in Baldwin Hills. They spoke for about six minutes, and then Rossi turned off her phone. 'He's on the way.'

I said, 'You sure you want to go to the scene?'

'Of course.'

Pike glanced at her in the rearview. 'It gets back to the brass that you're involved, it's over for you.'

Rossi took her Browning from under the seat and clipped it onto her waistband. 'I'm going.'

We scorched up the Harbor Freeway to the San Diego, the speedometer pegged at a hundred ten, Pike gliding the Jeep between and around traffic that seemed frozen in space. We drove as much on the shoulder as the main road, and several times Pike stood on the brakes, bringing us to screaming, sliding stops before he would once more stomp the accelerator to rocket around lane-changers or people merging off an entrance ramp. I said, 'We can't help anybody if we're piled up on the side of the road.'

Pike went faster.

Hawthorne slipped past, then Inglewood, and then we were off the freeway and climbing through the southern edge of Baldwin Hills along clean, wide residential streets lined with spacious postwar houses. Baldwin Hills is at the southwestern edge of South Central Los Angeles, where it was developed in the late forties as a homesite for the affluent African-American doctors and dentists and lawyers who served the South-Central community. At one time it was called the black Beverly Hills, though in recent years the community has diversified with upwardly mobile Hispanic, Asian, and Anglo families. Rossi's phone beeped, and she answered, mumbling for maybe ten seconds before ending the call. 'Dan just got off the freeway. They're three minutes behind us, and he's got a black-and-white behind him.'

We used Pike's Thomas Brothers map to find our way through the streets, watching for turns and scoping the area. Mothers were pushing strollers and children were playing with dogs and everyone was enjoying a fine summer day. I said, 'We're almost there.'

We were two blocks from Walter Lawrence's home when a tan Aerostar van passed us going fast in the opposite direction and Pike said, 'That's Kerris. Three others on board.'

Rossi and I twisted around, trying to see. 'Louise Earle's in the back. Looks like Lawrence and someone else, too.' Louise Earle looked scared.

Rossi said, 'The other guy is probably one of Kerris's security people.'

Pike jerked the Jeep into a drive and did a fast reversal. I said, 'Did they make us?'

Pike shook his head. The Aerostar turned a far corner, but it hadn't increased its speed, and its driving seemed even. We went after them, Pike hanging back. In cases like this there are always two choices: You can let them know that you're there, or you can hide from them. If they know that you're there they might get nutty and start shooting. As long as they're not shooting, you're better off. Louise Earle and Walter Lawrence would be better off, too. Rossi unfastened her seat belt and leaned forward between me and Joe, better to see. 'Don't crowd them, Joseph. Let's give them room.'

Pike pursed his lips. 'I know, Angela.' Nothing like a backseat driver in a pursuit situation.

Rossi got on her phone again and told Tomsic where we were and what we were doing. She didn't cut the circuit this time, but kept up a running flow of information so that Tomsic knew where we were at all times. I said, 'Can he get in front of them?'

'No. He's west of the hills and behind us. He's calling in more black-and-whites.'

I glanced at Rossi, but she seemed impassive. The brass would know now, for sure.

We followed the van down out of the residential area onto Stocker Boulevard, then started climbing again almost at once, leaving the residential area behind as we wound our way through dry, undeveloped hills dotted with oil pumpers and radio towers. I had hoped that they would turn into the city, but they didn't. They were heading into a barren place away from prying eyes.

We followed them deeper into the hills, staying well back, catching only glimpses of their dust trail so that we wouldn't be seen, and as the peaks rose around us Rossi's cell phone connection became garbled and our link to Tomsic was broken. She tossed the phone aside. 'I lost him.'

Pike said, 'He knows about where we are.'

630

'About.'

Maybe a half mile ahead of us the van turned up the side of a hill along a gravel service road, making its way toward two great radio towers. We could see the towers, and what was probably a maintenance shed at their bases, and another car parked there. I said, 'They're going to kill them. They couldn't kill them at the house with so many people on the street, but they're going to do them here.'

Rossi craned her head out the window. 'If we take the road up after them, they'll see us coming a mile away.'

Pike slapped the Jeep into four-wheel drive, and we left the road, heading first down into a gully, then up. We lost sight of the towers and the van, but we watched the ridgeline and followed the slope of hills and we did what we could until we came to an elevated pipeline that we could not cross. Pike said, 'Looks like we're on foot.'

Pike and I were wearing running shoes, but Angela Rossi was wearing dress flats. I said, 'Going to be a hard run.'

She said, 'Fuck it.'

She threw her jacket into the backseat, took her Browning from its holster, then kicked off her shoes and set out at a jog. Barefoot. The ground was rough and bristling with stiff dried grass and foxtails and must have hurt, but she gave no sign.

The hill was steep and the going was slow. The soil was loose and brittle, and the dessicated grass did not help bind it together. Our feet sunk deep and every step caused a minor landslide, but halfway up the hill we saw the tops of the towers, and pretty soon after that the roof of the shed. We went down to our hands and knees and eased our way to the ridge. The Aerostar was parked next to a bronze Jaguar. Kerris was already out of the van and moving toward the shed. He'd left the van's driver side door open. The same black security guard I'd seen at Green's party came out of the shed. The van's side door slid open and a younger guy with a very short crew cut pushed out. Walter Lawrence climbed out after him, but I guess he wasn't moving fast enough because the crew cut took his arm and yanked, and Mr Lawrence stumbled sideways to fall in a little cloud of dust. The black guy ignored all of that and opened the Jag's trunk to lift out two shovels and a large roll of plastic. Rossi said, 'They're going to execute these people.'

Pike said, 'Yes.'

I edged higher on the ridge. 'They'll bring them inside the building. Maybe we can work our way around to the backside of the slope and come up behind the building without being seen.' I didn't think Kerris would just shoot them in the open, even out here in the middle of nowhere.

Pike started backwards with Rossi behind him when the crew cut leaned into the van and said something to Louise Earle. I guess she didn't want to get out, because he reached in and pulled. He had her by the upper arm and it must've hurt. She tried swatting at him like you might a fly, but it did no good. That's when Walter Lawrence scrambled up out of the dust and grabbed the crew cut's jacket and tried pulling him away. Defending his woman. The crew cut guy put a hand on Walter Lawrence's face and pushed. Walter Lawrence flailed backwards and fell again, landing flat on his back, and the crew cut guy took a steel Smith & Wesson 9mm from beneath his left arm, pointed it at Walter Lawrence, and fired one shot.

The shot sounded hollow and faraway, and Mrs Earle screamed just as Elliot Truly stepped out of the maintenance shed.

34

Pike worked the Python out of his waist holster and pushed it in front him, lining up on the crew cut.

Rossi said, 'We're too far.'

'If they point a gun at her, Joe.' Ignoring Rossi.

'I'm on it.'

Rossi said, 'Can he make this shot?'

We were more than a hundred yards from them. It was a very long shot for a four-inch barrel, but Pike could brace his hand on the ground, and he was the finest pistol shot I've ever seen.

Truly waved his arms, raising hell with Kerris and the guy with the crew cut, and the guy with the crew cut put away his gun. Truly did some more waving, then went back into the maintenance shed. Kerris raised hell with the crew cut too, then he and the black guy lifted Mrs Earle by the arms and dragged her past Walter Lawrence's body to the shed. The crew cut went over to the shovels and plastic, and didn't look happy about it.

I said, 'We don't have much time.'

We crabbed back down beneath the ridgeline and trotted around the side of the hill until we had the maintenance shed between us and the van. The shed was at the base of the north tower, and its structure formed a kind of latticework around the shed and would provide cover between the shed and the Jaguar. We moved fast, but with every passing second I was frightened that we'd hear the second shot. I guess we could've just started yelling and let them know we were here, but they had already committed murder; Mrs Earle would probably catch the first shot.

When the shed was between us and the van, we crept up the hill to the rear of the base of the north radio tower. I said, 'Rossi and I will take the shed. You take the guy at the van.'

Pike slipped away to the edge of the shed, then disappeared among the girders at the base of the radio tower.

I looked at Rossi. 'You ready?'

She nodded. Her stockings were shredded, her feet torn and bleeding and clotted with dirt and little bits of brown grass. Her nice suit pants were ripped.

The maintenance shed was a squat cinderblock and corrugated metal building built against the base of the north tower. Inside, there would be tools and parts and paint for maintaining the towers and adjusting the repeater antennas. There were no windows, but doors were built into the front and back. Truly had probably been here for a while and had opened the doors for the air. The door nearest the cars was wide and tall so you could move oversized parts and equipment in and out, but the rear door, the door by the tower, was a people door.

Rossi and I slipped up to the side of the shed, then crept toward the door. We listened, but all we could hear was Mrs Earle crying. I touched Rossi, then pointed to myself, then the door, telling her that I was going to risk a look. She nodded. I went down onto my hands and knees, edged forward, and peeked inside. Mrs Earle was on the floor, tied, and Kerris and Truly were standing together just inside the far door. Truly looked nervous, like he didn't want to be there. The black guy wasn't inside; he'd probably gone back to help the crew cut with the shovels. I was still looking at them when the guy with the crew cut walked past the side of the shed with the shovel and the plastic and a sour expression and saw us. He did a classic double take, said, 'Hey!' then dropped the shovels and plastic to claw for his gun when I shot him two times in the chest. I said, 'Get Mrs Earle.'

Rossi rolled past into the door with me behind her when we heard three shots from the front of the shed. Kerris grabbed Truly and pushed him in the way and fired fast four times. Rossi said, 'Shit.'

Truly was looking confused and Mrs Earle was staring at us with wide, frightened eyes, and I was scared that if I tried to hit Kerris I would hit her. I fired high and Kerris fell back, scrambling through the door, firing as he went. Truly turned to run after him, and when he did he turned square into Kerris and was kicked backwards by one of the rounds, and then Kerris was gone. There was shouting out front, Kerris and the black guy, and more firing. The black guy was yelling, 'I'm hit! Oh, Holy Jesus, I'm hit!'

Rossi went to Mrs Earle and I went to Truly. Truly was trying to get up and not having a good time of it. The bullet had hit him maybe three inches to the right of his sternum, and a flower of red was blooming on his shirt. He said, 'I think I've been shot.'

Rossi was untying Mrs Earle. I said, 'Are you all right?'

Mrs Earle was still crying. 'They shot Mr Lawrence.'

Rossi helped her up, telling her that she had to stand, that she had to move to the side, out of the way, telling her that everything was going to be okay. The lies you tell someone when you need them to cooperate because their life depends on it. Truly said, 'Am I going to die?'

I tore off my shirt and bundled it and pressed it to his chest. 'I don't know.'

I pulled off his belt and wrapped it around his chest and the shirt and buckled it tight. He said, 'Oh, God, that hurts.'

There were more shots by the cars and running footsteps, and then Joe Pike slipped through the door. Maybe six shots slammed into the door and the walls and through the open doorway. Maybe seven. Pike said, 'Those Glocks are something.'

Rossi duck-walked over. 'What's the deal out front?'

Joe said, 'The black guy's punched out. Kerris is behind the Jaguar. I don't know about the crew cut.'

Rossi nodded toward the rear. 'Forget him.'

I said, 'Can we get to Kerris?'

Pike made a little shrug. 'He's got a clean field of fire at us. We could go back the way we came, maybe, and work our way around.' He glanced at Truly. 'Take about twenty minutes to work around behind the Jag.'

I turned Truly's face so that he looked at me. 'You hear that, Elliot? You're bleeding and we're pinned down in here and Kerris is doing the pinning.'

Truly opened his mouth, then closed it. He blinked at me, then shook his head. 'Kerris kidnapped these people. He shot that old man. I didn't know anything about it.'

Rossi said, 'Bullshit.'

I shook Truly's face. 'Stop lying, you idiot. Stop worrying about incriminating yourself, and start worrying about dying.'

He shook his head. His eyes filled with tears, and the tears tumbled out and ran down into his hair.

I said, 'It's you and Kerris and the black guy and the guy with the crew cut. Is there anyone else up here?'

He shook his head again. 'No.' A whisper.

'Is anyone else supposed to come up here?'

The crying grew worse and became a cough. When he coughed, pink spittle blew out across his chin and the chest wound made a wheezing sound.

I said, 'Tell Kerris to give it up. If Kerris gives it up, we can get you to a hospital.'

Truly's face wrinkled from the pain and he yelled, 'Kerris! Kerris, it's over. I need a doctor!' It wasn't much of a yell.

Kerris didn't answer.

Elliot Truly yelled, 'Goddammit, Kerris, enough of this, would you, please?! I'm dying! I've got to get to a doctor!' He coughed again, and this time a great red bubble floated up from his mouth.

Rossi duck-walked over. She said, 'You're fucked, Elliot. Your man outside is in for murder and he's looking to save himself. He's got to kill us and this woman to do that, and he doesn't give a damn if you live or die.'

Truly moaned. 'Oh, God.'

Rossi leaned closer to him. 'Maybe you'll make it, but maybe you won't. We still might get Kerris, though, and the sonofabitch who put you into this spot. Give him up, Elliot. Tell us what we want to hear.'

Truly squeezed his eyes shut, but still the tears came out. 'It was Jonathan.'

Rossi smiled. It was small, and it was personal.

I said, 'Everything that's happened, it's so Jonathan can take over Teddy's companies, isn't it?'

Truly tried to nod, but it didn't look like much. 'Not at first. At first, Jonathan was just going to defend him, like anyone else.'

'But Teddy got scared.'

Truly coughed, and more bubbles came up. 'Oh, God, it hurts. God, it hurts so bad.'

I said, 'Did Teddy kill his wife?'

Truly wet his lips to answer, and made his lips red. 'Yes. He denied it at first, but Jonathan knew. You can always tell. You know when they did it.'

Rossi frowned at me and nodded. You see?

Truly said, 'Then he just admitted it. I'm not sure why, but he did, just out of the blue one night when we were going over his story. Jonathan and I were alone with him and he started to cry and he admitted that he killed her. That changed everything. Jonathan advised him to negotiate a plea, but Teddy wouldn't do that. He was scared of going to prison, and he begged Jonathan not to quit the case. He said that he'd do anything rather to go to prison.'

'Even give away everything he owned.'

Another nod. 'That was Jonathan's price.'

Rossi said, 'All that stuff about Pritzik and Richards. That was bullshit?'

'Jonathan and Kerris and I put it together. Jonathan had the idea of a straw man, and Kerris came up with Pritzik and Richards, and I knew Lester. We just put it together.' He started coughing again, and this time a great gout of blood bubbled up and he moaned. I put my hands on the compress and leaned on it. He said, 'I don't want to die. Oh, God, please Jesus, I don't want to die. Please save me.'

I wiped the blood off his face and forced open his eyes and said, 'You're a piece of shit, Truly, but I'm going to save you, do you hear? Just hang on, and I will get you to a hospital. Do you hear me?'

He nodded. 'Uh-hunh.'

'Don't die on me, you sonofabitch.'

He moaned, and his eyes rolled back.

I checked on Mrs Earle, and made sure that she was behind as much metal as possible, and then Rossi and I went over to Pike. Pike was peering through a split in the door jamb. 'He got a shotgun from the van. He's talking on his cell phone.'

'Great. Probably calling for reinforcements.'

Pike glanced at Rossi. 'Be real nice if Tomsic happened to find us about now.'

Rossi shrugged. 'Let's all hold our breaths.'

I edged past Pike and looked through the split. Kerris was behind the Jaguar with the shotgun. The black guy was lying on his side between the Jag and the van, and Mr Lawrence was on his back a few yards behind him. The black guy was probably unconscious, but he might've been dead. I yelled, 'Come on, Kerris. There's three of us and one of you. Don't be stupid.'

The shotgun boomed twice, slamming buckshot into the corrugated metal about eighteen inches above my head. Mrs Earle made a kind of moaning wail, and Rossi dived across the doorway, popping off caps to force Kerris down.

Pike looked at me. 'I don't think he's scared of the odds.'

'Guess not.'

Rossi edged toward the door and stopped just shy of the jamb, squinting out into the sun. She said, 'Hey, the old man's still alive.'

Mrs Earle stopped wailing. 'Walter?'

I went back to the split and saw Walter Lawrence slowly roll onto his belly, then push up to his knees before falling onto his face.

Mrs Earle started for the door, but Pike pulled her down. 'Stay back, ma'am. Please.'

'But Walter needs help.' She said it loudly, and Pike put his hand over her mouth.

'Don't draw attention to him. If Kerris sees him he's a dead man.'

Her eyes were wide, but she nodded.

Walter Lawrence pushed up again, then looked around as if what he was seeing was new and strange. He saw the guy in the red knit shirt about ten feet in front of him and he saw the guy's pistol, a nice blue metal automatic, lying in the dust. He looked past the guy in the knit shirt and almost certainly saw Kerris hiding behind the Jaguar, pointing the shotgun at us. Walter Lawrence was behind Kerris, and since Kerris was looking at us, he wasn't looking at Walter Lawrence. Mr Walter Lawrence began crawling for the pistol. I said, 'Rossi.'

'I see him.'

I watched through the split jamb, and could see the hills and the pumpers and the rough service roads below, and as I watched a dark sedan appeared on the road between the pumpers, heading our way, kicking up a great gray roostertail of dust. Rossi saw it, too. I said, 'Is that Tomsic?'

She ejected her Browning's clip, checked the number of bullets left, then put it back in her gun. 'I can't tell.'

I glanced at Pike and Pike shrugged. Guess it didn't matter to him. Guess he figured the more the merrier.

Walter Lawrence crept toward the gun like a drunken infant, weaving on his hands and knees, bloody shirt hanging loose and sodden between his arms. He reached the pistol and sat heavily, but he did not touch the gun. As if simply reaching it had taken all of his energy. Rossi said, 'In a couple of seconds we're going to be able to hear the car. If Kerris looks that way, the old man's dead.'

I looked at Pike and Pike nodded. I took a breath, and peered out the split again. Kerris had taken up a position behind the Jaguar's front end. You could see about a quarter of his face behind the left front tire. The tire was probably a steel-belted Pirelli. Might be able to shoot through it, but it wasn't much of a target. 'Kerris? Truly's dying. He needs a doctor.'

'It's the cost of doing business.' All heart.

I stood. 'Listen, Kerris! Maybe we can work something out.' I sprinted past the open door to the other side of the shed. When I flashed past the door, the shotgun boomed again, but the buckshot hit the wall behind me.

Pike said, 'Lucky.'

I yelled, 'I didn't sign on to this job to get killed, and neither did Pike. You want the old lady, we just want to go home. You hear what I'm saying?' I hopped past the door in the opposite direction. Kerris fired twice more, once behind me through the doorway and once high through the wall. Maybe I could just keep running back and forth until he ran out of ammo.

Kerris said, 'Bullshit, Cole. I checked out you and your partner, remember? You aren't built that way.'

Another boom, and this time the number four slammed through the wall just over Joe's back.

I crawled across him to the split again and looked out. Walter Lawrence had once more focused on the gun. He leaned forward from the waist, picked it up, then held it as if he had never held a gun before in his life. Maybe he hadn't. He cupped it in both hands and pointed it at Kerris, but the gun wavered wildly. He lowered the gun. I yelled, 'I'm serious, Kerris. What's all this to me?'

'If you're so goddamned serious, throw out your guns and come out.'

'Forget that.'

'Then let's wait it out.'

The car was close, now, and if I strained I thought that I might hear it. Walter Lawrence raised the gun again. Rossi said, 'That's Tomsic!'

I yelled, 'Okay, Kerris. Let's talk.'

I stepped into the door, and as I did Mr Walter Lawrence pulled the trigger. There was a loud BANG and his shot slammed into the Jaguar's rear fender and Kerris jumped back from the wheel, yelling, 'Sonofa-bitch!'

Walter Lawrence fired again, and again the shot went wide, and Kerris swung the shotgun toward him but as he did Angela Rossi shouted, 'No!' and she and Joe Pike and I launched out the door, firing as fast as we could.

Kerris brought the shotgun back, pulling the trigger *BOOM-BOOM-BOOM-BOOM* as our bullets caught him and lifted him, and then slammed him into the soft gray earth, and then the noise was gone and it was over and there was only the sound of Louise Earle crying.

35

Mr Walter Lawrence fell onto his back and kept trying to right himself the way a turtle might, clawing at the air with his arms and legs. I took the gun from him and told him to lie still, but he wouldn't until Louise Earle hurried out from the shed and made him.

Linc Gibbs and Dan Tomsic pulled up in a cloud of dry gray dust, then ran over with their guns out. Tomsic said, 'Who's this?'

'One of the good guys. Get an ambulance, for Christ's sake. We've got another wounded in the shed.'

Linc Gibbs made the call while Tomsic ran for the first aid kit that every cop keeps in his trunk. The crew cut had put one high into the left side of Mr Lawrence's chest. His shirt and jacket were soaked red, and he felt cold to the touch. The blood loss was extreme. When Tomsic came with the kit, we put a compress bandage over the wound and held it in place. Mrs Earle held it. While Tomsic was working with the bandage he glanced at Angela Rossi. 'You okay, Slick?'

She made an uncertain smile. 'Yeah.'

When Mr Lawrence was bandaged we ran into the shed, but Elliot Truly was dead. Tomsic looked close at Truly as if he wanted to be sure of what he was seeing. 'Is this who I think it is?'

'Unh-huh.'

'Sonofabitch.'

Gibbs had them send a medivac helicopter, and while we waited, we secured the scene. There wasn't much to secure. Both the guy with the crew cut and the guy in the knit shirt were dead. Kerris was dead, too. Tomsic said, 'Do all of these guys work for Green?'

'Kerris was his chief investigator. I think these other two worked for Kerris. I saw the black guy at Green's home.'

Tomsic shook his head and stared at the bodies. 'Man, you really wrack'm up.'

I frowned at him. 'Do you have a spare shirt in your car?' My shirt was still a bloody wad on Elliot Truly's chest.

'Think I might have something.' Most cops keep a spare shirt for just such occasions.

He had a plain blue cotton dress shirt still in its original plastic bag stowed in his trunk. It had probably been there for years. 'Thanks, Tomsic.' When I put it on, it was like wearing a tent. Two sizes too big.

The medivac chopper came in from the north and settled to a rest well away from the radio towers. Two paramedics hustled out with a stretcher and loaded Mr Lawrence into the helicopter's bay. They told us that they were going to lift him to Martin Luther King, Jr. Hospital, which would be a five-minute flight, and Mrs Earle wanted to go. They refused to take her until Angela Rossi volunteered to go with her. Lincoln Gibbs told Rossi that we would pick her up at the hospital.

When the helicopter had lifted away and disappeared over the hills, Gibbs looked at me and Pike, and said, 'Well?' The first of the black-and-whites was just now kicking up dust on the roads below.

'Green's people got to LeCedrick Earle. They offered him money and an early out from prison if he could get his mother to change her story. He hadn't spoken to her in six years, but he called and told her that the guards and the other prisoners were beating him because she was defending the police. Green's people went to her also, and helped convince her that it was real, and that the only way they could save LeCedrick was if she changed her story so that they could get him away from the guards.'

Gibbs nodded. 'Figured it had to be something like that. Figured she wouldn't do it for money.'

Tomsic said, 'Will she say that on the record?'

'Yes. And we've got something else, too.'

They looked at me.

'Truly made a dying declaration that Teddy Martin admitted murdering his wife, and that Jonathan Green conspired with Truly and Kerris to fabricate false evidence against Pritzik and Richards.'

Tomsic smiled, and Lincoln Gibbs made a little whistle. Gibbs said, 'Truly said that to you?'

'Pike and Rossi heard it, too. Mrs Earle might've heard it, but I'm not certain that she did.'

Gibbs went back to his car and spoke on his cell phone for a time. As the black-and-whites rolled up, Tomsic met them and told them to hang around. There wasn't anything for them to do until the detectives who would handle the scene arrived. Gibbs came back in a few minutes and said, 'Is that your Jeep on the other side of the hills?'

Pike said, 'Mine.'

'Okay. We'll pick up Rossi and Mrs Earle at MLK and go see Sherman.'

I spread my arms. 'Like this?'

Tomsic was already walking to his car. 'The shirt looks great on you. What's your beef?'

'It looks like I'm wearing a tent.'

Pike's mouth twitched.

I said, 'Hey, Gibbs.'

He looked back.

'How about I pick up Mrs Earle? It might be easier for her.'

He stared at me for a short moment, and then he nodded. 'We'll meet you at Sherman's.'

A black-and-white brought us to Pike's Jeep, and we drove directly to the MLK emergency trauma center. Mr Lawrence was in surgery, and Rossi and Mrs Earle were in the waiting room. I sat next to Mrs Earle and took her hands. 'We need to go see the district attorney. We need to tell her what we know about all of this. Do you see?'

She looked at me with clear eyes that were free of doubt or equivocation. 'Of course. I knew that we would.'

The four of us drove to Anna Sherman's office in Pike's Jeep. Mrs Earle rode with her hands in her lap and her head up. I guess she was thinking about LeCedrick. We did not listen to the radio during this time, and perhaps we should have. Things might've worked out differently if we had.

It was just after three that afternoon when Louise Earle, Angela Rossi, and I were shown into Anna Sherman's office. The bald prosecutor, Warren Bidwell, was there, along with another man I hadn't seen before, and Gibbs and Tomsic.

Sherman greeted us, smiling politely at Louise Earle and giving me a kind of curious neutrality, as if the meeting in Greenblatt's parking lot had never happened. I guess that they had told her what to expect.

Sherman offered coffee, which everyone declined, and as we took our seats she passed close to me and whispered, 'Great shirt.'

I guess that they'd told her about the shirt, too.

Anna Sherman asked Mrs Earle if she would mind being recorded, and if she would like to have an attorney present.

Mrs Earle said, 'Am I going to be arrested?'

Anna Sherman smiled and shook her head. 'No, ma'am, but it's your right, and some people feel more comfortable.'

Mrs Earle raised her hands. 'Oh, Lord, no. I don't care for all those lawyers.'

Tomsic grinned big time at that one. Even Bidwell smiled. Sherman said, 'Do you mind if we record?'

'You can record whatever you want. I don't care who hears what I have to say.' Her jaw worked, and for a moment she looked as if she was going to cry again. 'You know, those things I said about LeCedrick and the officer wasn't true.' She looked at Angela. 'I want to apologize for that.'

642

Angela Rossi said, 'It's okay.'

Mrs Earle said, 'No, it is not. I am so ashamed that I don't know what to do.' She looked back at Sherman. 'They said that the most horrible things were happening to my boy. They said that he would surely die in that place unless I helped get him out of there.'

Anna Sherman turned on the recorder. 'Who is "they," Mrs Earle?'

Mrs Louise Earle went through her part of it first, telling how she received the first phone call that she'd had from LeCedrick in six years, how he'd pleaded with her that his life was in danger there in the prison, that he'd called again, crying this time, begging her to help and saying that he'd hired an attorney named Elliot Truly who wanted to come speak with her. She told us how Truly and Kerris had come to the house, confirming the horror stories that LeCedrick had claimed, and convincing her that the fastest way to get LeCedrick moved from harm's way was to claim that the police had framed him those six years ago, just as LeCedrick had always said. She said that Truly helped her work out what to say.

Anna Sherman took notes on a yellow legal pad even though the recorder was running. Bidwell was taking notes, too. Sherman said, 'Did Jonathan Green take part in any of these conversations?'

'No, ma'am.'

Bidwell said, 'I saw you and Green together at a news conference.'

'That's right. When Mr Truly said it was time to say my piece, he drove me over to meet Mr Green.'

'Did you and Mr Green talk about what you were going to say?'

Louise Earle frowned. 'I don't think so.' She frowned harder, trying to remember. 'I guess we didn't. I guess he knew from Mr Truly. He just said to say it to the newspeople as direct and as honest as I could.'

Gibbs leaned forward. 'He said for you to be direct and honest?'

Sherman shook her head. 'Green's smart.' She drew a line across her pad. 'Okay. Let's hear what you have.'

I told them how Rossi and I had gone to see LeCedrick, and what we had learned from him, and how Kerris and his people had gotten to Mrs Earle first and how we had followed them to the pumping fields west of Baldwin Hills, and what happened there. I told them what Truly had said as he lay dying. I said, 'Truly confirmed everything that Mrs Earle and LeCedrick said. He tied in Jonathan Green, and stated that it was Green who directed the fabricating of phony evidence implicating Pritzik and Richards.'

Bidwell put down his pad. 'Why would Green do that?'

I handed him the hard copy printout of the contracts between Jonathan Green and Theodore Martin. 'These are copies of confidential retainer agreements between Green and Teddy Martin. They have an amended agreement that gives Jonathan Green ownership and control of

643

most of Teddy's businesses.' Anna Sherman stared at me without emotion as I said it.

Bidwell flipped through the sheets, frowning. 'How in hell did you come by these?'

I shrugged. 'You just find things sometimes.'

Sherman smiled, still without emotion.

Bidwell passed the pages to her. 'Inadmissable.'

Anna Sherman took the pages but didn't look at them. The neutral smile stayed. She said, 'You have a dying declaration from Elliot Truly implicating Jonathan Green in the falsification of evidence.'

I nodded. 'We do.'

'Who heard it besides you?'

Rossi said, 'I did. So did Joe Pike.'

Sherman looked at Louise Earle. 'Did you hear it, Mrs Earle?'

Louise Earle looked uncertain. 'I don't think so. They put me behind all this metal. There was shooting, and I thought Mr Lawrence was dead.'

Anna Sherman patted her hand. 'That's all right.'

Bidwell said, 'So what we've got is a dying declaration witnessed by three people who have an interest in attacking Jonathan Green.'

Rossi said, 'What in hell does that mean?' She stood. 'We're giving it to you on a plate, and you're saying it's not enough?'

Bidwell crossed his arms and rocked.

Anna Sherman looked at the third guy. He hadn't said anything, and now he was staring at her. She stood and said, 'It's not the best, but I want to move on this. I am confident that these people are telling the truth, and that Jonathan Green is guilty of these crimes.'

Rossi said, 'Truly said something else, too.'

Everyone looked at her.

'He said that Theodore Martin admitted killing his wife.'

Anna Sherman smiled again, and Bidwell leaned forward.

'That's why the agreement was amended. Teddy said that he'd pay anything for Green to save him, and Green went for everything. Teddy put almost all of his personal and corporate holdings into escrow as payment to Green.'

Bidwell snatched up the pages and flipped through them again.

I said, 'There's also a second amendment that releases several million dollars in holdings back to Teddy Martin. I figure it's because Teddy thought he could get bail, and if he got it he was planning to skip.'

Rossi said, 'Truly confirmed that.'

Anna Sherman leaned forward just like Bidwell now, but she wasn't smiling anymore. 'Truly said Teddy was planning to skip?'

Rossi and I answered at the same time. 'Yes.'

Bidwell ran out of the room. The third guy angrily slapped his hands and said, 'Sonofabitch!'

I said, 'What?'

Anna Sherman slumped back in her chair and looked terribly tired. 'Theodore Martin was granted bail this morning at ten o'clock.'

36

Theodore 'Teddy' Martin was granted bail in the amount of five hundred thousand dollars at ten that morning under a nine-nine-five motion made by Jonathan Green on the defendant's behalf in the Los Angeles Superior Court. The nine-nine-five was granted, according to the presiding judge, due to the revelation of 'evidence consistent with innocence.' Namely, the evidence found by one Elvis Cole linking Pritzik and Richards to the kidnapping of Susan Martin. The same evidence that Elliot Truly declared to have falsified as he bled to death in a maintenance shed in the Baldwin Hills.

Lincoln Gibbs and Anna Sherman got on the phones in a mad scramble to ascertain Teddy's whereabouts. Calls were made to Green's office, Teddy's business manager, and Teddy's home. Radio cars were sent to all three locations. Both Green's office and the business manager denied any knowledge of Teddy's whereabouts, and there was no answer at his home. The radio car reported that his home appeared empty, and that a Hispanic housekeeper had responded to their knock and said that 'Mr Teddy' was not and had not been home. Sherman grew so angry that she slammed her phone and cursed, and Mrs Earle said, 'What's going on?'

I said, 'Teddy jumped bail.'

Sherman snapped, 'We don't know that.'

I picked up the amended retainer agreement and flipped to the list of Teddy's personal and corporate possessions. Teddy Jay Enterprises owned a Cessna Citation jet aircraft. It was listed among the properties transferred to Jonathan Green's control, but what does that matter when you're running for your life? Stealing jets isn't much when you compare it to killing people.

Anna Sherman was yelling into the phone at someone in Jonathan Green's office when I held the amendment in front of her with my finger pointing to the jet. She saw the listing, then said, 'Call you back,' and hung up. 'Where does he keep it?'

'I don't know.'

Sherman called Green's business manager again and demanded to know where Teddy housed the jet. She was yelling, and the business manager probably got his nose out of joint because of it, and he probably made the mistake of asking if she had a court order. Sherman went ballistic. Her face turned purple and a webwork of veins stood out on her forehead, and Gibbs said, 'Lord, Anna. You'll have a stroke.'

Anna Sherman shouted into the phone that if the business manager didn't cooperate she would have him arrested within the hour for accessory after the fact and conspiracy. It worked. The business manager told her, and Anna Sherman repeated the information as he gave it. 'Van Nuys airport. Skyway Aviation.' She also repeated a phone number, which Dan Tomsic copied.

Gibbs, Tomsic, Rossi, and I watched Anna Sherman dial Skyway, identify herself, and ask to speak with whoever was in charge. Mrs Earle was watching, too, but you could tell that it wasn't as important to her. Bidwell was arranging a ride back to the hospital for her. The Skyway manager came on the line, and Anna Sherman identified herself again. She asked as to the status of Theodore Martin's Citation jet, then asked several follow-up questions. We knew the answers from her expression. Lincoln Gibbs yelled, 'That sonofabitch,' and kicked the couch. Tomsic sat and put his face in his hands, as if he'd played a long, close game and given it everything and lost in the end. After maybe six minutes Anna Sherman hung up and looked at us with an ashen, strained face. 'Theodore Martin boarded his airplane at approximately eleven-forty this morning, and the jet departed at exactly eleven-fifty-five. His pilot filed a typical IFR flight plan to Rio de Janeiro.' Anna Sherman sat in her chair with her hands in her lap and put her head back. 'He's gone.'

Mrs Louise Earle looked as if she was about to cry. 'Did I do something wrong?'

Angela Rossi stared at her for a moment, then put her arm around Mrs Earle's shoulders. 'No, ma'am. No, you didn't. He just left. It happens all the time.'

Sherman took a deep breath, then sat forward and picked up the phone again. Only this time there wasn't any urgency to it. 'I'll notify the FBI and ask them to speak to the State Department. He's still in the air. Maybe we can work something out with the Brazilians.'

Bidwell said, 'We don't have reciprocal extradition with Brazil.'

Sherman snapped, 'Maybe we can work something out.'

I said, 'You going to do anything about Green?'

Anna Sherman stared at me for maybe six seconds, then she put down the phone. 'Oh, yes. Yes, I'm definitely going to do something about Mr Green.'

Bidwell said, 'You want to file an arrest warrant?'

Anna Sherman was looking at Angela Rossi. 'Yes, we'll file an arrest warrant. I saw Judge Kelton downstairs. Look him up and have it signed.' Arrest warrants had to be signed by a judge.

Bidwell started toward the door. 'I'll call Green's office and set it up. How much time do you want to give him to turn himself in?' Often in cases like this, the attorney is notified that a warrant has been issued and is allowed to turn himself in.

Anna Sherman shook her head, still looking at Angela Rossi. 'To hell with that. We're going to go over there and arrest his ass.'

Angela Rossi smiled. So did everyone else.

I said, 'You guys mind if I tag along?'

Lincoln Gibbs was pacing now. Grinning and anxious to take action, sort of like a leopard sensing that a hunt was on. 'No sweat.'

Rossi wanted to come, too, but Lincoln Gibbs told her no. She was still suspended, and an administrative action could be taken against her for violating her suspension.

Sherman and Bidwell made their calls and drafted their documents, and one hour and ten minutes later they were ready to pay a visit to Mr Jonathan Green, Attorney to the Stars. Mrs Louise Earle had already been returned to the hospital. Rossi walked out with us, but in the lobby she had to go one way and we another. A radio car was going to take her home.

Rossi put out her hand and we shook. 'I want to thank you.'

'No problem.'

'No, I mean it.'

'I understand.'

'I'll call Joe.'

I said, 'So long, Rossi.'

We smiled at each other and then she walked away.

Gibbs and Tomsic and I crowded into Anna Sherman's car and drove to Jonathan Green's office on Sunset Boulevard. A couple of uniforms in a radio car followed us. A district attorney almost never accompanied the police on an arrest, but then neither did freelance private eyes. I guess this was just too good to pass up.

We double-parked in front of his building, jamming up the westbound flow on Sunset, and walked in past the receptionist and the security guys in their blazers. A blond security guy with a red face tried to make a deal about stopping us to see the warrant, but Dan Tomsic said, 'You've gotta be kidding,' and motioned at the uniforms to walk the guy out of the way.

We took the elevator up to the fourth floor and Sherman said, 'You've been here before. Which way?'

I showed them to Green's office. Green had not been notified of Elliot Truly's death, nor of the deaths of his other people, nor had it yet hit the news. As we walked through the halls, lawyers and legal assistants and secretaries and clerks appeared in their doors. Jonathan Green's secretary stood as we approached, and I said, 'Knock knock knock, Chicken Delight!'

She looked at Anna Sherman. 'May I help you?'

Anna Sherman said, 'No.' We trooped past the secretary and through the door and into Green's office. Green and the two lesser attorneys and the videographer and three people I'd never seen before were seated around his conference table with their jackets off and their sleeves rolled. The videographer and his sound tech were seated in the background, the camera on the floor, sipping coffee and talking between themselves. Guess there's only so much you can do with endless footage of lawyers sitting around tables. Jonathan Green looked at us without a great deal of surprise and said, 'Doors are made for knocking.'

I said, 'Not bad. I was kinda hoping you'd say, "What's the meaning of this?"'

Anna Sherman smiled sweetly. 'Sorry for the intrusion, Jonathan. But we're here to arrest you on the charges of tampering with evidence, obstruction of justice, conspiracy to commit murder, and murder.'

The videographer's eyes got big and his jaw dropped. I waved at his camera. 'Better turn it on. You don't want to miss this.' The videographer jumped across the sound tech for his camera, spilling both his coffee and hers.

Anna Sherman turned to Lincoln Gibbs. 'Lieutenant, please inform Mr Green of his rights and take him into custody.'

Lt. Lincoln Gibbs handed the warrant forms to Jonathan, then recited his rights. Jonathan didn't interupt, and didn't bother to examine the forms. He sat with a kind of half-smile, as if he had anticipated these events. Maybe he had. When Gibbs finished with the rights, he said, 'Would you stand, sir? I have to handcuff you.' Polite.

Jonathan submitted without complaint. He said, 'Anna, this is the most flagrant case of judicial manipulation I've ever seen. I'll have you before the bar for this.'

Anna Sherman said, 'Teddy Martin has jumped bail and is on his way to Brazil. Elliot Truly, Stan Kerris, and two other men in your employ are dead. Elliot Truly supplied a dying declaration implicating you in the manufacture of false evidence, as well as the murder of James Lester and the kidnapping of Louise Earle.'

Jonathan Green said, 'That's absurd. I don't know what you're talking about.' He angled his face toward the camera when he said it.

She said, 'That's why we have trials, Jonathan. To determine the facts.'

Lincoln Gibbs took Green by the arm and guided him to the door. Jonathan Green turned back just long enough to say, 'We won't get to trial, Anna.' He smiled when he said it, and his smile was confident and without fear. 'I guess you believe you have reason to do this, but for the life of me I can't imagine what it might be.' He angled toward the video camera again. 'I look forward to seeing your proof, and I hope for your sake that this isn't some ugly form of harassment.'

Gibbs and Tomsic escorted him out, the videographer scurrying ahead of them to capture every moment of the arrest and departure.

I stood with Sherman, watching them go, and wondered at Jonathan Green's lack of concern. I was thinking that maybe he was crazy, or arrogant, or brimming with the fatal flaw of hubris, but you never know.

Maybe he was just used to winning.

37

Theodore Martin's flight from the country was covered throughout the evening by every one of the local Los Angeles television stations, effectively eliminating regular programming. Live news remote teams assaulted Skyway Aviation, Angela Rossi's home, Jonathan Green's office, and spokespeople for both the LAPD and the District Attorney's office. Angela Rossi did not return home that night, and so was unavailable for comment. She picked up her boys and spent the night with a friend. The Skyway people were available, however, and were more than a little surprised by the army of microwave vans and news teams who invaded their otherwise quiet world.

The Skyway employees who were interviewed included the flight operations manager, a young female flight dispatcher, and an even younger male line attendant. The line attendant was a seventeen-year-old kid name Billy Galovich who washed the planes, pumped them full of jet fuel, and pushed them in and out of a hangar with a little tractor. The sum total of his involvement in Teddy Martin's escape was that he had towed out Teddy's Citation, fueled it, then greeted the pilot, a very nice Hispanic man who introduced himself as Mr Garcia. I counted fourteen interviews with Billy Galovich that evening, and then I stopped counting.

The flight dispatcher's claim to fame was that she had taken the call from Teddy Martin, who personally ordered that his Citation be readied for flight. The dispatcher's name was Shannon Denleigh, and she related that Mr Martin told her that his pilot would be a man named Mr Roberto Garcia, and that Mr Garcia would be along directly. She said that she informed the flight operations manager, a Mr Dale Ellison, of the call and then she left the premises to have her nails done. I stopped counting her interviews at sixteen. Dale Ellison related that Mr Garcia arrived moments later, preflighted the Citation, and filed his flight plan. He said that Mr Garcia was an amiable, friendly man who identified himself as a flight officer with Air Argentina who picked up corporate charters to earn extra money. I didn't bother to count the number of times that Dale Ellison was interviewed, but it was plenty.

Reports of Jonathan Green's arrest and the charges against him were interspersed with the coverage of Teddy's flight, but when the newspeople discovered that the Citation was still in the air, the real show began. Reporters and cameras descended upon the FAA and the various Flight Operations Centers between Los Angeles and Rio. The Citation's path was charted, and its progress was depicted on a global map. It was kind of like watching the beginning of *Casablanca*. Every network put a little clock in the corner of their picture, counting down the time until the Citation landed. Crime and show business had merged.

Foreign bureau reporters flocked to the Rio de Janeiro airport, and Teddy Martin's landing was covered live even though it was after midnight in Rio and you really couldn't see anything. The Citation taxied to a private flight service facility for corporate jets where it was met by Brazilian authorities and a small army of newspeople. A spokesman for the Brazilian authorities said that Mr Martin would be questioned as to his plans, but thereafter would be free to go. Teddy Martin pushed through the cameras with his face covered, ignoring the shouting reporters. He reached the flight service facility's door, then apparently changed his mind and paused to make a short statement. Teddy Martin said, 'Please don't interpret my flight from California as indicative of guilt. I promise you, I swear to you all, that I did not murder my wife. I loved her. I left because I am convinced that I could not and would not get a fair and just hearing. I do not know why they are doing this to me.' He disappeared into the building and must have slipped out by some prearranged and secret manner because he was not seen again.

I went to bed at twenty minutes after one that night, and still the networks were on the air, rehashing the landing, replaying the interviews, offering taped 'live' coverage of something that was no more alive than a nightmare.

38

The phone rang several times throughout the night. I stopped answering and let the machine get the calls after I realized that they were reporters, looking for yet another comment. I finally unplugged the phone.

I slept late the next morning and woke to a quiet house. The cat was sleeping on the foot of my bed and the finches were waiting on the deck rail and no one was trying to shoot me, which was good, but for the first time in many days I felt the emptiness of Lucy's absence, which wasn't.

My involvement with Angela Rossi and Louise Earle and the events in their lives seemed to be at an end or, if not ended, then certainly diminished. Anna Sherman wanted to interview me in greater detail, but she would speak to Rossi first, then Gibbs and Tomsic. It might be days before we could get together.

I got out of bed, took a shower, then ate a bowl of granola and cottage cheese and sliced peaches. I drank a glass of nonfat milk. I phoned Martin Luther King Hospital, asked about Mr Lawrence, and was told that he was doing well even though he was listed in critical condition. The nurse remembered me, and told me that Mrs Earle was still there, asleep in the waiting room. She had been there throughout the night. I called a florist I know and sent flowers, addressing them to Mrs Earle as well as to Mr Lawrence. I hoped that they would brighten her day.

At twenty minutes after eleven my phone rang again, and this time I answered. Life in the fast lane. Joe Pike said, 'Are you looking at this?'

'What?'

'Turn on your television.'

I did.

Jonathan Green was surrounded by reporters on the steps of the Superior Court Building. The network legal analyst was saying that Green had been arraigned at ten A.M., had posted minimal bail, and was now about to make a statement. The two lesser attorneys were behind him, as was an older, gray-haired African-American attorney named Edwin Foss. Foss was a criminal defense attorney of Green's stature who had made his reputation defending a transient who had shot four people to death while

653

robbing an AM-PM Minimart. The murders had been caught on videotape, but Foss had still managed to gain an acquittal. I guess he had convinced the jury that it was reasonable to doubt what they had seen.

Edwin Foss whispered in Jonathan's ear, then Jonathan stepped to the microphones and made his statement. His tone was somber and apologetic, and Foss kept a hand on Jonathan's shoulder as he spoke. Guidance. Green said, 'No one is more surprised by Theodore Martin's actions than me. I have believed in his innocence from the beginning, and I still believe him to be an innocent man. I believed then, and believe now, that the evidence against Theodore Martin was planted by unscrupulous officers involved in the investigation. Teddy, if you can hear these words, I urge you to return. Justice will prevail.'

Pike said, 'You think Teddy's tuned in, down there in Rio?'

'Shh.'

Green said, 'I pledge my full cooperation to those investigating the charges that have been made against me. I will aid in uncovering whatever wrongdoing has occurred, if any, and in the prosecution of anyone in my employ who has conspired to breech the canon of ethics by which I have lived my life. I state now, publicly and for the record, that I have behaved honorably and within the law. I have done no wrong.'

Green's attorney again whispered something in Green's ear and gently pulled him away from the microphones. The reporters shouted questions, but Green's attorney waved them off and said that there would be no questions.

I turned off the television and said, 'This guy is something. He's already doctoring the spin.'

Pike didn't respond.

'You don't think he can beat this, do you?'

There was a pause, then Pike hung up. Guess he didn't have an answer. Or maybe he didn't want to think that it was possible.

I made an early lunch for myself, then brought the phone out onto the deck and called Lucy Chenier at her office. She had heard about Jonathan's arrest and Teddy's flight on the national news, but she didn't seem particularly anxious to hear the inside dirt. When I described the events beneath the radio towers, she told me that she was late for a meeting. Great. Anna Sherman called later that afternoon and asked me to come to her office the following day to make a statement. I did, and spent three hours in the Criminal Courts Building being interviewed by Sherman, Bidwell, and three LAPD detectives whom I had not previously met. Pike came in as I was leaving. Sherman told me that Mrs Earle had been interviewed the day before.

Two days after my interview, Mr Walter Lawrence was taken off the critical list. His prognosis was excellent. I went to see him and brought more flowers. Mrs Earle was still there, and told me that she planned to visit LeCedrick. It would be the first time that she'd seen him in the six years that he had been at Terminal Island. I offered to drive her.

Teddy's flight and Green's arrest stayed in the headlines. 'Teddy Sightings' were a regular feature in the tabloids, which reported on various occasions that Teddy was now living in a palatial Brazilian mansion that had been built by a famous Nazi war criminal, that Teddy had been seen in the company of Princess Diana, and that Teddy was gone for good because he had been abducted by short gray aliens with large heads. The California State Bar Association announced that it was launching an investigation into Jonathan Green's conduct independent of that by the Los Angeles Police Department and the District Attorney's office. Green said that he welcomed the opportunity to clear his name and would cooperate fully.

Jonathan Green and his attorney appeared regularly on local television news, local radio talk shows, and in the L.A. *Times*. Reports from 'unnamed sources' began surfacing that Elliot Truly had made a secret deal with Teddy, unknown to Mr Green. Leaks 'close to the prosecution' were quoted as saying that computer files found at Elliot Truly's home confirmed such an agreement. Other sources leaked that Truly had had several meetings with Teddy while Teddy was in jail to which Mr Green was not privy. Carefully worded public opinion polls charted a swing in the belief of Jonathan Green's involvement from 'absolutely' to 'probably' to 'uncertain.'

Eleven days after the events beneath the radio tower, the LAPD Internal Affairs Division announced that it had completed its investigation of Detective Angela Rossi and had found there to be no evidence either in the LeCedrick Earle matter (LeCedrick Earle himself had recanted his claims against her) or that she had manufactured or planted evidence against Theodore Martin. The story was given two inches on page nineteen of the *Times*, and the same public opinion polls indicated that seventy-three percent of the public still believed that she was a corrupt cop who had framed LeCedrick Earle (even though he now denied it) and who had 'probably' mishandled evidence against Teddy Martin. She was returned to active duty with her partner, Dan Tomsic.

I listened to the news and followed the investigations with a growing sense of unease. Jonathan Green signed a two-million-dollar contract with a major book publisher to publish his version of the story. He appeared on *Larry King Live* and *Rivera Live*, and each time he presented himself as a victim. I was offered many jobs, but I declined them. The press still called, though with less frequency, and I avoided them. I listened to talk radio and gained weight, as if I felt a hunger that I couldn't satisfy.

The days grew warm again, and I decided to refinish the deck. It had been almost eight years since I'd last stained and sealed the deck, and the wood was showing its age. Joe offered his help, and we spent the core of each day sanding and staining and sealing. We listened to music as we worked, but from time to time we turned to the news. Twenty-three days after the events beneath the radio tower, the California Bar quietly closed its investigation, saying that all evidence pointed to wrongdoing by Elliot Truly and not by Jonathan Green. Twenty-five days after the tower, the District Attorney's office dropped all charges against Jonathan Green save one count of tampering with evidence. I was on a ladder beneath the deck when we heard the news, and Pike said, 'He's getting away with it.'

I went inside and called Anna Sherman, who said, 'It's the best we can do.' Her voice was faraway and sounded lost.

I said, 'This is crap. You *know* he was behind it.'

'Of course.'

'He set up Truly just like he set up Rossi and Pritzik and Richards. He ordered Lester's murder. They were going to kill Louise Earle. He did his best to destroy the life and career of a police officer who did nothing worse than do her job.'

She didn't say anything for a time, and then she said, 'He knows how to play the game, Elvis. What can I tell you?' Then she hung up.

Twenty-eight days after the towers, Pike and I finished sealing the deck. It was slick and gleaming and smelled of marine-grade varnish. After the varnish had cured, we put the deck chairs and the Weber and the little table back, and sat in the sun drinking cold Falstaff. We sat for a while, and then Pike said, 'Say something.'

I looked at him.

'You haven't said anything for three days. You've said next to nothing for almost two weeks.'

'Guess I'm getting like you.'

I smiled at him, but he didn't smile back.

I finished my Falstaff, crimped the can, then put it carefully onto the shining deck. Little rings of condensation beaded on the thick varnish. I said, 'I'm not sure that I want to do this anymore.'

'Be an investigator?'

I nodded.

'What do you want to do?'

I shrugged.

'You want to stop being what you've been for almost fifteen years because Jonathan Green is getting away with murder?' He frowned when he said it. Like maybe he was disappointed.

I spread my hands. 'I guess that's it. Elvis Cole, sore loser.'

Pike shook his head.

I went inside, brought out two fresh Falstaffs, and gave him one. I said, 'What would you say if I told you that I was thinking about moving to Louisiana to be closer to Lucy?'

Pike sipped some of the Falstaff, then gazed out at the canyon, then wet his lips and nodded. 'I'd say that I'd miss you.'

I nodded.

'I'd say that if that's what you needed to do, that I would help any way that I could.'

I nodded again.

'You talk to her about it?'

'Not yet.'

Pike shook his head. 'You're something.'

Four hours later Pike was gone and I was cooking a very nice *puttanesca* sauce when I decided to call Lucy Chenier. I was most of the way through a bottle of California merlot. In the course of my life I've been shot, sapped, slugged, stabbed with a broken beer bottle, and I've faced down any number of thugs and miscreants, but talking to Lucy about moving to Louisiana seemed to require fortification. She answered on the third ring, and I said, 'Guess who?'

'Have you been drinking?' Don't you hate smart women?

'Absolutely not.' Giving her affronted. Giving her shocked. Then I said, 'Well, maybe a little.'

She sighed. 'I heard on the news that the charges against Green were reduced. How's Angela?'

'Not great, but not bad, either. The public still thinks that she's rotten, but IA cleared her.'

'How nice for her children.'

'Green kept himself insulated so that there was always plausible deniability.'

'What about Truly's dying declaration?' I had told her about Truly weeks ago. 'That's legitimate evidence.'

'It is, but since it was witnessed only by me and Angela and Joe, the powers that be view it as questionable. Because I resigned from Green's employ, and because he accused Rossi, the powers that be feel that a jury would discount our version of events.'

She didn't say anything for a time, and then she said, 'Well, in this case the powers that be are probably right.'

I nodded, but she probably couldn't see it. 'I don't believe Truly had a secret agreement with Teddy Martin. Green fabricated that, just as he fabricated the business about Pritzik and Richards.'

'I'm sure you're right.'

'Truly was telling the truth.'

'I'm sure of that, too.'

I didn't say anything. I was staring at the bubbles rising in the sauce and my shoulders felt tight and I was wishing that I hadn't drunk all the wine.

Lucy said, 'It hurts, doesn't it?'

I moved my tongue, trying to scrub away the wine's taste. 'Oh, God, yes.'

'You try so hard to make things right, and here's this man, and he's oozing through the system in a way that keeps things wrong.'

'He is defiling justice.' Defiling. That was probably the merlot talking.

She said, 'Oh, Studly.' I could see her smile. 'The law is not about justice. You know that.'

I finished the merlot and turned off the sauce. It was thick with chunks of tomatoes and black olives and raisins. I had cooked it without being hungry. Maybe I just wanted to give myself something worthwhile to do. 'Of course I know, but it should be.'

Lucy said, 'The law is an adversarial contest that defines justice as staying within the rules and seeing the game to its conclusion. Justice is reaching a conclusion. It has very little to do with right and wrong. The law gives us order. Only men and women can give us what you want to call justice.'

I took a deep breath and let it out. 'God, Lucille, I wish you were here.'

'I know.' Her voice was soft and hard to hear. Then she said, 'You're still the World's Greatest Detective, honey pie. They can't take that away from you.'

It made me smile.

Neither of us spoke for a time, and then Lucy said, 'Do you remember Tracy Mannos at Channel Eight? We met her at Green's party.'

'Sure. The program manager.'

'She called me last week. She arranged for the network affiliate here in Baton Rouge to shoot a test tape of me, and after she saw it she offered me a job as an on-air legal commentator.'

I said, 'In Baton Rouge?'

'No, Elvis. Out there. In Los Angeles.'

I couldn't say anything. The merlot seemed to be rushing through my ears.

Lucy said, 'It's more money, and we would be closer to you, but it's such a big move.' You could hear her uncertainty.

I said, 'You'd come to Los Angeles?'

'There's so much to think about. There's Ben. There's my house and my friends. I'm not sure what to do about Richard.'

'Please say yes.' It came out hoarse.

She didn't say anything for a time. 'I don't know just yet. I need to think about it.'

'I told Joe that I was thinking about moving to Baton Rouge.'

Another pause. 'Are you?'

'Yes.'

'Would you?'

'Yes.'

'Why?'

'You know why, Lucille. I love you.'

She didn't speak for another moment, and when she did her voice seemed lighter, somehow more at ease. 'I need to think.'

'Call me tomorrow.'

'I may not know tomorrow.'

'Call me anyway.'

She said, 'I love you, Studly. Always remember that.'

Lucille Chenier hung up, and I lay on my kitchen floor and smiled at the ceiling, and not very much later I knew that I had found the last and final way to bring Jonathan Green to justice.

Or, at least, a close approximation.

39

I called Eddie Ditko first. He came over that night, coughing and wheezing, but happy to eat spaghetti with the *puttanesca* sauce and listen to my account of the events in the maintenance shed while he recorded my every word. He grinned a lot while I talked, and said that he could guarantee a bottom half of the front-page position for the story. He said, 'Man, the shit's gonna hit the fan when this comes out.'

'That's the idea.'

When Eddie was gone, I called Tracy Mannos, who put me in touch with Lyle Stodge at twenty minutes after ten. Lyle and Marcy anchored the eleven P.M. newscast as well as the five. Lyle was only too happy to talk to me, and only too happy to accept my offer of an interview. He said, 'We've been hoping to get you for a comment on all of this! Can you make the eleven o'clock?'

'Nope.'

'How about tomorrow at five?'

'I'll be there.' The five o'clock newscast had the larger audience.

I phoned every person who had interviewed me in print or on radio or television, or who had wanted to interview me. I spent most of the night and part of the next morning on the phone, and everybody was happy to talk to me. I called both Peter Alan Nelsen and Jodi Taylor, and asked if they could put me in touch with any of the major network and cable news people, and of course they could. Even *Daily Variety* wanted an interview. Everybody wanted to know if I had been duped by Theodore Martin, and everybody wanted to know what had happened in the maintenance shed, and everyone still considered me the hero of the defense effort, just the way Jonathan had hoped when he had staged the news conferences with his hand on my shoulder. I told them that I would be happy to tell them exactly what happened, especially if we were on the air live.

By three the following afternoon, I had completed eleven interviews, and had provided each interviewer with a copy of Green's amended retainer agreement with Theodore Martin. Seven other interviews were scheduled, and more would be forthcoming. I had copies for them, too.

At twelve minutes after three, I parked in a red zone outside Jonathan Green's Sunset Boulevard building and went inside. I shoved past the receptionist and ran up the stairs and barged past the army of clerks and assistants and minions. There was a noticeable absence of blue-blazered security guards, but I guess those few who hadn't been killed in Baldwin Hills had been fired. All the better for Green to separate himself from Kerris.

The *Inside News* videographer and his sound technician were talking to a slim woman by the coffee machine when I went past. The videographer's eyes went wide when he saw me, and the sound tech dropped her coffee. The videographer said, 'What are you doing here?'

I grabbed him by the arm and pulled him along. 'Do you have tape in that thing?'

'Sure.'

'You're going to love this.'

The sound tech scrambled after us.

Jonathan Green's office occupied the entire east end of the fourth floor. An efficient-looking woman in her early forties tried to tell me that I couldn't go in, but I ducked around her and hit the door, only the door wouldn't open. The woman said, 'You stop that! You stop that before I call the police!'

The sound tech said, 'You have to buzz it open.'

I said, 'Where?'

The sound tech hurried to the woman's desk and pressed the buzzer. The sound tech was grinning.

I kicked open the door and stormed in and found Jonathan Green on the phone. The two lesser attorneys were with him, along with a younger man with a notepad. Somebody's secretary. The smaller of the lesser attorneys fell over a chair trying to get out of my way. Green said, 'I'm calling the police!'

I pulled the phone out of his hands and tossed it aside. I said, 'Here's the bad news, Jonathan: You've become my hobby. I know what Truly knew, and I am telling it to anyone who will listen.'

Green maneuvered to keep his desk between us. His face had grown white. 'The police are on their way! I'm warning you!'

I threw a copy of the retainer agreement at him. 'I'm also passing out copies of this. The *Examiner* is going to print it in this evening's edition.'

Green looked at it without touching it and shook his head. 'This means nothing. For all anyone knows you wrote it yourself. It isn't admissible.'

'Not in a court of law, Jonathan. But we're going to try you in the court of public opinion.' I shoved his desk, and Jonathan jumped backward. 'I will hound you, and I will not stop. I will tell everyone that it was you who falsified the evidence, and you who ordered James Lester killed, and

you who attempted to take the life of Louise Earle.' I started around the
end of the desk, and Jonathan scrambled in the opposite direction.

'You can't do that! I'll get a restraining order!'

'What's that to a tough guy like me?'

'No one will believe you!'

'Sure they will, Jonathan. I am the World's Greatest Detective,
remember? Above reproach. Trustworthy.'

Jonathan glared at the lesser attorneys and yelled, 'Don't just stand
there! Do something!'

The larger lesser attorney ran out the door.

'I will keep this alive until the DA can finally build a case or until you
are driven out of business. I will haunt you like a bad dream. I will come
to your house and follow you into restaurants and send videotapes of my
interviews to your clients.'

He drew himself up into a vision of outrage. 'We have laws against
that, you idiot! That's libel! That's slander! You won't get away with it!'

I looked at the videographer. 'Are you getting this?'

The videographer was all smiles. 'Hell, yes! What an ending!'

I jumped across the desk and punched Jonathan Green hard in the
mouth one time. He floundered backwards and went over his chair and
landed on his ass. The smaller lesser attorney shouted, 'Oh, my God,' and
then he ran, too.

Jonathan Green said, 'You hit me! You actually laid hands on me!' He
felt his mouth, then looked at his red fingers and started crying. 'You
broke my teeth!'

I walked over to Jonathan Green, looked down at him, and said, 'So
sue me.'

And then I walked out.